OF

LOVE

AND

LIFE

❖

OF
LOVE
AND
LIFE

Three novels selected and condensed
by Reader's Digest

CONDENSED BOOKS DIVISION

The Reader's Digest Association Limited, London

The Reader's Digest Association Limited

11 Westferry Circus, Canary Wharf, London E14 4HE

www.readersdigest.co.uk

ISBN 0-276-42557-X

For information as to ownership of copyright in the material of this book, and acknowledgments, see last page.

CONTENTS

Cocktails
for Three
Madeleine Wickham

❧

CANDICE: kind, honest and trusting, but racked with guilt about the past.

ROXANNE: glamorous and self-confident; in love with a married man she hopes will one day be hers.

MAGGIE: a high-achiever, capable and efficient, but worried about the changes motherhood will bring.

Three very different women but the very best of friends. Surely nothing can come between them?

❧

Chapter One

CANDICE BREWIN PUSHED OPEN the heavy glass door of the Manhattan Bar and felt the familiar swell of warmth, noise, light and clatter rush over her. It was six o'clock on a Wednesday night and the bar was already almost full. Waiters in dark green bow ties were gliding over the pale polished floor, carrying cocktails to tables. Girls in slippy dresses were standing at the bar, glancing round with bright, hopeful eyes. In the corner, a pianist was thumping out Gershwin numbers, almost drowned by the hum of metropolitan chatter.

It was getting to be too busy here, thought Candice. When she, Roxanne and Maggie had first discovered the Manhattan Bar, it had been a small, quiet, almost secretive place to meet. They had stumbled on it by chance, desperate for somewhere to drink after a particularly fraught press day. It had then been a dark and old-fashioned-looking place, with tatty bar stools and a peeling mural of the New York skyline on one wall. The patrons had been few and silent—mostly tending towards elderly gentlemen with much younger female companions. Candice, Roxanne and Maggie had boldly ordered a round of cocktails and then several more—and by the end of the evening had decided, amid fits of giggles, that the place had a certain terrible charm and must be revisited. And so the monthly cocktail club had been born.

But now, newly extended, relaunched and written up in every glossy magazine, the bar was a different place. These days a young, attractive after-work crowd came flocking in every evening. Really, thought Candice, handing her coat to the coat-check woman and receiving an art deco silver button in return, they should find somewhere else.

Somewhere less busy. At the same time, she knew they never would. They had been coming here too long; had shared too many secrets over those distinctive frosted martini glasses. Anywhere else would feel wrong. On the first of every month, it had to be the Manhattan Bar.

There was a mirror opposite, and she glanced at her reflection, checking that her short cropped hair was tidy and her make-up—what little there was of it—hadn't smudged. She was wearing a plain black trouser-suit over a pale green T-shirt—not exactly the height of glamour, but good enough.

Quickly she scanned the faces at the tables, but couldn't see Roxanne or Maggie. Although they all worked at the same place—the editorial office of the *Londoner*—it was rare they made the walk to the bar together. For a start, Roxanne was a freelance, and at times only seemed to use the office to make long-distance calls, arranging the next of her foreign jaunts. And Maggie, as editor of the magazine, often had to stay for meetings later than the others.

Not today, though, thought Candice, glancing at her watch. Today, Maggie had every excuse to slip off as early as she liked.

She walked towards the tables and, spotting a couple getting up, stepped quickly forward. The young man had barely made it out of his chair before she was sliding into it and smiling gratefully up at him. You couldn't hang about if you wanted a table at the Manhattan Bar. And the three of them always had a table. It was part of the tradition.

Maggie Phillips paused outside the doors of the Manhattan Bar, put down her bulky carrier bag full of bright, stuffed toys, and pulled unceremoniously at the maternity tights wrinkling round her legs. Three more weeks, she thought, giving a final tug. Three more weeks of these bloody things. She took a deep breath, reached for her carrier bag again and pushed at the glass door. As soon as she got inside, the noise and warmth of the place made her feel faint. She grasped for the wall and stood quite still, blinking away the dots in front of her eyes.

'Are you all right, my love?' enquired a voice to her left. Maggie swivelled her head and, as her vision cleared, made out the kindly face of the coat-check lady.

'I'm fine,' she said, flashing a tight smile. She began to struggle out of her coat, aware of the coat-check lady's appraising gaze. For pregnancy wear, her black Lycra trousers and tunic were about as flattering as you could get. But still there it was, right in front her. A bump the size of a helium balloon. Maggie handed over her coat and met the coat lady's gaze head-on.

If she asks me when it's due, she thought, I swear I'll smother her with Tinky Winky.

'When's it due?'

'The 25th of April,' said Maggie brightly. 'Three weeks to go.'

'Your first, is it,' she added, with no hint of interrogation in her voice.

So it's that obvious, thought Maggie. It's that clear to the rest of the world that I, Maggie Phillips—or Mrs Drakeford as I'm known at the clinic—have barely ever touched a baby. Let alone given birth to one.

'Yes, it's my first,' she said.

'I had four myself,' the woman said. 'Three girls and a boy. And each time, those first few weeks were the most magical time of all. You want to cherish those moments, love. Don't wish it all away.'

'I know,' Maggie heard herself saying. *I don't know!* she yelled silently. I don't know anything about it. I know about page layout and editorial ratios and commissioning budgets. Oh God. What am I doing?

'Maggie!' A voice interrupted her and she wheeled round. Candice's cheerful face smiled back at her. 'I thought I saw you! I've nabbed a table.'

'Well done!' Maggie followed Candice through the throng, aware of the curious glances following her. No one else in the bar was pregnant. No one was even fat. Everywhere she looked she could see girls with flat stomachs and stick legs and pert little breasts.

'OK?' Candice had reached the table and was carefully pulling out a chair for her. Biting back a retort that she wasn't ill, Maggie sat down.

'Shall we order?' said Candice. 'Or wait for Roxanne?'

'Oh, I dunno.' Maggie gave a grumpy shrug. 'Better wait, I suppose.'

'Are you OK?' asked Candice curiously. Maggie sighed.

'I'm fine. I'm just sick of being pregnant. Being prodded and patted and treated like a freak.'

'A freak?' said Candice in disbelief. 'Maggie, you look fantastic!'

'Fantastic for a fat woman.'

'Fantastic full stop,' said Candice firmly. 'Listen, there's a girl across the road from me who's pregnant at the moment. I tell you, if she saw the way you look, she'd throw up in jealousy.'

Maggie laughed. 'Candice, I adore you. You always say the right things.'

'It's true!' Candice reached for the cocktail menu. 'Come on, let's have a look, anyway. Roxanne won't be long.'

Roxanne Miller stood in the ladies' room of the Manhattan Bar, leaned forward and carefully outlined her lips in cinnamon-coloured pencil. She pressed them together, then stood back and studied her reflection critically, starting with her best features. Good cheekbones. Blue eyes a little bloodshot, skin tanned from three weeks in the Caribbean. Bronzy-blonde hair tumbling down from a beaded comb in her hair. She was dressed, as she so often was, in a white T-shirt. In her opinion, nothing showed off a tan better than a plain white T-shirt. She put her hairbrush away and smiled, impressed by her own reflection in spite of herself.

There was a sound from the door and her head jerked round.

'Roxanne!' Maggie was coming towards her, a wide smile on her face, her nut-brown bob shining under the spotlights.

'Darling!' Roxanne beamed, and gaily thrust her make-up bag into a larger Prada tote. 'I was just beautifying.'

'You don't need it!' said Maggie. 'Look at that tan!'

'That's Caribbean sun for you,' said Roxanne cheerfully.

'Don't tell me,' said Maggie. 'I don't want to know. It's not even approaching fair. Why did I never do a single travel feature while I was editor? I must have been mad!' She jerked her head towards the door. 'Go and keep Candice company. I'll be out in a moment.'

As she entered the bar, Roxanne saw Candice sitting alone, reading the cocktail menu, and an involuntary smile came to her lips. Candice always looked the same. Her skin always looked well scrubbed and glowing, her hair was always cut in the same neat crop. And she always looked up with the same wide, trusting eyes. No wonder she was such a good interviewer, thought Roxanne fondly. People must just tumble into that friendly gaze.

'Candice!' she called, and strode up to the table. She kissed Candice twice. 'Have you ordered?'

'I'm just looking,' said Candice, gesturing to the menu. 'I can't decide between a Summer Sunset or an Urban Myth.'

'Have the Urban Myth,' said Roxanne. 'A Summer Sunset is bright pink and comes with an umbrella.'

'Does it?' Candice wrinkled her brow. 'Does that matter? What are you having?'

'Margarita,' said Roxanne. 'I lived on Margaritas in Antigua.' She reached for a cigarette, then remembered Maggie and stopped.

'So—how was it?' said Candice. 'Any toy boys this time?'

'Enough to keep me happy,' said Roxanne, grinning wickedly at her. 'One return visit in particular.'

'You're terrible!' said Candice.

'On the contrary,' said Roxanne, 'I'm very good. That's why they like me. That's why they come back for more.'

'What about your—' Candice broke off awkwardly.

'What about Mr Married with Kids?' said Roxanne lightly.

'Yes,' said Candice, colouring a little. 'Doesn't he mind . . . ?'

'Mr Married with Kids is not allowed to mind,' said Roxanne. 'Mr Married with Kids has got his wife, after all. Fair's fair, don't you think?' Her eyes glinted at Candice as though to forbid any more questions. Roxanne always discouraged talk of her married man and resolutely refused to divulge his identity. Candice and Maggie had jokingly speculated between themselves that he must be somebody famous—a politician, perhaps—and certainly rich, powerful and sexy. Whether she was really in love with him, they were less sure. She was always so flippant about the affair—it was as though she were using him, rather than the other way round.

'Look, I'm sorry,' said Roxanne, reaching again for her cigarettes. 'Foetus or no foetus, I'm going to have to have a cigarette.'

'Oh, smoke away,' said Maggie, coming up behind her. 'I'm sure it can't be worse than pollution.' As she sat down, she beckoned to a cocktail waitress. 'Hi. Yes, we're ready to order.'

As the fair-haired girl in the green waistcoat came walking smartly over, Candice stared curiously at her. Something about her was familiar. Candice's eyes ran over the girl's wavy hair; her snub nose; her grey eyes, shadowed with tiredness. Where on earth had she seen her before?

'Is something wrong?' said the girl, politely, and Candice flushed.

'No. Of course not. Ahm . . .' She opened the cocktail menu again and ran her eyes down the lists. 'A Mexican Swing, please.'

'A Margarita for me,' said Roxanne.

'Oh God, I don't know what to have,' said Maggie.

'A Virgin Mary?' suggested Candice.

'Definitely not.' Maggie pulled a face. 'Oh, sod it. A Shooting Star.'

'Good choice,' said Roxanne. 'Get the kid used to a bit of alcohol inside its system. And now . . .' She reached inside her bag. 'It's present time!'

'For who?' said Maggie. 'Not for me. I've had *heaps* of presents today. Far too many. Plus about five thousand Mothercare vouchers . . .'

'A Mothercare voucher?' said Roxanne disdainfully. 'That's not a present!' She produced a tiny blue box. 'This is a proper present.'

'Tiffany?' said Maggie incredulously. 'Really? Tiffany?' She opened the box and carefully took something silver from its tiny bag. 'I don't believe it! It's a rattle!' She shook it, and they all smiled with childish delight.

'Let me have a go!' said Candice.

'You'll have the most stylish baby on the block,' said Roxanne. 'If it's a boy, I'll get him cuff links to match.'

'It's wonderful,' said Candice, staring admiringly at it. 'It makes my present seem really . . . Well, anyway.' She put the rattle down and started to rummage in her bag. 'It's here somewhere . . .'

'Candice Brewin!' said Roxanne accusingly, peering over her shoulder. 'What's that in your bag?'

'What?' said Candice, looking up guiltily.

'More tea towels! And a sponge.' Roxanne hauled the offending items out of Candice's bag. There were two blue tea towels and a yellow sponge, each wrapped in cellophane and marked 'Young People's Cooperative'.

'How much did you pay for these?' demanded Roxanne.

'Not much,' said Candice. 'Hardly anything. About five pounds.'

'Which means ten,' said Maggie. 'What are we going to do with her? Candice, you must have bought their whole bloody supply, by now!'

'Well, they're always useful, aren't they, tea towels?' said Candice flushing. 'And I feel so bad, saying no.'

'Exactly,' said Maggie. 'You're not doing it because you think it's a good thing. You're doing it because if you don't, you'll feel bad.'

'Well, isn't that the same thing?' retorted Candice.

'No,' said Maggie. 'One's positive, and the other's negative. Or . . . something. Oh God, I'm confused now. I need a cocktail.'

'Who cares?' said Roxanne. 'The point is, no more tea towels.'

'OK, OK,' said Candice, hurriedly stuffing the packets back in her bag. 'No more tea towels. And here's my present.' She produced an envelope from her bag and handed it to Maggie. 'You can take it any time.'

There was silence round the table as Maggie opened it and took out a pale pink card. 'An aromatherapy massage,' she read out disbelievingly. 'You've bought me a massage.'

'I just thought you might like it,' said Candice. 'Before you have the baby, or after.' Maggie looked up, her eyes glistening slightly.

'You know, that's the only present anyone's bought for me. For *me*, as opposed to the baby.' She gave Candice a hug. 'Thank you, my darling.'

'We'll really miss you,' said Candice. 'Don't stay away too long.'

'Well, you'll have to come and see me!' said Maggie. 'And the baby.'

'In your country manor,' said Roxanne sardonically. 'Mrs Drakeford At Home.' She grinned at Candice, who tried not to giggle.

When Maggie had announced, a year previously, that she and her husband Giles were moving to a cottage in the country, Candice had believed her. She had pictured a quaint little dwelling somewhere in the middle of a village.

The truth had turned out to be rather different. Maggie's new house,

The Pines, had turned out to be situated at the end of a long, tree-lined drive. It had eight bedrooms and a billiards room and a swimming pool. Maggie, it had turned out, was secretly married to a millionaire.

'You never told us!' Candice had said accusingly as they'd sat in the vast kitchen, drinking tea. 'You never told us you were rolling in it!'

'We're not rolling in it!' Maggie had retorted defensively. 'It just . . . *looks* bigger because it's in the country.' This remark she had never been allowed to forget.

'It just looks bigger . . .' Roxanne began now, snorting with laughter.

'Oh, shut up, y'all,' said Maggie good-naturedly. 'Look, here come the cocktails.'

The blonde-haired girl was coming towards them, holding a silver tray on the flat of her hand. Three glasses were balanced on it. One a Margarita glass, frosted round the rim, one a highball decorated with a single fanned slice of lime, and one a champagne flute adorned with a strawberry. The girl set the glasses down on their paper coasters, added a silver dish of salted almonds, and discreetly placed the bill to one side of the table. As she stood up, Candice looked again at her face. She knew this girl from somewhere. But from where?

'Thanks very much,' said Maggie.

'No problem,' said the girl, and smiled—and as she did so, Candice knew, in a flash, who she was.

'Heather Trelawney,' she said aloud, before she could stop herself. And then, as the girl's eyes slowly turned towards her, she wished with all her soul that she hadn't.

'I'm sorry,' began the girl puzzledly. 'Do I—' She stopped and peered at Candice. Then suddenly her face lit up. 'Of course!' she said. 'It's Candice, isn't it? Candice . . .' She wrinkled her brow. 'Sorry, I've forgotten your last name.'

'Brewin,' said Candice in a frozen voice, barely able to utter the syllables. As she saw Heather frowning thoughtfully, Candice flinched, waiting for the jolt of recognition, the anger and recriminations. Why had she not just kept her stupid mouth shut? But as Heather's face cleared, it was obvious that she recognised Candice as nothing but an old school acquaintance. Didn't she know? thought Candice incredulously.

'Candice Brewin!' said Heather. 'That's right! I should have recognised you straightaway.'

'How funny!' said Maggie. 'How do you two know each other?'

'We were at school together,' said Heather. 'It must be years since we've seen each other.' She looked again at Candice. 'You know, I thought there was something about you, when I took your order. But, I don't know. You look different, somehow. I suppose we've all changed since then.'

'I suppose so,' said Candice. She picked up her glass and took a sip, trying to calm her beating heart. 'So, Heather,' she said quickly, 'have you been working here long?'

'Only a couple of weeks,' said Heather. 'It's a nice place, isn't it? But they keep us busy.' She glanced towards the bar. 'Speaking of which, I'd better get on. Good to see you, Candice.'

She began to move off, and Candice felt a jolt of alarm.

'Wait!' she said. 'We haven't caught up properly.' She swallowed. 'Why don't you . . . sit down for a minute?'

'Well, OK,' said Heather after a pause. 'But I can't be long. We'll have to pretend I'm advising you on cocktails or something.'

'We don't need any advising,' said Roxanne. 'We are the cocktail queens.' Heather giggled.

'I'll just see if I can find a chair,' she said. 'Back in a tick.'

As soon as she had walked away, Maggie turned to Candice.

'What's wrong?' she hissed. 'Who is this girl? You're staring at her as though you've seen a bloody ghost!'

'Is it that obvious?' said Candice in dismay. She picked up her cocktail with a shaking hand and took a gulp. 'Cheers, everybody.'

'Never mind bloody cheers!' said Maggie. 'Who is she?'

'She's—' Candice rubbed her brow. 'I knew her years ago. We were at school together. She—she was a couple of years below me.'

'We know all that!' said Maggie impatiently. 'What else?'

'Hi!' Heather's bright voice interrupted them, and they all looked up guiltily. 'I found a chair at last.' She set it at the table and sat down. 'So—what are you up to now?' she said to Candice.

'I'm a journalist,' said Candice.

'Really?' Heather looked at her wistfully. 'I'd love to do something like that. Do you write for a newspaper?'

'A magazine. The *Londoner*.'

'I know the *Londoner*!' said Heather. 'I've probably even read articles you've written.' She looked round the table. 'Are you all journalists?'

'Yes,' said Maggie. 'We all work together.'

'God, that must be fun.'

'It has its moments,' said Maggie. 'Some better than others.'

There was a brief silence, then Candice said, with a slight tremor in her voice, 'And what about you, Heather? What have you done since school?'

'Oh well . . .' Heather gave a quick little smile. 'It was all a bit grim, actually. I don't know if you know—but the reason I left Oxdowne was my father lost all his money.'

'How awful!' said Maggie. 'What—overnight?'

'Pretty much,' said Heather. 'Some investment went wrong. The stock markets or something. They couldn't afford school fees any more. Or the house. It was all a bit horrendous. My dad got really depressed over it, and my mum blamed him . . .' She broke off awkwardly. 'They split up.'

Maggie glanced at Candice for a reaction, but her face was averted. She had a cocktail stirrer in her hand and was stirring her drink, round and round.

'And what about you?' said Maggie cautiously to Heather.

'I kind of lost it, too, for a bit.' Heather gave another quick little smile. 'You know, one minute I was at a nice fee-paying school with all my friends. The next, we'd moved to a town where I didn't know anyone, and my parents were arguing all the time, and I went to a school where they all gave me a hard time for talking posh.' She sighed. 'I mean, looking back, it was quite a good comprehensive. I should have just stuck it out and gone on to college . . . but I didn't. I left as soon as I was sixteen.' She pushed back her thick, wavy hair. 'My dad was living in London by then so I moved in with him and got a job in a wine bar. And that was it, really. I never did a degree, or anything.'

'What a shame,' said Maggie. 'What would you have done, if you'd stayed on?'

'Oh, I don't know,' said Heather. She gave an embarrassed little laugh. 'Done something like you're doing, maybe. Become a journalist, or something. I started a creative writing course once, at Goldsmiths', but I had to give it up.' She looked round the bar and shrugged. 'I mean, I do like working here. But it's not really . . . Anyway.' She stood up. 'I'd better get going, or André will kill me. See you later!'

As she walked away, the three of them sat in silence, watching her. Then Maggie turned to Candice, and said carefully, 'She seems nice.'

Candice didn't reply. Maggie looked questioningly at Roxanne, who raised her eyebrows.

'Candice, what's wrong?' said Maggie. 'Is there some history between you and Heather?'

'Darling, speak to us,' said Roxanne.

Candice said nothing, but continued stirring her cocktail, faster and faster and faster, until the liquid threatened to spill over the sides of the glass. Then she looked up at her friends.

'It wasn't the stock markets,' she said in a flat voice. 'It wasn't the stock markets that ruined Frank Trelawney. It was my father.'

Heather Trelawney stood by the entrance to the kitchen, watching Candice Brewin's face through the crush of people. Gordon Brewin's daughter, large as life, sitting at the table with her friends. With her nice haircut and her good job, and money for cocktails every night. Oblivious of what suffering her father had caused. Unaware of anything except herself.

Because she'd come out all right, hadn't she? Of course she had. Good-Time Gordon had been very clever like that. He'd never used his own money. Only other people's. Other poor saps, too greedy to say no. Like her poor, reckless, stupid dad. At the thought, Heather's chin tightened and her hands gripped her silver tray harder.

'Heather!' It was André, the head waiter, calling from the bar. 'What are you doing? Customers waiting!'

'Coming!' called back Heather. She picked up her tray and walked smartly to the bar, never once taking her eyes off Candice Brewin.

'They called him Good-Time Gordon,' said Candice. 'He was there at every single party. Life and soul.' She took a gulp of her cocktail. 'And every school function. I used to think it was because he was proud of me. But all the time, he just wanted to pick up new contacts to do business with. Frank Trelawney wasn't the only one. He got to all our friends, all our neighbours.' Her hand tightened around her glass. 'They all started popping up after the funeral. Some had invested money with him, some had lent him money and he'd never paid it back . . . It was horrendous. These people were our friends. And we'd had no idea.'

Roxanne and Maggie glanced at each other.

'So how do you know Heather's father was involved?' said Maggie.

'I found out when we went through the paperwork,' said Candice blankly. 'My mother and I had to go into his study and sort out the mess. It was . . . just awful.'

'How did your mum take it?' asked Maggie curiously.

'Terribly,' said Candice. 'Well, you can imagine. He'd actually told some people he needed to borrow money from them because she was an alcoholic and he wanted to put her through rehab.'

Roxanne snorted with laughter, then said, 'Sorry.'

'I still can't talk to her about it,' said Candice. 'In fact, I think she's pretty much persuaded herself it never happened. If I even mention it, she gets all hysterical . . .'

'You've never even mentioned any of this before,' said Maggie.

'Yes, well,' said Candice shortly. 'I'm not exactly proud of it.'

She closed her eyes as unwanted memories of that dreadful time after his death came flooding back into her mind. It had been at the funeral that she'd first noticed something wrong. Friends and relatives, clumped in little groups, had stopped talking as soon as she came near. Everyone had seemed to be in on one big secret. As she'd passed one group, she'd heard the words, '*How* much?'

Then the visitors had started arriving, ostensibly to pay their condolences. But sooner or later the conversation had always turned to money. To the five or ten thousand pounds that Gordon had borrowed. To the investments that had been made. Even Mrs Stephens, their cleaning lady, had awkwardly brought up the subject of a hundred pounds, loaned some months ago and never repaid.

At the memory of the woman's embarrassed face, Candice felt her stomach contract with humiliation; with a hot, teenage guilt. She still felt as though she were somehow to blame. Even though she'd known nothing about it; even though there was nothing she could have done.

'And what about Frank Trelawney?' said Maggie.

'He was on a list of names in the study,' she said. 'He'd invested two hundred thousand pounds in some venture capital project which folded after a few months. At first I didn't know who Frank Trelawney was. It was just another name. But it seemed familiar . . . And then I suddenly remembered Heather Trelawney leaving school with no warning. It all made sense.' She bit her lip. 'I think that was the worst moment of all. Knowing that Heather had lost her place at school because of my father.'

'You can't just blame your father,' said Maggie gently. 'This Mr Trelawney must have known there was a certain risk.'

'I always used to wonder what happened to Heather,' said Candice, as though she hadn't heard. 'And now I know. Another life ruined.'

'Candice, don't beat yourself up about this,' said Maggie. 'It's not your fault. You didn't do anything!'

'I know,' said Candice. 'Logically, you're right. But it's not that easy.'

'Have another drink,' advised Roxanne. 'That'll cheer you up.'

'Good idea,' said Maggie, and drained her glass. She lifted her hand and, on the other side of the room, Heather nodded.

Candice stared at Heather as she bent down to pick up some empty glasses from a table and wipe it over, unaware she was being watched. As she stood up again, Heather gave a sudden yawn and rubbed her face with tiredness, and Candice felt her heart contract with emotion. She had to do something for this girl, she thought suddenly. She had to absolve her guilt for at least one of her father's crimes.

'Listen,' she said, as Heather began to approach the table. 'They haven't got a new editorial assistant for the *Londoner* yet, have they?'

'Not as far as I know,' said Maggie in surprise. 'Why?'

'Well, what about Heather?' said Candice. 'She'd be ideal. Wouldn't she?'

'Would she?' Maggie wrinkled her brow.

'She wants to be a journalist, she's done creative writing . . . she'd be perfect! Oh, go on, Maggie!' Candice looked up, to see Heather approaching. 'Heather, listen!'

'Do you want some more drinks?' said Heather.

'Yes,' said Candice. 'But . . . but not just that.' She looked at Maggie entreatingly. Maggie gave her a mock glare, then grinned.

'We were wondering, Heather,' she said, 'if you'd be interested in a job on the *Londoner*. Editorial assistant. It's pretty low-ranking, and the money's not great, but it's a start in journalism.'

'Are you serious?' said Heather. 'I'd love it!'

'Good,' said Maggie, and took a card from her bag. 'This is the address, but it won't be me processing the applications. The person you need to write to is Justin Vellis.' She wrote the name on the card and handed it to Heather. 'Just write a letter about yourself, and pop in a CV. OK?'

Candice stared at her in dismay.

'Great!' said Heather. 'And . . . thanks.'

'And now I suppose we'd better choose some more cocktails,' said Maggie cheerfully. 'It's a tough old life.'

When Heather had departed with their order, Maggie grinned at Candice and leaned back in her chair.

'There you are,' she said. 'Feel better now?' She frowned at Candice's expression. 'Candice, are you OK?'

'To be honest, no!' said Candice, trying to stay calm. 'I'm not! Is that all you're going to do? Give her the address?'

'What do you mean?' said Maggie in surprise. 'What's wrong?'

'I thought you were going to give her the job!'

'What, on the spot?' said Maggie. 'Candice, you must be joking.'

'Or an interview . . . or a personal recommendation, at least,' said Candice. 'If she just sends in her CV like everyone else, there's no way Justin will give her the job! He'll appoint some awful Oxford graduate.'

'Like himself,' put in Roxanne with a grin.

'Exactly! Maggie, you know Heather hasn't got a chance unless you recommend her. Especially if he knows she's anything to do with me!' Candice flushed slightly. It was only a few weeks since she had broken up with Justin, the features editor who was taking over from Maggie as acting editor. She still felt a little awkward, talking about him.

'But, Candice, I can't recommend her,' said Maggie simply. 'I don't know anything about her. And neither, let's face it, do you.'

Candice stared into her drink miserably, and Maggie sighed.

'Candice, I can understand how you feel, truly I can,' she said. 'But you can't just leap in and procure a job for some woman you hardly know, just because you feel sorry for her.'

'And what would be wrong with that?' said Candice with a sudden fierceness. 'What's wrong with giving people a boost every so often if they deserve it? You know, we three have had it very easy, compared to the rest of the world.' She gestured round the table. 'We've got good jobs, and happy lives, and we haven't the first idea what it's like to have nothing.'

'Heather doesn't have nothing,' said Maggie. 'She has good looks, she has a brain, she has a job, and she has every opportunity to go back to college if she wants to. It's not your job to sort her life out for her. OK?'

'OK,' said Candice after a pause.

'Good,' said Maggie. 'Lecture over.'

An hour later, Maggie's husband Giles arrived at the Manhattan Bar. He stood at the side of the room, peering through the throng—then spotted Maggie's face. She was clutching a cocktail, her cheeks were flushed pink and her head was thrown back in laughter. Giles smiled fondly at the sight and headed towards the table.

'Man alert,' he said cheerfully as he approached. 'Kindly cease all jokes about male genitals.'

'Giles!' said Maggie, with slight dismay. 'Is it time to go already?'

'We don't have to,' said Giles. 'I could stay for a drink or two.'

'No,' said Maggie after a pause. 'It's OK, let's go.'

It never quite worked when Giles joined the group. Not because the other two didn't like him—and not because he didn't make an effort. He was always genial and conversation flowed nicely. But it just wasn't the same. He wasn't one of them. Well—how could he be? thought Maggie. He wasn't a woman.

'I've got to go soon, anyway,' said Roxanne, draining her glass and putting her cigarettes away. 'I have someone to see.'

'Would that be Someone?' said Maggie with a deliberate emphasis.

'Possibly.' Roxanne smiled at her.

'I can't believe this is it!' said Candice, looking at Maggie. 'We won't see you again till you've had the baby!'

'Don't remind me!' said Maggie, flashing an over-cheerful smile.

She pushed back her chair and gratefully took the hand Giles offered. They all slowly made their way through the crowds to the coat-check, and surrendered their silver buttons.

'And don't think you're allowed to give up on the cocktail club,' said

Roxanne. 'We'll be round your bed in a month's time, toasting the babe.'

'It's a date,' said Maggie, and suddenly felt her eyes fill with easy tears. 'Oh God, I'm going to miss you guys.'

'We'll see you soon,' said Roxanne, and gave her a hug. 'Good luck, darling.'

'OK,' said Maggie, trying to smile. She suddenly felt as though she were saying goodbye to her friends for ever.

'Maggie doesn't need luck!' said Candice. 'She'll have that baby licked into shape in no time!'

'Hey, baby,' said Roxanne, addressing Maggie's stomach humorously. 'You are aware that your mother is the most organised woman in Western civilisation?' She pretended to listen to the bump. 'It says it wants to have someone else. Tough luck, kid.'

'And listen, Candice,' said Maggie. 'Don't let Justin lord it over you just because he's in charge for a few months. I know it's a difficult situation for you . . .'

'Don't worry,' said Candice at once. 'I can handle him.'

'Justin the bloody Wunderkind,' said Roxanne. 'You know, I'm glad we can all be rude about him now.'

'You always were rude about him,' pointed out Candice. 'Even when I was going out with him.'

'Well, he deserves it,' said Roxanne, unabashed. 'Anyone who comes to a cocktail bar and orders claret is obviously a waste of space.'

'Candice, they can't seem to find your coat,' said Giles. 'But here's yours, Roxanne, and yours, darling. I think we should get going, otherwise it'll be midnight before we get back.'

'Right, well,' said Maggie in a shaky voice. 'This is it.'

'We'll see each other soon,' said Candice. 'I'll come and visit.'

'And I'll come up to London.'

'You can bring the baby up for day-trips,' said Candice. 'They're supposed to be the latest accessory.'

'I know,' said Maggie, giving a little laugh. She leaned forward and hugged Candice. 'You take care.'

'And you,' said Candice. 'Good luck with . . . everything. Bye, Giles,' she added. 'Nice to see you.'

Giles opened the glass door of the bar, and after one final backwards glance, Maggie walked out into the cold night air. Roxanne and Candice watched silently through the glass as Giles took Maggie's arm and they disappeared down the dark street.

'Just think,' said Candice. 'In a few weeks, they won't be a couple any more. They'll be a family.'

'So they will,' said Roxanne. 'A happy little family, all together in their huge, fuck-off happy house.' Candice glanced at her.

'Are you OK?'

'Of course I'm OK!' said Roxanne. 'Just glad it isn't me! The very thought of stretch marks . . .' She gave a mock shudder then smiled. 'I've got to shoot off, I'm afraid. Do you mind?'

'Of course not,' said Candice. 'Have a good time.'

'I always have a good time,' said Roxanne, 'even if I'm having a terrible time. See you when I get back from Cyprus.' She kissed Candice briskly on each cheek and disappeared out of the door. Candice watched her hailing a taxi and jumping in; after a few seconds, the taxi zoomed off down the street.

Candice waited until it had disappeared, then, feeling like a naughty child, swivelled round to face the bar again. Her heart was thumping,

'I've found your coat!' came the voice of the coat-check lady. 'It had fallen off its hanger.'

'Thanks,' said Candice. 'But I've just got to   .' She swallowed. 'I'll be back in a moment.'

She hurried through the press of people, feeling light and determined. Maggie and Roxanne meant well, but they were wrong. They didn't understand. They couldn't see that this was the opportunity she'd unconsciously been waiting for ever since her father's death. This was her chance to make things right. It was like . . . a gift.

Heather was behind the bar, polishing a glass and laughing with one of the waiters. Fighting her way through the crowds, Candice made her way to the bar and waited patiently, not wanting to interrupt.

Eventually Heather looked up and saw her—and to Candice's surprise, a flash of hostility seemed to pass over her features. But it disappeared almost at once, and her face broke into a welcoming smile.

'What can I get you?' she said. 'Another cocktail?'

'No, I just wanted a word,' said Candice. 'About this job.'

'Oh yes?'

'If you like, I can introduce you to the publisher, Ralph Allsopp,' said Candice. 'No guarantees—but it might help your chances. Come to the office tomorrow at about ten.'

'Really?' Heather's face lit up. 'That would be wonderful!' She put down the glass she was polishing and took Candice's hands. 'Candice, this is really good of you. I don't know how to thank you.'

'Well, you know,' said Candice awkwardly. 'Old schoolfriends and all that . . .'

'Yes,' said Heather, and smiled sweetly. 'Old schoolfriends.'

Chapter Two

AS THEY REACHED THE MOTORWAY, it began to rain. Giles turned on Radio Three and a glorious soprano's voice filled the car. After a few notes, Maggie recognised the piece as 'Dove Sono' from The *Marriage of Figaro*. As the music soared over her, Maggie felt foolish tears coming to her eyes, in sympathy with the fictitious Countess. A good and beautiful wife, unloved by her philandering husband, sadly recalling moments of tenderness between them.

Maggie blinked a few times and took a deep breath. This was ridiculous. Everything was reducing her to tears at the moment.

'Did you have a good send-off?' asked Giles.

'Yes, lovely,' said Maggie. 'Heaps of presents. People are so generous.'

'And how did you leave it with Ralph?'

'I told him I'd call him after a few months.'

'I still think you should have been honest with them,' said Giles. 'I mean, you know you've no intention of going back to work.'

Maggie was silent. She and Giles had discussed at length whether she should return to work after the baby was born. On the one hand, she adored her job and felt that there were still things she wanted to achieve in her career. On the other, the image of leaving her baby behind and commuting to London every day seemed appalling. And after all, what was the point of living in a house in the country and never seeing it?

The fact that she had never actually wanted to move to the country was something that Maggie had almost managed to forget. Giles had been desperate for his future children to have the rough-and-tumble, fresh-air upbringing which he had enjoyed. 'London isn't healthy for children,' he had pronounced. And although Maggie had pointed out that the London streets were full of perfectly healthy children; that parks were safer places to ride bicycles than country lanes; that nature existed even in cities, Giles had still not been persuaded.

Then, when he'd started applying for the details of country houses, she'd found herself weakening. On a wonderfully sunny day in June, they'd gone to look at The Pines. The drive had crackled under the wheels of their car; the swimming pool had glinted in the sun, the lawns had been mowed in light and dark green stripes. After showing them round the house, the owners had poured them glasses of Pimm's and invited them to sit under the weeping willow, then tactfully moved away. And Giles had looked at Maggie and said, 'This could be ours, darling. This life could be ours.'

And now that life was theirs. Except it wasn't so much a life yet as a large house which Maggie still didn't feel she knew very well. On working days, she barely saw the place. At the weekends, they often went away, or up to London to see friends. But things would be different when the baby arrived, she told herself. The house would really become a home. Maggie put her hands on her bump and felt the squirming, intriguing movements beneath her skin. Then, with no warning, something hard jabbed into her ribs. A heel, perhaps, or a knee. It jabbed again and again, as though desperate to break out. Maggie closed her eyes. It could be any time now, her pregnancy handbook had advised her.

At the thought, her heart began to thump with a familiar panic, and she began quickly to think reassuring thoughts. Of course, she was prepared for the baby. She had a nursery full of nappies and cotton wool; tiny vests and blankets. The Moses basket was ready on its stand; the cot had been ordered from a department store. Everything was waiting.

But somehow she secretly still didn't feel quite ready to be a mother. She almost didn't feel *old* enough to be a mother. Which was ridiculous, she told herself firmly, bearing in mind she was thirty-two years old.

'You know, I can't believe it's really happening,' she said. 'Three weeks away. That's nothing! And I haven't been to any classes, or anything . . .'

'You don't need classes!' said Giles. 'You'll be great! The best mother a baby could have.'

Maggie bit her lip. 'I don't know. I just feel a bit . . . unprepared.'

'What's to prepare?'

'Well, you know. Labour, and everything.'

'One word,' said Giles firmly. 'Drugs.'

Maggie giggled. 'And afterwards. You know, looking after it. I've never even *held* a baby.'

'You'll be fantastic!' said Giles at once. 'Maggie, if anyone can look after a baby, you can. Come on.' He flashed a smile at her. 'Who was voted Editor of the Year?'

'I was,' she said, grinning proudly in spite of herself.

'Well then. And you'll be Mother of the Year, too.' He reached out and squeezed her hand, and Maggie squeezed gratefully back. Giles's optimism never failed to cheer her.

'Mum said she'd pop round tomorrow,' said Giles. 'Keep you company.'

'Oh good,' said Maggie. She thought of Giles's mother, Paddy—a thin, dark-haired woman who had, unaccountably, produced three huge, cheerful sons with thick, fair hair. Giles and his two brothers adored their mother—and it had been no coincidence that The Pines was in the next-door village to Giles's old family home. At first, Maggie had been slightly discomfited at the proximity of their new house to her in-laws. But, after all, her own parents were miles away, in Derbyshire, and it would be useful to have at least one set of grandparents around.

'She was saying, you'll have to get to know all the other young mums in the village,' said Giles.

'Are there many?'

'I think so. Sounds like one long round of coffee mornings.'

'Oh good!' said Maggie teasingly. 'So while you slave away in the City I can sip cappuccinos with all my chums.'

'Something like that.'

'Sounds better than commuting,' said Maggie. 'I should have done this years ago.' She closed her eyes and imagined herself in her kitchen, making coffee for a series of new, vibrant friends with cute babies dressed in designer clothes. Roxanne and Candice would come down from London and they would all drink Pimm's while the baby gurgled happily on a rug. They would look like something from a lifestyle magazine. In fact, maybe the *Londoner* would run a piece on them. *Former editor Maggie Phillips and her new take on rural bliss.* It was going to be a whole new life, she thought happily. A whole wonderful new life.

The brightly lit train bounced and rattled along the track, then came to an abrupt halt in a tunnel. The lights flickered, went off, then went on again. A group of partygoers began to sing 'Why are we waiting', and the woman across from Candice tried to catch her eye and tut. But Candice didn't see. She was staring at her reflection in the window opposite, as memories of her father rose painfully through her mind.

Good-Time Gordon, tall and handsome, always dressed in an immaculate navy blazer. He'd been a charming man, with vivid blue eyes and a firm handshake. Everyone who met him had admired him. Her friends had thought her lucky to have such a fun-loving father.

And then he'd died, and the horror had begun. Now Candice could not think of him without feeling sick, humiliated; hot with shame. He'd fooled everybody. Every word he'd ever uttered now seemed double-edged. Had he really loved her? Had he really loved her mother? The whole of his life had been a charade—so why not his feelings, too?

Hot tears began to well up in her eyes and she took a deep breath.

She didn't usually allow herself to think about her father. In the midst of those dreadful days full of pain and confusion, she'd walked into a hairdresser's and asked to have all her long hair cropped off. As the lengths of hair had fallen onto the floor, she'd felt as though her connections with her father were, in some way, being severed.

But of course, it wasn't as easy as that. She was still her father's daughter and she was still the beneficiary of all his shady dealings. Other people's money had paid for her clothes and her skiing trips and the little car she'd been given for her seventeenth birthday. The thought of it still made her feel sick with anger; with self-reproach. But how could she have known? She'd only been a child. And her father had managed to fool everybody. Until his car crash, halfway through her first year at university. His sudden, horrific, unexpected death.

Candice felt her face grow hot all over again. Despite everything, she still felt grief for her father. A searing, angry grief—not only for him, but for her innocence; her childhood. She grieved for the time when all she'd felt for her father was love and pride. Before everything had suddenly darkened and become coated in dishonesty.

After his death, there hadn't been nearly enough money left to pay everyone back. Most people had given up asking; a few had taken her mother to court. It had been several years before everyone was finally settled and silenced. But the damage had never been properly repaired. The consequences to people's lives could not be settled so quickly.

Candice's mother Diana had moved away to Devon, where no one had heard of Gordon Brewin. If Candice ever tried to bring up the subject of her father, Diana would refuse to talk about it. Several years after moving to Devon she had begun a relationship with a mild-mannered, elderly man named Kenneth—and he now acted as a protective buffer. He was always present when Candice visited, ensuring that conversation never ventured beyond the polite and inconsequential. And so Candice had given up trying to get her mother to confront the past. There was no point—and at least Diana had salvaged some happiness in her life. But she rarely visited her mother any more. The fact that Diana wouldn't admit the truth, even to her own daughter—slightly sickened Candice.

As a result, she had found herself shouldering the entire burden of memories herself. She would not allow herself to forget or deny. And so she had learned to live with a constant guilt; a constant, angry shame. It had mellowed a little since those first nightmare years; she had learned to put it to the back of her mind and get on with her life. But the guilt had never quite left her.

Tonight, however, she felt as though she'd turned a corner. Perhaps she couldn't undo what her father had done. Perhaps she couldn't repay everyone. But she could repay Heather Trelawney—if not in money, then in help and friendship. Helping Heather as much as she possibly could would be her own private atonement.

As she got off the tube at Highbury and Islington, she felt light and hopeful. She briskly walked the few streets to the Victorian house where she had lived for the last two years, let herself in at the front door and bounded up the flight of stairs to her first-floor flat.

'Hey, Candice.' A voice interrupted her as she reached for her Yale key, and she turned round. It was Ed Armitage, who lived in the flat opposite. He was standing in the doorway of his flat, wearing ancient jeans and eating a Big Mac. 'I've got that Sellotape, if you want it back.'

'Oh,' said Candice. 'Thanks.'

'Give me a sec.' He disappeared into his flat, and Candice leaned against her own front door, waiting. She didn't want to open her door and find him inviting himself in for a drink. Tonight, to be honest, she wasn't in the mood for Ed.

Ed had lived opposite Candice for as long as she'd lived there. He was a corporate lawyer at a huge City law firm, earned unfeasibly large amounts of money, and worked unfeasibly long hours. The very thought of it made Candice feel sick. It was pure greed that drove him so hard, she thought. Nothing but greed.

'Here you are,' said Ed, reappearing. He handed her the roll of tape and took a bite of his Big Mac. 'Want some?'

'No, thanks,' said Candice politely.

'Not healthy enough?' said Ed, leaning against the banisters. His dark eyes glinted at her as though he were enjoying his own private joke. 'What do you eat, then? Quiche?'

'Yes,' said Candice. 'I suppose I eat quiche.' Why couldn't Ed just make polite small talk like everyone else? she thought. Why did he always have to look at her with those glinting eyes, waiting for an answer—as though she were about to reveal something fascinating? It was impossible to relax while talking to him. No idle comment could go unchallenged.

'Quiche is cholesterol city. You're better off with one of these.' He gestured to his hamburger, and a piece of slimy lettuce fell onto the floor. To Candice's horror, he picked it up, and popped it in his mouth.

'See?' he said as he stood up. 'Salad.'

Candice rolled her eyes. Really, she felt quite sorry for Ed. He had no life outside the office. No friends, no girlfriend, no furniture even. She had once popped across to his flat for a drink in order to be neighbourly—and discovered that Ed possessed only one ancient leather chair, a wide-screen TV and a pile of empty pizza boxes.

'So, have you been sacked or something?' she said sarcastically. 'I mean, it's only ten o'clock. Shouldn't you be hammering out some deal somewhere?'

'Since you ask, I'll be on gardening leave as from next week,' said Ed.

'What?' Candice looked at him uncomprehendingly.

'New job,' said Ed. 'So I get to spend three months doing sod-all. It's in my contract.'

'Three months?' Candice wrinkled her brow. 'But why?'

'Why do you think?' Ed grinned complacently. 'Because I'm bloody important, that's why. I know too many little secrets.'

'Are you serious?' Candice stared at him. 'So you don't get paid for three months?' Ed's face creased in a laugh.

'Of course I get paid! These guys love me! They're paying me more to do nothing than I used to get working my arse off.'

'But that's immoral!' said Candice. 'Think of all the people in the world desperate for a job. And you're getting paid to sit around.'

'That's the world,' said Ed. 'Like it or slit your wrists.'

'Or try to change it,' said Candice.

'So you say,' said Ed. 'But then, we can't all be as saintly as you, Candice, can we?'

Candice stared furiously at him. How did Ed always manage to wind her up so successfully? 'I've got to go,' she said abruptly.

'By the way, your man's in there,' said Ed. 'Ex-man. Whatever.'

'Justin?' Candice stared at him. 'Justin's in the flat?'

'I saw him letting himself in earlier,' said Ed, and raised his eyebrows. 'Are you two back together again?'

'No!' said Candice.

'Now, that's a shame,' said Ed. 'He was a really fun guy.' Candice gave him a sharp look. On the few occasions that Ed and Justin had met, it had been clear that the two had absolutely nothing in common.

'Well, anyway,' she said abruptly, 'I'll see you around.'

'Sure,' said Ed, shrugging, and disappeared back into his flat.

Candice took a deep breath, then opened her front door, her head whirling. What was Justin doing there? And more to the point, what the hell was he still doing with a key to her flat?

'Hi?' she called. 'Justin?'

'Candice.' Justin appeared at the end of the corridor. He was dressed, as ever, in a smart suit which verged on trendy, and holding a drink. His dark curly hair was neatly glossed back and his dark eyes glowed in the lamplight; he looked to Candice like an actor playing the role of a moody intellectual.

'I apologise for dropping in unannounced,' he said.

'Glad to see you've made yourself at home,' said Candice.

'I expected you back earlier,' said Justin, in a slightly resentful tone. 'I won't be long—I just thought we should have a little chat.'

'What about?'

Justin said nothing, but solemnly ushered her into the sitting room. Candice felt herself prickling with annoyance. Justin had a unique ability to make it seem as though he was always in the right and everyone else was in the wrong.

When they'd first met, of course, he had dazzled her. He had arrived at the *Londoner* fresh from a year's experience on the *New York Times*, with the reputation of a huge intellect and a barrage of impressive connections. When he had asked her out for a drink she had felt flattered. She had drunk copious quantities of wine and gazed into his dark eyes, and had listened admiringly to his views—half persuaded by everything he said, even when she would normally have disagreed. After a few weeks he had begun to stay the night at her flat every so often. Then his flat-share in Pimlico had fallen apart and he had moved in with her.

It was really then that things had gone wrong, thought Candice. Her hazy admiration had melted away as she saw him in close proximity—taking three times longer than herself to get ready in the mornings; claiming proudly that he couldn't cook and didn't intend to learn; expecting the bathroom to be clean but never once cleaning it himself. She had come to realise the full extent of his vanity and the strength of his arrogance. For in his own mind, Justin was destined for great things. His ambition was almost frightening in its strength; it drove him like a steamroller, flattening everything else in his life.

Even now, Candice couldn't be sure which had been hurt most when she had ended the relationship—his feelings or his pride? He had almost seemed more sorrowful for her than anything else, as though she'd made a foolish mistake which he knew she would soon regret. However, so far she hadn't regretted her decision for an instant.

'So,' she said as they sat down. 'What do you want?'

Justin gave her a tiny smile. 'I wanted to come and see you,' he said, 'to make sure you're absolutely OK about tomorrow.'

'Tomorrow?' said Candice blankly. Justin smiled at her again.

'Tomorrow, as you know, is the day I take over as acting editor of the *Londoner*. Effectively, I'll be your boss. I wouldn't want any . . . problems to arise between us.'

Candice stared at him. 'Problems?'

'I realise it may be a rather difficult time for you,' said Justin smoothly. 'My promotion coinciding with the break-up of our relation-ship. I wouldn't want you feeling at all vulnerable.'

'Vulnerable?' said Candice in astonishment. 'Justin, it was me who ended our relationship! I'm fine about it.'

'If that's the way you want to see it,' said Justin kindly. 'Just as long as there are no bad feelings.'

'I can't guarantee that,' muttered Candice.

She watched as Justin swirled his glass of whisky. He looked as though he were practising for a television ad, she thought. Or a *Panorama* profile: 'Justin Vellis: the genius at home'. A giggle rose through her, and she clamped her lips together.

'Well, I mustn't keep you,' said Justin at last, and stood up. 'See you tomorrow.'

'Can't wait,' said Candice, pulling a face behind his back. As they reached the door she paused. 'By the way,' she said casually, 'do you know if they've appointed a new editorial assistant yet?'

'No, they haven't,' said Justin, frowning. 'In fact, I'm a bit pissed off about that. Maggie's done absolutely nothing about it. Just disappears off into domestic bliss and leaves me with two hundred CVs to read.'

'Oh dear, poor you,' said Candice innocently. 'Still, never mind. I'm sure someone'll turn up.'

Roxanne took another sip of her drink and calmly turned the page of her paperback. He had said nine thirty. It was now ten past ten. She had been sitting in this hotel bar for forty minutes, ordering Bloody Marys and sipping them slowly and feeling her heart jump every time anyone entered the bar. Around her, couples and groups were murmuring over their drinks; in the corner, an elderly man in a white tuxedo was singing 'Someone to watch over me'.

How many hours of her life had she spent like this? Waiting for a man who was often late and half the time didn't show up at all? There was always an excuse, of course. Another crisis at work, perhaps. An unfore-seen encounter with a member of his family. Once, she'd been sitting in a London restaurant, waiting for their third anniversary lunch—only to see him entering with his wife. He'd glanced over at her with a helpless expression, and she'd been forced to watch as he and his wife were ush-ered to a table. To watch, with pain eating like acid at her heart, as his wife sat frowning at him, obviously bored by his company.

He'd later told her that Cynthia had bumped into him on the street and insisted on joining him for lunch. The next weekend, to make up, he'd cancelled everything else and taken Roxanne to Venice.

Roxanne closed her eyes. That weekend had been an intoxication of happiness. She'd known a pure single-minded joy which she'd never since experienced. They had walked hand in hand through dusty ancient squares; along canals glinting in the sunshine; over crumbling bridges. They'd drunk Prosecco in Piazza San Marco, listening to Strauss waltzes. They'd made love in the old-fashioned wooden bed at their hotel, then sat on their balcony watching the gondolas ride past.

They hadn't mentioned his wife or family once. For that weekend, four human beings simply hadn't existed. Gone, in a puff of smoke.

Roxanne opened her eyes. She no longer allowed herself to think about his family. Down that road lay pain; self-reproach; indecision. Down that road lay the knowledge that she would never have him to herself. That she was wasting the best years of her life on a man who belonged to another woman. The mother of his children.

A familiar pain seared Roxanne's heart and she drained her Bloody Mary, placed a twenty in the leather folder containing her bill and stood up in an unhurried motion, her face nonchalant. She strode on out of the bar and through the hotel foyer.

'Taxi, madam?' said the doorman as she emerged into the cold night air.

'Thanks,' said Roxanne, and forced herself to smile brightly, hold her head high. So she'd been stood up, she told herself firmly. So what was new? It had happened before and it would happen again. That was the deal when the love of your life was a married man.

Candice sat in the office of Ralph Allsopp, publisher of the *Londoner*, biting her nails and wondering where he was. She had hesitantly knocked on his door that morning, praying that he was in. When he'd opened the door, holding a phone to his ear, and gestured her in, she'd felt a spurt of relief. First hurdle over.

But before she'd been able to launch into her little speech, he'd put the phone down, said, 'Stay there', and disappeared out of the room. That was about ten minutes ago. Now Candice was wondering whether she should have got up and followed him. That was the sort of gumption Ralph Allsopp liked in his staff. He admired dynamic, energetic people, prepared to work hard and take risks. The worst crime a member of his staff could possibly commit was to be feeble.

'Feeble!' would come his roaring voice from the top floor. 'Bloody feeble!' And all over the building, people would pull their chairs in, stop chatting about the weekend, and begin typing.

But those who made the grade, Ralph treated with the utmost respect. As a result, staff tended to join Allsopp Publications and stay for years. Even those who left to become freelance or pursue other careers would keep in touch; pop in for a drink and float their latest ideas past Ralph's enthusiastic ear. It was a sociable, relaxed company. Candice had been there five years and had never considered leaving.

She leaned back in her chair now and looked idly around Ralph's desk—legendary for its untidiness. Two wooden in-trays overflowed with letters and memos; a telephone was perched on a pile of books. As she looked at it, the phone began to ring. She hesitated for a second, wondering if she ought to answer someone else's phone—then imagined Ralph's reaction if he came in to see her just sitting there, letting it ring. 'What's wrong, girl?' he'd roar. 'Afraid it'll bite you?'

She picked up the receiver. 'Hello,' she said. 'Ralph Allsopp's office.'

'Is Mr Allsopp there?' enquired a female voice.

'I'm afraid not,' said Candice. 'May I take a message?'

There was a pause, then the voice said, 'This is Mr Davies's assistant, Mary, calling from the Charing Cross Hospital. Please could you tell Mr Allsopp that Mr Davies is unfortunately unable to make the two o'clock appointment, and wondered if three would be convenient instead.'

'Right,' said Candice, scribbling on a piece of paper. 'OK. I'll tell him.'

She put the phone down and looked curiously at the message.

'So! My dear girl.' Ralph's breezy voice interrupted her, and she gave a startled jump. 'What can I do for you? Here to complain about your new editor already? Or is it something else?'

Candice laughed. 'Something else.'

She watched as he made his way round to the other side of the desk, and thought again what an attractive man he must have been when he was younger. He was tall—at least six foot three—with dishevelled greying hair and intelligent, gleaming eyes. He must be in his fifties now, she guessed—but still exuded a relentless, almost frightening energy.

'You just got this message,' she said, handing him the bit of paper.

'Ah,' said Ralph, scanning it expressionlessly. 'Thank you.'

Candice opened her mouth to ask if he was all right—then closed it again. It wasn't her place to start enquiring about her boss's health. She had intercepted a private call; it was nothing to do with her.

'I wanted to see you,' she said instead, 'about the editorial assistant's job on the *Londoner*.'

'Oh yes?' said Ralph, leaning back in his chair.

'Yes,' said Candice, garnering all her courage. 'The thing is, I know somebody who I think would fit the bill.'

'Really?' said Ralph. 'Well, then, invite him to apply.'

'It's a girl,' said Candice. 'And the thing is, I don't think her CV is that spectacular. But I know she's talented. I know she can write. And she's bright, and enthusiastic . . .'

'I'm glad to hear it,' said Ralph mildly. 'But you know, Justin's the one you should be talking to.'

'I know,' said Candice. 'I know he is. But—' She broke off, and Ralph's eyes narrowed.

'Now, look,' he said, leaning forward. 'Is there going to be trouble between you two? I'm quite aware of the situation between you, and if it's going to cause problems . . .'

'It's not that!' said Candice at once. 'It's just that he's very busy. It's his first day, and I don't want to bother him. He's got enough on his plate. In fact . . .' She felt her fingers mesh tightly together in her lap. 'In fact, he was complaining yesterday about having to read through all the applications. And after all, he is only *acting* editor . . . So I thought perhaps—'

'What?'

'I thought perhaps you could interview this girl yourself?' Candice looked entreatingly at Ralph. 'She's downstairs in reception.'

'She's *where*?'

'In reception,' said Candice falteringly. 'She's just waiting—in case you say yes.'

Ralph stared at her, an incredulous look on his face. Then suddenly his face broke into a laugh. 'Send her up,' he said. 'Since you've dragged her all this way, let's give the poor girl a chance.'

'Thanks,' said Candice. 'Honestly, I'm sure she'll be—' Ralph raised a hand to stop her.

'Send her up,' he said. 'And we'll see.'

Maggie Phillips sat alone in her magnificent Smallbone kitchen, sipping coffee and staring at the table and wondering what to do next. She had woken that morning at the usual early hour and had watched as Giles got dressed, ready for his commute into the City.

'Now, you just take it easy,' he'd said, briskly knotting his tie. 'I'll try to be home by seven.'

'OK,' Maggie had said, grinning up at him. 'Give the pollution my love, won't you.'

'That's right, rub it in,' he'd retorted. 'You bloody ladies of leisure.'

As she'd heard the front door slam, she'd felt a delicious feeling of freedom spread through her body. No work, she'd thought to herself. No work! She could do what she liked.

She'd come downstairs and made herself some breakfast and eaten it, reading the paper and admiring the garden out of the window. That had taken her until eight thirty. Then she'd gone back upstairs, run a bath and lain in it for what seemed like at least an hour. When she emerged, she discovered she'd been in there for twenty minutes.

Now it was nine thirty. The day hadn't even begun yet, but she felt as though she'd been sitting at her kitchen table for an eternity. How was it that time—such a precious, slipping-away commodity in London—seemed here to pass so slowly?

Maggie closed her eyes, took another sip of coffee and idly reached for her pregnancy handbook. 'At this point the pains will become stronger,' she found herself reading. 'Try not to panic. Your partner will be able to offer support and encouragement.' Hastily she closed the book and pushed it behind the breadbin, where she couldn't see it. She poured herself another cup of coffee. At that moment, the doorbell rang. Maggie heaved herself out of her chair and walked through the hall to the front door. There on the front step was her mother-in-law, dressed in a Puffa jacket, a stripy shirt and a blue corduroy skirt, straight to the knee.

'Hello, Maggie!' she said. 'Not too early, am I?'

'No!' said Maggie, half laughing. 'Not at all. Giles said you might pop round.' She leaned forward and awkwardly kissed Paddy.

Although she had been married to Giles for four years, she still did not feel she had got to know Paddy very well. They had never once sat down for a good chat—principally because Paddy never seemed to sit down at all. She was a thin, energetic woman, always on the move. Always cooking, gardening, running someone to the station or organising a collection.

She smiled and handed Maggie a cake tin. 'A few scones,' she said. 'Some raisin, some cheese.'

'Oh, Paddy!' said Maggie, feeling touched. 'You shouldn't have.'

'It's no trouble,' said Paddy. 'I'll give you the recipe, if you like. They're terribly easy to rustle up. Giles always used to love them.'

'Right,' said Maggie after a pause, remembering her one disastrous attempt to make a cake for Giles's birthday. 'That would be great!'

'And I've brought someone to see you,' said Paddy. 'Thought you'd like to meet another young mum from the village.'

'Oh,' said Maggie in surprise. 'How nice!'

Paddy beckoned forward a girl in jeans and a pink jersey, holding a baby and clutching a toddler by the hand.

'Here you are!' she said proudly. 'Maggie, meet Wendy.'

As Candice tripped down the stairs to reception she felt elated with her success. Powerful, almost. It just showed what could be achieved with a little bit of initiative. She arrived at the foyer and walked quickly to the chairs where Heather was sitting, dressed in a neat black suit.

'He said yes!' she said, unable to conceal her triumph. 'He's going to see you!'

'Really?' Heather's eyes lit up. 'What, now?'

'Right now! I told you, he's always willing to give people chances.' Candice grinned with excitement. 'All you've got to do is remember everything I told you. Lots of enthusiasm. Lots of drive.'

'OK.' Heather tugged nervously at her skirt. 'Do I look all right?'

'You look brilliant,' said Candice. 'And one more thing. Ralph is sure to ask if you've brought an example of your writing.'

'What?' said Heather in alarm. 'But I—'

'Give him this,' said Candice, handing a piece of paper to Heather.

'What?' Heather gazed at it incredulously. 'What is it?'

'It's a short piece I wrote a few months ago,' said Candice. 'On how ghastly London transport is in summer. It was never used in the magazine, and the only other person who read it was Maggie.' She lowered her voice. 'And now it's yours. Look—I've put your by-line at the top.'

'"London's Burning",' read Heather slowly. '"By Heather Trelawney."' She looked up, eyes dancing. 'I don't believe it! This is wonderful!'

'You'd better read it over quickly before you go in,' said Candice. 'He might ask you about it.'

'Candice . . . this is so good of you,' said Heather. 'I don't know how I can repay you.'

'Don't be silly,' said Candice at once. 'It's a pleasure.'

'But you're being so kind to me. Why are you being so kind to me?' Heather's grey eyes met Candice's with a sudden intensity, and Candice felt her stomach give a secret guilty flip. She stared back at Heather and, for a heightened instant, considered telling Heather everything.

Then, almost as she was opening her mouth, she realised what a mistake it would be. What an embarrassing situation she would put Heather—and herself—in by saying anything. It might make her feel better but to unburden herself would be selfish. Heather must never find out that her motives were anything but genuine friendship.

'It's nothing,' she said quickly. 'You'd better go up. Ralph's waiting.'

Paddy had insisted on making the coffee, leaving Maggie alone with Wendy. Feeling suddenly a little nervous, she ushered Wendy into the sitting room and gestured to the sofa.

'Do sit down,' she said. 'Have you . . . lived in the village long?'

'A couple of years,' said Wendy, dumping her huge holdall on the floor and sitting down on Maggie's cream sofa.

'And . . . do you like living here?'

'S'all right, I suppose. Jake, leave that alone!'

Maggie looked up and, with a spasm of horror, saw Wendy's toddler reaching up towards the blue Venetian glass bowl Roxanne had given them as a wedding present.

'Oh gosh,' she said, getting to her feet. 'I'll just . . . move that, shall I?' She reached the glass bowl just as Jake's sticky fingers closed around it. 'Thanks,' she said politely to the toddler and quickly withdrew the bowl from his grasp and placed it on top of the tallboy.

'They're monsters at this age,' said Wendy. 'When are you due?'

'Three weeks,' said Maggie, sitting back down. 'Not long now!'

'You might be late,' said Wendy.

'Yes,' said Maggie after a pause. 'I suppose I might.'

Wendy gestured to the baby on her lap. 'I was two weeks late with this one. They had to induce me in the end.'

'Oh,' said Maggie. 'Still—'

'Then he got stuck,' said Wendy. 'His heartbeat started to fall and they had to use forceps.' She met Maggie's eye. 'Twenty-nine stitches.'

'Dear God,' said Maggie. 'You're joking.' Suddenly she thought she might faint. She took a deep breath and forced herself to smile at Wendy. Get off the subject of childbirth, she thought. Anything else at all. 'So—do you . . . work at all?'

'No,' said Wendy, staring at her blankly. 'Jake! Get off that!' Maggie turned, to see Jake balancing precariously on the piano stool. He gave his mother a murderous stare and began to bang on the piano keys.

'Here we are!' Paddy came into the room, carrying a tray. 'I opened these rather nice almond biscuits, Maggie. Is that all right?'

'Absolutely,' said Maggie.

'Only I know what it's like when you've planned all your meals in advance, and then someone else comes and disrupts your store cupboard.' She laughed, and Maggie smiled feebly back. She suspected that Paddy's idea of a store cupboard and her own were somewhat different.

'I've got some squash for Jake somewhere,' said Wendy. Her voice suddenly rose. 'Jake, pack it in or you won't get a drink!' She deposited the baby on the floor and reached for her holdall.

'What a pet!' said Paddy, looking at the baby wriggling on the floor. 'Maggie, why don't you hold him for a bit?' Maggie stiffened in horror.

'I don't think—'

'Here you are!' said Paddy, picking the baby up and putting him in Maggie's awkward arms. 'Isn't he a poppet?'

Maggie stared down at the baby in her arms. What was wrong with her? She felt nothing towards this baby except distaste. It was ugly, it smelt of stale milk and it was dressed in a hideous pastel Babygro. The baby opened his blue eyes and looked at her, and she gazed down, trying to warm to him. He began to squirm and chirrup, and she looked up in alarm.

'He might need to burp,' said Wendy. 'Hold him upright.'

'OK,' said Maggie. With tense, awkward hands, she shifted the baby round and lifted him up. He screwed up his face and for an awful moment she thought he was going to scream. Then his mouth opened, and a cascade of warm regurgitated milk streamed onto her jersey.

'Oh my God!' said Maggie in horror. 'He's thrown up on me!'

'Oh,' said Wendy dispassionately. 'Sorry about that. Give him to me.'

'Never mind,' said Paddy briskly, handing Maggie a muslin cloth. 'You'll have to get used to this kind of thing, Maggie! Won't she, Wendy?'

'Oh yeah,' said Wendy. 'You just wait!'

Maggie looked up from wiping her jersey to see Paddy and Wendy both looking complacently at her. *We've got you*, their eyes seemed to say. Inside, she began to shiver.

'Wanta do a poo,' Jake announced, wandering over to Wendy's side.

'Good boy,' she said. 'Just let me get the potty out.'

'Dear God, no!' cried Maggie, getting to her feet. 'I mean—I'll make some more coffee, shall I?'

In the kitchen she flicked on the kettle and sank into a chair, shaking. She didn't know whether to laugh or cry. Was this really what motherhood was all about? And if so, what the hell had she done? She closed her eyes and thought of her office at the *Londoner*. Her organised, civilised office. She hesitated, glancing at the door—then picked up the phone and quickly dialled a number.

'Hello?' As she heard Candice's voice, Maggie exhaled with relief. Just hearing those friendly, familiar tones made her relax.

'Hi, Candice! It's Maggie.'

'Maggie!' exclaimed Candice in surprise. 'How's it going? Are you all right?'

'Oh, I'm fine,' said Maggie. 'You know, lady of leisure . . .'

'I suppose you're still in bed, you lucky cow.'

'Actually,' said Maggie gaily, 'I'm hosting a coffee morning. I have a real-live Stepford mum in my living room.' Candice laughed, and Maggie felt a warm glow of pleasure steal over her. Thank God for friends, she thought. Suddenly the situation seemed funny. 'You won't *believe* what happened just now,' she added, lowering her voice. 'I'm sitting on the sofa, holding this pig-ugly baby, and the next minute—'

'Actually, Maggie,' interrupted Candice, 'I'm really sorry, but I can't chat. Justin's holding some stupid meeting and we've all got to go.'

'Oh,' said Maggie, feeling a stab of disappointment. 'Well . . . OK.'

'But we'll talk later, I promise.'

'Fine!' said Maggie brightly. 'It doesn't matter at all. I was just calling on the off chance. Have a good meeting.'

'I doubt that. Oh, but before I go, there's something I must tell you!' Candice's voice grew quieter. 'You remember that girl, Heather, we saw last night? The cocktail waitress?'

'Yes,' said Maggie. 'Of course I do.'

'Well, I introduced her to Ralph,' said Candice. 'And he was so impressed, he offered her the job on the spot. She's starting as editorial assistant next week!'

'Really?' said Maggie in astonishment. 'How extraordinary!'

'Yes,' said Candice, and cleared her throat. 'Well, it turns out she's . . . she's very good at writing. Ralph was really impressed with her work. So he's decided to give her a chance.'

'Typical Ralph,' said Maggie. 'Well, that's great.'

'Isn't it fantastic? I can't tell you what this means to me. It's as though I'm finally making amends for what my father did.'

'Then I'm really glad for you,' said Maggie more warmly. 'I hope it all works out well.'

'Oh, it will,' said Candice. 'Heather's a really nice girl. In fact, we're having lunch today, to celebrate.'

'Right,' said Maggie wistfully. 'Well, have fun.'

'We'll toast you. Look, Mags, I've got to run. Talk soon.' And the phone went dead.

Maggie stared at the receiver for a moment, then slowly replaced it. Already, within twenty-four hours, office life had moved on without her. But what did she expect? She gave a sigh and looked up, to see Paddy standing in the doorway, watching her with a curious expression.

'Oh,' said Maggie guiltily. 'I was just talking to an old colleague about a . . . a work matter. Is Wendy all right?'

'She's upstairs, changing the baby's nappy,' said Paddy. 'So I thought I'd give you a hand with the coffee.'

Paddy went to the sink, turned on the tap, then turned round and smiled pleasantly.

'You know, you mustn't cling onto your old life, Maggie.'

'What?' said Maggie in disbelief. 'I'm not!'

'You'll soon find you put down roots here. You'll get to know some other young families. But it does require a bit of effort. It's a different way of life down here.' Paddy gave a tight little smile. 'After a while, you may find you have less in common with some of your London friends.'

'Possibly,' Maggie said, smiling back at Paddy. 'But I'll make every effort to keep in touch with my old friends. There's a threesome of us who always meet up for cocktails. I'll certainly carry on seeing them.'

'Cocktails,' said Paddy, giving a short laugh. 'How glamorous.'

Maggie felt a sudden stab of resentment. What business of hers was it what kind of life she led? 'Yes, cocktails,' she said, and smiled sweetly at Paddy. 'My own personal favourite is Sex on the Beach. Remind me to give you the recipe some time.'

Chapter Three

THE DOORBELL RANG and Candice jumped, despite the fact that she'd been sitting still on the sofa, waiting for Heather's arrival, for a good twenty minutes. She nervously headed towards the front door. As she opened it, she gasped in surprise, then laughed. All she could see was a huge bouquet of flowers. Yellow roses, carnations and freesias nestling in dark greenery, wrapped in gold-embossed cellophane.

'These are for you,' came Heather's voice from behind the bouquet.

'This is so kind of you!' said Candice, taking the bouquet from Heather and giving her a hug. 'You really shouldn't have.'

'Yes I should!' said Heather. Her eyes met Candice's earnestly. 'Candice, look at everything you're doing for me. A job, a place to stay . . .'

'Well, you know,' said Candice awkwardly, 'I do have two bedrooms. And if your other place was grim . . .'

It had been purely by chance that, during their lunch together, Heather had happened to start talking about the flat where she lived. As she had talked, making light of its awfulness, Candice had suddenly hit on the idea of asking Heather to move in with her—and to her delight, Heather had agreed on the spot.

'It was like a hovel,' said Heather. 'Six to a room. Utterly sordid. But this place . . .' She put down her suitcases and walked slowly into the flat. 'Is this all yours?'

'Yes,' said Candice. 'At least, I had a flatmate when I first moved in, but she moved out, and I never got round to—'

'It's a palace!' interrupted Heather. 'Candice, it's beautiful!'

'Thanks,' said Candice, flushing in pleasure. 'I . . . well, I like it.'

She was secretly rather proud of her attempts at home decoration. She'd spent a long time the previous summer stripping down the brown swirly wallpaper left by the previous occupant of the flat and covering the walls in a chalky yellow paint.

'Look—the flowers I brought go perfectly with your walls,' said Heather. 'That's a good omen, don't you think?'

'Absolutely!' said Candice. 'Well, let's get your luggage in and you can see your room.'

She picked up one of Heather's cases and hefted it down the hall, then opened the first bedroom door.

'Wow,' breathed Heather behind her. It was a large room, decorated simply, with lavender walls and thick cream-coloured curtains. In the corner was a huge, empty oak armoire; on the night-stand beside the double bed was a pile of glossy magazines.

'This is fantastic!' said Heather. 'I can't believe this place.' She looked round. 'What's your room like? Is it this door?'

'It's . . . fine,' said Candice. 'Honestly . . .'

But Heather was too quick for her. She had already opened the door, to reveal a much smaller room, furnished with a single bed and a cheap pine wardrobe.

'Is this yours?' she said, then looked back at the lavender-painted room. 'That one's yours, isn't it?' she said in surprise. 'You've given me your room!'

She seemed astonished—almost amused—and Candice felt herself flush with embarrassment. She had felt so proud of her little gesture but now, looking at Heather's face, she realised it had been a mistake. Heather would, of course, insist on swapping back. The whole incident would bring an awkwardness to their arrangement.

'I just thought you'd want your own space,' she said, feeling foolish. 'I know what it's like, moving into someone else's home—sometimes you need to get away. So I thought I'd give you the bigger room.'

'I see,' said Heather. 'Well—if you're quite sure.' She beamed at Candice. 'It's very good of you. I'll love being in here.'

'Oh,' said Candice, half relieved, half discomfited. 'Right. Well . . . good. I'll leave you to unpack, then.'

41

'Don't be silly!' said Heather. 'I'll unpack later. Let's have a drink first.' She reached into her holdall. 'I brought some champagne.'

'Flowers *and* champagne!' Candice laughed. 'Heather, this is too much.'

'I always drink champagne on special occasions,' said Heather. 'And this occasion is very special indeed. Don't you agree?'

As Candice popped the champagne in the kitchen, she could hear the wooden floorboards of the sitting room creaking slightly as Heather moved about. She filled two champagne flutes then took them into the sitting room. Heather was standing by the mantelpiece gazing up at a framed photograph. As she saw her, Candice's heart began to thump. Why hadn't she put that photograph away? How could she have been so stupid?

'Here,' she said, handing Heather a glass of champagne. 'Here's to us.'

'To us,' echoed Heather, and took a sip. Then she turned back to the mantelpiece, picked up the photograph and looked at it.

'This is you, isn't it?' said Heather. 'How old were you?'

'About eleven,' said Candice, forcing a smile.

'And are these your parents?'

'Yes,' said Candice, trying to keep her voice casual. 'That's my mother, and—' she swallowed '—and that's my father. He died a while back.'

'Oh, I'm sorry,' said Heather. 'He was a handsome man, wasn't he?' She smiled. 'I bet he spoiled you rotten when you were a kid.'

'Yes,' said Candice, and attempted a laugh. 'Well—you know what fathers are like . . .'

'Absolutely,' said Heather. She gave the photograph one last look, then replaced it on the mantelpiece. 'Oh, this is going to be fun,' she said suddenly. She put her arm affectionately round Candice's waist. 'The two of us, living together. It's going to be such fun!'

At midnight that night, after a four-course dinner and more than her fair share of a bottle of divine Chablis, Roxanne arrived back at her suite at the Aphrodite Bay Hotel, to find her bed turned down, the lights dimmed and a message light blinking on her telephone. Kicking off her shoes, she sat down on the bed and pressed the message button.

'Hi, Roxanne? It's Maggie. Hope you're having a good time, you lucky cow—and give me a call some time.' Roxanne grinned and was about to pick up the phone, when the machine beeped again, indicating a second message.

'No, you dope, I haven't had the baby,' came Maggie's voice again. 'This is something else. Ciao.' Roxanne reached for the phone and pressed three digits.

'Hello, Nico?' she said as the phone was answered. 'I'll be down in a minute. I just have to make a quick call.' She pointed her toes, admiring her tan against her pink-polished toenails. 'Yes, order me a Brandy Alexander. See you in a moment.' She dialled Maggie's number.

'Hello?' said a sleepy voice.

'Giles!' said Roxanne, and guiltily looked at her watch. 'Oh God, it's late, isn't it? Sorry! I didn't think. It's Roxanne. Were you asleep?'

'Roxanne,' said Giles blearily. 'Hi. Where are you?'

'Give it to me!' Roxanne could hear Maggie saying in the background. There was a scuffling noise, and then Maggie's voice came down the receiver. 'Roxanne! How are you?'

'Hi, Mags,' said Roxanne. 'Sorry I woke Giles up.'

'Oh, he's OK,' said Maggie. 'He's already fallen asleep again. So, how's life in Cyprus?'

'Bearable,' drawled Roxanne. 'A paradise of blazing sun, blue waters and five-star luxury. Nothing to speak of.'

'I don't know how you stand it,' said Maggie. 'I'd complain to the management if I were you.' Then her voice grew more serious. 'Listen, Roxanne, the reason I called—have you spoken to Candice recently?'

'Not since I came out here. Why?'

'Well, I rang her this evening,' said Maggie, 'and that girl was there.'

'Which girl?' said Roxanne.

'Heather Trelawney. The waitress in the Manhattan Bar, remember?'

'Oh yes,' said Roxanne. 'The one Candice's father ripped off.'

'Yes,' said Maggie. 'Well, you know Candice got her the editorial assistant job on the *Londoner*?'

'Really?' said Roxanne in surprise. 'That was quick work.'

'Apparently she went to see Ralph the next morning, and made some special plea. God knows what she said.'

'Oh well,' said Roxanne. 'She obviously feels very strongly about it.'

'She must do,' said Maggie. 'Because now this girl's moved in with her.'

'Moved in with her? But, I mean, she hardly knows her!'

'I know,' said Maggie. 'Exactly. Don't you think it seems a bit . . .'

'Mmm,' said Roxanne. 'Sudden.'

There was silence down the line, punctuated by crackles and Giles coughing in the background.

'I just have a bad vibe about it,' said Maggie eventually. 'You know what Candice is like. She'll let anyone take advantage of her.'

'Yes,' said Roxanne slowly. 'You're right.'

'So I was thinking—maybe you could try and keep tabs on this girl? There's not much I can do . . .'

'Don't worry,' said Roxanne. 'As soon as I get back, I'll suss it out.'

'Good,' said Maggie. 'I'm sure I'm worrying about nothing. It'll probably all turn out fine. But . . .' She paused. 'You know.'

'I do,' said Roxanne. 'And don't fret. I'm on the case.'

The next morning Candice woke to a sweet, mouth-watering smell wafting through the air. She sat up, groaning slightly at the heaviness of her head. Champagne always got her like that. She stood up, put on a robe, and tottered down the hall to the kitchen.

'Hi!' said Heather, looking up from the stove, with a beam. 'I'm making pancakes. Do you want one?'

'Pancakes?' said Candice. 'I haven't had pancakes since . . .'

'Coming right up!' said Heather, and opened the oven. Candice stared in amazement, to see a pile of golden-brown pancakes, warming gently in the oven's heat.

'This is amazing,' she said, starting to laugh. 'You can stay.'

'You don't get pancakes every day,' said Heather with mock severity. 'Only when you've been good.'

Candice giggled. 'I'll make some coffee.'

A few minutes later, they sat down at Candice's marble bistro table, each with a pile of pancakes, sugar and lemon juice, and a steaming mug of coffee.

'This is delicious,' said Candice, her mouth full of pancake. 'Heather, you're an utter star.'

'It's a pleasure,' said Heather, smiling modestly down at her plate.

Candice took another bite of pancake and closed her eyes, savouring the pleasure. To think she'd actually had some last-minute qualms about inviting Heather to live with her. It was obvious that Heather was going to make a wonderful flatmate—and a wonderful new friend.

'Well, I guess I'd better go and get ready.' Candice looked up to see a sheepish grin flash across Heather's face. 'Actually, I'm a bit nervous about today.'

'Don't be,' said Candice at once. 'Everyone's very friendly. And remember I'll be there to help you.' She smiled at Heather, filled with a sudden affection for her. 'It'll all go fine, I promise.'

Half an hour later, as Candice brushed her teeth, Heather knocked on the bathroom door.

'Do I look OK?' she asked nervously, as Candice appeared. Candice gazed at her, feeling impressed and a little taken aback. Heather looked incredibly smart and polished. She was wearing a red suit over a white T-shirt and black high-heeled shoes.

'You look fantastic,' said Candice. 'Where's the suit from?'

'I can't remember,' said Heather vaguely. 'I bought it years ago, when I had a windfall.'

'Well, it looks great,' said Candice. 'Just give me a sec and we'll go.'

A few minutes later, she ushered Heather out of the flat and banged the door shut. Immediately, Ed's front door swung open and he appeared on the landing clutching an empty milk bottle.

'Well, hello there!' he said, as though in surprise. 'Fancy bumping into you, Candice!'

'What a coincidence,' said Candice.

'Just putting the milk out,' said Ed, his eyes glued on Heather.

'Ed, we don't have a milkman,' said Candice, folding her arms.

'Not yet, we don't,' said Ed, and waved the milk bottle at Candice. 'But if I put this out as bait, maybe I can lure one this way. It works for hedgehogs. What do you think?'

He put the milk bottle down on the floor, looked at it for a moment, then moved it a little towards the stairs. Candice rolled her eyes.

'Ed, this is my new flatmate, Heather. You may have heard her arrive last night.'

'Me?' said Ed innocently. 'No, I heard nothing.' He stepped forward, took Heather's hand and kissed it. 'Enchanted to meet you, Heather.'

'You too,' said Heather.

'And may I say how delightfully smart you look?' added Ed.

'You may,' said Heather, dimpling at him.

'You know, you should take a few tips from Heather,' said Ed to Candice. 'Look—her shoes match her bag. Very chic.'

'Thanks, Ed,' said Candice. 'But the day I take sartorial tips from you is the day I give up wearing clothes altogether.'

'Really?' Ed's eyes gleamed 'Is that a move you're planning in the near future?'

Heather giggled. 'What do you do, Ed?' she asked.

'He does nothing,' said Candice. 'And he gets paid for it. What is it today, Ed? Loafing around the park? Feeding the pigeons?'

'Actually, no,' said Ed, his eyes glinting in amusement. 'Since you ask, I'm going to go and look at my house.'

'What house?' said Candice suspiciously. 'Are you moving away?'

'I've inherited a house,' said Ed. 'From my aunt.'

'Of course you have!' said Candice. 'Obviously. Some people inherit debts; Ed Armitage inherits a house.'

'Dunno what I'm going to do with it,' said Ed. 'It's down in Monkham. Bloody miles away.'

'Where's Monkham?' said Candice, wrinkling her brow.

'Wiltshire,' said Heather. 'I know Monkham. It's very pretty.'

'I suppose I'll sell it,' said Ed. 'But then, I'm quite fond of it. I spent a lot of time there when I was a kid . . .'

'Sell it, keep it . . . who cares?' said Candice. 'What's an empty property here or there? It's not like there are people starving on the streets.'

'Or turn it into a soup kitchen,' said Ed. 'A home for orphans. Would that satisfy you, St Candice?' He grinned, and Candice scowled at him.

'Come on,' she said to Heather. 'We'll be late.'

The editorial office of the *Londoner* was a long, large room with windows at each end. It held seven desks—six for members of editorial staff and one for the editorial secretary, Kelly. At times it could be a loud and noisy place to work; on press day it was usually mayhem. As Candice and Heather arrived, however, the room was full of the usual midmonth, Monday morning lethargy.

Candice stood at the door to the room, grinned encouragingly at Heather, and cleared her throat. 'Everybody,' she said, 'this is Heather Trelawney, our new editorial assistant.'

A murmur of hung-over greetings went round the room, and Candice smiled at Heather. 'They're very friendly really,' she said. 'I'll introduce you properly in a moment. But first we should find Justin . . .'

'Candice,' came a voice behind her, and she jumped. She turned round to see Justin standing in the corridor. He was dressed in a dark purple suit, holding a cup of coffee and looking harassed.

'Hi!' she said. 'Justin, I'd like you to . . .'

'Candice, a word,' interrupted Justin tersely. 'In private. If I may.'

'Oh,' said Candice. 'Well . . . OK.'

She glanced apologetically at Heather, then followed Justin to the corner by the photocopying machine. As he turned round, the expression on his face was distinctly unfriendly. Candice folded her arms and stared back at him defiantly.

'Yes?' she said, wondering if she'd made some horrendous gaffe in the magazine without realising. 'Is something wrong?'

'Where were you on Friday?'

'I took the day off,' said Candice.

'In order to avoid me.'

'No!' said Candice. 'Of course not! Justin, what's wrong?'

'What's wrong?' echoed Justin. 'OK, tell me this, Candice. Did you or did you not go over my head to Ralph last week simply in order to secure a job for your little friend?' He jerked his head towards Heather.

'Oh,' said Candice, taken aback. 'Well, not on purpose. It just . . . happened that way.'

'Oh yes?' A tense smile flickered across Justin's face. 'That's funny. Because the way I heard it was that after our discussion the other night, you went straight up to Ralph Allsopp and told him I was too busy to process the applications for editorial assistant. Is that what you told him, Candice?'

'No!' said Candice, feeling herself colouring. 'At least . . . I didn't mean anything by it! It was just—'

She broke off, feeling slightly uncomfortable. Although—of course—she'd been acting primarily to help Heather, she couldn't deny that it had given her a slight *frisson* of pleasure to have outwitted Justin.

'How do you think that makes me look?' hissed Justin furiously.

'Look, it's no big deal!' protested Candice. 'I just happened to know someone who I thought would be good for the job, and you'd said you were busy—'

'And you happened to see a neat way to sabotage my position on day one,' said Justin, with a little sneer.

'No!' said Candice in horror. 'God, is that the way you think my mind works? I would never do anything like that!'

'Of course you wouldn't,' said Justin.

'I *wouldn't*!' said Candice, and glared at him. She felt a movement at her arm and looked up in surprise. 'Oh, hello, Heather.'

'I thought I'd come and introduce myself,' said Heather brightly. 'You must be Justin.'

'Justin Vellis, acting editor,' said Justin, holding out his hand.

'Heather Trelawney,' said Heather, shaking it firmly. 'I'm so delighted to be working for the *Londoner*. I've always read it, and I look forward to being part of the team.'

'Good,' said Justin shortly.

'I must just also add,' said Heather, 'that I love your tie. I've been admiring it from afar.' She beamed at Justin. 'Is it Valentino?'

'Oh,' said Justin, taken aback. 'Yes, it is. How . . . clever of you.'

'I love men in Valentino,' said Heather.

'Yes, well,' said Justin, flushing very slightly. 'Good to meet you, Heather. Ralph's told me about the high quality of your writing and I'm sure you're going to be an asset to the team.'

He nodded at Heather, glanced at Candice, then strode away. The two girls looked at each other, then started to giggle.

'Heather, you're a genius!' said Candice. 'How did you know Justin had a thing about his ties?'

'I didn't,' said Heather, grinning. 'Just call it instinct.'

'Well, anyway, thanks for rescuing me,' said Candice. 'You got me out of a tight corner there.' She shook her head. 'God, Justin can be a pain.'

'I saw you arguing,' said Heather casually. 'What was the problem?' She looked at Candice, and a curious expression came over her face. 'You weren't arguing about . . . me, were you?'

Candice felt herself flush. 'No!' she said hastily. 'No, of course we weren't! It was . . . something else completely. It really doesn't matter.'

'Well—if you're sure,' said Heather, and gazed at Candice with luminous eyes. 'Because I'd hate to cause any trouble.'

'You're not causing trouble!' said Candice, laughing. 'Come on, I'll show you your desk.'

Maggie was in her bedroom, sitting by the rain-swept window and staring out at the muddy green fields disappearing into the distance. Fields and fields, as far as the eye could see. Proper, old-fashioned English countryside. And twenty acres of it belonged to them.

That first October weekend after they'd moved in, she'd made a point of walking to the furthest point of the plot and looking back towards the house—greedily taking in the swath of land that now belonged to her and Giles. The second weekend it had rained, and she'd huddled inside by the Aga. The third weekend, they'd stayed up in London for a party.

The phone rang and she looked at her watch. It would be Giles, wanting to know what she had been doing with herself. She had told herself—and him—that she would go up to the attic bedrooms today and plan their redecoration. In fact, she had done nothing more than go downstairs, eat some breakfast and come back upstairs again. She felt heavy and inert, unable to galvanise herself into action.

'Hi, Giles?' she said into the receiver.

'How are you doing?' said Giles cheerily. 'It's lashing it down here.'

'Fine,' said Maggie, shifting uncomfortably in her chair. 'It's raining here, too.'

'You sound a bit down, my sweet.'

'Oh, I'm OK,' said Maggie gloomily. 'My back hurts, it's pissing with rain and I haven't got anyone to talk to. Apart from that, I'm doing great.'

Suddenly she felt a tightening across the front of her stomach, and drew in breath sharply.

'Maggie?' said Giles in alarm.

'It's OK,' she said. 'Just another practice contraction.'

'I would have thought you'd had enough practice by now,' said Giles, and laughed merrily. 'Well, I'd better shoot off. Take care of yourself.'

'Wait,' said Maggie, suddenly anxious for him not to disappear off the line. 'What time do you think you'll be home?'

'It's bloody frantic here,' said Giles, lowering his voice. 'I'll try to make it as early as I can. I'll ring you a bit later and let you know.'

'OK,' said Maggie disconsolately. 'Bye.'

After he'd rung off she slowly put the receiver down and felt suddenly bereft, like a child at boarding school. Ridiculously, she felt as though she wanted to go home. But this was her home. Of course it was. She was Mrs Drakeford of The Pines. She got to her feet and lumbered wearily into the bathroom, thinking that she would have a warm bath to ease her back. It would be something to do.

She stepped into the warm water and leaned back, just as her abdomen began to tighten again. Another bloody practice contraction. Hadn't she had enough already? As she closed her eyes, she remembered the section in her pregnancy handbook on false labour. 'Many women,' the book had said patronisingly, 'will mistake false contractions for the real thing.'

Not her, thought Maggie grimly. She wasn't going to have the humiliation of summoning Giles from the office and rushing excitedly off to the hospital, only to be told kindly that she'd made a mistake. You think *that's* labour? the silent implication ran. Ha! You just wait for the real thing! Well, she would. She'd wait for the real thing.

Roxanne reached for her orange juice, took a sip and leaned back comfortably in her chair. She was sitting at a blue and green mosaic table on the terrace of the Aphrodite Bay Hotel, overlooking the swimming pool and, in the distance, the beach. A final drink in the sunshine before her flight back to England. She took another sip and closed her eyes.

'You are enjoying the sun,' came a voice beside her and she looked up. Nico Georgiou was pulling a chair out and sitting down at the table. He was an elegant man in his middle years, always well dressed; always impeccably polite. The more reserved of the two Georgiou brothers.

She had met them both on her first trip to Cyprus, when she had been sent to cover the opening of their new hotel, the Aphrodite Bay. Since then, she had never stayed anywhere else in Cyprus and, over the years, had got to know Nico and his brother Andreas well. Between them, they owned three of the major hotels on the island, and a fourth was currently under construction.

'I adore the sun,' said Roxanne, smiling. 'And I adore the Aphrodite Bay.' She looked around. 'I can't tell you how much I've enjoyed my stay here.'

'And we have, as always, enjoyed having you,' said Nico. He lifted a hand and a waiter came rushing to attention.

'An espresso, please,' said Nico, and glanced at Roxanne. 'And for you?'

'Nothing else, thanks,' said Roxanne. 'I have to leave soon.'

'I know,' said Nico. 'I will drive you to the airport. I want to talk to you, Roxanne.'

'Really?' said Roxanne. 'What about?'

Nico's coffee arrived and he waited for the waiter to retreat before he spoke again. 'You have been to visit our new resort, the Aphrodite Falls?'

'I've seen the construction site,' said Roxanne. 'It looks very impressive. All those waterfalls.'

'It will be impressive,' said Nico. 'It will be unlike anything previously seen in Cyprus.'

'Good!' said Roxanne. 'I can't wait till it opens.' She grinned at him. 'If you don't invite me to the launch party you're in trouble.'

Nico laughed, then said, 'The Aphrodite Falls is a very high-profile project. We will be looking for a . . . a dynamic person to run the launch and marketing of the resort. A person with talent. With energy. With contacts in journalism . . .' There was silence, and Nico looked up. 'Someone, perhaps, who enjoys the Mediterranean way of life,' he said slowly, meeting Roxanne's eyes. 'Someone, perhaps, from Britain?'

'Me?' said Roxanne disbelievingly. 'You can't be serious.'

'I am utterly serious,' said Nico. 'My brother and I would be honoured if you would join our company.'

'But I don't know anything about marketing! I don't have any qualifications, any training—'

'Roxanne, you have more intelligence and flair than any of these so-called qualified people,' said Nico, gesturing disparagingly. 'We would provide accommodation for you,' he said, leaning forward. 'The salary would be, I think, generous.'

'Nico—'

'And, of course, we would expect you to continue with a certain amount of travel, to other comparable resorts. For . . . research purposes.'

Roxanne looked at him suspiciously. 'Has this job been tailor-made for me?'

A smile flickered over Nico's face. 'In a way . . . perhaps yes.'

'I see.' Roxanne stared into her glass of orange juice. 'But . . . why?'

There was silence for a while—then Nico said, 'You know why.'

A strange pang went through Roxanne and she closed her eyes, trying to rationalise her thoughts. The sun was hot on her face; in the distance she could hear children shrieking excitedly on the beach. 'Mama!' one of them was calling, 'Mama!' She could live here all year round, she thought. Wake up to sunshine every day. Join the Georgiou family for long, lazy celebration meals—as she once had for Andreas's birthday.

And Nico himself. Courteous, self-deprecating Nico, who never hid his feelings for her—but never forced them on her either. Kind, loyal Nico; she would die rather than hurt him.

'I can't,' she said, and opened her eyes to see Nico gazing straight at her. The expression in his dark eyes made her want to cry. 'I can't leave London.' She exhaled sharply. 'You know why. I just can't—'

'You can't leave him,' said Nico, and, in one, quick movement, drained his espresso.

Something was ringing in Maggie's mind. A fire alarm. An alarm clock. The doorbell. Her mind jerked awake and she opened her eyes. Dazedly, she glanced at her watch on the side of the bath and saw to her astonishment that it was one o'clock. She'd been in her bath for almost an hour, half dozing in the warmth. She stood up, reached for a towel, and began to dry her face and neck before getting out.

Halfway out of the bath another practice contraction seized her and in some kind of terror, she clung onto the side of the bath, willing herself not to slip over. As the painful tightness subsided, the doorbell rang again downstairs, loud and insistent.

'Bloody hell, give me a minute!' she yelled. She wrenched angrily at a towelling robe on the back of the door, wrapped it round herself and padded out of the room.

She headed for the front door, already knowing from the thin shadowy figure on the other side of the frosted glass that her visitor was Paddy. Barely a day went by without Paddy popping in with some excuse or other—a knitted blanket for the baby, a cutting from the garden, the famous recipe for scones. 'She's keeping bloody tabs on me!' Maggie had complained, half jokingly, to Giles the night before. On the other hand, Paddy's company was better than nothing.

'Maggie!' exclaimed Paddy, as soon as Maggie opened the door. 'So glad to have caught you in. I've been making tomato soup, and, as usual, I've made far too much. Can you use some?'

'Oh,' said Maggie. 'Yes, I should think so. Come on in.' As she stood aside to let Paddy in, another contraction began—this one deeper and more painful than the others. She gripped the door, biting her lip, waiting for it to pass.

'Maggie, are you all right?' said Paddy sharply.

51

'I'm fine,' said Maggie, breathing normally again. 'Just a practice contraction.'

'A what?' Paddy stared at her.

'They're called Braxton-Hicks contractions,' explained Maggie patiently. 'It's in the book. Perfectly normal in the last few weeks.' She smiled at Paddy. 'Can I make you a cup of coffee?'

'You sit down,' said Paddy, giving Maggie an odd look. 'I'll do it. Maggie, you don't think this could be it?'

'What?' Maggie stared at Paddy and felt a little plunge of fear. 'Labour? Of course not. I'm not due for another two weeks. And I've been having practice contractions like this all week. It's . . . it's nothing.'

'Shall I run you up to the hospital, just to make sure?'

'No!' said Maggie at once. 'They'll just tell me I'm a stupid woman and send me home again. I'm just . . .' But she couldn't manage the rest of her sentence. She held her breath, waiting for the pain to pass. When she looked up, Paddy was standing up and holding her car keys.

'Maggie, I'm no expert,' she said cheerfully, 'but even I know that wasn't a practice contraction.' She smiled. 'My dear, this is it. The baby's coming.'

'It can't be,' Maggie heard herself say. She felt almost breathless with fright. 'It can't be. I'm not ready.'

It was raining, a soft slithery rain, when Roxanne emerged from London Underground at Barons Court. The skies were dark with clouds, the pavements were wet and slimy. It felt, to Roxanne, like the middle of winter. She picked up her case and began to walk briskly along the street. It seemed hardly believable that only a few hours ago she'd been sitting in the blazing heat of the sun.

Nico had driven her to the airport in his gleaming Mercedes. He had, despite her protestations, carried her suitcase into the airport terminal for her and ensured that everything was in order at the check-in desk. Not once had he mentioned the job at the Aphrodite Falls. Instead he had talked generally, about politics and books, and his planned trip to New York—and Roxanne had listened gratefully, glad of his tact. Only as they'd been about to bid farewell to one another had he said, with a sudden vehemence, 'He is a fool, this man of yours.'

'You mean I'm a fool,' Roxanne had responded, trying to smile. Nico had shaken his head silently, then taken her hands.

'Come back to visit us soon, Roxanne,' he'd said in a low voice. 'And . . . think about it? At least think about it.'

'I will,' she had promised, knowing that her mind was already made up. Nico had scanned her face, then sighed and kissed her fingertips.

'There is no one like Roxanne,' he'd said. 'Your man is very lucky.'

Roxanne had smiled back at him, and laughed a little, and waved cheerfully as she went through the departure gate. Now, with rain dripping down her neck, she felt less cheerful. London seemed a grey, unfriendly place. What was she living here for, anyway?

She reached her house and felt inside her bag for her keys. Her tiny little flat was on the top floor, with what estate agents described as far-reaching views over London. By the time she reached the top of the stairs, she was out of breath. She unlocked the door to her flat, pushed it open, and stepped over a pile of post. Quickly she went into the little kitchen and switched on the kettle, then wandered back into the hall. She picked up her mail and began to flip through it, dropping all the uninteresting bills and circulars back onto the floor. Suddenly, at a handwritten white envelope, she stopped. It was a letter from him.

With cold hands, still wet from the rain, she tore it open.

My darling Rapunzel,

As many apologies as I can muster for Wednesday night. Will explain all. Now as my deserved punishment—must wait jealously for your return. Hurry home from Cyprus. Hurry, hurry.

The letter ended, as ever, with no name but a row of kisses. Reading his words, she could suddenly hear his voice; feel his touch on her skin; hear his warm laughter. She sank to the floor and read the letter again and again, devouring it greedily with her eyes. Then eventually she looked up, feeling in some strange way restored. The truth was, that there was no conceivable alternative. She couldn't stop loving him; she couldn't just move to a new country and pretend he didn't exist. And the fact that he was rationed, the fact that she could not have him properly, simply made her crave him all the more.

The phone rang and, with a sudden lift of hope, she reached for the receiver. 'Yes?' she said lightly, thinking that if it was him, she would get in a taxi and go to him straightaway.

'Roxanne, it's Giles Drakeford.'

'Oh,' said Roxanne in surprise. 'Is Maggie all—'

'It's a girl,' said Giles, sounding more emotional than she'd ever heard him. 'It's a girl. Born an hour ago. A perfect little girl. Six pounds eight. The most beautiful baby in the world.' He took a deep, shuddering breath. 'Maggie was . . . fantastic. She was so quick, I only just made it in time. God, it was just the most amazing experience. We've decided we're going to call her Lucia. Lucia Sarah Helen. She's . . . she's perfect. A perfect little daughter.' There was silence. 'Roxanne?'

'A daughter,' said Roxanne, in a strange voice. 'Congratulations. That's . . . that's wonderful news.'

'I can't talk long,' said Giles. 'To be honest, I'm bloody shattered. But Maggie wanted you to know.'

'Well, thanks for calling,' said Roxanne. 'And congratulations again. And s-send all my love to Maggie.'

She put the phone down and looked at it silently for a minute. Then, with no warning at all, she burst into tears.

Chapter Four

THE NEXT DAY DAWNED BRIGHT and clear, with the smell of summer and good spirits in the air. On the way to the office, Roxanne stopped off at a florist and chose an extravagantly large bunch of lilies for Maggie from an illustrated brochure entitled 'A New Arrival'.

'Is it a boy or a girl?' enquired the florist, typing the details into her computer.

'A girl,' said Roxanne. 'Lucia Sarah Helen. Isn't that pretty?'

'LSH,' said the florist. 'Sounds like a drug.' Roxanne gave the woman an annoyed glance and handed her a Visa card. 'They'll go out this afternoon,' added the woman, swiping the card. 'Is that all right?'

'Fine,' said Roxanne, and imagined Maggie sitting up like one of the women in the brochure, in a crisp white bed, rosy-cheeked and serene. A tiny sleeping baby in her arms, Giles looking on lovingly, and flowers all around. Deep inside her she felt something tug at her heart.

'If you could just sign there,' said the florist, passing a slip of paper to Roxanne, 'and write your message in the box.' Roxanne picked up a Biro and hesitated.

Can't wait to mix Lucia her first cocktail, she wrote eventually. *Much love and congratulations to you both from Roxanne.*

'I'm not sure that'll fit on the card,' said the florist doubtfully.

'Then use two cards,' snapped Roxanne, suddenly wanting to get away from the sickly scent of flowers. As she strode out of the shop, a petal fell from a garland onto her hair like confetti, and she brushed it irritably away.

She arrived at the editorial office a little after nine thirty, to see Candice sitting cross-legged on the floor sketching something out on a piece of paper. Sitting next to her was the blonde-haired girl from the Manhattan Bar. For a few moments Roxanne gazed at them, remembering Maggie's phone call. Was this girl really trouble? She looked outwardly innocuous, with her freckled snub nose and cheerful smile. But there was also, Roxanne noticed, a firmness to her jaw when she wasn't smiling, and a curious coolness to her grey eyes.

As she watched, the blonde girl looked up and met Roxanne's gaze. Her eyes flickered briefly, then she smiled sweetly.

'Hello,' she said. 'You probably don't remember me.'

'Oh yes I do,' said Roxanne, smiling. 'It's Heather, isn't it?'

'That's right. And you're Roxanne.'

'Roxanne!' said Candice, looking up, eyes shining. 'Isn't it wonderful news about the baby?'

'Fantastic,' said Roxanne. 'Did Giles call you last night?'

'Yes. He sounded absolutely overwhelmed, didn't you think?' Candice gestured to the piece of paper. 'Look, we're designing a card for the art department to make up. Then we'll get everyone to sign it. What do you think?'

'It's an excellent idea,' said Roxanne, looking fondly at her. 'Maggie'll love it.'

'I'll take it down to the studio,' said Candice, standing up. 'I won't be long.'

When she'd gone, there was silence. Roxanne gave Heather an appraising look and Heather stared back innocently.

'So, Heather,' said Roxanne at last, in a friendly tone. 'How are you enjoying the *Londoner*?'

'It's wonderful,' said Heather. 'I feel so lucky to be working here.'

'And I gather you're living with Candice now?'

'Yes, I am,' said Heather. 'She's been so incredibly kind.'

'Has she?' said Roxanne pleasantly. 'Well, you know, that doesn't surprise me at all. Candice is a very kind, generous person. She finds it very difficult to say no to people.'

'Really?' said Heather.

'Oh yes. I'm surprised you haven't picked that up.' Roxanne nonchalantly examined her nails for a moment. 'In fact, her friends—including myself—sometimes get quite worried about her. She's the sort of person it would be so easy to take advantage of.'

'Do you think so?' Heather smiled at Roxanne. 'I would have thought Candice could take pretty good care of herself. How old is she now?'

Well, thought Roxanne, almost impressed. She certainly gives as good as she gets. 'So,' she said, abruptly changing the subject, 'I gather you've never worked on a magazine before.'

'No,' said Heather unconcernedly.

'But you're a very good writer, I hear,' said Roxanne. 'You obviously impressed Ralph Allsopp at your interview.'

To her surprise, a faint pink flush began to creep up Heather's neck. Roxanne stared at it with interest.

'Well, Heather,' she said. 'Lovely to meet you again. We'll be seeing lots of each other, I'm sure.'

She watched as Heather sauntered away into Justin's office, noticing that Justin looked up with a smile as Heather entered. Typical male, she thought acidly. He'd clearly already been seduced by Heather's smile.

Roxanne stared through the window at Heather, trying to work her out. She was young, she was pretty, and probably talented to some degree. At face value, a lovely girl. So why did she make Roxanne's hackles rise? The consideration passed through Roxanne's mind that she might simply be jealous of Heather—and immediately she dismissed it.

As she stood, staring, Candice came back into the office, holding a colour page proof.

'Hi!' said Roxanne, smiling warmly at her. 'Listen—fancy a quick drink after work?'

'I can't,' said Candice regretfully. 'I promised Heather I'd go shopping with her. I'm going to find a present for Maggie.'

'No problem,' said Roxanne lightly. 'Another time.'

She watched as Candice went into Justin's office, grinned at Heather and started talking. Justin immediately began to gesture, frowning, at the page proof—and Candice nodded earnestly and began to gesture herself. As they both stared, engrossed, at the proof, Heather slowly turned and met Roxanne's eyes coolly through the window. For a moment, they simply stared at each other—then Roxanne abruptly turned away and strode out of the office. She didn't wait for the lift but hurried up the stairs and along the corridor to Ralph Allsopp's office.

'Janet!' she said, stopping at his elderly secretary's desk. 'Can I see Ralph for a moment?'

'He's not in, I'm afraid,' said Janet. 'Not in at all today.'

'Oh,' said Roxanne, subsiding slightly. 'Listen, Janet,' she said. 'Can I ask you something?'

'You can ask,' said Janet. 'Doesn't mean you'll get.'

Roxanne grinned, and lowered her voice slightly. 'Has Ralph said anything to you about this new editorial assistant, Heather?'

'Not really,' said Janet. 'Just that he was giving her the job.'

Roxanne frowned. 'But when he interviewed her. He must have said something.'

'He thought she was very witty,' said Janet. 'She'd written a very funny article about London Transport.'

'Really?' Roxanne looked at her in surprise. 'Was it really any good?'

'Oh yes,' said Janet. 'Ralph gave me a copy of it to read.' She leafed through a pile of papers on her desk and produced a piece of paper. 'Here. You'll like it.'

'I doubt that,' said Roxanne. She glanced at the piece of paper, then put it in her bag. 'Well, thanks.'

'And do give my love to Maggie when you speak to her,' added Janet fondly. 'I do hope motherhood isn't too much of a shock for her.'

'A shock?' said Roxanne in surprise. 'Oh no. Maggie'll be fine.'

A voice calling her name dragged Maggie from a vivid, frenzied dream. She opened her eyes and blinked a few times disorientatedly at the bright overhead light.

'Maggie?' Her eyes snapped into focus, and she saw Paddy, standing at the end of her hospital bed, holding an enormous bunch of lilies. 'Maggie, dear, I wasn't sure if you were asleep. How are you feeling?'

'Fine,' said Maggie in a scratchy voice. 'I'm fine.' She tried to sit up, wincing slightly at her aching body. 'What time is it?'

'Four o'clock,' said Paddy, looking at her watch, 'just gone. Giles will be along any moment.'

'Good,' whispered Maggie. Giles, along with all the other visitors, had been ejected from the ward at two o'clock so that the new mothers could catch up on some rest. Maggie had lain tensely awake for a while, waiting for Lucia to cry, then had drifted off to sleep. But she didn't feel rested. She felt bleary and unfocused; unable to think straight.

'And how's my little granddaughter?' Paddy looked into the plastic cradle beside Maggie's bed. 'Asleep like a lamb. What a good little baby!'

'She was awake quite a lot of the night,' said Maggie, pouring herself a glass of water with shaking hands.

'Was she?' Paddy smiled fondly. 'Hungry, I expect.'

'Yes.' Maggie looked through the glass of the crib at her daughter. She didn't seem real. None of it seemed real. Nothing had prepared her for what this would be like, thought Maggie. Nothing.

The birth itself had been like entering another, alien world, in which her body responded to some force she had no control over. In which her dignity, her ideals, her self-control and self-image were obliterated. She had wanted to object; to call a halt to the whole proceedings. But it had been too late. There was no alternative but to grit her teeth and do it.

Already the hours of pain were fading from her memory. In her mind the whole event seemed to have kaleidoscoped around those last few minutes—the actual delivery of the baby. And that, thought Maggie, had been the most surreal moment of all. The delivery of another, living, screaming human being from inside her. Looking around the maternity ward at the faces of the other mothers, she could not believe how calmly they seemed to be taking this momentous, extraordinary event. Or perhaps it was just that they'd all done it before. None of the other women on the ward was a first-time mother. They all dandled their little bundles with accustomed ease. During the night, she had heard the girl in the bed next to hers joking with the midwife on duty about her baby.

'Greedy little bugger, isn't he?' she'd said, and laughed. 'Won't leave me alone.' And Maggie had felt tears pouring down her face as she tried to persuade Lucia to feed. What was wrong with her? she had thought as, yet again, Lucia sucked for a few seconds, then opened her mouth in a protesting shout. As the baby's squawks had become louder, a midwife had appeared, looked at Maggie and pursed her lips with disapproval.

'You've let her get too wound up,' she'd said. 'Try to calm her down.'

Flushed with distress and humiliation, Maggie had tried to soothe a flailing, wailing Lucia. But Lucia's screams had become louder and louder. With a sigh of impatience, the midwife had eventually reached for her. She had laid the baby on the bed, wrapped her up tightly in a blanket and lifted her up again. And almost immediately, Lucia's cries had ceased. Maggie had stared at her own baby, peaceful and quiet in someone else's arms, and had felt cold with failure.

'There,' the midwife had said more kindly. 'Try again.' Stiff with misery, Maggie had taken the baby from her. She had held Lucia to her breast and, almost magically, the baby had begun to feed contentedly.

'That's more like it,' the midwife had said. 'You just need a bit of practice.' She had waited a few minutes, then had looked more closely at Maggie's red-rimmed eyes. 'Are you OK? Not feeling too down?'

'Fine,' Maggie had said automatically, and forced herself to smile brightly at the midwife. 'Honestly. I just need to get to grips with it.'

'Good,' the midwife had said. 'Well, don't worry. Everyone has trouble at first.'

She'd glanced at Lucia, then left the flowery cubicle. As soon as she'd gone, tears had begun to pour down Maggie's face again.

'These lilies arrived for you just as I was leaving,' Paddy was saying now. 'Shall we find another vase, or shall I take them back to the house?'

'I don't know,' said Maggie. 'Did . . . did my mother call?'

'Yes,' said Paddy, beaming. 'She's coming down tomorrow. Unfortunately she couldn't take today off. Some crucial meeting.'

'Oh,' said Maggie, trying not to let her disappointment show. After all, she was a grown woman. What did she need her mother for?

'And look, here's Giles!' said Paddy. 'I'll go and fetch us all a nice cup of tea, shall I?' She laid the lilies on the bed and walked off briskly.

Maggie watched as mother and son greeted each other. Then, as Giles approached her bed, she tried to compose her features into light-hearted friendliness. The truth was, she felt dissociated from him, unable to communicate on anything but a surface level. In a matter of twenty-four hours she had moved into a new world without him. By the time the message had got to him at work, she had been well into the throes of labour. He had arrived just in time for the last half-hour and, although he could claim to have been present at his daughter's birth, she felt that he would never fully understand what she had been through.

'Did you have a nice sleep?' Giles sat down on the bed and stroked Maggie's hair. 'You look so serene. I've been telling everyone how won-derful you were. Everyone sends their love.'

'Everyone?'

'Everyone I could think of.' He looked at the crib. 'How is she?'

'Oh, fine,' said Maggie lightly. 'She hasn't done much since you left.'

'Nice flowers,' said Giles, looking at the lilies. 'Who are they from?'

'I haven't even looked,' said Maggie. She opened the little envelope and two embossed cards fell out. 'Roxanne,' she said, laughing. 'She says she's going to mix Lucia her first cocktail.'

'Typical Roxanne,' said Giles.

'Yes.' As Maggie stared down at the message, she felt the treacherous tears pricking her eyes again. Hurriedly, she blinked and put the cards down on the bedside table.

'Here we are!' came Paddy's voice. She was carrying a tray of cups and accompanied by a midwife Maggie didn't recognise. Paddy put the tray down and beamed at Maggie. 'I thought perhaps, after your tea, you could give Lucia her first bath.'

'Oh,' said Maggie, taken aback. 'Yes, of course.'

She took a sip of tea and tried to smile back at Paddy. It hadn't occurred to her that Lucia would need a bath. What was wrong with her?

'Has she fed recently?' said the midwife.

'Not since lunchtime.'

'Right,' said the midwife cheerfully. 'Well, maybe you'd like to feed her now. Don't want to leave her too long.'

A renewed stab of guilt went through Maggie's chest and her face flushed. 'Of course,' she said. 'I'll . . . I'll do it now.'

Aware of everyone's eyes on her she reached into the crib, picked up Lucia and began to unwrap the tiny cellular blanket.

'Let me hold her for a moment,' said Giles suddenly. 'Let me just look at her.' He picked Lucia up, nestling her comfortably into the crook of his arm. As he did so, she gave an enormous yawn, then her tiny screwed-up eyes suddenly opened. She stared up at her father, her little pink mouth open like a flower.

'Isn't that the most beautiful sight?' said Paddy softly.

'Can I have a little look?' said the midwife.

'Of course,' said Giles. 'Isn't she perfect?'

'Such a healthy colour!' said Paddy.

'That's what I was wondering about,' said the midwife. She placed Lucia on the bed and unbuttoned her sleepsuit. She stared at Lucia's chest, then looked up at Maggie. 'Has she always been this colour?'

'Yes,' said Maggie, taken aback. 'I . . . I think so.'

'She's got a tan,' said Giles, and laughed uncertainly.

'I don't think so,' said the midwife, and frowned. 'Someone should have picked this up. I think she's got jaundice.'

Maggie stared at the midwife and felt her heart begin to thump. They'd lied to her. They'd all lied. Her baby wasn't healthy at all.

'Is it very serious?' she managed.

'Oh no! It'll clear up in a few days.' The woman looked up at Maggie's face and burst into laughter. 'Don't worry, sweetheart. She'll live.'

Ralph Allsopp sat on a bench outside the Charing Cross Hospital. On his lap was a greetings card he had bought from the hospital shop, depicting a crib and a winsome, grinning baby. *My dear Maggie*, he had written shakily inside the card. Then he had stopped and put the pen down, unable to write any more. He felt ill. Not from the disease itself: that had crept up quietly. It had tiptoed around him, setting up camp wherever it could find a foothold, letting him remain unaware of its presence until it was too late. Now, of course, he knew it all. He had had his disease explained to him carefully by three separate doctors. Each had looked him straight in the eye with a practised, compassionate expression; had mentioned counselling and hospices and Macmillan Nurses—then, after a pause, his wife. It had been taken for granted that his wife and family would be told; that his staff would be told; that the world would be told. It had been taken for granted that this dissemination of information was his task; his choice; his responsibility.

And it was this responsibility which made Ralph feel ill. It was too much. Whom to tell. What to tell. For the moment the words were out of his lips, everything would change. His life would no longer be his own. It would belong to those he loved. And therein lay the problem; the heartache. To whom did those last months, weeks, days, belong?

By speaking now, he would grant the rest of his life to his wife, to his three children, to the closest of his friends. And so it should be. But by speaking now, it seemed to him, his last months would at once be placed under a magnifying glass, allowing no secrets. He would be obliged to play out the remainder of his life in conventional, noble fashion. For, after all, cancer patients were not adulterers, were they?

Feeling a sudden shaft of determination, Ralph picked up his pen again. *A new little light in the world*, he wrote in the baby card. *With many congratulations and love from Ralph.* He would buy a magnum of champagne, he suddenly decided, put the card in with that and send the whole lot by special delivery. Maggie deserved something special.

He sealed the envelope, stood up stiffly and looked at his watch. Half an hour to go. A taxi was cruising slowly along the street and he hailed it. As it moved off through the thick evening traffic, he stared out of the window. People were bad-temperedly barging past one another as they crossed the road and he gazed at them, relishing the normality of their expressions after the guarded looks of the doctors. He would hold on to that normality for as long as possible, he thought fiercely.

He got out of the taxi at a corner and walked slowly along the street to the house in which she lived. As he looked up he could see all her windows lit up and uncurtained in a brilliant, defiant blaze. His unwitting Rapunzel in her tower, unaware of what the future held. A dart of pain went through his heart and, for a moment, he desperately wanted to tell her. To hold her tight and weep with her into the small hours.

But he would not. He would be stronger than that. He quickened his pace and arrived at her front door. He pressed the buzzer and after a few moments the front door was released. Slowly he climbed the stairs, arrived at the top and saw her waiting at her front door. She was wearing a white silk shirt and a short black skirt and the light from behind was burnishing her hair. For a few moments he just stared at her.

'Roxanne,' he said eventually. 'You look . . .'

'Good,' she said, and her mouth curved in a half-smile. 'Come on in.'

The gift shop was small and quiet and sweetly scented—and practically empty. Candice walked around, looking doubtfully at sampler cushions and mugs saying 'It's a Girl!' She stopped by a shelf of stuffed toys, picked up a teddy bear and smiled at it. Then she turned it over to look at the price and, as she saw the ticket, felt herself blanch.

'How much?' said Heather, coming up behind her.

'Fifty pounds,' said Candice in an undertone.

'Fifty quid?' Heather stared at the teddy incredulously, then began to laugh. 'That's outrageous! It hasn't even got a nice face. Come on. We'll go somewhere else.'

As they walked out of the shop, Heather took Candice's arm in hers, and Candice felt herself blush slightly with pleasure. She could hardly believe it was only a week since Heather had moved in with her. Already they felt like old friends. Every night, Heather insisted on cooking a proper supper and opening a bottle of wine; every night she had another entertainment planned. One evening she had given Candice a facial, another evening she'd brought home videos and popcorn; the next, she'd brought home an electric juicer and announced she was setting up a juice bar in the kitchen. By the end of that evening they'd produced approximately one glass of warm juice—but they'd both been in fits of giggles. Even now, remembering it, Candice felt a giggle rising.

'What?' said Heather, turning towards her.

'The juicer.'

'Oh God,' said Heather. 'Don't remind me.' She paused by the entrance to a big department store. 'What about in here? There must be a baby department.'

'Oh, that's a good idea,' said Candice.

'In fact, I'm just going to slip off,' said Heather. 'I've got something I need to buy. So I'll see you in the baby department.'

'OK,' said Candice, and headed for the elevator. It was seven o'clock at night, but the shop was as crowded as though it were the middle of the day. As she arrived at the baby department, a row of little embroidered dresses took her eye and she began to leaf through the rack.

'Here you are!' Heather's voice interrupted her and she looked up.

'That was quick!'

'Oh, I knew what I wanted,' said Heather, and flushed slightly. 'It's . . . actually, it's for you.'

'What?' Puzzled, Candice took the paper bag Heather was holding out to her. 'What do you mean, it's for me?'

'A present,' said Heather. 'You've been so good to me, Candice. You've transformed my life. If it weren't for you, I'd be . . . well. Something quite different.'

Candice stared back at her wide grey eyes and felt suddenly shamefaced. If Heather only knew the real reason for Candice's generosity;

knew the trail of guilt and dishonesty that lay behind their friendship. Would she still be standing there, looking at Candice with such candid, friendly eyes? Feeling suddenly sick at her own deceit, Candice ripped the bag open and drew out a slim silver pen.

'It's not much,' said Heather. 'I just thought you'd like it. For when you're writing up your interviews.'

'It's beautiful,' said Candice, feeling tears coming to her eyes. 'Heather, you really shouldn't have.'

'It's the least I can do,' said Heather. She took Candice's arm and squeezed it. 'I'm so glad I ran into you, that night. There's something really . . . special between us. Don't you think? I feel as if you're my closest friend.' Candice looked at her, then impetuously leaned forward and hugged her. 'I know your other friends don't like me,' came Heather's voice in her ear. 'But . . . you know, it doesn't matter.'

Candice withdrew her head and looked at Heather in surprise.

'What do you mean, my other friends don't like you?'

'Roxanne doesn't like me.' Heather gave a quick little smile. 'Don't worry about it. It doesn't matter.'

'But this is awful!' exclaimed Candice, frowning. 'Why don't you think she likes you?'

'I might have got it wrong,' said Heather at once. 'It was just a look she gave me . . . Honestly, Candice, don't hassle about it. I shouldn't have said anything.' She flashed a quick grin. 'Come on, choose one of these dresses, and then let's go and try on some proper clothes.'

'OK,' said Candice. But as she began to pick up the baby dresses again, her face was creased in a frown.

'Look, now I feel terrible!' said Heather. 'Please, Candice, forget I said anything. I'm probably just sensitive. I probably got it all wrong.'

Roxanne lay happily on the sofa in a T-shirt, listening to low, jazzy music and, in the background, the sounds of Ralph cooking in the kitchen. He always cooked the supper—partly because he claimed to enjoy it, and partly because she was useless at it. She associated some of their happiest moments together with meals that he had cooked, after sex. Those were the times she cherished the most, she thought. The times when she could almost believe that they lived together; that they were a normal couple.

Of course, they weren't a normal couple. Perhaps they never would be. Roxanne's thoughts flicked to Ralph's youngest son Sebastian. Sweet little Sebastian, the accident. And still only ten years old. Ten years, five months and a week.

Roxanne knew Sebastian Allsopp's age to the minute. His older brother and sister were in their twenties, safely off in their own lives. But Sebastian was too young to bear the turmoil of a divorce. Not until he was eighteen, Ralph had said once. Eighteen. Another seven years, six months and three weeks. In seven years she would be forty.

Sebastian had been four years old that night when she and Ralph had first danced together. A poppet in pyjamas, sleeping in his bed, while she looked into his father's eyes and realised with a sudden urgency that she wanted more of them. That she wanted more of him. She'd been twenty-seven, then. Ralph had been forty-six. Anything in the world had seemed possible.

Roxanne closed her eyes, remembering. It had been at the first night of a star-laden visiting production of *Romeo and Juliet* at the Barbican. Ralph had been sent two complimentary tickets and, at the last minute, had wandered into the editorial office of the *Londoner*, looking for a second taker. When Roxanne had jumped at the chance, his face had registered slight surprise. He had, he'd later confessed, always thought of her as a glossy, materialistic girl—bright and talented but with no real depth. When he turned to her at the end of the play to see her face streaked unashamedly with tears, he'd felt a lurch of surprise and an unexpected liking for her. Then, when she'd pushed her hair back off her brow, wiped her eyes and said, with her customary spirit, 'I'm bloody parched. How about a cocktail?' he'd thrown back his head and laughed. He'd produced two invitations for the post-performance party—which he hadn't been intending to use—had called his wife and told her that he would be a little later than he'd thought.

He and Roxanne had stood at the edge of the party, drinking Buck's Fizz and talking about the play. Then a jazz band had struck up and the floor had crowded with couples. And after hesitating a second, Ralph had asked her to dance. As soon as she'd felt his arms around her and looked up into his eyes, she'd known. She'd simply known.

A familiar spasm, half pain, half joy, went through Roxanne at the memory. She would always remember that night as one of the most magical in her life. Ralph had disappeared off to make a phone call that she hadn't allowed herself to think about. Then he had returned to the table at which she was sitting, trembling with excitement. He had sat down opposite her, had met her eyes and said slowly, 'I was thinking about going on somewhere from here. A hotel, perhaps. Would you . . . care to join me?' Roxanne had stared at him silently for a few seconds, then had put down her drink.

She had intended to play it cool, but the moment they had got into their taxi, Ralph had turned to her, and she had found herself gazing back with an almost desperate longing. As their lips met she had thought, with a brief flash of humour, Hey, I'm kissing the boss. And then his kiss had deepened and her eyes had closed and her mind had lost its capacity for coherent thought. A capacity which had only returned in the morning, as she woke up in a Park Lane hotel with an adulterous man nineteen years her senior.

'Glass of wine?' Ralph's voice interrupted her, and she opened her eyes to see him gazing fondly down at her. 'I could open the bottle I brought.'

'Only if it's properly cold,' she said suspiciously.

'It is cold,' said Ralph, smiling. 'I put it in the fridge when I got here.'

'It'd better be,' said Roxanne. She sat up and hugged her knees as he went back out to the kitchen. A minute later Ralph returned with two glasses full of wine.

'Why weren't you in the office today, by the way?' said Roxanne. She lifted her glass. 'Cheers.'

'Cheers,' replied Ralph. He took a long sip, then said easily, 'I had a meeting with my accountant all morning and into lunch. It didn't seem worth coming in.'

'Oh, right,' said Roxanne, and took a sip of wine. 'Slacker.'

A half-smile flickered across Ralph's face and he lowered himself slowly into a chair. Roxanne stared at him and frowned slightly.

'Are you OK?' she said. 'You look knackered.'

'Bit of a late night last night,' said Ralph, and closed his eyes.

'Oh well,' said Roxanne cheerfully. 'In that case, you don't get any sympathy from me.'

Candice took another swig of wine and gazed round the packed restaurant. 'I can't believe how full it is!' she said. 'I had no idea late-night shopping was such a big thing.'

Heather laughed. 'Have you never been shopping in the evening before?'

'Of course. But I didn't realise what a . . . party atmosphere there was here. You know, I might suggest to Justin that we do a piece on it. We could come down, interview some people, take some photographs . . .'

'Good idea,' said Heather, and sipped at her wine. In front of her was a paper menu and a pen that their waiter had left behind, and Heather idly picked it up. She began to doodle on the menu. Candice watched her, slightly mesmerised, slightly drunk. They had had to wait half an hour for a table, during which time they had consumed a gin and tonic each and half a bottle of wine. Somehow she seemed to be drinking more quickly than Heather.

'It's funny, isn't it?' said Heather, looking up suddenly. 'We're so close and yet we don't really know each other.'

'I suppose not,' said Candice, and grinned. 'Well, what do you want to know?'

'Tell me about Justin,' said Heather. 'Do you still like him?'

'No!' said Candice, then laughed. 'I suppose I can stand him as an editor. But I don't have any . . . feelings for him. I think that was all a huge mistake.'

'Really?' said Heather lightly.

'When I first met him, I thought he was incredibly clever and wonderful. But he's not. Not when you actually listen to what he's saying.' She took another gulp of wine. 'He just likes the sound of his own voice.'

'And there's no one else on the horizon?'

'Not at the moment,' said Candice. 'And I can't say I mind.'

'So . . . men aren't important to you?'

'I don't know,' said Candice, laughing a little. 'I suppose the right one would be.' She watched as Heather picked up the bottle of wine, replenished Candice's glass, then looked up, her eyes shining with intensity.

'So what is?' she asked softly. 'What means most to you in the world? What do you . . . treasure?'

'What do I treasure?' Candice repeated the question thoughtfully. 'I don't know. My family, I suppose. Although my mother and I aren't that close any more. And my friends.' She looked up with a sudden certainty. 'I treasure my friends. Roxanne and Maggie especially.'

'Your friends.' Heather nodded. 'Friends are such important things.'

'And my job. I love my job.'

'But not for the money,' probed Heather.

'No! I don't care about money!' Candice flushed slightly. 'I hate materialism. And greed. And . . . dishonesty.'

'You want to be a good person.'

'I want to try.' Candice gave an embarrassed little laugh. 'What about you? What do you treasure?'

There was a short silence, and a curious expression flitted across Heather's face. 'I've learned not to treasure anything much,' she said eventually, and gave a quick smile. 'Because you can lose it all overnight, with no warning. One minute you have it, the next you don't.' She snapped her fingers. 'Just like that.'

Candice stared at her in guilty misery, suddenly wanting to talk more; perhaps even reveal the truth.

'Heather . . .' she said hesitantly. 'I've . . . I've never—'

'Look!' interrupted Heather brightly. 'Here comes our food.'

Roxanne took a last mouthful of pasta, put down her fork and sighed. She was sitting opposite Ralph at her tiny folding dining table, the lights were dim and Ella Fitzgerald was crooning softly in the background.

'That was bloody delicious.' Roxanne hugged her stomach. 'Aren't you eating yours?'

'Go ahead.' Ralph gestured to his half-full plate, and, wrinkling her brow slightly, Roxanne pulled it towards her.

'No appetite?' she said. 'Or is it still your hangover?'

'Something like that,' said Ralph lightly.

'Well, I'm not going to let it go to waste,' said Roxanne, plunging her fork into the pasta. 'I always miss your cooking when I go away.'

'Do you?' said Ralph. 'What about all those five-star chefs?'

Roxanne pulled a face. 'Not the same. They can't do pasta like you.' She tilted her dining chair back so that it rested against the sofa, took a sip of wine and comfortably closed her eyes. 'In fact, I think it's very self-ish of you not to come and cook me pasta every night.' She took another sip of wine, then another. Then, as the silence continued, she opened her eyes. Ralph was gazing at her, a curious expression on his face.

'I am selfish,' he said at last. 'You're right. I've treated you appallingly selfishly.'

'No you haven't!' said Roxanne, giving a little laugh. 'I'm only joking.'

For a while they were both silent. Then Ralph, almost casually, said, 'Suppose in a year's time you could be doing anything. Anything at all. What would it be?'

'In a year's time,' echoed Roxanne, feeling her heart start to beat a little more quickly. 'Why a year?'

'Or three years,' said Ralph, making a vague gesture with his wine glass. 'Five years. Where do you see yourself?'

'Well, I . . . I don't know,' said Roxanne, and took a sip of wine, trying to stay calm. What was going on? She and Ralph, by tacit agreement, never discussed the future; never talked about their own situation.

In the early days, she had tearfully insisted on hearing about his wife, about his family; about every last detail. She had shaken with misery and humiliation each time he'd left; had thrown accusations and ultima-tums at him to no avail. Now she behaved almost as though each evening were a one-off; a self-contained bubble. It was simple self-preservation. That way she could pretend—at least to herself—that she was conducting the relationship on her own terms.

She looked up to see Ralph still waiting for an answer, and felt her stomach give a little flip. He was staring straight at her, his eyes glisten-ing slightly, as if her answer really mattered to him.

'In a year's time?' she said lightly. 'If I could be anywhere, I think I'd like to be lying on a white beach somewhere in the Caribbean—with you, naturally.'

'Glad to hear it,' said Ralph, his face crinkling into a smile.

'But not just you,' said Roxanne. 'A posse of attentive waiters in white jackets would see to our every need. Then, as if by magic, they would discreetly disappear, and we'd be left on our own in the magical sunset.'

She broke off and took a sip of wine, then, after a short silence, looked up. As she met Ralph's eyes, her heart was thumping. Does he realise, she thought, that what I have just described is a honeymoon?

Ralph was staring at her with an expression she'd never seen in his eyes before. Suddenly he took hold of her hands and drew them up to his lips.

'You deserve it,' he said roughly. 'You deserve it all, Roxanne.' She gazed at him, feeling a hotness growing at the back of her throat. 'I'm so sorry for everything,' he muttered. 'When I think what I've put you through . . .'

'Don't be sorry.' Roxanne blinked hard, feeling tears smarting at her eyes. She drew him close across the table and kissed his wet eyes, his cheeks, his lips. 'I love you,' she whispered, and felt a sudden swell of painful, possessive happiness inside her. 'I love you, and we're together. And that's all that counts.'

Chapter Five

THE HOSPITAL WAS A LARGE, Victorian building, with well-tended gardens at the front and a fenced area for children to play in. As Roxanne and Candice got out of the car and began to walk along the path towards the main entrance, Roxanne started laughing.

'Typical Maggie,' she said. 'Even the hospital's a picture postcard. She couldn't have her baby in some grim London hellhole, could she?'

They strode into the reception area and spoke to a friendly woman at a desk, who tapped Maggie's name into a computer.

'Blue Ward,' she said. 'Follow the corridor round as far as you can go, then take the lift to the fifth floor.'

As they walked along the corridors, Candice pulled a face.

'I hate the smell of hospitals,' she said. 'Horrible places. I think if I ever had a baby, I'd have it at home.'

'Of course you would,' said Roxanne. 'With panpipes playing in the background and aromatherapy candles scenting the air.'

'No!' said Candice, laughing. 'I'd just . . . I don't know. Prefer to be at home, I suppose.'

'Well, if I ever have a baby, I'll have it by Caesarean,' said Roxanne drily. 'Full anaesthesia. They can wake me up when it's three years old.'

They arrived at the lift and pressed the fifth-floor button. As they began to rise, Candice glanced at Roxanne. 'You look tired,' she said. 'Are you feeling OK?'

'I'm great,' said Roxanne, and tossed her hair back. 'Never better.'

But as they rose up in the lift, she stared at her tinted reflection in the lift doors. She did look tired. Since that night with Ralph she had found it difficult to sleep; impossible to wrench her mind away from their conversation and what it had meant. Impossible to stop hoping.

Of course, Ralph had said nothing definite. He had made no promises. After that one short conversation, he had not even referred to the future again. But something was going on; something was different. As they'd said goodbye, he'd stared at her for minutes without speaking. It was as though he was coming to the hardest decision of his life.

She knew it was a decision that couldn't be hurried, but the stress of this constant uncertainty was unbearable. And they were both suffering because of it—Ralph looked tired and strained. She'd glimpsed him the other day at the office, and had realised with a shock that he was actually losing weight. What mental hell he must be going through. And yet if he would only make up his mind and take courage, the hell would be over for good.

Once again, a surge of painful hope rose through her. She shouldn't allow herself to think like this. But after six years of refusing to hope or even think about it, her mind was now gorging itself on fantasy. Ralph would leave his wife. They would both be able to relax; to enjoy each other. They would set up house together. Perhaps they would even—

There she stopped herself. She could not let herself go that far; she had to keep some control on herself. After all, nothing had been said. But surely that conversation had meant something? Surely he was at least thinking about it?

And she deserved it, didn't she? She bloody well deserved it, after everything she'd been through. An unfamiliar resentment began to steal over her. Over the past few days, having let her mind break out into fantasy land, she had discovered that beneath the joyous hope there was a darker flip side. An anger that she had suppressed for too many years. Six whole years of waiting and wondering and grabbing moments of happiness where she could. It had been too long.

The lift doors opened and Candice looked up at Roxanne.

'Well, here we are,' she said, and gave a little smile. 'At last.'

'Yes,' said Roxanne, and exhaled sharply. 'At last.'

They walked out of the lift and towards a swing door marked 'Blue Ward'. Candice hesitantly pushed the door open. The room was large, but divided into cubicles by floral curtains. Candice raised her eyebrows at Roxanne, who shrugged back. Then a woman in a dark blue uniform, holding a baby, approached them.

'Are you here to visit?' she said, smiling.

'Yes,' said Roxanne. 'Maggie Drakeford.'

'Oh yes,' said the woman pleasantly. 'In the corner.'

Roxanne and Candice advanced slowly down the ward. Finally, Candice pushed back the curtain of the last cubicle, and there she was, Maggie, sitting up in bed with a tiny baby in her arms. For a moment none of them said anything. Then Maggie gave a wide smile, held up the baby to face them and said, 'Lucia, meet the cocktail queens.'

Maggie had had a good night. As she watched Roxanne and Candice advance hesitantly towards the bed, eyes glued on Lucia's tiny face, she allowed herself to feel a warm glow of contentment. A bit of sleep, that was all. A bit of sleep every night, and the world changed.

The first three nights had been hell. Utter misery. She had lain stiffly in the darkness, unable to sleep while there was even the smallest chance that Lucia might wake. Even when she had drifted off to sleep, every snuffle from the tiny crib would wake her.

On the fourth night, at two in the morning, Lucia had refused to go back to sleep. She had cried when Maggie tried to place her in her cot and thrashed about when she tried to feed her. After a few minutes, a face had appeared round Maggie's curtain. It was a midwife Maggie had not met before, and at the sight of Lucia, she shook her head comically.

'Young lady, your mother needs her sleep!' she'd said, advancing inside the cubicle. She had looked at Maggie's shadowed face and sighed. 'This is no good. You look exhausted.'

'I feel a bit tired,' Maggie had admitted in a wobbly voice.

'You need a break.' The midwife had paused, then said, 'Would you like me to take her to the nursery?'

'The nursery?' Maggie had stared at her blankly. Nobody had told her about any nursery.

'I can keep an eye on her and you can have a sleep. Then, when she needs feeding, I can bring her back.'

Maggie had stared at the midwife, wanting to burst into tears with gratitude. 'Thank you. Thank you . . . Joan,' she had managed, reading the woman's name-badge in the dim light. 'Will she be all right?'

'She'll be fine!' Joan had said reassuringly. 'Now, you get some rest.'

As soon as she had left the cubicle, wheeling Lucia's crib, Maggie had fallen into the first relaxed sleep she'd had since Lucia's birth. She had woken at six, feeling almost restored, to see Lucia back in the cubicle again, ready for feeding.

Since then, Joan had appeared at Maggie's bedside each night, offering the services of the nursery—and Maggie had found herself guiltily accepting every time. She felt she should be with Lucia twenty-four hours a day, as all the books recommended. Anything less was failure. And so she hadn't mentioned Joan to Giles or to Paddy—or, in fact, to anyone.

Now she smiled at Roxanne and Candice and said, 'Come on in and sit down. It's so good to see you.'

'Mags, you look wonderful!' said Roxanne. She embraced Maggie in a cloud of scent, then sat down on the edge of the bed. She was looking thinner and more glamorous than ever, thought Maggie. And for an instant, Maggie felt a twinge of jealousy. She'd imagined that straight after the birth she would regain her old figure, but her stomach was still frighteningly flabby and she had no energy to exercise it.

'So, Mags,' drawled Roxanne, looking round the ward. 'Is motherhood all it's cracked up to be?'

'Oh, you know.' Maggie grinned. 'Not too bad. Of course, I'm an old hand now.'

'Maggie, she's beautiful!' Candice looked up with shining eyes. 'And she doesn't look ill at all.'

'She's not, really,' said Maggie. 'She had jaundice, and it's taken a while to clear up. It just meant we had to stay in hospital a bit longer.'

'Can I hold her?' Candice held out her arms and, after a pause, Maggie handed the baby over.

'She's so light,' breathed Candice.

'Very sweet,' said Roxanne. 'You'll be making me broody in a moment.'

Maggie laughed. 'Now, that would be a miracle.'

'Do you want to hold her?' Candice looked up at Roxanne, who rolled her eyes comically.

'If I must.'

She had held scores of babies before that aroused in her no feeling other than tedium. Roxanne Miller did not coo over babies, she yawned over them. She was famous for it. But as she looked into the sleeping face of Maggie's baby, Roxanne felt her defences begin to crumble; found herself thinking thoughts she had never let herself think before. She wanted one of these. Oh God. She actually wanted one. The thought frightened her, exhilarated her. She closed her eyes and imagined herself holding her own baby. Ralph's baby. The picture made her almost sick with hope, and with fear. She was treading on forbidden ground.

'So, what do you reckon, Roxanne?' said Maggie, looking at her amusedly. Roxanne stared at Lucia a few seconds longer, then forced herself to look up with a nonchalant expression.

'Very nice, as babies go. But I warn you, she'd better not pee on me.'

'I'll take her back,' said Maggie, smiling, and a ridiculous thud of disappointment went through Roxanne.

'Here you are then, Mummy,' she drawled, handing the bundle back.

'Oh, Maggie, I brought you these,' said Candice, rescuing the bouquet of flowers that she'd deposited on the floor.

'They're lovely,' said Maggie, smiling. 'Thank you.' Candice looked round the cubicle. 'Have you got a vase?'

Maggie pulled a doubtful face. 'There might be one in the corridor. Or one of the other wards.'

'I'll find one.' Candice put the flowers on the bed and headed out of the ward. When she'd gone, Maggie and Roxanne smiled at each other.

'So—how are you?' asked Maggie.

'Oh, fine,' said Roxanne. 'You know, life goes on . . .'

'How's Mr Married with Kids?' asked Maggie cautiously.

'Still got kids,' said Roxanne lightly. 'Still married.' They both laughed, and Lucia stirred slightly in her sleep. 'Although . . . you never know,' Roxanne couldn't resist adding. 'Changes may be afoot.'

'Really?' said Maggie in astonishment. 'You're not serious?'

'Who knows?' A smile spread over Roxanne's face. 'Watch this space.'

'You mean we might actually get to meet him?'

'Oh, I don't know about that.' Roxanne's eyes flashed in amusement. 'I've got used to him being my little secret.'

Maggie smiled at her, then said, 'Tell me about the outside world. What have I been missing?'

'Oh God, I don't know,' said Roxanne lazily. 'I never know the gossip. I'm always away when things happen.'

'What about that girl of Candice's?' said Maggie, suddenly frowning. 'Heather Whatsername. Have you met her again?'

'Yes, I saw her at the office. Didn't exactly warm to her.' Roxanne pulled a face. 'Bit sickly sweet.'

'I don't know why I got so worked up about her,' said Maggie ruefully. 'Pregnancy paranoia. She's probably a lovely girl.'

'Well, I wouldn't go that far. But I tell you what—' Roxanne sat up and reached for her bag. 'She can certainly write.'

'Really?'

'Look at this.' Roxanne pulled a sheet of paper from her bag. 'I got it from Janet. It's actually very funny.'

She watched as Maggie read the first two lines of the piece, frowned, then scanned further down to the end.

'I don't believe it!' she exclaimed as she looked up. 'Did she really get a job at the *Londoner* on the strength of this piece?'

'I don't know,' said Roxanne. 'But you've got to admit, it's on the nail.'

'Of course it is,' said Maggie drily. 'Everything Candice writes is on the nail.'

'What?' Roxanne stared at her.

'Candice wrote this for the *Londoner*,' said Maggie. 'I remember it. Word for word. It's her style and everything.'

'I don't believe it!'

'No wonder Ralph was impressed,' said Maggie, rolling her eyes. 'God, Candice can be an idiot sometimes.'

Candice had taken longer than she had expected to find a vase, and had struck up a conversation with one of the midwives on another ward. As she finally made her way back to the ward, she saw Roxanne and Maggie staring at her, ominous expressions on their faces.

'So,' said Roxanne. 'What do you have to say for yourself?'

'What?' said Candice.

'This,' said Maggie, producing the piece of paper with a flourish. Candice stared at it in bewilderment—then, as she realised what it was, a flush spread over her cheeks.

'Oh, that,' she said. 'Well . . . Heather didn't have any examples of her writing. So I—' She broke off awkwardly.

'So you thought you'd supply her with an entire portfolio?'

'No!' said Candice. 'Just one little piece. Just . . . you know.' She shrugged defensively. 'Something to get her started. For God's sake, it's no big deal.'

Maggie shook her head. 'Candice, it's not fair. It's not fair on Ralph, it's not fair on all the other people who applied for the job . . .'

'It's not fair on Heather, come to that,' put in Roxanne. 'What happens when Justin asks her to write another piece just like that one?'

'He won't! And she's fine. You know, she has got talent. She can do the job. She just needed a chance.'

There was silence—then Maggie said, 'And she's living with you.'

'Yes.' Candice looked from face to face. 'What's wrong with that?'

'Is she paying you rent?'

'I . . .' Candice swallowed. 'That's our business, don't you think?'

She had not yet mentioned rent to Heather—nor had Heather ever brought the subject up. In her heart she had always assumed that Heather would offer to pay something, at least—but then even if she didn't, Candice thought with a sudden fierceness, what was the big deal? It wasn't as if she was desperate for the money.

'Of course it is,' said Roxanne. 'As long as she isn't using you.'

'*Using* me?' Candice shook her head disbelievingly. 'After what my father did to her family?'

'Candice—'

'No, listen to me,' said Candice. 'I owe her one. OK? I owe her one. So maybe I got her this job under slightly false pretences, and maybe I'm being more generous to her than I normally would. But she deserves a break.' Candice felt her face growing hot. 'And I know you don't like her, Roxanne, but—'

'What?' said Roxanne in outrage. 'I've barely spoken to her!'

'Well, she has the impression you don't like her.'

'Maybe she doesn't like *me*. Had you thought of that?'

'Why wouldn't she like you?' retorted Candice indignantly.

'I don't know! Why wouldn't I like her, for that matter?'

'This is ridiculous!' cut in Maggie. 'Stop it, both of you!'

At her raised voice, Lucia gave a sudden wriggle and began to wail, plaintively at first, then more lustily.

'Now look what you've done!' said Maggie.

'Oh,' said Candice, and bit her lip. 'Sorry. I didn't mean to lose it like that.'

'Neither did I,' said Roxanne. She squeezed Candice's hand. 'Don't get me wrong. I'm sure Heather's a great girl. We just worry about you.'

'You're too nice,' put in Maggie, then winced. The others turned and, in appalled fascination, watched her putting Lucia to her breast.

'Does it hurt?' said Candice, watching Maggie's face involuntarily screw up in pain.

'A bit,' said Maggie. 'Just at first.' The baby began to suck and gradually her face relaxed. 'There. That's better.'

'Bloody hell,' said Roxanne, staring at Maggie's breast. 'Rather you than me.' She pulled a face at Candice, who gave a sudden giggle.

'She likes a drink, anyway,' she said, watching Lucia greedily sucking.

'Like her mother,' said Roxanne. 'Speaking of which . . .' She reached into her bag and, after some rummaging, produced a silver cocktail shaker.

'No!' exclaimed Maggie in disbelief. 'You haven't!'

'I told you we'd toast the baby with cocktails,' said Roxanne.

'But we can't,' said Maggie, giggling. 'If somebody sees us, I'll get thrown out of the Good Mother club!'

'I thought of that, too,' said Roxanne. With a straight face, she reached into the bag again and produced three little baby bottles. She unscrewed each of the bottles, placed them in a row on the bedside table, picked up the cocktail shaker and gave it a good shake as the other two watched in amazement. Then she removed the lid of the cocktail shaker and solemnly poured a thick white liquid into each of the bottles.

'What is it?' said Candice, staring at it.

'Not milk, surely?' said Maggie.

'Pina Colada,' said Roxanne airily.

At once, Candice and Maggie exploded into giggles. Pina Colada was a standing joke between them—ever since that first uproarious night at the Manhattan Bar, when Roxanne had announced that if anyone ordered Pina Colada she was disowning them.

'I mustn't!' wailed Maggie, trying not to shake. 'I mustn't laugh. Poor Lucia.'

'Cheers,' said Roxanne, handing her a baby bottle.

'To Lucia,' said Candice.

'Lucia,' echoed Roxanne, holding her bottle up.

'And to you two,' said Maggie, smiling at Roxanne and Candice. She took a gulp and closed her eyes in delight.

'The thing is,' said Candice, taking a slurp, 'that actually, Pina Colada is bloody delicious.'

'It's not bad, is it?' said Roxanne, sipping thoughtfully. 'If they could just call it something classier . . .'

'Talking of alcohol, Ralph Allsopp sent us a magnum of champagne,' said Maggie. 'Wasn't that nice of him? But we haven't opened it yet.'

'Great minds think alike,' said Roxanne lightly.

'Mrs Drakeford?' A doctor's cheerful head popped round the side of the curtain and grinned at them all. 'Mrs Drakeford, I'm one of the paediatricians. Come to check up on little Lucia.'

'Oh,' said Maggie weakly. 'Ahm . . . come in.'

'I'll take your . . . milk, shall I?' said Roxanne and reached for Maggie's baby bottle. 'Here. I'll leave it on your bedside table for later.'

'Thanks,' said Maggie trying not to laugh.

'Maybe we'd better go,' said Candice.

'OK,' whispered Maggie.

'See you soon,' said Roxanne. She downed her Pina Colada in one and thrust the empty bottle back into her bag.

'Lucia's gorgeous,' said Candice, and bent over the bed to kiss Maggie. 'And we'll see you soon.'

'At the Manhattan Bar,' put in Roxanne. 'First of the month. You think you'll be able to make it, Maggie?'

'Absolutely,' said Maggie, and grinned at her. 'I'll be there.'

As Candice arrived home that evening, her cheeks were flushed with happiness and she still felt giggles rising whenever she thought of the baby bottles full of Pina Colada. She also felt more emotional than she had been expecting to. The sight of Maggie and her baby had stirred her deep inside; more than she had been aware at the time. Now she felt overflowing with affection for both her friends.

The only awkward moment had been over Heather—and that, thought Candice, was because they didn't understand. Maggie and Roxanne had never felt her secret, constant guilt—so they couldn't know what it was like to feel that guilt alleviated. They couldn't understand the lightness she had felt inside over the past few weeks; the sheer pleasure it gave her to see Heather's life falling into place.

Besides which, neither of them had really met Heather properly. They had no idea what a warm and generous person she was; how quickly the friendship between them had developed. Maggie and Roxanne behaved as though having Heather living in her flat were a huge disadvantage. In fact, the opposite was true. Heather wasn't a disadvantage, thought Candice affectionately. She was a life-enhancer.

As she closed the front door behind her, she could hear Heather's voice in the kitchen. She sounded as though she might be on the phone, and Candice advanced cautiously down the corridor, not wanting to disturb Heather's privacy. A few feet before she reached the kitchen, she stopped in slight shock.

'Don't give me any of your grief, Hamish!' Heather was saying, in a low, tense voice so far from her usual bubbling tones that Candice barely recognised it. 'What the fuck is it to you?' There was a pause, then she said, 'Yeah, well maybe I don't care. Yeah well, maybe I will!' Her voice rose to a shout and there was the sound of the phone slamming down. Out in the hall, Candice froze in panic. Please don't come out, she thought. Please don't come out and see me.

Feeling absurdly guilty, she tiptoed a few feet back down the hall, opened the front door again, then banged it shut. 'Hi!' she called brightly. 'Anyone in?'

Heather appeared at the kitchen door and gazed at Candice appraisingly, without smiling.

'Hi,' she said at last. 'I was on the phone. I expect you heard.'

'No!' said Candice. 'I've only just got in.' She felt herself flushing.

'Men,' said Heather after a pause. 'Who needs them?'

Candice looked up in surprise. 'Have you got a boyfriend?'

'Ex-boyfriend,' said Heather. 'Utter bastard. You don't want to know.'

'Right,' said Candice awkwardly. 'Well—shall we have some tea?'

'Why not?' said Heather, and followed her back into the kitchen.

'By the way,' said Heather, as Candice reached for the tea bags, 'I needed some stamps, so I got some from your dressing table. You don't mind, do you? I'll pay you back.'

'Don't be silly!' said Candice. 'And of course I don't mind. Help yourself.' She laughed. 'What's mine is yours.'

'OK,' said Heather casually. 'Thanks.'

Roxanne arrived back at her flat cold and hungry, to see a cardboard box waiting outside the front door. She stared at it, bewildered, then opened the door and gave it little shoves with her foot until it was inside. She shut the front door, flicked on the lights, then crouched down and looked at the box more closely. The postmark was Cyprus and the writing on the label was Nico's.

Smiling a little, Roxanne ripped open the box, to see row upon row of bright orange tangerines, still with their green leaves attached to the stalks. She picked one up, closed her eyes, and inhaled the sweet, tangy, unmistakable scent. Then she reached for the handwritten sheet lying on top of the tangerines.

My dearest Roxanne,
  A small reminder of what you are missing, here in Cyprus. Andreas and I are still hoping you will reconsider our offer.
  Yours as ever,
  Nico.

For a moment, Roxanne was quite still. Then she looked at the tangerine consideringly, threw it into the air and caught it. Bright and sweet, sunny and appealing, she thought. Another world altogether. But her world was here. Here in the soft London rain, with Ralph.

After all the visitors had left the ward and Lucia had settled to sleep, Maggie lay awake trying to quell her feelings of panic.

The paediatrician had been very complimentary about Lucia's progress. The jaundice had completely gone, she was putting on weight well, and all was as it should be.

'You can go home tomorrow,' he'd said, 'I expect you're sick of this place.'

'Absolutely,' Maggie had said, and had smiled weakly at him. 'I can't wait to get home.'

Later, Giles had arrived to visit—and when she'd told him the good news, had whooped with delight.

'At last! What a relief. You must be thrilled. Oh, darling, won't it be great, having you home again?' He'd leaned forward and hugged her so tightly she could hardly breathe, and her spirits had, for a moment, lifted to something near euphoria.

But now, lying in the dark, she could feel nothing but fear. In ten days, she had become used to the rhythm of life in hospital. She had become used to the feeling of security: the knowledge that, if disaster struck, there was always a button to press, a nurse to summon. She had become used to Joan wheeling Lucia off at two in the morning and returning at six.

She exhaled sharply, then switched on her night light, glanced at Lucia's sleeping face, and poured herself a glass of water.

'Can't sleep?' A young midwife poked her head round the curtain. 'I expect you're excited about going home.'

'Oh yes,' said Maggie again, forcing a smile onto her face. 'Can't wait.'

The midwife disappeared and she stared miserably into her glass of water. She couldn't tell anyone how she really felt. She couldn't tell anyone that she was scared of returning to her own home, with her own baby. They would think she was absolutely mad. Perhaps she was.

Late that night, Candice awoke with a start and stared into the darkness of her room. A sound was coming from the kitchen. Oh my God, she thought: a burglar. She lay quite still, heart thumping in panic—then slowly and silently she got out of bed, wrapped a dressing gown around herself and cautiously opened the door of her room.

The kitchen light was on. Did burglars usually put lights on? She hesitated, then padded out into the corridor. As she reached the kitchen, she stopped and stared in shock. Heather was sitting at the table, cradling a cup of coffee, surrounded by page proofs of the *Londoner*. As Candice stared, she looked up, her face drawn and anxious.

'Hi,' she said, and immediately looked back at the sheets of paper.

'Hi,' said Candice, staring at her. 'What are you doing? You're not working, surely?'

'I forgot all about it,' said Heather, rubbing her red eyes. 'I brought these pages home to work on over the weekend, and I completely forgot to do them. How can I be so *stupid*?'

'Well . . . don't worry,' said Candice. 'It's not the end of the world.'

'I've got to redo five pages by tomorrow,' said Heather, a note of desperation in her voice. 'And then I've got to put all the corrections onto the computer by the time Alicia arrives. I promised they'd be ready.'

'I don't understand,' said Candice, sinking onto a chair. 'Why have you got so much work?'

'I got behind,' said Heather. 'Alicia gave me a load of stuff to do, and I . . . I don't know, maybe I'm not as quick as everyone else. Maybe everyone else is cleverer than me.'

'Rubbish!' said Candice at once. 'I'll have a word with Alicia.' She had always liked Alicia, the earnest chief subeditor.

'No, don't,' said Heather at once. 'She'll just say—' She stopped abruptly and there was silence in the little kitchen.

'What?' said Candice. 'What will she say?'

'She'll say I should never have got the job in the first place,' said Heather miserably.

'What?' Candice laughed. 'Alicia wouldn't say that.'

'She already has,' said Heather. 'She's said it several times.'

'Are you serious?' Candice stared at her in disbelief.

Heather gazed back at her, as though debating whether to carry on, then sighed. 'Apparently a friend of hers applied for the job, too. Some girl with two years' experience on another magazine. And I got it over her. Alicia was a bit annoyed.'

'Oh.' Candice rubbed her nose, discomfited. 'I had no idea.'

'So I can't let her know I'm slipping behind. I've just got to manage.' Heather took a sip of coffee. 'Go back to bed, Candice. Honestly.'

'I can't just leave you!' said Candice. 'I feel terrible about this. I had no idea you were being worked so hard.'

'It's fine, really. Just as long as I get it all done by tomorrow morning'—Heather's voice shook slightly—'I'll be all right.'

'No,' said Candice. 'Come on, this is silly! I'll do some of this work. It won't take me nearly as long.'

'Really? Would you?' Heather looked up at her entreatingly. 'Oh, Candice . . .'

'I'll go in early and do the work straight onto the computer.'

'But . . . won't Alicia know you've been helping me?'

'I'll send the pages over to your terminal when I've finished them. And you can print them out.' Candice grinned. 'Easy.'

'Candice, you're a star,' said Heather, sinking back into her chair. 'And it'll just be this once, I promise.'

'No problem,' said Candice. 'What are friends for?'

The next day she went into work early and sat, patiently working through the pages Heather had been given to correct. It took her rather longer than she had expected, and it was eleven o'clock before she had perfected the final proof. She glanced over at Heather, gave her the thumbs up and pressed the button that would send the page electronically to Heather's computer terminal. Behind her she could hear Alicia saying, 'This page is fine, too. Well done, Heather!'

Candice grinned and reached for her cup of coffee. She felt rather like a schoolchild outwitting the teachers.

'Candice?' She looked up at Justin's voice and saw him standing at the door of his office. His brows were knitted together in a thoughtful frown—which he'd probably been practising in the bathroom mirror, she thought with an inward grin. After having lived with Justin and seen his little vanities close at hand, she couldn't take his studied facial expressions seriously any more. Indeed, she could barely take him seriously as an editor at all. He could throw as many long words as he liked around at meetings, but he would never be half the editor Maggie was.

'What is it?' she said, reluctantly getting out of her seat and going towards his office.

'Candice, I'm still waiting for the profile list you promised me,' said Justin as she sat down.

'Oh yes,' she said, and felt herself flush with annoyance. Trust Justin to catch her out. She'd meant to type up the list that morning, but Heather's pages had taken priority. 'I'm onto it,' she said.

'Hmm. This isn't the first piece of work you've been late with, is it?'

'Yes it is!' said Candice indignantly. 'And it's only a list. It's not exactly front-page editorial.'

'Hmm.' Justin looked at her thoughtfully and Candice felt herself stiffen with irritation.

'So, how are you enjoying being acting editor?' she said, to change the subject.

'Very much,' said Justin, nodding gravely. 'Very much indeed.' He put his elbows on the desk and carefully placed his fingertips together. 'I see myself rather as a troubleshooter,' said Justin. 'I intend to institute a series of spot checks in order to locate problems with the system.'

'What problems?' said Candice. 'Are there problems with the system?'

'I've been analysing the running of this magazine since I took power—'

Power! thought Candice scornfully.

'—and I've noticed several glitches which, frankly, Maggie just didn't pick up on.'

'Oh, really?' Candice folded her arms and gave him the least impressed look she could muster. 'So, you think, after a few weeks, you're a better editor than Maggie.'

'That's not what I said.' Justin paused. 'Maggie has, as we all know, many wonderful talents and qualities—'

'Yes, well, Ralph obviously thinks so,' put in Candice loyally. 'He sent her a magnum of champagne.'

'I'm sure he did,' said Justin, and leaned comfortably back in his chair. 'You know he's retiring in a couple of weeks' time?'

'What?'

'I just heard it this morning. Wants to spend more time with his family, apparently,' said Justin. 'It seems one of his sons is going to take over. He's coming in to meet us all next week.'

'Gosh,' said Candice, taken aback. 'I had no idea that was on the cards.' She frowned. 'Does Maggie know about this?'

'I doubt it,' said Justin, carelessly. 'Why should she? She's got other things to think about.' He took a sip of coffee, then glanced over her shoulder through the window at the editorial office. 'That friend of yours is doing well, by the way.'

'Who, Heather?' said Candice, with a glow of pride. 'Yes, she is good, isn't she? I told you she would be.'

'She came to me with an excellent idea for a feature the other day,' said Justin. 'I was impressed.'

'Oh yes?' said Candice. 'What's the idea?'

'Late-night shopping,' said Justin. 'Do a whole piece on it.'

'What?' Candice stared at him.

'We'll run it in the lifestyle section. Take a photographer down to a shopping mall, interview customers . . .' Justin frowned at her flabbergasted expression. 'What's wrong? Don't you think it's a good idea?'

'Of course I do!' exclaimed Candice. 'But . . .' She broke off feebly. What could she say without looking as though she wanted to get Heather into trouble?

'What?'

'Nothing,' said Candice slowly. 'It's . . . it's a great idea.'

Heather stood by the coffee machine with Kelly, the editorial secretary. Kelly was a sixteen-year-old girl with a thin, bright-eyed face, always eager for the latest gossip.

'You were working hard this morning,' Kelly said, pressing the button for hot chocolate. 'I saw you, typing hard!' Heather smiled, and leaned against the coffee machine. 'And sending lots of things to Candice, weren't you?' added the young secretary.

Heather's head jerked up. 'Yes,' she said carefully. 'How could you tell?'

'I heard your email pinging away,' said Kelly. 'The two of you, pinging away all morning!' She laughed merrily, and picked up her polystyrene cup full of hot chocolate.

'That's right,' said Heather after a pause. 'How observant of you.' She pressed the button for white coffee. 'You know what all that email was?' she said in a lower voice.

'What?' said Kelly interestedly.

'Candice makes me send all my work to her to be checked,' whispered Heather. 'Every single word I write.'

'You're joking!' said Kelly. 'Why does she do that?'

'I don't know,' said Heather. 'I suppose she thinks I'm not up to scratch, or something . . .'

'Bloody nerve,' said Kelly. 'I wouldn't stand for it.' She blew on her hot chocolate. 'I've never liked Candice very much.'

'Really?' said Heather. 'Kelly—what are you doing at lunchtime?'

Roxanne sat opposite Ralph at her little dining table and looked accusingly at him across her mound of beef stroganoff.

'You've got to stop cooking me such nice food,' she said. 'I'm going to be fat now.'

'Rubbish,' said Ralph, taking a sip of wine and running a hand down Roxanne's thigh. 'Look at that. You're perfect.'

'That's easy for you to say,' said Roxanne. 'You haven't seen me in a bikini.'

'I've seen you in a lot less than a bikini.' Ralph grinned at her.

'On the beach, I mean!' said Roxanne impatiently. 'Next to all the fifteen-year-olds. There were scores of them in Cyprus. Horrible skinny things with long legs and huge brown eyes.'

'Can't stand brown eyes,' said Ralph obligingly.

'You've got brown eyes,' pointed out Roxanne.

'I know. Can't stand them.'

Roxanne laughed and leaned back in her chair, lifting up her feet so that they nestled in Ralph's lap. As he reached down and began to massage them, she felt again the light tripping sensation in her heart; the lift of hope, of excitement. Ralph had arranged this meeting as an unexpected extra treat; a few days ago he had surprised her with a bouquet of flowers. It wasn't her imagination—he was definitely behaving differently. A sudden fizz of hope rose through Roxanne.

'How did the trip go, by the way?' he added, stroking her toes. 'I never asked. Same old thing?'

'More or less,' said Roxanne. She reached for her wine and took a sip. 'Oh, except you'll never guess what. Nico Georgiou offered me a job.'

'A job?' Ralph stared at her. 'In Cyprus?'

'At the new resort he's building. Marketing manager or something.' Roxanne looked provocatively at Ralph. 'He's offering a very good deal. What do you think? Shall I take it?'

Over the years, she had often teased him like this. She would mention job opportunities in Scotland, in Spain, in America—some genuine, some fabricated. The teasing was partly in fun—and partly from a genuine need to make him realise that she was choosing to be with him; that she was not staying with him simply by default. But today, it was almost a test. A way of getting him to talk about the future again.

'He even sent me a box of tangerines,' she added, gesturing to the fruit bowl, where the tangerines were piled up in a shiny orange pyramid. 'So he must be serious. What do you think?'

What she expected was for him to grin, and say, 'Well, he can sod off,' as he usually did. But Ralph stared at her as though she were a stranger —then, eventually, cleared his throat and said, 'Do you want to take it?'

'For God's sake, Ralph!' said Roxanne, disappointment sharpening her voice. 'I'm only joking! Of course I don't want to take it.'

'Why not?' He was leaning forward, looking at her with an odd expression on his face. 'Wouldn't it be a good job?'

'I don't know!' exclaimed Roxanne. 'Since you ask, I expect it would be a marvellous job.' She reached for her cigarettes. 'And they're *desperate* to have me.'

'So—what did you say to them?' said Ralph, meshing his hands together as though in prayer. 'How did you leave it?'

'Oh, the usual,' said Roxanne. 'Thanks, but no thanks.'

'So you turned it down.'

'Of course I did!' said Roxanne, giving a little laugh. 'Why? Do you think I should have said yes?'

There was silence, and Roxanne looked up. At Ralph's tense expression she felt a sudden coldness inside her.

'Maybe it's time for you to move on. Take one of these opportunities up.' Ralph reached for his glass of wine with a trembling hand and took a sip. 'I've held you back far too long. I've got in your way.'

'Ralph, don't be stupid!'

'Is it too late to change your mind?' Ralph looked up. 'Could you still go to them and say you're interested?'

Roxanne stared at him in shock.

'Yes,' she said eventually. 'I suppose I could, in theory . . .' She swallowed, scarcely able to believe they were having this conversation. 'Are you going to tell me I should? Do you want me to take this job?'

There was silence, then Ralph looked up. 'Yes,' he said. 'I do. I think you should take it.'

There was silence in the room. This is a bad dream, thought Roxanne. 'I . . . I don't understand,' she said at last, trying to stay calm. 'Ralph, what's going on? You were talking about the future. You were talking about Caribbean beaches!'

'I wasn't, you were.'

'You *asked* me!' said Roxanne furiously. 'Jesus!'

'I know I did. But that was . . . dreaming. Idle fantasies. This is real life. And I think if you have an opportunity in Cyprus, then you should take it.'

'Fuck the opportunity!' She felt close to tears, and swallowed hard. 'What about you and me? What about that opportunity?'

'There's something I need to tell you,' said Ralph abruptly. 'There's something that will . . . make a difference to you and me.' He stood up, walked to the window, then, after a long pause, turned round. 'I'm planning to retire, Roxanne,' he said without smiling. 'To the country. I want to spend more time with my family.'

At first Roxanne didn't comprehend what he was saying. Then, as his meaning hit her, she felt a stabbing pain in her chest.

'You mean it's over,' she whispered, her mouth dry. 'You mean you've had your fun. And now you're off to . . . to play happy families.'

There was silence.

'If you want to put it that way,' said Ralph eventually, 'then yes.' He met her eyes, then looked away quickly.

'No,' said Roxanne, feeling her whole body starting to shake. 'No. I won't let you. You can't.' She flashed a desperate smile at him. 'It can't be over. Not just like that.'

'You'll go to Cyprus,' said Ralph, a slight tremor in his voice. 'And you'll make a wonderful new life for yourself. Away from all . . . all this.' He lifted a hand to his brow and rubbed it. 'It's for the best, Roxanne.'

'You don't want me to go to Cyprus. You don't mean it. Tell me you don't mean it.' She felt out of control, almost dizzy. 'You're joking . . .'

'No, Roxanne. I'm not joking.'

'But you love me!' Her smile grew even wider; tears began to drip down her cheeks. 'You love me, Ralph.'

'Yes,' said Ralph in a suddenly choked voice. 'I do. I love you, Roxanne. Remember that.'

He stepped forward, took her hands and squeezed them hard against his lips. Then, without saying anything, he turned, picked up his coat from the sofa and left.

Through a sea of pain, Roxanne watched him go; heard the front door shut. For a second she was silent, white-faced, quivering slightly. Then with a trembling hand she reached for a cushion, held it up to her face with both hands and screamed silently into it.

Chapter Six

MAGGIE LEANED AGAINST A FENCE and closed her eyes, breathing in the clean country air. It was mid-morning, the sky was bright blue and there was a feel of summer about the air. In her previous life, she thought, she would have felt uplifted by the weather. But today, standing in her own fields, with her baby asleep in the pram beside her, she felt pale and drained through lack of sleep. Lucia was waking every two hours, demanding to be fed. She could not breastfeed her in bed, because Giles, with his demanding job, needed to sleep. And so she seemed to be spending the whole night sitting in the rocking chair in the nursery, falling into a doze as Lucia fed, then waking with a start as the baby began to wail again. As the greyness of morning approached, she would rouse herself, pad blearily into the bedroom, holding Lucia in her arms.

'Good morning!' Giles would say, beaming sleepily from the big double bed. 'How are my girls?'

'Fine,' Maggie said every morning, without elaborating. For what was the point? It wasn't as if Giles could feed Lucia; it wasn't as if he could make her sleep. And she felt a certain dogged triumph at her own refusal to complain; at her ability to tell Giles that everything was going wonderfully, and see him believe her. She had heard him on the phone, telling his friends, in tones of pride, that Maggie had taken to mother-hood like a duck to water. Then he would come and kiss her warmly and say that everyone was amazed at how competent she was. 'Mother of the Year!' he said one evening. 'I told you so!' His delight in her was transparent. She couldn't spoil it all now.

So she would simply hand Lucia to him and sink into the bed, almost wanting to cry in relief. Those half-hours every morning were her salva-tion. She would watch Giles playing with Lucia and feel a warm glow creep over her; a love so strong, it was almost painful.

Then Giles would get dressed and kiss them both, and go off to work, and the rest of the day would be hers. Hours and hours, with nothing to do but look after one small baby. It sounded laughably easy.

So why was she so tired? She felt as if she would never shift the fog of exhaustion that had descended on her. Things that would have seemed mildly irritating before the birth now reduced her to tears; minor hitches that would once have made her laugh now made her panic.

The day before, she had taken all morning to get herself and Lucia dressed and off in the car to the supermarket. She had stopped halfway to feed Lucia in the Ladies', then had resumed and joined the queue—at which point Lucia had begun to wail. Maggie had tried to soothe Lucia, but her cries had grown louder and louder. Finally the woman in front had turned round and said, 'He's hungry, poor little pet.'

To her own horror, Maggie had heard herself snapping, 'It's a she! And she's not! I've just fed her!' Almost in tears, she had grabbed Lucia from the trolley and run out of the shop, leaving a trail of astonished glances behind her.

Now, remembering the incident, she felt cold with misery. How com-petent a mother could she be if she couldn't even manage a simple shop-ping trip? A memory of her old life rose in her mind—so tantalising it made her want to sink down on the ground and weep. And immediately, as if on cue, Lucia began to cry. Maggie felt the familiar weariness steal over her.

'OK, my precious,' she said aloud. 'Let's get you back inside.'

It was Giles who had suggested that she take Lucia outside for a walk that morning, and, seeing the cloudless blue sky outside, she had thought it a good idea. But now, pushing the pram back through resis-tant layers of thick mud, the countryside seemed nothing but a battle-ground. By the time she arrived at the back door, her face was drenched in sweat.

'Right,' she said, taking Lucia out of the pram. 'Let's get you changed, and feed you.'

Did talking to a four-week-old baby count as talking to oneself? she wondered as she sped upstairs. Was she going mad? Lucia was wailing more and more lustily, and she found herself running along the corridor to the nursery. She placed Lucia on the changing table, unbuttoned her snow suit and winced. Lucia's little sleeping suit was sodden.

'OK,' she crooned. 'Just going to change you . . .' She quickly unbuttoned the sleeping suit, cursing her fumbling fingers. Lucia's wails were becoming louder and louder, with a little catch of breath in between.

'I've just got to change you, Lucia,' Maggie said, trying to stay calm. She quickly pulled apart Lucia's wet nappy, threw it on the floor and reached for another one. But the shelf was empty. A jolt of panic went through her. Where were the nappies? Suddenly she remembered taking the last one off the shelf before setting off for her walk; promising herself to open a new box and restock the shelf. But she hadn't.

'OK,' she said, pushing her hair back off her face. 'OK, keep calm.' She lifted Lucia off the changing table and placed her on the safety of the floor. Lucia's screams became incomparably loud. The noise seemed to drive through Maggie's head like a drill.

'Lucia, please!' she said, feeling her voice rise dangerously. 'I'm just getting you a new nappy, OK? I'll be as quick as I can!'

She ran down the corridor to the bedroom, where she had dumped a new box of nappies, and began to rip hastily at the cardboard. At last she managed to get the box open—to discover the nappies were snugly encased in plastic cocoons.

'Oh God!' she said aloud, and began to claw frenziedly at the plastic. Eventually her fingers closed over a nappy and she pulled it out. She ran back down the corridor to find Lucia in wailing paroxysms.

'OK, I'm coming,' said Maggie breathlessly. 'Just let me put your nappy on.' She bent down over Lucia and fastened the nappy around her as quickly as she could—then, with the baby in one arm, scrambled to the rocking chair. She reached with one hand under her jumper to unfasten her bra, but the catch was stuck. With a tiny scream of frustration, she placed Lucia on her lap and reached with the other hand inside her jumper as well, trying to free the catch; trying to stay calm. Lucia's screams were getting higher and higher.

'I'm coming!' cried Maggie, jiggling hopelessly at the catch. 'I'm coming as quick as I can, OK!' Her voice rose to a shout. 'Lucia, be quiet! Please be quiet! I'm coming!'

'There's no need to scream at her, dear,' came a voice from the door.

Maggie's head jerked up in fright—and as she saw who it was, she felt her face drain of colour. There, watching her, lips tight with disapproval, was Paddy Drakeford.

Candice stood, holding a cup of coffee, peering at her computer screen over the shoulder of the computer engineer and trying to look intelligent.

'Hmm,' said the engineer eventually, and looked up. 'Have you ever had any virus-screening programs installed?'

'Ahm . . . I'm not sure,' said Candice, and flushed at his glance. 'Do you think that's what it is, a virus?'

'Hard to tell,' said the engineer, and punched a few keys. Candice looked at her watch. It was already eleven thirty. She had called out a computer engineer believing he would fix her machine in a matter of minutes, but he had arrived an hour ago, started tapping and now looked like he was settled in for the day. She had already called Justin, telling him she would be late, and he had 'Hmm'd' with disapproval.

'By the way, Heather says, can you bring in her blue folder,' he'd added. 'Do you want to have a word with her? She's right here.'

'No, I've . . . I've got to go,' Candice had said hastily. She had put down the phone, exhaled with relief, and sat down, her heart thudding. This was getting ridiculous. She had to sort her own mind out; to rid herself of the doubt that was growing inside her over Heather.

Outwardly, they were as friendly as ever. But Candice had started to wonder. Were the others right? Was Heather using her? She had still paid no rent, neither had she offered to. She had barely thanked Candice for doing that large amount of work for her. And she had blatantly stolen Candice's late-night shopping idea and presented it as her own.

Candice knew that she should confront Heather on the matter and listen to what Heather had to say. Perhaps, reasoned a part of her brain, it had all been a misunderstanding. But she couldn't quite bring herself to. The thought of appearing to accuse Heather filled her with horror. Things had been going so well between them—was it really worth risking a scene just over one little idea? And so for more than a week she had said nothing, and had tried to forget about it. But there was a bad feeling inside her stomach that would not go away.

'Do you ever download from the Internet?' said the engineer.

'No,' said Candice. Then she thought for a second. 'Actually, yes. I tried to once, but it didn't really work. Does that matter?'

The engineer sighed, and she bit her lip, feeling foolish. Suddenly the doorbell rang and she breathed out in relief.

'Excuse me,' she said. 'I'll be back in a minute.'

Standing in the hall was Ed, wearing an old T-shirt, shorts and espadrilles. 'So,' he said with no preamble. 'Tell me about your flatmate.'

'There's nothing to tell,' said Candice, flushing defensively in spite of herself. 'She's just . . . living with me. Like flatmates do.'

'I know that. But where's she from? What's she like?' Ed sniffed past Candice. 'Is that coffee?'

'Yes.'

'Your flat always smells so nice,' said Ed. 'Like a coffee shop. Mine smells like a shit-heap.' He leaned further into the flat and sniffed longingly. 'Come on, Candice. Give me some coffee.'

'Oh, all right,' said Candice. 'Come in.'

'I saw your friend leaving this morning without you,' said Ed, following her into the kitchen, 'and I thought—aha. Coffee time.'

'Don't you have any plans today?' said Candice. 'Properties to visit? Daytime TV to watch?'

'Don't rub it in,' said Ed. 'This bloody gardening leave is driving me nuts. I'm bored.'

'You obviously don't have any inner resources,' said Candice.

'No,' said Ed. 'Not a one. I went to a museum yesterday. A *museum*. Can you believe it?'

'Which one?' said Candice.

'I dunno,' said Ed. 'One with squashy chairs.' Candice rolled her eyes and turned away to fill the kettle. Ed grinned

'So, you haven't told me about Heather,' he said, sitting down. At the name, Candice felt a spasm inside her stomach, and looked away.

'What about her?'

'How do you know her?'

'She's . . . an old friend,' said Candice. She poured hot water into the cafetière and a delicious smell filled the kitchen.

'Oh yeah? Well, if she's such an old friend, how come I never saw her before she moved in? How come you never even mentioned her?'

'Because . . . we lost touch, all right?' said Candice, feeling rattled. 'Why are so you interested, anyway?'

'I don't know,' said Ed. 'There's something about her that intrigues me.'

'Well, if she intrigues you so much, why don't you ask her out?' said Candice curtly.

'Maybe I will,' said Ed, grinning.

There was a sharp silence in the kitchen. Candice handed Ed his cup of coffee and he took a sip. 'You wouldn't mind, would you, Candice?' he added, eyes gleaming slightly.

'Of course not!' said Candice at once. 'Why should I mind?'

'Ahem.' The voice of the computer engineer interrupted them and they both looked up.

'Hi,' said Candice. 'Have you found out what's wrong?'

'A virus,' said the engineer. 'It's got into everything, I'm afraid.'

'Oh,' said Candice in dismay. 'Well—can you catch it?'

'Oh, it's already long gone,' said the engineer. 'These viruses are very slick. In and out before you know it. All I can do now is try to repair the damage it's left behind.' He shook his head reprovingly. 'And in future, Miss Brewin, I suggest you try to protect yourself a little better.'

Maggie sat at her kitchen table, stiff with humiliation. At the Aga, Paddy lifted the kettle and poured scalding water into the teapot, then turned round and glanced at the Moses basket by the window.

'She seems to be sleeping nicely now. I expect all that screaming wore her out.'

The implied criticism was obvious, and Maggie flushed. She couldn't bear to look Paddy in the eye. You try! she wanted to scream. You try keeping calm after nights and nights of no sleep. But instead she stared silently down at the table. Just keep going, she told herself, and clenched her hands in her lap. Keep going till she's gone.

After arriving on the scene in the nursery, Paddy had left her alone to breastfeed and she had sat in misery, feeling like a punished child. She arrived downstairs, holding Lucia, to find that Paddy had tidied the kitchen and mopped the floor. She knew she should have felt grateful—but instead she felt reproved. A good mother would never have let her kitchen descend into such a sordid state.

'Here you are,' said Paddy, bringing a cup of tea over to the table. 'Would you like some sugar in it?'

'No, thanks,' said Maggie. 'I'm trying to keep tabs on my weight.'

'Really?' Paddy paused. 'I found I needed to eat twice as much when I breastfed, otherwise the boys would have gone hungry.' She gave a short little laugh and Maggie felt a spasm of irrational hatred for her. What was she saying now? That she wasn't feeding Lucia properly?

'And how are the nights going?' said Paddy.

'Fine,' said Maggie shortly, and took a sip of tea.

'Is Lucia settling into a routine?'

'Not particularly,' said Maggie. 'But actually, these days they don't recommend bullying babies into routines.' She looked up and met Paddy's gaze. 'They recommend feeding on demand and letting the baby settle into its own pattern.'

'I see,' said Paddy. 'Well, it's all changed since my day.'

Maggie took another gulp of tea and stared fixedly out of the window.

'It's a shame your parents couldn't visit for a little longer,' said Paddy. A spasm of pain went through Maggie and she blinked hard. Did the woman have to twist *every* knife? Her parents had visited for two days while Maggie was in hospital—then, reluctantly, had had to leave. Both still worked—and the drive from Derbyshire to Hampshire was a long one. Maggie had smiled brightly as they'd left, had promised she would visit soon. But in truth their parting had hit her harder than she'd expected. The thought of her mother's kindly face could still sometimes reduce her to tears. And here was Paddy, reminding her of the fact.

'Yes, well,' she said. 'They're busy people.'

'I expect they are.' Paddy took a sip of tea. 'Maggie—'

'What?' Reluctantly, Maggie turned her head.

'Have you thought about having any help with the baby? A nanny, for example?'

Maggie stared at her, feeling as though she'd been hit in the face. So Paddy really did think she was an unfit mother; that she couldn't care for her own child without paid help.

'No. I'd rather look after my child myself,' said Maggie in a trembling voice. 'I may not do it perfectly, but . . .'

'Maggie!' said Paddy. 'Of course I didn't mean—' She broke off, and Maggie looked stiffly away. There was silence in the kitchen, broken only by Lucia's sleeping snuffles.

'Perhaps I should go,' said Paddy. 'I don't want to get in your way.'

'OK,' said Maggie, giving a tiny shrug.

She watched as Paddy gathered her things together, shooting Maggie the odd anxious glance.

'You know where I am,' she said. 'Bye bye, dear.'

'Bye,' said Maggie, with careless indifference.

She waited as Paddy walked out of the kitchen and let herself out of the front door; waited as the car engine started and the gravel crackled under the wheels. And then, when the car had disappeared completely and she could hear nothing more, she burst into sobs.

Roxanne sat on a wooden bench, her shoulders hunched and her face muffled in a scarf, staring across the road at Ralph Allsopp's London home. It was a narrow house in a quiet Kensington square with black railings and a blue front door. A house that she'd seen the outside of too many times to count; a house that she'd cursed and wept at and stared at for hours—and never once stepped inside.

At the beginning, years ago, she had secretly used to come and sit outside the house for hours. She would station herself in the square garden with a book and stare at the façade behind which Ralph and his family lived, wondering if today she would catch a glimpse of her, or of him, or of any of them.

For, at that time, Cynthia had still spent most of her time in London—and Roxanne had quite often seen her coming up or down the steps with Sebastian. Cynthia Allsopp, with her elegant, oblivious face. And her little son Sebastian, with his innocent Christopher Robin haircut. Roxanne would sit and stare at them as they came down the steps and got into the car or walked off briskly down the road. The sight never failed to appal her; to fascinate her—and, ultimately, to depress her. Because Cynthia was his wife. That elegant, soulless woman was his wife. And she, Roxanne, was his mistress. His tawdry, tacky mistress. That initial excitement of seeing them—the feeling of power, almost— had always given way to a black, destructive devastation.

And yet she'd been unable to stop coming back until the day when Ralph had come down the steps, glanced towards the garden square, and had seen her. She'd immediately hunched down, praying that he wouldn't give her away; that he would remain cool. To his credit, he had done. But he had not been cool on the phone that evening. He had been angry—more angry than she'd ever known him. She'd pleaded with him, reasoned with him; promised never to set foot in the square again. And she'd kept that promise.

But now she was breaking it. Now she didn't give a fuck who saw her. She reached into her pocket for her cigarettes and took out her lighter. The irony was, of course, that now, years later, it didn't matter. Cynthia had decamped to the country manor and only came up for the Harrods sale. And Sebastian rode his little ponies, and everyone was happy. And that was the life Ralph was choosing over her.

Roxanne inhaled deeply on her cigarette. She wasn't going to cry any more. For the past two weeks, she'd sat at home, drinking vodka and staring out of her window, sometimes crying, sometimes shaking, some- times silent. She'd left the answering machine on and listened to mes- sages mount up like dead flies.

Candice had left countless messages, and so had Maggie—and she had almost been tempted to phone back. Of all people, those were the ones she'd wanted to talk to. She'd even picked up the receiver once and begun to dial Candice's number. And then she had stopped, unable to think of what she would say. How she would halt the flow once she'd begun. It was too big a secret. Easier to say nothing.

They, of course, had assumed she was abroad. 'Or perhaps you're with Mr Married,' Maggie had said in one of her messages, and Roxanne had actually found herself half laughing, half crying. Dear Maggie. If she only knew. 'But we'll see you on the first,' Maggie had continued anxiously. 'You will be there, won't you?'

Roxanne looked at her watch. It was the 1st of the month. It was six o'clock. In half an hour's time they would be there. The two faces—at this moment—dearest to her in the world. She stubbed out her cigarette, stood up and faced Ralph Allsopp's house square-on.

'Fuck you,' she said out loud. Then she turned and strode away, her heels clicking loudly on the wet pavement.

Ralph Allsopp lifted his head from the chair he was sitting in and looked towards the window. Outside, the sky was beginning to darken and the streetlights of the square were beginning to come on. He reached for a lamp and switched it on, and the dim room brightened.

'Is there a problem?' said Neil Cooper, glancing up from his papers.

'No,' said Ralph. 'I just thought I heard something. Probably nothing.' He smiled. 'Carry on.'

'Yes,' said Neil Cooper. He was a young man, with a severe haircut and a rather nervous manner. 'Well, as I was explaining, I think your easiest option, in this instance, is to add a short codicil to the will.'

'I see,' said Ralph. 'And can I draw that up now?'

'Absolutely,' said the lawyer, and clicked his pen expectantly. 'If you give me, first of all, the name of the beneficiary?'

There was silence. Ralph closed his eyes, then opened them and exhaled sharply. 'The beneficiary's name is Roxanne,' he said, and his hand tightened slightly round the arm of his chair. 'Miss Roxanne Miller.'

Maggie sat at a plastic table in a Waterloo café and took another sip of tea. Her train had arrived in London an hour ago, and originally she had thought she might take the opportunity to go shopping. But, having made her way off the train, the very thought of shops and crowds had exhausted her. Instead, she had come in here and ordered a pot of tea and had sat, immobile, ever since. She felt shell-shocked by the effort it had taken to get herself here.

Lucia had been awake for most of the previous night, with what she could only suppose was colic. She had paced up and down the bedroom as far away as possible from Giles, trying to soothe the baby's cries. Then Giles had left for work, and instead of crawling back into bed she had spent the entire remainder of the day preparing for her evening out.

She had decided to wash her hair, hoping the blast of the shower would wake her up. Lucia had woken up as she had started to dry it and she had been forced to carry on while simultaneously rocking Lucia's bouncy chair with her foot. For once, the situation had struck her as comical, and she had made up her mind to tell the other two about it that evening. Then she had opened her wardrobe, wondering what to wear—and her spirits had immediately sunk. She still fitted into none of her pre-pregnancy clothes. A whole rail of designer clothes was hanging in front of her, and they might as well not have existed.

As she'd stared at herself in the mirror—large, dumpy and pale-faced with fatigue—she'd suddenly felt like cancelling the whole thing. How could she walk into the Manhattan Bar looking like that? She sank down onto her bed and buried her head in her hands, feeling easy tears rising.

But, after a while, she had wiped her face and told herself not to be silly. She wasn't going up to London to pose. She was going to be with her two best friends. They wouldn't care what she looked like. Taking a deep breath, she had stood up and approached her wardrobe again. She assembled a well-worn outfit in unadventurous black, and placed it on the bed, ready to put on at the last moment. She didn't want to risk any spillages from Lucia.

At two o'clock, Paddy rang the doorbell and Maggie let her in with a polite greeting. Ever since that day when Paddy had interrupted her, there had been a certain distance between them. Paddy had offered to babysit for Maggie's evening out, and Maggie had politely accepted—but no warmth of feeling had flowered between them.

As Paddy came into the house she scanned Maggie's face with a frown, then said, 'My dear, you look very tired. Are you sure you want to go all the way up to London, just for a few cocktails?'

Count to ten, Maggie told herself. Count to ten. Don't snap.

'Yes,' she said eventually, and forced herself to smile. 'It's . . . it's quite important to me. Old friends.'

'Well, you look to me as if you'd do better with an early night,' said Paddy, and gave her short little laugh. Immediately, Maggie had felt herself tense up all over.

'It's very kind of you to babysit,' she'd said. 'I do appreciate it.'

'Oh, it's no trouble!' Paddy had said. 'Anything I can do to help.'

'Right.' Maggie had taken a deep breath, trying to stay calm; to be pleasant. 'Well, let me just explain. The expressed milk is in bottles in the fridge. It needs to be warmed up in a saucepan. If she cries, she might need her colic drops. They're on the—'

'Maggie.' Paddy had lifted her hand with a little smile. 'Maggie, I've raised three children of my own. I'm sure I can manage little Lucia.'

Maggie had stared back, feeling snubbed. 'Fine,' she'd said at last, in a trembling voice. 'I'll just get ready.' And she'd run upstairs, suddenly not wanting to go to London at all. Wanting to tell Paddy to go away and to spend the evening alone, rocking her baby.

Of course she had done nothing of the sort. She had brushed her hair, put on her coat, imagining that she could already hear Lucia crying; telling herself not to be so foolish. But as she had come downstairs, the crying had got louder. She had run into the kitchen and felt her heart stop as she saw a wailing Lucia being comforted by Paddy.

'What's wrong?' she'd heard herself say as the doorbell rang.

'Nothing's wrong!' Paddy had said, laughing. 'That'll be your taxi. Now you go off and have a nice time. Lucia will calm down in a minute.'

Maggie had stood, stricken, staring at her daughter's red, crumpled face. 'Maybe I'll just take her for a moment—' she'd began.

'Honestly, dear, she'll be fine! No point hanging about and confusing her. We'll go for a nice walk round the house in a moment, won't we, Lucia? Look, she's cheering up already!'

And sure enough, Lucia's cries had tailed off into silence. She gave a huge yawn and stared at Maggie with blue, teary eyes.

'Just go,' Paddy had said gently. 'While she's quiet.'

'OK,' Maggie had said numbly. 'OK, I'll go.'

Somehow she had made herself walk out of the kitchen, through the hall to the front door. As she'd closed it behind her, she'd thought she could hear Lucia sobbing again. But she hadn't gone back. She'd forced herself to keep going, to get in the taxi and ask for the station; she'd even managed to smile brightly at the ticket officer as she'd bought her ticket. It was only as the train to Waterloo pulled out of the station that tears had begun to fall down her cheeks, ruining her carefully applied make-up.

Now she rested her head in her palms and thought, with disbelief, how much things had changed in her life. There was no point even attempting to convey to Candice and Roxanne quite how much physical and emotional effort it had taken for her to be here this evening. No one who was not herself a mother would believe what she had gone through. And so, in some way, that meant they would never quite understand how highly she prized their friendship. How important their little threesome was to her.

Maggie sighed, and reached into her bag for a compact to check her reflection, wincing at the dark shadows under her eyes. Tonight, she decided, she would have as much fun as she possibly could. Tonight would make up for it all. Tonight she would talk and laugh with her dearest friends, and return—perhaps—to something like her former self.

Candice stood in front of the mirror in the Ladies', applying her make-up for the evening. She should have been looking forward to the evening out—a chance to see Roxanne and Maggie again, a chance to relax—but she felt unable to relax while she was still so confused about Heather. Another week had gone by and still she had said nothing. She had not mentioned any of the matters troubling her, and neither had Heather. And so the unresolved situation remained and the niggling feeling remained in her stomach.

The door opened, and she looked up to see Heather coming in, dressed smartly in a violet-coloured suit.

'Hi, Heather,' she said, and flashed an automatic little smile.

'Candice.' Heather's voice was full of distress. 'Candice, you must hate me. I feel so awful!'

'What about?' said Candice. 'What are you talking about?'

'About your idea, of course,' said Heather, and looked at her with earnest grey eyes. 'Your late-night shopping feature.'

Candice stared at her and felt a thud of shock. She pushed back her hair and swallowed. 'Wh-what do you mean?' she said, playing for time.

'I've just seen the features list for July. Justin's put down that feature as though it was my idea.' Heather took hold of Candice's hands and grasped them tightly. 'Candice, I told him it was your idea in the first place. I don't know where he got the thought that it was mine.'

'Really?' Candice gazed at Heather, her heart thumping.

'I shouldn't have said anything about it,' said Heather apologetically. 'But I just happened to mention it and Justin got really enthusiastic. I told him it was your idea—but he can't have been listening.'

'I see,' said Candice. She felt hot with shame; with a drenching guilt. How could she have doubted Heather so readily? It was Maggie and Roxanne, she thought with a sudden flicker of resentment. They'd turned her against Heather

'You know, I could tell there was bad feeling between us. But I had no idea what it was. I thought maybe I'd done something in the flat to annoy you . . . And then I saw the list and I realised.' Heather met Candice's eyes steadily. 'You thought I'd stolen your idea, didn't you?'

'No!' said Candice at once, then flushed. 'Well, maybe . . .' She bit her lip. 'I didn't know what to think.'

'You have to believe me, Candice. I would never do that to you. Never!' Heather hugged Candice. 'You've done everything for me. I owe you so much . . .' When she pulled away, her eyes were glistening slightly, and Candice felt her own eyes well up in sympathy.

'I feel so ashamed,' she whispered. 'I should never have suspected you. I might have known it was bloody Justin's fault!' She gave a shaky laugh and Heather grinned back.

'Let's go out tonight,' Heather said. 'Friends again.'

'Oh, that would be great,' said Candice. She wiped her eyes, and grinned ruefully. 'But I'm meeting the others at the Manhattan Bar.'

'Oh well,' said Heather lightly. 'Another time, perhaps . . .'

'No, listen,' said Candice, seized by a sudden fierce affection for Heather. 'Come with us. Come and join the gang.'

'Really?' said Heather cautiously. 'You don't think they'd mind?'

'Of course not! You're my friend—so you're their friend too.'

'I'm not sure about that,' said Heather. 'Roxanne—'

'Roxanne loves you! Honestly, Heather.' Candice met her gaze. 'Please come. It would mean a lot to me.'

'Candice, are you sure about this?'

'Of course!' Candice gave Heather an impetuous hug.

'OK.' Heather beamed. 'I'll see you downstairs, shall I? In about . . . fifteen minutes?'

'Fine,' smiled Candice. 'See you then.'

Heather stepped out of the Ladies' and looked around. Then she headed straight for Justin's office and knocked.

'Yes?' he said.

'I wondered if I could see you for a moment,' said Heather.

'Oh yes?' Justin smiled. 'Any more wonderful ideas for the magazine?'

'No, not this time.' Heather pushed back her hair and bit her lip. 'Actually . . . it's a bit of an awkward matter.'

'Oh,' said Justin in surprise, and gestured to a chair. 'Well, come on in.'

'I don't want to make a fuss,' said Heather apologetically, sitting down. 'In fact, I'm embarrassed even mentioning it. But I had to talk to somebody . . .' She rubbed her nose and gave a little sniff.

'My dear girl!' said Justin. 'What's wrong?' He got up from his chair, walked round behind Heather and shut the door. Then he walked back to his desk. 'If you've got any kind of problem, I want to know,' said Justin. 'Whatever it is. That's what I'm here for.'

There was silence in the little office.

'Can this remain completely confidential?' said Heather at last.

'Of course!' said Justin. 'Whatever you say will remain between these four walls—' he gestured '—and our two selves.'

'Well . . . OK,' said Heather doubtfully. 'If you're absolutely sure . . .' She took a deep shuddering breath and looked up beseechingly at Justin. 'It's about Candice.'

Chapter Seven

THE MANHATTAN BAR WAS HOLDING a Hollywood Legends night, and the glass door was opened for Maggie by a beaming Marilyn Monroe look-alike. Maggie walked into the foyer a few paces, staring at the vibrant scene before her, then closed her eyes and let the atmosphere just pour over her for a second. The buzz of people chatting, the jazzy music in the background, the scent of cigarette smoke and designer fragrances wafting past. As she opened her eyes, a happiness began to well up inside her. She had not realised quite how much she'd missed it all. After the silence and mud of the fields, after the constant wearying wailing of Lucia, this warm noisy bar was like coming home.

She surrendered her coat to the coat-check, took her silver button and turned towards the throng. At first she thought she must be the first to arrive. But then, suddenly, she spotted Roxanne. She was sitting alone at a table in the corner, a drink already in front of her. As she turned her head, unaware she was being watched, Maggie's stomach gave a small lurch. Roxanne's eyes, usually so full of wit and verve, were dull and unseeing, as though nothing around her interested her.

'Roxanne!' Maggie called, and began to make her way to the table, threading through the crowds of people. 'Roxanne!'

'Maggie!' Roxanne's face lit up and she stood up, holding her arms out. The two women embraced for slightly longer than usual; as Maggie pulled away, she saw that Roxanne's eyes were glistening with tears.

'Roxanne, are you OK?' she said cautiously.

'I'm fine!' said Roxanne at once. She flashed a bright smile and reached into her bag for her cigarettes. 'How are you? How's the babe?'

'We're all fine,' said Maggie slowly. She sat down, staring at Roxanne's trembling hands as she scrabbled for her lighter.

'And Giles? How's he enjoying being a father?'

'Oh, he loves it,' said Maggie drily. 'All ten minutes a day of it.'

'Not exactly a New Man, then, our Giles?' said Roxanne, lighting up.

'You could say that,' said Maggie. 'Roxanne are you OK? Seriously.'

Roxanne looked at her through a cloud of smoke. Her blue eyes were full of pain; she seemed to be struggling to keep control.

'I've been better,' she said eventually. 'Thanks for all your messages, by the way. They really kept me going.'

'Kept you going?' Maggie stared at her, aghast. 'Roxanne, what's going on? Where have you been?'

'I haven't been anywhere.' Roxanne gave a wobbly smile. 'I've been at home, drinking lots of vodka.'

'Roxanne, what the hell's happened?' Maggie's eyes sharpened. 'Is it Mr Married?'

Roxanne looked for a moment at the still-burning end of her cigarette, then stubbed it out with a suddenly vicious movement.

'You know I said watch this space? Well, you needn't have bothered.' She looked up. 'Mr Married is out of the picture. His choice.'

'Oh my God,' whispered Maggie. She reached for Roxanne's hands across the table. 'God, you poor thing. The bastard!'

'Hello there!' A cheery voice interrupted them and they both looked up. Scarlett O'Hara was smiling at them, notebook in hand. 'May I take your order?'

'Not yet,' said Maggie. 'Give us a few minutes.'

'No, wait,' said Roxanne. 'I'd like another double vodka and lime.' She smiled at Maggie. 'Vodka is my new best friend.'

'Roxanne—'

'Don't worry! I'm not an alcoholic. I'm an alcohol-lover. There's a difference.'

Scarlett disappeared, and the two friends looked at each other.

'I don't know what to say,' said Maggie, and her hands clenched the table. 'I feel like going over to wherever he lives, and—'

'Don't,' cut in Roxanne. 'It's . . . it's fine, really.' Then, after a pause, she looked up with a glint in her eye. 'What, out of interest?'

'Scraping his car,' said Maggie fiercely. 'That's where it hurts them.' Roxanne threw back her head and roared with laughter.

'God, I've missed you, Maggie.'

'You too,' said Maggie. 'I've been looking forward to this evening like a little kid. Counting off the days!'

'I would have thought there was no room in your grand country life for us any more,' said Roxanne, grinning slyly at her. 'Aren't you too busy going to hunt balls and shooting things?' Maggie gave her a wan smile, and Roxanne frowned. 'Seriously, Maggie. Is it all OK? You look pretty beat-up.'

'Thanks a lot.'

'You're welcome.'

'Here you are!' The voice of Scarlett O'Hara interrupted them. 'One double vodka with lime.' She put the glass down and smiled at Maggie. 'And can I get you anything?'

'I'll have a Jamaican Rumba, please.'

'And a Margarita for me,' said Roxanne. 'Can't have you starting on the cocktails without me,' she added, at Maggie's look. As the waitress retreated, she looked appraisingly at Maggie. 'So, come on. What's it like, being Mummy Drakeford of The Pines?'

'Oh, I don't know,' said Maggie, after a pause. She picked up a silver coaster and stared at it, twisting it round and round in her fingers. Part of her yearned to confide in someone. But another part of her couldn't bring herself to admit such defeat, even to Roxanne. She was used to being Maggie Phillips: editor of the *Londoner*, clever and organised and always on top of things. Not Maggie Drakeford, a pale, fatigued, disillusioned mother who couldn't even bring herself to go shopping.

And how could she begin to explain how these feelings of weariness and depression were bound up inextricably with a love; a joy so intense it could leave her feeling faint? How could she convey the fact that during some of her happiest moments she was, nevertheless, in tears of exhaustion?

'It's different,' she said eventually. 'Not quite how I imagined it.'

'But you're enjoying it.' Roxanne's eyes narrowed. 'Aren't you?'

There was silence. 'I'm enjoying it, of course I am,' Maggie began after a while. 'Lucia's wonderful, and . . . and I love her. But at the same time—' She broke off and sighed. 'Nobody can have any idea what it's—'

'Look, there's Candice,' interrupted Roxanne. 'Sorry, Maggie. Candice!' She peered through the throng. 'What's she doing?'

Maggie turned in her seat and followed Roxanne's gaze.

'She's talking to someone,' she said, wrinkling her brow. 'I can't quite see who . . .' She broke off in dismay. 'Oh no.'

'I don't believe it,' said Roxanne slowly. 'I don't believe it! She's brought that bloody girl.'

'Come on!' Candice smiled at Heather and took her hand, pulling her forward. She felt buoyant tonight; overflowing with good spirits and affection. Towards Heather, towards Maggie and Roxanne; even towards the waitress dressed as Doris Day who crossed their path, forcing them to stop. 'Isn't this fun?' she said, turning to Heather. 'Just think, a few weeks ago it would have been you, dressing up.'

'Until you rescued me from my sad waitressing life,' said Heather, squeezing Candice's hand. 'My own Princess Charming.' Candice laughed, and pushed on through the crowds.

'Hi!' she said, arriving at the table. 'Isn't it busy tonight!'

'Yes,' said Roxanne, looking at Heather. 'Overpopulated, one might say.'

'You remember Heather, don't you?' said Candice cheerfully, looking from Roxanne to Maggie. 'I thought I'd ask her along.'

'Evidently,' muttered Roxanne.

'Of course,' said Maggie brightly. 'Hello, Heather. Nice to see you again.' She hesitated, then moved her chair round to make space at the little table.

'Here's another chair,' said Candice. She sat down and smiled at her two friends. 'So, how are you both? How's life, Roxanne?'

'Life's just fine,' said Roxanne, and took a gulp of her vodka.

'And you, Maggie? And the baby?'

'Yes, fine,' said Maggie. 'Everything's fine.'

'Good!' said Candice.

There was an awkward silence. Maggie glanced at Roxanne, who was sipping her vodka, stony-faced. Candice smiled encouragingly at Heather, who grinned nervously back.

'So, are you enjoying working for the *Londoner*, Heather?' said Maggie politely.

'Oh yes,' said Heather. 'It's a great place to work. And Justin's a wonderful editor.'

Roxanne's head jerked up. 'That's what you think, is it?'

'Yes!' said Heather. 'I think he's fantastic!' Then she looked at Maggie. 'Sorry, I didn't mean—'

'No,' said Maggie, after a pause. 'Don't be silly. I'm sure he's doing marvellously.'

'Congratulations on the birth of your baby, by the way,' said Heather. 'I gather she's very sweet. How old is she?'

'Seven weeks,' said Maggie, smiling.

'Oh right,' said Heather. 'And you've left her at home, have you?'

'Yes. With my mother-in-law.'

'Is it OK to leave them that young?' Heather spread her hands apologetically. 'Not that I know anything about babies, but I once saw a documentary saying you shouldn't leave them for the first three months.'

'Oh, really?' Maggie's smile stiffened. 'Well, I'm sure she'll be fine.'

'Oh, I'm sure she will!' Heather blinked innocently. 'I don't know anything about it, really. Look, here comes a waiter. Shall we order?' She picked up her cocktail menu, looked at it for a second, then lifted her eyes to meet Roxanne's.

'And what about you, Roxanne?' she said sweetly. 'Do you think you'll ever have children?'

By the time the others were all ordering their second cocktails, Roxanne was on her fifth drink of the evening. She had eaten nothing since lunchtime, and the potent combination of vodka and Margaritas was beginning to make her head spin. But it was either keep drinking, and try somehow to alleviate the tension inside her, or scream. Every time she looked up and met Heather's wide-eyed gaze she felt acid rising in her stomach. How could Candice have fallen for her smooth talk?

She glanced up, met Maggie's eye over her cocktail and rolled her eyes ruefully. Maggie looked about as cheerful as she felt. What a bloody disaster.

'I don't actually think much of this place,' Heather was saying dismissively. 'There's a really great bar in Covent Garden I used to go to. You should try it.'

'Yes, why not?' said Candice. 'We could probably do with a change.'

'Maybe,' said Maggie, and took a sip of her cocktail.

'That reminds me,' said Heather, suddenly bubbling over with laughter. 'Do you remember that school trip to Covent Garden, Candice? Where we all got lost and Anna Staples got her shoulder tattooed?'

'No!' said Candice, her face lighting up. 'Did she really?'

'She had a tiny flower done,' said Heather. 'It was really cute. But she got in terrible trouble. Mrs Lacey called her in, and she'd put a plaster over it. So then Mrs Lacey said, "Is something wrong with your shoulder, Anna?"' Heather and Candice both dissolved into giggles, and Roxanne exchanged disbelieving looks with Maggie.

'Sorry,' said Candice, looking up with bright eyes. 'We're boring you.'

'Not at all,' said Roxanne. She took out a packet of cigarettes and offered it to Heather.

'No, thanks,' said Heather. 'I always think smoking ages the skin.' She smiled apologetically. 'But that's just me.'

There was silence as Roxanne lit up, blew out a cloud of smoke and looked through it at Heather with dangerously glittering eyes.

'I think I'll go and check on Lucia,' said Maggie, and pushed her chair back. 'I won't be a minute.'

The quietest place to call from was the foyer. Maggie stood by the glass door looking out onto the street, watching as a group of people in black tie hurried past. She felt flushed, hyped up by the evening and yet exhausted. After all the preparation, all the effort, she was not enjoying herself as much as she had hoped. As she leaned against the wall and took out her mobile phone, she found herself wishing she were at home, away from Candice's hateful friend and her insensitive comments, away from the bright lights and the pressure to sparkle.

'Hello?'

'Hi! Paddy, it's Maggie. I just thought I'd see how things were going.'

'All's well,' said Paddy briskly. 'Lucia's been coughing a little, but I'm sure it's nothing to worry about.'

'Coughing?' said Maggie in alarm.

'I wouldn't worry,' said Paddy. 'Giles will be back soon, and if there's any problem, we can always send for the doctor.' A thin cry came from the background; a moment later, Maggie felt a telltale dampness inside her bra. Oh shit, she thought miserably. Shit shit.

'Do you think she's OK?' she asked, a perilous wobble in her voice.

'Really, dear, I wouldn't worry. You just enjoy yourself.'

'Yes,' said Maggie, on the verge of tears. 'Thanks. Well, I'll call later.' She clicked off the phone and leaned back against the wall, trying to breathe deeply; trying to gain some perspective. A cough was nothing to worry about. Lucia was fine with Paddy. This was her one night off; she was entitled to enjoy herself and forget about her responsibilities.

But suddenly it all seemed irrelevant. Suddenly the only person she wanted to be with was Lucia. A single tear ran down her face and she brushed it away roughly. She had to get a grip on herself. She had to go back in there and make an effort to be entertaining company.

Perhaps if it had just been the three of them, she thought miserably, she would have confided in the others. But she couldn't with Heather there. Heather with her constant snide little comments. She made Maggie feel middle-aged; the frump among the glamour girls.

'Hi!' A voice interrupted her and her head jerked up in shock. Heather was standing in front of her, an amused look on her face. 'Baby OK?'

'Yes,' muttered Maggie.

'Good.' Heather shot her a patronising smile and disappeared into the Ladies'. God, I hate you, thought Maggie. I *hate* you, Heather Trelawney. Oddly enough, the thought made her feel a little better.

As soon as Heather had disappeared to the Ladies', Roxanne turned to Candice and said, 'What the hell did you have to bring her for?'

'What do you mean?' said Candice in surprise. 'I just thought it would be fun for us all to get together.'

'Fun? You think it's fun listening to that bitch?'

'What?' Candice stared at her incredulously. 'Roxanne, are you drunk?'

'Maybe I am,' said Roxanne. 'But to steal a phrase, she'll still be a bitch in the morning. Didn't you *hear* her? "I always think smoking ages the skin. But that's just me.'" Roxanne's voice rose in savage mimicry. 'Stupid little cow.'

'She didn't mean anything by it!'

'Of course she did! Jesus, can't you see what she's like?'

Candice took a few deep breaths, trying to stay calm. Then she looked up. 'You've had it in for Heather from day one, haven't you?'

'Not at all.'

'You have! You told me not to get involved with her, you gave her a nasty look at the office . . .'

'Oh, for God's sake,' said Roxanne impatiently.

'What's she ever done to you?' Candice's voice rose above the chatter. 'You haven't even *bothered* to get to know her . . .'

'Candice?' Maggie arrived at the table and looked from face to face. 'What's wrong?'

'Heather,' said Roxanne.

'Oh,' said Maggie, and pulled a face. Candice stared at her.

'What, so you don't like her either?'

'I didn't say that,' said Maggie at once. 'I just think it would have been nice if the three of us could have . . .' She was interrupted by Roxanne coughing.

'Hi, Heather,' said Candice miserably.

'Hi,' said Heather pleasantly. 'Everything all right?'

'Yes,' said Candice, her cheeks aflame. 'I think I'll just . . . go to the loo. I won't be a minute.'

'Well,' said Maggie awkwardly. 'Shall we all order another cocktail?'

'Yes,' said Roxanne. 'Unless you think cocktails age the skin, Heather?'

'I wouldn't know,' said Heather politely.

'Oh, really?' said Roxanne, her voice slightly slurred. 'That's funny. You seem to know about everything else.'

'Is that so?'

'Anyway,' said Maggie hastily. 'There's a full one here.' She picked up a highball, filled with ice and an amber-coloured liquid. 'Whose is this?'

'I think it was supposed to be mine,' said Heather. 'But I don't want it. Why don't you have it, Roxanne?'

'Have your lips touched the glass?' said Roxanne. 'If so, no, thanks.'

Heather stared at her for a tense moment, then shook her head, almost laughing. 'You really don't like me, do you?'

'I don't like users,' said Roxanne pointedly.

'Oh, really?' said Heather, smiling sweetly. 'Well, I don't like sad old lushes, but I'm still polite to them.'

Maggie gasped and looked at Roxanne.

'What did you call me?' said Roxanne very slowly.

'A sad old lush,' said Heather, examining her nails. She looked up and smiled. 'A sad—old—lush.'

For a few seconds, Roxanne stared at her, shaking. Then, very slowly and deliberately, she picked up the highball full of amber liquid. She stood up and held the glass up to the glittering light for a moment.

'You wouldn't,' said Heather scathingly.

'Oh yes she would,' said Maggie. There was a moment of still tension as Heather stared disbelievingly up at Roxanne—then, with a sudden flick of the wrist, Roxanne up-ended the cocktail over Heather's head. The icy drink hit her straight in the face and she gasped, then spluttered furiously, brushing crushed ice out of her eyes.

'Jesus Christ!' she spat, getting to her feet. 'You're a fucking . . . nutcase!' Maggie looked at Roxanne and broke into giggles. At the next table, people began to nudge each other.

'Hope I haven't aged your skin,' drawled Roxanne, as Heather angrily pushed past. They both watched as Heather disappeared out of the door, then looked at each other and burst into laughter.

'Roxanne, you're wonderful,' said Maggie, wiping her eyes.

'Should have done it at the beginning of the evening,' said Roxanne. 'Looks like the party's over. Let's get the bill.'

Candice was washing her hands when Heather burst into the Ladies'. Her hair and face were drenched, the shoulders of her jacket were stained, and she had a murderous expression on her face.

'Heather!' said Candice, looking up in alarm. 'What's happened?'

'Your bloody friend Roxanne, that's what!'

'What?' Candice, stared at her. 'What do you mean?'

'I mean,' said Heather, her jaw tight with anger, 'that Roxanne tipped a whole fucking cocktail over my head. She's crazy!' She headed towards the brightly lit mirror, reached for a tissue and began to blot her hair.

'She tipped a *cocktail* over your head?' said Candice disbelievingly. 'But why?'

'God knows!' said Heather. 'All I said was, I thought she'd had enough to drink. I mean, how many has she had tonight? I just thought maybe she should move onto the soft stuff. But the moment I suggested it, she went berserk!' Heather met Candice's eye in the mirror. 'You know, I reckon she's an alcoholic.'

'I can't believe it!' said Candice. 'I don't know what she can have been thinking of. Heather, I feel awful about this! And your poor jacket . . .'

'I'll have to go home and change,' said Heather. 'I'm supposed to be meeting Ed in half an hour.'

'Oh,' said Candice, momentarily distracted. 'Really? For a . . .' She swallowed. 'For a date?'

'Yes,' said Heather, throwing a piece of sodden tissue into the bin. 'God, look at my face!' Heather sighed. 'Oh, I don't know, maybe I was tactless. Maybe I should have kept my mouth shut.'

'No!' exclaimed Candice, feeling fresh -indignation on Heather's behalf. 'God, don't blame yourself! You made every effort, Heather. Roxanne just—'

'She's taken against me all along,' said Heather, looking at Candice with distressed eyes. 'I've done my best to be friendly . . .'

'I know,' said Candice, her jaw firming. 'Well, I'm going to have a little word with Roxanne.'

'Don't argue!' said Heather, as Candice strode towards the door of the Ladies'. 'Please don't argue over me!' But her words were lost as the door closed behind Candice with a bang.

Out in the foyer, Candice saw Roxanne and Maggie at the table, standing up. They were leaving! she thought incredulously. Without apologising, without making any effort whatsoever . . .

'So,' she said, striding towards them. 'I hear you've been making Heather feel welcome in my absence.'

'Candice, she had it coming,' said Maggie, looking up. 'She really is a little bitch.'

'Waste of a good drink, if you ask me,' said Roxanne. She gestured to the green leather folder containing the bill. 'Our share's in there. I've paid for the three of us. Not for her.'

'I don't believe you, Roxanne!' said Candice furiously. 'Aren't you sorry? Aren't you going to apologise to her?'

'Is she going to apologise to me?'

'She doesn't have to! It was you who poured the drink over her! Bloody hell, Roxanne!'

'Look, just forget it,' said Roxanne. 'Obviously you can see nothing wrong in your new best friend—'

'Well, maybe if you'd made more of an effort with her, and hadn't just taken against her for no good reason—'

'No good reason?' exclaimed Roxanne in an outraged voice. 'You want to hear all the reasons, starting with number one?'

'Roxanne, don't,' said Maggie. 'There's no point.' She picked up her bag. 'Candice, can't you understand? We came to see you. Not her.'

'What, so we're a little clique, are we? No one else can enter.'

'No! That's not it. But—'

'You're just determined not to like her, aren't you?' Candice stared at them with a trembling face. 'I don't know why we bother to meet up, if you can't accept my friends.'

'Well, I don't know why we bother to meet up if you're going to sit chatting about school all night to someone we don't know!' said Maggie, with a sudden heat in her voice. 'I made huge sacrifices to be here, Candice, and I've hardly spoken a word to you all evening.'

'We can talk another time,' said Candice defensively. 'Honestly—'

'I can't!' cried Maggie. 'I don't have another time. This was my time!'

'Well, maybe I'd talk to you a bit more if you weren't so bloody gloomy,' Candice heard herself snapping. 'I want to have fun when I go out, not just sit like a misery all night.'

There was an aghast silence.

'See you,' said Roxanne remotely. 'Come on, Maggie.' She took Maggie's arm and, without looking again at Candice, led her away.

Candice watched them walk through the noisy crush of people and felt a cold shame spread through her. Shit, she thought. How could she have said such an awful thing to Maggie? How could the three of them have ended up yelling so aggressively at each other?

Her legs suddenly felt shaky and she sank down onto a chair, staring miserably at the wet table, the chaos of ice and cocktail glasses and— like a reprimand—the bill in its green folder.

'Hi there!' said a waitress dressed as Dorothy from *The Wizard of Oz*, stopping at the table. She briskly wiped the table and removed the debris of glasses, then smiled at Candice. 'Can I take your bill for you? Or haven't you finished?'

'No, I've finished, all right,' said Candice dully. 'Hang on.' She opened her bag, reached for her purse and counted off three notes. 'There you are,' she said, and handed the bill to the waitress. 'That should cover it.'

'Hi, Candice?' A voice interrupted her, and she looked up. It was Heather, looking clean and tidy, with her hair smoothed down and her make-up reapplied. 'Have the others gone?'

'Yes,' said Candice stiffly. 'They . . . they had to leave.'

'You had a falling-out, didn't you?'

'Kind of,' said Candice, and attempted a smile.

'I'm really sorry,' said Heather. 'Truly.' She squeezed Candice's shoulder, then looked at her watch. 'I've got to go, I'm afraid.'

'Of course,' said Candice. 'Have a good time. And say hello to Ed,' she added as Heather walked off, but Heather didn't seem to hear.

'Your bill,' said the waitress, returning the green folder.

'Thanks,' said Candice. She pocketed the slip of paper and got up from the table, feeling weary with disappointment. How could everything have gone so wrong? How could the evening have ended like this?

Chapter Eight

THE NEXT MORNING, Candice woke with a cold feeling in her stomach. She stared up at the ceiling, trying to ignore it, then turned over, burying her head in the duvet. But the chill persisted; would not leave her. She had argued with Maggie and Roxanne, her brain relentlessly reminded her. As recollections of the evening began to run through her head, she squeezed her eyes tight shut, but she could not avoid the images—the iciness in Roxanne's eyes; the shock in Maggie's face. How could she have behaved so badly? How could she have let them leave without sorting it out?

At the same time, as pieces of the evening resurfaced in her head, she felt a lingering resentment begin to lift itself off the lining of her mind. A slow self-justification began to pervade her body. After all, what crime had she really committed? She had brought along a friend, that was all. Perhaps Heather and Roxanne had not hit it off, perhaps Maggie had wanted to have a cosy tête-à-tête. But it wasn't her fault things hadn't worked out. She shouldn't have snapped at Maggie—but then, Maggie shouldn't have called Heather a bitch.

With a small surge of annoyance, Candice swung her legs out of the bed and sat up, wondering if Heather had already had her shower. And then it hit her. The flat was silent. Candice walked to the door of her room. She pushed it open and waited, listening for any sounds. But there were none—and Heather's bedroom door was ajar. Candice walked towards the kitchen, and as she passed Heather's room, looked in. It was empty, and the bed was neatly made. The flat was empty.

Candice glanced at the clock on the kitchen wall. Seven twenty. Heather could have got up extremely early, she told herself, putting on the kettle. Or she could have stayed out all night with Ed.

An indeterminate spasm went through Candice's stomach, and she shook her head crossly. It was none of her business what Ed and

Heather did, she told herself firmly. If he wanted to ask her out, fine. And if Heather was desperate enough to want to spend the evening with a man who thought 'gourmet' meant three pizza toppings, fine again.

She walked briskly back into the bathroom, peeled off her nightshirt and stepped under the shower—noticing, in spite of herself, that it hadn't been used that morning. Quickly she lathered herself with a rose-scented gel marked 'Uplifting', then turned the shower on full hot blast to wash away the bubbles, the cold feeling in her stomach, her curiosity about Heather and Ed. She wanted to rinse it all away; to emerge refreshed and untroubled.

By the time she came back into the kitchen in her robe, there was a pile of post on the mat and the kettle had boiled. Very calmly, she made herself a cup of camomile tea and began to open her letters, deliberately keeping till last the mauve envelope at the bottom of the pile.

A credit card bill—higher than usual. Heather's arrival had meant more treats, more outings, more expenditure. A bank statement. Her bank balance also seemed rather higher than usual and she peered at it, puzzled, for a while, wondering where the extra money had come from. Then, shrugging, she stuffed it back into its envelope and moved on. A letter exhorting her to enter a prize draw. And then, at the bottom, the mauve envelope; the familiar loopy handwriting. She stared at it for a moment, then ripped it open, knowing already what she would find.

Dear Candice, wrote her mother. *Hope all is well with you. The weather is moderately fine here. Kenneth and I have been on a short trip to Cornwall. Kenneth's daughter is expecting another baby . . .*

Candice read to the end of the letter, then put it back into the envelope. The same anodyne words as ever, the same neutral, distancing tone. A familiar flame of hurt burned briefly within Candice, then died. She had read too many such letters to let this one upset her. *I don't care*, flashed through her head as she put the letters in a neat pile on the counter. *I don't care*. She took a sip of camomile tea, then another. She was about to take a third when the doorbell rang.

She pulled her robe more tightly around her, cautiously walked to the front door and opened it.

'So,' said Ed, as though continuing a conversation begun three minutes ago, 'I hear one of your friends tipped a cocktail over Heather last night.' He shook his head admiringly. 'Candice, I never knew you ran with such a wild set.'

'What do you want?' said Candice.

'An introduction to this Roxanne character for a start,' said Ed. 'But a cup of coffee would do.'

'What's wrong with you?' said Candice. 'Why can't you make your own bloody coffee? And anyway, where's Heather?' Immediately the words were out of her mouth, she regretted them.

'Interesting question,' said Ed, leaning against the door frame. 'The implication being—what? That Heather should be making my coffee?'

'No!' snapped Candice. 'I just—' She shook her head. 'It doesn't matter.'

'You just wondered? Well . . .' Ed looked at his watch. 'To be honest, I have no idea. She's probably on her way to work by now, wouldn't you think?' He raised his eyes and grinned innocently.

Candice stared back at him, then turned on her heel and walked back into the kitchen. She flicked the kettle on, then sat down and took another sip of camomile tea.

'I have to thank you, by the way,' said Ed, following her in. 'For giving me such sound advice.' He reached for the cafetière and began to spoon coffee into it. 'You want some?'

'No, thank you,' said Candice coldly. 'And what did I give you advice about?'

'Heather, of course. You were the one who suggested I ask her out.'

'Yes,' said Candice. 'So I was.'

There was silence as Ed poured water into the cafetière. Don't ask, she told herself firmly. Don't ask. He's only come round to brag.

'So—how was it?' she heard herself saying.

'How was what?' said Ed, grinning.

Candice felt a flush come to her cheeks. 'How was the evening?' she said in deliberate tones.

'Oh, the *evening*,' said Ed. 'The evening was lovely, thank you.'

'Good.' Candice gave an uninterested shrug.

'Heather's such an attractive girl,' continued Ed musingly. 'Nice hair, nice clothes, nice manner . . .'

'Glad to hear it.'

'Barking mad, of course.'

'What do you mean, "barking mad"?' said Candice bad-temperedly.

'She's screwy,' said Ed. 'You must have noticed.'

'Don't be stupid.'

'Being her oldest friend and all,' said Ed, taking a sip of his coffee. 'Or perhaps you hadn't noticed.'

'There's nothing to notice!' said Candice.

'If you say so,' said Ed, and Candice stared at him in frustration. 'Of course, you know her better than I do. But, in my opinion—'

'I'm not interested in your opinion!' cut in Candice. 'What do you know about people, anyway? All you care about is fast food and money.'

'Is that so?' said Ed, raising his eyebrows. 'The Candice Brewin Analysis. And in what order do I rate these two staples of life? Do I put money above fast food? Fast food above money? Even stevens?'

'Very funny,' said Candice sulkily. 'You know what I mean.'

'No,' said Ed after a pause. 'I'm not sure I do.'

'Oh, forget it,' said Candice.

'Yes,' said Ed, a curious look on his face. 'I think I will.' He put his coffee mug down and walked slowly towards the door, then stopped. 'Just let me tell you this, Candice. You know about as much about me as you do about your friend Heather.'

He strode out of the kitchen and down the hall, and, in slight dismay, Candice opened her mouth to say something; to call him back. But the front door banged closed and she was too late.

As she arrived at work a couple of hours later, Candice paused at the door of the office and looked at Heather's desk. It was empty and her chair was still tucked in. Heather had obviously not turned up yet.

'Morning, Candice,' said Justin, walking past towards his office.

'Hi,' said Candice absently, still staring at Heather's desk. Then she looked up. 'Justin, do you know where Heather is?'

'Heather?' said Justin, stopping. 'No. Why?'

'Oh, no reason,' said Candice at once, smiling. 'I was just wondering.'

'You keep pretty close tabs on Heather, don't you, Candice?'

'What's that supposed to mean?'

'You supervise a lot of her work, is that right?'

'Well,' said Candice, after a pause. 'I suppose I sometimes . . . check things for her.'

'Nothing more than that?'

Candice stared back at him and felt herself flush a guilty red. Had Justin realised that she'd been doing most of Heather's work for her?

'Maybe a bit more,' she said. 'Just a helping hand occasionally.'

'I see,' said Justin. He looked at her appraisingly. 'Well, I think Heather can probably do without your little helping hand from now on. Would you agree?'

'I . . . I suppose so,' said Candice, taken aback by his harsh tone. 'I'll leave her to it.'

'I'm glad to hear it,' said Justin. 'I'll be watching you, Candice.'

'Fine!' said Candice, feeling rattled. 'Watch me all you like.'

A phone began to ring in Justin's office and, after a final glance at Candice, he strode off.

How had Justin worked out that she'd been helping Heather so much? And why was he so hostile about it? All she'd been trying to do, after all, was help. She frowned, and began to walk slowly towards her own desk. As she sat down, a new, worrying thought came to her. Was her own performance suffering as a result of helping Heather?

'People.' Justin's voice interrupted her thoughts and she swivelled round in her chair. He was standing at the door to his little office, looking round the editorial room with a strange expression on his face. 'I have some rather shocking news for you all.' He paused and waited for everyone in the office to turn away from what they were doing and face him. 'Ralph Allsopp is extremely ill,' he said. 'Cancer.'

There was silence, then someone breathed, 'Oh my God.'

'Yes,' said Justin. 'It's a bit of a shock for everyone. Apparently he's had it for a while, but no one else knew. And now it's . . .' He rubbed his face. 'It's quite advanced. Quite bad, in fact.'

There was another silence.

'So . . . so that's why he retired,' Candice heard herself saying, in a faltering voice. 'He knew he was ill.' As she said the words, she suddenly remembered the message she'd once taken from Charing Cross Hospital, and a coldness began to drip down her spine.

'He's gone into hospital,' said Justin. 'But apparently it's spread everywhere. They're doing all they can, but . . .' He tailed off and looked around the stunned room. He appeared genuinely distressed by the news, and Candice felt a sudden flash of sympathy with him. 'I think a card would be nice,' he added, 'signed by us all. Cheerful, of course . . .'

'How long do they think he's got?' asked Candice awkwardly. 'Is it . . .' She halted, and bit her lip.

'Not long, apparently,' said Justin. 'I think from what Janet said, it'll be a matter of weeks. Or even . . .' He broke off.

'Jesus Christ!' said Alicia shakily. 'But he looked so . . .' She broke off and buried her head in her hands.

'I'll phone Maggie and let her know,' said Justin soberly. 'And if you can all think of anyone else who would like to be informed . . . Freelancers, for example.'

'Roxanne,' said somebody.

'Exactly,' said Justin. 'Maybe somebody should phone Roxanne.'

Roxanne flipped over on her sun lounger, stretched out her legs and felt the heat of the evening sun warm her face like a friendly smile. She had arrived at Nice airport at ten that morning and had immediately taken a taxi to the Paradin Hotel. Gerhard, the general manager, was an old friend and had managed to find her a spare room at a vastly reduced rate. She didn't want much, she had insisted. A bed, a shower, a place by the pool. A place to lie with her eyes closed, feeling the healing, warming sun on her body. A place to forget about everything.

She had lain all day on a sunbed under the blistering sunshine, oiling herself sporadically and taking sips from a pitcher of water. At six thirty she looked at her watch and felt a lurch of amazement that only twenty-four hours before, she'd been in the Manhattan Bar, about to descend into the evening from hell.

If she closed her eyes, Roxanne could still summon up the thrill she'd felt as she'd seen the first piece of crushed ice hit that little bitch in the face. But it was a faded thrill; an excitement that even at the time had been overshadowed by disappointment. She had not wanted to argue with Candice. She had not wanted to end up in the cold evening air, drunk and alone and miserable.

Maggie had abandoned her. After the two of them had walked out of the bar, both flushed and buoyed up with adrenalin from the argument, Maggie had looked at her watch and said reluctantly, 'Roxanne . . .'

'Don't go,' Roxanne had said. 'Come on, Maggie. This evening's been so shitty. We've got to redeem it somehow.'

'I've got to get back,' Maggie had said. 'It's already late—'

'It's not!'

'I have to get back to Hampshire.' Maggie had sounded genuinely upset. 'You know I do. And I have to feed Lucia, otherwise I'll burst.' She'd reached for Roxanne's hand. 'Roxanne, I'd stay if I could—'

'You could if you wanted to.' There had been a childish wobble in Roxanne's voice; she'd felt a sudden cold fear of being left alone. First Ralph, then Candice. Now Maggie. Turning to others in their lives. Preferring other people to her. She'd looked down at Maggie's warm hand clasping hers, adorned with its huge engagement sapphire and had felt a surge of jealousy. 'OK then, go,' she'd said savagely. 'Go back to hubby. I don't care.'

'Roxanne,' Maggie had said. 'Roxanne, wait.' But Roxanne had wrenched her hand away and tottered down the street, knowing that Maggie would not run after her. Knowing that Maggie had no choice.

She had slept for a few hours, woken at dawn and made a snap decision to leave the country; to go anywhere as long as it had sunshine. She didn't have Ralph any longer. Perhaps she didn't even have her friends any longer. But she had freedom and contacts and a good figure for a bikini. She would stay here as long as she felt like it, then move on. Perhaps even further afield than Europe. Forget Britain, forget it all.

Roxanne sat up on her sun lounger, lifted her hand and watched in pleasure as a white-jacketed waiter came walking over. That was service for you, she thought with pleasure.

'Hello,' she said. 'I'd like a club sandwich, please. And a freshly squeezed orange juice.' The waiter scribbled on his pad, then moved off again, and she sank comfortably back onto her sun lounger.

Roxanne stayed at the Paradin for two weeks. The sun shone every day, and the pool glistened, and her club sandwich arrived fat and crisp and delicious. She did not vary her routine, did not talk to her fellow guests and did not venture beyond the hotel portals more than once. She felt remote from everything but the sensation of sun and sand and the sharp tang of the first Margarita of the evening.

Only occasionally would flashes of pain descend upon her, so great that she could do nothing but close her eyes and wait for them to pass. One night, as she sat at her corner table in the bar, the band struck up a song that she used to listen to with Ralph—and with no warning she felt a stabbing in her chest that brought tears to her eyes. But she sat quietly, allowing the tears to dry on her cheeks. And then the song ended, and another began, and her Margarita arrived. And by the time she'd finished it, she was thinking of something else completely.

After two weeks she woke up and strode to her window and felt the first stirrings of ennui. She felt energetic and restless; suddenly the confines of the hotel seemed narrow and limited. She had to get away, she thought suddenly. Much further away. Without pausing to reconsider, she reached for her suitcase and began to pack.

By the time she kissed Gerhard farewell in the hotel foyer, she had booked herself a seat on a flight to Nairobi and called her friends at the Hilton. A week at half-rate and concessions on a two-week safari. She would write the whole thing up for the *Londoner*.

The flight was only half full, and after some discussion with the girl at the check-in desk, Roxanne managed to get herself an upgrade. She strode onto the plane with a satisfied smirk on her face and settled comfortably into her wide seat. As the flight attendants demonstrated the safety procedures, she reached for a complimentary copy of the *Daily Telegraph* and began to read the front-page stories.

They were on the runway now, and moving more quickly; the roar of the engines was getting louder, almost deafening. The plane picked up speed and then, with a tiny jolt, lifted into the air. At that moment Roxanne turned the page again, and felt a mild surprise. Ralph was staring back at her, in stark black and white. Then, as she realised what page she was on, her face grew rigid with disbelief.

Ralph Allsopp, read the obituary title. *Publisher who brought life to defunct magazine the 'Londoner'*.

'No,' said Roxanne in a voice that didn't sound like hers. 'No.' Her hands were shaking so much, she could barely read the text.

Ralph Allsopp, who died on Monday . . .

Pain hit Roxanne like a hammer. She stared at his picture and felt herself start to shudder, to retch. With useless hands, she began to tug at her safety strap. 'No,' she heard herself saying. 'I've got to go.'

'Madam, is everything all right?' A stewardess appeared in front of her, smiling frostily.

'Stop the plane,' said Roxanne. 'Please. I've got to go. I have to go back. It's an emergency.' She swallowed hard, trying to keep calm. 'Please. Just turn the plane round!'

'We can't do that, I'm afraid,' said the stewardess, smiling slightly.

'Don't you fucking laugh at me!' Roxanne's voice rose to a roar; suddenly she couldn't keep control of herself any more. 'Don't laugh at me!' Tears began to course down her face in hot streams.

'I'm not laughing!' said the stewardess in surprise. She glanced at the crumpled page in Roxanne's hand and her face changed. 'I'm not laughing,' she said gently. She crouched down and put her arms round Roxanne. 'You can fly back from Nairobi,' she said quietly into Roxanne's hair. 'We'll sort it out for you.' And as the plane soared higher and higher into the clouds, she knelt on the floor, ignoring the other passengers, stroking Roxanne's thin, sobbing back.

Chapter Nine

THE FUNERAL WAS NINE DAYS LATER, at St Bride's, Fleet Street. Candice arrived early, to find groups of people clustering outside, exchanging the same numb, disbelieving looks they'd been exchanging all week. The whole building had been silenced by the news that Ralph had died only two weeks after being admitted into hospital. People had sat blankly at their computers, unable to believe it. Many had wept. Then, while they were all still shell-shocked, the phones had started ringing and the flowers had started to arrive. And so they had been forced to put on brave faces and start dealing with the messages pouring in; the expressions of sympathy and the curious enquiries about the future of the company.

Ralph's son Charles had been glimpsed a few times, pacing the corridors with a stern look on his face. He had been at the company for such a short time, no one knew what he was like, beneath the good looks and the expensive suit. As he had toured the offices directly after his father's death, there had been a chorus of murmured sympathy; shy comments about what a wonderful man Ralph had been. But no one dared to ask him what his plans for the company were. Certainly not until after the funeral. And so business had carried on as usual, with heads down and voices low and a feeling of slight unreality.

Candice shoved her hands in her pockets and went to sit alone on a bench. The news of Ralph's death had brought back her own father's death with a painful vividness. She could still remember the disbelief she'd felt; the shock, the grief. And then, just as she'd felt she was levelling out and beginning to cope, the descent into nightmare had begun. Roughly, Candice brushed a tear from her eye and stared at the ground, blinking hard. There was no one she could share these memories and emotions with. Her mother would change the subject immediately. And Roxanne and Maggie were out of the picture. Nobody had heard from Roxanne for weeks. And Maggie . . . Candice winced. She had tried to call Maggie, the day after the announcement of Ralph's death. She had wanted to apologise; to share the shock and grief. But as she'd said, falteringly, 'Hi, Maggie, it's Candice,' Maggie had snapped back, 'Oh, I'm interesting now, am I? I'm worth talking to, am I?'

'I didn't mean . . .' Candice had begun helplessly. 'Maggie, please . . .'

'Tell you what,' Maggie had said. 'You wait until Lucia's eighteen, and call me then. OK?' And the phone had been slammed down.

Candice flinched again at the memory, then forced herself to stand up. She brushed down her coat and prepared to walk over to Heather, who was in a corner comforting a weeping Kelly. Then, as her gaze passed over the gates, she stopped. Coming in, looking more suntanned than ever, her bronzy-blonde hair cascading down over a black coat, was Roxanne. She was wearing dark glasses and walking slowly, almost as though she were ill. At the sight of her, Candice's heart contracted and tears stung her eyes. If Maggie wouldn't make up, Roxanne would.

'Roxanne,' she said, hurrying forward, almost tripping over herself. She reached her and looked up breathlessly. 'Roxanne, I'm so sorry about the other night. Can we just forget it ever happened?'

Roxanne was silent, then in a husky voice—as though with a huge effort—said, 'What are you talking about, Candice?'

'At the Manhattan Bar,' said Candice. 'We all said things we didn't mean—'

'Candice, I don't give a shit about the Manhattan Bar,' said Roxanne roughly. 'You think that's important now?'

'Well—no,' said Candice, taken aback. 'I suppose not. But I thought . . .' She broke off. 'Where've you been?'

'I went away,' said Roxanne. 'Next question?' Her face was inscrutable behind her dark glasses. Candice stared at her, discomfited.

'How . . . how did you hear the news?'

'I saw the obituary,' said Roxanne. 'On the plane.' With a quick, jerky gesture, she opened her bag and reached for her cigarettes. 'On the fucking plane.'

'God, that must have been a shock,' said Candice.

Roxanne looked at her for a long while, then simply said, 'Yes. It was.' With shaking hands, she tried to light her cigarette, flicking and flicking as the flame refused to catch light. 'Stupid thing,' she said, her breaths coming more quickly. 'Bloody . .'

'Roxanne, let me,' said Candice, taking the cigarette from her. She felt taken aback by Roxanne's obvious lack of composure. Had she been very close to Ralph? She had known him for a while—but then, so had everybody. Candice looked puzzled as she lit the cigarette and handed it back to Roxanne.

'Here you are,' she said, then stopped. Roxanne was gazing transfixed at a middle-aged woman with a neat blonde bob and a dark coat who had just got out of a black mourner's car. A boy of around ten got out and joined her on the pavement, then a young woman and, after a moment, Charles Allsopp.

'Oh,' said Candice curiously. 'That must be his wife. Yes, of course it is. I recognise her.'

'Cynthia,' said Roxanne. 'And Charles. And Fiona. And Sebastian.'

'How old is he?' said Candice, gazing at them. 'The little one?'

'I don't know,' replied Roxanne, and gave an odd little laugh. 'I've . . . I've stopped counting.'

The Allsopps turned, and, led by Cynthia, began to head towards the church. As they passed Roxanne, Cynthia's gaze flickered towards her, and Roxanne stuck her chin out firmly.

'Do you know her?' said Candice curiously.

'I've never spoken to her in my life,' said Roxanne.

'Oh,' said Candice, and lapsed into a puzzled silence. Around them, people were beginning to file into the church. 'Well . . . shall we go in?' said Candice eventually. She looked up. 'Roxanne?'

'I can't,' said Roxanne. 'I can't go in there.'

'What do you mean?'

'I can't do it.' Roxanne's voice was a whisper. 'I can't sit there. With all of them. With . . . her.'

'With who?' said Candice. 'Heather?'

'Candice,' said Roxanne in a trembling voice, and pulled off her sunglasses. 'Will you get it through your bloody head that I don't care about your stupid little friend?'

Candice stared back at her in pounding shock. Roxanne's eyes were bloodshot and there were dark grey shadows beneath them, unsuccessfully concealed by a layer of bronze make-up.

'Roxanne, what is it?' she said desperately. 'Who are you talking about?' She followed Roxanne's stare and saw Cynthia Allsopp disappearing into the church. 'Are you talking about *her*?' she said, wrinkling her brow in incomprehension. 'You don't want to sit with Ralph's wife? But I thought you said . . .' Candice tailed off, and looked slowly at Roxanne's haggard face. 'You're not . . .' She stopped. 'You can't mean . . .' She raised her eyes to meet Roxanne's and, as she saw the expression in them, felt her stomach flip over. 'Oh my God.' She swallowed. 'Ralph.'

'Yes,' said Roxanne, without moving. 'Ralph.'

Maggie sat on the sofa in her sitting room, watching the health visitor scribbling in Lucia's little book. The others would all be at the funeral now. Ralph's funeral. She couldn't quite believe it. This had to be one of the worst periods in her life, she thought dispassionately. Ralph was dead. And she had fallen out with both her best friends.

She could hardly bear to remember that evening at the Manhattan Bar. So many hopes had been pinned on it—and it had ended so terribly. She still felt raw whenever she remembered Candice's cruel remarks. She had travelled back to Hampshire that evening drained with exhaustion and in tears. When she'd arrived home it had been to find Giles holding a fretful Lucia, clearly at his wits' end, and Lucia frantic for a feed. She felt as though she'd failed them both; failed everybody.

'So, how was it?' Giles had said as Lucia started ravenously feeding. 'Mum said you sounded as though you were having a good time.' And Maggie had stared at him numbly, unable to bring herself to admit that the evening had been a disaster. So she'd smiled, and said, 'Great!' and had sunk back in her chair, grateful to be home again.

Since then, she had been out only infrequently. She was getting used to her own company; was starting to watch a great deal of soothing daytime television. On the day she'd heard the news about Ralph she'd sat and wept in the kitchen for a while, then reached for the phone and dialled Roxanne's number. But there was no reply. The next day, Candice had rung, and she'd found herself lashing out angrily; not wanting to, but unable to stop herself retaliating with some of the hurt she still felt. Obviously Candice thought she was a miserable, boring frump. She had slammed down the receiver on Candice and felt a moment of powerful adrenalin. Then, a moment later, the tears had begun to fall.

'Solids at four months,' the health visitor was saying. 'Baby rice is widely available. Then move on to apple, pear, anything simple. Cooked well and puréed.'

'Yes,' said Maggie. She felt like an automaton, sitting and nodding and smiling at regular intervals.

'And what about you?' said the health visitor. 'Are you feeling well in yourself?' Maggie stared at the woman, and felt her cheeks flame scarlet. She had not expected any questions about herself.

'Yes,' she said eventually. 'Yes, I'm fine.'

'Is husband nice and supportive?'

'He does his best,' said Maggie. 'He's . . . he's very busy at work, but he does what he can.'

'Good,' said the health visitor. 'And are you getting out much?'

'A fair bit,' said Maggie defensively. 'It's difficult, with the baby . . .'

'Yes,' said the health visitor. She smiled sympathetically, and took a sip of the tea Maggie had made her. 'What about friends?'

The word hit Maggie like a bolt. To her horror, she felt tears springing to her eyes.

'Maggie?' said the health visitor. 'Are you all right?'

'Yes,' said Maggie, and felt the tears yet again begin to course down her face. 'No.'

A pale sun shone as Roxanne and Candice sat in the courtyard of St Bride's, listening to the distant strains of 'Hills of the North, Rejoice'. Roxanne gazed ahead, unseeingly, and Candice stared up at the gusting clouds, trying to work out whether she and Maggie had been incredibly blind, or Roxanne and Ralph had been incredibly discreet. Six years. It was unbelievable. Six years of complete and utter secrecy.

What had shocked Candice the most, as Roxanne had told her story, was how much the two had obviously loved each other. How deep their relationship had been, beneath all Roxanne's jokes, all her flippancy. 'But what about all your toy boys?' Candice had faltered at one point— to be met by a searing blue gaze.

'Candice,' Roxanne had said, almost wearily, 'there *were* no toy boys.'

Now, in the stillness, Roxanne inhaled deeply on her cigarette and blew a cloud of smoke into the air.

'I thought he didn't want me any more,' she said, without moving her head. 'He told me to go to Cyprus. To have a new life. I was utterly . . . devastated. All that bullshit about retiring.' She stubbed out her cigarette. 'He must have thought he was doing me a favour. He must have known he was dying.'

'Oh, he knew,' said Candice without thinking.

'What?' Roxanne turned and stared at her. 'What do you mean?'

'Nothing,' said Candice, wishing she'd kept her mouth shut.

'Candice, what do you mean? Do you mean . . .' She paused, as though trying to keep control of herself. 'Do you mean you knew Ralph was ill?'

'No,' said Candice. 'I . . . I took a message once, from the Charing Cross Hospital. It was meaningless. It could have been anything.'

'When was this?' asked Roxanne in a trembling voice.

'I don't know,' said Candice, flushing. 'A while ago. A couple of months.' She looked up at Roxanne and flinched under her gaze.

'And you said nothing,' said Roxanne disbelievingly. 'You didn't even mention it to me. Or Maggie.'

'I didn't know what it meant!'

'Didn't you guess?' Roxanne's voice harshened. 'Didn't you *wonder*?'

'I . . . I don't know. Maybe I wondered a bit—' Candice broke off and ran a hand through her hair.

'You knew Ralph was dying and I didn't.' Roxanne shook her head distractedly as though trying to sort out a welter of confusing facts.

'I didn't know!' said Candice in distress. 'Roxanne—'

'You knew!' cried Roxanne. 'And his wife knew. And the whole world knew. And where was I when he died? In the South of France. By the fucking pool.'

Roxanne gave a little sob and her shoulders began to shake. Candice gazed at her in horrified silence.

'I should have known,' said Roxanne, her voice thick with tears. 'I could see something was wrong with him. He was thin, and he was losing weight, and he . . .' She broke off, and wiped her eyes roughly. 'But you know what I thought? I thought he was stressed out because he was planning to leave his wife. And all the time he was dying. And . . .' She paused disbelievingly. 'And you knew.'

In dismay, Candice tried to put her arm round her, but Roxanne shrugged it off.

'I can't stand it!' she said desperately. 'I can't stand that everyone knew but me. You should have told me, Candice.' Her voice rose like a child's wail. 'You should have told me he was ill!'

'But I didn't know about you and Ralph!' Candice felt tears pricking her own eyes. 'How could I have known to tell you?' She tried to reach for Roxanne's hand, but Roxanne was standing up, moving away.

'I can't stay,' she whispered. 'I can't look at you. I can't take it—that you knew and I didn't.'

'Roxanne, it's not my fault,' cried Candice, tears running down her face. 'It's not my fault!'

'I know,' said Roxanne huskily. 'I know it's not. But I still can't bear it.' And without looking Candice in the eyes, she walked quickly off.

Maggie wiped her eyes and took a sip of hot, fresh tea.

'There you are,' said the health visitor kindly. 'Now don't worry, a lot of new mothers feel depressed to begin with. It's perfectly natural.'

'But I've got nothing to be depressed about,' said Maggie. 'I've got a loving husband and a great big house, and I don't have to work. I'm really lucky.'

She looked round her large, impressive sitting room: at the grand piano, the fireplace stacked with logs; the French windows leading out onto the lawn. The health visitor followed her gaze.

'You're quite isolated out here, aren't you?' she said thoughtfully. 'Any family nearby?'

'My parents live in Derbyshire,' said Maggie, closing her eyes. 'But my mother-in-law lives a few miles away.'

'And is that helpful?'

Maggie opened her mouth, intending to say 'Yes'. 'Not really,' she heard herself say instead.

'I see,' said the health visitor. 'You don't get on particularly well?'

'We do . . . but she just makes me feel like such a failure,' said Maggie, and as the words left her mouth she felt a sudden painful relief. 'She does everything so well, and I do everything so . . .' Tears began to stream down her face again. 'So badly,' she whispered.

'I'm sure that's not true.'

'It is! I can't do anything right!' Maggie gave a little shudder. 'I didn't even know I was in labour. Paddy had to *tell* me I was in labour. I felt so . . . so stupid. And I don't keep the house tidy, and I don't make scones—and I got rattled changing Lucia's nappy, and Paddy came in and saw me shouting at her . . .' Maggie wiped her eyes and gave a huge sniff. 'She thinks I'm a terrible mother.'

'I'm sure she doesn't—'

'She does! I can see it in her eyes every time she looks at me. She thinks I'm useless.'

'I don't think you're useless.' Maggie and the health visitor both started, and looked round. Paddy was standing at the door, her face flushed. 'Maggie, where did you get such a dreadful idea?'

Paddy had arrived at the house and had found the door on the latch. As she'd walked through the hall, she'd heard Maggie's voice, raised in emotion, and, with a sudden jolt of shock, had heard her own name. She had told herself to walk away—but instead had drawn nearer the sitting room, unable to believe what she was hearing.

'Maggie, my darling girl, you're a wonderful mother!' she said now, in a trembling voice. 'Of course you are.'

'No one understands!' said Maggie, wiping her blotchy face. 'Everyone thinks I'm bloody superwoman. Lucia never sleeps . . .'

'I thought you said she was sleeping well,' said the health visitor.

'I know,' cried Maggie in anguish. 'I said that because everyone seems to think that's what she should be doing. But she's not sleeping. And I'm not sleeping either. Giles has no idea . . . no one has any idea.'

'I've tried to help,' said Paddy, and glanced defensively at the health visitor. 'I've offered to baby-sit, I've tidied the kitchen . . .'

'I know,' said Maggie. 'And every time you tidy it you make me feel worse. Every single time you come round . . .' She looked at Paddy. 'Every time, I'm doing something else wrong. When I went up to London you told me I should have an early night instead.' Tears began to pour down her face again. 'My one night off.'

'I was worried about you,' said Paddy, her face reddening in distress. 'I could tell you were exhausted; I didn't want you to make yourself ill.'

'Well, that's not what you said.' Maggie looked up miserably. 'You made me feel like a criminal.' Paddy stared at her for a few silent moments, then sank heavily down onto a chair.

'Perhaps you're right,' she said slowly. 'I didn't think.'

'I'm grateful for everything you've done,' muttered Maggie. 'I am, really. But . . .'

'It sounds like you could do with more emotional support,' said the health visitor, looking from Paddy to Maggie. 'You say your husband's got a very demanding job?'

'Yes, he's very busy,' said Maggie, and blew her nose. 'It's not fair to expect him—'

'Nonsense!' cut in Paddy crisply. 'Giles is this baby's father, isn't he? Then he can share the burden.' She gave Maggie a beady look. 'Anyway, I thought all you women were into New Men these days.'

Maggie gave a shaky laugh. 'I am, in principle. It's just that he works so hard—'

'So do you! Maggie, you must stop expecting miracles of yourself.'

Maggie flushed. 'Other women manage,' she said, staring at the floor.

'Other women manage *with help*,' said Paddy. 'Their mothers come to stay. Their husbands take time off. Their friends rally round.' She met the health visitor's eye. 'I don't think any husband ever died from losing a night's sleep, did he?'

'Not to my knowledge,' said the health visitor, grinning.

'You don't have to do it all,' said Paddy to Maggie. 'You're doing marvellously as it is. Much better than I ever did.'

'Really?' said Maggie, and raised a shaky smile. 'Even though I don't make scones?'

Paddy was silent. She looked down at little Lucia, sleeping in her basket, then raised her eyes to meet Maggie's.

'I make scones because I'm a bored old woman,' she said. 'But you've got a lot more in your life than that. Haven't you?'

As people began to pour out of the church, Candice looked up. She felt bruised from Roxanne's powerful anger. She didn't want to see anyone, she thought, and got up to leave. But as she was walking away, Justin suddenly appeared from nowhere and tapped her on the shoulder.

'Candice,' he said coldly. 'A word, please.'

'Oh,' said Candice, and rubbed her face. 'Can't it wait?'

'I'd like you to come and see me tomorrow. Nine thirty.'

'OK,' said Candice. 'What's it about?'

Justin gave her a long look, then said, 'Let's speak tomorrow, shall we?'

'All right,' said Candice, puzzled. Justin nodded curtly, then walked on into the crowds.

Candice stared after him, wondering what on earth he was talking about. The next moment, Heather appeared at her side.

'What did Justin want?' she said casually.

'I've no idea. He wants to see me tomorrow. He was very cloak-and-dagger about it. Probably his latest genius idea about something.'

'Probably,' said Heather. She looked at Candice consideringly for a moment, then grinned. 'Tell you what, let's go out tonight,' she said. 'Have some supper somewhere nice. We could do with some fun after all this misery. Don't you think?'

'Absolutely,' said Candice. 'I feel pretty wrung out, to tell you the truth.'

'Really?' said Heather thoughtfully. 'I saw you and Roxanne earlier. Another row?'

'Kind of,' said Candice. An image of Roxanne's haggard face passed through her mind and she winced. 'But it . . . it doesn't matter.' She looked at Heather's friendly smile and suddenly felt uplifted. 'It really doesn't matter.'

The next morning, as Candice got ready for work, there was no sign of Heather. She smiled to herself as she made a cup of coffee. They had sat in a restaurant until late the night before, eating pasta and drinking red wine and talking. They seemed to see life in exactly the same way; to hold the same values; to share the same sense of humour.

Heather had drunk more than Candice and, as their bill had arrived, had almost tearfully thanked Candice for everything she'd done for her. Then she'd laughed at herself. 'Look at me, completely out of it as usual. Candice, if I don't wake up in the morning, just leave me. I'll need the day off to recover!' She'd taken a sip of coffee then added, 'And good luck with your meeting with Justin. Let's hope it's something nice!'

Candice finished her coffee, tiptoed to Heather's room and listened. There was no sound. She grinned, picked up her bag and left the flat. It was a crisp morning, with the feel of summer in the air, and she walked along briskly, wondering what Justin wanted to see her about.

As she arrived at work she saw that his office was empty. She went to her desk and immediately switched on her computer—then, validated, turned round to chat with whoever was about. But Kelly was the only one in the office, and she was sitting at her desk, furiously typing, not looking up for a second.

'I saw you at the funeral,' said Candice. 'It seemed very moving.' Kelly gave Candice a strange look.

'Yeah,' she said, and carried on typing.

'I didn't make it to the actual service,' continued Candice. 'But I saw you going in with Heather.'

To her surprise, a pink tinge spread over Kelly's face.

'Yeah,' she said again. She typed for a bit longer, then stood up. 'I've just got to . . .' she said, bit her lip and walked out of the room. Candice watched her go in puzzlement, then turned back to her computer.

At nine twenty-five, Justin appeared at the door of the editorial office, still in conversation with someone in the corridor.

'OK, Charles,' he was saying. 'Thanks for that. Much appreciated. Yes, I'll keep you posted.' He lifted his hand in farewell, then came into the room and met Candice's eye.

'Right,' he said. 'In you come.'

He ushered Candice to a chair, then closed the door behind her.

Slowly he walked round his desk, sat down and looked at her.

'So, Candice,' he said eventually, stopped, and gave a sigh. 'Tell me, how long have you been working for the *Londoner*?'

'You know how long!' said Candice. 'Five years.'

'That's right,' said Justin. 'Five years. And you've been happy here?'

'Yes,' said Candice. 'Of course I have. Justin—'

'So you'd think, wouldn't you, that in all that time, a degree of . . . trust would have built up. You'd think that a satisfied employee would have no need to resort to . . . dishonesty.' Justin shook his head solemnly and Candice stared at him, trying to work out what he was getting at.

'Justin,' she said calmly. 'What are you talking about?'

Justin stared at her, then sighed. 'I'm talking about expenses, Candice. I'm talking about claiming false expenses.'

'Really?' said Candice. 'Who's been doing that?'

'You have!'

The words seemed to hit Candice in the face like a slap. 'What?' she said, and heard herself give an incongruous giggle. 'Me?'

'You think it's funny?'

'No! Of course not. It's just . . . ridiculous! You're not serious.'

'Oh, come on!' said Justin. 'Stop this act. You've been caught, Candice.'

'But I haven't done anything!' said Candice, her voice coming out more shrilly than she had intended. 'I don't know what you're talking about!'

'So you don't know about these?' Justin reached into his desk drawer and produced a pile of expense claim forms with receipts attached. 'Haircut at Michaeljohn,' he read from the top form. 'Are you telling me that's a legitimate editorial expense?'

'What?' said Candice, flabbergasted. 'I didn't submit that!' Justin was turning to the next page. 'A beauty morning at Manor Graves Hotel.' He turned again. 'Lunch for three at the Ritz.'

'That was Sir Derek Cranley and his publicist,' said Candice. 'I had to give them lunch to get an interview. They refused to go anywhere else.'

'And Manor Graves Hotel?'

'I've never even been to Manor Graves Hotel!' said Candice, almost laughing. 'And I wouldn't claim something like that! This is a mistake!'

'So you didn't sign this hotel receipt and fill in this claim form.'

'Of course not!' said Candice incredulously. 'Let me see.'

She grabbed the piece of paper, looked at it, and felt her stomach flip over. Her own signature stared up at her from a receipt she knew she'd never signed. An expenses claim form was neatly filled in—in what looked exactly like her handwriting. Her hands began to tremble.

'A total of one hundred and ninety-six pounds,' said Justin. 'Not bad, in a month.'

Suddenly a cold feeling came over Candice. Suddenly she remembered her bank statement; the extra money which had seemed to come out of nowhere. The extra money—which she hadn't bothered to question. She looked quickly at the date on the hotel receipt—a Saturday, six weeks ago—and again at the signature. It looked like hers, but it wasn't.

'Perhaps it doesn't seem like a big deal to you,' said Justin. Candice looked up to see him standing by the window, facing her. 'Fiddling expenses.' He made a careless gesture. 'One of those little crimes that doesn't matter. The truth is, Candice, it does matter.'

'I know it matters!' spat Candice in frustration. 'Don't bloody patronise me! I know it matters. But I didn't do it, OK?' She took a deep breath, trying to keep calm.

'So what are these?' Justin pointed to the expense forms.

'Someone else must have filled them in. Forged my signature.'

'And why would they do that?'

'I . . . I don't know. But look, Justin! It isn't my handwriting. It just looks like it!' She flipped quickly through the pages. 'Look at this form compared to . . . this one!' She thrust the pages at Justin but he shook his head.

'You're saying somebody—for a reason we have yet to ascertain—forged your signature.'

'Yes!'

'And you knew nothing about it.'

'No!' said Candice. 'Of course not!'

'Right,' said Justin. He sighed as though disappointed by her reply. 'So when the expenses came through a week ago and you found a load of unexplained money in your account, you naturally pointed out the mistake and returned it straightaway.'

He looked at her evenly and Candice stared back dumbly. Why hadn't she queried the extra money? How could she have been so stupid?

'For God's sake, Candice, you might as well admit it,' said Justin wearily. 'You tried to fleece the company and you got caught.'

'I didn't!' said Candice, feeling a sudden thickness in her throat. 'Justin, you *know* I wouldn't do something like that.'

'To be honest, Candice, I feel at the moment as though I don't know you very well at all,' said Justin.

'What's that supposed to mean?'

'Heather's told me all about your little power trips over her,' said Justin. 'I'm surprised she didn't make an official complaint.'

'What?' said Candice in astonishment. 'Justin, what the hell are you talking about?'

'All innocent again?' said Justin sarcastically. 'Come on, Candice. We even spoke about it the other day. You admit you've been supervising all Heather's work. Using your power over her to intimidate her.'

'I've been *helping* her!' said Candice in outrage. 'My God! How can you—'

'She told me how badly you treated her after she presented her feature idea to me.' Justin's voice harshened. 'You just can't stand the fact that she's got talent, is that it?'

'Of course not!' said Candice, flinching at his voice. 'Justin, you've got it all wrong! It's twisted! It's—'

Candice broke off and gazed at Justin, trying to marshal her thoughts. Nothing was making sense. Nothing was making—

She stopped, as something hit her. The receipt for the Michaeljohn haircut. That was hers. Her own private receipt, from her own pile of papers on the dressing table in her bedroom. No one else could have—

'Oh my God,' she said slowly.

She picked up one of the expense forms, gazed at it again and slowly felt herself grow cold. Now that she looked closely, she could see the hint of another handwriting beneath the veneer of her own. Like a mocking wave, Heather's handwriting was staring up at her. She looked up, feeling sick.

'Where's Heather?' she said in a trembling voice.

'On holiday,' said Justin. 'For two weeks. Didn't she tell you?'

'No,' said Candice. 'No, she didn't.' She took a deep breath. 'Justin, I think . . . I think Heather forged these claims.'

'Oh really?' Justin laughed. 'Well, there's a surprise.'

'No.' Candice swallowed. 'No, really. You have to listen to me—'

'Candice, forget it,' said Justin impatiently. 'You're suspended.'

'What?' Utter shock drained Candice's face of colour.

'The company will carry out an internal investigation, and a disciplinary hearing will be held in due course,' said Justin. 'In the meantime, until the matter is resolved, you will remain at home on full pay.'

'You . . . you can't be serious.'

'As far as I'm concerned, you're lucky not to be fired on the spot! Candice, what you did is fraud,' said Justin.

Candice's eyes smarted with disbelieving, angry tears. 'You're treating me like a criminal, after . . . everything. I mean, we lived together for six months, didn't we? Doesn't that count for *anything*?'

At her words, Justin gave her an almost triumphant look.

He's been waiting for me to say that, thought Candice in horrified realisation. He's been waiting for me to grovel.

'So you think I should make an exception for you because you used to be my girlfriend,' said Justin. 'You think I might do you a special favour and turn a blind eye. Is that it?'

Candice stared at him, feeling sickened.

'No,' she said, as calmly as she could manage. 'Of course not.' She paused. 'But you could . . . trust me.'

There was silence as the two stared at each other and, for an instant, Candice thought she saw the old Justin looking at her—the Justin who would have believed her. Then he reached into his desk drawer.

'As far as I'm concerned,' he said coldly, 'you've forfeited my trust. And everybody else's. Here.' He looked up and held out a black plastic bin bag. 'Take what you want and go.'

Half an hour later, Candice stood on the pavement outside the glass doors, holding her bin bag and flinching at the curious gazes of passersby. It was ten o'clock in the morning. For most people the day was just beginning. People were hurrying to their offices; everyone had somewhere to go. Candice swallowed and took another step forward, trying to look as though she was standing here on the pavement with a bin bag on purpose. But she could feel her calm face slipping; could feel raw emotion threatening to escape. She had never felt so vulnerable; so frighteningly alone.

As she'd come back into the editorial office, she'd managed to hold her head up high and, above all, had refused to look guilty. But it had been difficult. Everyone obviously knew what had happened. She could see heads looking up at her, then quickly looking away; faces agog with curiosity; with relief that it wasn't them. With a new member of the Allsopp family in charge of the company, the future was uncertain for everybody. At one point she'd caught Alicia's eye and saw a genuine flash of sympathy before Alicia, too, looked away. Candice didn't blame her. No one could afford to take any chances.

She'd shaken the bin bag open with trembling fingers. She had never felt so sordid, so humiliated. Around the room, everyone was working silently at their computers, which meant they were all listening. Candice had opened her top desk drawer and looked at its familiar contents. Notebooks, pens, old disks, a box of raspberry tea bags.

'Don't take any disks,' Justin had said, passing by. 'And don't touch the computer. We don't want any company information walking out with you.'

'Just leave me alone!' Candice had snapped savagely, tears coming to her eyes. 'I'm not going to *steal* anything.'

Now, standing outside on the hard pavement, a hotness rose to her eyes again. They all believed she was a thief. And why shouldn't they? The evidence was convincing enough. Candice closed her eyes. She still felt dizzy at the idea that Heather had fabricated evidence about her. That Heather had, all the time, been plotting behind her back. Her mind scurried backwards and forwards, trying to work it all out. But she could not think straight while she was fighting tears.

'All right, love?' said a man in a denim jacket, and Candice's head jerked up.

'Yes, thanks,' she muttered, and felt a small tear escape onto her cheek. Before he could say anything else she began walking along the pavement, not knowing where she was going. In a shop window she glanced at her reflection and was shocked at the sight. Her face was white, and busy with suppressed tears. She had to get home, she thought frantically. She would take off her suit, take a bath, hide away like a small animal in a hole until she felt able to emerge.

At the corner she reached a telephone box. She pulled open the heavy door and slipped inside. Maggie, she thought frantically, picking up the receiver. Or Roxanne. They would help her. One of them would help her. Roxanne or Maggie. She reached to dial, then stopped. Not Roxanne. Not after the way they'd parted at Ralph's funeral. And not Maggie. Not after that awful phone call.

A cold feeling ran down Candice's spine and she leaned against the cool glass of the kiosk. She couldn't call either of them. She'd lost them both. Somehow she'd lost her two closest friends in the world.

She stepped out of the telephone box onto the street, shifted her bin bag to the other hand and looked around confusedly, as though resurfacing from a tunnel. Then she began to walk again in a haze of misery, barely aware of where she was going.

As Roxanne came up the stairs, holding a loaf of bread and a newspaper, she heard the telephone ringing inside her flat. Let it ring, she thought. Let it ring. There was no one she wanted to hear from. Slowly she reached for her key, inserted it into the lock of the front door and opened it. She closed the door behind her, put down the loaf of bread and the newspaper, and reached for the receiver. 'Yes?'

'Am I speaking to Miss Roxanne Miller?' said a strange male voice.

'Yes,' said Roxanne. 'Yes, you are.'

'Good,' said the voice. 'Let me introduce myself. My name is Neil

Cooper and I represent the firm of Strawson and Co. I'm telephoning you in connection with the estate of Ralph Allsopp.'

'Oh,' said Roxanne. Hearing his name unexpectedly on other people's lips still took her by surprise; still sent shock waves through her body.

'Perhaps I could ask you to come into the office?' the man was saying, and Roxanne's mind snapped into focus. Ralph Allsopp. The estate of Ralph Allsopp.

'Oh God,' she said, and tears began to run freely down her face. 'He's gone and left something to me, hasn't he? The stupid, sentimental bastard. And you're going to give it to me.'

'If we could just arrange a meeting . . .'

'Is it his watch? Or that crappy ancient typewriter.' Roxanne gave a half-laugh in spite of herself.

'Shall we say half past four on Thursday?' the lawyer said.

'Look,' Roxanne said. 'I don't know if you're aware, but Ralph and I weren't exactly . . .' She paused. 'I'd rather stay out of the picture. Can't you just send whatever it is to me? I'll pay the postage.'

There was silence down the line, then the lawyer said, more firmly, 'Half past four. I'll expect you.'

Candice became aware that her steps were, unconsciously, taking her towards home. As she turned into her street she stopped at the sight of a chugging taxi outside her house. She stood still, staring at it—then stiffened as Heather appeared, coming out of the front door. She was wearing jeans and a coat and carrying a suitcase. As Candice stared at her she felt herself falter in confusion.

Was she really accusing Heather—this cheery, warm-hearted friend—of deliberately setting her up? Logically, the facts drew her to that conclusion. But as she gazed at Heather, everything in her resisted it. Could there not be some other plausible explanation? she thought frantically.

As she stood transfixed, Heather turned as though aware of Candice's gaze and gave a slight start of surprise. For a few moments the two girls stared at each other silently. Heather's gaze ran over Candice, taking in the bin bag, her flustered face, her bloodshot eyes.

'Heather.' Candice's voice sounded hoarse to her own ears. 'Heather, I need to talk to you.'

'Oh yes?' said Heather calmly.

'I've just been . . .' She paused, barely able to say the words aloud. 'I've just been suspended from work.'

'Really?' said Heather. 'Shame.' She smiled at Candice, then turned and got into the taxi.

Candice stared at her and felt her heart begin to pound.

'No,' she said. 'No.' She began to run along the pavement, her breath coming quickly, her bin bag bouncing along awkwardly behind her. 'Heather, I . . . I don't understand.' She reached the taxi door just as Heather was reaching to close it, and grabbed hold of it.

'Let go!' snapped Heather.

'I don't understand,' said Candice. 'I thought we were friends.'

'Did you?' said Heather. 'That's funny. My father thought your dad was his friend, too.'

Candice's heart stopped. She stared at Heather and felt her face suffuse with colour. 'When . . . when did you find out?' Her voice was strangled; something like cotton wool seemed to be blocking her airway.

'I didn't have to find out,' said Heather scathingly. 'I knew who you were all along. As soon as I saw you in that bar.' Her voice harshened. 'My whole family knows who you are, Candice Brewin.'

Candice stared at Heather speechlessly. Her legs were trembling; she felt almost dizzy with shock.

'And now you know how I felt,' said Heather. 'Now you know what it was like for me. Having everything taken away, with no warning.' She gave a tiny, satisfied smile. 'So—are you enjoying it? Do you think it's fun, losing everything overnight?'

'I trusted you,' said Candice numbly. 'You were my friend.'

'And I was fourteen years old!' spat Heather with a sudden viciousness. 'We lost everything. Jesus, Candice! Did you really think we could be friends, after what your father did to my family?'

'But I tried to make amends,' said Candice. 'I tried to make it up to you.' Heather shook her head, and wrenched the taxi door out of Candice's grasp.

'Heather, listen!' said Candice. 'Don't you understand?' She leaned forward. 'I was trying to make it up to you. I was trying to help you.'

'Yes, well,' said Heather coldly. 'Maybe you didn't try hard enough.'

She gave Candice one final look, then slammed the door.

'Heather!' said Candice. 'Heather, wait! Please. I need my job back.' Her voice rose in desperation. 'You have to help me! Please, Heather!'

But Heather didn't even turn round. A moment later the taxi zoomed away up the street.

Candice watched it go in disbelief, then sank shakily down onto the pavement, the bin bag still clutched in her hand. A couple passing by with their dog looked at her curiously, but she didn't react. She was oblivious to the outside world, oblivious to everything except her own thudding shock.

Chapter Ten

THERE WAS A SOUND BEHIND HER and Candice looked up. Ed was standing at the door of the house, gazing at her. He looked serious, almost stern.

'I saw her getting all her stuff together,' he said. 'I tried to call you at work, but they wouldn't put me through.' He took a couple of steps towards her, and looked at the bin bag lying in a crumpled heap on the ground. 'Does that mean what I think it does?'

'I've been . . . suspended,' said Candice, barely able to manage the words. 'They think I'm a thief.'

'So—what went wrong?'

'I don't know,' said Candice, rubbing her face wearily. 'I don't know what went wrong. You tell me. I just . . . All I wanted, all along, was to do the right thing. And what happens?' She looked up at him. 'I lose my job, I lose my friends . . . I've lost everything, Ed. Everything.'

Two tears spilled onto her cheeks, and she wiped them away with the sleeve of her jacket. Ed looked at her consideringly for a moment.

'It's not so bad,' he said. 'You haven't lost your looks. If that's of any interest to you.' Candice stared at him, then gave a shaky giggle. 'And you haven't lost—' He broke off.

'What?'

'You haven't lost me,' said Ed, looking straight at her. 'Again—if that's of any interest to you.'

There was a taut silence.

'I . . .' Candice swallowed. 'Thanks.'

'Come on.' Ed held out his hand. 'Let's get you inside.'

'Thanks,' she whispered and took his hand gratefully. 'Thanks, Ed.'

They trudged up the stairs in silence. As she arrived at the front door of her flat Candice hesitated, then pushed it open. Immediately she had a feeling of emptiness. Heather's coat was gone from the stand in the hall; her bedroom door was ajar and the wardrobe visibly empty.

'Is everything still there?' said Ed behind her. 'If she's stolen anything we can call the police.'

Candice walked a few steps into the sitting room and looked around. 'I think everything's still here,' she said. 'Everything of mine, anyway.'

132

'Well, that's something,' said Ed. 'Isn't it?'

Candice didn't reply. She walked over to the mantelpiece and looked silently at the photograph of herself, her mother and her father. Smiling into the sun, innocently happy, before any of it happened. Her breath began to come more quickly; something hot seemed to rise through her, burning her throat, her face, her eyes.

'I feel so . . . stupid,' she said. 'I feel so completely stupid.' Tears of humiliation began to run down her cheeks and she buried her face in her hands. 'I believed every bloody thing she said. But she was lying. Everything she said was . . . lies.'

Ed leaned against the door frame, frowning.

'So—what—she had it in for you?'

'She had it in for me all along.' Candice looked up and wiped her eyes. 'It's a . . . it's a long story.'

'And you had no idea.'

'I thought she liked me. I thought we were best friends. She told me what I wanted to hear and I fell for it.'

'Come on, Candice,' said Ed. 'You can't just blame yourself. She fooled everyone. Face it, she was good.'

'You weren't fooled by her though, were you?' retorted Candice. 'You told me you thought she was mad.'

'I thought she was a bit weird,' said Ed, shrugging. 'I didn't realise she was a psycho.'

'She must have been plotting all along. From the moment she walked in the door with all those flowers. Pretending to be so sweet and grateful. Always so . . .' She swallowed hard. 'In the evenings, we used to sit on this sofa together watching the telly. Doing each other's nails. I'd be thinking what a great friend she was. And what was Heather thinking?' Candice looked bleakly at Ed. 'What was she really thinking?'

'Candice—'

'She was sitting there, hating me, wasn't she? Wondering what she could do to hurt me.' Fresh tears began to fall down Candice's face. 'How could I have been so *stupid*? I did all her bloody work for her, she never paid me a penny rent . . . and I kept thinking I still owed her! I kept feeling guilty about her.' Candice wiped her streaming nose. 'You know what she told them at work? She said I was bullying her.'

'And they believed her?' said Ed incredulously.

'Justin believed her.'

'Well,' said Ed. 'That figures.'

'I tried to tell him,' said Candice, her voice rising in distress. 'I tried to explain. But he wouldn't believe me. He just looked at me as though I was a . . . criminal.' She broke off into a shuddering silence.

'You need a stiff drink,' said Ed. 'Have you got any drink in the house?'

'Some white wine,' said Candice after a pause. 'In the fridge.'

'White wine? What is it with women and white wine?' Ed shook his head. 'Stay here. I'm going to get you a proper drink.'

Candice sat on the sofa, head buried in her hands, her eyes closed and her mind a whirl of images and memories. Heather's innocent smile and gushing words. Heather asking her what meant most to her in the world. And her own pride and delight in her new friend; her idealistic belief that she was atoning for her father's crimes.

'I was a fool,' she muttered aloud. 'A gullible, stupid—'

'Stop talking to yourself,' came Ed's voice from above her. 'And get that inside you,' he added, holding out a glass of transparent liquid.

'What is it?' she said suspiciously, taking it.

'Grappa. Wonderful stuff. Go on.' He nodded at the glass and she took a gulp, then gasped as the fiery liquid hit her mouth.

'Bloody hell!' she managed, her mouth tingling with pain.

'Like I said.' Ed grinned. 'Wonderful stuff. Go on, have some more.'

Candice braced herself, and took another gulp. As the alcohol descended inside her, a warm glow began to spread through her body and she found herself smiling up at Ed.

'There's plenty more,' said Ed, replenishing her glass from the bottle in his hand. 'And now,' he added, reaching for the phone, 'before you get too comfortable, you've got a call to make.' He plonked the phone in her lap and grinned at her.

'What?' said Candice, confused.

'Phone Justin. Tell him what Heather said to you—and that she's scarpered. Prove she's a nutcase.' Candice gazed up at him and, gradually, realisation descended on her.

'Oh my God,' she said slowly. 'You're right! That changes everything, doesn't it? He'll have to believe me!' She took another gulp of grappa, then picked up the receiver. 'OK. Let's do it.' Briskly she dialled the number and, as she heard the ringing tone, felt a surge of excitement.

'Hello,' she said, as soon as she got through, 'I'd like to speak to Justin Vellis, please.'

'I'll just check for you,' said the receptionist. 'May I say who's calling?'

'Yes,' said Candice. 'It's . . . it's Candice Brewin.'

As she heard Justin's phone ringing, Candice felt a pang of apprehension. She glanced at Ed, leaning against the arm of the sofa, and he gave her the thumbs up.

'Justin Vellis.'

'Hi, Justin,' said Candice, winding the telephone cord tightly around her fingers. 'It's Candice.'

'Yes,' said Justin. 'What do you want?'

'Listen, Justin.' Candice tried to speak quickly but calmly. 'I can prove that what I said in your office was true. Heather's admitted she set me up. She's got a vendetta against me. She yelled at me in the street!'

'Oh, really?' said Justin.

'Yes. And now she's cleared out of the flat with all her stuff. She's just disappeared.'

'So what?'

'So, isn't that a bit suspicious?' said Candice. 'Come on, think about it.'

There was a pause, then Justin sighed. 'As I recall, Heather's gone on holiday. Hardly suspicious.'

'She hasn't gone on holiday!' cried Candice in frustration. 'She's gone for good. And she admitted she'd got me into trouble on purpose.'

'She actually said that she'd forged your handwriting?'

'No,' said Candice. 'Not exactly in those words. But she said—'

'Candice, I'm afraid I don't have time for this,' interrupted Justin coolly. 'You'll have an opportunity to state your case at the hearing. But please don't telephone me again. I'll be telling reception not to put through your calls.'

'Justin, how can you be so bloody obtuse?' yelled Candice. 'How can you—'

'Goodbye, Candice.' The phone went dead and Candice stared at it in disbelief.

'Let me guess,' said Ed, taking a gulp of grappa. 'He apologised and offered you a pay rise.'

'He doesn't believe me,' said Candice. 'He doesn't bloody well believe me.' Her voice rose in outrage. 'How *can* he believe her over me?'

She rose to her feet, letting the phone fall to the ground with a crash, and strode to the window. She was shaking with anger, unable to keep still. 'Who the hell does he think he is, anyway?' she said. 'He gets a bit of temporary power, and suddenly he thinks he's running the whole bloody company. It's pathetic.'

'Tiny dick, obviously,' said Ed.

'Not tiny,' said Candice, still staring out of the window. 'But fairly meagre.' She turned round, met Ed's eyes and gave a bursting gasp of laughter. 'God, I can't believe how furious I am.'

'Neither can I,' said Ed in impressed tones. 'Angry Candice. I like it.'

'I feel as though—' She shook her head, smiling tightly as though suppressing more laughter. Then a tear ran quickly down her face.

'So what do I do now?' she said more quietly. She wiped the tear away and exhaled. 'The hearing won't be for weeks. So what do I do in the meantime? I can't even get back into the building. They took my security card away.'

There was silence for a few seconds, then Ed put down his glass of grappa and stood up. 'Come on,' he said. 'Let's get out of here. Go to my aunt's house.'

'What?' She looked at him uncertainly. 'The house you inherited?'

'Change of scene. You can't stick in this flat all day.'

'But . . . it's miles away, isn't it? Wiltshire or somewhere.'

'So what?' said Ed. 'Plenty of time.'

'I don't know.' Candice rubbed her face. 'I'm not sure it's a good idea.'

'Well, what else are you going to do all day? Sit around and go crazy?'

There was a long pause.

'You're right,' said Candice eventually. 'I mean, what else am I going to do?' She looked up at Ed and felt a sudden euphoria at the thought of escaping. 'You're right. Let's go.'

At midday, Giles knocked on the bedroom door and waited until Maggie sleepily lifted her head.

'Someone to see you,' he said softly. Maggie rubbed her eyes and yawned as he advanced into the room, holding Lucia in his arms. The room was bright with sunshine and she could smell coffee. And she didn't feel tired. She grinned and stretched her arms high above her head. What a wonderful place bed was, she thought happily.

'Oh, I feel good!' she said, and sat up, leaning against a mound of pillows. 'I feel fantastic. Except I'm bursting with milk . . .'

'I'm not surprised,' said Giles, handing Lucia to her and watching as Maggie unbuttoned her nightshirt. 'That's fourteen hours you've been asleep.'

'Fourteen hours,' said Maggie wonderingly, as Lucia began to feed. 'Fourteen hours. I can't remember the last time I slept for more than . . .' She shook her head. 'And I can't believe I didn't wake up.'

'You've been a noise-free zone,' said Giles. 'I turned all the phones off and took Lucia out for a walk. We only got back a few minutes ago.'

'Did you?' Maggie looked down at Lucia's little face and smiled, with a sudden tenderness. 'Isn't she pretty?'

'She's gorgeous,' said Giles. 'Like her mother.'

He came and sat down on the bed, and watched them both in silence. After a while, Maggie looked up at him.

'And how was she during the night? Did you get much sleep?'

'Not much,' said Giles ruefully. 'She doesn't like that cot much, does she?' His gaze met Maggie's. 'Is that what it's been like, every night?'

'Pretty much,' said Maggie after a pause.

'I don't understand why you never told me. We could have got help, we could have—'

'I know.' Maggie bit her lip. 'I just . . . I don't know. I couldn't face admitting how awful it was.' She hesitated. 'You thought I was doing so well, and you were so proud of me. If I'd told you it was a nightmare . . .'

'I would have said sod the baby, let's send it back,' said Giles promptly and Maggie giggled.

'Thanks for taking her last night,' she said.

'Maggie, don't *thank* me,' said Giles, almost impatiently. 'She's my child too, isn't she? I've got just as much right to curse her at three o'clock in the morning as you have.'

'Bloody baby,' said Maggie, smiling down at her.

'Bloody baby,' echoed Giles. 'Bloody silly Mummy.' He shook his head in mock disapproval. 'Lying to the health visitor. I don't know. You could get put in prison for that.'

'It wasn't lying,' said Maggie. 'It was . . .' She thought for a moment. 'It was spin.'

'Good PR, you mean.'

'Exactly,' said Maggie, giving a self-mocking smile. '"Life with my new baby is utter bliss," commented Ms Phillips.' She stared at Lucia's tiny, sucking face, then looked up seriously at Giles. 'I thought I had to be like your mother. But I'm nothing like your mother.'

'You're not as bossy as my mother,' said Giles, pulling a face. 'She gave me a real earful about my responsibilities. She can be pretty fearsome when she wants to, my mum.'

'Good,' said Maggie, grinning.

'Which reminds me,' said Giles. 'Would Madam like breakfast in bed?'

'Madam would *adore* breakfast in bed.'

'And what about Mademoiselle? Shall I take her with me or leave her?'

'You can leave Mademoiselle,' said Maggie, stroking Lucia's head. 'I'm not sure she's quite finished her own breakfast.'

When Giles had gone she lay back comfortably against the pillows, staring out of the window at the fields beyond the garden. A bright sun was beating down and wind was ruffling the long green grass. The countryside at its most idyllic.

'What do you think?' she said, looking down at Lucia. 'You like rustic? You like cows and sheep? Or cars and shops? You choose.'

Lucia looked at her intently for a moment, then screwed up her tiny face in a yawn.

'Exactly,' said Maggie. 'You don't really give a toss, do you?'

'*Voilà!*' Giles appeared at the door holding a tray on which reposed a glass of orange juice, a cafetière full of steaming coffee, a plate of warm croissants and a pot of apricot conserve. He looked at Maggie silently for a second, then put the tray down on a table.

'You look beautiful,' he said.

'Yeah, right,' said Maggie, flushing slightly.

'You do.' He came towards the bed, plucked Lucia from Maggie's arms and placed her carefully on the floor. He sat down on the bed and stroked Maggie's hair, her shoulder; then, very gently, her breast. 'Any room in that bed for me, do you think?'

Maggie stared back at him and felt her well-rested body respond to his touch.

'Could be,' she said, and smiled self-consciously.

Slowly Giles leaned forward and kissed her. Maggie closed her eyes in delight and wrapped her arms round his body, losing herself in delicious sensation. Giles's lips found her ear lobe, and she gave a little moan of pleasure.

'We could make number two,' came Giles's voice in her ear. 'Wouldn't that be lovely?'

'What?' Maggie stiffened in horror. 'Giles . . .'

'Joke,' said Giles. She pulled away, to see him laughing at her. 'Joke.'

'No!' said Maggie, her heart still thudding. 'That's not a joke! That's not even . . . not even half funny. It's . . . It's . . .' Suddenly she found herself giggling. 'You're evil.'

'I know,' said Giles, and nuzzled her neck. 'Aren't you glad you married me?'

Ed's car was a navy-blue convertible. As he bleeped it open, Candice stared at it in disbelief.

'I didn't know you had a . . . what is this?'

'BMW,' said Ed.

'Wow,' said Candice. 'So how come I've never seen you in it?'

Ed shrugged. 'I don't drive a lot.'

'So why have you got a flash car like this if you never drive?'

'Come on, Candice.' He grinned disarmingly. 'I'm a boy.'

Candice laughed in spite of herself, and got into the car. Immediately she felt ridiculously glamorous. As they drove off, her hair began to blow about her face. They stopped at a traffic light and Candice watched a girl of about her own age cross the road. She was dressed smartly and obviously hurrying back to the office. Back towards a secure job; a trusting environment; a secure future. At the beginning of the day she'd been just like that girl, thought Candice. Oblivious and trusting. And in a matter of hours it had all changed.

'I'll never be the same again,' she said, without quite meaning to. Ed swivelled in his seat and looked at her.

'What do you mean?'

'I'll never be so . . . trusting. I was a stupid, gullible fool. What a bloody disaster. What a bloody . . .'

'Candice, don't get like that,' said Ed. 'Don't tear yourself to bits. What you did, helping Heather—it was a . . . a generous, positive thing to do. If Heather'd been a different person, maybe it would have worked out fine.'

'I suppose so,' muttered Candice after a pause.

'It wasn't your fault she was a nutter, was it?'

'But I was so bloody   idealistic about the whole thing.'

'Of course you were,' said Ed. 'That's what makes you . . . you.'

There was a sudden stillness between them. Candice gazed back into Ed's dark, intelligent eyes and felt a faint tinge in her cheeks. Then, behind them, a horn sounded. Without speaking, Ed put the car into gear and drove off, and Candice sat back in her seat and closed her eyes, her heart thumping.

When she opened her eyes again, they were on the motorway. The sky had clouded over a little and the wind had become too strong to allow talking. Candice struggled up to a sitting position and looked about. There were fields, and sheep, and a familiar country smell. Her legs felt stiff and her face dry from the wind, and she wondered how much further away it was. As though reading her mind, Ed signalled left and turned off the motorway.

'Are we nearly there?' shouted Candice. He nodded, but said nothing more. They passed through a village and the car swung off the main road up a narrow track. They bumped along for two miles or so, then Ed turned in at a gate and the car crackled down a sloping drive. Candice gazed ahead of her in disbelief.

They were approaching a low, thatched cottage, turned slightly away from them as though too shy to show its face. The walls were painted a soft apricot and the window frames were turquoise. From inside a window she caught a splash of lilac. Round the corner she could see several brightly painted pots clustering outside the wooden front door.

'I've never seen anything like it,' Candice said in astonishment. 'It's like a fairy tale.'

'What?' said Ed. He switched the engine off and looked around with a suppressed gleam. 'Oh, yes. Didn't I say? She was a painter, my aunt. Liked a bit of colour.' He opened the car door. 'Come and see inside.'

The front door opened onto a low hall; a bunch of dried flowers hung from a low beam.

'That's to warn tall bastards,' said Ed. He glanced at Candice, who was peering into the flagstoned kitchen. 'What do you think? You like it?'

'I love it,' said Candice. 'When you said a house, I imagined . . . I had no idea.'

'I stayed here quite a bit,' said Ed. 'When my parents were splitting up. I used to sit in front of that window, playing with my trains. Sad little git, really.'

'How old were you?' said Candice.

'Ten,' said Ed. 'The next year, I went away to school.'

He turned away, staring out of the window. Somewhere in the house, a clock was still ticking; outside was a still, country silence.

Candice looked at a framed sampler on the wall. *Absence makes the heart grow fonder.* Next to it was a charcoal drawing of a shell, and below that a child's painting of three fat geese in a field. Looking more closely, Candice saw the name 'Edward Armitage' written in a teacher's hand in the bottom left-hand corner.

'You never told me it was like this,' she said, turning round. 'You never told me it was so . . .' She spread her hands helplessly.

'No,' said Ed. 'Well, you never asked.'

'So what happened to my breakfast,' murmured Maggie, lying in the crook of Giles's arm. Lazily he shifted and opened one eye.

'You want breakfast, *too*?'

'You bet I do. You don't get off that lightly.' Maggie sat up to allow Giles to move, then flopped back onto the pillows and watched as he reached for his T-shirt. Halfway through putting it on, he stopped.

'I don't believe it!' he whispered. 'Look at this!' Maggie sat up and followed his gaze. Lucia was fast asleep on the carpet, her little hands curled into fists.

'Well, we obviously didn't disturb her,' she said with a giggle.

'How much did that cot cost?' said Giles ruefully. He tiptoed past Lucia, lifted the tray of breakfast off the table and presented it to Maggie. 'Madam.'

'Fresh coffee, please,' she said at once. 'This is lukewarm.'

'The management is devastated,' said Giles. 'Please accept this complimentary glass of orange juice and array of fine croissants with our humblest apologies.'

Giles took the cafetière and headed out of the room. Maggie sat up, pulled open a croissant and spread it thickly with the amber-coloured conserve. She took a huge bite and then another, savouring the buttery taste, the sweetness of the jam. Simple food had never tasted so delicious. She felt as though her taste buds, along with everything else, had been temporarily dulled and then sprung back to life.

'This is more like it,' said Giles, coming back into the room with fresh coffee. He sat down on the bed, and smiled at Maggie. 'Isn't it?'

'Yes,' said Maggie, and took a gulp of tangy orange juice. She looked out of the window at the green fields, shining in the sunshine like an English paradise, and felt a momentary pull towards them. Brambles and weeds, she reminded herself. Cows and sheep. Or cars and shops and taxis. Bright lights. People.

'I think,' she said casually, 'I might go back to work.' She took a sip of grainy, delicious coffee and looked up at Giles.

'Right,' he said cautiously. 'To your old job? Or . . .'

'My old job,' said Maggie. 'Editor of the *Londoner*. I miss it.' She took another sip of coffee. 'I can still take a few months more maternity leave, and then we can hire a nanny and I can go back.'

Giles was silent for a few minutes. Cheerfully, Maggie finished her first croissant and began to spread jam on the second.

'Maggie . . .' he said eventually. 'Are you sure about this? It would be hard work.'

'I know. And so is being a full-time mother.'

'And you think we could find a nanny . . . just like that?'

'Thousands of families do,' said Maggie. 'I don't see why we should be any different.'

Giles frowned. 'It would be a very long day. Up on the train, all day at work, back again . . .'

'I know. It would if we carried on living here.' Maggie looked at Giles and smiled. 'And that's why we're moving back to London.'

'What?' Giles stared at her. 'Maggie, you're not serious.'

'Oh yes I am. Lucia agrees, too, don't you, sweetheart? She wants to be a city girl, like me.'

'Maggie . . .' Giles swallowed. 'Darling, aren't you overreacting just a tad? All our plans have always been—'

'Your plans,' put in Maggie mildly.

'But with my mother so close, and everything, it seems crazy to—'

'Your mother agrees with me.' Maggie smiled. 'Your mother, in case you didn't know, is a star.'

There was silence as Giles gazed at her in astonishment. Then, suddenly, he threw his head back and laughed.

'You women! You've been plotting behind my back, haven't you?'

'Maybe.' Maggie smiled wickedly.

'You'll be telling me next you've sent for house details in London.'

'Maybe,' said Maggie after a pause, and Giles guffawed.

'You're unbelievable. And have you spoken to them at work?'

'Not yet,' said Maggie. 'But I'll phone the new chap today. I want to catch up with what's been going on, anyway.'

'And do I have a role in any of this?' said Giles.

'Hmmm.' Maggie looked at him consideringly. 'You could make some more coffee, if you like.'

Candice and Ed sat outside in the sunshine, side by side on the front doorstep, drinking instant coffee out of oddly shaped pottery mugs.

'You know the really stupid thing?' said Candice. 'I still feel guilty. I still feel guilty towards her.'

'Heather?' said Ed in amazement. 'After everything she did?'

'Almost *because* of everything she did. If she could hate me that much . . .' Candice shook her head. 'What does that mean about what my father did to her family? He must have utterly ruined their lives.'

'Well, I don't know a lot about guilt,' said Ed. 'Being a lawyer.' He took a sip of coffee. 'But one thing I do know is that you have nothing to feel guilty about. *You* didn't rip off Heather's family. Your father did.'

'I know,' said Candice after a pause. 'You're right. In my head, I know you're right. But . . .' She took a sip of coffee and sighed miserably. 'I've got everything wrong, haven't I?' Carefully she put down her coffee cup and leaned back against the painted door frame. 'I mean, these last few weeks, I was so happy. I really thought Heather and I were . . .' Candice gave a shamefaced laugh. 'We just got on so well . . . And it was silly things. Like . . .' She gave a little shrug. 'One time she gave me a pen.'

'A pen?' said Ed, grinning.

'Yes,' said Candice defensively. 'A pen.'

'Is that all it takes to win your heart? A pen?' Ed put down his coffee and reached into his pocket.

'No! Don't be—' Candice stopped as Ed produced a scruffy old Biro.

'Here you are,' he said, presenting it to her. 'Now do you like me?'

'You think I'm a fool, don't you?' Candice said, feeling a flush come to her cheeks. 'You think I'm just a stupid—'

'I don't think you're stupid.'

'You despise me.'

'You think I despise you.' Ed looked at her without the glimmer of a smile. 'You really think I despise you, Candice.'

Candice looked up into his dark eyes. And as she saw his expression, she felt a sliding sensation, as though the ground had fallen away from beneath her; as though the world had swung into a different focus. She stared silently at Ed, unable to speak; scarcely able to breathe.

For an endless, unbearable time, neither of them moved. Then, very slowly, Ed leaned towards her, his eyes still pinned on hers. He raised one finger and ran it down her cheek. He touched her chin and then, very gently, the corner of her mouth. Candice gazed back, transfixed by a longing so desperate it was almost fear.

Slowly he leaned closer, touched her ear lobe, softly kissed her bare shoulder. His lips met the side of her neck and Candice shuddered, unable to control herself, unable to stop herself wanting more. And then, finally, he bent his head and kissed her, his mouth first gentle, then urgent. They paused, and looked at each other, not speaking; not smiling. As he pulled her, determinedly, to her feet and led her into the house, up the stairs, her legs were as staggery as those of a newborn calf.

She had never made love so slowly; so intensely. The world seemed to have dwindled to Ed's two dark eyes, staring into hers, mirroring her own hunger; her own gradual, unbelieving ecstasy. As she'd come to orgasm, she'd cried out in tears, at the relief of what seemed like a lifetime's tension. Now, sated, she lay in his arms, gazing up at the ceiling.

'Are you asleep?' said Ed after a while. His hand caressed her stomach and she felt a fresh, undeserved delight run through her body.

'No.'

'I've wanted you ever since I've known you.'

There was a pause, then Candice said, 'I know.'

'Did you . . . want me?' he said.

'I want you now,' said Candice, turning towards him. 'Is that enough?'

'It'll do,' said Ed, and pulled her down to kiss him.

Much later, as the evening sun crested the hills, they wandered downstairs. 'There should be some wine somewhere,' said Ed, going into the kitchen. 'See if you can find some glasses on the dresser.'

Yawning slightly, Candice went into the adjoining parlour. A pine dresser in the corner was covered with colourful crockery, postcards of paintings, and thick, bubbled glasses. As she went towards it, she passed a writing desk, and glanced down as she did so. A handwritten letter was poking out of the tiny drawer, beginning, 'Dear Edward'.

Curiosity overwhelmed her. She struggled with herself for a few moments—then glanced back at the door and pulled the letter out a little further.

Dear Edward, she read quickly. *Your aunt was so pleased to see you last week; your visits do her the power of good. The last cheque was much appreciated and so generous. I can hardly believe—*

'Found them?' Ed's voice interrupted Candice, and she hastily stuffed the letter away.

'Yes!' she said, grabbing two glasses off the dresser. 'Here we are.' As Ed entered the room she looked at him anew.

'You must miss your aunt,' she said. 'Did you . . . visit her much?'

'A fair bit.' He shrugged. 'She was a bit gaga by the end. Had a nurse living in and everything.'

'Oh,' said Candice casually. 'That must have been pretty expensive.'

A faint colour came to Ed's cheeks. 'The family paid,' he said, and turned away. 'Come on. I've found some wine.'

They sat outside, sipping wine, watching as the sun grew lower and a breeze began to blow. As it got chillier, Candice moved closer to Ed on the wooden bench and he put an arm round her. Her mind floated absently for a while, landed on Heather and quickly bounced away again, before the flash of pain could catch light from her thoughts. No point thinking about it, she told herself. No point reliving it all.

'I don't want to go back,' she heard herself saying.

'Then let's stay the night,' said Ed, and his arm tightened round Candice's shoulders. 'It's my house. We can stay as long as we like.'

Chapter Eleven

IT WAS THREE DAYS LATER that Maggie got round to ringing Charles Allsopp about coming back to work. She waited until Paddy arrived for morning coffee, then handed Lucia to her, together with a load of house details.

'I want to sound businesslike,' she explained. 'No wailing babies in the background.'

Maggie waited until Paddy had carried Lucia off to the sitting room, then dialled the number of Allsopp Publications.

'Hello, yes,' she said, as soon as the phone was answered. 'Charles Allsopp, please. It's Maggie Phillips.' Then she beamed in pleasure. 'Yes, I'm fine, thanks, Doreen. Yes, she's fine, too. An absolute poppet.'

Paddy, from inside the sitting room, caught Maggie's eye and gave her an encouraging smile. This, she thought, is what the real Maggie was like. Confident and cheerful and in command. Thriving on a challenge.

'I'll miss you,' she murmured to Lucia, letting the baby grasp her finger and tug at it. 'I'll miss you. But I think you'll be happier. Don't you?' Paddy reached for one of the estate agents' house details and began to read the descriptions.

'Yes, I look forward to it, too, Charles,' she could hear Maggie saying in the kitchen. 'And I'll be in contact with Justin. Oh, could you? Well, thank you. And I look forward to our meeting. Yes. Bye.' She looked up, caught Paddy's eye and gave the thumbs up. 'Oh, hello, Justin,' she said 'Just wondering how it's all going?'

Paddy tickled Lucia's little tummy and watched in pleasure as the baby began to chortle. 'Are you going to be clever like your mummy? Are you going to be—'

'What?' Maggie's voice came ripping out of the kitchen, and both Paddy and Lucia jumped. 'You did *what*?'

'Goodness,' said Paddy. 'I wonder . . .'

'And she didn't have any explanation?' Maggie stood up and began to pace furiously about the kitchen. 'Oh, she did. And you followed that up, did you?' Maggie's voice grew colder. 'I see. And nobody thought to consult me?' There was a pause.

'Yes, I am challenging your authority!' shouted Maggie. 'To be frank, you don't deserve any!' She thrust the phone down and said angrily, 'Wanker!' Then she picked up the phone again and jabbed in a number.

'Oh dear,' said Paddy faintly. 'I wonder what—'

'Come on,' said Maggie in the kitchen, drumming her nails on the table. 'Come on, answer the phone. Candice, where the hell are you?'

Candice was lying in the garden of the cottage, staring up at the leaves above her. The early summer sun was warm on her face, but she was cold inside as thoughts she had tried to put from her mind during the last few days came crowding in.

She had been suspended from work. She had been publicly branded dishonest. And she had ruined the two friendships that meant most to her in the world. A sharp wave of pain went through Candice and she sat up, trying to escape her thoughts, wondering what Ed was doing. He had disappeared mysteriously that morning, muttering something about a surprise.

They had been down at the cottage for four days now, but it felt as though it could have been weeks. They had done little but sleep and eat and make love, and lie on the grass in the early summer sun. Their only forays into the local village had been to buy essentials: food, soap and toothbrushes. Neither had brought any spare clothes, but in the spare room Ed had found a pile of colourful T-shirts advertising a screen-printing exhibition, and, for Candice, a wide-brimmed straw hat decorated with a bunch of cherries. They had not spoken to a soul, had not even read a paper. It had been a haven; a place of sanctuary and healing.

But although her body was well rested, thought Candice, her mind was not. She could push the thoughts from her brain, but they only came rushing back in when she wasn't expecting it. She felt bruised and humiliated. And her mind constantly circled around Heather.

'Candice!' Ed's voice interrupted her thoughts and she stood up, shaking her stiff legs. He was coming towards her, a strange look in his eye. 'Candice,' he said, 'don't get angry—but I've got someone to see you.'

'What?' Candice stared at him. 'What do you mean, someone to see me?' Her gaze shifted over his shoulder but she could see no one.

'He's in the house,' said Ed. 'Come on.'

'Who is?' said Candice, her voice truculent.

Ed looked at her steadily. 'Someone I think you need to speak to,' he said.

'Who? Who is it? Oh God, I know who it is,' she said at the door, her heart pounding. 'It's Justin, isn't it?'

'No,' said Ed, and pushed the door open.

Candice peered into the gloom and saw a young man of about twenty standing by the dresser in the kitchen. She stared at him in puzzlement.

'Candice,' said Ed, 'this is Hamish.'

'Hamish?' said Candice wrinkling her brow. 'You're . . .' She stopped as a memory surfaced in her mind like a bubble. 'Oh my God. You're Heather's ex-boyfriend, aren't you?'

'No, I'm not,' said Hamish. 'I'm her brother.'

Roxanne sat in the office of Strawson & Co, sipping tea out of a bone china cup and wishing that her hand wouldn't shake every time she put it down. There was a smooth, thickly carpeted silence about the place; an air of solid opulence and respectability which made her feel flimsy and cheap, even though she was wearing one of the most expensive, sober outfits she possessed.

'I'm so glad you decided to come,' said Neil Cooper.

'Yes, well,' said Roxanne shortly. 'Curiosity won in the end.'

'It often does,' said Neil Cooper, and picked up his own cup.

He was much younger than Roxanne had expected, and had an earnest, guarded expression on his face, as though he didn't want to disappoint her. As though he didn't want to let down the hopes of the gold-digging mistress. A flash of humiliation passed through Roxanne and she put down her cup.

'Look,' she said, more aggressively than she'd intended. 'Let's just get this over with, shall we? I wasn't expecting anything, so whatever it is, I'll just sign for it and leave.'

'Yes,' said Neil Cooper carefully. 'Well, it's not quite as simple as that. If I can just read to you a codicil which the late Mr Allsopp added to his will shortly before dying . . .'

He reached for a black leather folder, opened it and shuffled some papers together, and Roxanne stared at his calm, professional face in sudden realisation.

'Oh God,' she said, in a voice which shook slightly. 'He really has left something to me, hasn't he? Something serious. What is it? Not money.'

'No,' said Neil Cooper with a tiny smile. 'Not money.'

'We're fine for money,' said Hamish, taking a sip of tea from the mug Ed had made. 'In fact, we're pretty loaded. After my parents split up, my mum remarried this guy Derek. He's . . . well, he's stinking rich. He gave me my car . . .' He gestured out of the window, to where a new Alfa Romeo was sitting smartly on the gravel next to Ed's BMW. 'He's been really good to us. Both of us.'

'Oh,' said Candice. She rubbed her face, trying to marshal her thoughts. She was sitting across the table from Hamish, and every time she looked up at him she could see Heather in his face. Heather's little brother. She hadn't even known Heather had a brother. 'So . . . so why was Heather working as a cocktail waitress?'

'It's the kind of thing she does,' said Hamish. 'She starts something like an art course or a writing course and then she drops out and takes some crummy job so we all feel bad.'

'Oh,' said Candice again. She felt slow and very stupid, as though her brain had overloaded on information.

'I knew she'd gone to live with you,' said Hamish. 'And I thought she might do something stupid. I told her the two of you should just talk about it. You know—work it out. But she wouldn't listen.' He paused, and looked at Candice. 'I really didn't think she'd go as far as . . .' He broke off, and took another sip of tea.

'So . . . she really hated me,' said Candice.

'Oh God,' said Hamish. 'This is . . .' He was silent for a time, then looked up. 'Not you,' he said. 'Not you as a person. But . . .'

'But what I represented.'

'You have to understand. What your dad did—it split up our family. My dad was wrecked. He went a bit crazy. And my mum couldn't cope with it, so . . .' Hamish broke off for a few moments. 'And it was easy to blame your dad for everything. But now I look back, I think maybe it would have happened anyway. It wasn't like my parents had such a great marriage.'

'But Heather didn't agree?' said Candice tentatively.

'Heather never saw the whole picture. She was away at school, so she didn't see my parents rowing the whole time. She thought they had the perfect set-up. You know: big house, perfect marriage . . . Then we lost all our money and they split up. And Heather couldn't deal with it. She went a bit . . . screwy.'

'So when she saw me in the Manhattan Bar . . .'

'Candice, let me get this straight,' said Ed, leaning forward. 'Both of you knew about what your dad had done—but neither of you ever mentioned it?'

'Heather behaved as if she had no idea!' said Candice defensively. 'And I didn't say anything to her because I didn't want her to think I was helping her out of pity. I wanted to . . .' She flushed slightly. 'I really wanted to be her friend.'

'I know,' said Hamish. He met Candice's eyes. 'For what it's worth, I think you were probably the best friend she ever had. But of course she wouldn't have seen that.'

'Do you know where she is now?' Candice said apprehensively.

'No idea,' said Hamish. 'She disappears for weeks. Months. But she'll turn up eventually.'

Candice swallowed. 'Would you . . . would you do me a favour?'

'What?'

'Come and tell Justin, my boss, what Heather's really like? Tell him that she set me up?'

There was a long pause.

'No,' said Hamish at last. 'No, I won't. I love my sister, even if she is a bit—' He broke off. 'I'm not going to go into some office and tell them she's a conniving, crazy bitch. I'm sorry.' He looked at Candice, then pushed his chair back with a scraping sound. 'I have to get going.'

'Yes,' said Candice. 'Well . . . thanks for coming.'

'I hope everything works out,' said Hamish, shrugging slightly.

Ed followed him out, then after a few minutes came back into the kitchen as the Alfa Romeo disappeared up the track. Candice stared at him, then said incredulously, 'How did you find him?'

'Heather told me her family lived in Wiltshire. I looked them up and paid them a visit.' Ed gave a rueful grin. 'To be honest, I was half hoping to find her there, too. Catch her out.'

Candice shook her head. 'Not Heather.'

Ed sat down beside Candice and took her hand. 'But anyway. Now you know.'

'Now I know. Now I know I was harbouring a psychopath.' Candice smiled at him, then buried her head in her hands. Tears began to ooze out of the corners of her eyes.

'What?' said Ed in alarm. 'Oh, Jesus. I'm sorry. I should have warned you. I shouldn't have just—'

'It's not that.' Candice looked up and wiped her eyes. 'It's what Hamish said about me being a good friend.' She stared straight ahead, her face trembling slightly. 'Roxanne and Maggie were the best friends I ever had. They tried to warn me about Heather. And what did I do?' She took a deep, shuddering breath. 'I got angry with them. I was so . . . besotted with Heather, I would rather lose them than hear the truth.'

'You haven't lost them!' said Ed. 'I'm sure you haven't.'

'I said some unforgivable things, Ed. I behaved like a—'

'So call them.'

'I tried,' said Candice miserably. 'Maggie put the phone down on me. And Roxanne is furious with me. She thinks I was keeping Ralph's illness a secret from her, or something . . .'

'Well, it's their loss,' said Ed. 'It's their bloody loss.'

'It's not, though, is it?' said Candice. 'It's mine.'

Roxanne stared at Neil Cooper, feeling a whooshing in her head. For the first time in her life, she thought she might faint.

'I . . . that can't be right,' she managed. 'There must be . . .'

'To Miss Roxanne Miller,' repeated Neil Cooper deliberately, 'I leave my London house. Fifteen Abernathy Square, Kensington.' He looked up from his folder. 'It's yours. To live in, sell—whatever you prefer. We can provide you with advice on the matter if you like. But obviously there's no hurry to decide. In any case, it will all take a while to go through.'

Roxanne stared back at him, unable to speak; unable to move. Ralph had left her his house. He'd sent a message to her—and to the world—that she had meant something. That she hadn't been a nothing. He'd almost . . . legitimised her.

'I . . .' Roxanne stopped. 'I'm sorry,' she gulped, as tears suddenly began to stream down her face. 'Oh God. It's just I never expected . . .'

Sobs were overtaking her; she was powerless to stop them. Furiously she scrabbled for a tissue, trying to control herself.

'It's just . . .' she managed eventually, 'a bit of a shock.'

'Of course it is,' said Neil Cooper diplomatically, and hesitated. 'Do you . . . know the property?'

'Only the outside,' said Roxanne, wiping her eyes. 'I know every blasted brick of the outside. But I've never been inside.'

'Well. If you would like to visit it, that can be arranged.'

'I . . . No. I don't think so. Not yet.' Roxanne blew her nose, and watched as Neil Cooper made a note on the pad in front of him.

'What about . . .' she began, then stopped, almost unable to say the words. 'The . . . the family. Do they know?'

'Yes,' said Neil Cooper. 'Yes, they do.'

'Are they . . .' Roxanne took a deep breath. 'Do they hate me?'

'Miss Miller,' said Neil Cooper earnestly, 'there's no need for you to concern yourselves with the other members of the Allsopp family. Let me just reassure you that Mr Allsopp's will was very generous to all parties concerned.' He paused, and met her gaze. 'But his bequest to you is between you and him.'

There was a pause, then Roxanne nodded. 'OK,' she said quietly. 'Thanks.'

'If you have any further questions . . .'

'No,' said Roxanne. 'No, thanks. I think I'd just like to go and . . . digest it all.' She stood up and met the young man's eyes. 'You've been very kind.'

Neil Cooper adroitly opened the door for her and stood aside, and Roxanne walked into the hall to see a man in a navy-blue overcoat standing at the reception desk.

'I'm sorry,' he was saying. 'I am rather early . . .'

Roxanne stopped in her tracks. At the desk, Charles Allsopp looked up, saw Roxanne and froze. There was an instant of silence as they stared at each other—then Roxanne turned away, trying to keep calm.

'Well, thank you very much,' she said to Neil Cooper in a voice which trembled with nerves. 'I'll . . . I'll be in touch. Thanks very much.' And without looking him in the eye she began to walk towards the exit.

'Wait.' Charles Allsopp's voice halted her in her tracks. 'Please.'

Roxanne stopped and very slowly turned round, aware that her cheeks were flushed; that her mouth was lipstickless and reddened; that her legs were still shaking. But she didn't care. And suddenly, as she met his gaze, she wasn't nervous. Let him say what he liked. He couldn't touch her.

'Are you Roxanne Miller?'

'I really think,' said Neil Cooper, 'that for all parties concerned . . .'

'Wait,' said Charles Allsopp. 'All I wanted was to introduce myself. That's all.' He hesitated—then slowly held out his hand. 'How do you do. My name's Charles Allsopp.'

'Hello,' said Roxanne after a pause. 'I'm Roxanne.'

Charles nodded gravely and Roxanne found herself wondering how much he knew about her; whether Ralph had said anything to his eldest son before he died.

'I hope they're looking after you,' said Charles, glancing towards Neil.

'Oh,' said Roxanne, taken aback. 'Yes. Yes, they are.'

'Good,' said Charles Allsopp, and looked up at an elderly lawyer descending the stairs into the hall. 'Well, I must go,' he said. 'Goodbye.'

'Goodbye,' said Roxanne awkwardly, watching as he walked towards the stairs. 'And . . . and thanks.'

Outside, on the pavement, she leaned against a wall and took a few deep breaths. She felt confused; euphoric; shattered with emotion. Ralph had left her his house: the house she'd spent obsessive hours staring at. It was hers. A house worth a million pounds was hers. The thought made her feel tearful, almost sick. She hadn't expected Ralph to leave her anything. She hadn't expected Charles Allsopp to behave so politely to her. The world was suddenly being nice to her and she didn't know how to react.

Roxanne reached inside her bag for her cigarettes, and as she did so, felt the vibrating motion of her mobile phone. She hesitated, then took the phone out and half reluctantly put it to her ear.

'Hello?'

'Roxanne! Thank God.' Maggie's voice crackled urgently down the line. 'Listen, have you spoken to Candice recently?'

'No,' said Roxanne. 'Is something wrong?'

'That little twerp Justin has suspended her from work. Some nonsense about expenses.'

'*What?*' exclaimed Roxanne, her mind snapping into focus.

'And she's disappeared. No one knows where she is. She isn't answering her phone . . . she could be dead in a ditch somewhere.'

'Oh my God,' said Roxanne, her heart thumping. 'I had no idea.'

'Hasn't she called you, either? When did you last speak to her?'

'At the funeral,' said Roxanne. She paused. 'To be honest, we didn't part on good terms.'

'The last time I spoke to her was when she phoned up to apologise,' said Maggie miserably. 'I snapped at her and put the phone down.'

There was a subdued silence.

'Anyway,' said Maggie. 'I'm coming up to London tomorrow. Breakfast?'

'Breakfast,' agreed Roxanne. 'And let me know if you hear anything.' She switched off her phone and began to walk on, her face clouded with sudden worry.

At eleven o'clock the next morning, Maggie and Roxanne stood outside Candice's front door, fruitlessly ringing the bell. After a while, Maggie bent down and peered through the letterbox into the communal hall.

'There's a load of letters piled up on the table,' she reported.

'Addressed to Candice?'

'I can't see. Possibly.' Maggie dropped the letterbox flap, stood up and looked at Roxanne. 'God, I feel shitty.'

'I feel awful,' agreed Roxanne. She sank down onto the front step, and Maggie sat down beside her. 'I gave her such a hard time at Ralph's funeral. I was just . . . oh, I don't know. Beside myself.'

'Of course you were,' said Maggie at once. 'It must have been a terrible time.'

Her voice was sympathetic, but again she felt a *frisson* of shock at the idea of Roxanne and Ralph as lovers. Roxanne had told her everything on the journey from Waterloo to Candice's flat, and for at least five minutes Maggie had been utterly unable to speak. How could two people be friends for such a long time and one of them have a secret as big as that? How could Roxanne have talked about Ralph so normally, without once giving their relationship away? Of course it was understandable, of course she hadn't had any choice, but even so, Maggie felt hurt; as though she would never look at Roxanne in quite the same way.

'It was as if I'd finally found someone to blame,' said Roxanne, staring bleakly ahead. 'So I took it all out on her.'

'It's a natural reaction,' said Maggie after a pause. 'You feel grief, you need a scapegoat.'

'Perhaps it is,' said Roxanne. 'But Candice, of all people . . .' She closed her eyes briefly. 'How could I have blamed Candice?'

'I know,' said Maggie shamefacedly. 'I feel the same. I can't believe I slammed the phone down on her. But I just felt so hurt. Everything seemed so awful . . .' She looked at Roxanne. 'I can't tell you what these last few weeks have been like. I honestly think I lost it for a bit.'

There was a short silence.

'I had no idea,' said Roxanne eventually. 'You always looked so . . . in control. It all seemed so perfect.'

'I know,' said Maggie. 'I was stupid. I couldn't bear to admit how terrible I felt to anyone. Not to Giles, not to anyone.' She paused. 'Actually that's not true. I was going to tell you about it once. That night at the Manhattan Bar.' She gave a rueful smile. 'You know, that night has to be one of the worst in my life. I felt fat, I was exhausted, I was guilty at leaving Lucia . . . Then we all end up arguing with each other. It was . . .' She gave a short laugh. 'It was one to forget.'

'God, I feel terrible.' Roxanne looked miserably at Maggie. 'I should have realised you were depressed. I should have called. Visited.' She bit her lip. 'Some friend I've been. To both of you.'

'Come on,' said Maggie. 'You've had it worse than either of us.'

She put an arm round Roxanne's shoulders and squeezed them. For a while they were both silent. A postman arrived, looked at them oddly, then reached past them to post a bundle of letters through the letterbox.

'So, what do we do now?' said Roxanne finally.

'We go and put Justin on the spot,' said Maggie. 'He's not going to get away with this.' She stood up and brushed down her skirt. 'Let's find a taxi.'

'That's a nice suit, by the way,' said Roxanne, looking up at her. Then she frowned. 'In fact, now I come to think of it, you're looking very good all over.' She surveyed Maggie's silk, aubergine-coloured suit; her simple white T-shirt; her gleaming nut-brown hair. 'Have you just had your hair cut?'

'Yes,' said Maggie, a half-smile coming to her face. 'This is a whole new me. New hair, new clothes, new lipstick. I went shopping yesterday afternoon. Spent a bloody fortune, I might add.'

'Good for you,' said Roxanne. 'That's a fantastic colour on you.'

'I just have to avoid hearing any crying babies,' said Maggie, pulling Roxanne to her feet. 'Or I'll leak milk all over the jacket.'

'Oooh.' Roxanne pulled a face. 'You didn't have to tell me that.'

'The joys of motherhood,' said Maggie cheerfully, and began to stride ahead to the corner. If someone had told her a few weeks ago, she thought, that she'd be *laughing* about breastfeeding, she just wouldn't have believed them. But then, neither would she have believed that she'd be wearing a suit two sizes bigger than normal and feeling good in it.

As they got out of a chugging taxi outside the Allsopp Publications building, Maggie tilted her head back and stared at it. The building where she'd spent most of her working life looked as familiar as ever— and yet different. In just a few weeks it seemed, almost imperceptibly, to have changed.

'This is so strange,' she murmured as Roxanne swiped her security card and pushed open the glass doors to reception. 'I feel as if I've been away for years.'

'Ditto,' muttered Roxanne. She looked at Maggie. 'Ready?'

'Absolutely,' said Maggie. The two grinned at each other, then, side by side, walked into the foyer.

'Maggie!' exclaimed Doreen at the reception desk. 'What a surprise! Don't you look well? But where's the baby?'

'At home,' said Maggie, smiling. 'With my mother-in-law.'

'Oh! What a shame! You should have brought her in! Little pet.' Doreen nudged the girl sitting next to her at the desk—a shy-looking redhead whom Maggie didn't recognise. 'This is Maggie who I was telling you about,' she said to the girl. 'Maggie, this is Julie. Just started on reception yesterday.'

'Hello, Julie,' said Maggie politely. 'Doreen, I'm here to see Justin. Could you give him a quick call?'

'I don't think he's in,' said Doreen in surprise. 'He and Mr Allsopp have gone off somewhere together. I'll just check.' She pressed a button and said, 'Hello, Alicia? Doreen here.'

'Damn!' said Maggie, and looked at Roxanne. 'It didn't even occur to me he wouldn't be in.'

'Back in about an hour, apparently,' said Doreen, looking up.

'So what do we do?' said Roxanne.

'We wait,' said Maggie firmly.

An hour later, Justin was still not back. Maggie and Roxanne sat on leather chairs in the foyer, leafing through old copies of the *Londoner* and looking up every time the door opened. Some of those entering were visitors who gave them polite looks; others were members of staff who came over to greet Maggie warmly and ask where the baby was.

'The next time someone asks me that,' Maggie muttered to Roxanne, as a group of marketing executives walked off to the lifts, 'I'm going to say it's in my briefcase.'

Roxanne didn't answer. She was transfixed by a photograph of Candice she had just come across in an old issue of the *Londoner*. *Staff writer Candice Brewin investigates the plight of the elderly in London's hospitals*, read the caption. And next to it, Candice's round face stared out.

Roxanne gazed down at the familiar picture as though for the first time, and felt a pain in her chest at the innocence of Candice's expression. She didn't look like a hard-hitting reporter. She looked like a child.

'Roxanne?' said Maggie curiously. 'Are you OK?'

'We should have seen it coming,' said Roxanne in a trembling voice. 'We knew that little bitch was up to no good. We should have . . . I don't know.' She rubbed her face. 'Warned Candice, or something.'

'What could we have done?' said Maggie. 'We didn't know anything. Let's face it, it was nothing more than instinct. We just didn't like the girl.'

'We should have been there for her,' said Roxanne in a low, fierce voice. 'I'll never forgive myself for shutting her out. Or you, for that matter.' She looked up at Maggie. 'I should have been there for you when you were feeling down.'

'You weren't to know,' said Maggie. 'How could you have known?'

'But that's my point!' said Roxanne urgently. 'We shouldn't keep secrets . . . or . . . or put on acts for each other. None of us should ever feel we have to struggle through on our own.' She gazed at Maggie with blue eyes suddenly glittering with tears. 'Maggie, ring me next time. If it's the middle of the night, or . . . whenever it is, if you're feeling low, ring me. I'll come straight over and take the baby for a walk. Or Giles. Whichever one you want off your hands.' She grinned, and Maggie gave a giggle. 'Please,' said Roxanne seriously. 'Ring me, Maggie. Don't pretend everything's fine when it isn't.'

'I won't,' said Maggie, blinking away her own tears. 'I'll . . . I'll ring you, I promise. Maybe even when things *aren't* bad.' She smiled briefly, then hesitated. 'And next time you have a six-year-long affair with the boss—you tell me too, all right?'

'It's a deal.' Impulsively, Roxanne leaned forward and hugged Maggie tightly. 'I've missed you,' she murmured. 'Come back to London soon.'

'I've missed you too,' said Maggie, her throat blocked with emotion. 'God, I've missed you all. I feel as though—'

'Shit,' said Roxanne, staring over her shoulder. 'Here they come.'

Maggie swivelled round and saw Justin walking along the pavement towards the glass doors of the building. He was talking enthusiastically to Charles Allsopp at his side. 'Oh God!' she said in dismay and turned back to Roxanne. She gave a huge sniff and lifted her hands to her eyes. 'Quickly. Do I look all right? Has my make-up run?'

'A bit,' said Roxanne, leaning forward and quickly wiping away a smudge of eyeliner. 'How about mine?'

'It looks fine,' said Maggie, peering intently at her face. 'All intact.'

'That's waterproof mascara for you,' said Roxanne lightly. 'Copes with sea, sand, strong emotions . . .' She broke off as the glass doors swung open. 'Here they are. What are we going to say?'

'Don't worry,' said Maggie. 'I'll do the talking.' She stood up, smoothing her skirt down, and took a deep breath. 'Right,' she said, glancing nervously at Roxanne. 'Here goes. Justin!' she exclaimed, raising her voice and taking a step forward. 'How are you?'

Justin turned at the sound of Maggie's voice as though he'd been scalded. As he saw her, his face fell spectacularly—then repositioned itself in an expression of delight.

'Maggie!' he said. 'What a charming surprise.'

'I thought I'd just pop in and see how things were going,' said Maggie, smiling back.

'Great!' said Justin with forced enthusiasm. 'What a marvellous idea!'

'So this is the famous Maggie Phillips,' said Charles Allsopp, giving her a friendly smile and extending his hand towards her. 'Maggie, I'm Charles Allsopp. Congratulations on the birth of your baby. It must be a very exciting time for you.'

'Thank you,' said Maggie pleasantly. 'And, yes, it is.'

'I have to say though, not a day goes by without my being asked when you're coming back to the *Londoner*.'

'Really?' said Maggie, allowing herself a tiny, satisfied glance at Justin's crestfallen face. 'Well, I'm very glad to hear it. And let me tell you, I'm intending to return to work in a matter of weeks.'

'Good,' said Charles Allsopp. 'I'm delighted.'

'Charles, this is Roxanne Miller,' said Justin in a loud, attention-seeking voice. 'One of our regular freelancers.'

'Miss Miller and I have already met,' said Charles after a tiny pause, and gave Roxanne a friendly little smile. 'Now, may I offer the two of you a cup of tea? A drink?'

'Very kind,' said Maggie in a businesslike manner. 'But I'm afraid this visit isn't social. I'm actually here on an unfortunate matter. The suspension of Candice Brewin. I was a little perturbed to hear about it.'

'Ah,' said Charles Allsopp, and glanced at Justin. 'Justin?'

'It was completely justified,' said Justin defensively. 'The fact is, Candice has been found to be defrauding the company. If you don't think that's a serious offence, Maggie—'

'Of course I do,' said Maggie calmly. 'But I can't believe Candice is capable of doing such a thing.'

'I've got the evidence in my office,' said Justin. 'You can see it with your own eyes if you like.'

'Fine,' said Maggie, and gestured towards the lifts. 'Let's see it.'

As Maggie strode through the door of the editorial office, she felt suddenly proprietorial. Here was her magazine; here was her team. It was almost as though she were coming home.

'Hi, Maggie,' said Alicia casually as she walked past, then did a double-take. 'Maggie! How are you! Where the hell's that bump gone?'

'Damn,' said Maggie in mock alarm. 'I knew I was missing something.' There was a giggle round the office. Bright-eyed faces looked up from desks, glanced at Justin and back to Maggie.

'I'm only popping in briefly,' said Maggie. 'Just a quick hello.'

'Well, good to see you,' said Alicia. 'Bring the baby next time.'

'Will do,' said Maggie cheerily, then turned and walked into Justin's office where he, Charles and Roxanne were waiting. She pulled the door shut behind her and for a few moments there was silence.

'I have to say,' said Charles eventually to Maggie, 'I'm a little unclear as to why you're here. The evidence against Candice seems, I'm afraid, fairly strong. And she will, of course, be given a chance at the hearing . . .'

'Hearing?' said Maggie impatiently. 'You don't need a hearing to sort this out.'

'Here we are,' said Justin, producing from a drawer a pile of photocopied forms, each headed with Candice's name. His voice sharpened slightly with triumph. 'What do you make of these?'

Maggie ignored him. 'Did you hear her explanation?' she asked Charles.

'Some story about being set up by one of her colleagues?' He wrinkled his brow. 'It seems a little fanciful.'

'Well, frankly, the idea that Candice Brewin is capable of fraud is even more fanciful!' exclaimed Roxanne.

'You're her friend,' said Justin scathingly. 'You would defend her.'

'Correct me if I'm wrong,' retorted Roxanne, 'but you're her ex-boyfriend. You *would* get rid of her.'

'Really?' said Charles in surprise. He frowned, and looked at Justin. 'You didn't tell me that.'

'It's irrelevant,' said Justin, flushing. 'I behaved in a completely fair and impartial way.'

'On the contrary,' said Maggie. 'If you ask me, you behaved in a high-handed and irresponsible way. You took the word of Heather Trelawney—a girl who has been at the company for a matter of weeks—over that of Candice, who's worked here for, what, five years? You fell for this ridiculous story of office bullying—did you ever actually see it going on with your own eyes? You took at face value these expenses claims—'

Maggie picked one up and dropped it dismissively on the desk. 'But I'm a hundred per cent sure that if they were analysed, they would be shown to be an imitation of Candice's handwriting, not the real thing.' She paused, letting her words sink in. 'I would say, Justin, that not only have you shown a partisan and improper haste to get rid of a talented employee, but that your lack of judgment has cost the company substantially in terms of lost time, disruption and damaged morale.'

'There were witnesses to the bullying,' said Justin, leafing through his papers. 'There was definitely a . . . Yes.' He pulled out a sheet of paper. 'Kelly Jones.' He stood up, stalked to the door and called, 'Kelly? Could you step in here a moment, please? Our secretary,' he added to Charles. 'Heather said she had witnessed some of Candice's unpleasant behaviour.'

As the sixteen-year-old girl came into the office, a hot pink blush spread over her face. She stood by the door, her gaze steadily fixed on the floor.

'Kelly,' said Justin. 'I'd like to ask you about Candice Brewin and Heather Trelawney.'

'Yes,' whispered Kelly.

'Did you ever see any unpleasantness between them?'

'Yes,' said Kelly after a pause. 'I did.'

Justin shot a pleased glance around the room.

'Could you tell us a little more?' he said.

'I feel really bad about it now,' added Kelly miserably, twisting her hands together. 'I was going to come and say something before. But I didn't want to . . . you know. Cause trouble.'

'Never mind that,' said Justin kindly. 'What were you going to say?'

'Well, just that . . .' Kelly hesitated. 'Just that Heather hated Candice. Really . . . hated her. And she knew Candice was going to get in trouble, even before it happened. It was expenses, wasn't it?' Kelly looked up nervously. 'I think maybe Heather had something to do with it.'

'I see,' said Charles Allsopp heavily and looked at Justin. 'I would say, at the very least, this matter could have done with a little further investigation before action. What do you think, Justin?'

'I . . . I . . . I utterly agree,' said Justin in a furious, stammering voice. 'Obviously there has been some . . . some gross misrepresentation of the facts . . .' He shot an angry look at Kelly. 'Perhaps if Kelly had come to me sooner . . .'

'Don't blame *her*!' said Roxanne. 'It's you who got rid of Candice!'

'I think what we need in this case is a . . . a full and thorough investigation,' said Justin, ignoring her. 'Clearly some errors have been made—' he swallowed. 'And clearly some . . . some clarification of the situation is needed. So what I suggest is that as soon as Heather gets back—'

'She isn't coming back,' said Kelly. 'She's gone to Australia.'

'For good?' said Justin, his voice rising in disbelief.

'I don't know,' said Kelly, flushing. 'But she's not coming back here. She . . . she gave me a goodbye present.'

'The sweetheart,' said Roxanne.

Charles Allsopp shook his head disbelievingly.

'This is ludicrous,' he said. 'Utterly—' He stopped himself and nodded at the blushing girl. 'Thank you, Kelly. You can go now.'

As the door closed behind her, he looked at Maggie. 'What we must do, straightaway, is contact Candice and arrange a meeting. Could you do that, Maggie? Ask her to come in as soon as possible. Tomorrow, perhaps.'

'I would do,' said Maggie. 'But we don't know where she is.'

'What?' Charles stared at her.

'She's disappeared,' said Maggie soberly. 'She isn't answering the phone. We're actually rather alarmed.'

'Christ!' said Charles in dismay. 'This is all we need. Has anyone called the police?'

'Not yet,' said Maggie. 'But I think perhaps we should.'

'What a bloody fiasco,' said Charles. For a moment or two he was silent. Then he turned to Justin, his face stern. 'Justin, I think the two of us need to have a little talk.'

'Ab-absolutely,' said Justin. 'Good idea.' He reached for his desk planner with a trembling hand. 'Ahm . . . when were you thinking of?'

'I was thinking of now,' said Charles curtly. 'Right now, upstairs in my office.' He turned to the others. 'If you'll excuse me . . .'

'Absolutely,' said Maggie.

'Go right ahead,' said Roxanne, and grinned maliciously at Justin.

When the two of them had left, Roxanne and Maggie sank heavily onto chairs and looked at each other.

'I feel absolutely . . . shattered,' said Maggie. She lifted her hands to her head and began to rub her temples.

'I'm not surprised!' said Roxanne. 'You were fantastic. I've never seen anything like it.'

'Well, I think I made my point,' said Maggie, giving a satisfied smile.

'Made your point? I tell you, after your performance, Charles will be welcoming Candice back with the whole red carpet treatment.'

'If we find her,' Maggie said.

'If we find her,' echoed Roxanne, and looked soberly at Maggie. 'Were you serious about calling the police?'

'I don't know.' Maggie sighed. 'To be honest, I'm not sure the police can actually do anything. They'll probably tell us to . . .'

There was a sound at the door, and she stopped mid-sentence. Outside the glass panel of the door, the new receptionist Julie was peering in anxiously. As Maggie beckoned, she cautiously opened the door.

'Sorry to bother you,' she said, looking from face to face.

'That's OK,' said Maggie. 'What is it?'

'There's somebody downstairs to see Justin,' said Julie nervously. 'Doreen wasn't sure if he was in a meeting or not.'

'He is, I'm afraid,' said Maggie. 'And he may be some time.'

'Right.' Julie paused. 'So what should I say to the person?'

'What do you think?' said Maggie, glancing at Roxanne. 'Shall I see them myself?'

'I don't see why you should,' said Roxanne, stretching her arms above her head. 'You're not here to work. You're on maternity leave, damn it.'

'I know,' said Maggie. 'But even so . . . it might be important.' She looked at Julie. 'Do you happen to know what the name was?'

There was a pause as Julie consulted her little piece of paper.

'She's called . . . Candice Brewin.' Julie looked up. 'Apparently she used to work here or something?'

Candice stood by the reception desk, trying desperately to fight the impulse to run out of the door and never return. Her legs were trembling, her lips were dry, and every time she thought of having to face Justin she felt as if she might vomit. But at the same time, there was a determination inside her like a thin steel rod. I have to do this, she told herself yet again. If I want my job back, my integrity back—I have to do this.

That morning at the cottage, she had woken up feeling a strange lightness inside her. A sense of release, almost. For a while she had stared silently up at the ceiling, trying to place this new sensation.

And then it had hit her. She didn't feel guilty any more. It was as though a burden that she'd unconsciously been carrying for years had been lifted, and suddenly she was able to stretch her shoulders; to enjoy the sensation of freedom. The guilt she'd been carrying for her father's crimes was gone.

Deliberately she had tested herself by bringing Heather to the forefront of her mind; waiting for the flash of guilt. It was such an automatic reaction, she had got used to it over the years. But this morning there had been nothing. A new absence inside her. A numbness.

She had lain still and silent, marvelling at her transformation. Now she was able to view Heather with uncluttered eyes; to view the whole relationship between them in a different way. She had owed Heather nothing. Nothing. As Ed shifted beside her in bed, Candice had felt clear-headed and cool.

'Morning,' he'd murmured sleepily and leaned over to kiss her.

'I want my job back,' she'd replied, staring straight at the ceiling. 'I'm not waiting for any hearing. I want my job back, Ed.'

'Good,' he'd said, and kissed her ear. 'Well, go and get it.'

They'd eaten breakfast and packed up the cottage almost silently, as though to chat would be to destroy the mood; the focus. As they'd driven back to London, Candice had sat tensely, staring straight ahead. Ed had taken her home, waited while she changed into the smartest outfit she possessed, then had driven her here. Somehow she'd managed to stride confidently into the foyer and ask for Justin. Somehow she'd got that far.

But now, standing on the marble floor, flinching under Doreen's curious gaze, her confidence was evaporating. What exactly was she going to say to Justin? What if he wouldn't listen?

'Yes,' said Doreen, looking up. 'It's as I thought. Justin is in a meeting at the moment.'

'Oh,' said Candice in a trembling voice. 'I see.'

'But you've been asked to wait here,' said Doreen coldly. 'Someone will be down presently.'

'What for?' said Candice, but Doreen merely raised her eyebrows.

Candice felt her heart pound with fright. Perhaps they were going to charge her. Perhaps they were going to bring the police in. She should never have come, she thought frantically.

At the back of the foyer, there was a ping as the lift arrived at the ground floor. Candice felt her stomach lurch in panic. Then the lift doors opened and her face went numb with shock. It couldn't be. There, in front of her, was Maggie, coming out of the lift, her hazel eyes looking ahead anxiously. And, behind her, Roxanne, her face taut, almost stern with worry.

They stopped as they saw Candice and there was a tense silence as the three gazed at each other.

'It's you,' whispered Candice at last.

'It's us,' said Roxanne, nodding. 'Isn't it, Maggie?'

Candice stared at her friends' unsmiling faces through a haze of fear. They hadn't forgiven her.

'I . . . Oh God. I'm so sorry.' Tears began to stream down her face. 'I'm so sorry. I should have listened to you. I was wrong and you were right. Heather was . . .' She swallowed desperately. 'She was a . . .'

'It's OK,' said Maggie. 'It's OK, Candice. Heather's gone.'

'And we're back,' said Roxanne, and started to walk towards Candice with glittering eyes. 'We're back.'

Chapter Twelve

THE GRAVE WAS PLAIN AND WHITE; almost anonymous-looking among the rows in the suburban, functional cemetery. She stared at the plainly engraved name, chiselled into the stone in capital letters. The name she'd been ashamed of for all her adult life.

Candice clutched her bunch of flowers more tightly and walked towards her father's grave. She hadn't been to visit it for years. Neither, judging by its state, had her mother. Both of them too consumed by anger, by shame, by denial. Both wanting to forget the past.

But now, staring at the stone, Candice felt a sense of release. She felt as though, in the last few weeks, she had handed all the guilt back to her father. And in return she was beginning to be able to forgive him. After years of feeling nothing for him but shame and hatred, she was starting to recall her father in a different light; to remember all those good qualities which she'd almost forgotten. His wit, his warmth. His ability to put people at their ease; his generosity; his impulsiveness. His sheer enjoyment of the good things in life.

Gordon Brewin had caused a lot of misery in his life. But he had also given a lot of people a great deal of pleasure. And he had given her a magical childhood. For nineteen unsullied years, right up until his death, she had felt loved, secure and happy. Nineteen years of happiness. That was worth something, wasn't it?

With shaky legs, Candice took a step nearer the grave. He hadn't been an evil man, she thought. Only a man with flaws. A happy, dishonest, generous man with too many flaws to count. As she stared at his name, etched in the stone, hot tears came to her eyes and she felt again a childish, unquestioning love for him. She bent down, placed the flowers on his grave and tidied the edges of the plot. She stood up and stared at it silently for a few moments. Then she turned abruptly and walked away, back to the gates where Ed was waiting for her.

'**W**here's the other godmother?' said Paddy, bustling up to Maggie in a rustle of blue flowery crepe. 'She's not going to be late, is she?'

'On her way, I'm sure,' said Maggie calmly. She fastened a final button on Lucia's christening robe and held her up to be admired. 'What do you think?'

'Oh, Maggie,' said Paddy. 'She looks an angel.'

'She does look rather fine, doesn't she?' said Maggie, surveying the frothing trail of silk and lace. 'Roxanne, come in here and see your goddaughter!'

'Let's have a look,' said Roxanne, and sauntered into the room. She was wearing a tightly fitted black and white suit, and a stiff, wide-brimmed hat with a curling ostrich feather. 'Very nice,' she said. 'Very nice indeed. Although I'm not sure about that bonnet affair. Too many ribbons.'

Maggie gave a little cough. 'Actually,' she said, 'Paddy very kindly made this bonnet, to match the christening robe. And I rather like the ribbons.'

'All my boys wore that robe when they were christened,' put in Paddy proudly.

'Hmm,' said Roxanne, looking the robe up and down. 'Well, that explains a lot.' She met Maggie's eye and, without meaning to, Maggie gave a snort of laughter.

'Paddy,' she said, 'do you think the caterers have brought napkins, or should we have provided them?'

'Oh dear,' said Paddy, looking up. 'Do you know, I'm not sure. I'll just pop down and check, shall I?'

When she'd left the bedroom, there was silence for a while. Maggie popped Lucia under her baby gym on the floor and sat down at the dressing table to do her make-up.

'Budge up,' said Roxanne presently, and sat down next to her on the wide stool. She watched as Maggie hastily brushed shadow onto her eyelids and stroked mascara onto her lashes.

'Glad to see you still take your time with your maquillage,' she said.

'Oh, absolutely,' said Maggie, reaching for her blusher. 'We mothers enjoy nothing more than spending an hour in front of the mirror.'

'Slow down,' said Roxanne. 'I'll do your lips. Properly.' She swivelled Maggie's face towards her, then reached for a lipstick and a lip brush.

'Listen here, Lucia,' she said as she brushed the colour on. 'Your mother needs time to put on her lipstick, OK? So you just give her time. You'll realise why it's important when you're a bit bigger.' She finished, and handed Maggie a tissue. 'Blot.'

Maggie pressed her lips slowly on the tissue, then drew it away from her mouth and looked at it.

'God, I'm going to miss you,' she said. 'I'm really going to . . .' She exhaled sharply and shook her head. 'Cyprus. I mean, I can't see you living in Cyprus!' said Maggie. There was a long pause, then she said reluctantly, 'Well, perhaps I can. If I try hard.'

'I'll be back at least every month,' said Roxanne. 'You won't know I'm gone.' Her blue gaze met Maggie's in the mirror. 'And I meant what I said, Maggie. I still stand by it. If you ever feel down, if you're ever depressed—ring me. Whatever time it is.'

'And you'll fly back,' said Maggie, laughing.

'I'll fly back,' said Roxanne. 'That's what you do for family.'

As Ed turned into the drive of The Pines, he gave an impressed whistle. 'So this is the house she's *selling*? What the hell's wrong with it?'

'She wants to live in London again,' said Candice. 'They're going to live in Ralph's house. Roxanne's house. Whatever.' She looked anxiously in the mirror. 'Do I look all right?'

'You look like a cherub,' said Ed, leaning over to kiss her. 'Baby face.'

'I'm not supposed to be the baby! I'm supposed to be the godmother.'

'You look like a godmother, too.' Ed opened his door. 'Come on. I want to meet your friends.'

As they crunched over the gravel, Roxanne turned and beamed at Candice. Then her gaze shifted to Ed and her eyes narrowed appraisingly.

'Jesus Christ,' muttered Ed to Candice. 'She's checking me out with her bloody X-ray vision.'

'Don't be silly! She loves you already.' Candice strode breathlessly towards Roxanne and hugged her. 'You look fantastic!'

'And so do you,' said Roxanne. 'You look happier than you have for a long time.'

'Well . . . I feel happy,' said Candice, and glanced shyly at Ed. 'Roxanne, this is—'

'This is the famous Ed, I take it.' Roxanne's gaze swivelled and her eyes gleamed dangerously. 'Hello, Ed.'

'Roxanne,' replied Ed. 'Delighted to meet your hat. And you, of course.' Roxanne inclined her head pleasantly and surveyed Ed's face.

'I have to say, I thought you'd be better looking,' she said eventually.

'Yup. Easy mistake to make,' said Ed, unperturbed. 'A lot of people make it.' He nodded confidentially at Roxanne. 'Don't let it worry you.'

There was a short silence, then Roxanne grinned. 'You'll do,' she said. 'You'll do nicely.'

'Hey, godmothers!' came Maggie's voice from the front door. 'In here! I need to give you this sheet on what your duties are.'

'We have duties?' said Roxanne to Candice, as they walked together across the gravel. 'I thought we just had to be able to pick out silver.'

'And remember birthdays,' said Candice.

'And wave our magic wands,' said Roxanne. 'Lucia Drakeford, you *shall* go to the ball. And here's a pair of Prada shoes to go in.'

The church was thick-walled and freezing, despite the heat of the day outside, and Lucia wailed lustily as the unheated water hit her skin. When the ceremony was over, Candice, Roxanne and Lucia's god-father—an old university friend of Giles—posed together for photographs in the church porch, taking turns to hold her.

'I find this very stressful,' muttered Roxanne to Candice through her smile. 'What if one of us drops her?'

'You won't drop her!' said Candice. 'Anyway, babies bounce.'

'That's what they say,' said Roxanne ominously. 'But what if they forgot to put the India rubber in this one?' She looked down at Lucia's face and gently touched her cheek. 'Don't forget me,' she whispered, so quietly that not even Candice could hear. 'Don't forget me, little one.'

'OK, that's enough pictures,' called Maggie eventually, and looked round the crowd of milling guests. 'Everyone, there's champagne and food at the house.'

'Well, come on then,' said Roxanne. 'What are we waiting for?'

Back at The Pines, a long trestle table had been laid out on the lawn and covered with food. A pair of ladies from the village were serving champagne and offering canapés, and a Mozart overture was playing from two speakers lodged in trees. Roxanne and Candice collected their drinks, then wandered off, a little way from the main crowd.

'Delicious,' said Candice, taking a sip of icy cold champagne. She closed her eyes and let the warm summer sun beat down on her face, feeling herself expand in happiness. 'Isn't this lovely? Isn't it just . . . perfect?'

'Nearly perfect,' said Roxanne, and gave a mysterious grin. 'There's just one more thing we have to do.' She raised her voice. 'Maggie! Bring your daughter over here!'

As Candice watched in puzzlement, she reached into her chic little bag, produced a miniature of brandy and emptied it into her champagne glass. Then she produced a sugar lump and popped that in, too.

'Champagne cocktail,' she said, and took a sip. 'Perfect.'

'What is it?' Maggie joined them, holding Lucia, her eyes bright and her cheeks flushed with pleasure. 'Didn't it all go well? Wasn't Lucia good?'

'It was beautiful,' said Candice, squeezing her shoulder. 'And Lucia was an angel.'

'But it's not quite over,' said Roxanne. 'There's one more vital ceremony that needs to be performed.' Her voice softened slightly. 'Come here, Lucia.'

As the others looked on in astonishment, Roxanne dipped her finger into the champagne cocktail and wetted Lucia's brow.

'Welcome to the cocktail club,' she said.

For a few moments there was silence. Maggie stared down at her daughter's tiny face, then looked up at the others. She blinked hard a few times, then nodded. Then, without speaking, the three turned and slowly walked back across the grass to the party.

MADELEINE WICKHAM

When I met Madeleine Wickham in London's Covent Garden on a cold, frosty January day, she arrived laden down with shopping bags from Hobbs, Karen Millen and French Connection. 'The shops were just too tempting,' she said with a grin, 'but at least most of the bags have SALE written on them so I won't have to hide them away when I get home!'

Home for Madeleine and her husband, Henry, is a four-bedroomed, detached cottage in Tadworth, Surrey, close to the school where Henry teaches and where Freddy, the eldest of their two sons, is a pupil. 'I've lived in London for most of my life,' she told me, 'but we have just moved to the country and we are all enjoying every minute of it. One of the things I love most about it is that we have this wonderful stable door out of the kitchen, and, in the morning I can stand there and watch Henry taking Freddy to school, walking down the country lane, hand-in-hand. It's lovely.'

Madeleine Wickham wrote her first best-selling novel, *The Tennis Party*, aged twenty-four, while working as an editorial assistant on a magazine. 'I just got an idea and started writing in the evenings and at weekends,' she says. 'I wasn't sure what I wanted to do as a career, but I didn't have any expectations of becoming a novelist.' Now, six years later, she has just finished her seventh novel, *Sleeping Arrangements*, which will be published in the summer. Apart from moving house, looking after the children and completing her novel, she has also found time to write and submit a film script to Hollywood. 'This year has just been unbelievable,' she says. 'I feel very lucky.' But it is not just down to luck. Madeleine has worked hard to achieve her success and takes a couple of months to structure each novel. 'You can't just sit and wait for inspiration to hit you,' she tells me. 'I map out the plot and characters extensively.. I always have something to refer back to and that stops me from drying up.' Madeleine is a keen observer of human nature and creates a real sense of drama in her novels by thinking through a 'what if' scenario for her characters. 'I think: what would be the most cringing, toe-curling thing that could happen to this person and create tension in the story? In *Cocktails for Three* I started with Candice's and Heather's stories, and the question of just how far you should go to try to make amends for the past? But then I thought it would be more interesting to have a contrast of different characters and their stories. And I have always loved the idea of girls meeting up, supporting each other and keeping tabs on each other's lives, especially over glamorous cocktails.'

It was the end of the interview, but the mention of cocktails reminded me that I had not yet asked the one question I was dying to know the answer to: what is Madeleine's favourite cocktail? 'I dither between very alcoholic and very subtle. But, I have to say, my absolute favourite is a Bellini—champagne and fresh peach juice, preferably drunk in Venice!'

Jane Eastgate

Kristin Hannah

Angel Falls

Mikaela Campbell has a secret: a glamorous past life her husband and two children know nothing about. Now, through a terrible accident, the truth about those distant days is about to be exposed. And Mikaela will have to choose whether or not to take up her old life again or turn her back on it once and for all.

CHAPTER 1

IN NORTHWEST WASHINGTON STATE, great granite mountains reach for the misty sky, their peaks inaccessible even in this age of helicopters and high-tech adventurers. The trees in this part of the country grow thick as an old man's beard and block out all but the hardiest rays of the sun. Only in the brightest months of summer can hikers find their way back to the cars they park along the sides of the road.

Deep in the black and green darkness of this old forest lies the tiny town of Last Bend. To visitors—there are no strangers here—it is the kind of place they'd thought to encounter only in the winding tracks of their imaginations. When they first walk down the streets, folks swear they hear laughter. Then come the memories—some real, some manufactured images from old movies and *Life* magazine. They recall how their grandmother's lemonade tasted . . . or the creaky sound of a porch swing gliding quietly back and forth on a muggy summer's night.

Last Bend was founded fifty years ago, when a big, broad-shouldered Scotsman named Ian Campbell gave up his crumbling ancestral home in Edinburgh and set off in search of adventure. Somewhere along the way—family legend attributed it to Wyoming—he took up rock climbing, and spent the next ten years looking for two things: the ultimate climb and a place to leave his mark.

He found what he was looking for in Washington's North Cascade mountain range. Close to the mighty Mount Baker he bought a hundred acres of prime pastureland; then he bought a corner lot on a gravel road that would someday mature into the Mount Baker Highway. He built his town along the pebbly, pristine shores of Angel Lake and christened it Last Bend, because he thought the only home worth having was worth searching for, and he'd found his at the last bend in the road.

It took him some time to find a woman willing to live in a moss-chinked log cabin without electricity or running water, but find her he did—a fiery Irish lass with dreams that matched his own. Together they fashioned the town. She planted Japanese maple saplings along Main Street and started a dozen traditions—Glacier Days, the Sasquatch race, and the Halloween haunted house on the corner of Cascade and Main.

In the same year that the Righteous Brothers lost that lovin' feeling, Ian and Fiona Campbell began to build their dream home: a huge log house that sat on a small rise in the middle of their property. On some days, when the sky was steel blue, the glaciered mountain peaks seemed close enough to touch. Towering Douglas firs rimmed the carefully mowed lawn, protected the orchard from winter's frozen breath. Bordering the west end of their land was Angel Creek, a torrent in the still gloaming of the year, a quiet gurgling creek when the sun shone high and hot in the summer months. In the wintertime they could step onto their front porch and hear the echo of Angel Falls.

Now the third generation of Campbells lived in that house. Tucked tightly under the sharply sloped roofline was a young boy's bedroom. It was not unlike other little boys' rooms in this media-driven age—Corvette bed, Batman posters tacked to the uneven log walls, Goosebumps books strewn across the shag-carpeted floor.

Nine-year-old Bret Campbell lay quietly, watching the digital clock flick red numbers into the darkness: 5:30 . . . 5:31 . . . 5:32.

Halloween morning.

At precisely 5:45, he flipped the covers back and climbed out of bed. Careful not to make any noise, he pulled the grocery sack from underneath his bed and unpacked it.

There was no light on, but he didn't need one. He'd stared at these clothes every night for a week. His Halloween costume. A sparkly pair of hand-me-down cowboy boots that they'd picked up at The Emperor's New Clothes used-clothing shop, a fake leather waistcoat from the Dollar-Saver thrift shop, a pair of felt chaps his mom had made, a plaid flannel shirt and brand-new Wrangler jeans from Zeke's Feed and Seed, and best of all, a shiny sheriff's star and gun belt from the toy store. His daddy had even made him a kid-sized lariat.

He stripped off his pj's and slipped into the outfit, leaving behind the gun belt, guns, chaps and lariat. Those he wouldn't need now.

He *felt* like a real cowboy. He went to his bedroom door, peeking into the shadowy hallway. He tiptoed out and peered down at the other two bedrooms. Both doors were closed, and no light slid out from underneath. Of course, his sixteen-year-old sister, Jacey, was asleep. It was Saturday, and she always slept until noon. Dad had been at the hospital all night with a patient, so he'd be tired this morning, too. Only Mom would be getting up early, and she'd be in the barn, ready to go, at six o'clock.

He pushed the flash button on his Darth Maul watch: 5:49.

'Yikes.' He bounded down the stairs. Feeling his way through the darkened kitchen, he hit the ON button on the coffeepot and headed for the front door, opening it slowly.

On the porch, he was spooked by the black shape of a man, but in the second after he saw the outline, he remembered. It was the pumpkin-headed farmer he and Mom had made last night.

Bret jumped off the porch; then he ran up the driveway. At the empty guest cottage he zagged to the right and clambered up the slippery grass pasture.

A single floodlight lit up the huge, two-storey barn his granddad had built. Bret had always been in awe of the famous grandfather he'd never met. The stories of Granddad's adventures had been told and retold for as long as Bret could remember, and he wanted to be just like him. That's why he was up so early on this Halloween morning. He was going to convince his overprotective mother that he was ready to go on the Angel Falls overnight trail ride.

He grabbed the cold iron latch on the barn door and swung it open. Horses nickered softly and moved around in their stalls, thinking it was feeding time. He flicked the lights on and hurried down the wide cement aisle towards the tack room. He struggled to pull his mom's jumping saddle off the wooden tree. He dropped it twice before he figured out how to balance it on his arm. With the girth dragging and clanging behind him, he headed to Silver Bullet's stall.

There, he stopped. Jeez, Bullet looked bigger this morning.

Granddad would *never* chicken out.

Bret took a deep breath and opened the stall door.

It took him lots of tries, but he finally got the saddle up on the horse's high back. He even managed to tighten the girth. Not enough, maybe, but at least he'd buckled the strap.

He led Bullet to the centre of the arena. The lights overhead cast weird shadows on him and Bullet, reminding him that it was Halloween. Bullet dropped her head and snorted, pawing at the ground.

Bret tightened his hold on the lead rope. 'Whoa, girl,' he said softly, trying not to be afraid.

The barn door shuddered, then let out a long, slow creaking sound. Wood scraped on cement and the door opened.

Mom stood in the doorway. Behind her, the rising sun was a beautiful purplish colour. He couldn't quite see her face, but he could see her silhouette, black against the brightness, and he could hear the steady *click-click-click* of her boot heels on the concrete. She paused, tented one hand across her eyes. 'Bret? Honey, is that you?'

Bret led Bullet towards Mom, who stood at the edge of the arena. She was wearing a long brown sweater and black riding pants; her boots were already dusty. She was staring at him—one of those Mommy looks—and he sure wished she'd smile.

He yanked hard on the rope and brought the mare to a sudden stop—just the way they'd taught him in the 4-H rural youth training programme. 'I saddled her myself, Mom.' He stroked Bullet's velvet-soft muzzle. 'I tightened up the saddle just like I'm s'posed to.'

'You got up early—on Halloween—and saddled my horse for me. Well, well.' She bent down and tousled his hair. 'Hate to let me be alone for too long, eh, Bretster?'

'I know how lonely you get.'

She laughed, then knelt down in the dirt. His mom never worried about getting dirty, and she liked to look her kids in the eyes. At least, that's what she said. She pulled the worn, black leather glove off her right hand and smoothed the hair from Bret's face. 'So, young Mr Horseman, what's on your mind?'

That was another thing about his mom. You could *never* fool her. 'I want to go on the overnight ride to Angel Falls with you this year. Last year you said maybe later, when I was older. Well, now I'm a whole year older, and I can saddle a big old Thoroughbred by myself.'

Mom sat back on her heels. Some dirt must have got in her face, because her eyes were watering. 'You're not my baby boy any more, are you?'

He plopped onto her bent legs, pretending that he was little enough to still be held in her arms. She gently took the lead rope from him, and he wrapped his arms round her neck.

She kissed his forehead and held him tightly. It was his favourite kind of kiss, the kind she gave him every morning at the breakfast table.

'Well, I guess any kid big enough to saddle this horse is ready to go on an overnight ride. I'm proud of you, kiddo.'

He let out a loud 'Whoopee!' and hugged her. 'Thanks, Mom.'

'No *problema*.' She gently eased away from him and got to her feet. 'Now I've got to work Bullet for an hour or so before Jeanine gets here to worm the horses. I've got a zillion things to do today before we go trick-or-treating.'

'Can I stay and watch you ride?'

'OK, but no talking and no getting off the fence.'

He grinned. 'You just *have* to tell me the rules again, don't you?'

She laughed. Turning her back to him, she tightened the girth and bridled the mare. 'Go and get me my helmet, will you, Bretster?'

He ran back to the tack room. At the chest marked MIKE'S STUFF, he bent down and lifted the lid, rummaging until he found the dusty black velvet-covered helmet. Tucking it under his arm, he let the lid drop shut and ran back into the arena.

Mom was already on Bullet. 'Thanks, sweetie.' She leaned down and took the helmet.

By the time Bret reached his favourite spot on the arena fence, Mom was already easing Bullet towards the path that ran along the wall. He watched as she went round and round. She pushed Bullet through her warm-up: walk, trot, extended trot, and canter. Bret watched as horse and rider became a blur of motion.

He knew instantly when Mom had decided it was time to jump. He'd watched so many times he knew the signs, although he couldn't have said what they were. He just *knew* that she was going to head for the first two-foot jump.

Just like he knew something was wrong.

He leaned forward. 'Wait, Mommy. The jump is in the wrong place. Someone musta moved it . . .'

But she didn't hear him. Bullet was fighting her, lunging and bucking as she tried to rein the mare down to a controlled canter.

'Whoa, girl. Slow down. Calm down.'

Bret heard the words as Mom flew past him. He wanted to yell, but Mom was already at the fence. Bret's heart was hammering in his chest. *Somethingiswrong.* The words jammed together in his mind, growing bigger and uglier with every breath.

Silver Bullet bunched up and jumped over the fake brick siding with ease.

Bret heard his mom's whoop of triumph and her laugh.

He had a split second of relief.

Then Silver Bullet stopped dead.

One second Mom was laughing, and the next, she was flying off the horse. Her head cracked into the barn post so hard the whole fence

175

shook. And then she was just lying there in the dirt, her body crumpled like an old piece of paper.

There was no sound in the big, covered arena except his own heavy breathing. Even the horse was silent, standing beside her rider as if nothing had happened.

Bret slid down the fence and ran to his mom. He dropped to his knees beside her. Blood trickled down from underneath her helmet, smearing in her short black hair.

He touched her shoulder, gave her a little shove. 'Mommy?'

The bloodied hair slid away from her face. That's when he saw that her left eye was open.

Bret's sister, Jacey, was the first to hear his scream. She came running into the arena, holding Dad's big down coat around her. 'Bretster—' Then she saw Mommy, lying there. 'Oh my God! *Don't touch her!*' she yelled at Bret. 'I'll get Dad.'

Bret couldn't have moved if he'd wanted to. He just sat there, staring down at his broken mommy, praying for her to wake up, but the prayers had no voice; he couldn't make himself make any sound at all.

Finally Daddy ran into the barn. Bret popped to his feet and held his arms out, but Daddy ran right past him. Bret stumbled backwards so fast, he hit the fence wall. He couldn't breathe enough to cry. He just stood there, watching the red, red blood slither down his mommy's face. Jacey came and stood beside him.

He knelt beside her, dropping his black medical bag into the dirt. 'Hang on, Mikaela,' he whispered. Gently he removed her helmet— should Bret have done that?—then Daddy opened her mouth and poked his fingers between her teeth. She coughed and sputtered, and Bret saw blood gush across his daddy's fingers.

'Hang on, Mike,' his dad kept saying, over and over again, 'hang on. We're all here . . . Stay with us . . .'

Stay with us. That meant don't die . . . which meant she *could* die.

Dad looked up at Jacey. 'Call nine one one—*now!*'

It felt like hours they all stood there, frozen and silent. Finally red lights cartwheeled through the darkness; sirens screamed; an ambulance skidded through the loose gravel.

Blue-uniformed paramedics came running into the barn dragging a bumping, clanking bed on wheels behind them. Bret's heart started beating so loud he couldn't hear. He backed away, hitting the fence so hard it knocked him dizzy. He covered his ears and shut his eyes and prayed as hard as he could.

She is dying.

Memories rush through her mind in no particular order, some tinged with the sweet scent of roses after a spring rain, some smelling of the sand at the lake where she tasted the first kiss that mattered. Too many come wrapped in the iridescent, sticky web of regret.

They are moving her now, strapping her body to a strange bed. She can hear her husband's voice, the soft, whispering love sounds that have guided her through the last ten years of her life, and though she can hear nothing from her children—her babies—she knows they are here, watching her. More than anything in the world, she wants to say something to them, even if only a sound, a sigh—something . . .

Warm tears leak from the corners of her eyes, slide behind her ears. She wishes she could hold them back, swallow them, so that her children won't see, but such control is gone, as distant and impossible as the ability to lift her hand for a final wave.

Then again, maybe she isn't crying at all. Maybe it is her soul, leaking from her body in droplets that no one will ever see

CHAPTER 2

WHEN HE WAS YOUNG, Liam Campbell hadn't been able to get out of Last Bend fast enough. Everywhere he went, he was compared to his larger-than-life dad, and he fell short. Even at home, he felt invisible. His parents were so in love, there simply wasn't much room left over for a boy who read books and longed to be a concert pianist.

To his utter astonishment, he had been accepted at Harvard. By the time he'd finished his undergraduate studies, he'd learned that he wasn't good enough to be a concert pianist. The best player at Last Bend, even the best player at Harvard, wasn't good enough. So he'd tucked that youthful dream aside and turned his attention to medicine. If he wasn't talented enough to entertain people with his hands, he believed he was caring enough to heal them.

He graduated at the top of his class and took a job that stunned and appalled his Ivy League classmates—at an AIDS clinic in the Bronx. It was the early days of the epidemic and people were terrified of the

disease. But Liam believed that there, amid true suffering, he would discover the man he was meant to be.

In hallways that smelt of death and despair, he made a difference in
patients' lives, but he never once got to say, 'You'll be fine. You're cured.'
Instead, he dispensed medicines that didn't work and held hands that
got weaker and weaker. He wrote out death certificates until he could
no longer hold a pen without horror.

When his mother died of a sudden heart attack, he came home and
tended to the father who, for the first time, needed his only son. Liam
had always meant to leave again, to find his own place in the world, but
then he'd met Mikaela . . .

Mike.

With her, at last, he had found his place in the world.

Now he was in the hospital, waiting to hear whether she would live . . .

They had been here for only a few hours, but it felt like for ever. His
children were in the waiting room—he could picture them, huddled
together, weeping. Though he longed to be with them, he knew that if
he looked at his children now, he would break, and the tears that fell
from his eyes would scald them all.

'Liam?'

He spun towards the voice. Dr Stephen Penn, the chief of neurology,
stood before him. Though he was Liam's age—just turned fifty—
Stephen looked old now, and tired. They had played golf together for
years, he and Stephen, but nothing in their relationship had prepared
them for this moment.

He touched Liam's shoulder. 'Come with me.'

They walked side by side down the austere corridor and turned into
the ICU. Liam noticed the way the trauma nurses wouldn't look at him.
It was humbling to know how it felt to be the 'next of kin'.

At last they entered a glass-walled private room, where Mikaela lay in
a narrow bed. She looked like a broken doll, hooked up to machines—
ventilators, IVs, monitors that tracked everything from her heart rate to
her intracranial pressure. The ventilator breathed for her, every breath a
rhythmic *thwop-whoosh-clunk* in the quiet room.

'The—*her*—brain is functioning, but we don't know at what level
because of the meds.' Stephen produced a straight pin and poked
Mikaela's small, bare feet, saying nothing when she failed to respond. He
conducted a few more tests, which he knew Liam could assess along
with him. Quietly he said, 'The neurosurgeon is on board, just in case,
but we haven't identified anything surgical. We're hyperventilating her,
controlling her pressure and temperature. Barring development of any

bleeding . . . well, you know we're doing everything we can.'

Liam closed his eyes. For the first time in his life, he wished he weren't a doctor. He didn't want to understand the reality of her condition. They had a state-of-the-art medical centre and some of the best doctors north of San Francisco, all drawn here by the quality of life. But the truth was, there wasn't a damn thing that could be done for her right now.

He didn't mean to speak, but he couldn't seem to hold it all inside. 'I don't know how to live without her . . .'

When Stephen turned to Liam, a sad, knowing expression filled his eyes. For a split second he wasn't a specialist, but just a man, a husband, and he understood. 'We'll know more tomorrow, if . . .' He didn't finish the sentence; it wasn't necessary.

If she makes it through the night.

'Thanks, Steve,' Liam said, his voice barely audible above the whirring of the machines and the steady *drip-drip-drip* of the IVs.

Stephen started to leave but paused at the doorway and turned back. 'I'm sorry, Liam.' Without waiting for a response, he left the room. When he came back, there were several nurses with him. Together they wheeled Mikaela out of the room for more tests.

Courage, Liam thought to himself, wasn't a hot, blistering emotion held only in the hands of men who joined the Special Forces and jumped out of planes and scaled unnamed mountains. It was a quiet thing— ice-cold more often than not—the last tiny piece you found when you thought that everything was gone. It was facing your children at a time like this, holding their hands and brushing their tears away when you were certain you hadn't the strength to do it. It was going on, one bitter breath at a time.

He put his own fear away and focused on the things that had to be done. Tragedy, he'd learned, came wrapped in details—insurance forms that had to be filled out, suitcases that had to be packed *in case*, schedules that needed to be altered. If he did all of this without making eye contact with another human being, well, that was the way it had to be. He called Rosa Luna—Mike's mother, who lived on the eastern side of the state—and left an urgent 'Call me' message on her answering machine. Then, unable to put it off any longer, he walked down to the waiting room in the hospital's lobby.

Jacey was sitting in one of the red vinyl chairs by the gift shop, reading a magazine. Bret was on the floor, idly playing with the toys the hospital staff kept in a plastic box.

Liam's hands started to shake. He crossed his arms tightly and stood there. *Help me, God*, he prayed; then he forced his arms to his sides and strode into the area. 'Hi, guys,' he said softly.

Jacey lurched to her feet. The magazine she'd been reading fluttered to the floor. Her eyes were swollen and red-rimmed; her mouth was drawn into a tremulous line. 'Daddy?'

Bret didn't stand. He wiped his moist eyes and tilted his little chin upwards. 'She's dead, isn't she?' he said in a voice so dull and defeated that Liam felt the grief well up inside him again.

'She's not dead, Bretster,' he said, feeling the hot sting of tears. *Damn*. He'd promised himself that he wouldn't cry; they needed his strength now. He pinched the bridge of his nose for a second, then knelt down beside his son and scooped him into his arms, holding him tightly.

Jacey knelt beside Liam and pressed her cheek against his shoulder. He slipped an arm round her, too.

'She's in bad shape right now,' he said slowly, searching for each word. How could you tell your children that their mother could die? 'She's suffered a pretty severe head injury. She needs our prayers.'

Bret wiggled closer to Liam. His body started to shudder; tears dampened Liam's lab coat. When Bret looked up, he was sucking his thumb.

Liam didn't know what to do. Bret had stopped sucking his thumb years ago, and here he was, huddled against his dad like a boy half his age, trying desperately to comfort himself.

Liam knew that from now on, his children would know that dark and terrifying truth, the one that he and Mike had tried so hard to keep from them: the world could be a frightening place. Sometimes a single moment could change everything, and people—no matter how much you loved them—could die.

The hours of their vigil dripped into one another and formed a day.

Finally it was evening. Liam sat in the waiting room with his children, each of them watching the wall clock's slow, black hands. It had been hours since anyone had spoken.

At eight o'clock they heard footsteps coming down the hallway towards them. Liam tensed instantly. *Please, don't let it be bad news.*

Jacey's boyfriend, Mark Montgomery, swept into the quiet room, bringing with him a swell of energy. 'Jace?' he said, his voice too loud. 'I just heard.'

Jacey ran into his arms, sobbing against his chest. Finally she drew back and looked up at him. 'We haven't gotten to see her yet.' Mark led her to the sofa. Together they sat down. Jacey leaned against him. The quiet flutter of their whispery voices floated through the room.

Liam went to Bret and hugged him, cradling his son in his arms, carrying him back to the chair. And still they watched the clock.

Just before nine o'clock, Stephen came into the room.

Liam eased Bret onto the floor. Then he stood up and went to Stephen.

'The same,' Stephen said softly. 'There's nothing more we can do for her tonight. We just have to wait and see.' He lowered his voice then, speaking with a friend's concern. 'Take your children home, Liam. If anything happens, I'll call you.'

Liam knew that Stephen was right, but the thought of walking into that empty, empty house . . .

Stephen patted him on the shoulder, then turned and left.

Liam took a deep breath. 'Come on, kids. It's time to go home. We'll come back in the morning.'

Jacey stood up. 'Home?' She looked terrified. Liam knew that she didn't want to walk into that house, either.

Mark glanced at her, then at Liam. 'A bunch of us were going to the haunted house. Maybe you want to come?'

Jacey shook her head. 'No, I need to stay—'

'Go, Jace,' Liam said softly. 'Think of something else for an hour or two. We can't help her this way. I'll call you if anything happens.'

He could see the war going on within her; she wanted to go and she wanted to stay. Finally she turned to Mark, and said, 'OK. Maybe just for a few minutes.'

Mark took Jacey's hand in his and led her out of the room.

'Daddy?' Bret said after she'd left. 'I'm hungry.'

'Jesus, Bretster, I'm sorry. Let's go home.'

Bret popped his thumb back in his mouth and got to his feet. He looked small and pathetic. For the first time, Liam noticed the clothes his son was wearing—plaid flannel shirt, fake leather waistcoat with a tin sheriff's star pinned on the chest, crisp Wrangler jeans, and cowboy boots. A costume. The haunted house.

Halloween.

Liam had a sudden flash of memory—Mike staying up late at night to finish the chaps that went with the costume. 'You want to drive over to Angel Glen and go trick-or-treating?'

Bret sucked his thumb; then slowly he shook his head.

Liam understood. It was Mommy who always organised Halloween. 'OK, kiddo. Let's go.'

Together they walked outside, into the cold, crisp October night. The air smelt of dying leaves and rich, black earth.

They climbed into the car and drove home. The garage door, when it opened, cut a whining, scraping hole in their silent cocoon.

Liam took his son's hand and led him into the house. They talked in fits and starts—about what, Liam couldn't have said.

If only it weren't so damn quiet.

Make Bret dinner.

There, focus on that.

The phone rang. Mumbling something to Bret, Liam stumbled into the kitchen and answered it.

'Hi, Liam. It's Carol. I just heard . . . So sorry . . .'

And so it began.

Liam sagged against the log wall, hearing but not listening. He watched as Bret went into the living room and lay on the sofa. There was the *hm-click* of the television as it came on. The *Rugrats*. Screamingly loud. Bret stared dry-eyed at his least favourite cartoon. One that only last week he'd said was 'for babies'.

After Liam hung up, he stood in the empty kitchen wondering what to fix Bret for dinner. The phone rang again. This time it was Marion from the local 4-H chapter. He tossed out a jumbled explanation, thanked her for her prayers, and hung up.

He didn't make it five feet before the phone rang again. This time he ignored it and went into the living room, where he knelt beside his son. 'What do you say we order pizza?'

Bret popped the thumb out of his mouth. 'Jerry doesn't deliver on Halloween. Not after the Monroes tee-peed his truck last year.'

'Oh.'

'It's stir-fry night, anyway. Mommy and me put the chicken in its sauce last night. It's marinatin'.'

'Stir-fry.' Chicken and veggies. How hard could it be? 'You want to help me cook it?'

'You don't know how.'

'I can figure it out. Come on. We'll do it together.' He helped Bret off the sofa and followed him into the kitchen. When Bret was settled on a kitchen stool, Liam went to the fridge and got out the plastic bags full of veggies and the marinated chicken. After some searching, he found the cutting board and a big knife.

He started with the mushrooms.

'Mommy doesn't put 'shrooms in it. I don't like 'em.'

'Oh.' Liam put the mushrooms back in the bag and reached for the broccoli.

The phone rang.

'Damn it.' Liam slammed down the knife and waited until the ringing stopped.

Then came Bret's quiet voice. 'What if that was the hospital . . . or Jacey?'

Liam winced. 'I'll answer it from now on.' He started to chop up the broccoli.

The phone rang again. Liam reluctantly picked it up. It was Mike's friend, Shaela, from the Saddle Club, wondering if there was anything she could do.

Liam found the electric wok. 'Thanks, Shaela,' he said in the middle of her sentence, and hung up. Then he plugged in the wok and poured a cup of oil into it.

'That's a lot of oil,' Bret said with a frown as the phone started ringing again.

'I like it crispy.' Liam answered the phone—Mabel from the horse-rescue programme—and repeated what he'd told everyone else. By the time Mabel said, 'I'm sorry' for the fourth time, Liam almost screamed. He appreciated the calls—truly—but they made it all too real. And now the damn oil was popping and smoking.

'Daddy—'

He hung up on Mabel in the middle of a word. 'Sorry, Bretster. Sorry.' He tossed the chicken and marinade into the oil. It splattered everywhere. Tiny drops of scalding oil hit his cheeks and stung.

Swearing, he went back to the broccoli.

The phone rang again, and he cut his finger.

Bret screamed, 'Daddy, you're bleeding!'

Riiiiing . . . riiiiing . . .

The smoke detector went off, *buzzzzzz*. Liam reached for the phone and knocked the wok with his hip. Greasy chicken and burning oil and smoke flew everywhere.

It was Myrna from Lou's Bowl-O-Rama, wondering if there was anything she could do.

When Liam hung up, he was breathing so hard he felt dizzy. He saw Bret, backed against the cold fridge, his whole body shaking.

Liam didn't know if he wanted to scream or cry or run. Instead, he knelt in front of Bret, blood dripping from his forefinger. 'I'm sorry, Bretster. But it's OK.'

'That's not how Mommy cooks.'

'I know. I guess I'll have to learn.'

'We'll starve.'

He put his hands behind Bret's head and stared into his son's eyes, as if by pure will he could make Bret feel safe. 'We won't starve. Now, how about we go to town for dinner?'

Bret looked up at him. 'I'm gonna go change my clothes, OK?'

Liam hugged him. It was the only thing he could think of to do.

Bret was crying, softly, silently, and Liam felt as if his own heart would break at the pathetic silence of those tears.

Jacey came home earlier than Liam expected, looking wan and tired. She hardly said a word; instead, she kissed his cheek and headed up to her room.

When he was pretty sure that both kids were asleep, Liam went to Mikaela's office. He opened the door and flicked on the light.

The first thing he noticed was her fragrance, soft and sweet as new-fallen rain. Her desk was scattered with piles of papers. If he closed his eyes, he could imagine her sitting at that desk, a cup of steaming French Roast coffee in her hand, her gaze glued to the computer screen as she wrote letter after letter on behalf of animals that were being neglected.

On an ordinary day she would have looked up at him, her beautiful eyes filled with compassion. *'There's a mare in Skykomish so starved she can't stand up. Can we take in one more?'*

Downstairs, he went to the big picture window that framed the pastures below. The horses couldn't be seen now on this black night, but they were out there. A dozen horses that Mikaela had saved. They'd arrived, broken and starved, but Mike healed them, one by one then gave them away to good homes. Mike had such a tender heart. It was one of the things he loved most about her.

But when was the last time he'd told her that? He wished he could remember. She was his sun and his moon, his whole world.

He slumped on the overstuffed down sofa.

She could die . . .

No. He wouldn't let his mind wander down that road. Mike would wake up soon, any minute now.

But the road beckoned him anyway. He closed his eyes, remembering everything about her, and when he opened his eyes, she was there, beside him on the couch. She was wearing the ratty, torn old Levi's that he was always threatening to throw away, and a black chenille boat-neck sweater that could have fitted a woman twice her size.

He wished he could reach for her, kiss the fullness of her lower lip, but he knew that she wasn't really there. He couldn't hold the grief inside him any more; he couldn't be strong. At last, he leaned back on the sofa, and he cried.

'Daddy?' The small, hesitant voice floated down the stairs.

Liam wiped the tears from his eyes. He rose to his feet, crossed the room, and climbed the stairs.

Bret stood at the top. 'I couldn't sleep, Daddy.'

Liam scooped Bret into his arms and carried him up to the master bedroom, tucking him into the bed that was too big without Mike in it. He curled against his son.

'She was lookin' at me, Dad.'

Liam tightened his hold on Bret. 'When you saw Mommy, her eyes were open. Is that what you mean?'

'She was lookin' right at me, but . . . she wasn't there.'

'She was just too hurt to close her eyes, and now she's too hurt to open them.'

'Can I see her tomorrow?'

Liam thought about how she looked—her face battered and swollen and discoloured, a nasogastric tube snaking up one nostril. Some things, once seen, could never be forgotten, and they could taint a memory for ever. 'No, kiddo, I don't think so. It's against hospital policy to let a child into intensive care. You can see her as soon as she gets moved to the regular ward.'

Bret said quietly, 'But that's how dead looks in the movies.'

'She's *not* dead. She's just . . . resting for a while. Like Sleeping Beauty.'

'Did you try kissin' her?'

It took Liam a long time to answer. He knew he would remember this moment for ever, and that's how long it would hurt. 'Yeah, Bretster. I tried that.'

Liam stayed in bed until Bret fell asleep; then he cautiously extricated himself and went downstairs to pour himself a drink.

The phone rang.

He ignored it. The answering machine clicked on. He wasn't ready to hear Mike's soft, throaty voice. 'You have reached the Campbell residence and the winter office of Whatcom County's horse-rescue programme. No one is available right now.'

When the message clicked off, another voice came on. '*Hola*, Dr Liam. This is Rosa. I am returning—'

Liam picked up the phone. 'Hello, Rosa.'

'Dr Liam. This is you? I am sorry not to call earlier, but I was working the dinner shift this ni—'

'Mike's had an accident,' he said quickly. Then, taking a deep breath, he told his mother-in-law everything.

A pause slid through the lines. 'I will be there tomorrow.'

'Thank you,' he said, not realising until that moment how much he needed her help in this. 'I'll arrange for a plane ticket.'

'No. It will be quicker if I drive. I will leave first thing in the morning. Will she . . .?'

Make it through the night.

'We hope so.' He answered the unfinished question.

'Dr Liam?' Another pause, then a soft, 'Pray for her. More than medicines and machines, she will need God now. You pray for her.'

'Every minute, Rosa. Every minute.'

When he hung up the phone, he went to his bedroom. *This* was where Mikaela belonged—in this room she'd once painted fire-engine red just for fun, the one that now had gold moons and stars and suns stencilled on its white walls and a chiffon-draped canopy bed that she said made her feel like Candice Bergen in *The Wind and the Lion*. Unfortunately, it made him feel like Candice Bergen, too, but so what? She loved their room, and so he'd crawled into their bed every night and thanked God that she wanted him there. Him, an ordinary man whose only claim to the extraordinary was the depth of his love for a woman.

Rosa Elena Luna walked towards the small altar in her living room and lit two votive candles. She sank to her knees on the linoleum floor and clasped her hands, staring at the figurine of the Virgin Mary as she began to pray. But the words didn't ease this ache in her chest.

She grabbed hold of the rickety table leg and pulled herself up. For the first time in many years she wanted to call William Brownlow.

He would be no help, of course. She hadn't seen him in several years. Sunville was a small town, but even in so small a place, they travelled in different circles. He owned a modest apple orchard—not a powerful, wealthy man—but compared with Rosa, he might as well have been a Kennedy. Though he had fathered Mikaela, he had never been a father to her. He had another family, a lily-white one. He might have spent fifteen years in Rosa's bed, but every moment had been stolen from his wife and legitimate children.

Rosa stood in the darkened living room. Here and there, watery moonlight peeked through the worn, tattered curtains, illuminating the garage-sale sofa, the fake wood-grain end tables, the religious paintings on the walls. Mikaela and Liam had often tried to get Rosa to move from this house, or to accept the money to repair it, but she always refused them. She was afraid that if she left, she would forget the mistakes God wanted her to remember.

It had all started here, in this house she never should have accepted—a present from a man who loved her. In those days, she had still believed he would leave his wife.

Bad love. It was the heart of this house. It had purchased every nail and paid most of the bills. She had always known that she would pay for these sins. No amount of confession could cleanse her soul, but this . . . She'd never imagined this.

'Please, God,' she said, 'save *mi hija*.'

With a tired sigh, she walked into her small bedroom, pulled her only suitcase out of the closet, and began to pack.

CHAPTER 3

THE BEDSIDE PHONE rang at six o'clock the next morning. Liam had been dreaming—a good dream, in which he and Mikaela were sitting on the porch swing, listening to the children's distant laughter. For a second, he could feel the warmth of her hand in his; then he noticed the boy sleeping quietly beside him, and it all came rushing back.

His heart was clattering like a secondhand lawn mower as he reached for the phone.

It was Sarah, the head nurse from the hospital. Mikaela had made it through the night.

Liam leaned carefully over Bret and hung up the phone. He crawled out of bed, showered, then went to wake his children.

Within an hour, the three of them were on their way to the hospital. Liam settled the kids in the waiting room, then went to the ICU.

He went to Mikaela's bedside, hoping—absurdly—to find her sitting up, smiling . . . But the room was deathly still; she hadn't moved.

She looked worse. The right side of her face was swollen almost beyond recognition. Both eyes were hidden beneath puffy discoloured flesh. Clear plastic tubing invaded her left nostril.

The team of specialists arrived. They examined her, tested her, and talked among themselves. Liam waited silently.

Truth is, Liam, we don't know why she's not waking up.

Some of the best doctors in the country, and that was all they could say. Just wait and hope. Pray she lives another day, then another day after that. Pray she wakes up on her own . . .

Although Liam hadn't really expected a medical miracle, he'd certainly hoped for one. Even a radical surgery would be better than this . . .

It was 11.00am when Liam walked slowly towards the waiting room. He allowed himself a moment's pause before he turned into the alcove beyond the nurses' station.

Jacey stood at the window with her back to him. Bret was on a gold sofa, his small body curled into the foetal position, his eyes squeezed shut. Again today he was sucking his thumb.

Liam prayed for strength. 'Hi, guys,' he said.

Jacey spun to face him. Her long black hair—normally manicured to teenaged perfection—hung limply along her arms. Silver tear marks streaked her pale cheeks. Her eyes were red and swollen, and in them he saw the agonising question.

'She's still alive,' he said.

Jacey brought a shaking hand to her mouth. She was trying not to cry in front of her younger brother. 'Thank God.'

Liam went to the sofa and scooped Bret onto his lap. 'Sit down, Jace,' he said. She sat down beside them, reaching for Liam's hand.

Bret snuggled closer and opened his eyes. Tears rolled down the boy's pink cheeks. 'Can we see her today?'

Liam drew in a deep breath. 'Not yet. Yesterday I told you that her head was hurt, but there's . . . a little more to it than that. She's in a very deep sleep. It's called a coma, and it's the body's way of healing itself. You know how when you have the flu, you sleep all the time to get better? It's like that.'

Jacey's colourless lips trembled. 'Will she wake up?'

Liam flinched. Any answer felt like a lie. 'We hope so. She needs us to believe in her. When she's ready, she'll wake up.'

Bret wiped his eyes. 'Fix her, Daddy.'

'The docs are doing everything they can right now, Bretster, but she's asleep.'

'Like Sleeping Beauty,' Jacey said to her little brother.

Bret burst into tears. 'Sleeping Beauty was asleep for a hundred years!'

Liam pulled Bret into his arms and held on to his son tightly. Jacey scooted closer and hugged them both.

When Liam felt Bret's tiny shudder, and the warm, wet rush of his daughter's tears, he buried his face in his son's hair.

And he prayed.

There were too many cars in the hospital parking lot. Absurdly, that was Rosa's first thought as she drove into the Ian Campbell Medical Center that afternoon.

She gazed at the small figurine of the Virgin Mary anchored to the beige plastic dashboard. Then she got out of the car and walked towards the hospital. The electronic doors whooshed open; the bitter, astringent smell of stale, medicated air assaulted her.

'I am here to see Dr Liam Campbell,' she said at the front desk.

'I'll page him,' the receptionist answered.

Rosa heard her son-in-law's name echo through the halls. A few minutes later, she watched him walk towards her.

He looked tired and beaten. He was a tall man, although you didn't notice that most of the time. He just didn't seem to take up that much space. But he had the heart of a lion. Rosa had never known anyone who loved as completely as her son-in-law.

'*Hola*, Dr Liam,' she said.

'Hello, Rosa.' In his green eyes, she saw a harrowing sadness.

'Is she still alive?' Her voice was barely a whisper.

He nodded.

'Ah. Thank God. You will take me to see her now?' she said, her fingers toying nervously with her bag.

Liam looked away. His sandy blond hair was clumpy and tousled, as if he'd forgotten to wash it. 'I wish . . .' His voice, always quiet and carefully modulated, was now as thin as a strand of silk thread. 'I wish I could spare you this, Rosa,' he finished.

'Let us go,' was all she could say.

They walked down one hallway after another. Finally Liam stopped at a closed door. He touched her shoulder. It was a brief, comforting touch, but it surprised her. They were not that free with each other. That he wanted to comfort her, in the midst of his own pain, moved her deeply.

'She doesn't look good, Rosa. Do you want to go in alone?'

She meant to say yes, *thought* she'd said yes, but she heard herself say no. Liam nodded and followed her into the room.

When she saw her daughter, Rosa stopped and drew in a sharp breath. '*Dios mío.*'

Mikaela lay in a narrow bed—a child's bed with silver railings. All around her machines hissed and beeped. Her beautiful face was scratched and bruised and swollen, her eyes hidden beneath puffy black folds of flesh.

Rosa leaned over the railing and touched her daughter's cheek. The skin felt bloated, hard to the touch, like a balloon overfilled with air. She was silent for many minutes. 'My little girl,' she said at last. 'That must have been quite a fall you took.'

'We don't know how much she can hear . . . or if she can hear at all,' Liam said. 'We don't know . . . if she'll wake up.'

Rosa looked up at him. At first she was stung by his words. But then she realised it was the doctor in him speaking. He was a man of science; he believed in evidence. Rosa was a woman of faith, and a long, hard life had taught her that truth almost never revealed itself to the human eye. 'Do you remember when you all went to Hawaii last summer?'

He frowned. 'Of course.'

'When you got home, Jacey called me. She had been surfing, and she got into trouble. The board, it hit her on the head, and when she was under water, she did not know up from down.' She noticed the way Liam's fingers tightened around the bed rail, and she understood. 'Do not be afraid, Dr Liam. Mikaela is like Jacey. She is lost in a place she cannot understand. She will need us to guide her home. All we have is our voices, our memories. We must use these to show her the way.'

Liam's gaze softened. 'I'm glad you're here, Rosa.'

'Sí. It is hard to be alone for something like this.'

He flinched at the word 'alone', and she knew what he was thinking. That without his wife, there would be a lifetime of alone. And one thing Rosa knew about Liam—he loved his Mikaela. Loved her in the bone-deep way that most women long for and only a handful ever find.

Rosa couldn't help wondering if Mikaela understood her good fortune. Or if, in some dark, forbidden corner of her heart, there grew the untamed remains of an old, bad love.

Rosa knew how deep the roots of that love had gone into her daughter's heart, and she knew, too, that sometimes first love went to seed, growing in wild disarray until there was no room for anything—or anyone—else.

Rosa moved into the small cottage beside the main house, set her few personal items in the bathroom, and stocked the refrigerator with iced tea and a loaf of bread. There was no point in doing more; she planned on spending all her time with the children or Mikaela.

The next morning, after Liam left for the hospital, Rosa made the children a hot breakfast and tried to take them to school.

Not yet, Grandma, please.

She had not the heart to deny them. She granted their wish for one more day at the hospital, but after that, she said, they must go to school.

The waiting room was no place for children day upon day.

They drove the few miles to the medical centre. Rosa settled the kids in the waiting room, then she hurried to Mikaela's room in the ICU.

The small room still frightened her—there were so many unfamiliar noises and machines. At the bedside, she gazed down at her beautiful, broken child. 'I guess it does not matter how old we get, you will always be my little girl, *sí, mi hija?*' She gently stroked Mikaela's unbruised cheek. The skin was swollen and taut, but Rosa thought she could feel a little more softness in the flesh than had been there yesterday.

She picked up the brush from the bedside table and began pulling it through Mikaela's hair. 'I am still not used to this short hair of yours, even though it has been many years like this. When I close my eyes, I still see my *niña*, with hair streaming like spilt ink down her back.'

Rosa's thoughts turned to the bleak days when her daughter had been so unhappy that she'd chopped off her own hair with a pair of drugstore scissors. Mikaela had been waiting for *him*. Waiting and waiting for a man who never showed up, and when she realised that he had no intention of returning, she'd cut off her lovely hair—the thing he liked best about her.

You cannot make yourself ugly. That's what Rosa had said when she'd seen what Mikaela had done, but what she'd meant was, *He isn't worth this broken heart of yours.* She hadn't said that; she was the last person in the world who should dare to devalue a woman's love for the wrong man.

She had thought that Mikaela would get over him, and that when she did, she would one day grow her hair long again.

Yet still, Mikaela's hair was as short as a boy's.

'No,' Rosa said aloud, 'I will not think about him. I will think instead about my little girl. You were so bright and beautiful and funny. Always you make me laugh.

'And you had such big dreams. Remember? You used to pin all those *fotografías* up on your bedroom wall, pictures of faraway places. I used to say to you, "Where do you get such big dreams, Mikita?" And do you remember your answer?'

She stroked her daughter's hair gently. 'You told me, "I have to have big dreams, *Mamá*. I have them for both of us."'

'It broke my heart when you said that.' Rosa's hand stilled. She couldn't help remembering how her daughter's swollen dreams had shrivelled years ago beneath the hot California sun.

'I am the one with big dreams now, *querida*. I dream that you will sit up in this bed and open your eyes, that you will come back to us.' Her voice cracked, fell to a throaty whisper. 'I am the carrier of my dreams now . . . and yours, too, Mikita. I am dreaming for both of us.'

That afternoon, Stephen called Liam and Rosa into his office.

'The good news is, she has stabilised. She's off the ventilator and breathing on her own. She's being fed intravenously. We've moved her out of the ICU to a private room on Two West.'

Liam barely heard the words. He knew that whenever a doctor said, 'The good news is,' there was a hell of a right hook coming.

Rosa stood near the door. 'She is breathing. This is life, sí?'

Stephen nodded. 'Yes. The problem is, we don't know why she isn't waking up. She's healthy, stable. Her brain activity is good. By all measures, she should be conscious.'

Rosa asked, 'How long can a person sleep like this?'

Stephen hesitated. 'Some people wake up in a few days, and some stay in a coma for years and never wake up. I wish I could tell you more.'

'Thanks, Steve.' Liam rose to his feet and went to Rosa, gently taking her arm. 'Let's go and see her.'

Rosa nodded. Together they left Stephen's office and headed for Mikaela's new room.

Once inside, Liam went to the window and shoved it open. Turning, he went to his wife's bedside and gently touched her swollen cheek. 'It's winter, baby. You went to sleep in the fall, and already it's winter. How can that be, in only three days?' He swallowed hard. His life flashed before him, an endless calendar of weeks without her. Thanksgiving, Christmas, Easter.

Rosa came up beside him. 'You must not give up hope, Dr Liam. She will be one of the lucky ones who wake up.'

Liam had given his mother-in-law the gift of ignorance. He'd told her that a bad outcome was possible, but he'd made it sound improbable. Now he didn't have the strength for subterfuge. Brain damage, paralysis, even a lifetime of coma; these were the possibilities.

He drew in a deep breath and exhaled slowly. 'I won't *ever* give up, Rosa. But I need . . . something to pin my faith on, and right now my colleagues aren't giving me much to work with.'

'Faith in God will be your floor. Do not be afraid to stand on it.'

He held a hand up. 'Not now, Rosa. Please . . .'

'If you cannot speak to God, then at least talk to Mikaela. She needs to be reminded she has a life out here. Now it is up to love to bring her back.'

Liam turned to Rosa. 'What if my love doesn't bring her back?'

'It *will* bring her back.' Rosa gazed up at him. 'She needs you now more than ever. She needs you to be the light that guides her home. This is all you should be thinking about now.'

'You're right, Rosa.' Then, stronger, 'You're right.'

'And what you talk about is *importante, sí?* Talk to her about the things that matter.' She moved towards him. Her mouth was trembling as she said, 'I have slept through my life, Dr Liam. Do not let my daughter do the same thing.'

Bret made it past lunchtime without screaming, but now he could feel the temper tantrum building inside him. At first he'd just been crabby; then he'd ripped the head off his action figure and thrown the brand-new *People* magazine in the garbage.

He was tired of being in this waiting room, tired of being ignored.

No one seemed to care that Bret was always by himself. Jacey's friends came at lunchtime, and it didn't bother her one bit to leave her little brother alone while she went to the cafeteria. Even Grandma and Daddy seemed to have forgotten all about him.

Bret went to the sofa again and tried to interest himself in drawing, but he couldn't do it. Instead, he picked up the nearest crayon—black—and went to the wall. In bold, sweeping letters, he wrote: *I hate this hospital.* When he finished, he felt better. Then he turned round and saw Sarah, the head nurse, standing in the doorway.

'Oh, Bret,' she said softly, giving him that 'poor you' look.

He waited for her to say something else, maybe to come in and yell at him, but all she did was turn round and walk away. A few minutes later, he heard his dad's name ringing out through the hospital paging system.

He dropped the crayon on the floor and went back to the sofa

'Bretster?'

Dad's voice. Bret's cheeks burned. Slowly he turned.

Dad was standing there, holding a bucket and a sponge. He set the bucket down and crossed the room in a few big steps; then he sat down on the coffee table in front of Bret.

'I know, Daddy.' He tried not to cry, but he couldn't help himself. 'I'm sorry.'

Dad wiped Bret's tears away. 'I'm sorry we left you alone, Bretster. There's so much going on . . . I'm sorry.'

Bret drew in a great gulping breath. 'I shouldn't've of written on the walls, Daddy. I'm sorry.'

Dad almost smiled. 'I know you want to see your mom, kiddo. It's just . . . She doesn't look good. Her face is pretty bruised up. I thought it would give you bad dreams.'

Bret thought about how she'd looked, with her eye open, staring at him, and he shuddered. He wiped his eyes and whispered, 'When dead people have their eyes open, can they see you, Daddy?'

193

'She's *not* dead, Bret. I swear to you.' He sighed heavily. 'Do you want to come down and see your mom?'

Bret sniffed and wiped his upper lip. That image of Mommy flashed through his mind again, and when he saw it, his heart did a little *kathump*. 'No,' he said. 'I don't wanna see her.'

Dad pulled him into a hug, and Bret felt himself slowly, slowly relaxing. The hug felt so good. He clung to his dad for a long, long time.

Then, finally, Daddy said, 'Well, pal, I guess you'd better start washing that wall. I don't think it's fair to make the custodians do it.'

Bret scooted back. On wobbly legs, he got to his feet and went over to the bucket. When he picked it up, soapy water splashed over the rim and hit his trouser legs. Holding on to the handle with both hands, he carried the bucket to the wall. He plunged the sponge into the water, squeezed it almost dry, and started cleaning up his mess.

It wasn't even a minute later that Dad was beside him, crouching down. He grabbed a second sponge and wrung it out.

Dad smiled at him, right at eye level. 'I guess this is sort of a family mess, don't you think?'

At dinnertime Rosa took the children home. Liam knew he should have gone with them, but he couldn't leave Mikaela. It was as simple as that.

He stared down at his wife. She was lying on her side now; the nurses had turned her. 'I hired Judy Monk to take care of your horses. They all seem to be doing great. And the vet said Scotty's colic is all cleared up.'

He reached for the box he'd brought from home. 'I brought you a few things.' He lifted the box from the chair and brought it to the bedside table. He pulled out a beribboned bag of scented potpourri. 'Myrtle down at the drugstore told me this brand was your favourite.' He poured the multicoloured clippings into a small glass bowl. The soft scent of vanilla wafted upwards. Then he pulled out a collection of family photographs and layered them along the windowsill—just in case she opened her eyes when none of them were there.

He set a tape player on another table and popped in a cassette—Madonna's 'Crazy for You'—to remind her of the old days. Then he pulled out a sweater of Bret's, one he'd outgrown long ago. He smoothed it over her shoulder, tucking the tiny Shetland-wool arms round her. If anything could reach her, it would be the never-to-be-forgotten smell of her little boy.

Memories tiptoed into this quiet room. He remembered the first time he'd seen Mikaela. It had been here, in this very hospital, where she had been a nurse. He'd come home for his mother's funeral and found his father—the great Ian Campbell—suffering from Alzheimer's. When the inevitable slide to death began, Ian had been moved into the medical centre that bore his name.

That was when Liam had met Mikaela. She'd been young then—only twenty-five—and the most beautiful woman he'd ever seen.

'Did you know how much I longed to talk to you?' he said softly, leaning towards her. 'You were sitting by my dad's bedside. Do you remember that day? I didn't say anything. I just stood in the doorway, listening to the way you talked to my father.'

He sat down in the chair by the bed and coiled his fingers around hers. 'Do you remember what you said to me? "Do you talk to him?" you asked me. I was so embarrassed. I said, "No one really talks to my dad any more." And you said, "Then you should. He needs to know you care."'

Care. It was such a little word. Like *love* or *hate*. Up until that moment, Liam and his father hadn't spent much time *caring*.

'You gave him back to me, you know. You taught me to talk to him, and in those last weeks there were moments when he saw me, moments when he knew who I was and why I was there. The day before he died, he held my hand and told me he loved me for the first and only time in my life. You gave me that, Mikaela.'

He stood up and leaned over the bed rail. He slowly released her hand and touched her swollen cheek. 'I love you, Mike, with everything inside me. I'll be here; waiting for you, for the rest of our lives.' His voice broke. He gave himself a minute, then kissed her forehead, whispering, 'For ever.'

Then he sat back down, holding her hand again.

CHAPTER 4

FOR FOUR WEEKS, Mikaela had seen only darkness.

By the end of the first week, Liam and the children had learned the age-old truth that life went on. As much as they wanted the world to stop for them, it didn't. Amazingly, the sun still rose in a world without Mikaela, and hours later, it set. Thanksgiving came and went, and in the last week in November, the first snow fell.

Liam had learned that it was possible to appear to move forward when you were really standing still. As the coma dragged on, he'd had no choice. The kids went back to school, Rosa knitted enough sweaters and blankets to cover everyone in town, and eventually he began seeing patients again. He left the office at two o'clock every afternoon and sat by Mike's bed until dinnertime. Some days Jacey showed up, some days she didn't. Bret hadn't yet found the courage to visit his mother, but Liam knew he would.

Liam stood at his office window, staring out. Next door, the snow was beginning to stick to Mrs Peterson's picket fence. Very soon the last elementary-school bell would ring; children would begin to gather at Turnagain Hill, dragging their sledges and inner tubes along the snow-slicked street.

She loved the snow, his Mikaela. She loved mittens with fake fur trim and black angora cowled hoods that turned an ordinary housewife into Grace Kelly. She loved watching her children eat soup at the kitchen table while snow melted from their hair and slid down their pinkened cheeks.

A knock at the door. 'Doctor?' His nurse, Carol Audleman, pushed the partially open door and stepped into the small, darkened room. 'Marian was your last patient for the day.'

He smiled tiredly, knowing she would see the weariness in his face, wishing he could change it.

'Midge called around noon. She left a lasagne and salad on your kitchen table.'

That was something Liam had learned. People didn't know how else to help, so they cooked. This town had banded together to help the Campbells through this, and they would remain at the ready for a long time.

'Thanks, Carol.' Liam reached for his down parka, grabbing it off the hook on the wall. Shrugging out of his white coat, he carefully laid it over the chairback and followed Carol out of the office, past the empty waiting room. At the door he patted her shoulder, then went out into the cold.

He drove to the hospital and pulled into the parking lot. The medical centre was unusually quiet today. Snow covered everything now, turning the cars into white humps. He parked in his spot and reached under the seat for the two things he'd brought: a photo album and a small, wrapped box. He headed for the hospital, forcing himself to plunge into the antiseptic environment that used to be as welcoming to him as his own living room, but now brought him instantly to despair.

He nodded hellos to the familiar faces but never stopped. Too many of the doctors and nurses no longer believed that Mikaela would wake up or, if she did, that she wouldn't be *Mikaela* any more.

He paused at the closed door to Mikaela's room, gathering his strength, then turned the knob and went inside. As always, the first sight of her was difficult; she lay as still as death on the metal-railed bed. Her chest rose and fell with deceptive regularity as she breathed. The only sign of life. He could see that her hair had been recently washed—it was still a little damp. The nurses took extra care of Mikaela; she'd been one of them. They'd even exchanged the hospital-issue gown for a soft, hand-sewn version.

He settled into the chair beside her bed. 'Heya, Mike,' he said, putting new potpourri in the dish on the bedside table. Bayberry this week, to let her know that Christmas was on its way.

Bit by bit, he carried out his daily ritual—the potpourri, the careful placement of one of the kids' shirts on Mikaela's chest, the music that seeped softly from the tape machine in the corner: *The Eagles' Greatest Hits*, to remind her of high school; *The Phantom of the Opera*, to remind her of the time they'd gone to Vancouver to see the show. He did everything he could think of to engage her senses and remind her that life was still here, that *they* were still here, her loving family, waiting for her to join them once again.

He took hold of her foot and began gently manipulating it in the way the physiotherapists had taught him. 'It was a quiet day at the office, Mike,' he said in a throaty voice, the only kind he seemed able to manage when he was beside her. 'Jimmy McCracken came in again— this time with a marble stuck up his nose. And old Mrs Jacobsen had another migraine. Of course, she really just wanted to talk.'

In a gentle stream of words, he poured himself into her, his heart and soul. He talked and talked and talked, all the while searching desperately for some movement, some blink of the eye or flutter in her hand that would tell him that the heat of his voice reached the cold darkness of her world.

'Heya, Mike, I'll bet you thought I forgot our anniversary.' He started to reach for the photo album on the bedside table, but at the last second he drew his hand back.

It was a collection of pictures from last Christmas. He suddenly saw the album as a wound that, once torn open, would only seep infection and cause more pain. Instead, he glanced down at the box in his lap.

It had been wrapped for almost two months and hidden in his office. He'd been so excited on the day he'd decided what to give her for their tenth anniversary.

'I got us tickets on the Concorde, Mike. Paris . . .' *For New Year's.* His voice cracked. For years they'd talked about Paris, dreamed about New Year's at the Ritz. Why had it taken him so long to get tickets?

He stood and grabbed the bed rail, lowering it. The railing fell with a clattering whine and clunked into the bottom position. Slowly he climbed into bed with her. Tucking one arm behind her head, he drew her close, being careful not to pull out her IV.

He held on to her lifeless hand, squeezing gently so that she would know he was there. 'Help me, Mike. Squeeze my hand, blink your eyes. Do *something.* Show me how to reach you.'

'Dad?'

For a second, Liam thought his wife had spoken. He turned to see Jacey standing in the open doorway. She was holding a cake.

'Hi, honey.' He climbed awkwardly out of the bed and slumped into his chair.

She moved towards him, her long black hair swinging gently against her flannel shirt. Her face was winter pale, and what little colour her cheeks might have produced was sucked clean away by the sight of her mother. 'It's your tenth anniversary. You and Mom always made such a big deal out of it . . .' Her words fell away, and he knew she was looking to him for reinforcement.

It was difficult, but he nodded and smiled. 'You're right. She would have wanted us to celebrate.'

Jacey set the cake on the table by the bed. It was a round, two-layered affair with pink butter-cream frosting—the same cake that Suzie Sanman at the Lazy Susan Bake Shop had concocted for them every year. Only this year, instead of the normal HAPPY ANNIVERSARY, MIKE AND LIAM, it was blank on top. Liam wondered how long Suzie had spent trying to think of something festive and hopeful to write before she gave up.

Jacey moved closer to the bed and leaned over her mother. 'Happy anniversary, Mom.' She brushed a lock of hair from Mikaela's face. 'Can you believe it has been ten years since we married Liam?' She turned and smiled at him. 'How is she today?'

Liam shrugged. 'The same.'

Jacey swiped a finger along the side of the cake, drawing up a big glob of pink frosting. She held it beneath Mikaela's nose. 'Can you smell the cake, Mom? It's Suzie's best, with real Grand Marnier. Just the way you liked—*like*—it.'

The tiny fissure in her voice was almost more than Liam could bear. 'Here, pull up a chair. How was school today?'

Jacey tucked a long strand of hair behind her ear. 'Good. I aced the math test.'

'Of course you did.'

She looked at him, then turned away. He noticed the quick, nervous way she bit down on her lip.

'What's the matter, Jace?'

It was a minute before she answered. 'The winter dance is coming up. Mark asked me if I wanted to go.'

'You know it's OK. Whatever you want to do is fine.'

'I know, but . . .'

He turned to her. 'But what?'

She wouldn't meet his gaze. 'Mom and I were going to go into Bellingham to get a dress. She . . .' Her voice snagged on emotion and fell to a whisper. 'She said she'd never been to a prom, and she wanted me to look like a princess.'

Liam couldn't imagine his beautiful wife sitting at home on prom night. How come *he* didn't know that about her? It was another of his wife's secrets. 'Come on, Jace. It'll break her heart if she finds out you didn't go.'

She looked away, then softly said, '*If* she wakes up.'

Liam wanted, just once, to hold Jacey and say, *I'm scared, too. What if this is it . . . or what if she wakes up and doesn't know us . . . or if she never wakes up at all?* But those were his fears, and it was his job to keep the lights on for his family. 'Jacey, your mother *is* going to wake up. We have to keep believing that. She needs us to keep believing. This is no time to go soft on her.'

She looked at him. 'I heard you last night. You were talking to Grandma about Mom. You said no one knew why she didn't wake up. After Grandma left, I heard you crying.'

'Oh.' He sagged forward in his chair. There was no point in lying to her. It had been a bad night, the kind where his armour felt as if it were crafted of cellophane. Remembering their anniversary had done him in. He'd sat at the elegant Steinway in the living room, aching to play again, to recapture the music that had once lived inside him. But ever since the accident, the music that had sustained him through so much of his life had simply vanished, and now there was only this aching emptiness.

He gave Jacey the only truth he could. 'Sometimes it grabs so hard I can't breathe. I sort of fall through the floorboards of my fear, but I always land here, at her bedside, holding her hand and loving her.'

Jacey looked down at her mother again. This time tears flooded her eyes. 'I want to tell her I'm sorry for all the times she looked sad and I didn't care.'

'She loves you and Bret with all her heart and soul, Jacey. You *know* that. And when she wakes up, she's going to want to see those dance photos. If you don't go, we'll be eating macaroni and cheese out of a box for months. No one can hold a grudge like your mother.' He smiled gently. 'Now, I may not know much about shopping for girl stuff in Bellingham, but I know about style because Mike has bucketloads. Remember the dress your mom wore to the Policemen's Ball last year? She went all the way to Seattle for that dress, and to be honest, it cost more than my first car. You'd look perfect in it.'

'The Richard Tyler. I forgot all about it.'

'I know I'm not as good at this as your mom, but—'

Jacey threw her arms round him. 'She couldn't have done any better, Daddy. Honest.'

Liam turned to his wife, forced a smile. 'You see what's happening, Mike? You're forcing me to give fashion advice to Jacey. Hell, the last time I picked out my own clothes, bell-bottoms were in fashion.'

'Dad, they're in fashion again.'

'See? If you don't wake up soon, I might authorise that eyebrow piercing she's been asking for.'

They sat there for the next hour, talking to each other and to the woman lying motionless in the bed before them. They talked as if it were a normal day, hoping all the while that some snippet of their conversation would sneak through Mike's darkness and remind her that she wasn't alone.

At almost four o'clock the bedside phone rang, jangling through one of Jacey's stories.

Liam reached for the phone and answered, 'Hello.'

He listened for a minute, then said, 'I'll be right along,' and hung up. He turned to Jacey. 'I've got to go back to the clinic to see a patient. You want to come?'

'Nope. Grandma's going to pick me up here after doing some errands.'

'OK.' Liam scooted back in his chair. He stood up and leaned over his wife. 'I've got to go, Mike, but I'll be back soon. I love you, honey.' He leaned closer and kissed her slack lips, whispering, 'For ever.'

When Liam turned the car engine over before leaving the clinic, the radio came on. It was playing the first Christmas song of the season, 'Silent Night'.

He clicked the radio off, fast.

Snow pattered against the windshield, blurring the outside world.

The windshield wipers came on with a *ka-thump ka-thump ka-thump*, making exactly the same sound as a heart beating.

He put the car in gear and drove slowly out of the parking lot. If Mike were home, they'd probably build a snowman after dinner. Or maybe they'd drive to Turnagain Hill and go sledging.

But Liam knew there would be no sledging, no snowmen, no hot cocoa. He and the kids would think of such things, perhaps even talk about doing them, but in the end, as they'd done for the past four weeks, they would come together in that big house in the middle of the snowy field and go their separate ways. They would eat dinner together, then do the dishes, the four of them. Then they would try to watch television together—*Wild Discovery* or maybe a sitcom—but gradually they would drift apart. Jacey would burrow into her room and talk on the phone. Bret would settle in front of his computer and play loud fast-paced games that required his full attention, and Rosa would knit.

Liam would float from room to room doing nothing, trying to keep his mind blank. More often than not, he ended up in front of the grand piano in the living room, wishing the music was still in his heart and in his fingers, but knowing that it was gone. As he stood there he could almost hear the squeaky joint of the antique bench, with its needlepoint seat, as Mike would sit down beside him.

'Tips are welcome,' he'd say, just as he'd said a thousand times on a thousand nights.

'Here's a tip for you, piano man,' she'd answer. 'Get your wife to bed or miss your chance.'

He downshifted and turned left, passing beneath the rough-hewn arch his dad had constructed years ago. In some distant part of his mind he heard the gentle clanking of the iron sign that hung suspended from the arch, the one that read ANGEL FALLS RANCH.

He pulled into the garage, turned off the engine, and sat there, hands planted on the wheel. He didn't look at the album and present he'd tossed in the back seat, but he knew they were there.

Finally he got out of the car and headed into the house. At the end of the hallway, a light glowed faintly orange.

Thank God for Rosa.

He was still a little awkward around her, uncomfortable. She was so quiet, like one of those Cold-War spies who'd learned to walk without making a sound. Sometimes he caught her staring at him, and in her dark eyes he saw a sadness that went clear to the bone.

When he reached the living room, he stood in the shadows, watching Rosa and Bret play a game of Yahtzee. He wished he didn't notice how quiet Bret was. There was none of the clapping or whistling or 'All right!'s' that used to be his son's natural soundtrack.

Rosa looked up and saw him. '*Hola,* Dr Liam.'

He'd told her a dozen times to please, please call him Liam, but she wouldn't do it. 'Who's winning?'

'My grandson, of course. He takes advantage of my fading eyesight.'

Liam smiled. 'Don't listen to her, Bret. Your grandma sees everything.'

'You would like to join us, *sí*?'

'I don't think so.' He ruffled Bret's hair—a substitute for time and intimacy, he knew—but it was all he could manage.

Bret's disappointment was obvious. 'You sure, Dad?'

'I'm sure, buddy. Maybe later.'

Bret sighed. 'Yeah, right.'

Liam headed towards the stairs.

'Dr Liam, wait.' Rosa stood up in a single, fluid motion and followed him into the dining room. There, in the dark, quiet room, she stared up at him. 'The children . . . They are much quiet today. I think something is—'

'It's our tenth wedding anniversary,' he blurted. 'The kids knew I'd bought Mike tickets to Paris.'

'Oh. *Lo siento.*' Something close to a smile breezed across her mouth and disappeared. 'She is lucky to have you, Dr Liam. I do not know if I have ever told you this.'

It touched him deeply, that simple sentiment from this woman who spoke so rarely. 'Thanks, Rosa, I—' His voice dried up.

'Dr Liam.' Her soft voice elongated the vowels in his name and turned it into music. 'Come play Yahtzee with us. It will help.'

'No. I need . . .' A bad start. There were so many things he needed. 'I have something to do upstairs. Jacey needs to borrow one of Mike's dresses for the winter dance.'

She leaned closer and he had an odd sense that she wanted to say something more, but she turned away and headed back to the game.

Liam went into the kitchen and poured himself a drink. The Crown Royal burned down his throat and set his stomach on fire. Holding the drink tightly, he moved up the wide staircase to the first floor. He could hear music seeping from beneath Jacey's closed door.

With a glance down the hallway, he turned into his bedroom and flicked on the light. The door to Mike's walk-in closet seemed to magnify before his eyes. He hadn't ventured into it since the day of the accident, when he'd naively packed her a suitcase full of things she might need at the hospital.

He crossed the room and paused at the closet; then he reached for the knob and twisted. A floor-length mirror along the end wall caught his image and threw it back: a tall, lanky man with unkempt hair. On either side of him, clothes were hung on colourful plastic hangers. The ivory plastic of Nordstrom's designer departments hung clustered in one area. Her evening clothes.

He began unzipping the bags, one at a time, looking for the dress Mike had worn to the Policemen's Ball. At about the sixth bag, he reached inside, and instead of finding a gown of silk or velvet as he'd expected, he found a pillowcase, carefully hung on a trouser hanger.

Frowning, he eased it from the bag. It was an elegant white silk affair, not the kind of pillowcase they used at all. On one end was a monogram: *MLT.*

Mikaela Luna . . . Something.

His heart skipped a beat. This was from her life *before.*

He should turn away, zip this bag up, and forget its very existence. He knew this because his hands had started to sweat and a tickling unease was working its way down his spine. But he couldn't do that. Over the years, he'd collected so many questions, stroked them in his mind every time she'd said, '*Let's not go there, Liam. The past isn't something that matters now.*'

The past mattered, of course. Liam had been willing to pretend otherwise because he loved his wife—and because he was afraid of who or what had caused the deep well of her sorrow—but the moment he touched the pillowcase, he was lost. The past they'd all ignored was here; it had lived with them all these years, hidden inside a Nordstrom bag in his wife's closet. And like Pandora, he simply had to look.

He felt strangely detached as he walked back into his bedroom and sat down on his big, king-sized four-poster bed, dragging the pillowcase up beside him. He stared down at it for a long time, weighing the danger, knowing that sometimes there was no way to undo what had been done, and that some secrets were composed of acid that, once spilled, could burn through the fragile layers of a relationship. Still, the lure of finally knowing was too powerful to resist.

He turned it upside-down and watched as photographs, newspaper clippings and official-looking documents, all bent and yellowed, fluttered onto the duvet. The last thing to fall out was a wedding ring with a diamond as big as a dime. Liam stared at it so long his vision blurred, and then he was seeing another ring, a thin gold band. '*No diamonds, Liam,*' she'd said softly, and though he'd heard the catch in her voice, he'd paid it no mind. He'd thought how nice it was that she didn't care about such things.

The truth was, she'd already had diamonds.

Turning away from the diamond ring, he saw a photograph—an eight-by-ten full-colour glossy print. It was half covered; all he could see was Mikaela in a wedding dress. The groom was hidden behind a carefully cut-out newspaper article. He wanted to pick it up, but his hands were shaking too badly.

He hardly recognised Mikaela. Her wavy black hair was drawn up in a sleek, elaborate twist, and make-up accentuated the catlike tilt of her eyes, turned her lips into the kind of mouth that fuelled a thousand male fantasies. The sleeveless gown she wore was unlike the conservative cream-coloured suit she'd worn for her second wedding. There were oceans of pearls and beads sewn into the silky sheath—so many that the dress appeared to be made of crushed diamonds and clouds. Not a thing of this earth at all.

She, his *wife*, was a woman he'd never seen before, and that hurt, but the pain of it was nothing compared to the way he felt when he looked at her smile. God help him; she'd never smiled at Liam like that, as if the world were a shining jewel that had just been placed in the palm of her hand.

Slowly he reached for the picture and picked it up. The newspaper clipping fell away, and he saw at last the groom's face.

Julian True.

For a dizzying moment, Liam couldn't breathe. He could actually *feel* the breaking of his heart.

'Jesus Christ,' he whispered, not knowing if the words were a curse or a prayer.

She'd been married to Julian True, one of the most famous movie stars in the world.

'Daaaaad! Dinner's ready!'

Liam rose unsteadily to his feet and walked away from the pictures on the bed. Closing the door behind him, he went down the stairs, drawing a heavy breath before he turned into the dining room.

Bret was already at the rough-hewn trestle table. Jacey sat beside him, just now putting the chequered napkin in her lap. 'Hi, Dad,' she said with a smile.

She looked so much like Mike that he almost stumbled.

Rosa came round the corner carrying a glass bowl of salad. 'Good, good, you are here. Have a seat, Dr Liam,' she said as she plonked the bowl onto the table and took her own place.

Liam forced his dry mouth to smile. He tried to act as if this were a normal dinner—at least as normal as their meals had become in the past month—but he was weary and the veneer had worn thin.

'Dad?'

He looked up from the chicken enchiladas. 'Yeah, Jace?'

'Did you find that dress for me?'

'Yeah, honey, I found it. I'll give it to you after dinner. Maybe you and Grandma can practise fixing up your hair.'

She smiled. 'Thanks, Dad.'

Dad. The word had a hook that drew blood.

Jacey had called him that almost from the start. She'd been a little bit of a thing back then, a four-year-old with jet-black pigtails and ears that seemed so big she'd never grow into them.

She'd called him Dad for so long he'd forgotten that there was another father out there, another man who could lay claim to both his wife's and daughter's hearts.

'Dad. *Dad*.' Bret was staring at him. 'You're gonna take me to basketball tryouts, aren't you?'

'Of course, Bretster.'

Bret nodded and started talking to Jacey. Liam tried to pay attention, but he couldn't do it. A single sentence kept running through his mind: *She was married to Julian True.* He saw that Rosa was staring at him, her dark eyes narrowed and assessing. He was seized by a sudden fear that she knew what he'd found, that she'd talk about Mikaela's past now, tell him more than he wanted to know.

'I thought maybe we could watch a movie together,' she said. 'The children have rented *Dumb and Dumber*. They say it will make us laugh.'

The idea of Rosa's watching *Dumb and Dumber* brought a smile. 'Thank you, Rosa,' he answered. 'But not tonight.'

'There is something wrong,' she said, eyeing him.

He looked at Rosa for a long, desperate minute, knowing that if he sat here any longer, feeling Rosa's sympathy like a warm fire on a cold, cold night, he'd ask the question: Did she ever love me, Rosa?

He stood suddenly, heard his chair crash to the floor. When he spun round, he found himself staring into the silvered plane of an antique mirror. The image blurred and twisted before his eyes, until for a flashing second it wasn't even himself he saw. It was a younger man, blindingly handsome, with a smile that could sell a million movie tickets. 'I need to go to the hospital.'

'But—' Rosa began. Liam could see shock on the children's faces.

'Now,' he said, grabbing his coat off the hook on the wall. 'I need to see my wife.'

The emergency room was bustling with people tonight; the bright hallways echoed with voices and footsteps. Liam hurried to Mike's room.

She lay there like a broken princess in someone else's bed, her chest steadily rising and falling.

'Ah, Mike,' he murmured, moving towards her. He sat in the chair, drew close. She was still beautiful.

'I fell in love with you the first second I saw you,' he said, curling his hand round hers, feeling the warmth of her flesh. He hadn't known who she was. How could he? He'd never been one to read celebrity magazines. Even then he'd known she was running from something—or someone. It was obvious. But what did he care? He knew what he wanted: Mikaela and Jacey and a new life in Last Bend. And every day that she stayed with him was a blessing.

He closed his eyes and culled memories, brushing some aside and savouring others. The first time he'd kissed her. The day Bret had been born and they'd put him in Liam's arms, and Mike had whispered softly that life was good. The day he'd asked her to marry him.

That was the one that hurt.

They'd been at Angel Falls, stretched out on a blanket beside a still, green pool of water. There had been tears in her eyes when she told him she was pregnant.

He had known to tread carefully. It had been difficult, when all he wanted to do was to laugh with joy, but he'd touched her cheek and asked her quietly to marry him.

'I've been married before,' she'd answered, a single tear sliding down her pink cheek.

'OK.' That's what he'd said, all he'd said.

'I loved him with all my heart and soul,' she'd said. 'I'm afraid I'll love him until I die.'

'I see.'

But she was the one who could see. She'd known she was breaking his heart. She turned and knelt beside him. 'There are things I can't tell you—ever. Things I won't talk about.'

'I didn't care about all that, did I, Mike?' he said now. 'I was forty years old, and until I met you, I had given up on love. Did you know that? I had grown up in a great man's shadow; I knew that everyone I met compared me to the famous Ian Campbell, and beside him, I was an agate pushed up alongside a diamond.

'Then I met you. I thought at last I'd found someone who wouldn't compare me all the time. But you'd already had a diamond, hadn't you, Mike? And I was still just an ordinary agate . . .'

But he hadn't told her any of this when he asked her to marry him. All he'd said was that he loved her, and that if she could return even a piece of his love, they'd be happy.

He'd known that she wanted it to be true, just as he'd known she didn't completely believe it. *'I will never lie to you, Liam, and I'll never be unfaithful. I will be as good a wife as I can be.'*

'I love you, Mike,' he'd said, watching her cry.

'And I love you.'

He'd thought that over the years she'd learned to love him, but now he was seized by doubt. Maybe she cared for him. Only that.

'You should have told me, Mike,' he said, but even as he said the words, he heard the lie echoing within them. She couldn't have told him. She was right in that, at least. The knowing was unbearable.

'I found the pillowcase,' he said, leaning close. 'The pictures, the clippings. I know about . . . him.'

He squeezed her hand. 'I guess I know why you didn't tell me. But it hurts, Mike. God, it hurts. How could I ever measure up to Julian True?'

She blinked.

Liam gasped and sat bolt upright. 'Mike, can you hear me? Blink if you can hear me.' He hit the nurses' button.

Within seconds, Sarah came bustling into the room, already out of breath. 'Dr Campbell, is she—'

'She blinked.'

Sarah came closer to the bed, studying Mike first, and then Liam. She checked each machine, one by one; then she moved to stand by Liam. 'I think it was a reflex. Or maybe—'

'It *wasn't* my imagination, damn it. She blinked.'

'Maybe I should call for Dr Penn.'

'Do it,' he said, without looking up.

He let go of Mike's hand for just long enough to hit the PLAY button on the tape recorder. Music swept into the room, songs from the *Tapestry* album by Carole King.

Liam held her hand again, talking to her, saying the same thing over and over again. He was still talking, begging, when Stephen came into the room, examined Mike, and then quietly left.

Liam talked until his throat was dry and there were no more pleas left inside him. Then he slumped back down into the chair and bowed his head. *Please, God, help her.* But deep inside he knew. It hadn't been God who'd helped Mikaela blink. It was a name—just that after all these weeks. Just a simple name. When she heard it, she responded.

Julian True.

*She is floating in a sea of grey and black. There is the smell of something . . .
flowers . . . a music she can almost recognise.*

*She longs to touch the music, but she has no arms, no legs, no eyes. All she
can feel is the thudding beat of her heart. Fast, like a baby bird's, and she can
taste the metallic edge of fear.*

'You should have told me.'

*It is the voice she's come to know, soft and soothing, and she knows that
somewhere, some time, she knew it, but here there is no before, there is no
now. There is just the dark, the fear, the helpless longing for something.*

'Julian.'

*Julian. The word seems to sink deep, deep inside her. It makes her heart
beat faster, and she wants to reach for it, hold it against her chest.*

*Julian. In the black rubble of her life it is connected to another word, one
she remembers.*

Love.

CHAPTER 5

THE NEXT MORNING, Rosa was finishing the last of the breakfast dishes
when the phone rang . . . and rang . . . and rang. Frowning, she went to
the bottom of the stairs and yelled up for Dr Liam to answer it.

In the other room, the answering machine clicked on. 'Rosa? Are you
there? Pick up the phone. It's me, Liam.'

She threw the damp dishrag over her shoulder and raced back into
the kitchen to answer. '*Hola*,' she said.

'Have the kids left for school?' he asked.

'*Sí*. Bret's bus just left.'

'Good. Come to the hospital.'

'Is Mikaela—'

'The same. Just hurry. Please, Rosa. Hurry.'

'I am leaving.'

He didn't even say goodbye before she heard the dial tone buzzing in
her ear. Rosa snagged her car keys from the hook near the phone and
grabbed her bag and coat.

Outside, it was snowing lightly—not much, but enough to make an old woman like her drive slowly. All the way to the hospital she tried to be hopeful, but Dr Liam had sounded upset.

She parked in one of the vacant visitor spots and hurried into the hospital. At the closed door to Mikaela's room, she offered a quick prayer to the Virgin; then she opened the door.

Everything looked the same. Mikaela lay in the bed, on her back this morning. Liam was sitting in the chair by the bed. He was wearing the same clothes from yesterday. Shadows rimmed his eyes.

'You slept here last night,' she said, frowning. 'Why—' The look in his eyes was so cold and unfamiliar that she bit her sentence in half. 'Dr Liam?'

'Julian True.'

Rosa gasped. She grabbed hold of the metal bed rail. Her legs felt like warming butter. '*Cómo?*'

'You heard me. I said his name.'

She brought a trembling hand to her chest. 'Why do you say this name to me now?'

'Last night, when I was looking for Mike's dress, I found a pillowcase hidden in the closet.' He rose from the chair and moved towards her. 'It was filled with pictures and newspaper clippings . . . and a huge diamond ring.'

'Forget this, Dr Liam. It is old news.'

'Watergate is old news, Rosa. This is something else—and do you know how I know this?'

'How?'

'I said his name to Mikaela. That's all, just his name, and she blinked.'

'She blinked?'

'Yes.'

And just that quickly, she saw the anger leave her son-in-law's eyes. Without it, he looked old and tired and afraid.

'All this time,' he said quietly, 'I've been talking to her, holding her hand. Why? Because you made me *believe* that love would reach her. But it wasn't my love that reached her, Rosa. Or yours, either. It was just a man's name.'

'*Madre de Dios.*' She stared down at her sleeping daughter. 'Mikita, are you hearing us, *querida?* Blink if you can.'

Liam sighed. 'She's hearing us. We've just been saying the wrong things.' He sidled in close beside her and gently placed his hand on top of hers. 'Maybe it's not about our love for *her.* Maybe it's about her love for *him.*'

'Don't—'

'Talk to her about Julian. Remind her how much she loved him. Maybe that will help her come back to us.'

Rosa turned and gazed up at him. 'That is very dangerous.' She could only imagine how much this was hurting him, this good man who loved so deeply.

'It's her *life*,' he said at last. 'We have to do everything to reach her.'

Rosa wished she could disagree. 'I will try this,' she said. 'But only if you remember always that she married *you*.'

He looked as if he was going to say something; in the end, he turned and walked to the window.

She stared at him. 'Y-You are not going to stay in the room for this, Dr Liam? It will be most hurtful.'

He didn't turn round. His voice, when he found it, was low and scratchy, not his sound at all. 'I'm staying. I think it's time I got to know the woman I love.'

Rosa stood beside the bed, clasping the silver St Christopher's medallion at her throat. Slowly she closed her eyes.

For fifteen years she had not allowed herself to remember those days. That's how she thought of them—*those days*—when he had breezed into their airless life and changed everything.

She pulled up an image of Mikaela—twenty-one years old, bright brown eyes, flowing black hair, a vibrant flower in a hot, desolate farming town where migrant workers lived eight to a room in shacks without indoor plumbing. A town where the line between the 'good' folks and the Mexicans was drawn in cement. And Mikaela—a bastard half Mexican—wasn't fully welcomed in either world.

It had been the full heat of summer, that day he came into their lives. Mikaela had just finished her second and final year at the local junior college. She'd received an academic scholarship to Western Washington University in Bellingham, but Rosa had known that her daughter wanted something bigger. Cambridge. Harvard. The Sorbonne. But they both knew that girls like her didn't make it to schools like that.

It was Rosa's fault that Mikaela had felt so alone as a young girl. For years, Mikaela waited for her father to acknowledge her in public. Then had come the dark, angry years, when she hated him and his perfect white-bred children. The years when she wrote trash about him in women's lavatories all over town, when she prayed to God that just once his blue-eyed, blonde-haired cheerleader daughter would know how it felt to *want*. In time that phase had passed, too, and left Mikaela with a deeper loneliness.

Rosa opened her eyes. She could feel Liam behind her. She took a deep breath and began. 'You remember the first day you met him, *querida*, your Julian True?'

Mikaela sucked in a sharp breath; her eyelids fluttered.

A limousine, sleek and black and impossibly shiny, slid past the front window of Joe's Get-It-While-It's Hot diner. Mikaela and Rosa raced to the window. It was high noon in the first week of July, and the storefronts all wore the crackled, faded look of exhaustion. The limousine pulled up in front of City Hall and parked. Then the doors opened, all of them at once, like a huge, enamelled beetle unfurling its wings. Strangers in black suits and sunglasses emerged from the car, one after another. And then he appeared.

A shiver of recognition moved through the crowd of people that had gathered near the limo.

'Oh my God, it's Julian True,' someone whispered.

He stood with the casual, unaffected elegance of one who is used to the stares of strangers. Tall and lean, with long, sunstreaked hair that covered half his face, he looked like a rebellious angel cast down from the heavens. He wore a loose black T-shirt and a pair of ragged Levi's that were tattered and ripped out at the knees. Whatever blue dye had once been woven into the denim had long ago bleached to a foamy white.

The crowd surged towards him, crying out. One sound, one name rose from the confusion.

Julian True . . . It's him . . . Julian True in Sunville.

Then came the requests: Here! Sign my shirt . . . my notebook . . . my napkin.

Rosa turned to whisper something to Mikaela, but the words caught in her throat. Her daughter looked . . . mesmerised. Rosa moved away from the window and went back to work. Mikaela headed for the lunch counter and began refilling the sugar jars.

Suddenly the bell above the front door jingled, and he was standing there, in the diner, beneath the lazily whirring overhead fan.

Mikaela dropped the half-empty sugar jars on the table. Her cheeks turned bright pink.

He gave Mikaela a smile. It was the old cliché, sun erupting through the clouds, a bolt of electric-blue lightning from the black sky. Eyes the colour of shaved turquoise looked at Mikaela as if she were the only woman in the world.

'C-Can I help you?'

His smile held the tattered edge of exhaustion. 'Well, darlin',' he said in that world-famous Texas drawl, as thick and sweet as corn syrup, 'we've been travellin' for hours, and any minute that doorway's gonna fill up with every thirteen-year-old girl between here and Spokane. I was hopin' a pretty little thing like you could round me up a beer and a sandwich and show me where I could eat it in peace.'

'We were at the diner,' Rosa said, 'both of us working the lunch shift. And then *he* appeared. Ah, the way he looked at you, as if you were the only woman in the world. He was like no one we had ever seen before.

'You thought I was too old to understand what you were thinking, my Mikaela, but I could see it in your eyes. You thought you were Cinderella and here . . . here was a prince.

'He started calling you Kayla almost from the start. Kayla of the midnight hair—that was his nickname for you. I hated that he would give you a *gringa* name, and that you would take it . . . but it did not matter what I thought.

'When he first kissed you, you told me it felt like you'd jumped off a skyscraper. I said that such a fall could kill a girl. Remember your answer? You said, "Ah, *Mamá*, but sometimes it is worth it to fly."'

Rosa leaned down and touched Mikaela's face. 'I watched you fall in love with him, this man with the face of an angel. I knew there would be fireworks at the start of it. I knew, too, that there would be pain at the end of it. Enough to last a lifetime.'

Rosa gave her daughter a small, sad smile. 'You laughed and told me not to worry. You promised that you would not make my mistake. But I knew, *querida*. I saw it in your eyes. You already had.'

Rosa turned round suddenly, and Liam realised that she had stopped talking. 'She has not blinked again, Dr Liam.'

He crossed the short distance to the bed. This time, when he looked down at his wife, he saw a stranger. *Kayla*. He picked up her hand, held it gently. 'She never told me any of this, Rosa. Why did I let her keep such secrets?'

Rosa stood beside him, her head angled close to his shoulder. 'You come from money,' she said simply. 'You are a doctor—from Harvard. You cannot understand what life is like for people like us. Mikaela had such big dreams, but no way to make them come true. Even her own papá—he did not show her any love at all.' She turned to him. 'I first came to Sunville to pick apples when I was a little girl. *Mi padre*, he died when I was eleven. There was no money to buy medicines, and no doctor to help him. Sometimes I can still remember the pickers' camps—especially when the air smells of ripe fruit. I can smell the tin-roofed shack where we lived, ten people in a room this size.

'I found my way out with a man. He wasn't *my* man—that was my great sin—but I didn't care. I loved him. *Madre de Dios*, I loved him in the desperate way that women like me always love another woman's husband.' She leaned over the bed rail and gazed down at Mikaela. 'I am afraid I taught my daughter that a woman will wait for ever for the man she loves.'

Liam could tell by the sad end note of Rosa's sentence that she was finished. She turned and looked up at him again.

'Perhaps now you will think badly of me—'

'Ah, Rosa, don't you think I know how it feels to love someone who belongs to another?'

'She *married* you.'

'Yes, and she stayed with me, and we built something. But I always knew. Deep down I knew. There was a part of Mike's heart that was off limits to me. I didn't even know her.'

Rosa didn't say anything.

'Keep talking to her, Rosa. You left off when she fell in love with him.'

She frowned. 'The rest of the story—it is filled with much pain for her. Maybe it will make the coma worse.'

'Pain is a powerful stimulus. Maybe even stronger than love. We can't give up yet. Talk to her.'

Rosa drew in a deep breath. It went against her every instinct to talk about these things in front of Dr Liam. But then she thought about the blinking of her daughter's eyes. Maybe . . .

'You loved him so much, my Mikita. Loved him in the way that only young girls can. He swept you off your feet—it wasn't hard, not when you ached so badly to fly. He took your heart and your virginity . . . and then he left you.'

Rosa brushed the hair from her daughter's forehead. 'I watched you wait for him, day after day, night after night. You stood at the diner's window, waiting for a car to drive up.'

Rosa remembered those days in brutal detail. Every time she'd looked into her daughter's eyes, she'd known what would happen. Slowly, before Mikaela knew to guard against it, she would begin to shrink. Rosa knew it would go on, the slow chipping away of self-confidence, until only a shadow of Mikaela was left.

'When you asked me, I told you that it would go away, this love of yours. But we both knew it was a lie. And then it happened. A *milagro*. He came back for you.

'I could not believe it when he asked you to marry him, *mi hija*. He took you out of Sunville and gave you the world. From that moment you were someone who mattered. You were in every newspaper, on the television all the time. You turned into a woman I'd never seen before, this Kayla of the midnight hair.'

Rosa's voice fell away. She turned to Liam. 'After that come the years I do not know about. She kept secrets from me, too. I read in the tabloid newspaper about Julian's drinking, about his other women, but Mikaela told me none of this. All I remember is when she called me—it was the day after Jacey's first birthday party. She sounded tired and broken, my little girl, when she told me that it was over.' Rosa sighed. 'Mikaela was only twenty-three, but she was not young any more.'

Liam made a sound—part sigh, part moan—and there was such a sadness in it.

Rosa wished she were the kind of woman who could go to him, hold him in this moment that was tearing at his heart. 'I am sorry, Dr Liam,' she said.

He rose from the chair and went to the bed. 'Help us, Mike,' he said. 'Let us know you're still there. We all miss you—me, Rosa, Jacey, Bret . . . Julian.'

'Help us, Mike. Let us know you're still there.'

The voice, familiar and unfamiliar at the same time, keeps asking questions she can't answer, in words she doesn't truly understand.

But then there is that one sound again.

'Julian.'

She tries desperately to extract a memory, just one, but the shallow, rocky soil of her mind gives up nothing.

If only she could open her eyes.

'Miss you . . .'

These are words she understands, and they hurt. Miss. It is about being alone and afraid. Yes, she understands.

Please, God, she prays. Help me.

'She's crying. Jesus Christ.' Liam reached for a tissue and gently wiped her eyes. 'Mike, honey, can you hear me?'

She didn't respond, but those terrible silver tears kept falling. He punched the nurses' button and ran for the door. When he saw Sarah, he yelled for her to get Dr Penn. Then he went back into the room and bent over his wife, stroking her damp cheeks, whispering the same words to her over and over again. 'Come on, baby. Come on back to us.'

Stephen Penn appeared in the doorway, out of breath. 'What is it, Liam?'

He looked up at his friend. 'She's crying, Steve.'

Stephen went to the side of the bed and stared down at Mikaela. She was as still as death, her cheeks pale, but the trail of moisture glittered promiselike in the dim lighting. He produced a straight pin from his pocket. Gently lifting her bare foot in his palm, Stephen stuck the sharp tip into the tender flesh.

Mikaela jerked her foot back. A broken moan escaped her lips.

Stephen laid her foot down again and covered it with the blanket. Then he looked at Liam. 'The coma's lightening. It doesn't necessarily mean . . .' He paused. 'You know what it does and doesn't mean. But maybe something reached her. Whatever you're doing, keep doing it.'

It was way past bedtime when Bret heard the knock on his door. He was sitting on the floor of his bedroom, playing Diddy Kong racing on his Nintendo 64.

The door opened, and Dad poked his head in. 'Come on, kiddo. It's bedtime. Close up the game and get your fangs washed.'

Bret turned off the television and hurried down the hall. In his bathroom he brushed his teeth really good; then he went back into his room.

Dad was already in bed under the covers, with a book open in his lap. It was one of Mike's favourite books. *The Lion, the Witch and the Wardrobe*. Bret got into bed, snuggling up close. 'Is that the lion book?'

'You bet.'

Bret curled up next to his dad and listened to the story. It calmed him down, listening to his dad's deep, steady voice.

It felt like only a few minutes later that Dad shut the book and set it on the table by the lamp.

Dad took Bret in his big, strong arms and held him tightly. 'I think you should visit Mommy. It's important now.'

Dad had never said that before—that it was *important* that Bret see her. All along, Bret had thought that he didn't matter.

He felt the tears he'd been holding back. They came out of him like a waterfall, burning down his cheeks. He held on to his daddy as hard as he could.

Dad drew back, wiped the tears from Bret's face. 'I think she misses you visiting her.' He stroked Bret's hair.

Dad said quietly, 'It's not a scary place. Just a plain old room with a plain old bed. I wouldn't lie to you, Bret. Your mom looks just like she used to, only she's sleeping.'

'You *swear* she's alive?'

'I swear it. She needs to hear your voice, Bretster. I know she has been missing her favourite boy in the whole world.'

For the first time, Bret wondered if maybe *he* could wake her up. After all, he was her favourite boy and she loved him more than the whole world. She always told him that. Maybe all this time she'd been waiting to hear him. He wiped his nose with his sleeve and stared at Dad through a blurry screen of tears. 'I could go and see her tomorrow before school.'

Dad's voice was quiet now, a little shaky. 'That'd be great.'

The next morning Bret bounced in his seat all the way to the hospital. Last night he'd dreamed of his mommy for the first time. In his dream, she woke up when he gave her the Mommy Kiss. *That's* what she'd been waiting for, all this time. The Mommy Kiss.

At the hospital, he held Daddy's hand and dragged him down the hallway to her room. The first thing he saw was the baby bed, with the silver side rails. Not a grown-up bed at all. There were no lights on; the room was painted in dull grey shadows.

And there was Mommy, lying in the bed. Slowly he moved towards her. She looked pretty, not broken at all. He could imagine her waking up . . . Just like that, she'd sit up in bed, open her eyes, and see Bret.

'How's my favourite boy in the whole world?' she'd say, opening her arms for a hug.

'You can talk to her, Bret.'

He let go of his dad's hand and moved closer to the bed, climbing up the silver rails until he was leaning over his mom. Then, very slowly, he gave her the Mommy Kiss, exactly the way she always gave it to him: a kiss on the forehead, one on each cheek, then a butterfly kiss on the chin. At last he whispered, 'No bad dreams,' as he kissed the side of her nose.

She lay there, unmoving.

'Come on, Mommy. Open your eyes. It's me. Bret.'

Still nothing.

He slid off the bed and turned, looking up at his dad through a blur of tears. 'She didn't wake up, Daddy.'

His dad looked like he was going to cry. It scared Bret. 'I know,' he said, 'but we have to keep trying.'

Liam pushed back from his desk. Today he faced a crucial choice. He had been grappling with it ever since Mike first blinked. He had no doubt that the decision he made would lay the groundwork for the rest of his life. He grabbed his coat and walked out of his office.

Outside, the sudden plunge in temperature was exactly what Liam needed to clear his mind. The sound of children's laughter rode high in the still, clean mountain air. He followed it to Mr Robbin's llama farm. His frog pond, settled comfortably in a flat patch of the pasture, had been turned by Mother Nature into a beautiful silver skating rink. Suzie Sanman was stationed at the picnic table, heating pots of milk on a camp stove, and Mayor Comfort was roasting hot dogs over an open fire.

Liam could see Bret skating with his friends. Rosa was sitting on one of the benches near the pond, alone.

He greeted his friends and neighbours as he made his way through the crowd, pretending not to notice their surprise at seeing him there. Beside Rosa, he sat down. Wordlessly, she scooted sideways to make more room for him.

'Life goes on, eh, Rosa?' Liam said softly.

'*Sí.*'

She handed him a paper coffee cup; the moist heat felt good against his lips. 'She is not doing well, Rosa. I've said Julian's name to her so many times, I'm afraid I'll accidentally say it at dinner. I thought maybe Bret would be the key, but he's visited every day after school, and . . . nothing.'

'She needs a little more time, maybe.'

'Time isn't her friend right now. I think—'

His pager went off, bleating from its place on his belt. He reached down and pulled out the small black unit.

It was an emergency message from Stephen Penn.

'Oh God,' he said. 'It's Mike.'

Rosa shoved her keys at him. 'Take my car. It is right there.'

He snatched the keys. 'My car's in the office lot. The keys are in the visor. Get Bret and Jacey. This could be—'

'I know what it could be. We'll be right behind you.'

'Cardiac arrest.'

Liam slumped in his chair.

Stephen didn't look away. 'I don't know what to tell you, Liam. Her heart just stopped. We got it going again in no time, but it could be an indicator. I think it might be time to prepare yourself and the kids for the end.'

The end. He wished he'd never said that to a patient of his, but he knew that he had.

'What will you tell the kids?'

'I don't know. How do you tell a nine-year-old that it's time to say goodbye to Mommy?'

Liam got to his feet and made his way out of Penn's office.

The corridor was too bright; the light stung his glazed eyes. In the waiting room, Jacey stood at the window, with Mark beside her. Rosa sat perched on the very edge of the sofa. Bret—still in his skating coat and Gore-Tex bib overalls—stood pressed against the wall. His little cheeks were candy-apple red.

When Jacey saw Liam, she let go of Mark's hand and took a cautious step towards him. 'Daddy?'

He couldn't tell them. Not here, at least—not beneath these cold strips of fluorescent lighting.

He didn't look at Rosa as he spoke. 'She's OK. Mom's OK. She had a little trouble with her heart, is all. It skipped a few beats, but everything is OK now.'

'Can I see her?' Jacey asked.

'Only for a minute or two. Ironically, she needs her rest.'

Jacey nodded and headed for the door.

Bret looked up at him. 'Is she awake?'

Liam touched his son's cold cheek. 'No, honey, she's not.'

Bret backed into the wall. 'I don't wanna see her.'

Liam didn't know what to do.

'Hey, Bretster,' Mark said, moving towards them. 'I promised to get you a soda and some Gummi Bears. How about now?'

Bret's face broke into a relieved smile. 'Can I, Dad?'

Liam felt like a coward for taking the easy road, but he nodded. He reached into his pocket and pulled out a couple of dollar bills. 'Here you go, but don't be too long.'

Bret took the money and fisted it. ''Kay.' Then he followed Mark out of the room.

At last Liam turned to Rosa. He could tell by the wary look in her eyes that she had been waiting for this moment.

She sat stiff as a fence post. 'It is bad, sí?'

Liam sat down beside her on the hard vinyl sofa. He said simply, 'Her heart stopped.'

Rosa drew in a sharp breath and crossed herself. '*Dios mío.*'

'They revived her easily—and quickly, which is important.'

'There must be something you can do. Some medicine—'

Liam sighed. 'We're going to have to try something else, Rosa. Something a little more extreme. She's not responding to our voices. And I don't think we have a lot of time.'

'What are you thinking?' Rosa asked.

He heard the worry in her voice, and he knew that she knew what he was going to say. 'I'm going to call Julian and ask him to come see her. Talk to her.'

She gasped. 'You cannot! He is . . . dangerous.'

'You think he was physically violent to her?'

'No, no. The danger is in how much she loves—*loved*—him.' She twisted round so they were face to face. 'You do not have to do this, Liam. God will waken Mikaela if that is His plan. You need to take care of *su familia*. That man, he could ruin everything.'

He wondered if she realised that she'd used his name. Strangely, that little intimacy comforted him as no touch ever could. 'You and I, Rosa, we're not kids. We know how easy it is to do the wrong thing. This is probably the clearest moment I've had in all my fifty years. I can call Julian and give my wife a chance at life. Or I can not call Julian and know that I was so afraid of losing Mikaela's love that I let her die.'

Rosa's eyes filled with tears.

'I won't be able to look myself—or my children—in the eye if I let fear keep me from doing what's right. I am going to call Julian True. There's a phone number for his agent in the pillowcase.'

Rosa reached out, placed her hands on top of his. 'Does my Mikita know how lucky she is to have you?'

Liam knew he shouldn't ask it, but he couldn't help himself. 'Did she love me, Rosa?'

She squeezed his hands. 'Of course.'

'Like she loved him?'

Rosa paused, and in that heartbeat's hesitation, Liam saw the harrowing truth. '*Sí*,' she answered with a smile that was too bright, too fast.

Liam sighed. 'Then I guess we have nothing to worry about.'

CHAPTER 6

BEVERLY HILLS. Two words, each unremarkable enough on its own, but like champagne and caviar they combined to form the ultimate expression of the good life. In this pastel pocket of Los Angeles, stardust from nearby Hollywood gilded even the mundane. Images of Beverly Hills were famous around the world: pink hotels with poolside phones, valet parking at the post offices, restaurant tables that couldn't be bought for any amount of money—ah, but a whisper of fame could get you seated in an instant. It was a city where last names were unnecessary among the chosen few: Harrison, Goldie, Brad, Julian.

Even in the rarefied perfection of this most trimmed and tucked and glamorised of cities, Julian True was special. Not just a star, but a superstar, a nova who showed no sign of burning out.

He'd come to Hollywood like thousands of young men before him, with nothing more than a handsome face and a dream. He'd wanted to be someone who mattered, and he knew it would happen. Things had always come easily to him—attention, women, invitations, everything—and he took what came easily.

Today he was flying high. The screening of his new film, *The Bad Boys of C Company*, had gone better than he'd hoped. Better than anyone had hoped. Julian had earned his twenty million. He'd given the studio a sure-fire hit.

A hit. Two of the sweetest words possible.

He pushed a little harder on the accelerator. The Ferrari responded instantly, following the winding, stop-and-go traffic into Century City. There, he pulled up in front of a grand high-rise building and parked at a metered spot.

A doorman rushed out, held the door open. 'Good evening, Mr True.'

Julian patted his pocket, found it empty. *Damn.* He was so used to other people picking up the tab, he regularly left his wallet at home. 'I don't have any money with me, kid. I'll tell Val to tip you, OK?'

'S-Sure, Mr True. And thank you.'

Julian followed the doorman through the ornate marble-panelled lobby to the elevator.

At the penthouse, the doors opened. Julian's agent, Val Lightner, lounged in the open doorway, waiting for his most famous client.

'Hey, Juli,' Val said, lifting his martini glass in a salute that upset his precarious balance. He staggered against the door frame. 'The phones have been ringing off the hook since the screening. If you were any hotter, you'd need asbestos underwear.' He grinned lazily and pushed a long, cornsilk-blond lock of hair away from his face. 'Come on in, superstar.'

Julian followed Val into the apartment, where a raucous party was in full swing. Movie stars mingled with wannabes; you could tell them apart by the eyes. The stars looked confident; the wannabes looked desperate, starvelings standing at a banquet table where they'd never be fed.

The place had no paintings, no knick-knacks, no rugs. Val had bought the unit, picked a few things to sit on, and called it home. But then, Val didn't need to decorate. In this town, failure to do what you could easily afford had a cachet all its own.

'I need a drink,' Julian said to no one in particular, and within seconds someone handed him a drink. It didn't matter what was in the glass, as long as it had a kick. He downed it, knowing that every pair of eyes was on him. And why not? He was on top of the world. He moved through the crowd, laughing and talking.

Val had drifted into the bedroom. Julian found him snorting a line of coke off the table by the bed. There was a woman beside him wearing nothing but a pair of lacy red panties. Val turned, grinning sleepily. 'Hey, Jules, say hi to May Sharona. She wanted to talk to you about a part in—' He cupped the woman's perfect right breast in his hand. 'What movie were you interested in, doll?'

The woman was talking now. Julian could see her painted lips moving, but he didn't listen. He'd heard it all before.

'I'm going to another party,' Julian said, without looking at the woman. 'This one's dead.'

Val angled up to a swaying sit. 'Whassa matter? I have more coke in the bathroom.'

'No, thanks.'

'No? *No?*' Val grabbed his martini glass from the end table. He sauntered unsteadily across the room. 'Hey, before you go, I gotta message for you. Someone called the office, looking for you. A doctor. He said he needed to talk to you about Mikaela Luna. How's *that* for a blast from the past?'

'A doctor. Is she hurt?'

'I dunno. He just wanted you to call him.'

Julian felt a fluttering in his chest. *Kayla*. Of all the women he'd known, he'd loved her the most. 'Where's the number?'

'I told Susan to leave it on your answering machine.'

'Thanks,' Julian answered, distracted by a sudden onslaught of memories. His first love. Kayla. He hadn't heard from her in so long he'd almost forgotten her. Almost.

Val raised his glass. 'The missing Mrs True. The press loved her.' He paused, looked blearily at Julian. 'And so did you.'

Liam sat at his desk. He didn't bother to leaven the silence by playing one of the CDs stacked by the stereo.

The intercom buzzed. His nurse's staticky voice came through the small black box. 'You're not going to believe this, Doctor. But there's a man on the phone who says he's Julian True.'

Liam's heart skipped a beat. 'I'll take it.'

'Do you think it's the real—'

'Patch him through, Carol.'

The red light on line one started flashing. Liam took a deep breath, stabbed the button, and picked up the phone. 'This is Dr Campbell.'

There was a pause, and then, 'Dr *Liam* Campbell?'

Even through the impersonal medium of the phone lines, Liam would have recognised the voice. 'This is he.'

'This is Julian True. You left a message with my agent, Val Lightner, regarding Mikaela Luna—'

'She's been injured.'

'Oh God. How bad?'

'She's in a coma.'

Another pause crackled through the lines, and Liam realised that Julian was on a carphone. 'What can I do? I'll pay for her hospital bills, and—'

'She doesn't need your money, Mr True. I called you because . . . well, she shows some response to your name. I . . . *we* . . . thought that maybe if she heard your voice—'

'You think she'll wake up for me?'

Liam was unprepared for the pain that came with that simple question. 'We think there's a chance.'

'I can be there tomorrow. Where is she?'

'In the Ian Campbell Medical Center in Last Bend, Washington. About sixty miles east of Bellingham. When you get there, ask for me. I'll be in my office.'

'OK. Uh . . . how does she look? I mean, I need to be prepared.'

It was a perfectly human question, nothing wrong with it, so why did Liam feel suddenly angry? His answer was barely audible along the crackling line. 'She looks as beautiful as you probably remember.'

In the living room, there were candles on every windowsill and table-top. The candelabra on the grand piano was a blaze of flickering golden light. Liam heard the soft patter of Rosa's slippered feet on the stairs.

'*Buenas noches*, Rosa,' he said.

She reached the bottom of the stairs and turned towards him. '*Buenas noches,* Dr Liam.'

'What's with all the candles, Rosa? Is this all for Mike?'

She shook her head. He could see the worry carved onto her face. 'It is for you that I light these candles, Dr Liam. For you and the children. I spoke to Carol today. She told me that Julian True called you.'

'He'll be here tomorrow.'

Her mouth puckered with disapproval.

'Follow me,' he said, and led her to the sofa.

She sat stiffly, her gaze riveted on her lap.

He sat beside her, leaning forward in the hope that it would make her look at him. 'I'm afraid of him, too, Rosa. But I love her. I can't let her go without trying everything possible.'

Rosa sighed heavily. 'You cannot understand bad love.'

'Julian True married her, Rosa. He must have loved her.'

'There is love . . . and *love*. The good love, like what you have for my Mikaela, does not let a young girl run off alone with a tiny baby. It does not stay hidden for years and years. It does not leave you cold in the winter in bed all by yourself.'

Liam looked away. Candlelight reflected all round the room, a thousand tiny golden drops against the night-tarnished windowpanes.

Rosa leaned over and touched Liam's hands. 'When he comes here, you cannot tell Jacey who he is. This is *muy importante*. We cannot let him hurt our precious girl.'

Liam told himself that Mikaela should be the one to reveal her secrets to Jacey. 'You're right, Rosa. We won't say anything yet.'

Yet even as he said the words, he knew it was the wrong thing to do.

The town looked like a damn movie set. Julian stared through the limousine's smoked-glass windows. He couldn't remember ever seeing a place this . . . cute.

He lowered the privacy screen so he could talk to the driver. 'We're looking for the Country Haus Bed and Breakfast. It's probably right next door to the Drift On Inn.'

'I've got the address, sir.'

The driver turned onto Glacier Street. Halfway down the road they came to a barricade. Cars were parked behind the orange dividers. The driver started to turn the car round.

'Wait.' Julian hit the window control and peered out.

Off to the right there was a huge field, coated in white. In the middle of it was a large frozen pond. Cars ringed its perimeter; their golden headlights turned the place into an outdoor Madison Square Garden. There were people everywhere—kids and adults—all skating in the same direction.

He noticed a small concession stand set up just a few feet from the car. A woman was making hot chocolate on a camp stove. Some men were roasting hot dogs over an open-pit fire.

'The only thing missing is Jimmy Stewart.' Julian drew his head back in and raised the window. 'Go on. Take me to the hotel.'

They pulled up alongside a huge Victorian house that sat on a corner lot, its roof covered in drifts of snow. A white picket fence cut the large lot into a pretty, bite-sized piece. Next to the open gate was an etched wooden sign that read WELCOME TO OUR COUNTRY HAUS.

Julian stepped out of the car. His breath clouded in front of his face. 'Bring the bags in,' he said, already moving, his tennis shoes crunching through the hard crust of snow.

The door swung open before he even reached the porch. A grey-haired, heavyset woman in a floral dress and plaid apron stood in the doorway. 'It *is* you! The girls and I didn't dare hope.' She dissolved into giggles.

Even though he was tired, he flashed her The Smile. It never hurt to schmooze the fans. 'Hello, darlin'.'

She clapped her hands together. 'Darling—ooh eee. Wait till I tell Gertrude. I made you shortbread, just in case. I read in the *Enquirer* that it's your favourite.'

'You're an angel straight from heaven,' he said, though in truth, he couldn't remember what in the hell shortbread was. 'Now, if you wouldn't mind, I've had a long trip and I'm tired. I'd sure appreciate it if you'd show me to my room.'

'Of course.' She scuttled around like a dung beetle and hopped up the narrow staircase. Julian could hear the driver banging up behind them with his garment bag.

On the first floor, the woman went to the end of the landing and opened a door, revealing a big, airy bedroom that exceeded the weight limit on ruffles.

'It's the honeymoon suite,' she said, beaming. 'I'm Elizabeth, by the way, but you can call me Lizbet.'

'Lizbet. Charming.' He poked his head into the room and frowned. 'I'm sorry, Lizbet, but where's my bathroom?'

'Down the hall. Third door on the left.'

He turned slowly to face her. 'You're saying I have to *share* a bathroom with other people?'

'Ordinarily that would be true, but ski season hasn't started yet. You're our only guest. So, really, it's like a private bathroom.'

'Except that I need to pack a lunch to get to it.'

She puffed up. 'Well, really—'

'I'm sorry. That was just a joke. The room is fine. Give my driver a room, too, would you? Then I'll buy up all the rest. I'd like to have the place to myself.'

'Of course.' Backing away from him, she smiled until the last possible moment, when she turned and disappeared.

He sat down on the end of the bed. The springs squeaked and moaned beneath his weight. 'Unpack my bags, will you?' he said to the driver, flopping back on the bed.

Liam left his office at five o'clock and drove to the medical centre. Once there, he went to the small corner office that he shared with Tom Granato, a general practitioner.

He knew the instant that Julian True arrived at the hospital. A flurry of sounds came through the door of his small office; footsteps speeded up; whispers turned up in volume.

Sarah appeared at the door, opening it without even a knock. Her face was flushed a bright pink, and she was grinning. 'Dr Campbell, there's a man here to see—'

'Julian True.'

She sucked in a surprised breath. 'How did you know?'

'Magic.'

'He says he's here to see Mikaela.'

'Send him in.'

Sarah bobbed a quick nod and disappeared.

And so it began. Liam tried to steady his nerves.

The door opened. The man standing in the open doorway smiled— just that—and Liam felt ill. The photographs didn't do Julian justice; no lens could capture the magnetic power of that face.

'I'm Julian True,' he said unnecessarily.

Liam rose slowly to his feet. 'Hello, Julian. I'm glad you could come. I'm Liam Campbell. I wanted—'

'Can I see her now?'

Liam sighed. He didn't know why he'd wanted to put it off; it wasn't as if Julian was going to leave. Still, the thought of bringing them together made him feel sick. 'Follow me.'

He led Julian down the hallway towards Mikaela's room. Slowly he opened the door.

Julian pushed past him and went to the bed. He stared down at Mikaela for a long time. 'What happened?'

'She fell off a horse and hit her head on a fence post.'

'How long has she been like this?'

'A little more than a month.'

Julian brushed a strand of hair from her eyes. 'Heya, Kayla. It's Jules.' Then he looked up. 'What do I do?'

Liam felt like Grandpa Walton giving advice to Robert Redford about how to talk to a woman. 'Just talk to her, Julian.' Liam's voice fell to a whisper. 'She sometimes responds to stories from the past.'

'And my name. She responded to my name, right?'

It took an incredible effort to answer. 'Yes.'

Julian dragged a chair over to the bed. 'Leave us alone for a while, will you, Doc? Heya, Kayla. It's me, Jules.'

She didn't respond.

Liam let out a shaky breath. He realised he'd been afraid she would simply wake up, just like that, when she heard Julian's voice.

Julian took her hand in his. 'Kayla, honey . . .'

Liam couldn't stand the sight of Julian touching her, so he turned and walked out of the room. In the hall, he leaned back against the wall.

It wasn't until almost a full minute had passed that he realised he hadn't told Julian that he was Mike's husband.

Julian had never been any good at writing his own lines.

The woman lying before him looked beautiful, like a sleeping princess. He half expected her to sit up, smiling, and say, 'Hey, Jules, what took you so long?'

At the imagined sound of her voice, the years fell away. Julian hadn't thought about her in ages, but now, looking at her, he could recall clearly how it had felt to love her and to be loved by her.

He closed his eyes; memories floated to the surface. 'Remember the beginning, Kay? I fell so far in love with you it felt like I was drowning.'

He tried to remember how they'd fallen out of love. It had been so deep, that well of their emotion, how had they drifted apart? Yet even as he wondered, he knew.

She'd wanted him to grow up. It sounded absurdly simple, but that was the core of it. She had wanted him to make sacrifices for their family. But he'd been twenty-three years old. Barely ready to be a husband, completely unprepared to be a father. All he'd wanted was fun . . . and so he'd drawn back, taken the careless path he knew so well, the road lined with women whose names could never be remembered and parties that never died.

It felt as if a door had opened. Beyond it, he saw a glimpse into himself, past the golden boy, past the star, all the way back to the lonely boy he'd once been. In all the years between then and now, he'd never really loved anyone. This woman, Kayla, had been the closest. His love for her had been the best of him, and he'd turned his back on it.

He stared down at her face, studying the lovely half-moon curl of her black eyelashes, the pale puffiness of her lips.

What could he say to this woman whom he knew so well and yet didn't really know at all? This woman whose heart he'd broken with the ease of a child smashing an out-of-favour toy?

Tears seared his eyes. He couldn't believe it. He hadn't cried in years. Except when they paid him to, of course.

'You'd love this, Kay. *Me*, crying.'

He rested his chin on the cold silver bed rail and gazed down at her, noticing for the first time the plain gold band on the ring finger of her left hand.

'Oh my God,' he whispered. 'You're *married*?'

Liam parked in front of the Country Haus Bed and Breakfast. The last thing in the world he wanted to do right now was talk to Julian True, but he had no choice. When he looked up, Julian was standing beside the car. The idiot was wearing a black T-shirt and jeans. He had to be freezing.

Liam reached over and unlocked the door.

Julian slid into the seat. 'It's cold out there.' Smiling, he turned to Liam. 'I'm glad you called. The thought of spending the evening in that bathroomless room, watching one of three speckled television channels, was more than I could bear. What do you say we get a drink?'

Offhand, Liam could think of at least thirty-two-hundred things he'd rather do. 'Sure.' He started the car again. In an awkward silence they drove through town.

Liam parked in front of Lou's Bowl-O-Rama and got out of the car. 'Follow me.'

The bowling alley was predinner-hour quiet. No one was using any of the four bowling lanes. The owner, Lou Padinsky, stood behind the counter, wiping it down with a soggy grey rag. When he saw Liam, he flashed a grin that made the cigarette in his mouth droop. 'Howdy, Doc.'

Liam nodded. 'Get us a couple o' beers, willya, Lou?'

'Sure thing, Doc.' Lou slapped the rag across his shoulder and turned towards the beer taps.

Liam led Julian to a booth at the back of the bowling alley. As they sat down across from each other, Liam was glad they'd come here. First off, the lighting was poor, and God knew he didn't need to see the younger man's face in good light. Second, there wouldn't be a bunch of look-e-loos wandering through the place and getting all hot and bothered about a genuine movie star in Last Bend. He hoped that Julian felt out of place in a joint like this, but truthfully, Liam figured that a man like Julian never felt out of place.

He stared at the younger man, remembering all the things he'd learned about Julian. The Internet was great for that sort of thing. He knew, for example, that Kayla True had 'disappeared' one day. He'd learned, too, that Julian and Mike had been blessed in the beginning, a genuine Hollywood superstar couple, but something—some reports said drugs, some said other women—had tarnished their star. And that the four-times-married Julian True was one of the highest-paid actors in the world.

Lou waddled towards the table and set down two schooners.

Julian flashed the man a bright smile. 'Thanks.'

Lou started to answer, then stopped. 'Hey, you look like that guy Julian True. You hear that a lot?'

'All the time.'

Lou turned to Liam. 'And how's that beautiful wife of yours?'

'She's OK. Thanks, Lou.'

Lou headed back towards the lunch counter, humming as he went.

Liam took a sip of beer.

Julian leaned back, sliding his arms across the top of the booth's settee. Liam had the impression of a golden lion stretching in the sun. 'I didn't expect her to be so . . .' He didn't finish.

'She's better than she was. Earlier this week, she blinked.'

'Jesus.' Julian's eyes narrowed. 'A blink. That's good, huh?'

'It's better than nothing.'

'Well, it was awful good of you to call me. We don't have doctors like you at Cedars-Sinai.'

'I'm her husband.'

'*You?*'

Liam refused to let the tone upset him. 'We've been married for ten years. I'm sure you noticed the wedding ring.'

Julian rolled his eyes and his hand shot in the air. 'Hey, Lou. Bring me a pack of Marlboros, willya?'

Lou grinned and grabbed a packet. Hurrying over to the table, he dropped them in front of Julian, with a book of matches. 'It's nice to see a smoker in Last Bend. We're dying out.'

'Nice imagery, Lou. Thanks.' Julian opened the packet, extracted a cigarette and lit it up. Smoke swirled across his face, but through the cloud Liam could see those blue eyes studying him. Julian reached for his beer and took a long drink, then set it down. 'You must really love her—to call me, I mean.'

'I do,' Liam said quietly.

Julian leaned back again. 'This place reminds me of that dump of a diner where Kayla used to work.'

'Really?'

He smiled. 'God, she was beautiful. And those good Christian folks in Sunville treated her like trash.'

'She said she never fitted in.'

'Who the hell would want to? But it hurt her, you know. Kay would have done *anything* to belong somewhere.'

'You mean, like marry you?'

Julian didn't smile this time. 'Or you. I can see why she came to this town. And she needed someone like you . . . after me.'

Liam couldn't stop the question; it burned on his tongue, left a bitter taste. 'What happened between you two?'

Julian sighed. 'You know how it is. We were in love, and then we weren't. Hell, I was twenty-three years old. I didn't know who I wanted to be.' He looked away, took another long drag on the cigarette, then exhaled. 'When she left, she said she'd wait for me to come and get her. For ever—that's how long she said she'd wait.'

Liam wished he couldn't see it so clearly. He sipped his beer, studying Julian over the frosted rim. 'What about your daughter? Why didn't you ever contact her?'

Julian flinched, and Liam thought, My God, he never even thought about Jacey. He got on a plane, rushed up here, and never once remembered that he had a child here.

'She was so little when I last saw her. To be honest, I don't know what I feel about her. I'm sure we'll work it all out when I meet her.'

Liam couldn't fathom the kind of man who could be so careless with a young girl's heart. At least the man could *look* ashamed. 'She doesn't know you're her father.'

'What? Kay never told her?'

'Do you want to tell her yourself?'

'*Me?* No.'

God help him, Liam was relieved. 'It's a small town. I don't want her to find out—'

'I won't say anything. If word gets around, I'll say I'm here for the Make-A-Wish Foundation. Please, Liam, let's wait and see what happens with Kayla, OK? I mean, if she doesn't wake up . . .'

'OK,' Liam said, watching Julian closely. 'We'll wait.'

The next morning, Liam woke up early and rolled quietly out of bed, being careful not to wake Bret, who was sleeping peacefully beside him. He showered quickly, jammed some clothes from his closet into a duffle bag, and headed downstairs. On the kitchen table he left a 'Have a good day' note for Rosa and the kids.

Dawn crept through Last Bend like a slow reckoning. Thin bands of pink light crested the trees. The storefronts were all black.

He drove to the hospital, parked, and went to Mikaela's room. He flicked on the lights and went immediately to draw open the curtains.

Then, very slowly, he turned round.

She was as still as always, her pale face slack, her arms tucked gently along her sides. He'd been afraid Julian had already woken her.

Now, for the first time, it felt important—essential, even—that Liam be the one to reach her.

'Heya, Mike,' he whispered, starting the music. Today he chose something by Andrea Bocelli, to remind her of the sad, aching sweetness of life. At her bedside, he set down the duffle bag and unzipped it, extracting a navy cashmere sweater, the one she'd bought for him on their last trip to Vancouver. Very gently, he placed it on her chest.

'Can you smell me, Mike? *Me?*' He took hold of her hand. 'I don't know why I never thought to bring one of my own sweaters before. Last night I woke up in a cold sweat, thinking that very question. I thought of everyone you loved, except me. You always said that was my greatest strength—that I thought of everyone before I thought of myself. But it's my weakness, too, and we both know that.'

He brought her arm up and kissed the back of her hand. 'I let everyone else feed you memories because I was afraid of the power they held. I was afraid of . . . breaking. I still am, I guess, but I can't let another day pass without going through that fear. It seems that all I can think about is you and Julian. There's a whole part of you I never knew, and knowing that makes me feel lost. Like our life together wasn't real.'

He stroked her hair, noticing the trembling in his hand.

'But we were lovers, Mike. And I'll never forget how beautiful it feels to have you in my arms. We can be lovers again if you'll just open your eyes and look at me. I love you. Always. I love you.'

Very slowly he leaned down and kissed her forehead, murmuring, 'For ever.'

Julian woke up with a deadly hangover. It was inevitable, of course. There was nothing to do in this Norman Rockwell town except sit in your room, watch one of three channels, and drink. Last night he'd spent at least two hours trying to get Val on the phone. At every busy signal, he'd taken a swig of Scotch.

Groggily, he turned onto his side and reached for the telephone, punching in Val's office number. Susan, the receptionist, answered on the second ring, 'Lightner and Associates.'

Julian angled to a sit. 'Is Val in?'

'Hi, Julian. Just a second.'

Val came on. 'Juli, how goes it in the Great White North?'

'I saw Kayla yesterday.'

'I sorta figured that. How is she?'

He tried to put into words how he'd felt yesterday, but as always, this kind of honesty was difficult. 'It was weird, Val. There she was, unconscious. I didn't know what to do. They said she'd responded to memories, and so I started talking about us.' He laughed. 'You know me, I can't remember yesterday, and there I was remembering the first time I kissed her. I felt . . . something.'

'So, what's the deal? You want to stay longer, is that it?'

Julian was vaguely disappointed. He wished they could talk, just this once, about something that mattered. 'She really loved me, Val. I guess that's what I remembered most. How it felt to be loved.'

'Every woman you meet adores you.'

'That's not the same thing, is it?' he asked softly.

Val was quiet, and Julian wondered if his agent had really listened this time. 'No, I guess it's not. So, what are you going to do with all this rampant emotion?'

That wasn't something Julian had thought about. 'Well, nothing, I guess. She's married.'

'She's *what*?'

Julian jerked the phone away from his ear. Val's tone of voice was so high that dogs were probably barking all over town. 'You heard me. She's married. To the doctor who called me.'

Through the lines came the unmistakable sound of a cigarette firing up, then a whoosh of smoke exhaled into the receiver. 'Does he love her?'

'Yes. Her hospital room is a shrine to their life together. The nurse told me that he sits by her side for hours every day.'

'So he's the real deal, cape and all. A superhero who loves his wife enough to call *you*—her first husband—to help wake her up. The press'd have a field day.' Val fell quiet for a minute, an uncharacteristic display of thoughtfulness. 'You'd better be very careful here, Jules.'

Julian knew Val was right. Kayla was a part of his past. But when he'd touched her, he'd remembered their love, and the remembering had made him feel . . . lonely.

'Julian? You're coming back now, right? I mean, tomorrow you're scheduled for Leno—'

Julian hung up. Hollywood felt far away suddenly, a sepia-toned photograph next to the technicolour memories of his first love. He swung his legs over the side of the bed and stood up, making his unsteady way down the hallway to the bathroom.

He showered in the world's smallest white Fibreglass shower stall, then dressed in faded Levi's and a black T-shirt. He grabbed the coat he'd bought yesterday at that lightning rod of fashion, Zeke's Feed and Seed. Shrugging into it, he flipped up the collar and left his room hurrying downstairs. He pounded on his driver's door. 'Come on, let's go!'

Lizbet popped out of the kitchen and met him in the foyer. She looked like she'd been dipped in flour and was ready for the fryer. 'Goodbye, Mr True. Will we see you for lunch?'

'I don't know. Bye, Lizbet.' He opened the front door and saw a dozen teenage girls standing beyond the white picket fence. The second he appeared, they screamed his name.

He grinned lazily. 'Well, hello, ladies. Good to see y'all.'

They crammed together, a centipede in cheerleader outfits and bare legs, giggling.

He bounded down the steps. 'What have we here? The Last Bend welcomin' committee? Such pretty gals, too. I'm honoured.'

'Will you sign my autograph book, Mr True?' asked one of the girls. Her saucer-round cheeks were bright red.

'It'd be my great pleasure.' He pulled a pen out of his pocket and started signing autographs.

'Tonight's the winter prom, Mr True. I don't suppose you'd like to stop by?' one of the girls asked, dissolving into a fit of laughter before she finished the sentence.

He planted a hand against his heart. God, he loved this. 'Why, I'll bet a girl as pretty as you already has a date.'

'Yeah, Serena,' someone yelled. 'You've already got a date. How about going with me, Mr True?'

He was about to answer the silly question when he saw her, off in the back of the group, smiling but not giggling, not asking for his autograph.

His jaded heart skipped a beat. Maybe two.

She was beautiful—Hollywood beautiful—this tall, thin, black-haired girl with eyes as soft as melted bittersweet chocolate. Midnight-black hair fell like a waterfall of ink down her back. It had to be her.

He pushed through the crowd and sidled up to the dark-haired girl. His heart was beating hard. 'And who are you, darlin'?'

'I'm Jacey.'

Juliana Celeste. J.C.

His daughter. He was too stunned to speak. For the first time, she was real; not a faded image of a baby in a crib, but a young girl who'd grown up without him.

'Mr True?' She blushed prettily. 'W-What are you doing in Last Bend?'

'I'm . . . uh . . . here . . . for the Make-A-Wish Foundation, visitin' sick folks at the hospital.'

'My mom is sick. She's in a coma. Maybe you could visit her.'

'I'd be happy to. Why, I'll do it right now.'

'I'm here, Mr True!' The driver's voice lifted above the giggling.

The girls instantly drew back, showing a respect he hadn't seen in Hollywood in a long time. All except Jacey. She stood there, staring up at him through eyes that were suddenly sad.

He looked down at her, trying to memorise her face for a moment longer; then he went to the limo. He refused to look back, but when he was in the car, he finally turned, gazing at her through the smoked glass.

A new and alien emotion unfolded in Julian's chest, making it difficult to breathe.

Shame.

Night fell like sudden blindness, obliterating the last pink rays of the setting sun. Liam turned away from the window and stared at his daughter.

Jacey stood in front of a full-length mirror, staring at her reflection. Her hair had been swept back from her face and coiled into a thick black mass, accented with four glittering pink crystal butterflies. The sleek lavender gown fitted her perfectly.

She looked so grown up. He couldn't help feeling a brush of sadness, as if he'd already lost his little girl. Tears glazed her dark eyes, and he knew she was thinking of her mother.

'She would be so proud of you,' he said. 'You look beautiful.'

'Thanks, Dad.' She took his hand, squeezed it.

Holding hands, they went downstairs. A few minutes later, Rosa ushered Mark into the living room. He was wearing a navy-blue tuxedo with a ruffled white shirt and a lavender bow tie.

'Oh, Jacey,' Mark said, moving towards her, 'you look great.'

She smiled. 'Thanks, Mark.'

Upstairs, Bret poked his head over the railing and started singing at the top of his lungs, 'Here comes the bride, all fat and wide—'

'Bret!' Liam yelled, biting back a laugh. 'Stop it.'

Bret scampered down the stairs, skidding into place beside his sister. She elbowed him in the shoulder. 'Thanks a lot, Rugrat.'

Bret looked up at her. Rosa had scrubbed his little face to a polished shine. 'Really, you look pretty.'

'Thanks, kiddo.'

Liam said, 'OK, folks, photo op,' and then he snapped enough pictures for a *Town and Country* layout. He knew he was prolonging the moment—as if Mikaela would magically walk through that door if he could just extend this scene a little longer.

'Enough, Dad,' Jacey said, laughing. She disentangled herself from Mark's arm and went to Liam.

'I know,' she said softly, 'she'll want to see all the pictures. Every angle, every pose. That's why I'm bringing my camera in my bag. I'll take pictures of everything.'

He pulled her into his arms and held her close. Then he drew back and smiled down at her. 'Now go and have a good time.'

Jacey kissed Rosa and Bret goodbye, then hurried out of the door.

Liam stood at the window, watching them drive away. *There she goes, Mike.* In ordinary times, he would have turned to his wife now and taken her in his arms. She would have been crying.

Only right now he was the one who felt like crying. And there was no one there to hold him. With a sigh, he went into the living room and turned on the television.

Julian knew it was the wrong thing to do. Dangerous, even, but he couldn't help himself. In truth he didn't even try. Self-control had never been his strong suit. He couldn't have said exactly why he wanted to go to the prom, but he'd never been one to get caught up in reasons. He wanted to go. That's all that mattered.

In his overdecorated bedroom, he dressed carefully, as if he were headed to the Oscars, instead of some backwoods high-school dance. A black silk T-shirt and black pleated Armani trousers. Instead of bothering his driver, he walked the three blocks to Angel Falls High School. When he got there, his cheeks were numb from the cold and he desperately needed a smoke.

At the auditorium, he paused, took a deep breath, and opened the double doors. The gym had been turned into a cheesy tropical paradise. False palm trees clustered around a patch of gold shag carpeting; beside it, a dozen tuxedoed boys and ball-gowned girls formed a line for pictures. Against the far wall, a band played some hard-edged song that was almost familiar.

He knew the moment he'd been recognised. Dancing stopped. The kids eased away from him, forming a whispering, pointing funnel towards the dance floor.

He looked around, smiling his big, overpractised smile until he saw her. She was on the dance floor with her date. Even from this distance Julian could see that they were staring at him.

He moved through the crowd in the way he'd learned long ago; head up, smile planted, making eye contact with no one.

The song ended, and another began. The love theme from *Titanic*, the movie.

He stopped beside Juliana—J.C., he reminded himself—and held out his hand. 'May I have this dance?'

The crowd gasped. Her date—a big, good-looking kid in a ridiculously cheap tux—looked confused.

Jacey turned to the boy. 'Do you mind?'

'Uh . . . no.'

Julian swept her into his arms and began dancing. The crowd closed in on them, talking so loudly it was hard to hear the music.

'Why me?' she whispered.

He smiled. 'Why not? So, J.C. of the midnight hair, tell me about yourself. Do you get good grades? Have lots of friends? Practise safe sex?'

She laughed, a throaty bar-room sound that was exactly like Kayla's. 'You sound like my dad—not that he'd ask about my sex life.'

Something about the way she said it—*dad*—while she was smiling up at him . . . well, it pinched his heart.

It seemed odd, but he'd never thought about that word until today. *Dad*. Such a solid, dependable, grown-up word. Even now, with his daughter in his arms, Julian couldn't really imagine being someone's dad.

'Mr True? Did you hear me?'

He laughed easily. 'Sorry, I was thinking about something. So, what do kids in this town do for fun?'

She shrugged. 'The usual stuff. Skiing, ice-skating, bowling, horseback riding. In the summer we hang out at Angel Lake. There's a cool rope swing off a big madrona tree at Currigan Point.'

It sure as hell wasn't 'the usual' in Los Angeles, not for a celebrity's kid, anyway. If J.C. had grown up with Julian, she'd have spent her life behind iron gates and sheltered by bodyguards.

For the first time, he understood what Kayla had asked of him all those years ago. She'd used words like *rehab* and *safety*, but what she'd wanted was a normal life for their daughter.

Just that. A normal life.

It was something Julian had never wanted. But now, as he held this daughter who was and wasn't his, he wondered about the price he'd paid for his fame.

It struck him hard, left him breathless, the sudden realisation of how deeply he'd failed his daughter. He wasn't J.C.'s father. She had a man at home who'd loved her, who knew if she'd worn braces or snored in her sleep, who'd been there to pick her up when she fell down.

Even though he was smart enough to know the truth—that he wasn't this girl's father and never would be—he couldn't help wishing, dreaming, that things could be different.

The song came to an end. Sadly he leaned down and kissed her cheek. Then he did what he did best: he walked away.

Liam was in the living room, nursing a watered-down Scotch, when he heard the car drive up.

Immediately he tensed. He'd been sitting here for hours, thinking about the decision he and Julian had made. The more he considered it, the more he saw how reckless and dangerous it was to withhold the truth in a town as small as this. Gossip moved like bees from one backyard flower to the next, over picket fences and through telephone lines.

The bottom line was this: Liam hated deceiving Jacey. He couldn't quite believe that deceit was ever really in a person's best interest. Now, every time he looked at her, he felt the heavy, ugly curtain of this lie between them.

The front door swung open and she breezed into the room. Her cheeks were a deep rosy pink, and her espresso-dark eyes were shining.

He knew then that he couldn't tell her now, not on this night that should hold only magical memories.

'Hi, Dad,' she said dreamily.

'How was it?'

She swept over to the couch and dipped down like a hummingbird, planting a feather-light kiss on his cheek. 'Totally awesome. Perfect. I took *tons* of pictures for Mom.' She stifled a yawn.

'She'll want to see every one.'

Smiling, she spun round and floated towards the stairs. He followed along behind her, turning off lights as he went.

At her bedroom door, she stopped and grinned at him. 'Guess what happened.'

He brushed a lock of hair from her eyes. 'What?'

'Julian True showed up at the prom. He asked me to dance. *Me*. He called me Jacey of the midnight hair. I'll remember this night for ever.'

Liam's hand froze against her cheek. 'But—'

'Good night, Dad.' She kissed his cheek and went into her room, closing the door.

He stood there a long, long time. Then slowly he knocked on her door. When she answered, he tried to find a smile. 'I just got an emergency call—don't worry, it's not about Mom—but I have to run to the hospital. I'll be right back.'

She smiled dreamily; he could tell that she was barely listening. 'OK. Drive safely.'

He nodded and closed the door. Anger seeped through him, rising steadily. He raced down to the garage and jumped into his car.

He found Julian on the front steps of the bed and breakfast, smoking a cigarette.

Liam skidded to a stop and jumped out of the car. He took a deep, stinging breath of icy air. 'What in the hell were you thinking?'

Julian looked up. The cold was cruel to his face, leeched the colour from his cheeks. 'I had to see her.'

Liam lost his hold on anger. There was a wealth of sadness in Julian's eyes, a look of pure defeat. *Of course* he'd had to see her.

'She's beautiful, Liam. The spitting image of Kayla. And when I looked at her, I couldn't see anything of me.'

Liam didn't know what to say. He could tell that Julian had never really considered his daughter before, what it meant to have fathered a child. A young girl.

Julian took a last drag on his cigarette, then stabbed it out in a cushion of new snow. It hissed and sent up a thread of smoke. 'I didn't tell her. I can't imagine I ever could.'

Liam took a step forward. 'Why not?'

'How could I make a man like you understand?' He sighed; a cloud of breath puddled in front of his face. 'I break everything I touch.' He tried to smile. 'I think I've only just realised that. I don't want to hurt J.C.'

Liam felt as if he'd finally glimpsed something real in Julian, and he couldn't help pitying the younger man.

Julian got slowly to his feet. 'Don't tell her, Liam. Please, don't . . .'

Later Liam would wonder what had got to him—the sad regret in Julian's eyes or his own fear of wounding Jacey's tender heart. Whatever it was, he found himself saying, 'OK, Julian.'

CHAPTER 7

The WATER IS NOW *a beautiful aqua blue. She is at the bottom of a swimming pool, staring up. Her limbs feel heavy; the water resists her movements, but she has learned that if she really concentrates, focuses all of her will, she can lift her fingers and wiggle her toes. She knows that at some time, long ago, this would have been next to nothing, something the tiniest newborn can do, but to her, in this pool of endless clear blue water, it is everything.*

She is floating up through the water, rising, rising, her body weightless. The water moves easily aside for her and buoys her.

As she reaches the surface, the water slides away from her face. She gasps, breathing in the sweet, pine-scented air; then she is reaching for the shadow in front of her.

She opens her eyes and immediately cries out. The light is so bright, she cannot stand the brightness.

'She opened her eyes. Oh my God, Mike. We're here.'

She takes a deep, calming breath and opens her eyes again. The shadows spin in front of her, waving like mirages on a desert highway; then, slowly, slowly, they begin to take shape. There are three people around her—men.

Julian. She sees him, sees those beloved blue eyes staring down at her. She reaches out for him, meaning to touch his face in the gentlest caress, but her control is shot, and she slaps him hard across the cheek. She means to laugh at the surprise on his face, but instead she bursts into tears.

She tries to talk. It hurts, burns. Still, she pushes a sound up her cracked, broken throat, and when the word comes out, mangled and unfamiliar, she weeps even harder. 'Ju . . . li . . . an.'

'I'm here, baby,' he says in the voice she remembers so well, the voice that seems connected to the tender cords in her heart. 'Kayla, baby, are you there? Squeeze my hand.'

It seemed to take her hours to focus, but when she did, she saw him staring down at her, and she felt a rush of joy. 'You came back.'

Another man leaned towards her. On the front of his white coat, it read DR LIAM CAMPBELL. 'Hi, Mike.'

She frowned and tried to turn her head to look for Mike. It tired her and she gave up. She tried to remember how she got here, but there was nothing. She remembered every moment of her life up to when she said goodbye to Julian. After that, there was a complete and utter blankness. It terrified her. 'I . . . don't . . . where . . .'

'You're in the hospital,' someone says.

'Juliana,' she croaked. 'Where's my baby?'

'Baby?' Julian turned to the other man. 'What's going on?'

Something was wrong. She'd been hurt, she realised suddenly. Hurt. And they wouldn't answer her question about Juliana. Oh God . . .

The other man touched her face, and there was a gentleness in him that calmed her. She blinked up at his watery, out-of-focus face. 'Don't cry, Mike. Your daughter is fine.'

She trusted him. *Juliana's OK.* 'Who . . .'

'Don't rush it, sweetheart. Take it slowly.'

'Who . . . are you?' she asked at last.

Before he answered, she lost interest. Her head felt so heavy, so . . . broken. She sank back into the cool, blue water, back to the place where she was unafraid.

'Retrograde amnesia.'

Liam and Julian were seated in front of Stephen Penn's massive oak desk. The neurologist looked worn and tired.

Liam leaned forward. 'In post-traumatic—'

'Goddamn it, wait a sec.' Julian shot to his feet. He prowled the small office like a caged lion, repeatedly running his hand through his hair. 'I haven't had twenty years of college and I don't know what you two are talking about. What in the hell is retrograde amnesia?'

Stephen removed the small, circular spectacles from his face. 'At the moment of serious trauma, the brain stops accumulating memories. That's why a victim of serious brain injury rarely remembers the actual incident itself. More often than not, the last clear memory is one that happened days or weeks . . . or even years before. These are often powerful, significant memories—weddings, births, that sort of thing. It appears that Mikaela's mind is . . . trapped, some years ago. She seems to believe that Jacey is still a baby.' He paused. 'Clearly, she doesn't remember her life with Liam at all.'

'How long do you think the amnesia will last?' Liam asked, even though he knew the answer.

'There is no way of knowing,' Stephen said slowly. 'Although, chances are that she *will* remember. Long-term retrograde amnesia is rare.' His voice softened. 'But it does happen.'

'How can we help her?' Liam asked quietly.

'Right now she's afraid and confused. We want to tread very carefully. The mind is a fragile thing. We don't want to overwhelm her with frightening information. I think it's best if we let it come back naturally.'

Liam sighed. 'You're saying that the kids and I should stay away.'

'I'm sorry, Liam. I can only imagine how hard this is for you. But I think she needs some time to let her mind heal.'

Liam hung his head, staring down at the Oriental carpet so long that the colours smeared into one big bruise.

What was he going to tell his children?

Julian went to a payphone and called his agent. 'She woke up today,' he said when Val answered.

'No shit. How is she?'

'She's got amnesia. She doesn't remember anything of the last fifteen years. She thinks we're still married.'

'Are you saying—'

'She's still in love with me, Val. With none of the bad memories of our breakup.'

Val made a low, whistling sound. 'Jesus Christ, what did you do— script this? It's a fairy tale, and you're the prince. The press'll *love* it.'

Julian sagged against the wall. 'You don't get it. How am I going to tell her that I never came back for her, Val? . . . Val?'

His answer was a dial tone.

With a curse, Julian hung up the phone. For the first time since he'd got here, he was afraid.

As he drove home, Liam told himself it would be OK. He knew that retrograde amnesia was a common short-term side effect of brain injury.

Short-term. Those words were the ledge he tried to hold on to, but they kept crumbling beneath the weight of his fear.

What if she never remembered him or the kids?

He concentrated on breathing; it didn't seem like much, but if he didn't think about it, he stumbled into a place where panic was inches from his face.

Who are you?

Would he ever be able to forget those words? Forget the pain that knifed through him in that single horrifying moment when she'd said Julian's name . . . and then asked Liam who he was?

The snow was coming down fast. He didn't see his own driveway until he was practically on top of it. He put the car in four-wheel drive and lowered his speed, manoeuvring carefully into his garage.

At the garage door, he paused, taking a moment to collect himself; then he pushed into the house. 'Hello,' he called out. 'I'm home.'

He heard the scurrying sound of slippered feet on the hardwood floor. Rosa appeared, wearing one of Mike's old aprons over a black housedress. '*Buenas noches*,' she said.

'Where are the kids?'

She must have sensed something in his tone. She froze, her gaze stuck fast to his. 'Jacey will be home any *momento*. Bret is upstairs in the shower. Would you like—'

'Mike woke up today.'

She gasped. Her hand flew to her mouth. '*Dios mío*, it is a miracle. How is she?'

'She didn't recognise me, Rosa.' He could hear the terrible ache at the edge of his voice. 'Julian . . . She recognised Julian.'

Rosa's hand fell slowly to her side, where her fingers curled into a tight fist. 'What does this mean?'

'I could give you a bunch of technical explanations, but the bottom line is that her memory has failed. She seems to think she's twenty-three and still married to Julian. She thinks Jacey is still a baby.'

Rosa was staring at him with a familiar look. It was the look of a patient who'd just received devastating news. 'So she does not remember you or Bret?'

'No. We *hope* it's temporary.' He put the tiniest emphasis on the word *hope*. 'Usually people get their memories back.'

Rosa closed her eyes and let her head drop forward. 'This pain for you . . . I can barely imagine it.'

His throat felt tight. 'Yes.'

Finally she looked up, and her brown eyes—so like Mike's—were glazed with tears. 'What will you tell the children?'

Liam sighed. 'I can hardly think of it, Rosa.'

'*Sí*. They have been praying for this for so long. It will break their hearts to learn that she does not remember them.'

'I know. But it's a small town. Not a place where secrets keep.'

Secrets. Like a famous father a girl knew nothing about.

Rosa took a step towards him. 'Do not tell them yet. At least for this night. Give Mikita until tomorrow. Maybe then we will never have to tell the *niños* this terrible thing, *sí*?' She gazed at him. 'What did she say, my Mikita, when you told her about your marriage?'

He was caught off guard. 'We didn't tell her. Stephen thinks the truth might frighten her.'

Rosa seemed to think about that for a minute; then she shook her head. 'You men—you doctors—you do what you think is best. But I am her *mamá*, no? I have always taken care of my Mikaela. I will not stop now. I will need the *fotografías* you found.'

Liam tried to imagine what it must be like to have a mother like this. What a power it must grant a person in life to have a place where you could always land softly, even after the hardest hit. 'Rosa,' he said quietly, touching her hand. 'I don't know how I would have made it through this without you.'

Rosa took hold of his hands and held them tightly. 'You are stronger than you think you are, Liam. Now you are thinking that Mikaela does not need you, that she has forgotten you because she does not love you, but you are wrong. Her eyes may be open, but *mi hija* is still asleep. Give her time.'

She woke easily this time. No floating at the bottom of a swimming pool. She just opened her eyes. Strangers surrounded her bed. Some she'd seen before, some she hadn't. They were talking to her and to one another.

One by one, their faces came into focus, and the questions they were asking began to make sense. Dr Penn—the nice-looking man with the grey hair and white coat—smiled at her.

'Good morning, Mikaela. Do you remember me?'

'Penn,' she answered, her voice as cracked as old porcelain and nearly as fragile. Her throat still hurt. 'What . . . happened to me?'

'You fell off your horse and hit your head. You suffered quite a head injury. You've been in a coma.'

She wanted to ask questions, but she couldn't remember any of the words she needed.

'Don't worry, Mikaela. It'll all come back to you.' Stephen turned to the strangers. 'Let's go. She needs to rest.'

Wait. She tried to sit up. It was hard. Her right side felt weighted down, too weak to move easily. Her heart started beating too fast; her breathing broke into gasping bits. Before she could remember the right words to make them stay, they were gone.

The door to her room squeaked open and a new stranger appeared. She was a heavyset woman in a blue polyester trouser suit. Her fleshy face was creased into a bright smile. 'Good morning, Mikaela. How are we feeling today?'

She frowned. Her name was Kayla now. Everyone knew that. *Everyone.* So why did they all keep calling her Mikaela?

She tried to push a question past her disobedient tongue. The word she was searching for—*hello*—was bouncing around in her mind, but it disappeared before reaching her mouth.

'We removed the catheter last night. Do you remember? I thought you might like to try going to the bathroom by yourself.'

Mikaela gazed up at the woman. 'Who . . .? Where . . .?'

'I'm Sarah Fielding, honey,' she answered the unasked question. The nurse eased a plump arm behind Mikaela's head and gently tilted her upright. In spare, economical movements, she manoeuvred Mikaela to a sit, then helped her to a shaky stand. Mikaela clung to Sarah and tried to walk. She had to drag her right leg as they made their slow, shuffling way across the room.

'Do you think you can use the toilet by yourself, honey?'

Toilet. The word fluttered around for a second, then landed on the white porcelain seat beside her. *Toilet.* 'Yes,' she answered, gripping the counter unsteadily. She was shaking and breathing hard, but she could stand on her own.

'I'll be just outside if you need me.' Sarah backed away and half closed the door behind her.

Mikaela sank onto the cold seat. It burned when she urinated, so badly that she had to clamp a hand over her mouth to keep from crying out. When she was finished, she leaned forward and grabbed the counter again, dragging her reluctant body to an awkward stand.

Then she saw herself in the mirror. Her face was chalky pale. And her hair was short; it looked as if it had been cut with children's scissors.

But her hair was long—down to her waist. Julian wouldn't let her cut it.

Shaking, she leaned closer to the mirror, pressed her damp palms to the cold glass. There were tiny lines around her eyes and mouth, lines she'd never seen before. And there were grey hairs threaded through all that black.

She screamed.

The door burst open, and Sarah was there. 'What happened?'

Mikaela tottered around, her hands on her face. 'I'm . . . old. Oh God. What happened to me?'

'I'll get the doctor.'

Mikaela grabbed the woman's sleeve. 'I'm old . . . What happened?'

Sarah wrenched away. 'I'll be right back.' She ran from the room. The door slammed shut behind her.

Mikaela couldn't breathe; her knees felt weak. How long had she been lying in that bed? How long—

Dr Penn rushed into the room. A breathless, flushed Sarah waddled along behind him.

Mikaela looked at him and started to cry. 'How old am I?' In her mind, she screamed the question, but in truth it came out as a hacked-up whisper.

Dr Penn took her hand and held it. 'Calm down, Mike.'

'I'm *Kayla*.' This time she did scream. She clung to the doctor's hand, staring at him through a stinging veil of tears.

He touched her face so gently, as if he were a friend. 'Remember what I told you? You've been in a coma, Mike.'

Her mouth trembled. 'How long?'

'A little more than a month.'

The relief she felt at that was so stunning she laughed out loud. She meant to wipe her eyes, but she had no control. She smacked herself in the nose and laughed harder.

'It's OK,' Dr Penn said in a nice, even voice. 'Your emotions are off track right now, along with your motor skills. But there's no permanent damage. It'll all come back.'

She was still grinning as tears rolled down her cheeks and plopped onto her bare arm. She felt like an idiot, laughing and crying at the same time. 'How old . . . am I?'

He paused, glanced at Sarah, and then sighed as he looked back at Mikaela. 'You're thirty-nine.'

She couldn't breathe. Focusing on his grey eyes, she shook her head. 'No . . . no . . . I'm almost twenty-four. I got married two and a half years ago. Juliana just had her first birthday. I remember all this perfectly.'

'There are other things, other times, you can't remember yet. But it'll come back. Just give yourself a little time.'

It took all her strength of will to formulate one little sentence. 'I want to see my husband now.'

Dr Penn nodded. 'Just a minute.'

Mikaela climbed back into bed, where she felt safe. Julian would tell her the truth. He would tell her—

The door opened again. Only it wasn't Julian; it was another stranger. She shook her head. 'No more . . .'

Slowly he came up to the bed.

She frowned. She wanted to tell him to go away.

He touched her, grabbed her shoulders and pulled her gently towards him. She felt like a rag doll, sagging in his arms.

He stared at her and his eyes were so green. She'd never seen eyes that were so filled with comfort. It calmed her, the way he looked at her. 'For ever,' he whispered.

The word struck a chord deep, deep inside her. She felt her body go still, her heartbeat even out. The air in her lungs seemed to refill itself. The words—*for ever*—drifted through her, swirling, meaning something that she couldn't grasp; but it found no perch and fluttered away.

'Remember me,' he said, gently shaking her.

And all at once, she did. 'I do remember you,' she said quietly. 'You're the other doctor.'

He let go of her. It was so unexpected that she fell back into the mound of pillows. Those green eyes looked so sad.

'I'm sorry,' she whispered, though she had no idea what she'd done to wound this man. 'I just . . . want to see my husband.'

'OK,' he said softly. 'I'll go and get Julian.'

Liam walked into the room where Julian and Stephen Penn were waiting. He looked at Julian. 'She wants to see her husband.'

Julian turned to Dr Penn. 'What now? What am I supposed to tell her when she asks where I've been for fifteen years?'

'Tell her where you've been.' It was Liam's voice.

Julian spun to face him. 'Yeah, you'd like that.'

'*Like* that? I don't like you even being in the same room with her.' He moved towards Julian. 'If she asks you a direct question, I want you to answer truthfully. You can evade—but don't lie.'

'Maybe I shouldn't go and see her.' Julian's voice fell to a whisper that only Liam could hear. 'I'm afraid of hurting her.'

'That's the best news I've heard today.'

Julian waited, but Liam didn't say anything else. 'Well,' he said at last, 'I'll go and see her.'

He ducked out of the room and walked slowly down the hallway. Really slowly.

At her door, he paused. Forcing a bright smile, he opened the door. She was asleep.

He shut the door quietly and went to her bedside. She looked so peaceful, so beautiful.

Slowly she blinked awake. 'Jules? Is that you?'

He leaned over her. 'Heya, Kay.'

She worked herself up to a sit. 'Where's Juliana? I want to see my baby.'

'She'll be here soon. I promise.'

'I missed you,' she said with a smile, reaching for him in a jerky, uncontrolled movement. 'I knew you'd come back for us.'

He grabbed her hand and held it tightly. 'I missed you, too.' It surprised him, the truth of that simple statement. He *had* missed Kayla;

he'd missed the man he'd once been—the man he could have been with her at his side.

Her gaze focused on his face. 'You're older, too.'

He smiled uneasily.

'Julian, no one will tell me the truth. But I know you wouldn't lie to me. Please. I need to understand.'

'You have a few gaps in your memory, that's all. The docs say it'll all come back.' He leaned down and kissed her. She tasted just like he remembered, all sweet compliance and homecoming. When he kissed her, he felt complete.

'How could I forget fifteen years of loving you and Juliana? Tell me about us, Jules. Help me remember.'

'Ah, baby . . .' He would have done anything to erase the sorrow in her eyes. 'She's beautiful, Kay. The spitting image of you.'

She gazed up at him, her pale face as serious as he'd ever seen it. 'I remember when I left. Do you remember that, Jules?'

'I remember.'

'I remember packing my bags, buying a car—that green station wagon with the wood-grain side panels—and loading it up. I hardly took anything from our life together, not even your money. I was so sure you'd come for us quickly . . . I can remember waiting and waiting, but I can't remember ever seeing you again.'

He actually thought he might cry; that's how awful he felt. 'I'm sorry, baby. I'm so sorry.'

'How long, Jules?'

'H-How long what?'

'How long?'

He touched her soft, soft cheek. He was cornered; there was no way out of this except to lie—and that was pointless. 'Now,' he answered in a tired, broken voice. 'Just now.'

She frowned. 'Just now what? I'm thirty-nine years old. That means my—*our*—baby is sixteen. You don't mean . . .'

'Just now,' he repeated quietly.

Tears filled her eyes; her pain seemed to suck the air from the room. 'You mean you *never* came back for me? Never?'

He felt the sting of tears in his own eyes. 'I was young and stupid. I didn't know how special it was between us.'

'Never.' The single word slipped from her mouth, toneless and dead. 'No wonder I forgot.'

'Don't look at me like that.'

'Like what?'

'Like . . . I've broken your heart.'

She tried to wipe her eyes, but her effort was a failure. 'I guess you did that a long time ago—and, lucky me, I get to experience it twice. Oh, Jules.' She sagged into the pillows. 'I love you so much. But it's not enough, is it?' She closed her eyes. 'I wish I'd forgotten you.'

'Don't say that. Please . . .' He had hurt her again, as he'd known he would, and he regretted it more deeply than he would have thought possible. Suddenly he saw all the chances he'd lost. For the first time, he wanted the years back, wanted to have become the kind of man who knew how to love.

She rolled awkwardly onto her side. 'Go away.'

'Kayla, don't—'

'Go away, Julian. *Please.*'

If he'd had Liam's courage, he would have known what to say, but he was empty. He turned away and headed for the door.

'I want to see my daughter,' she said.

He nodded, saying nothing. Then he left.

She wanted to curl into a small, safe ball and close out the world again. *He never came back.*

She couldn't seem to grasp that. It broke her, pure and simple. For a long, long time she lay in her lonely bed, trying to wrap her arms round a truth that was too big to hold.

What had she been doing all these years? And what about her daughter? She remembered a pudgy, brown eyed toddler with a halo of jet-black curls. She remembered the feel of that baby in her arms, but after that, nothing. Fifteen blank years.

Without memories, there was no passage of time, no change, no growth. There was just this love for Julian, this runaway train of emotion that she could do nothing but ride.

He must have nearly killed her with his betrayal. She knew that because when she'd said the word *never*, she'd felt it in her heart and soul.

The door opened. 'Mikita, you are awake?'

'*Mamá!*'

Rosa stood in the doorway, smiling brightly. Mikaela gasped, brought a shaking hand to her mouth. Rosa's hair was snow-white now, her dark skin creased heavily round the eyes and mouth.

'Oh, *Mamá* . . .'

Rosa came up to her bedside. She touched Mikaela's cheek, said softly, 'A *milagro.*' Then she bent down and scooped Mikaela into a hug. 'I never think to see you smile again.' She drew back.

'What happened to me, *Mamá*?'

Rosa picked up a brush from the bedside table and began brushing Mikaela's short hair. 'You fell from a horse.'

'So they tell me. What in the hell was I doing on a horse?'

Rosa smiled. 'You remember the bad language, I am not happy to say. In the past years, you have become the good horse rider. It is something you love.'

Mikaela grabbed her mother's thin wrist. 'Tell me about Juliana.'

Rosa carefully set down the brush. Her bony fingers curled round the bed rail. 'We call her Jacey now, and she is everything you would wish for in a daughter.' She gazed down at Mikaela, her eyes glistening. 'She is beautiful and gifted and loving and *muy inteligente*. And popular—I have never heard the phone ring so much. Look around this room, Mikita, and tell me what you see.'

For the first time, Mikaela really looked. There were flowers and balloons everywhere; cards lined the tables and the windowsill. 'Are they all from Julian?'

Rosa made a sweeping gesture with her hand. 'Not from that one. They are from your friends. This is your home now, Mikaela. It is a wonderful place—not like Sunville at all. Every shop I go in, someone asks about you. The women, they bring food to the house every day. Here, *mi hija*, here you are much loved.'

Mikaela looked up at her mother through a stinging blur of tears. 'He never came for me, *Mamá*.'

'I know. This was hard on you before. Maybe it is even harder now. Then you remembered why you left him. Now I think maybe you forget.'

'I want to see my daughter.'

Rosa didn't answer for a moment. Then, softly, she said, 'It will wound her heart . . . this forgetfulness. Dr Liam wishes for you to have another day to remember, *sí*? You do not want to hurt her.'

Mikaela didn't know how she could survive the heartache seeping through her. 'I remember how it feels when a parent doesn't know you. I remember this from my father.'

'You have never called him this before.'

'I know.' She sighed tiredly. 'But calling him something else doesn't make him someone else, does it?'

'No.' Rosa reached into her pocket, pulling out a photograph. 'Here.'

Mikaela stared down at the picture—it was of Mikaela and Rosa and a beautiful young girl. They were standing in an unfamiliar room, beside a gorgeous, wonderfully decorated Christmas tree.

Mikaela's hungry gaze took in every detail about the girl—the brown eyes, the easy smile, the waist-length black hair. 'This is my Juliana—no, my *Jacey.*'

'*Sí.* The memories, they are in you, Mikaela. Place this *fotografía* next to your heart and sleep well. Your heart will remember what your mind forgets.'

Mikaela stared down into the eyes so like her own. Try as she might, she couldn't remember holding this little girl, or stroking her hair, or kissing her cheek. 'Oh, *Mamá,*' she whispered, and at last she cried.

Not long after lunch, Mikaela fell asleep.

She knew she was dreaming now. It was the first dream she'd had since waking, and there was a comforting familiarity in the sensation.

She was walking along a deserted gravel road. She came round a bend and saw a beautiful log house. A bank of grey clouds moved in suddenly, obliterating the sunshine, casting the house in shadow.

The front door opened for her.

She walked across the porch, into the house, and felt her way down the smooth wooden wall towards a staircase she somehow knew was there. At the bottom, she paused, listening. Somewhere in this cold, dark house a child was crying.

'*I'm coming.*' The words played across Mikaela's mind. She was moving again, running this time.

The cries became louder, more insistent. Mikaela had a fleeting, heartbreaking image of a little boy sucking his thumb. He was tucked back in a corner, waiting for his mommy to come for him.

But there were a hundred doors in front of her, and the hallway stretched for miles, fading out of focus at its end. She ran down the corridor, yanking open doors. Behind those doors lay nothing, yawning black rectangles spangled with starlight, breathing a cold winter wind.

All at once, the crying stopped. She was too late . . too late . . .

She woke with a start. The ceiling above her was made of white tiles, their pattern sharp and bright after the hazy quality of her dream.

The hospital.

There was a man standing by her window, wearing a white coat. He turned towards her, and she saw that it wasn't Dr Penn. It was the other one—what was his name? He was a tall man, with longish blond hair and a nice face. 'You need a haircut.' The words just popped out of her mouth, and she winced. What on earth had made her say that?

He ran a hand through his shaggy hair and smiled, but it was a sad smile. 'Yeah, I suppose I do. My wife cuts my hair.'

When he spoke, it sent a shiver through her. She frowned, studying him, trying to remember. Then it came to her. 'You're the voice,' she said softly. 'When I was asleep, I heard you.'

He smiled again. 'I didn't know if you'd be able to. It seemed like I talked for ever.'

For ever. Those words, they teased her, tickled some forgotten chord. 'Who are you?' she asked.

He studied her for a minute. 'Dr Liam Campbell.'

Somehow she knew that wasn't right. She knew without knowing that this was the man who'd played the endless stream of her favourite songs. He was the one who'd given her something to hang on to in all that darkness.

'No,' she said. 'Who are you? Who are you to me?'

Slowly he reached for her left hand. He caressed her fingers, so tenderly that her breath caught in her throat. 'This ring,' he said quietly. 'I put it on your finger ten years ago.'

She stared down at the ring. A wedding ring. 'You're . . .' She couldn't seem to form the word.

'I'm your husband.'

It was incomprehensible. 'But . . . Julian . . .'

'Julian was your first husband.'

She panicked. First a child, now a husband. How much had she forgotten? How much more was out there? She stared at him, shaking her head in denial. She wanted to say, 'It can't be,' but in the last few days she knew that anything could be. 'How could I forget such a thing? How could I have . . . no feeling for you at all?'

He flinched, and in that tiny expression of pain she knew it was true. 'Don't worry,' he said. 'It's OK not to remember.'

'I—I don't know what to say to you . . . Liam.' She tried out the name on her tongue, but nothing came with it. It was just a collection of vowels and consonants that had no meaning. She tried to smile at him, but it was a trembling failure. 'Tell me about our life together.' These were the words that slipped from her lips, but what she meant was, 'Make me love you again.'

He smiled. 'You were a nurse then. I first met you when you cared for my father.'

Over the bed rail their gazes met and held. She felt awkward suddenly, confused by this man who was both a stranger and her husband.

Husband.

'Kinda weird, huh?' he said with a crooked, nervous grin.

She smiled in return and leaned towards him, studying his face, searching for *something*, some vagrant memory. But there was nothing.

250

Still, he had the kindest eyes she'd ever seen. 'This must be hard on you,' she said softly.

'The coma was harder.'

Somehow she didn't think so. 'Did you call Julian?'

'Yes.'

'If you and I are married now, why would you do that?'

'I couldn't . . . wake you up. I sat here every day, holding your hand, talking to you, playing your favourite music. I did everything I could think of to reach you, but . . . day after day, you just lay there.' His voice fell to a throaty whisper. 'I knew I was losing you.'

'Why Julian?'

He let out a long, sighing breath. 'Because, Mikaela, I knew.'

She felt her heart skip a beat. 'Knew what?'

'That you never completely stopped loving him.'

For a heartbeat, she forgot to breathe. 'You loved me very much.' She could never remember feeling this way before, this awesome mixture of joy and sadness, this feeling of being loved deeply and completely. Julian's love wasn't like that. It was a blast of red-hot fireworks that exploded in technicolour around you, but left a cold, black sky behind.

'I still do,' he said, smiling down at her with a sadness that wrenched her heart.

'I must have loved you, too.'

He paused a moment too long before answering. 'Yes.'

And she knew. 'I stayed in love with Julian, didn't I? I hurt you,' she said softly, sadly. 'I'm sorry.'

There was more to say, and no way she could think of to say it all. How could you apologise for what you couldn't remember? Or, worse, for what you were afraid you were going to do all over again?

CHAPTER 8

IT BEGAN SIMPLY ENOUGH, with the whooshing sound of the electronic doors opening. Julian sat in the lobby, staring at the wall clock. The slim black hands seemed to be stuck at two forty-five. Liam was in with Kayla now, and he'd asked Julian to wait for him.

'Hey, Juli.'

Julian looked up and saw Val sauntering towards him. Instead of his usual faded jeans and movie T-shirt, his agent was wearing a black Hilfiger suit with a dyed-to-match silk shirt and tie. He hadn't bothered to remove the Ray Bans that shielded his eyes.

Julian would have smiled if he hadn't felt so bad. 'This is Last Bend, you idiot, not Cannes. The only designer they know around here is L. L. Bean.' He got to his feet and turned.

That's when he saw them. Outside, beyond the wall of windows that flanked the front doors, the vans and rental cars were already lining up. People in rumpled black clothes streamed out of those cars like locusts.

'He'd seen it enough times to know the sequence by heart. The media circus coming to town. 'Jesus, Val. What did you do?'

Val lifted his hands. 'You're white-hot, Juli. A few words whispered in a few ears and the story spread like wildfire.'

'Damn it, Val, I *told* you not to—' Julian stopped. It was too late. They'd seen him.

Reporters swarmed through the doorway, cameras stationed on their shoulders. Within seconds, Julian and Val were engulfed.

Julian had to get them out of here. He pushed through the crowd and headed out, into the freezing cold. The locusts followed, firing questions.

'Julian, is it true? Have you found your Cinderella?'

'How badly is she hurt?'

'Is she still beautiful?'

Julian held up his hands, forcing his trademark smile. 'I'm here for the Make-A-Wish Foundation, that's all.'

Val thumped him on the back—hard. 'He's too shy to tell you the truth. You all know that Juli's first wife, Kayla, was the love of his life. Unfortunately, they were too young . . .' He paused and glanced around.

Val had them—hook, line and sinker. Julian could see it in the reporters' feverish eyes, hear it in the sudden indrawn silence.

Julian's best intentions cracked under the strain. God help him, he couldn't let Val hog the spotlight. 'You can imagine how I felt when I heard that she'd had an accident,' Julian said. 'I was told that Kayla had suffered a serious head injury—'

'Is she brain-damaged?' someone shouted out.

Val took the reins of the story again. 'She was in a coma for a month. It looked hopeless. Then the doctors discovered that Kayla responded to only one thing—the sound of Julian's name.'

A gasp rippled through the crowd; they recognised the taste and feel of it. The story that had just been handed to them.

'Naturally, Julian raced up here,' Val said. 'He sat with her, day after day, talking to her, holding her hand.' He gave them a brilliant, here-comes-the-good-part smile. 'Yesterday she woke up. Julian was the first person she saw.'

One of the reporters spoke. 'Is she still in love with you, Julian?'

Instead of answering, Julian sighed. He looked round at the faces. These reporters were a reflection of his life. Funny, but he'd never realised that before. He had no life except that which was filmed. He'd traded everything real for the split second brightness of a camera's flash

Val grinned. 'You've got your headline, kids. "The Kiss of True Love wakes up Sleeping Beauty".'

As Liam walked out of Stephen's office, he heard his name paged over the hospital's system. He grabbed the nearest phone and punched in his code. The message was from Rosa. She was waiting for him in the lobby. It was an emergency.

He saw Rosa before she saw him. Even from a distance, he could see the way her mouth was drawn into an angry line.

Something was wrong.

Up close, he could see the worry lines etched round her eyes and mouth. 'Rosa?'

'You see what he has done?' She cocked her head towards the hospital's front doors, where a crowd was gathered round Julian. 'It is the big story, Dr Liam. They are saying on the radio that Julian brought his true love out of a coma.'

'Damn it.' Liam headed for the doors.

Reporters circled Julian, angled towards him like supplicants, microphones instead of prayer books in their outstretched hands.

'When will we get to interview Kayla?'

'When will we get a shot of the two of you?'

'Are you two going to get married again?'

Liam grabbed Julian by the arm and spun him round. He said in a quiet voice, 'I need to speak to you. Now.'

Julian had the grace to look embarrassed. 'Sure thing, Doc.' He threw the crowd a false smile. 'This here is Liam Campbell. He's Kayla's . . . doctor.'

The crowd had a dozen simultaneous questions. Liam ignored them. Hanging on to Julian's arm, he dragged him into the lobby, past Rosa, and into an empty examining room.

An instant later, the door opened and Rosa walked in.

'Hi, Rosa,' Julian said, then turned to Liam. 'I'm so sorry, Liam. I told my agent to keep the press away, but he ignored me. Really, I'm sorry. And believe me, they're like termites—once they infest your house, you have to deal with them. If I didn't talk to them, God knows what story they'd come up with.'

Liam looked at him. 'You've spoonfed them a romance, haven't you? With you as the hero of the piece, the white knight who pulled her back from the brink of death.'

'You have not heard the worst of it, Dr Liam,' Rosa said, shuffling towards the two men. 'When I was walking into the hospital, the reporters were asking about his daughter.'

Liam grabbed Julian by the shoulders. 'Tell me you protected her. Tell me you didn't say a word about your daughter.'

Julian winced. 'I protected her—honestly—but Val . . . He told them that she was a cheerleader at the high school.'

For the first time in his life, Liam punched a man. He drew back his fist and slammed it into Julian's pretty-boy jaw. Pain radiated up his arm.

He turned to his mother-in-law. 'You stay here with Mike. Keep the press away from her. I'll get the kids and be back as soon as I can. We'll come in through the back way.'

Please, let me get to her in time.

Liam glanced at the clock on the Explorer's dashboard: 3:05. Cheerleader practice ended five minutes ago. He pressed harder on the gas. At the entrance to the high school, the car hurtled down the driveway and into the parking lot.

He was too late. Already there was a crowd of reporters outside the school's front doors. Liam lurched out of the car and ran towards them. His heart was hammering.

'Jacey!' His voice was lost in the din.

Reporters circled the group of cheerleaders, making it impossible for Liam to get through. They were shouting out questions.

'Which one of you is Juliana?'

He heard Mrs Kurek, the cheerleader adviser, answer, 'There's no Juliana here. Now go away.'

Liam screamed his daughter's name, trying to push through the sardine-packed bodies. It was impossible.

'Which one of you has a mother in a coma?'

He knew that all it would take was a look at Jacey.

'There she is!'

The mob shifted, separated, and came back together round Jacey, cutting her off from everyone else with practised ease.

'Are you Kayla's daughter?'

'Are you Juliana?'

He could see that Jacey was afraid. 'I'm Jacey,' she answered softly. 'My mom's in a coma.'

A microphone flew at her face, almost hit her in the nose. 'How does it feel to be his daughter?'

Liam grabbed hold of the cameraman in front of him and shoved. The man stumbled sideways.

Liam surged through the opening. 'Jace, come here!'

Above the crowd, their gazes met. Liam saw the fear in his daughter's eyes. He tried to plough through the crush of bodies.

'How does it feel to be Julian True's daughter?' someone yelled out.

A hush fell. Jacey looked at Liam, her mouth open, her eyes widening in shock.

'My God, she doesn't know.'

'Move in, Bert. Get a shot of her face—*now!*'

'GET AWAY FROM HER!' Liam screamed the words. He threw himself forward, ramming people aside with his elbows.

At last he was at her side. He slipped an arm round Jacey and pulled her close. He could feel her trembling.

'She has no comment.' Liam heard the snarl in his voice; it came from a dark place deep inside him. He dragged a dazed Jacey through the crowd and helped her into the Explorer. The reporters followed them, still shouting questions.

Liam started the engine and hit the gas. The car surged forward on the slushy snow and spun out of the parking lot.

His heart was hammering, and there was a coppery fear taste in his mouth. He'd never felt so ashamed and defeated in his life. He had failed to protect her. The daughter he loved more than his own life had been hurt.

Jacey twisted round in her seat, watching the road behind them. 'They're not following us,' she said in a watered-down version of her ordinary voice.

Liam veered left onto the snowy forest service road that led to Angel Falls State Park. He chose this road because it appeared only on the most detailed maps of the area. No one would follow them here.

When they reached the end of the road, the empty parking lot was as pristine as a new sheet of paper. In the late afternoon it was dark in these deep woods. Liam parked near the information board, which told the story of these falls—discovered and named by Ian Campbell in honour of his beloved wife.

Liam took a deep breath and turned at last to his daughter. 'I couldn't get to you fast enough.'

She looked at him, her dark eyes confused. 'Is it true, Dad?'

'It's true. Your mom was married to Julian True.'

The colour faded from her cheeks. 'He's my father?'

Father. The word hit him like a blow to the larynx. 'Yes.'

He waited for her to say more, but she remained silent.

'I should have told you—'

'Is that why he's really in town? To see Mom?'

'Yes.'

'Did you know he was my father?'

He understood the question. She didn't want to believe that he had lied to her all these years. 'Mike told me that she'd been married too young, to a man who only wanted to party and have fun. I didn't know it was Julian. I found out the truth when I went looking for that dress you wore to the dance.'

'She wouldn't ever talk about my other dad. When I was little, she used to cry every time I asked about him, so I stopped asking. Jeez . . . Julian True.'

Liam tried not to be hurt by the tiny, hitching smile that tugged at her mouth. What teenager wouldn't be thrilled to find out that a famous movie star was her father?

'When was she going to tell me? When we colonise Mars?'

It had come faster than he'd expected, the anger. There was no way to excuse what Mike had done to her. 'I don't know when she was going to tell you,' he said at last.

He could see that she was close to crying. 'That's why he came to the prom—to dance with me—but he didn't say anything that mattered. How did he know Mom was hurt?'

'I called him. I . . . discovered that your mom responded to his name. I thought that if he talked to her, she might wake up, and it worked. She woke up yesterday.'

'Julian woke her up after all the hours you and I spent talking to her?'

Liam winced. 'Well—'

'Oh my God. What if . . .' This time she couldn't hold back the tears. She launched herself at Liam, landing in his arms as if she were a child again. She cried on his shoulder. 'I hate her right now, Dad.'

He touched her face. 'No. You're hurt and angry. But you could never hate your mom. She loves you, Jace.'

'What about you? She lied to you all these years, too.'

He sighed. 'Sometimes people lie to protect their loved ones. Maybe she thought . . . we couldn't handle the truth.'

Jacey sniffed, wiped her nose with the back of her hand. 'He didn't want me, did he? That's why he never called or wrote.'

Liam wanted to lie to her, but it was lies that had brought them to this sorry, painful place in their lives. 'I don't know Julian well enough to answer that,' he said. 'I'm sorry, Jace. For all of it.'

She gazed at him, tears sliding down her cheeks. 'I love you . . . Dad.'

He heard the tiny hesitation before she called him Dad. 'I love you, too, Jace. We're still a family,' he whispered. 'You remember that. Your mom loves you and Bret—Oh, my God. *Bret.*' He jerked back so hard his head hit the window.

'The reporters.' Jacey slid back into her seat and clamped the seat belt in place. 'It's three thirty. He's in music class.'

Bret was getting cranky. They'd been practising for the Christmas assembly for more than an hour, and he hated standing still. They were all in rows, all the fourth and fifth graders, standing side by side on three risers. The music teacher, Mrs Barnett, had organised them by height, which meant that the girls were next to the boys, and that was *always* a problem.

Mrs B. rapped her wooden pointer on the metal music stand. 'Come on, children. Let's try the last verse again.'

At the cue, Mr Adam started playing 'Silent Night'.

Bret couldn't remember a single word.

Katie elbowed him hard and said, 'Sing.'

He hit her back. 'Shut up.'

'Mrs Barnett,' she yelled. 'Bret Campbell isn't singing.'

Mr Adam's fingers stumbled on the keys. There was a confused jangle of notes, and then silence.

Slowly Mrs B. lowered her pointer. 'Now, Katherine, let's not pick on Bret. We all know that his mom just woke up and that it's been a hard time for the family.'

We all know that his mom just woke up.

Bret couldn't breathe. It couldn't be true. Dad would have told him if Mommy woke up. But Mrs B. said it . . .

Suddenly the door to the music room banged open and Jacey stood in the opening. Her face was all red and streaked, as if she'd been crying. 'Mrs Barnett,' she said, 'I need to take Bret home now.'

Mrs B. nodded. 'Go along, Bret.'

Bret went up to his sister. He felt very small all of a sudden, and his heart was beating so fast he felt dizzy. 'Is Mommy—'

'Come on, Bretster.' She dragged him out of the music room and down the hall. Outside, the Explorer was parked in the bus loading zone. Bret allowed himself to be loaded into the back seat like a bag of grain. Then Jacey jumped into the front seat and before Bret could even think of what to say, they were speeding through town.

Dad was driving way too fast. Bret wanted to ask something, to scream something, but it felt like Superman was squeezing his throat.

Dad pulled the car up to the back door of the hospital. He didn't even look at Bret, just at Jacey. 'Stay with your brother. Stay away from the lobby. I have to talk to Sam in Administration. I'll meet you in the cafeteria in ten minutes, OK?'

Jacey nodded.

Then Daddy was gone, running off ahead of them, and Jacey and Bret were walking down the empty hallway at the back of the hospital. Their footsteps echoed, and it was creepy.

She was dead. Bret was sure of it this time. When he got to his mommy's room, the bed would be empty and it would be too late for him to see her. He yanked away from his sister and ran towards his mother's room.

'Bret, come back!'

He ignored her and kept running. At his mom's room, he skidded to a stop and pulled the door open.

There was Mommy, lying in that old bed just like always. Asleep.

He shut the door quietly and went to Mommy's bed.

It still scared him, to see her like this. He heard the door open behind him, then the soft sound of his sister's footsteps. 'Come on, Bret. Dad told us to meet him in the cafeteria.'

'Just a sec.' He leaned a little closer and gave her the Mommy Kiss, just exactly how she always did it to him. A quick kiss on the forehead, one on each cheek, and a butterfly kiss on the chin, then a longer kiss on the right side of the nose. While his lips were brushed against her nose, he whispered the magic words, 'No bad dreams.'

Very slowly, she opened her eyes.

Bret almost fell off the bed.

She eased up to a sit and stared at him. He waited and waited, but she didn't smile. 'Well, hello, little boy.'

It was all wrong. It wasn't his mommy.

Bret opened his mouth; nothing came out. All this time he'd waited and prayed, and in every dream he had, his mom said the same thing when she woke up: *'How's my favourite boy in the whole world?'* And then she'd sweep him into her arms and hold him.

Tears burned his eyes.

The fake mommy looked around the room. Her gaze landed on Jacey, who was standing by the door, hugging herself and crying. 'How's my favourite girl in the whole world?'

A tiny sound escaped Bret then. He couldn't hold it all in. Those were *his* words—*his*—but she'd given them to Jacey.

RUN. That was all he could think. He tore out of the building and plunged into the darkening afternoon.

By the time he got to the highway, he was freezing, but he didn't care. He kept running.

'**W**e call her Jacey now.'

It was like looking into a mirror that reflected the past. Instinctively she wanted to reach out.

'Jacey,' she whispered, holding out her arms.

'Mom?' Jacey moved slowly towards her. Mikaela felt an odd reluctance in her daughter, but at last Jacey leaned over the bed rail. Mikaela wrapped her arms round Jacey, pulling her close.

When she drew back, Jacey was crying.

Mikaela touched her cheek. 'Don't cry. I'll get my memory back. You'll see.'

Jacey's eyes rounded. 'You lost your memory? That's why . . .' She glanced at the open door.

'I'm sorry. I have some gaps, is all.'

'Why didn't Dad tell me?'

'I think they asked Julian to hold off on that.'

'Juli— You don't remember Dad?' Jacey's voice was barely audible.

'Oh, I remember Julian—up to a point, anyway. Everything after I left him is kind of a blank. I think—'

'Oh, *perfect!*' Jacey stared at Mikaela as if she'd grown horns. 'I can't believe this.'

Mikaela frowned. 'You're mad at me.'

'My *dad* is Liam Campbell.' Jacey surged towards Mikaela. 'We fell in love with him a long time ago, when I was only four years old. He's been your husband for ten years. And you don't remember him. You only remember Julian, who never, *ever* called me or sent a birthday card or wanted to see me.'

Mikaela was confused. 'But Julian is your father . . .'

Jacey backed away. She seemed to be hanging on to composure by the thinnest thread. 'Oh, he's my father, all right. And thanks to your lies, I didn't know that until today.'

Mikaela felt like she'd been punched in the stomach. 'I never told you?'

'No.'

'Oh, Jacey.' Mikaela didn't know what to say. What kind of woman would do this to her daughter? 'Jacey, I—'

The door swung open. Sarah bustled into the room, rosy-cheeked and out of breath. 'Jacey, the receptionist just called. She saw Bret run out of the hospital. He wouldn't stop—'

'Bret! Oh, my God. It's my fault!' Jacey spun round the nurse and ran out of the room.

Mikaela looked helplessly at Sarah. 'Who's Bret?'

Sarah gave her a sad, knowing look. 'Get your rest, honey.'

Mikaela's heart beat too fast. The room spun round her, making her sick and dizzy. She grabbed Sarah's arm. 'Sarah . . . did you know me . . . before?'

'Of course. I hired you right out of nursing school.'

Mikaela released Sarah and sank into the mound of pillows. 'Was I a good person?'

Sarah gazed down at her, smiling softly. 'You have the pure heart of an angel, Mikaela. You were—and are—a good person.'

She wanted to believe it, but she couldn't. She'd lied to her daughter for all these years, and obviously she'd broken Liam's heart. For the first time, she wondered if this amnesia was a gift from God. A momentary respite that allowed a sinner to feel like a saint.

Liam tried not to think of everything that could go wrong on this dark December night, when God had seen fit to drop the temperature four degrees in the last thirty minutes. Or that Bret was alone out there, his precious nine-year-old son, still more baby than young man. Did Bret know how dangerous it was to walk along the side of the road when the streets were icy, when visibility was cut in half by the falling snow?

'Hang on, Bretster,' Liam whispered aloud. He leaned forward, peering through the obscured windshield. It was snowing so hard, the wipers were having trouble keeping up.

By now Bret would be freezing. He'd run off without his coat.

Liam slowed down from eight miles per hour to five. He had gone less than a quarter of a mile from the hospital. The distance to town stretched out before him, an endless, twisting path of darkness.

He forced his gaze to the right, into the black fields along the side of the highway. Bret wouldn't have crossed the road; he knew better than that. Liam was certain. His son wouldn't cross the road alone at night.

But would he take a ride with a stranger? Liam suppressed a horrified shudder.

The temperature gauge on the dashboard indicated that outside it had dropped another degree.

Liam concentrated on the little things: his foot on the gas, his hands on the wheel, his gaze on the side of the road. Up ahead, on the right side of the road, the county fairgrounds were a cluster of big metal buildings, barns, arenas and pavilions. The barn was awash in light; it stood out like a beacon against the blackness all around it.

Liam felt an electrifying strand of hope. It was one of Mike's favourite places, that barn. Only a few months ago, Bret had earned his first 4-H ribbon award there.

At the turnoff, he slowed. Perspiration itched across his brow, turned his hands cold and slick.

Any wrong choice would hurt. He turned onto the road and floored the accelerator, speeding down the bumpy road.

In the parking lot, he left the engine running and jumped out of the car, racing through the downy, ankle-deep snow. 'Bret?' he yelled. His cry echoed off the unseen mountains and bounced back at him, thin as a sheet of ice.

He flung the metal doors open. The well-lit barn was cavernous, a row of empty stalls. 'Bret?'

He ran from stall to stall, peering in each one.

He found Bret in the very last stall—the one Mike had used at last summer's Last Bend Classic horse show. Shivering and curled into a tiny ball, Bret was sucking his thumb.

Liam had never known a relief this big; it made it hard to move, to speak, to do anything except sweep down and pull his son into his arms. 'Oh, Bret,' he whispered brokenly, 'you scared me.'

Bret drew back. His cheeks were bright red and streaked with tears. 'I knew you'd find me, Daddy. I'm—' He burst into chattering, shivering tears.

'It's OK, baby,' he said, stroking his son's hair.

Bret blinked up at him. 'D-D-Daddy, she didn't even h-hug me.'

He touched Bret's cheek. 'I'm sorry, Bret. I should have told you the truth.'

'Sh-She's n-not my mommy, is she?'

'Yes,' he answered softly. 'She's your mom, but the accident broke something in her brain, and she can't remember some really important things.'

'L-Like me?'

'Or me. Or Jacey.'

'She remembered Jacey!'

'No. She'd heard about Jacey, and so she was able to figure out who she was. But she doesn't really remember.'

Bret wiped his eyes. 'So how come no one told her about me? I'm as important as Jace.'

Liam sighed. 'You're *everything* to her, Bret. You and Jacey are her whole world, and it hurt her so much to hear about Jacey. She cried and cried. I just couldn't tell her about you, too. I was hoping she'd remember on her own and then everything would be fine.'

Bret drew in a great, shuddering breath. Liam could tell he was trying to be a big boy. 'Will her memory get unbroken?'

Liam wanted to say, '*Of course*,' but in the last weeks he'd learned a thing or two about his children and himself. They were all strong enough to handle the truth. The only wound that festered was a lie. 'The doctors think she'll remember most things. Not every little thing, but the big things—like us—we think she'll get those back.'

'But you don't know for sure?'

'No. We don't know. But you know what?'

'What?'

'The love . . . I believe she'll remember all of that.'

Bret seemed to think about that for a long time. 'OK, Daddy.'

Liam smiled. Thank God for the resilience of a little boy's heart.

'Bret, there's something else we need to talk about.' Liam touched his son's face. 'You remember we told you a long time ago that Mommy had been married before?'

'Yeah. That's Jacey's other daddy.'

Liam swallowed hard. 'And did you know that Julian True was in town?'

'Hel-*lo*, Dad. Everyone knows that.'

Liam took a deep breath and jumped into the deep end. 'Actually, he's in town to visit Mom. Your mommy used to be married to him.'

Bret made a disbelieving sound. 'Yeah, right.'

'It's true, Bretster.'

Bret frowned. 'But you're my daddy and she's my mommy, right?'

'That's right.'

Bret seemed to turn it all over in his mind, this way and that. At last he said, 'OK.'

'OK?' Liam had expected tears, anger, something more traumatic than this quiet OK. Maybe Bret didn't understand.

'Yeah, OK. Sally Kramer's mom used to be married to Lonnie Harris down at the feed store, and Billy McAllister's dad used to be married to Gertrude at Sunny and Shear. My mom's ex-husband is way cooler than that.'

'You amaze me, Bret,' he answered softly. 'And I'm proud of you. This is all pretty hard for a little boy to understand.'

Slowly they got to their feet. Liam picked Bret up and carried him out of the barn. When he flicked off the lights, a crashing darkness descended, and he followed the Explorer's headlights through the falling snow. As soon as they were in the car, Liam called Rosa and Jacey and gave them the good news. Rosa offered to pick Jacey up from the hospital and meet Liam and Bret at home.

Bret leaned back in his seat. Even with the heat roaring through the vents, he was shivering. 'I'm sorry, Daddy.'

'It's OK. Sometimes a man has to get away to think.' He glanced at Bret. 'But next time, how about if you go into a room and slam the door shut?'

Bret almost smiled. 'OK. But I'm gonna slam it *really* hard.'

That evening the story broke. Pictures of 'Kayla' and Julian were splashed across television, each one scrutinised and commented upon, their life together cut up into bite-sized pieces for mass consumption. At eight o'clock, right after *Entertainment Tonight*, the phone rang for the first time. Liam made the mistake of answering it. Some woman from the saddle club was screeching about how it couldn't be true.

After that, the phone began ringing nonstop. Liam yanked the plug out of the wall.

He went through the motions of ordinary life—he ate dinner, washed the dishes, watched a little television with the kids, then tucked Bret into bed and read him a bedtime story.

He tried to act as if everything were normal, but all the while, he couldn't forget the images he'd seen on television tonight, or the quippy headlines that accompanied them: TRUE LOVE, AFTER ALL THESE YEARS; SLEEPING BEAUTY AWAKENS TO PRINCE CHARMING'S KISS.

Everywhere he looked, Liam saw photographs of a young, vibrant woman who was clearly in love. It was a woman he'd never seen. Kayla.

Now she was neither Kayla nor Mikaela. Without memories, she was a leaf, caught up in the swirling current of a dream, but soon she would land on earth. She would remember the years they'd spent together. He had to believe that.

But what then?

She would reach out for something solid, and the thing that would steady her, her anchor, would be her love for her children. That love was the cornerstone of her soul, and nothing—not even Julian—could separate her from Jacey and Bret.

In the end, Mike would stay married to Liam. When push came to shove, she would sacrifice her passion for her children's welfare.

The realisation brought no solace; instead, it weighed him down. He'd seen the way she looked at Julian.

He closed his eyes.

It was quiet, this falling apart of his life, as silent as the last beat of an old man's heart. A quiet, echoing thud, and then . . . nothing.

CHAPTER 9

MIKAELA DREAMED she was in the big log house.

She could hear the child crying again, and this time she was more afraid. She crossed the empty porch. Beside her a rocking chair squeaked and moved. She grabbed the doorknob and twisted, swinging the door open so hard it cracked against the interior wall.

'Hello?' Her voice was a reedy whisper.

The crying came again, louder this time.

She felt along the wall. This time she knew there was a light switch there, and when her fingers brushed it, the lights came on. An overhead chandelier crafted of deer antlers threw a soft, golden net across a deserted dining-room table. She had a quick, flashing image of herself sitting at that table. She heard a voice saying, *'So, kids, tell me about your day.'*

But there was no one there, just a trio of ghostly images.

'Where are you?' she called out.

The crying came again. She felt her way past the table, up the long, wide staircase made of split logs.

'Mo . . . mmy . . . Mo . . . mmy . . .'

She started to run, but this time there were no doors, no windows. She ran and ran, until the hallway ended in a blank wall.

'Where are you?' she screamed.

A door appeared in front of her.

Her hand was shaking as she reached for the brass knob. It turned easily. Inch by inch she pushed the door open. Behind it lay a box of perfect blackness.

And the quiet sound of a child crying.

She touched the rough-hewn wall, and a light came on.

The child was tucked in the corner. He was wearing a Seattle SuperSonics T-shirt. He looked up at her; his pale face was streaked with tears, his brown eyes magnified into pools of watery pain.

The boy from the hospital.

'Mommy?' he said.

'Bret,' she cried out, falling to her knees and taking him into her arms.

Then she woke up. Memories washed over and around her.

She said that one simple name over and over again.

Bret. Bret. Bret. The child she'd turned away from.

Her baby boy.

She reached for the phone, but before she dialled a number, she noticed the wall clock. It was three o'clock in the morning.

She couldn't call yet. She closed her eyes and leaned back into the pillows, letting the memories come again.

Mikaela woke with a start. She glanced at the clock: nine thirty.

'Damn it.' The kids were already at school.

She closed her eyes and thought of all the things she'd remembered last night.

Bret. Jacey. Her precious children.

And Julian. She remembered all the days and nights she'd waited by the phone for his call, the countless times she'd cried herself to sleep, waiting. Waiting . . .

And Liam. She remembered the hows and whys of her love for him . . . and how it had never been enough for her. She had grown to love him, but never had she fallen head over heels in love. In truth, she'd never allowed herself to; she saw that now. Deep down she'd kept a single candle burning for Julian's return.

She didn't know if she'd regretted it then—that was something she couldn't seem to remember. But she regretted it now, regretted it with a ferocity that was nearly desperation.

Whenever she closed her eyes—and sometimes even when she didn't—she saw the flickering reel of her whole life. In Last Bend, she'd found a place where she *belonged*. And the saddest part was, she was certain that she hadn't recognised that. Even as she'd volunteered for a dozen different charitable events and sat down to dinner at friends' houses and sipped punch with people after church, she'd always believed that she didn't belong. It was, she realised, an ugly bit of baggage that she'd carried here from her youth, and she'd been so busy hanging on to it that she'd failed to notice that the bags were empty.

She was so deep in thought, she didn't hear the knock at the door.

Rosa stood in the doorway. She wore a pair of crisply creased black trousers and a red sweater. In her arms she held a big leather book.

Mikaela manoeuvred herself to a sitting position. '*Recuerdo mi vida, Mamá*,' she said softly, not even bothering with hello.

Rosa went still, her wide brown eyes focused on Mikaela's face. 'You remember? All of it?'

'How's Bret . . . after yesterday?'

'A *milagro*.' Rosa moved towards the bed. Her smile was gentle. 'He is fine. This boy of yours, he has a hardy heart. And, of course, Dr Liam was there.'

Mikaela swallowed hard. 'Can I see the kids now?'

'Bret is on a field trip today. His class went eagle-watching at Rockport. It is the migration time. Jacey has a social studies presentation to give. It is half of her grade.'

Mikaela sagged back, disappointed. 'Life goes on, *eh, Mamá*?'

'It is for a short time only. I will bring them to your room this afternoon, *sí*?' Rosa handed Mikaela the book. 'This is for you.'

Mikaela touched the fine leather. '*Muy caro, eh, Mamá*?'

'Sometimes it is good to spend the money. Myrtle—your friend at the drugstore—she told me that you have wanted this for a long time.'

That was something Mikaela couldn't remember, but she did know that she'd been meaning to put together a family scrapbook for years. '*Gracias, Mamá*. It's beautiful.'

'Open it.'

Mikaela opened the book. The first page was a sheer piece of crinkled tissue, inset with dried violets. On a panel in the middle were the words 'Mikaela Conchita Luna True Campbell.'

It made her sound like she belonged on a throne. Slowly she turned the page, and there, alone against a sea of white paper, was a dogeared old black and white Kodak print.

It was a picture of her and her mother. In the background was the shack they'd lived in during apple harvest, twelve to a room, with no working bathroom. Those were the days that had shaped Mikaela's spirit, snipped the edges off her dreams.

For all of her life, Mikaela had been running away from these memories, as if with enough speed she could distance herself from the truth. Now, she was standing still at last and she saw the past for what it had been. She saw these photographs not as a child, rather as a mother.

But Rosa had had no choices. Without an education, a poor Hispanic woman who barely spoke the language had no way out, except . . .

She looked at her mother. 'I would have done it, too, *Mamá*.'

'Done what?'

'William. The house. If Jacey had crawled into my arms and looked at me with sad, hungry eyes, I would have done it, too.'

It was the first time Mikaela had ever seen her mother cry. 'I would give anything to have loved him less and myself more, but I cannot regret that my sin gave you a chance for something better.'

'I'm sorry it took me so long to say.'

Impatiently, Rosa wiped her eyes. 'Keep looking.'

Mikaela turned the next page, then the next, and saw the few photographs of her childhood.

Then came the wedding picture. Julian and Kayla.

Mikaela gasped. *This* she had hidden. She remembered that; this photograph had been in a pillowcase in her—

'Liam found these while I was in the coma,' she said in a dull voice.

Softly, sadly, '*Sí.*'

She could hardly imagine the pain it must have caused Liam to see her life in such vivid shots. She'd kept Julian hidden, both because no man could live up to such competition, and—if she was honest—because she couldn't give up this secret obsession she called true love. Maybe she'd been afraid that if she talked about Julian as if he were someone ordinary, just a first husband, she'd fall out of love with him. And the thought of that was more than she could bear.

Mikaela turned the pages slowly, mesmerised by the images of the life she'd led.

She had forgotten how young she was when she married Julian.

At first, in the pictures, she was bright and beautiful and always smiling, but as the photos accumulated, she saw how thin she'd grown, how jaded her look had become.

Mikaela sighed. 'Oh, *Mamá*.'

Rosa flipped through a few pages until she found the first pictures with Liam. 'You see it?'

'See what?'

'Your smile. It is coming back here.'

An aching sadness spread through Mikaela. 'Why didn't I love him, *Mamá*? I've made a mess of my life.'

Rosa laughed. 'You are young. It takes many years to truly make a mess of your life. This I know about.'

Mikaela turned to her. 'How will I fix it?'

Rosa's smile faded. 'Let me tell you something else I know. When you hide things away, and keep them secret, they have a power. Take your life apart, Mikita, look at it for once . . . and maybe you will be surprised at what you see.'

Mikaela counted the moments until she could see her children. After Rosa left, Mike had spent an hour with the physiotherapist, trying to relearn how to gracefully use a spoon.

Now it was nearly noon. She stood at the small window of her room, staring out at the parking lot below. The outdoor Christmas decorations were in place. It saddened her, this evidence of the coming holidays. Usually she was a Christmas addict, a whirling dervish who maniacally put up decorations and gathered her children round her on the sofa for the yearly viewings of *It's a Wonderful Life* and *Miracle on 34th Street*. But this year all she felt was a yawning sense of loss.

There was a knock at the door.

Mikaela turned so fast she stumbled. Her right leg was still weak. She clutched the windowsill to avoid falling.

Liam stood in the doorway. He looked awkward and uncertain, his tall, lanky body tilted to one side, his too-long hair falling across one eye. Quietly he closed the door behind him and moved into the room.

She could see the uncertainty in his eyes and she felt an overwhelming shame. She'd hurt him so much.

'Hello, Liam.' She wanted to say more, but she didn't know where to start. She didn't know if there even *was* a beginning that could take them where they needed to go.

He looked at her, still unsmiling. 'Rosa tells me that you've regained a huge chunk of your memories. That's great.' There was no enthusiasm in his voice, just a dull flatness that didn't sound like him at all.

She gazed up at him, noticing the network of lines that had gathered round his eyes, etched on by the trauma of her injury.

I love you, Liam. Those were the words he needed to hear. She could have said it—easily, in fact. She did love him; she always had. But it was a watery version that had more to do with comfort and friendship than with passion.

'I don't want to hurt you, Liam,' she said softly.

He smiled a sad and tired smile. 'I don't know what to say to you any more, Mike. It's like . . . treading water in the deep end.'

'Liam—'

He held up a hand. 'You could have told me more of the truth, you know. We might have had a chance if you had.'

Mikaela turned away from him and limped towards her bed, climbing in, pulling the sheets up to her chin, as if a little layer of cotton could shield her from his words. 'I know.'

A flash of anger darkened his green eyes, but it was gone almost before it began, replaced by a resignation that tore at her heart. 'Don't you know what it was like for me . . . loving you all these years, *knowing* it wasn't enough for you?'

'I only did it because I knew what it had been like for you, growing up in Ian's shadow. I didn't want you to always wonder about Julian. Same with Jacey. I thought Julian would be too big for a child to ever forget, and she needed you as a father so much.'

'I know all that, Mike.' He said her name softly. 'I just want to say this: no more lies. That's all I'm asking.' He touched her face with a gentleness that made her want to weep. 'Maybe you were right to hide the past from me. When I didn't know, I could pretend not to see the little things. I let you have your secrets and your silences and your sadnesses. Can you imagine what those silences would do to me now? I'd constantly be wondering, Is she thinking of *him*?'

He leaned towards her and held her face in his strong, steady hands, and very slowly he kissed her. In that one, tender touching of lips was all the heartache and desperation and joy of a deep and lasting love.

While she was still gasping for an even breath, he turned and left the room.

It was three o'clock. An hour until the kids would be here.

Mikaela lay in bed, staring dully at the television tucked up into the corner of the ceiling. In beautiful black and white images, *It's a Wonderful Life* unfolded.

It was nearing the end now. George Bailey—Jimmy Stewart—had just realised what the world was without him. He was tearing into that draughty old house now, breaking off the banister . . .

As always, Mikaela was crying, but this time she wasn't crying for George Bailey; she was crying for herself.

She threw the covers back and walked to the closet. There, sitting forlornly beneath a row of empty hangers, was a small brown leather suitcase. She reached down and picked it up with her left hand—the right one was still too weak to use—and dragged it to the bed, flipping it onto the mattress. Then she unlatched the small brass closures. The suitcase twanged open.

She ran her fingers across the clothing. It had to be Liam's doing, this artful arrangement of her favourite things. A black broomstick skirt and white turtleneck, with a matching tapestry waistcoat. The silver Concho belt she always wore with the skirt. A pair of black riding boots. Bra and panties. He'd even remembered her favourite gold hoop earrings. And all her make-up, even her hairbrush and perfume.

She couldn't help thinking how it must have been for him as he'd stood in her huge, walk-in closet, choosing clothing to go in a suitcase that might never be opened . . .

She would have grabbed anything to get out of that closet, stuffed mismatched clothing in a brown paper bag. But not Liam. No matter how much it hurt, he would have stood there thinking, choosing.

She stripped off the hospital gown and tossed it onto the moulded pink chair. It was difficult to dress herself—her right hand was barely any help at all—but she kept at it, pulling and tugging and strapping and buttoning until it was done.

Then she went into the bathroom and wet her hair, combing it back from her face. There was no way she could put on make-up, so she settled for pinching her cheeks.

She walked down the hall, with no idea where she was going. When she ended up at the hospital chapel, she realised she must have been heading there all along.

Kneeling in front of the utilitarian Formica altar, she stared up at the brass cross, then closed her eyes.

'Please, God, help me. Show me the way home.'

At first there was only darkness. Then a small, yellow ray of piercing sunlight. She heard voices as if from far away, a child's high-pitched giggle, a man speaking to her softly.

The memories came one after another, unconnected by time or space, just the random moments of life. She and Liam dancing at last year's Tex-Mex hoe-down . . . him drying the dishes while she washed them . . . him driving her to the feed store.

She'd remembered her marriage to Liam, but this was the first time she'd *felt* it.

She was afraid to open her eyes. 'More,' she pleaded. 'Show me more.'

Midnight Mass, last year. They were in the front row, wearing their Sunday best. She saw the four of them clearly, like strands of a rope, twisted together; they strengthened one another.

She felt as if she were looking at the moment from far, far away, through another woman's eyes. From a distance, she knew exactly what she was seeing. Love. Pure and simple.

Slowly she opened her eyes. The cross blurred in front of her. She stared down at the wedding ring on her left hand.

'Love.'

The realisation moved through her like an electrical shock.

See? You know what love is, Mikaela.

She heard the words as clearly as the ringing of a church bell. She opened her eyes and looked around. No one was there.

Slowly she smiled. The Virgin had spoken to her at last, after all these years of prayer.

Surprisingly, the Blessed Mother sounded exactly like Rosa.

Mikaela was back in her room, pacing, when the knock came.

Suddenly she was nervous. She had hurt them all so badly. What if her family didn't forgive her?

She shuffled away from the window and went to stand by the bed. The door opened, and Jacey stood in the doorway, looking as nervous as Mikaela felt.

Mikaela limped towards her daughter. With her weakened right hand she reached out and touched Jacey's cheek. 'Hello, Jace.'

'I'm sorry, Mom. I shouldn't have yelled at you.'

'Oh, baby.' Mikaela swallowed hard. 'Don't ever apologise for your feelings.' She moved closer. 'There are still a lot of gaps in my memory. I don't remember your first day at school, or when you lost your first tooth. But I remember that I love you. I love you more than my own life, and I can't believe how I've hurt you.'

Jacey's eyes filled with tears. She looked a little angry, a little sad. 'Why didn't you tell me about Julian?'

Mikaela had answered this question in her head so many times. Still, she was uncertain. Even now, after all that had happened, she didn't want to tell Jacey the whole truth.

'No more lies, Mom,' Jacey said.

'I know, *querida*. But I don't want to hurt you.'

'Tell me all of it.'

'I loved Julian too much. When I married him and moved to California, I became someone else, a *gringa* named Kayla True who had no past at all. Your *abuela* tried to tell me that he was no good for me, but I wouldn't listen. I lost myself. Not just the poor Hispanic girl I'd been, but more. *Me*.' She tried to smile but failed. 'Then I got pregnant. You brought me back to me. I knew what I wanted for you, even if I'd lost track of what I wanted for me. And Julian . . . well, he wasn't ready to be a father.'

Tears beaded Jacey's eyes. 'He didn't want me.'

Mikaela took a deep breath. There was nowhere to go now except forward. 'No.' She took Jacey's hands, held them tightly. 'But I wanted you and I wanted to give you the kind of childhood I hadn't known. So I left Julian.'

'But you loved him.'

'Yes.'

A tear streaked down Jacey's cheek and Mikaela forced herself not to wipe it away. Some tears were meant to fall, had to fall. This was one of the many truths she'd failed to see in her life.

Mikaela squeezed her daughter's hand. 'I know I've been dishonest with you and Liam, and I'll have to find a way to make that right. Together we are a family, and that's what we need to remember. We'll get through this hard time.'

'Are you coming home?'

Home. The word elicited a memory so clear, Mikaela could have pressed it under glass and framed it: *Liam is sitting at the piano playing her favourite song, 'A Time for Us'. She comes up behind him, touches his shoulder. 'Hey, piano man. Get your wife to bed or lose your chance.'*

He turns, smiles up at her, and it is there, in his eyes—the love, the welcome, the need that, until now, she has always taken for granted.

Mikaela laughed. She knew it was an inappropriate response, but she couldn't help herself. The joy inside her was so big. 'Come here, Jacey.' She opened her arms for a hug.

Jacey launched forward, landing in Mikaela's arms. 'Oh, Mom, I missed you. I was afraid—'

'Shh. I know.' Mikaela clung to her daughter. It felt so good.

Jacey drew back and smiled up at her. 'I love you, Mom.'

'Oh, Jace, I love you, too, and I'm so sorry for ev—'

The door burst open. Bret and Rosa stood in the doorway. Rosa shrugged. 'He thought that Jacey had enough time.'

Mikaela kissed Jacey's damp cheek and drew back.

Bret stood motionless, his arms belted to his sides. His mouth was trembling and there was fear in his eyes. This fear and uncertainty, he'd learned recently. The boy she'd raised was fearless.

She started to cry; there was no way to stop it. She knelt in front of him and opened her arms. 'So, how's my favourite boy in the whole world?'

He screamed, 'Mommy!' and flung himself into her waiting arms so hard that they toppled backwards.

She lay there on the ugly linoleum floor, squeezing her son until neither one of them could breathe.

'I love you, Bretster,' she whispered against his small pink ear. He buried his face in the crook of her neck. She felt, more than heard, him whisper back, 'I love you, too, Mommy.'

At last they drew apart and climbed awkwardly to their knees. Mikaela's weak right leg was trembling badly. She stayed kneeling, unable to let go of Bret's hand.

Over his head she looked at Rosa, who was crying now, too.

Mikaela sniffled. 'Too bad we can't sell all this water to the Californians.'

Bret giggled. It was what Liam always said when Mikaela cried over a stupid movie.

She smiled at her son. 'So, kiddo, what's new with you?'

'Sally May Randle has a crush on me. She smells bad, but she's sorta pretty.'

Mikaela laughed, mesmerised by the ordinariness of it, seized by a sudden hope. Maybe, with time, they could all find their way out of the woods and back onto the main road. 'Where's Daddy?' she asked Bret.

Bret bit his lip and didn't answer.

Rosa looked down at Mikaela. 'He did not come.'

'He's at home,' Bret said. 'I think he's sad 'cause you didn't remember him.'

Mikaela grabbed the bed rail and dragged herself to her feet. She looked at Rosa. 'Take the kids home, *Mamá*. I'll meet you there.'

Rosa frowned. 'What are you going to do, Mikita? The doctors say—'

'Please, *Mamá*.'

Rosa sighed. '*Sí*. But, Mikaela, stay away from the front doors. The reporters, they are waiting for you.'

Jacey moved towards Mikaela. 'I don't want to leave you, Mom.'

'There's nothing to be afraid of any more, honey. I'll be home soon.'

'You promise?'

Mikaela smiled. 'I promise.'

After they left, Mikaela decided not to bother checking out of the hospital. There would be time for technicalities tomorrow. She carefully packed up all the photographs from the bedside tables and windowsills. At the last minute, she folded up her hospital gown and placed it gently on top of the things in the suitcase—to remind her always of this time. She didn't ever want to forget any part of it. It was the coma that had saved her life. She prayed only that she had not woken up too late.

She'd been unconscious for a month. In reality, she had slept through the last fifteen years of her life.

Someone knocked at her door.

She froze, her heart thumping in her chest. Her gaze darted to the packed suitcase. *Please, don't let it be a nurse.*

Julian strode into the room, as if he belonged there. 'I started sneezing this morning. I think I'm developing an allergy to this Podunk town.' He grinned. 'You should see the hoopla on Main Street. Grown men are walking around in Sasquatch costumes.'

Glacier Days. She'd forgotten all about it.

In ordinary times, Liam would have been dressed in one of the bigfoot costumes. Every year he grumbled about his dignity, and every year he ran in the race for charity.

'Kayla?'

She limped towards Julian. When she was close enough to touch him, she stopped. Finally she saw him, the man and not the myth. She didn't need to see Liam and Julian side by side to recognise the difference between tinfoil and sterling silver.

'Oh, Julian,' she said, in a soft voice that held a lifetime's regret.

'I don't like the way you're looking at me.'

'Of course you don't. You want to be watched, not seen.' It was true, she realised. His was the magician's life, full of illusion, where only one man saw what was behind the curtain.

'Kayla, I've been doing a lot of thinking lately. I realised how much I've missed you.' He flashed her the grin she'd seen a million times, the one that used to curl her toes and make her heart lurch into overdrive. 'I know you've missed me, too.'

'Oh, Jules.' She sighed. It saddened her that she'd given up so much of her life waiting for this moment. As if they could simply ride off into the sunset together.

'What?' he asked, his voice uncharacteristically uncertain.

How did you tell a man that at last you'd learned true love wasn't a night of passionate sex under a sky lit up by fireworks, but an ordinary Sunday morning when your husband brought you a glass of water, two aspirins and a heating pad for your cramps?

She gazed up at him. 'I love Liam more than you can imagine, Jules. I only hope it's not too late to tell him that.'

'I know he loves you, Kayla.'

She felt an aching sadness. 'There is no Kayla, Jules. There never was.'

His voice was thick. 'It sounds like you're saying goodbye.'

'Oh, Jules, we said goodbye a long, long time ago. I'm only just now getting around to leaving.' She caressed his cheek, let her fingers linger there for a moment; then slowly she drew back her hand and headed for the door.

'Wait! You can't just walk out. The press are waiting at the front door. I'll go and make a statement, then pick you up at the back door and take you . . .' He paused, said softly, 'Home.'

She turned back to him. 'What will you tell them?'

He looked sad. 'I'll tell them the story's over. Sleeping Beauty found her prince. They might . . . follow you for a while.'

She smiled. 'And cover my glamorous life? After ten minutes, they'll realise that the ordinary life of a small-town doctor's wife is hardly front-page news.'

'I'll be right back with the limo. I'll meet you round the back.' He gave her a last, heavy look, then turned and left.

Mikaela reached for her suitcase, then decided to leave it in the closet. It was too unwieldy for her to carry, and it would only arouse suspicion. Empty-handed, she left her room. She kept her head down and made her slow, limping way down the hospital corridors.

When she opened the door, the first thing she noticed was the evergreen smell of Christmas. Green pine needles and fresh snow. A night sky filled with stars made her feel small. She smiled; she liked feeling small. It had been the wanting to feel big that had led her to Julian.

The limousine pulled up, the door opened and she got inside.

The limo crawled through town at the posted speed limit of ten miles per hour. Outside on this icy-cold night there were people everywhere, moving in grey clouds of exhaled breath, walking beneath banners that read, WELCOME TO GLACIER DAYS.

Julian couldn't take his eyes off Mikaela, although she rarely looked at him. She directed the driver out of town, onto a back road where trees outnumbered houses a thousand to one. They turned into a driveway, passing beneath an arch announcing ANGEL FALLS RANCH.

Acres of white pastures rolled away from the road on either side. At last the house came into view. It was a beautiful log structure set against the serrated black mountains. The car pulled up in front of the house and stopped. The driver—Julian could never remember his name—hurried round to their door.

'Thank you,' she said to the young man as she got out.

Julian realised that not once in all these days had he offered the driver those simple words. He got out of the car and stood beside Kayla. She shivered, and he put an arm round her.

'It's beautiful, isn't it?' she said, speaking of the house.

He looked down at her, only her. 'The most beautiful thing I've ever seen.'

Kayla turned to him. 'Come in with me, Jules. Meet your daughter.'

He searched her dark eyes. Still, as always, she expected the best of him. In all the world, she was the only one who had ever wanted him to reach for the man he could be.

He hated to hurt her again. 'You know I can't. If I walked through those doors, it would be a lie. We both know that. I don't want to do to Jacey what I did to you.'

She looked at him and tried to smile.

It broke his heart, that soft realisation in her beautiful eyes. 'Tell me you'll always love me,' he whispered.

She touched his cheek. 'I'll always love who we were.'

He felt and heard the continent that lay between his question and her answer. He reached down for her left hand. The plain gold band glittered in the pale glow of the limo's headlights. 'Do you still have the wedding ring I gave you?'

'Of course.'

'Give it to Jacey. Tell her that out here, somewhere, is a man who wishes he were different.'

'*Be* different, Jules. Come in with me. You know Liam, he'll make a place for you.'

'Liam's not the problem. I wish . . .' He couldn't say it.

'What do you wish?'

Somewhere a branch snapped in the breeze, and it sounded dangerously like the breaking of his own brittle heart. 'I wish I could love you the way he does.'

He didn't want her to answer, so he pulled her into his arms and kissed her for the last time. 'Goodbye . . . Mikaela.'

She turned away from him and limped through the snow. One last time she stopped and looked at him. 'Goodbye, Julian True.' It was spoken so softly, he wondered later if he'd imagined it.

The house smelt of evergreen boughs and baking apple pie. Mikaela paused in the doorway, breathing in the welcoming scent of *home*. Rosa and the kids were in the living room decorating a Christmas tree.

The kids didn't hear her come in, but Rosa did.

Her mother smiled and pointed upstairs.

Mikaela tiptoed through the kitchen and climbed the stairs. When she got to the top, she was out of breath.

Outside her bedroom she paused at the closed door, waiting for her heartbeat to slow. Finally she realised that it was nerves, not exertion, that had turned her heart into a set of drums.

Please, God, don't let it be too late.

She opened the door. Liam was standing by the bed. Last year's Sasquatch costume lay in a heap on the duvet.

'Liam?'

He turned and saw her. 'You should be at the hospital,' he said, looking awkward and uncertain.

'Tell me it's not too late.'

He looked confused. 'What do you mean?'

She came closer, laid her hand on his forearm. 'I wish I were smarter. I know there are words I need right now and I can't find them. For ten years I *wanted* to be the kind of wife you deserved. I just . . . couldn't.'

He stroked her hair, and she knew that the tenderness of his touch was as natural as breathing. 'I know that, Mike, but—'

'I love you,' she said. 'I want to grow old with you, Liam Campbell. I want to sit on our porch and sip lemonade and watch our children grow up and go on and have children of their own. I want to fix holiday dinners for all of us and watch our grandchildren learn to walk and talk and have them fall asleep in our arms.' She gazed up at him.

For the first time, she knew it was in her eyes, all the bits and pieces and scraps of love she'd collected over the years. Love, as pure and clean as rainwater, as complex as memories themselves. It was all for him, for this gentle, steady man who'd always been there for her.

'What about Julian?' he asked quietly.

For once, the beloved name hit the hard shell of her rib cage and clattered away. No piece of it reached the tender walls of her heart. 'It was real, what I felt for Jules; I'll never deny that. But it was a fragile love that didn't pass the test of time. When it broke apart, I held the pieces together, thinking—dreaming—that they'd magically fuse again. I was so busy holding them, I never noticed the emptiness in my hands.' Tears stung her eyes. 'I was a fool, Liam. And it took a smack on the head to make me see the truth. *You're* the one I love, and if you'll give me another chance, I'll love you until the day I die. You'll never, ever wonder again.'

'I've always loved you, Mike,' he said simply.

Tears were streaming down her cheeks now. 'I know.'

Slowly he smiled, and now it was in his eyes, too, that love they'd built together over all these years. 'I missed you. God, how I missed you.'

How was it that the profound simplicity of those words had the power to rock her world? Never again would she lose sight of what mattered—not for a day or an hour or even a minute. She would treasure every instant of her life from now on, for she knew something now, a deep truth that had eluded her all of her life. Love wasn't a great, burning brush fire that swept across your soul and charred you beyond recognition. It was simple, everyday moments, laid like bricks, one atop another, until they formed a foundation so solid that nothing could make them fall. Not wind, not rain . . .

Nothing.

She curled her arms round his waist and stared up at him through her tears. 'Here's a tip for you, piano man. Get your wife to bed.'

He laughed. 'I know, I know, or lose my chance.'

'You already lost your chance, Liam Campbell. You should have run when I was in a coma. Now you're stuck with me.' She pressed up onto her tiptoes and kissed him with years of pent-up passion. When she drew back, she whispered the words that had brought her through the darkness: 'For ever.'

KRISTIN HANNAH

Kristin Hannah originally set out to be a lawyer. Then, in 1985, her mother developed cancer, and during the hours she spent at her bedside, Kristin discovered her mother's love of romance novels. 'I was stunned. My mother was a true intellectual, and I, a college student, judged the books by their lurid covers. But my mother forced me to read them, and within the first few pages I was hooked. It wasn't long before we were collaborating on a romance. We had a ton of fun.'

Kristin Hannah did go on to practise law after her mother's death, but never lost the writing bug and had her first novel published in 1990. 'There was no one I wanted to call more than my mom,' she admits. Kristin has now given up the law and writes full-time. 'Most of my books are originally written longhand, on yellow legal pads. I don't know why that is, but I seem to enjoy writing in different locations rather than always at my computer.'

Kristin Hannah is married, with a thirteen-year-old son, and lives in the Pacific Northwest. 'Angel Falls is very similar to towns in which I've grown up,' she says. 'Right now, I live on a very small, very rural island. It's really beautiful—green hills and blue water and white-topped mountains. I always like to give my reader a sense of this part of the world. I consider the setting to be another character in the book.'

When I asked Kristin where the idea for *Angel Falls* came from she replied, '*Angel Falls* is pure fiction, although the themes of the book are very real and universal. I think many of us idealise certain times and people in our lives and every now and again we need to take time out to reassess our own lives. Thank God, I've never been faced with having a loved one in a coma, and the research necessary to bring that premise to life was extensive. But Mikaela's coma is somewhat metaphoric as well. How many of us believe that we've slept through our lives?'

Kristin Hannah is a writer who manages to engage her readers' emotions and I have often found myself reaching for a handkerchief when immersed in one of her novels. I asked her if she ever shed a tear when she was writing? 'No, I don't cry when I'm writing (unless it's going badly, of course!), but I do tap into many of the difficult, painful times in my past to access the emotions I need. All of my books are deeply personal to me and most of the really emotional peaks and valleys mirror some moment in my own life. But I'm lucky to have married my first true love—that was fifteen years ago and I'm still in love!'

She has recently finished her next novel, *Summer Island*, and is finally able to find some time to relax. 'Above all, I read. I don't suppose that surprises anyone. It's what got me into writing in the first place.'

Jane Eastgate

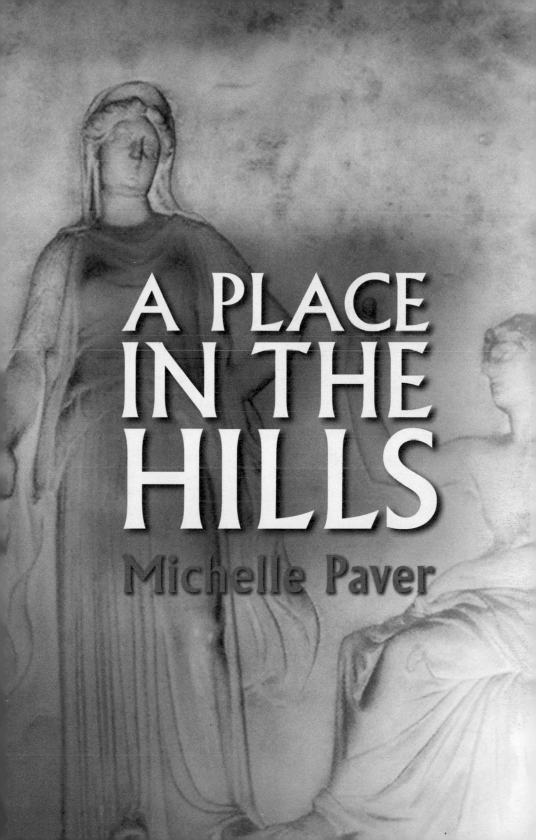

A PLACE
IN THE
HILLS

Michelle Paver

In the splendour of ancient Rome, the poet Cassius wrote passionately about the woman he loved and lost. Two thousand years later, in the foothills of the Pyrenees, archaeologist Antonia Hunt is determined to discover the identity of Cassius's mystery woman. But, as she gets nearer to the truth about Cassius, her own life becomes increasingly traumatic and she is in danger of losing everything she cares about.

PART ONE
CHAPTER ONE
Rome, March 24, 53 BC

IT WAS NOON on the Day of Blood when he first saw her.

The procession was nearing the doorway where he and Plautius were standing, and above the heads of the other onlookers Cassius had just glimpsed the Great Mother's effigy, lurching crazily towards them on the shoulders of her priests.

Rome wore a chaotically festive air that day. People thronged the narrow streets, and hung out of windows. It was the sort of spectacle which made educated men debate the nature of faith, and congratulate themselves on being above such foolishness. Besides, when else could you watch a barbarian mob howling through the streets of Rome, delirious on drugs and devotion and self-inflicted agony?

Afterwards, Cassius thought how incredible it was that in the crush he had managed to catch sight of her at all. He was to think of that a lot in the years to come. And of how different his life would have been if he hadn't glanced her way.

He had just picked a potsherd from the pavement, a fragment of a prayer lamp, and was turning it in his palm, when he saw her. She was standing in the doorway across the street. Like him, she held a fragment of pottery in her palm. She was frowning as she examined the reliefs.

'Pretty,' said Plautius, following his gaze.

'No,' Cassius replied. 'Beautiful.'

She was of medium height, and young, with straight dark hair and brows, and a chiselled mouth. He could tell from the way she wore her hair—in a simple horse-tail at the nape of the neck—that she was not yet married. He thought she must be some patrician miss who had come down from the Palatine for a little excitement. At her side stood a large, coarse-featured slave-girl in a brown wool tunic, whose job was obviously to shade her with a sun umbrella. And no doubt when the young mistress had tired of barbarian processions, a litter would emerge from a side street and carry her home.

Everything about the girl spoke of impeccable good breeding. Her dress was of some subtle blue-green stuff, belted at the waist and again beneath the breasts with a fine gilded cord; and she wore a dazzling white mantle. The heavy twisted chain about her neck had the sheen of real gold, no doubt about that, and on it she wore an amulet which intrigued him. A small crescent moon. Did that make her a believer in the Goddess? Surely not. She didn't look ecstatic as she studied that shard in her hand. Merely puzzled.

His gaze moved to her face, and he found with a start that she was watching him, and distinctly annoyed at being the object of his scrutiny.

He returned her stare for just long enough to prove that he wasn't disconcerted, then turned back to the procession and put her firmly from his mind. The day belonged to Plautius, his best and oldest friend. He would not allow some haughty little miss to interfere with that.

Suddenly the procession was upon them, and the girl disappeared behind a baying frenzy of eunuch priests. Flutes shrilled, cymbals clashed, and trumpets blared. Sunlight blazed off the towering silver form of the Mother on her saffron-painted litter.

'Make way for the Mother!' howled the believers, as they whirled about the Deity, in blood-spattered robes.

The street seemed as hot as Hades. The sunlight was a knife in the brain, the air thick with the smell of balsam and trampled roses, and the salty, metallic undertow of blood.

Next to him, Cassius felt Plautius sag. 'Are you all right?' he said in the old man's ear. 'If you like we can go—'

Plautius shook his head with an impatient frown, though when Cassius offered him his good arm, he leaned on it gratefully.

'Are you sure you wouldn't rather leave?' Cassius insisted.

'Quite sure,' Plautius told him. He was enjoying himself *immensely*, he said, hadn't observed the Syrian cult at such close quarters for years.

The Goddess's litter moved on, and the high priest, swaying dreamily in Her wake, drew level with them. At each step the eunuch lashed himself with a knotted scourge, shuddering in wide-eyed ecstasy as the whip hit his back, spattering the ladies in the crowd with blood.

The Day of Blood never failed to draw the upper classes. And who could blame them? This was *religion*. Painful, steaming, and intense.

'You know,' Plautius exclaimed, dragging him back to the present, 'after all these years I think I finally grasp the attraction of the Syrian cult. The blood washes away the believer's sins, thereby bringing him into closer communion with the Deity. And presumably the self-castration helps as well. Hm. An interesting idea. Enlightenment through suffering.'

Cassius bit back a smile. It was good to see his old friend so much in his element: observing, questioning, modestly enjoying the exercise of his powerful intellect.

But he, Cassius, why had *he* come? Why did he always come on this particular day, when he was not—or he didn't think he was—a believer? Was it to find out if maybe *this* time he would feel the presence of something higher and deeper than what he could only see and touch?

Just then the procession thinned to a straggle, and the girl across the street reappeared.

Still here? thought Cassius in irritation. Haven't you seen enough?

'She's someone's daughter, as I recall,' remarked Plautius.

'They usually are,' said Cassius drily.

'No, I mean to say—*a personage*.'

'Mm. She looks it. Out with the maid for a bit of excitement.' He shook himself as if to get rid of an unwelcome impression. 'Come along, old friend. Shall we go?'

'So soon?' said Plautius, trying not to look relieved.

'Well, I don't know about you, but I could do with a drink.'

Plautius's thin lips compressed into his version of a smile. 'My boy, you have read my mind.'

Cassius laughed. 'I haven't been a boy for decades, I'm thirty-three years old!'

'Ah, but to me you'll always be a boy, you know that!'

They turned to go.

'**P**roposition One,' Tacita's philosophy tutor had dictated to her that morning: 'the gods are indifferent to the world and have no effect upon it; *therefore* there is no point in worshipping them. Proposition Two: the gods determine all things; *therefore* man has no freedom of choice. Compare and contrast. With special reference—*if* you must—to this barbaric procession you're so intent upon witnessing.'

A randomly configured world, or the complete absence of free will. Watching the rapt faces of the believers, Tacita wondered if there wasn't anything in between. After all, what kind of compulsion makes a priest take a knife and cut off his own manhood, then walk through the streets carving up his back with a knotted scourge? He must believe in something, to do that. Mustn't he?

And she, Tacita—why was *she* here? To make notes for her next philosophy lesson? Or because she envied that priest his conviction, and wanted in some small way to experience it, or at least to understand?

'Not bad, for a soldier,' said Albia, her slave, nudging her arm.

Without seeming to, Tacita took in the tall, bearded officer across the street. She needn't have worried about being caught staring, for he was far too absorbed in watching the procession's approach.

His face was thoughtful, but she couldn't tell if he was amused, intrigued, or genuinely moved by what he saw. Perhaps he was a believer. Lots of soldiers were. Although it would be more unusual in an officer like him. With a practised eye, Tacita had already taken in the fact that he wore the gold ring of the equestrian class, and armour of tinned bronze and gilded hide beneath a cloak of fine white wool.

He was tall, with thick, dark-blond hair, and a short, straight beard clipped close to the strong line of the jaw. Beards were unusual in Rome, but perhaps he kept his out of convenience, as some career officers did.

Albia was right, it was a handsome face: high-browed and intelligent, though perhaps a little too grave. Maybe he was in pain, for his right arm was bandaged from elbow to wrist.

Then she noticed with surprise that the old man leaning on his good arm was—of all people—Lucius Faenius Plautius, the advocate. A friend of her father's. Or rather, a respected opponent in the courts.

'Quick!' hissed Albia. 'He's turning this way!' Wildly the slave looked round, then stooped and pressed a potsherd into her mistress's hand.

'What am I supposed to do with this?' said Tacita crossly.

'Just keep your eyes on it and look modest and intriguing. Trust me. I know what I'm doing.'

'No you don't.'

'Listen, mistress, you were the one who wanted to experience life. Well, there it is, all six-foot-something of it. Strongly built, nicely battle-scarred, and it's not as if he's a ranker, so that's all right.'

'He's a plebeian, though. No getting round that.'

'Yes, but compared to you, *everyone's* a pleb.'

With a sigh she studied the shard in her hand. Sometimes it was better to play along with her slave's little games. It tended to get them over sooner.

Besides, now that she came to examine it, the shard was interesting. A fragment of some largish vessel, perhaps a *kántharos* or some other type of drinking-cup, which bore a section of a finely moulded relief.

A deafening clash of cymbals made her jump. Across the street, the officer was still watching her. To her annoyance she felt herself blushing. Pointedly she returned his stare. Then she turned her head slowly and renewed her study of the procession.

When she glanced back again, the officer had gone. She felt let down—and angry with herself for feeling anything at all.

On the way home, Albia kept running off to look for the officer, then dashing back to check on her mistress, like a puppy let loose on its first walk. Then, as they approached the turning for Victory Hill, Albia gave a triumphant yelp and disappeared down a side street.

Moments later, Plautius and the officer emerged from the opposite side street. The old man saw Tacita stamping her foot and calling in vain, recognised her, and despite her protests, set off in chivalrous pursuit of the errant slave. Which, of course, was exactly what Albia had intended. And as no officer would leave a young girl of good breeding unattended in a crowded street, Tacita was forced to wait beside him until Albia should deign to reappear.

I will tan that girl's hide when I get my hands on her, she thought, gritting her teeth and trying to appear at ease. To further her irritation, the officer seemed disinclined to speak. Had he no manners whatsoever?

'So,' she said briskly, to break the silence, 'how long are you in Rome?'

'That depends on my orders,' he replied. 'But it'll be a couple of months at least.' Surprisingly, he had an educated voice, without a hint of a provincial accent.

'So you're up for a spot of big-city sophistication,' she remarked, letting a hint of scorn leach into her voice. 'Must be quite a change, after fighting Germans.'

'In fact,' said the officer, 'Germany isn't a bad guess. Perhaps I should return the favour and guess what you're doing down here.' He threw her a measuring glance. 'I'd say you were born and bred on the Palatine, and thought you'd amuse yourself with a look at the Syrian orgies. At a safe distance, of course. And no doubt on a pretty short leash.'

'What's that supposed to mean?'

He shrugged. 'Presumably you have a strict papa. Although I'm surprised you're not married at your age. You must be—what? Seventeen?'

'Sixteen.' That stung, for most of her friends had been married for years. But it was hardly her fault if her father couldn't find a man with blood pure enough to ally with his only daughter. 'So what about you?' she retorted sweetly. 'You must be—what, about twice my age?

Presumably you have a wife and several brats in some cosy little house down by the Meat Market?'

He looked amused. 'I'm not married. I'm a soldier.'

'I'd noticed.'

'And you are . . .'

'Not a soldier.'

One corner of his mouth went up. It was a good mouth, but it wasn't much of a smile. He didn't look as if he smiled very often.

The procession was far away by now, wending its way south towards the Porta Capena. At this distance, all that reached them was a discordant rumour of cymbals and harsh singing.

'So,' said the officer at last, 'was I right? Did you come down to see how the Syrians handle these things?'

'Something like that, I suppose.'

'What did you think of it? Did you find what you were looking for?'

She frowned. Abruptly, her talent for riposte deserted her. 'I don't know,' she said at last. 'I don't know why I came, or what I was looking for. I—don't know.'

Absurdly, she felt close to tears. She cast about for a change of subject. 'You're left-handed,' she said at random. He had ink stains on the fingers of his good hand.

'Then it was lucky for me that I sprained my right wrist, wasn't it?'

'I'm surprised you have ink stains at all. I didn't think soldiers had much time for writing.'

'I'm a poet.'

'You said you were a soldier.'

'Can't I be both?'

At last she felt on firmer ground. The doors had been flung open for ridicule, and that was something she could never resist. 'But of *course* you can,' she said with mock solemnity. 'At least, you can try. And you won't be alone, will you? Why, every officers' mess has its gaggle of hopeful scribblers. I've met your kind at my father's parties. You have—what shall we call them? *Literary aspirations?*' She said the phrase slowly, extracting every drop of sarcasm. 'Now let me see. I believe I can guess your background without being told. You're one of our New Men, aren't you? Your father was a citizen who made good out in the provinces. Probably somewhere in Narbonese Gaul?'

He nodded, his face expressionless.

'That's what I thought. And clearly the fond papa bought his son the best education he could afford: good local school, decent—albeit local—university. Perhaps even a bit of Greek on the cheap.'

'Quite right. Though we couldn't afford the grand tour to Athens.'

'Oh, couldn't you? *What* a pity. You don't know what you missed.'

'On the contrary. I think I do.'

That made her feel ashamed. But she'd started, so she soldiered on. She hadn't forgotten that crack about the leash. 'So. You thought that as you were in Rome, you'd take in a bit of the local colour. Perhaps to get some ideas for your next masterpiece.'

'That wasn't originally the reason.'

'But now it is?'

For the first time he looked her full in the face. 'Well,' he said softly, 'right now I'm certainly getting ideas.'

'That's coarse and impertinent,' she snapped, 'and hardly poetic.'

'What can I do? I'm a soldier.'

'I thought you were a poet.'

'And I thought you were a lady. It seems we're both wrong.'

At that moment, Plautius hurried up with an unrepentant Albia, and swamped them in a flurry of wheezy introductions. But she abruptly ceased to hear a word of what he was saying immediately after Plautius told her the officer's name. From then on, she was too appalled to hear anything except the thunder of her own blood in her ears.

'I'm a poet,' the officer had said in his offhand way. But if Tacita had known to whom she was speaking, she would have replied: No, you're not *a* poet—you're *The* Poet. You're Gaius Cassius Vitalis. We've all read you, we know you by heart. You're the man who broke all the rules of poetry, who isn't afraid to peel back his own skin and write what he feels, in words that fly up and sing like neat wine in the blood.

And *this* was the man she had been happily insulting to his face.

'I don't know what to say,' she said simply.

'Well, that's a first,' he remarked.

'I—didn't recognise you. I mean, I've never seen you before. I never managed to get to one of your readings.'

'I don't give many. I'm not often in Rome.' He paused, then added, 'Too busy fighting Germans, I suppose.'

She nodded slowly, accepting that as just punishment.

'But you've read my work?' he asked.

Again she nodded, pressing her lips together to prevent more ineptitudes escaping.

'Well?' he said. 'Are the—um, literary aspirations justified?'

Her chin went up. 'If you don't mind, I'd rather not tell you what I think. I see no point in trying to summarise a man's whole experience, when you've been doing that in your poems for years. How could I better them?' She thought she sounded both pompous and illogical, but to her surprise he only smiled.

'That's a novel approach to criticism. But I wasn't trying to catch you out. I wanted to know what you think.'

He sounded as if he meant it. And for an instant, he looked as surprised about that as she.

For the first time she met his glance.

His eyes were a startling light-filled grey, with an edge of smoky blue about the iris. Looking into them was like looking into his soul.

The breath caught in her throat. The sounds of the bustling street receded. She could not move. She had no idea how long they stood there. Plautius tapped the poet's shoulder, and murmured something about getting out of the sun.

Gaius Cassius Vitalis didn't seem to hear. His smile had vanished. She knew—she *knew*—that it was the same for him.

'Gaius,' the old man said uneasily. 'We really ought to be going.'

Tacita watched the poet slowly return to himself. He opened his mouth to speak. Then cleared his throat and started again. 'Will you—' he said to her. 'Will you—be at the Games next week?'

It was so unexpected that it caught her off guard, and her reply came out more tartly than she'd intended. 'That depends on how short they keep my leash.'

He took that gravely, in silence. But it had not been an idle question—it had cost him to ask—and she bitterly regretted her sharpness.

But by the time she had regained her wits, he had already turned and was walking away with the old man. 'I don't know,' she called after him. 'Maybe I will. I'll try.'

'Cassius,' said Plautius at his side. 'No.'

'Why?'

'You know why. She's a patrician and you're not.'

'I don't see wh—'

'Do you *know* who her father is? He's Publius Tacitus Silanus, for heaven's sake! One of the oldest clans in Rome, and not about to let anyone forget it. Strike first, think later, and pay for the funeral. That's his motto where the honour of the family is concerned.'

Cassius heard the words but he didn't understand them. He felt the paving stones beneath his feet, and the wind in his hair, and the sun on his face—all of it more intensely real than ever before in his life, and yet at the same time more bizarre and unintelligible. As if he were a stranger to the world, seeing it for the first time.

Glancing over his shoulder, Cassius watched her walk away up Victory Hill. Her back was very straight, and she did not turn round.

But she had said that she would try to get to the Games. That was what she had said.

'I'll see you there,' he called after her.

CHAPTER TWO
La Bastide, French Pyrenees, September 3, 1988

'*FUCK* ARCHAEOLOGY,' said Myles when he called Patrick the night before.

He was on speed again. Patrick could tell. He was talking too fast, with long breathy pauses in between.

'So I guess the dig's not going too well, huh?' Patrick had replied.

'Fuck knows,' said Myles, 'I haven't been down there for a week. Why should I? I'm a volunteer. And we haven't found a thing in eight weeks.'

'What, nothing at all?'

'A few bits of old flowerpot.'

'Did Romans have flowerpots?'

'How should I know? You can ask that prick of a supervisor when you get here, if you're so interested.'

'Right.'

'God, I hate it when you do that.'

'Do what?'

'Go all self-righteous on me. It's so *American*.'

'I'm not self-righteous. I was only wondering why, if this dig is such a fiasco, you still want me to come out, is all.'

'*Because*. I don't need a reason.'

And because Myles was Myles, Patrick was now on a plane to Toulouse, wondering what the hell he was getting himself into.

Because Myles, for all his crazy mood swings and bizarre public-school snobberies, was Patrick's best friend. The only person who had thrown him a lifeline in that first horrible week at Oxford, when the scholarship money hadn't come through in time, and the other freshers had congealed into cliques and repelled all comers.

That was when Myles, in his filthy Volkswagen Golf, had nearly flattened Patrick at an intersection, and after berating him for cycling on the wrong side of the road, had suggested they go for a curry. There he had got roaring drunk, and said, 'Listen, Paddy, or whatever your name is. You can't stay in hall, it'll be ghastly, you'll never meet anyone worth meeting. Why don't you take the spare room in my house?'

So Patrick did.

His friend's *house*, for Christ's sake. Myles's mother was some kind of high-flying attorney, who'd bought it as a reward when he scraped into Oxford at the third attempt. And it was to her 'weekend retreat' in the South of France that Patrick was now flying, having spent the past two months schooling horses at a riding stable, to save up the fare.

In the three years that Patrick had lived in the house in Norham Gardens, Mrs Passmore had never once visited her son. Nor had Myles's father, who was a surgeon. Nor had his stepfather, who was a judge. Myles said he didn't mind, but Patrick knew his friend better.

It still struck Patrick as odd that he should have a friend. After his mom walked out he had never seen the point. Why get attached to people? They only left. But somehow, Myles had slipped through the net.

'And I'll tell you another thing,' Myles had said. 'Dr Hunt is a prick. No getting round it. A twenty-four-carat prick of the first water.'

That had made Patrick laugh. To Myles, everyone was a prick. Including Myles. 'Myles, who cares? You don't want to be an archaeologist, you're going to be Director-General of the BBC.'

'And you, Paddy my boy, will be my own personal therapist, when I crack up from the strain.'

'So,' Patrick had said, 'you're not on this dig for the thrill of the find. So who is she?'

'I thought you'd never ask, old chum. Ah, the Vestal Virgin! *Yum yum yum!*'

With a *ping*, the sign for fastening seat belts lit up.

Patrick turned to gaze at the flawless sky. He bit his lip. From what Myles had told him, Antonia Hunt sounded like someone he could do without. Classy English girls put him on edge. They invariably patronised him when they learned that he was from Wyoming. 'Isn't that where cowboys come from?' they would say.

'So I guess Nerissa is a thing of the past, huh?' he had said to Myles.

A chuckle. 'God, you Yanks are so old-fashioned! It's so endearing.'

'I guess that means it's not goodbye to Nerissa.'

'What's wrong with keeping them both on their toes? Poor darling Toni hasn't a clue what's going on, so it can't possibly hurt her, and Nissa doesn't care one way or the other.'

From what Myles had told him about Nerissa, Patrick didn't like the sound of her, either. According to Myles, she was a dead ringer for the young Brigitte Bardot, and *serious* class. And on top of it all, she also happened to be Myles's stepsister. Which made her the daughter of the judge, from a previous marriage. Shit.

His stomach clenched. He was on his way to the South of France—the *South of France*, for Christ's sake. Grace Kelly and Cary Grant; cravats and croupiers and private yachts, and classy English girls with cool disparaging stares. Shit.

Get a grip, he told himself. You can do this. Set yourself more than you can do, and you'll do it. Right?

He had read that in a *Reader's Digest* when he was nine, the day after his mother walked out. He had been playing truant in the drugstore, numbly riffling the magazines, and wondering what he had done to make her leave. *Set yourself more than you can do.*

But what, the nine-year-old Patrick had asked, do I want to do? And then he knew. He wanted to end up the opposite of his father. He wanted to end up *not* humiliated, and *not* in a trailer home, and *not* a drunk.

As always when he thought of his father, he felt the familiar pain.

The only thing the poor guy ever wanted was to be proud of you. So what did you do? You broke his heart. And now you've got to live with that. Too late to make it better now.

The pretty stewardess came down the aisle. 'Bar's closing, sir. Last chance for another drink.' She gave him a brilliant smile.

Politely, he declined.

Still smiling, she leaned over to clear his tray-table.

She was mid-twenties, about his own age. Very pretty. And she'd been back twice already to check on him. If he made a move, they could have a coffee somewhere in the airport, and she would probably be available for a bout of what he and Myles called 'Teflon sex'. Fun for a couple of hours, and let's move right along. Which was exactly the way Patrick preferred it. Though of course there would be no time for anything like that today, for Myles would be waiting at the airport.

Myles wasn't.

Patrick stood around for an hour on the concourse, then he spent another twenty minutes trying to call the house at La Bastide. Eventually he got a ringing tone, but no one picked up.

Then he became seriously hungry. Tried to buy the smallest, plainest roll he could find at the airport café. Succeeded after a struggle, and wished he hadn't, for it was mind-blowingly expensive.

Another hour went by. He thought about getting a bus into Toulouse and finding a train. Gave up on the idea—and not just because it would probably swallow his entire month's spending money, all seventy-five pounds and fifty pence. He was beginning to realise that not speaking French was going to be a problem, for his high-school Spanish cut no ice with the French.

Why hadn't he learned French in high school? He could have, but he'd chosen Latin instead. 'With Latin, you're halfway there in most European languages,' his mother had airily assured him once, and he'd swallowed it whole, as he'd swallowed everything else she told him.

Looking back, that seemed like just another of her British tricks for tightening the cultural thumbscrews on her only son and her poor dumb hick of a husband.

Thanks, Mom. Wherever you are.

Myles Cantellow awoke with a start and stared at the ceiling, wondering, as he always did, where he was and who was beside him.

Ah, yes. You're at the mill with Toni.

Like the rest of the mill, her room was shabby and scantily furnished, but he found that endearing. Her mother—the Ageing Debutante, as he liked to call her—had stopped coming to La Bastide years ago, and neither Toni nor her father bothered much with their surroundings.

Toni lay on her side with her back to him, but he could tell from her breathing that she wasn't asleep. She hadn't enjoyed the sex. She hadn't said anything about it—she rarely did—but he could tell. He, on the other hand, was still coming down from somewhere among the chimney-stacks. Though there was no point in telling her that.

'I don't know about you,' he said quietly, 'but for me it wasn't that great.' He watched her turn to look at him. 'Maybe,' he added, 'I can only have good sex with women I don't like.'

She regarded him impassively, as she always did when he had hurt her. 'Maybe so,' she said at last.

'The trouble with you,' he said, 'is you lack the confidence to say what you feel.'

'The trouble with you,' she replied evenly, 'is that you'd use it against me if I did.'

He grinned. 'Paranoid.'

Her lip curled. 'Machiavelli.'

He was constantly amazed at how a girl like her, who could fearlessly contradict professors, and manage a team of volunteers like a four-star general, was going out with him. Myles Cantellow, fuckwit *extraordinaire*, and this summer's lucky recipient of a Gentleman's Third in Psychology, Philosophy, and Physiology—while she had a First in

Classics *and* a PhD, and was waiting to hear about a Cambridge lecture-ship which she was bound to get.

What the hell was she doing with him? If the roles had been reversed he wouldn't have given her the time of day. But they had been together now for just over two months, which was twice as long as any other relationship he'd ever had.

Sometimes he wondered if it was all the fault of her family. The Ageing Debutante must be pretty hard to take at the best of times, and so was Dr Hunt the Prick, still bumping along the bottom of the acade-mic world. Then there was the gorgeous dumb-blonde sister, Caroline, who had perfected the art of making Toni feel the ugly duckling.

With a family like that, no wonder escaping to Oxford had seemed like such a miracle to poor Toni. Once, in a fit of openness, she had told him how she had taken herself in hand in her first term there. Contact lenses, new clothes, a bit of make-up. It didn't sound like much to Myles, but obviously it meant a lot to her. Oh well, who was he to com-plain, when it meant that she'd never found the time or the courage to get a boyfriend? Lucky, lucky Myles. Although sometimes he felt sorry for her, stumbling across *him*, of all people, at her very first attempt.

He could have told her from the start that she was wasting her time with him. No one stayed with Myles Cantellow for long. They ended up hating him, and left. But when he thought about Toni leaving him, his chest hollowed out and he felt sick. To shake it off, he jumped out of bed and went naked to the chest of drawers.

In the mirror he saw her reflection watching him. He really liked the way she looked. The long, crinkly black hair. The pale skin.

His gaze shifted to his own face. He wasn't handsome, but women didn't seem to mind, so he didn't either. What he minded was that he was just *under* six feet tall, with a small girlish mouth, and hair that was too thin and too blond, when everyone knew that only dark men, like Patrick, got taken seriously.

'I don't know,' he said to Toni's reflection. 'Maybe you're frigid.'

She blinked. Absorbing the hurt without showing it. Her own pecu-liar response to pain.

'Maybe,' he went on, 'we should stop sleeping together.'

'If you like.'

Mission accomplished. Now she had something to think about while he was in Toulouse, and he'd got rid of the hollowness in his chest. 'I've got to go,' he said.

'You had to go an hour ago, when you came in. You should be at the airport by now.'

'Patrick can wait. He'll have to.' What Toni didn't understand was that it was crucial to be late to pick up his friend. Can't have Myles Cantellow hanging around looking keen now can we? Not when he's the one with the house and the public-school background and the villa in France, while Patrick's just some Yank from the middle of nowhere.

He gathered his spare change from the chest of drawers, along with his Amex card and the Roman coin his mother had given him when he got into university. He jammed the whole lot in his back pocket and said, 'I almost forgot. I won't be helping out at the Source any more. None of us will.'

That made her sit up. 'Why not?'

'Your father's pulling us off it. Didn't he tell you?'

'Wha—t?'

'He says there's no point in carrying on up there when we've only got three weeks left, and he needs everyone down on the main site, and anyway, the Source is obviously nothing to do with your fave Roman, and—oh, yes—he can't devote any more manpower to your childhood fantasy. Yup. I think that about covers it.'

He watched her take it all in. As he had known she would, she flicked a glance at the bedside cabinet, where her precious little secret was securely locked up: her own attempt at translating the Cassius *Poems*, along with a note of her screwball theories on the poet. It was all desperately heretical and personal, and secret—or so she thought. Poor Toni. He could screw her up about that too, any time he liked.

'Sometimes,' she said quietly, 'it feels as if he doesn't want me to succeed in anything I do.'

'Well, two cheers for you, Toni! You got there at last! Parents fuck you up. Didn't you know?'

Doubtfully, she met his eyes. It was amazing. She just didn't get it.

He paused in the doorway. 'I thought I'd take the Jeep instead of the Panda.' The Jeep was her father's, and looked so much cooler than the Panda, which belonged to his mother.

'OK by me,' she said.

'Oh, and by the way,' he added. 'About the sex—maybe we should keep trying a bit longer.'

If Myles was right about her father, thought Antonia as she pulled on shorts and a Peruvian cotton top and padded downstairs, she was going to be a good deal busier from now on. She would have to get up at least two hours earlier every day in order to put in time at the Source before joining the main dig.

The Source was her personal project. She had funded it from her savings, negotiated with the landowner for permission to dig, and designed the excavation strategy herself. She had first discovered the limestone cave as a child when she had stayed in the valley with her family. She had known immediately that it was a magic place and somehow had known that Cassius had been there too. Now, after years of waiting and hoping, she had finally won the chance to prove that 2,000 years ago, Cassius had lived in the valley of the Sarac, and had worshipped at the Source.

Contrary to what her father clearly believed, she wasn't doing it to prove him wrong. Quite the opposite. She wanted to get closer to Cassius because by doing that she got closer to solving the riddle, and fulfilling a pact she had made with her father sixteen years before. Together they would solve the riddle and become famous. Together. Once they did that, everything else would fall into place.

The kitchen was empty. Everyone was up at the main dig, or across the courtyard in the pot-shed. Not that there were very many of them. By any standards, the dig was woefully undermanned. Apart from herself and her father, there was only Myles and Nerissa (when they felt like it), Simon (because he needed the credits for his degree), and the ever-faithful Modge. It was hardly much of a team.

Maybe Daddy was right about the Source. Maybe they *should* just concentrate on what the university expected them to do. Keep on doggedly excavating the patch above the river, which had looked so promising as the site of a Roman villa. At least, it had looked promising from the aerial photos. But since the dig had begun, it was looking more and more likely that the Roman villa was not on the main site after all, but securely buried beneath the modern house *adjacent* to it. The beautiful little house with its elegant paved terrace, whose elderly Parisian owner only visited for a couple of weeks every year.

Judging by the mess on the kitchen table, her father had recently had lunch. Antonia snapped off the end of a loaf. If she hurried, she could reach the main site in under five minutes. Maybe her father wouldn't notice that she'd been gone for over two hours.

She reminded herself that it didn't matter if he *did* notice. She was twenty-four years old, she could do what she liked. So why did he still have this knack of making her feel in the wrong?

Hurrying out into the scullery, she almost fell over Modge.

The little girl had been studying her reflection in the mirror over the sink. To judge from her expression, she hated what she saw.

'Myles said I could go with him to the airport to meet Patrick,' she blurted out. 'He's gone to fetch the Jeep.'

Modge was on the verge of tears as she fought a losing battle to secure her ponytail with a plastic clip of fluorescent green. She wore an eye-popping lime-green T-shirt tucked into tight purple shorts which bit into her high, round midriff. The final *coup de grâce* was a *Star Trek* knapsack bulging awkwardly between her shoulder blades.

When she saw Antonia eyeing the knapsack, she shrugged it off and chucked it on the floor. 'Myles says only toddlers wear knapsacks,' she mumbled, 'but I *need* it! It's got my sunglasses and comic and some tissues and a bottle of water in case I get thirsty.'

Antonia hated to see the anxiety on the small sallow face. It wasn't fair. Why should it matter how an eight-year-old looked?

'Sometimes,' she said, 'I could clobber Myles.'

Modge's jaw dropped.

'Sometimes,' Antonia went on, 'I think he isn't a human being at all. I think he's a robot from outer space. Or maybe an android.'

Modge blinked. No one made fun of her half-brother.

'Come here, you,' said Antonia, pulling Modge towards her. 'You know,' she said, 'you'd feel better if you wore the T-shirt outside the shorts. Like this. And the way to wear a knapsack and not look like a toddler is to wear it over just one shoulder. There. Now you look radical.'

Modge threw her an uncertain look. 'Is that good?'

'Oh, yes. It's the ultimate in cool. Now how about losing that clip, and just using your usual one? Where is it, inside the knapsack? There. We know this one'll stay in place. But let's pep it up a bit, shall we?' She undid the ribbons from her own ponytail and tied them round Modge's. '*Et voilà*. A garnish of sapphire and silver—which, if I remember rightly, are the colours of the United Federation of Planets.'

Modge turned pink. '*Radical,*' she said.

Modge sat stiffly in the front of the Jeep and tried not to flinch at her half-brother's driving. When they nearly bumped into a lorry on the motorway, or lurched scarily as they rounded a bend, she sucked in her lips and struggled not to wince.

Earlier, as they were manoeuvring out of the courtyard at the mill, Myles had done something wrong to the gears, and the Jeep had continued going backwards when they should have gone forwards, and nearly backed into the wall. Antonia, watching from the porch, had laughed, and Modge had giggled, and Myles had nearly chucked her out.

He was quite capable of chucking her out at a petrol station, and leaving her there. Myles was capable of anything. He was *so* wicked. Modge longed to do something he'd admire.

'Cat got your tongue, Modge-Podge?' said Myles.

She gripped her seat, and wondered what he meant. It didn't sound very nice. Alfonse, the mill cat, would never do a thing like that. 'No,' she said carefully.

'Nervous about meeting your boyfriend again?'

'He's not my boyfriend.'

He laughed. 'Then why are you all togged up? Bells on your toes and ribbons in your hair.'

Her stomach turned over. Now that Myles had noticed the ribbons, she was desperate to take them off, for if he mentioned them to Patrick she would die. But if she *did* take them off, Antonia would be hurt, so it looked like she was stuck with them. Next to Patrick—and Myles when he wasn't being nasty—Antonia was her favourite person in the whole galaxy. Apart from Mummy, of course.

'Don't worry, Modge,' Myles said. 'I won't tell Patrick.'

She shot him a look. She'd heard *that* before.

Android, she told him silently in her head. It made her feel better.

They reached the airport. She was scared of airports, but knew better than to show it in front of Myles. She wanted to hold Myles's hand, but he was walking too fast, so she clutched her *Star Trek* pack and hurried after him.

'What's the time?' he said when they were inside, weaving through the crowds. He never wore a watch.

Modge consulted the Vulcan Time-Scanner on her wrist. 'Six minutes to three.'

Myles hooted. 'Oh, *man*! This time I've really done it, even for me! The poor bastard's plane got in at twelve.'

Modge's jaw dropped. Did he mean to say that they'd kept Patrick waiting for *three hours*?

Then suddenly there he was, and he was even handsomer than she remembered. And he didn't look in the slightest bit cross. He was laughing, and he gave Myles the sort of punch in the tummy which boys do when they're pleased to see each other. Myles was laughing too, and Modge could tell that he was trying not to show how incredibly pleased he was to see his friend. Shyly, she waited with her knapsack at her feet. She was so happy she wanted to cry.

Then Patrick reached down and hoisted his rucksack over one shoulder, *exactly* as Antonia had taught *her* to do. Casually, Modge did the same with hers.

Patrick looked down at her and grinned. A proper grin, as if he really was pleased to see her. 'Hi, Imogen,' he said.

By the time they were nearing the village of La Bastide, Patrick was fed up with France, Myles, and the British. But mostly with Myles.

'Well, it was your fault for flying to Toulouse instead of Perpignan,' Myles had said at the airport, as he chucked Patrick's rucksack in the Jeep. 'Perpignan's so much *nearer*, it's just down the road.'

'Yeah,' said Patrick drily, 'and British Airways is about twice as expensive as Air Express.'

Myles rolled his eyes. 'Oh, *money*! Is that all you think about?'

Knowing he was in the wrong made Myles drive even more appallingly than usual. Modge sat in the back gripping the edge of her seat, and Patrick concentrated on the scenery.

The South of France wasn't what he'd expected at all. He'd expected something like Beverly Hills. Palm trees and country clubs, and turquoise swimming pools. Instead he found himself in a harsh, lonely country of blinding silver rock and dusty thorn-scrub; a crazy geometry of dizzying gorges, towering pinnacles, and sun-baked uplands.

After about an hour and a half they reached a bridge across a fast-running river which foamed from the mouth of a narrow, steep-sided gorge. The entrance to the gorge was guarded by two massive, crazily leaning rock buttresses, several hundred feet high. Halfway across the bridge, Myles cut the engine. 'We're here. That's La Bastide up ahead.'

Beyond the bridge, the road veered sharply away from the mouth of the gorge and wound up to a jumble of Spanish-looking houses clinging to a steep hill. Patrick saw terracotta roofs, thick whitewashed walls, and tiny shuttered windows. Terraces of vines and olive trees occupied every spare inch in between. A small church squatted beside a capacious cemetery dotted with cypresses, and at the top of the hill, a ruined castle towered over the village. From there, a stony ridge ran in a long swooping curve to join the eastern buttress of the gorge.

'Our house,' said Myles, 'is Les Limoniers—the one just below the castle.' He pointed to a large whitewashed villa with sky-blue awnings, several terraces, and a garden of bougainvillea and lemon trees. 'The views are amazing. Best in the village.'

That figures, thought Patrick sourly, determined not to be overwhelmed.

He pointed to the slope beyond the bridge, where, just below the first house in the village, an area the size of three tennis courts had been cleared and staked out in squares. 'I guess that's the main site, huh?'

'Got it in one,' said Myles. 'The skinny shit shaking his head is our esteemed leader, Dr Hunt. The gawky redhead with the ponytail is Simon the Dork. And the blonde doing nothing in the shade is of course the luscious Nissa.'

The young Brigitte Bardot, thought Patrick with a sinking feeling.

'Tell you what,' said Myles, drumming his fingers on the steering wheel. 'You get out here with Modge-Podge and go and meet everyone, and I'll take your pack up to the house.'

Patrick opened his mouth to protest, but Myles cut him short. 'No time like the present, Patroclus. Go on—please.'

Patrick shot him a glance. His friend's eyes were bloodshot and jittery, and there was a thin sheen of sweat on his upper lip. He needed a hit.

Patrick gave a brisk nod, and opened the door. 'We'll catch you later. Come on, Imogen.'

The elder Dr Hunt turned out to have querulous grey eyes and a nicotine-stained beard which drew attention to a bitter mouth. He neither welcomed Patrick nor introduced him to the others, but merely gave him the briefest of handshakes, and told him to go and find his daughter, who would give him a site plan and a list of Do's and Don'ts.

'That would be Dr Hunt the younger?' Patrick said.

The thin lips became perceptibly thinner. Clearly, on this dig there was only *one* Dr Hunt.

Well, screw you, thought Patrick, watching him go. Out loud, he said to the blonde who had wandered over to inspect him: 'I guess I've just offended the Professor, huh?'

'Oh, don't mind him,' she said, 'he's just in a strop because he had a row with Toni. And by the way,' she took off her shades and favoured him with a cool smile, 'he isn't a professor. I know you Americans call everyone a professor, but over here they're not as common as they are in the States.'

Patrick nodded gravely.

She was extremely pretty in a feline sort of way, with large greenish-grey eyes and a flawless complexion tanned a beautiful honey-gold. She wore a wide straw hat and a short, floaty, flowered dress which seemed wildly out of place on a dig, but suited her smallness and femininity.

The tall redheaded guy had also wandered over. Hadn't Myles said this was Nerissa's boyfriend? Or maybe he just *wanted* to be her boyfriend. Whatever, he was welcome to her, so he could stop looking as if he'd just swallowed a lemon.

'So,' said Simon Toynbee, 'you're an American. Does that mean you don't speak French?'

'Well, I'm not sure about that as a definition,' Patrick said evenly, 'but yeah, it does.'

Simon tried not to look pleased. 'That'll set you back a bit.'

'Don't worry,' said Nerissa. 'We'll look after you.'

'Thanks,' said Patrick. 'In fact, your sister's been doing a pretty good job of that already.'

'Half-sister,' Nerissa put in sharply, with a glance at Modge. 'Same father, different mothers.'

At Patrick's side, the little girl flushed.

Patrick bit back his irritation. 'You know, it's getting kind of late. Why don't we let you finish up here and—'

'Yes, why don't you?' said Simon. 'Toni's probably down at the mill, you can check in with her.'

Shyly, Modge took his hand. 'Come along. I'll show you the way.'

Just before they reached the bridge, Modge took a side road on the left which Patrick hadn't noticed before, for it dropped steeply below the level of the parapet. They climbed down through pines, cypresses and oaks, and finally reached a dark ivy-choked ruin at the water's edge.

The Moulin de Sarac must once have housed a pretty wealthy miller, for it was built around a spacious courtyard, and reached through an impressive stone archway. It would have been magnificent about 400 years ago, but since then it had slipped a bit. The roof was a patchwork of moss and broken terracotta, half the outer wall had disappeared beneath a mountain of ivy, and the other half had subsided into the river.

The Gorges de Sarac, Patrick decided, was a truly horrible place. Above his head the black-streaked Roc shut out the sun. The riverbanks were choked with tumbled boulders and fallen trees, from which rose the sour tang of rottenness. If there were birds, Patrick couldn't see or hear any. He couldn't hear anything above the thunder of the river, which reverberated through the gorge.

'Hey, Modge,' he said suddenly, 'I'll bet Antonia wants to be by herself right now, after that row with her dad. What say we skip the mill and you show me the Source?'

They took a dirt road which branched off from the mill track and snaked steeply up the Roc, hugging a stony slope of sun-bleached thistles on which an occasional twisted olive tree struggled to survive.

It was a steep climb, but after ten minutes they rounded the buttress and left La Bastide behind. Suddenly Patrick found himself in a different world: harsher, wilder, and astonishingly remote.

He had always thought of Europe as a crowded place, but looking around, he couldn't see a single rooftop, or other sign of human occupation. All he could see were the splintered hills marching grimly towards the horizon, and the stark white brilliance of the Pyrenees.

After about a mile they came to an aluminium farm gate wedged open with a rock, and immediately after that, the track split. Modge told him that the left-hand fork, which was deeply rutted with tyre tracks, continued over the Roc to a farm called Le Figarol, where old Monsieur Panabière, who owned the Source, lived with his invalid wife. He was also the owner of the tiny terrace of vines ten yards down.

They continued up the right-hand track. The air grew hotter, dizzy with the scent of wild thyme. The cicadas were deafening.

After another few hundred yards, the track became a footpath. The rocks threw back the heat like a furnace, and Patrick wished he had kept his pack with him, and could have changed into a pair of shorts. When he left Oxford that morning it had been 'unseasonably cool'—as the British endearingly termed their lousy summers—so he was wearing jeans and a heavy cotton polo shirt.

Patrick was starting to feel bad about dragging Modge along. Even after he had relieved her of the *Star Trek* pack, her funny little face remained the colour of a ripe plum. But when he suggested that maybe she should wait under an olive tree while he carried on for a bit, she looked so crestfallen that he dropped it. The Source, she said, was a magic place, she absolutely *loved* it, and he would too.

They climbed further up the gorge, and as he got into his stride, the irritations of the day fell away. This was the same track—the *same track*, for Christ's sake—which the pilgrims had taken thousands of years before, when they had believed that the Source possessed healing powers. He had read about that on the plane. And the 'Fontaine del Bon Cristia', The Fountain of the Good Christ, was, by European standards, a pretty recent name, cobbled together by medieval Christians in an attempt to stamp out the last traces of paganism. The old name, which Modge said the locals still used, was 'La Source du Cheval'. The Spring of the Horse. Patrick wondered why they called it that. Up here you would need a mountain goat, not a horse.

They reached the end of the track. Ahead, a massive overhang framed a semicircle of pure darkness.

'See how it's a horseshoe shape?' panted Modge. 'There's a reason for that. Antonia told me. On Easter Day the Devil fought a terrible battle with St Pastou, and the Devil lost, and *leapt* on his horse and galloped up the gorge, and St Pastou chased after him. And just here, the Devil's horse gave a huge jump and left his hoof-print in the mountain. So St Pastou made a spring in the cave, to wash it clean again. Which means,' she added, 'that the cave is *actually* a giant hoof-print.'

Patrick went to the mouth of the cave, then stopped. Cold breath seemed to emanate from within. He felt strangely reluctant to enter. An interloper. Peering into the gloom, he saw that the cave was perhaps fifty feet deep, and roofed by stalactites which gave it a frozen, chaotic feel.

Narrowing his eyes to adjust to the dimness, he saw a thin black stream of water trickling from a narrow cleft in the back wall. It pooled in a small natural basin of rock, then seeped over the rim and disappeared down a crack in the floor.

Patrick thought of the poem he had read on the plane. *'I know a place in the hills where the gods walk the earth.'*

Standing before the darkness of the cave, he could believe it. At his back he heard the wind in the dry sage pods. He heard its velvet sighs in the oak at the cave mouth, and its deep marine soughing in the pine further down the track. And he could believe, as the pagans had believed, that a different spirit inhabited each plant.

'Would you mind awfully,' said a voice from the darkness of the cave, 'if you didn't come inside?'

Patrick's heart jerked.

'Sorry if I startled you,' said the voice, which was a girl's. 'But there's a grid in here, and if you don't know where to walk you might damage something.'

Patrick licked dry lips. For an instant, as her voice issued from the darkness, he had thought an oracle had spoken. He cleared his throat. Then he said hoarsely, 'I guess you'd be the second Dr Hunt?'

'Sorry, yes,' said the voice. 'I was in the side-chamber, that's why you didn't see me, and I was just finishing up, so I'd turned off the lamp to save gas. Modge, take this lot for me, will you?'

A girl emerged from the cave and handed Modge a trowel and a clipboard and some plastic bags with bits of rubble in them, while she rummaged in a knapsack hanging from her shoulder. Awkwardly she offered Patrick her other hand, but he was too startled to take it, and by the time he had regained his wits and extended his, she had dropped hers.

To his astonishment, he realised that she was nervous. He watched her brush the dust off her hands, drop her rucksack, stoop to retrieve it and brush the dust off it, then notice that she'd just dirtied her palms again and brush them off on the seat of her shorts, before once more extending her hand to him. This time he took it.

What the hell does a girl like this have to be nervous about? he thought in bemusement.

Myles had nicknamed her the Vestal Virgin, but that was all wrong. She didn't look Roman, she looked Minoan. He could picture her turning ceremonial cartwheels across a bull's back. Although before she did so, she would probably apologise to the bull.

She was tall, only a few inches shorter than he, with wide, straight shoulders, a narrow waist, and generous hips and bosom. Her colouring was clear and dramatic: pale skin, dark eyes, long dark hair with a kink to it. A wide mouth, and a fine straight nose with a high Grecian bridge.

The high priestess, he thought numbly.

And like a priestess, she was ablaze with colour. She wore wine-red shorts and a sleeveless top throbbing with zigzags of pure colour: emerald, sapphire, topaz and ruby. Her hair was tied back with a twist of satin ribbons—one the colour of ripe grapes, the other a deep, burning saffron—and from her ears hung tiny papier-mâché parrots. After the sun-bleached hues of the climb, so much richness hurt his eyes.

Belatedly, it occurred to him that he still had Modge's *Star Trek* bag dangling from one hand. He must look like an idiot. But Antonia Hunt didn't seem to notice. She was retrieving her specimens from Modge and packing them in her rucksack. Over her shoulder she said, 'Myles said you're from Wyoming?'

Patrick braced himself. But she surprised him by asking if that meant he'd learned Spanish in school.

'Uh-huh,' he replied warily.

'Lucky you,' she said with feeling. 'You'll probably get on far better with the locals than we do with our Parisian French.'

'You speak *Spanish*?' said Modge, looking up at him. 'Wow.'

Embarrassed, he took Antonia Hunt's now-bulging rucksack from her—in the teeth of her protestations that she could manage, honestly—and they started down the track.

'I'm sorry you had to hike all this way to find me,' she said.

'Well, in fact I wasn't—'

'—and I do hope you won't be bored out here. People often do get bored on a dig, you know, it's so much less exciting—I mean, less *immediately* exciting—than they expect. And I'm afraid we haven't had much luck on this one. In fact, none at all. We were hoping for traces of Roman occupancy, but it's been a huge disappointment.'

'That's OK with me,' he put in, when she paused for breath. 'I mean, I don't know much archaeology, but I've been on a couple of digs, so I know what to expect.'

'Oh, *have* you? But that's marvellous! I wish Myles had told me. We're crying out for experienced help.'

'I wouldn't say I was exactly—'

'You've no idea how hard it is to get *anyone* to help out here.'

Modge looked round at them and beamed, and skipped ahead with Antonia's clipboard in her arms.

Patrick still couldn't think of anything to say. He felt as if he'd been kicked in the chest. Luckily, Antonia Hunt was keeping up an edgy torrent of conversation enough for two.

She told him about the dig—about both digs—and he noticed that she was curiously self-deprecating about herself, and overgenerous when it came to her father. She even defended his decision to pull all the volunteers off the dig at the Source, when clearly it meant the world to her.

But strangely, when she started telling him about the Roman poet, Cassius, who she thought might be linked with the Source, she became a different girl. Focused, incisive, and not flustered at all. And she made no concessions whatsoever to Patrick as a non-classicist: he could either follow what she told him, or ask if he didn't, but until then, she would simply assume that he could keep up.

He liked her for that. It made a change from being patronised. But he didn't ask many questions. In fact, he didn't ask any. She was nothing like what he had expected.

What on earth was Myles playing at with a girl like this? Why didn't he stick with someone of his own kind, like Nerissa?

'So what do you think of the Source?' asked Antonia Hunt, cutting across his thoughts.

He wondered what to say. With anyone else he would have made some quip and left it at that. But with this girl he couldn't do that. For the first time since they had met, she was actually looking at him. Her face was slightly anxious, as if it really mattered what he thought.

That made Patrick feel curiously obliged to tell her the truth. 'I guess,' he began at last, searching for words, '"haunted" isn't the right expression for a place like that. It feels as if—as if something lives there. Or lived there once.' He shook his head. 'No, that's not right. I guess what I mean is, it's a place where the past feels very close.'

Her lips parted. 'That's so well put. That's exactly how it feels.'

Then she smiled at him. Not the quick edgy smile she had given him at the Source, but a wide, genuine smile that took his breath away.

'Come along, you two!' shouted Modge from further down the track.

'Coming!' Antonia Hunt called back, and started after the little girl.

Dimly, Patrick sensed the sun on his back and the smell of the wild thyme, and the breeze softly whipping the dust around his ankles.

Slowly he followed Antonia Hunt down the track.

To Patrick's relief, Myles noticed nothing when he and Modge finally reached Les Limoniers, having left Antonia Hunt at the mill.

Myles was in too good a mood to notice anything: restored, refreshed, and almost puppyish in his desire to show Patrick the room he had prepared for him. It was large and airy, and painted brilliant white, with a cool, blue-tiled floor, and a breathtaking view across the ridge towards the Roc de St Pastou.

Myles left Patrick to unpack, and went off to fetch the champagne he'd put on ice, and the *tarte Tatin* he'd bought in the village bakery, and the *pâté de sanglier*, which they would have to eat without bread, as he'd forgotten to buy any.

Patrick, emerging newly showered onto the terrace in shorts and a T-shirt, found the omission of the bread obscurely touching. It made him feel worse.

He sat in one of the wrought-iron chairs facing the mountains, and listened to Myles swapping jokes with Modge in the kitchen. After a while he leaned forward and put his elbows on the rail.

An overwhelming sense of danger swept over him. He had never felt like this. Not once. Not even close. It was terrifying. It felt as if someone had pulled away a scab and exposed his raw flesh to the burning sun.

You've got to get out of here, Patrick thought suddenly. Make some excuse, fall sick, it doesn't matter what. Just get out of here and go back to England. Myles will be furious, but what can he do?

For what's the alternative? Stay here, and steal your best friend's girl? Or sit back and watch him screw her up? Great choice. Oh, yeah.

You've got to get out of here fast.

CHAPTER THREE
Rome, March 31, 53 BC

CASSIUS HAD BEEN in a terrible mood all week.

He tried not to let it show when he was with Plautius, but the old man was too perceptive to be fooled for long.

Finally the evening came when Plautius took a little too much raisin wine, and made the mistake of congratulating Cassius on the 'honourable' course he had taken in avoiding another encounter with the daughter of Publius Tacitus Silanus. 'You did the right thing, my boy! The honourable thing. I'm proud of you.'

Cassius set his teeth, and barked at the freedman to refill his wine cup. He didn't need Plautius to tell him he was doing the right thing. What choice did he have? One glance at her father's house had been enough to tell him that anything else would be madness.

Three days after the Day of Blood, he had wandered up onto the Palatine and sought out the house. It was dusk—he had just got off duty—and compared to the din of the barracks, the Palatine Hill was like a tomb. Her father's house was in one of the quietest and most exclusive streets. Every brick, every tile, murmured discreetly of old money.

So of course he had been right to stay away. To bury himself in his duties and forget all about her. He only wished that Plautius didn't feel the need to applaud him so fulsomely to his face.

But unfortunately the old man did, so Cassius snapped at him, and then felt bad. Which prompted him to make amends by offering to take his friend's place at a poetry evening, when Plautius sprained his ankle getting out of the bath.

Ah, how the gods enjoy their little jokes! Who would have thought that Plautius, of all people, would be his undoing?

As Cassius had feared, the gathering turned out to be excruciatingly dull. The host was an elderly crony of Plautius's from the law courts, who had chosen to delight his friends by reading the unabridged version of his 'poetic discourse' on 'The Legends of the Deeps'. Plautius, who had been favoured with an advance copy, had generously pronounced it 'a fine, scholarly work on a sorely neglected theme'.

Not neglected enough, thought Cassius sourly. Stifling a yawn, he started counting the heads of the audience, for something to do.

She was two rows ahead of him, and across the aisle on his left. Sitting very straight and still, and staring in front of her with a rigid intensity which told him instantly that she knew he was behind her.

She wore a sleeveless gown of deep sapphire, the colour of a clear night sky just before the last light fades. Pearls in her ears, and the same gold half-moon at her breast.

Abruptly the reading came to an end, and there was a smattering of exhausted applause. People stood up, stretched, chatted, and began drifting towards the dining room.

Cassius watched her turn and make some appeal to the thickset, youngish man—her brother?—sitting beside her. *It's hot*, she seemed to be saying, fanning herself. *May I go outside for some air?*

The brother bestowed a gracious nod. Presumably he was eager to attain the dining room.

Still fanning herself, she rose and glided out onto the terrace.

What in Hades do I do now? wondered Cassius, his heart racing.

The sensible choice would be to say a swift goodbye to his host, and leave as rapidly as he could. That would also be the cowardly choice, and the cruel one. And discourteous, too. At the very least he ought to apologise for leading her on the other day at the procession.

Fool, said a waspish little voice inside his head. *You don't honestly believe that this has anything to do with courtesy?*

The garden was a pleasant place of smooth, sandy walks hedged with rosemary and box, and dimly illuminated by torches and moonlight. Which still left plenty of shadowy patches beneath the fruit trees.

He found her at the end of an arcade of mulberries.

She made no pretence at being surprised that he should have followed her outside, but merely drew back so that anyone passing the other end of the arcade would believe that he was alone.

'You weren't at the Games,' she said in a low voice.

'I had duties,' he lied.

'You said you'd be there.'

'Yes.'

'You were playing games with me.'

'No. No.'

Her face was grave, and he could see that she was trembling. Her hands were taut at her sides, clutching the stuff of her dress. 'I offended you,' she said abruptly. 'That day when we met. I was rude. I sneered at you.' Her chin went up. 'I'm sorry.'

'No,' he put in quickly. 'It's I who should apologise to you. I should have introduced myself, not led you on like that, it wasn't fair. That's why I came out here. To apologise.' Another lie. His cheeks darkened with shame. 'I had no idea,' he said, 'that you'd be here tonight. If I'd known, I wouldn't have come.' He realised how that must sound, and flushed anew.

She bowed her head. 'You've been avoiding me, haven't you?'

'Yes,' he said gently.

'Why?'

'You know why.'

Her head came up and she met his eyes. He felt himself sway.

'This is too dangerous,' he said. 'For both of us. You know that. You must go inside, now. Find your brother and make him take you home. At once. I'll wait here until you've gone.'

He stood back to let her pass, but she did not move. He watched her face turn pale. It tore his heart to see with what prickly dignity she strove to master her hurt. But at length a tear welled from her eye and spilled down her cheek.

'No,' he said. 'No. You mustn't cry.'

Without knowing what he did, he put out his hand and stopped the tear with his finger.

She stood perfectly still while he touched her cheek. Then, with a fine, proud gesture that was to stay with him for years, she twisted round with her back to him so that he wouldn't see more tears.

He stood with his fists at his sides, watching the silent rise and fall of her shoulders as she cried.

At last he reached out and turned her gently round, and drew her into his arms.

CHAPTER FOUR
La Bastide,
September 18–19, 1988

BEFORE PATRICK HAD COME to La Bastide, Antonia used to spend Saturday nights with Myles at Les Limoniers. Then on Sundays she would get up early, pull on her kimono, and wander out onto the terrace to watch the sun rise. But for the past fortnight she had been too self-conscious to wander around in her kimono. It embarrassed her to bump into Patrick after she had slept with Myles.

This particular Sunday morning, she lay in bed for longer than usual. Her face felt stiff with fatigue. Working at the Source as well as the main site was taking its toll. And last night had been late for everyone. Myles and Nerissa had insisted on driving twenty-five miles to Sainte Eulalie-les-Thermes for dinner at a three-star Michelin, and as Antonia's father refused to look after Modge, they had to take her with them. Modge spent the evening curled up asleep in the Panda, and Antonia spent the evening getting up to check on her.

It was after two when they returned to La Bastide. They dropped Simon and Nerissa at the mill, then drove up to Les Limoniers. Myles decided to watch the opening ceremony of the Olympics on TV. Patrick deposited the sleeping Modge in her room, then joined Myles in the sitting room. Antonia went to bed.

Now she lay watching the play of sunlight on the ceiling, while Myles whiffled into the pillow beside her.

Last night's redeeming feature, she thought, was that she had been asleep when he came in, so they didn't have sex. Then it occurred to her that this was not how one ought to feel about one's boyfriend. Maybe Myles was right, and she really was frigid. Or maybe they were just wrong for each other.

She felt too tired and too confused to deal with that now. And badly in need of a cup of coffee. She slid out of bed and pulled on shorts, a bra and a T-shirt. Then she twisted her hair into a plait, and padded downstairs.

Through the French windows she saw Modge and Patrick having breakfast on the terrace. Modge was shakily pouring Patrick a mug of coffee. She had already slopped a generous amount onto the table, but he pretended not to notice, though he swiftly took charge of his mug before she could spill that too. He thanked her gravely, and she sucked in her cheeks so as not to look too pleased.

Watching the little charade, Antonia wished Patrick liked her as much as he seemed to like Modge. Or even at all. But since his arrival he had avoided her whenever he could. On the dig he would listen politely to her instructions, then move away at the first opportunity. He never chatted or cracked jokes with her. And he never called her Toni. She didn't *like* her nickname, but she minded that he did not use it. 'Antonia' sounded so imperious; impossible to say without a drawl.

You botched things from the start, she told herself. That first day up at the Source, when you had to go rabbiting on like a demented school-marm. *'That's so well put. That's exactly how it feels.'* Who wouldn't feel patronised by that? You could hardly blame him for disliking her.

Why, then, did she sometimes get the feeling that he was protecting her? Like yesterday evening, when she had been digging for ten hours straight, and Myles was being particularly Myles-ish, and her father had decided to pick a fight with her about how to handle the next section. Patrick had wandered over and casually distracted them both, giving her a much-needed breathing space.

It didn't make sense. *He* didn't make sense.

She stepped out into the sunshine.

'Morning,' she said brightly, taking a chair opposite him.

'Hi, Antonia,' he said evenly.

This time, she resolved, it'll be different. I'll really try.

She watched him spread thick mountain honey on a brioche. He wore dusty jeans and a washed-out navy T-shirt. Bluish shadows beneath his eyes gave him a slightly bruised look.

She took a brioche from the basket. 'Myles is still asleep,' she said.

He gave a slow nod.

Well, full marks, Antonia. Ten out of ten for stating the obvious. And for making him feel like a gooseberry. She tried again. Asked him what he thought of the restaurant last night.

'OK. I guess . . . It went on a bit.'

'You're telling me. I was ready to go home an hour before we left.'

Again he nodded.

'*I* slept through the whole thing,' said Modge, pouring Antonia a mug of coffee and carrying it over to her.

'I know,' said Patrick with a smile. He had a nice smile. Antonia wished she got to see it more often.

'Patrick,' said Modge through a mouthful of brioche. 'Myles says you don't drink, but he's wrong. You *do* drink. I've seen you.'

He grinned at her. 'He means I don't drink alcohol.'

'Oh,' said Modge.

Antonia had wondered about that. Now she plucked up her courage and asked, 'Is that because you don't like it?'

He shook his head. Then he said simply, 'My dad was an alcoholic. It kind of put me off.'

'What's an alcoholic?' asked Modge.

'Someone who drinks too much and can't stop,' Patrick replied.

Modge looked at him with round eyes.

'That must have been rough,' Antonia ventured.

He thought for a moment. Then he said, 'My dad was all right.'

'I'm sorry,' she said quickly. 'I didn't mean—'

'I know you didn't,' he said with a slight smile.

They continued eating in awkward silence.

From the sitting room came the sound of someone knocking over a lamp and swearing savagely. Myles wandered out, yawning and rubbing his elbow. He threw himself onto a sun-lounger, stretched, and gave another tremendous yawn. 'Modge-Podge, save my life. Coffee, no milk, *tons* of sugar . . . Ah, you're an angel!'

Modge blushed.

'D'you know,' said Myles, 'I'm still so drunk I can't see straight? It'll be one hell of a hangover when it finally arrives.' He hooked his arm round Antonia's waist and pulled her down beside him.

She told him to let her go, as she had things to do.

'What can you possibly have to do at ten thirty on a Sunday morning?'

She improvised, and said she had to go to the Source.

He rolled his eyes. 'You know, Paddy, sometimes it's a bloody bore going out with a Vestal Virgin.'

'My name,' she said, 'is Antonia. Or Toni. You might try using one or the other now and again.'

'And mine's Imogen,' said Modge, plucking up her courage.

Myles chuckled. 'Who-ho! What's got into these two?'

Antonia tried to remove his arm from her waist.

'I've got a brilliant idea,' he said, tightening his grip. 'Let's go to Antibes and have drinks on the beach, then observe that hallowed Gallic tradition of a Sunday blowout somewhere good.'

'Yuk,' said Modge bravely. 'Last time we went to the beach I got stung by a jellyfish. I'm staying here.'

'Me too,' said Antonia. 'I've got the magnetometer for the day. I'm taking it up to the Source.'

'Stop sulking! Just because I called you a Vestal Virgin—'

'I'm not sulking, I just—'

'Yes you are.'

'I've never been to Antibes,' Patrick put in evenly. 'It sounds fun.'

'Now you've blown it,' Myles told him. 'Don't you know that fun and Vestal Virgins don't mix? Can't dance, can't get drunk. Never even swears. In fact, she has trouble letting go at all, don't you, my sweet?'

'Shut up, Myles,' snapped Antonia.

Patrick got to his feet. 'I think I'll take Imogen down to that bakery, or whatever you call it—'

'The *dépôt de pain*,' put in Modge.

'Right. We can pick up some stuff for this trip to the beach, in case we can't find a "good" enough restaurant.'

Modge leapt to her feet. 'Can I have *pain au chocolat* as well as *tarte Tatin*?'

'Sure you can,' said Patrick.

Myles laughed. 'Paddy, you're amazing! In one fell swoop you've restored family values *and* apple pie to us decadent Europeans.'

Patrick told him mildly to get lost.

'Where to, Patroclus?' Myles said with a smile. 'It's my terrace, isn't it?'

'It sure is,' said Patrick. His cheeks darkened.

'Patroclus?' Antonia snorted. 'No prizes for guessing who Achilles is supposed to be. Even if he is getting a bit thin on top.'

Myles's grin hardened. She would pay for that, but she didn't care.

Myles crossed his arms behind his head and lay back. 'Achilles the golden boy,' he murmured, 'that's me. A short life but a glorious one.'

'As if,' said Patrick drily. 'But you might not want to push that Achilles–Patroclus thing too far, buddy-boy. Those guys slept together, didn't they?'

'Wanker,' said Myles, chucking a brioche at him.

Patrick laughed and threw it back.

Myles dodged it like a cat. Then he got up and stretched, and wandered back into the house. 'Toni darling,' he called over his shoulder, 'when you've finished, come back to bed for a bit, there's a love.'

'I told you, I'm going up to the Source.'

'Oh, suit yourself!'

Modge ran off to find her sandals. Patrick hung back in the doorway. 'Listen,' he said suddenly. 'If you want help taking that magnetic thing up to the Source, I can do it before we go.'

She stared at him. He had never offered to help at the Source before. 'That's OK,' she said automatically, 'I'll take the Jeep.'

'But the road doesn't go all the way up. You'll have to carry it.'

'It's not heavy.'

He gave her a long look which she couldn't read.

It occurred to her that maybe he *wanted* to come to the Source. 'Sorry,' she said quickly, 'I didn't mean to stop you, if you wanted—'

'That's OK. I'd better go to Antibes with Myles.' He turned to go.

'Patrick,' she said suddenly. She felt herself blushing, for she didn't often call him by name. 'About your father . . .'

He waited, his face impassive.

'What I said about its being rough for you, I mean, about him being an alcoholic. I didn't mean to pry, or anything.'

'I know,' he said.

'Well. Anyway, I'm sorry.'

'You're always saying sorry,' he said. 'But you don't have anything to be sorry about.'

Before she could reply, he had turned and left the terrace. A few minutes later he appeared in the street below. She watched him walking down the hill, with Modge skipping round him like a puppy.

Myles sometimes teased him about the slight limp he'd acquired from a high-school football injury. According to Myles, it was something to do with a ligament in the knee, and surgery would fix it, but Patrick hadn't got round to having it done.

Watching him now, Antonia could detect no sign of a limp. She thought he moved well, with a kind of contained energy. She liked the way he moved. She liked him. And she wanted him to like her.

Myles had promised Modge that they would be back from Antibes by seven at the latest, and could have supper together on the terrace, with champagne for the grown-ups, and a *diabolo menthe*—her favourite—which he would make especially for her.

When there was still no sign of them by nine o'clock, Antonia gave

Modge a boiled egg and soldiers, and put her to bed in the spare room at the mill. Modge was subdued but not especially downcast. She was accustomed to being overlooked.

Antonia and her father ate a largely silent meal in the kitchen, then went their separate ways—he to work in his study, she to put in a few hours on her notes. At midnight she went to bed.

She was woken at two by her father's angry voice down in the courtyard. A door slammed. A girl laughed. A car horn hooted.

Antonia pulled on her kimono and stumbled downstairs.

She found her father standing in his pyjamas on the kitchen doorstep, blinking in the harsh porch light. Myles, Simon and Nerissa were slumped in the Panda, while Patrick sat behind the wheel, looking tired. Myles was yelling for Modge at the top of his voice. He was either very drunk or very high, or both.

'Over to you,' Dr Hunt muttered to her between clenched teeth before disappearing inside.

Antonia stifled a yawn. 'Myles, go home. It's two in the morning.'

'Where's *Modge*?' he cried. 'I've come to c'llect my sister!'

'Myles,' muttered Patrick. 'This was a mistake. Let's go home.'

'Fuck *off*, Paddy! I've come to c'llect *Modge*!'

'You'll do nothing of the sort,' snapped Antonia, 'so clear off! And that goes for Simon and Nerissa too. If you two can't come home at a decent hour you can jolly well stay at Myles's for a change. Now get lost.'

All four of them stared back at her.

She had a sudden image of herself—not in a short green kimono, but as a nagging housewife in a kitchen-sink melodrama.

Well, if you feel left out, she told herself angrily, it's your own fault. You could have gone with them to Antibes, there was nothing to stop you. But Myles is right, you're too much of a coward to have any fun.

Patrick started the engine, and Myles turned ostentatiously away. There would be trouble tomorrow.

Simon had slumped against the window and passed out. Nerissa sat beside Patrick, giggling helplessly, with one arm round his neck. Her thumb was gently rubbing the base of his throat.

As Patrick put the Panda into gear, he turned and looked at Antonia. 'I'm sorry,' he said. 'I didn't want this to happen.'

The Panda roared out of the courtyard in a spray of dust and gravel.

'I wonder,' said Myles as he rolled off Nerissa, 'what I'll have to do to make up with Toni. She was in a bit of a strop just now, wasn't she?'

Nerissa yawned and looked at her watch. Three o'clock in the morning.

Damn. If she didn't get some sleep soon, she'd look appalling.

'How would I know?' she murmured. She swung her legs over the side of the bed and stood up. 'I'm going for a Coke.'

She wandered naked into her own room, which she rarely used, now that she was seeing Simon. In a drawer she found a short slip of heavy oyster satin and slid it over her head, enjoying the slithery coolness against her skin. She couldn't understand girls who slept in an old T-shirt. Nerissa did not *own* a T-shirt.

Before leaving, she checked her appearance in the mirror. *'Nerissa Passmore has heavy strawberry-blonde hair, a small, firm body of supple porcelain, and eyes like agates in a sunlit river.'* That was how the review of her first film would begin. Men and women all over the world would gaze at her luminous image and cry, because she was so much more beautiful than they.

She got a Diet Coke from the fridge and curled up on the bench by the open window. She was halfway through the second paragraph of her review, when Patrick entered the kitchen. He wore a pair of cut-offs and nothing else, and he didn't see her until he had taken a Coke from the fridge and snapped the ring.

'Oh. Hi,' he said, his face expressionless.

She thought that was taking it a bit far, as she must look gorgeous: butterscotch-smooth legs curled beneath her, and one strap sliding obligingly off her shoulder.

She raised her Coke in a silent toast. 'So you couldn't sleep, either.'

He shook his head. He leaned against the fridge with his legs crossed at the ankles, holding the Coke can against his chest. He did not seem at all turned on by her, but she didn't mind. In fact she found it curiously restful. He was keeping his distance because she was sleeping with his best friend, which was fine for now. For now she was happy to lean back and admire the view.

He had long legs—a surprisingly rare feature in a man—and a fine, beautifully muscled torso. He would probably photograph well. In fact, they would look fantastic together. The fragile porcelain blonde and the tall, dark, angry-looking young man. Black and white film would be preferable to colour.

Myles wandered into the kitchen. He wore an orange T-shirt with a rip across the stomach, and no boxer shorts. Nerissa thought he looked absolutely disgusting.

He opened a bottle of Côtes du Roussillon, and rummaged in the drawer for a spliff. 'Are you chatting up my stepsister, Patroclus?'

'No,' said Patrick, 'I think she was chatting me up.'

Myles grinned. 'Don't hold it against her. The little baggage can't help herself.' Myles slapped her hard on the rump. 'Be off, you little strumpet. I'll be through in a minute. First I want a word with Patroclus.'

'OK, golden boy,' said Patrick, following Myles out onto the terrace. 'What's on your mind?'

Myles hitched himself up on the table and sat jiggling one foot, with the Côtes du Roussillon resting on his thigh. He inhaled deeply, then handed the spliff to Patrick. 'I was going to ask you the same thing. I've been getting waves of disapproval from you all evening. So I thought, if I'm in for a bollocking, I might as well get it over with.'

Patrick tilted back his head and blew a smoke ring at the stars, and handed back the spliff. 'Sorry. You're not going to get a bollocking.'

In the moonlight, Myles had stopped jiggling his foot. 'It's about Toni, isn't it?' he said suddenly.

Patrick's heart lurched. Thank Christ the light was too poor for Myles to see his face.

'Look,' said Myles. 'It isn't my fault. Toni's always working, and Nissa's so available! Jesus, you saw her just now, it's more than flesh and blood can stand!'

Patrick could find nothing to say to that.

'If you want to know,' Myles added, 'I've been thinking about straightening things out.'

'How?'

'Chucking Nissa, and making a go of it with Toni. That's what you think I should do, isn't it?'

Patrick made no reply.

'And that's not all,' Myles went on. 'This time I'm going to chuck the drugs, and cut back on the booze—'

'Oh, yeah, right!'

'No, I mean it! This time I really do.' He paused. 'I've got to get things sorted out, Patrick. Toni's part of that. She'll keep me on track.' He took a long pull at the bottle. 'But I need you to tell me how I do it.'

'How you do what?'

'How I straighten things out with Toni.'

I can't believe this is happening, Patrick thought. He felt dizzy, as if he was falling into the stars. 'I think,' he said at last, 'that your best chance with a girl like Antonia is to come clean with her. If you told her yourself, she'd probably forgive you.'

Shakily, Myles took another drag. 'No way. I *know* her.'

Patrick flinched.

'In many ways,' Myles went on, 'she's frighteningly naive. But deep down there's something strong about her. Something you don't mess with.'

Patrick was surprised, for he had felt that too.

'No, Paddy, she's not the forgiving kind. Nope. *Nyet*. No way, José.'

Patrick sighed. 'So what d'you want to do? You want me to go on covering for you while you go on two-timing your girl?'

Myles shrugged. 'Well yes, frankly, I'd have thought that was the least you could do.'

There was no reply to that. Myles never came out and said it, but at times he dropped a gentle reminder of what Patrick owed him.

Patrick said, 'You seem pretty sure that I'll play along.'

Myles's grin showed white in the moonlight. 'As sure as God made little green apples, Paddy me boy.'

'Why? I could tell Antonia any time I want and say—'

'Ah, but you won't. We both know that.'

'Why won't I?'

'Because you're my best friend.'

Patrick went quickly to the other end of the terrace. 'You don't believe in all that loyalty crap,' he said over his shoulder.

'No, but you do.'

Patrick did not reply.

Myles came to stand beside him. 'You won't tell Toni,' he said quietly.

Oh, but Patrick had thought about it. For two weeks he had thought of little else. Why *not* just march up to Antonia and say, *Listen, you're wasting your time with Myles. He's been screwing Nerissa for months.*

What stopped him wasn't only Myles. Antonia would get hurt, too. For Patrick knew his friend. If Antonia chucked Myles, as she would if she found out from someone else that he was screwing Nerissa, he would turn on her. He would find a way to hurt her. And hurting people was Myles's one, true, God-given talent.

Patrick glanced at his friend. 'Come clean with Antonia. It's the only way.'

'No.'

'Why not?'

Myles tossed the spliff into the garden, and they watched its red arc fade into the darkness. 'Because I'm not you, Patroclus. Sometimes I wish I were. But I'm not.'

Antonia couldn't sleep and sat at her desk, her notes spread before her. Her notes. Her secret. The one place where her thoughts had no limits.

It had started as a hobby, a distraction for a lonely undergraduate.

Since she met Myles, it had become a necessity. And at times it felt like her only link with Cassius.

During the day, as she trod a weary path between Myles's moods and her father's insecurities, there were moments when her mind would flash back to Cassius, and everything would be all right. It was as if the past—*his* past—was a wonderful peacock-coloured storybook, just waiting for her to turn the page and shed its light upon the present.

Tonight, she needed Cassius more than ever. She needed him to stop her thinking about Patrick.

'I didn't want this to happen,' Patrick had told her just before he drove off.

What hadn't he wanted to happen? Did he mean waking her up at two in the morning? Or did he mean whatever was going on between him and Nerissa?

What did he mean?

It had been easier when she thought he disliked her. But now what was she supposed to think? His offer to help at the Source; that remark he had made on the terrace. 'You're always saying sorry, but you don't have anything to be sorry about.'

This is wounded vanity, she told herself angrily. He's been avoiding you for a fortnight, so of course you can't stop thinking about him.

Then she remembered Myles, and felt bad. He was moody and impossible, but he needed her. He didn't deserve a girlfriend who disliked sex, and couldn't stop thinking about his best friend.

Gritting her teeth, she forced herself back to the poem she had been working on. The page before her was a mess, a jumble of crossings-out and bubbles of text shunted all over the place. To help herself back into the mood, she flicked to the Introductory Note she had already prepared: a layman's guide to Cassius.

'*Gaius Cassius Vitalis,*' she read, '*was born over 2,000 years ago, in 86 BC. The son of a prosperous farmer in the Roman province of Gallia Narbonensis, he grew up on an estate in the southeastern foothills of the Pyrenees—an estate he later immortalised in his poems, and which has been tentatively located in the valley of the Sarac. Unfortunately, all attempts to find the site of his villa, or the shrine mentioned in his poems, have come to nothing.*'

Here the text broke off, and was followed by a blank half-page. Full of optimism at the start of the summer, she had left space for the results of the dig.

Some hope. 'Come to nothing' still summed it up. Even that mention of a tentative location was a stretch. No one knew for sure if Cassius had grown up here. It was just supposition.

From the age of fourteen to eighteen he attended the University of Marseilles, where he met the diarist Lucius Faenius Plautius—who became a lifelong friend, and an essential biographical source for future generations. The young Cassius then joined the army, and for the next thirteen years he served with Pompey in Syria and Anatolia, then with Caesar in Gaul, Britain and Germany.

It was during the Anatolian campaign that he began writing poetry, and made a name for himself as a founder member of the Neoterici, the New Poets, whose immediacy and directness breathed new life into a stagnating art. To those who came after, Cassius was the standard-bearer, the first man in antiquity to write seriously about a love affair, and to acknowledge openly that one woman had been the ruling influence of his life. That woman is known to us only as the 'Lycaris' of the Poems: *a woman with whom he had a brief, passionate affair when he was thirty-three.*

Antonia sat back and studied the words on the page. To most people, they were heresy. For the simple fact was, no one these days believed that 'Lycaris' had ever existed. Everyone accepted that 'Lycaris' had only lived in the poet's mind. She was a literary conceit, a creation of his imagery: a way for him to explore the meaning of love. They were wrong.

Over the years, Antonia had had the argument with friends, colleagues, teachers, and her father. '*How* can you say he made her up?' she would cry. 'He didn't write fiction, he wrote from real life! "Lycaris"—whatever her name really was—was a living, breathing, flesh-and-blood woman! And he loved her, even when she broke his heart. He spent the rest of his life trying to fall out of love with her, it nearly tore him apart! We *know* all that, it's right there in the *Poems!*'

The answer was always the same. 'That's all very well, Antonia, but where's your evidence? What you're saying isn't scholarship, it's daydreams. You *want* to believe it, but where's your evidence?'

Of course, she had none. Only a belief as strong as it was unproven—and yet, that belief persisted. Her eyes returned to the page.

About the rest of his life we know tantalisingly little. We know that the affair with 'Lycaris' ended in heartbreak. Most people interpret this as meaning that his Muse departed suddenly, and he experienced a period of writer's block. Whatever the truth, we know that he left Rome in 53 BC, *and never returned.*

Thirteen years later, he fell victim to the bloody Terror which attended the death throes of the Republic. For reasons that remain unclear today, he incurred the wrath of Octavian, and was exiled to his estate in southeastern Gaul. There, to avoid the ignominy of the inevitable show trial, he took his own life.

His friend Plautius was with him when he died, and the old man's letter describing it is justly famous. 'When I'm gone,' Cassius said, 'I want you to make a libation to the Goddess. This must be for me and for Lycaris together, so that our spirits can meet after death.' Plautius asked how he might do this, for he didn't know Lycaris's true name—and without that, the Goddess would not hear the prayer. Then Cassius did an extraordinary thing. Instead of revealing her name, he set his old friend a riddle. 'In poculo veritas,' he said. 'The truth is in the cup.'

Today, the established view is that this riddle—which has baffled scholars for centuries—simply means that a poet must seek his inspiration in wine. So the riddle has been taken to mean: 'I seek the truth about Lycaris when I'm drunk—and so should you.'

Antonia sat straighter, rubbing the back of her neck.

A bat sped past the window: a silent velvet shadow tracking a trail of darkness across the stars.

Cassius, she thought, must have looked out at just such a view on his last night on earth, as he composed his riddle.

Although if you believed the 'established view', it was nothing more than an ironic word-game. 'Look for Lycaris in wine,' it told posterity. 'You won't find her anywhere else, for she never existed. I made her up.'

No, no, no! The 'established view' was all wrong. Cassius was not the man to bow out of life concocting ironic trifles. He was too direct and unflinching for that. The riddle had been important to him. 'Lycaris' had existed, and Cassius had loved her with all his heart.

Even if he had never written another poem, the one he wrote at the beginning of their affair had surely been proof of that.

One long look, and I was brought down.
She entered my blood. Although at the time
I didn't think she'd have me.
But when we met again,
how much we said to each other by moonlight!
The night wind bore our words away.
Then at last her breath yielded to mine,
and mine to hers. We were sheeted in fire.
And now like Pegasus I ride the stars,
I walk the spellbound moon.
The horse of darkness treads the sky
and I am with him, for I am immortal.
And she sleeps: her face as pale as fresh-cut marble
against my cloak.

Antonia put down her pencil and stared into the darkness. Compared with a love like that, what was the pallid, edgy dependency she had with Myles? How could she even think about Myles on a night like this?

Not Myles, and not Patrick, either. Especially not Patrick.

'Go to bed,' she said angrily, shuffling her papers into a pile.

In two weeks the dig would be over, and everyone would go their separate ways.

Two weeks, and she would never see Patrick again.

Two weeks, and it would all be over.

CHAPTER FIVE
A family tomb, Porta Capena, Rome, June 25, 53 BC

IN THE DARKNESS, Cassius made out the shadowy form of Albia on the bench in the little garden outside the tomb.

He and Faenio, his slave, made their way towards her through the cypresses. Although the moon was only in its first quarter, they had no trouble finding the path. After three months, they knew every stone.

Faenio joined Albia to keep watch, and Cassius made for the tomb, whose doorway showed as a faint, flickering oblong of light.

As he left them on the bench, Albia gave him an odd look, and he wondered why. An instant later he found out. As he reached the porch, something hard exploded against the doorpost, a hand's breadth from his temple. Straightening up, he brushed fragments of earthenware from his shoulders. The perfume of olive oil floated towards him on the warm night air, and he smiled. She had thrown a lamp.

'*Bastard!*' cried a voice from the shadows. 'Exactly *when* were you going to tell me that you've been recalled to Gaul?'

So that was it. 'Tonight,' he said evenly.

'Liar!'

'No. I was going to tell you tonight. That's the truth. I only heard yesterday myself.'

As his eyes adjusted to the gloom he made out her mantle, which she had flung across the flags. She herself was at the far end of the chamber, furthest from the remaining lamp. She was pacing up and down like a caged lioness. He thought she looked magnificent.

'Tacita,' he said quietly. 'You know I have to go. You know that.'

'No, I *don't* know it, because you haven't told me yet! I had to hear it from Albia's new man, of all people! A squid-seller!'

He bit back a smile. He wondered what galled her most: the fact that he hadn't told her sooner, or that she'd heard it from a fishmonger. 'It had to come some time,' he said, 'I've already stretched my stay in Rome far longer than I should.'

'I'm so very flattered.'

'They need me out there. I know the terrain.'

'Well, you would, wouldn't you? You're scarcely better than a peasant yourself.'

He went to her and drew her against him. He was surprised to find that she was trembling. She turned, and wrapped her arms tightly about his waist and buried her face in his chest.

'I'll be gone for six months at most,' he said into her hair.

'No,' she muttered, her voice muffled by his toga. 'At *most*, you'll be gone for ever. Those savages will slit your throat in the mountains and leave your bones for the buzzards to pick.' She drew a shuddering breath. 'And it's not even as if you *try* to stay alive! I've heard about the risks you take.'

That made him chuckle.

'What's funny?'

'You are. You berate me for taking risks, while trying to brain me with a lamp.'

'No jokes, Gaius. Not tonight.'

He tightened his hold on her. Gradually, the trembling ceased.

After a while she asked, 'How long before you leave?'

'A few weeks.'

She drew back a fold of his toga, and slipped his tunic off one shoulder. Then she bent her head, and he felt her warm breath on his skin. Her soft lips traced the line of his collarbone.

She opened her mouth and bit him as hard as she could.

With a cry he thrust her from him, and she staggered back against the wall and nearly fell.

'*Never* do that again!' he exclaimed. 'Are you all right? Ah, you're lucky I didn't hurt you!'

Shakily she wiped her mouth with her hand. 'As if you care!'

That gesture was pure Tacita: one moment a lady—and the next, as coarse as a street girl. He loved her for that.

He put a finger to his shoulder, and it came away dark with blood. 'Why?' he said.

Her chin went up. 'Now I've put my mark on you. You won't forget me when you're on campaign.'

'I'm not likely to forget you,' he replied.

He reached for her and put his hands on her shoulders. 'You're not going to lose me,' he said.

'Oh no? What if you're killed?'

'I won't be . . . But if I were, I'd still be with you.' He put his palm over her heart. 'In here.'

'Spoken like a poet! What good would you be to me there?'

He did not reply. She was in a strange mood tonight. Morbid and angry and vulnerable. It was his fault. The constant strain of the lies and the subterfuge was beginning to tell on her. No doubt his choice of trysting place hadn't helped, either. She was too young to meet in grave-yards. To have death thrust upon her at every turn.

'I'm sorry,' he said. 'I should never have brought you here.'

'You didn't bring me here. I brought myself.'

'Soon we won't have to do this at all. No more skulking in the shad-ows when we're married.'

He felt some of the tension leave her body. 'How do you propose to achieve that?' she asked over her shoulder.

'I'll find a way,' he said, taking her in his arms.

They kissed.

When at last they drew apart for breath, she touched the bite-mark on his shoulder. 'Does that hurt?'

'Yes.'

Slowly and deliberately she drew her fingernail through the congeal-ing blood, to reopen the wound.

'Now it hurts more,' he said.

'Good. It serves you right.' With both forefingers she gently parted the lips of the cut, then bent her head to his shoulder. 'Relax,' she mur-mured. 'You're tensing like a stallion.' Softly she blew into the cut. Then she pressed the edges back together, and sealed it with her tongue.

It felt like being attacked by a sharp-toothed creature of the night.

'There,' she whispered. 'Now part of my spirit will be inside you for ever.' She covered the wound with her hand. 'It will make a fine scar! A crescent moon, just like my amulet. From now on, wherever you go, you'll carry me with you.'

'I'll do that without a scar.'

'Fine words, poet. But this scar will last.'

Frowning, he searched her face. 'What's wrong? This isn't only about me returning to Gaul, is it?'

She met his eyes, and suddenly she looked very young. 'Gaius, I'm scared.'

'Of what?'

'I don't know. That's why I'm scared.'

'Tacita. Make sense. Tell me.'

She looked at him. 'Do you really believe that they'll let us grow old together?'

He did not reply.

'Do you believe,' she went on, 'that when our time comes, our sons and daughters will put our ashes in a single urn—'

'Tacita—'

'—and say the proper rites for us, so that our spirits can be together for eternity?'

'Yes,' he said. 'I believe all that.'

'Then you're a peasant!' she burst out. 'You say you don't believe in miracles, but you do! Deep down, in your heart, you do!'

'Perhaps.'

'*How* is it going to happen, Gaius? How? Do you plan to charm my father with that silver tongue of yours, and make him welcome a low-born provincial as a son-in-law?'

He flinched. 'It happens.'

'Not in my family.'

He knelt beside her. 'It will happen,' he said again.

She picked at the stuff of her dress. Then she said in a low voice, 'What do you expect me to do while you're away?'

'I expect you to wait for me.'

'And you think I will?'

'I know you will. Just as I know that when I return from Gaul, I'll deal with your family, and we'll be married.'

She nodded. Wanting to believe it. As he wanted to himself.

'Promise you'll wait for me, Tacita.'

She threw him a look. 'Why do you need me to promise?'

'I need something to keep me going in Gaul.'

'Oh well, in *that* case,' she said drily, 'I quite understand. What a prospect, stuck out in the back of beyond with all those barbarians.' She shuddered, and he knew that the worst was over. 'All right,' she said. 'I promise.'

He bent and kissed her gently on the lips.

'Come back alive,' she said against his mouth. 'You're no good to me as ashes.'

'I'll come back alive.'

CHAPTER SIX
La Bastide,
September 24, 1988

SHE'S GOING TO THINK you're crazy, Patrick told himself as he started down the street towards the mill. What do you think you're doing, seeking her out at the crack of dawn to apologise for something she's probably already forgotten?

But that kind of argument hadn't got him very far. It had been two days since the Panda had roared out of the courtyard in the early hours of the morning, and he could still see the look on her face.

But what, exactly, was he going to say when he found her? *'Listen, if you got the impression from Nerissa's little display the other night that I'm sleeping with her, you're wrong, and I really need you to know that.'*

Yeah, but *why* do you really need her to know that?

The noise of a car behind him shattered the early-morning calm. In disbelief he watched the Panda inch down the narrow street. 'Myles?'

'I know, I know, you can't believe your eyes,' muttered his friend as he cut the engine. 'A Cantellow awake and dressed before eight, it's a miracle. Though come to think of it, you're up pretty early, aren't you?'

Patrick shrugged:

'Look, Paddy. I need a favour. Take Modge for the day?'

'What?'

Myles jerked his head towards the back of the car, and Patrick saw the eight-year-old curled up asleep on the seat. She was still in her pyjamas. Myles must have scooped her straight out of bed.

'Myles, I can't. Not right now.'

'The thing is, I've got to go to Paris.'

'Paris?' Patrick was about to ask what the hell he thought he was doing, when suddenly he knew. There was only one thing that would get Myles out of bed before noon and take him all the way to Paris. He said, 'I thought you'd decided to kick that stuff.'

'It's *because* I have that I've got to do this! One last fling to get it out of my system.'

'Myles . . .'

'Go on. Be a friend and look after Modge.'

Patrick hesitated. If he said yes to Myles, it would mean waking Modge and taking her with him to the pot-shed. And he needed to see Antonia alone. On the other hand, his friend looked terrible. His face was drawn and glistening with sweat, and his glance skittered away from Patrick's.

Patrick sighed. 'I've got a better idea. We'll leave Modge with Antonia, and I'll come with you to Paris.'

'Don't be ridic—'

'You can't go by yourself. In this state you'll crash the car.'

'I'm not in a state!'

On the back seat, Modge stirred. Myles threw her a glance. 'Poor little cow. What did she do to deserve me?'

'Myles, don't do this. You don't need to go to Paris. You can give up that stuff right now.'

'Look after her, Paddy. That's all I ask.'

Patrick found Antonia alone, as he knew he would.

The pot-shed was a long barn on the opposite side of the courtyard, which the Hunts had rigged with light bulbs strung between the rafters. Three old stone sinks had been installed along the sides for washing and desalination, with four large trestle tables down the middle. These were covered with drying racks, washing-up bowls, scrubbing brushes, find trays and box files. The walls were covered in colour charts and notice boards. The notice boards were covered in lists.

Antonia sat at the far table in a shaft of dusty sunlight, gluing pieces of pottery back together. She wore emerald-green shorts and a sleeveless azure top of Indian cotton edged in scarlet. Her hair ribbons were the colours of raspberry and mint. A bird-of-paradise girl, thought Patrick, his heart pounding.

Modge, now thoroughly awake, called out, 'Antonia, look at me, I'm in pyjamas!'

Antonia raised her head. Wordlessly, she took in Patrick's presence.

I guess you didn't expect to see me here, he told her silently.

'Hello, Patrick,' she said. 'I'm afraid Myles isn't here.'

'I know,' he replied, disconcerted. 'I just saw him leave.'

'If it's my father you want, he—'

'No. In fact, I came to see you.'

She blinked.

Say your piece and get out of here.

Instead, he found himself asking if she wanted any help.

She gave him a puzzled look. 'Um—well. Thanks. If you like, you could label those shards over there.'

'Oh, good,' said Modge, 'I like labelling.' She fetched a tray, a stack of context sheets, the finds register, and a pot of white Indian ink. Patrick pulled up a couple of stools.

He struggled to concentrate while Modge showed him how to paint the context number onto each shard, and warned him sternly against labelling too near the edge, as that was *exactly* the place most likely to crumble—and once you'd lost the context number, that was *it*.

Across the table, Antonia went back to her reconstruction with the self-conscious absorption of a person who knows she is being watched.

Her movements were precise and delicate, and Patrick found them hypnotic. Carefully she dusted off each shard with a fine, soft brush. Then she painted the edges with a thin film of adhesive, slotting the shard into place. Finally, she smoothed the join with her fingertips, gently blowing away the last of the dust.

Patrick's mouth went dry.

To break the spell, he asked her what she was working on.

'It's a lamp.'

'And—you found that at the Source?'

'Yes.'

He had seen lamps like this in books. A flat disc-shaped chamber to hold the oil, with a stubby little nozzle for the flame. But this must have been a pretty small lamp, for he guessed that when it was completed, it would fit comfortably into her palm. That thought made his heart start to race all over again.

'I think she's a goddess,' she said. She held out a shard for him to see, and traced the profile of a woman with her finger. Patrick saw a straight Grecian nose, a mass of crinkly hair, and a dreamy archaic smile.

'Looks like a goddess,' he said hoarsely. 'Which one?'

She frowned. 'Not sure. Probably the Great Mother, Cybele. Or some sort of amalgam of her and the Moon Goddess. They were both pretty popular down here in southern Gaul. Or she might be the *triple* Moon Goddess, because of the three branches she's holding.'

Modge leaned over his shoulder, making him jump. 'That means she's three in one,' she said. 'Antonia told me. The Virgin of Spring, the Nymph of Summer, and the Crone of Winter. D'you get it? The new moon, the full moon, and the old moon . . . What's a virgin?'

'Uh . . .' said Patrick, 'a girl who isn't married yet.'

'Oh. Like me and Antonia.'

Antonia flicked him a glance, and smiled. It was not her usual polite social beam, but the genuine, heartbreaking smile she had given him on that first day up at the Source. It made him want to gather her to him and bury his face in the soft curve between her shoulder and throat.

She put down the shard, and went to the sink to wash her hands. Her bare feet made a soft whispering sound in the dust. Like a caress running the length of his spine. Now was the time for him to leave. Mutter some excuse and get the hell out of here.

He cleared his throat. 'So—what else have you found up there?'

'Not much,' she said over her shoulder. 'Quite a lot of fruit pips—pears, mostly. Wild pears were sacred to the Moon Goddess, because of their white blossom. And they were the sort of thing the peasants round here could have spared.'

'Right,' said Patrick. There was a pause.

'So,' said Antonia, still at the sink, 'where did Myles go?'

Patrick's head snapped up. 'He went to Paris.'

She turned. *'Paris?'*

'He—uh, he had to see a guy about something or other.'

He watched her take that in. She returned to her stool and sat down. 'You know,' she said, 'you don't have to cover for him.'

He coloured.

'I know about the—' she glanced at Modge—'substances.'

'What substances?' said Modge.

'Champagne,' said Patrick.

Modge shot him a disbelieving look.

'That's why he went, isn't it?' Antonia said. 'He's trying to get up the nerve to quit, and he thinks one last binge is going to help.'

He sighed. Then he said quietly, 'Is that why you stay with him? To help him quit?'

She raised her head and looked at him. 'I don't know,' she said at last. Then she added in a low voice, 'Sometimes I wonder why he stays with *me*. I mean, I don't like any of the things he likes.'

He watched her take another shard and start painting the edge with adhesive. This time her lips were pressed together, as if she was struggling for control.

That bastard, he thought. *Christ*, what does she see in him? If Myles had been there, Patrick would have grabbed him by the throat and beaten him to a pulp.

'You know,' she said with quiet intensity, 'sometimes I hate my role. The good girl. The boring one, who keeps everyone else in line.'

It wasn't hard to see what she meant. Over the years, she had boxed herself in. She had become the hotshot archaeologist, too focused on work to have any fun. Maybe she'd hoped that going out with Myles would change all that, but instead it had only made it worse. Because Myles had shown her how different she was from people like him.

He was surprised that she could be so open with him. Exposing her insecurities like a child. To leave now was out of the question. Not while she was in this strange, angry, self-denigrating mood. A mood he had helped to create.

Alfonse, the mill cat, nosed his way round the door.

'Modge,' said Patrick. 'Alfonse is looking kind of hungry. How about you take him to the kitchen and give him some breakfast?'

Modge snorted to indicate that she wasn't fooled in the least, but she scooped up the cat and staggered out. When she had gone, silence returned to the pot-shed like a settling of dust.

Antonia was gazing down at her tray of potsherds. She looked as if she was about to cry.

Patrick moved his stool nearer to hers. 'You are not boring,' he said. 'And you shouldn't feel bad just because other people act like jerks.'

Before she could think of a reply, he got to his feet and took the labelled shards to the storage trays in the corner, and started putting them away.

If I was Nerissa, she thought, watching his back, I'd ask him what he's thinking right now. It's as simple as that. Then I'd ask him to stay and talk. *Patrick,* I'd say, *I don't want you to go. I want you to talk to me. About you. I want to know everything. I want to know.*

So why don't you just ask? Because you're a coward. That's why. And because of Myles. She picked up a shard and went back to work.

But to her surprise, he didn't leave the pot-shed when he had finished, but returned with a fresh tray and sat opposite her, with a mutinous look on his face. For five minutes they worked in uneasy silence.

Then she took a deep breath, and asked what had made him try for Oxford. There now. What's so complicated about that?

He thought for a moment. 'I was working evenings on a dude ranch, and one time I got talking to this guest. Air-conditioning salesman. His wife was a teacher. She told me about some scholarship, and said, why don't you have a go? She said it was for Oxford, and I thought she meant Oxford, Connecticut.' He coloured, as if unused to talking about himself. 'It was kind of strange, really, because until then I hadn't even thought about going to college in the States, let alone England. But she kept on at me, and in the end I thought, what the hell? So I went for it.'

Slowly she nodded. Then she risked it. 'I bet your father was proud.'

He looked down at the shard in his hands. 'He never knew. He died before I heard I'd got the place.'

'I'm sorry. I didn't know.'

'That's OK. He knew I'd applied, and I guess he was proud about that.' His eyes became distant, remembering. 'Yeah. I guess he was. He even gave me a present. Me! We never gave each other presents. But he did. Couple of days after I told him I was trying for it, he came back from work with this pair of football boots. Top of the range, he said.' He shook his head. 'Poor guy. He really believed that. He thought they were the ultimate in cool.'

'And—they weren't?'

'Not even close. I couldn't wear them to football practice, because all the guys would have laughed at him.' He glanced at her. 'At *him*, you understand? It didn't matter about me. They'd be making fun of him. Their dads were mostly doctors and engineers. It was that kind of school. Another scholarship.' He paused. 'They knew all about his drinking, and that he worked on an assembly line making third-rate sports gear. Big laugh. I didn't want to give them something else to make fun of.'

'So—what happened then?'

'Oh, nothing much. He had to go into town, and he saw me on the field wearing my old boots, and he was hurt. He didn't say so, but he was.' He shrugged. 'That's it.'

She put down the shard she had been working on. 'But—did you explain?'

'Explain what? That he spent his life making crap?'

'No, that you were only trying to protect him.'

'No. I didn't tell him that.' He paused. 'I left it too late.'

'What do you mean?'

'Couple of days afterwards, he was standing in line at the canteen and he had a heart attack. End of story.' He forced a smile. 'So I guess the moral is, don't let the sun go down on a quarrel, huh?'

It was painful to see him trying to make light of it. 'It wasn't your fault,' she told him.

'That's what the doctors said.'

She watched him place the shard carefully in the finds tray, reach for another, and take up the paintbrush to begin painting on the context number. His hands were brown, with scratches on the backs from all the digging, and she noticed that he was left-handed.

As he flexed his wrist, the light caught the thick, raised vein snaking up his forearm. That's his life, thought Antonia. His blood, coursing just beneath the skin.

It looked frighteningly easy to cut. She wanted to cover it with her hand to protect it. To feel its smoothness and elasticity and strength.

She raised her eyes, and found with a shock that he was looking at her. His eyes were very blue, and filled with light.

'Antonia,' said Modge from the doorway, and they both jumped. 'When are we going to the Source?'

Antonia turned her head and stared blankly at the eight-year-old.

Patrick got to his feet. 'I'd better go,' he said.

She looked up at him. 'Yes,' she said at last.

But he stayed where he was, frowning down at her. 'Listen,' he said. 'Could you use some help up there?'

She opened her mouth to speak, then closed it again.

'Oh, *please*,' said Modge. 'He'd make an *incredible* difference. We've still got to do that whole strip at the back.'

She bit her lip. This is not a good idea, she thought. Then she told him, yes, they could do with some help. 'But . . . I'd better stay down here,' she added belatedly. 'My father. And . . . everything.'

'Yeah. You'd better do that.'

Eight hours later, Antonia straightened on her stool and told herself for the hundredth time that she was *not* going up to the Source to see how Patrick was getting on. All day she had forced herself to remain in the pot-shed, doggedly reconstructing the lamp. It was now as complete as it would ever be, and she was heartily sick of it.

She found her espadrilles under the table and went out for some air.

The courtyard was deserted. Simon and Nerissa had left an hour before, taking the jeep into Mazerans for a quiet dinner on their own. To judge from the clink of bottles coming from the kitchen, her father was already fixing himself a drink. She decided against joining him.

There was no sign of Patrick. Either he was still up at the Source, or else he'd finished for the day, and had gone back to Les Limoniers for a shower, and a peaceful evening on his own.

She wandered down to the river. Alfonse lay on his side on a boulder, lazily scrutinising the swallows. At her approach he raised his head an inch from the boulder, and twitched his tail like a miniature lion.

She sat beside him, and lobbed a pebble into the current.

He simply feels sorry for you, she told herself. That's why he's up at the Source now. He feels *sorry* for you.

She heard a trickle of gravel behind her and turned to see Modge picking her way between the rocks. Her fingernails were semicircles of dirt, and she had a smudge of black on her nose. Antonia sighed. For once, she didn't want Modge around. She didn't want anyone around.

Modge came and sat beside her, and tickled Alfonse's paws with a blade of grass. After a while she said, 'I'm hungry. Can I go and see what's in your fridge?'

"Course you can.'

But Modge made no move to go. Plainly she wanted Antonia to go with her. Antonia stayed where she was.

Eventually Modge got the hint and stood up, brushing the dust off her bottom. 'Patrick says, can you go to the Source as soon as possible?'

Antonia stared at her. 'What? You mean he's still up there?'

Modge nodded.

'But—didn't he bring you down? He can't have let you come all this way on your own?'

Modge shook her head. 'He came part of the way with me, then we met Monsieur Panabière on his tractor thingy and he gave me a lift the rest of the way, and Patrick went back to the Source.'

'But—do you know what Patrick wants?'

Modge gave an exaggerated shrug. 'He just said could you go to the Source as soon as possible. He didn't say why.'

Antonia pondered that. He must have a pretty good reason to ask her to make a two-mile hike at six o'clock in the evening. But she couldn't think what. Maybe he just wanted to see her? Her heart began to pound. But if that was the case, why didn't he come down to the mill?

Forty minutes later, she reached the Source. There was no sign of Patrick. She went inside.

She found him on his knees at the back of the main chamber. He was using a small trowel to work a patch in the final section, and he looked as if he'd been at it for hours. In the glow of the gas lamp the sweat gleamed on his shoulders. His dark hair flopped damply onto his forehead.

At her approach, he did not look up. 'I think we're onto something,' he said.

Afterwards, it struck Patrick as extraordinary that a discovery which would alter the entire course of his life should arrive without any kind of warning.

When his trowel first struck stone, he felt not the slightest premonition of its significance. He was working a patch of the cave floor about seven inches beneath the topsoil, and idly wondering what Myles was getting up to in Paris, when he came up against something hard. A rock, he thought absently.

Then he noticed how the complexion of the soil had changed. Instead of the heavy red dirt of the cave floor, he had reached a layer of dry mustard-coloured sand, which crumbled easily, like sugar.

Weird, he thought, pulling the lamp a little closer. Some kind of localised deposit from the glacier?

No. Not a deposit. It was *too* localised for that, only about the size of a beer crate. Could it have been placed there by human hands?

That was when he stopped whistling, and the adrenalin kicked in.

He put down his trowel, found a paintbrush in his rucksack, and used it to remove a small patch of dirt. Smooth, rust-coloured stone gleamed through yellow sand. His heart began to pound.

The urge to plunge in his hands and yank the thing out was almost overwhelming, but he knew that would be a disaster. The precise orientation of the find and the position of any associated objects, could be crucial to its interpretation. If he rushed it now, all that would be lost for ever. Antonia would never forgive him.

It was a physical effort to curb his eagerness: to uncover just a little at a time, then stop and take notes on the context pad. His progress was agonisingly slow.

He glanced at his watch. A little after five. Fortunately, Modge had wandered off for a rest at the mouth of the cave, and had no idea of what he had found. Some instinct prevented him from calling her over. Whatever this turned out to be, Antonia should see it first. But he needed to get Modge back to the mill with a message.

Half an hour later, he had torn himself away for long enough to put Modge safely into the hands of Monsieur Panabière, with strict instructions to tell Antonia to come as soon as she could. Then he returned to the cave and got back to work.

An endless time later, he had brushed away enough sand to make out the outline of the vessel. It was a goblet, lying on its side. He made out a graceful convex bowl, mounted on a short, slender stem and a small foot. Twin handles extended the length of the bowl in an elegant curve.

He could not breathe. It was the most beautiful thing he had ever seen.

Patrick gazed down at the crisply cut relief of a young man. The young man walked like a prince, with his head held high. His lips were parted in a smile of great serenity and joy, and one arm was raised, the palm turned outwards in the age-old sign of friendship. He looked as if he were welcoming whoever was on the other side of the cup—the side which still lay buried in the sand.

Patrick sat back on his heels, and for the first time, pain gripped his shoulders in a vice. He realised that he must have been working for hours, for beyond the cave mouth the sky had dimmed to a delicate translucent mauve. Already the cicadas were singing their night song: slower, sweeter, more musical than their noonday rasp. And from the shadowy cleft behind him came the voice of the spring: a constant, mysterious flow of words, just beyond the edge of human understanding.

He shook himself, and flexed his aching neck and shoulders. Then he went back to work.

Half an hour later, just as he was starting to dig down underneath the cup to free it, Antonia arrived. He put down his brush and wiped his forehead with the back of his hand.

When she saw the cup, her lips parted, but no words came. Silently she sank to her knees. He watched her put out a hand to touch it, then draw back. In the bluish light of the lamp her face was drained of colour, her lips chiselled in marble. Her face reminded him of the goddess on the terracotta lamp. He couldn't look at her for long.

'I think it's some kind of cup,' he said softly, to break the silence.

'It's a *kántharos*,' she replied, without taking her gaze from it. Like him, she spoke in a whisper, as if she feared to offend whatever his discovery had awakened. 'A Greek wine goblet. The Romans revived the style around the fall of the Republic.' She drew a deep breath.

'Should we dig it up now, or wait till it's light?'

'We'll do it now.' She glanced up at him, and smiled. 'I'll work all night, if that's what it takes to get this out of the ground.'

She would, too. Sometimes she didn't know when to stop. That was one of the things he loved about her.

He asked if she wanted to take over the digging, but to his surprise she shook her head.

'You do it. I'll take the notes.'

'Are you sure? It's your dig.'

'Positive. I don't dare touch it yet.'

In the end it didn't take all night, it took less than three hours. Gradually Patrick worked his way under the cup, until finally it was ready to be lifted from its bed of sand. He glanced at Antonia over his shoulder. 'Is there any special way I should do this?'

'No. Just lift it very carefully. And try not to let any of the sand inside fall out, there could be more finds in there. I'll empty it once we get back to the mill.'

Still he hesitated. 'Are you sure about this? If I don't do it right I could break it.'

'I don't think so. I think it's made of sardonyx. Hard as nails.'

'Sardonyx?'

She nodded. 'The Romans used it for making signet rings. It's incredibly rare to find an entire cup made of it. I've only ever seen one, in a museum in Paris.' She leaned closer. 'Yes, that's sardonyx, I'm sure of it.'

As she said it, a strange expression came over her face, as if an idea had just occurred to her. He threw her a questioning look, but she only shook her head. Obviously she wasn't ready to share it yet.

The *kántharos* came away from the sand with a suddenness he found shocking. It was intact and perfect in every respect. Holding it in both hands, he carried it to the middle of the cave and set it on the wooden crate which held the magnetometer. Antonia brought the lamp and hung it from one of the iron hooks in the roof.

The side of the *kántharos* which had lain face downwards was still crusted with sand. Carefully, Patrick began to brush it away. Antonia knelt beside him with her hands on her knees. He could feel the warmth of her body inches from his own. He could smell the faint minty perfume of her hair.

Little by little, he uncovered the polished relief of a horse. A splendid muscular neck. Taut, rounded haunches. The stallion trotted joyfully over a field of rippling acanthus. Its head was raised and its ears pricked, as if it was eager to reach the young man on the other side of the cup.

Then Patrick saw the great wings half-furled across its back. 'Antonia, look! It's Pegasus!'

He heard the sharp intake of her breath.

Gazing at the winged horse, he felt suddenly cold, as if some blind power had awakened, after an ageless sleep.

Maybe Antonia picked up something of what he was feeling, for suddenly she said in her normal archaeologist's voice, 'Let's check under the foot for inscriptions.'

He cleared his throat. 'Yeah. That's a good idea.'

'I'll lift it,' she said, 'and you take a look.'

'Shouldn't I do the lifting? It's heavy.'

'No, I'll hold it. I—can't bear to look. In case there's nothing there.'

Again he glanced at her. Her face was taut. Whatever she suspected, she still wasn't ready to share with him.

He put the lamp on the floor beside him, got down on one elbow, and started to brush the sand from the smooth, round base.

His hand froze. The underside of the foot bore three words, beautifully incised in crisp, authoritative Roman capitals. He said hoarsely, 'How did you know there'd be an inscription?'

'Oh God. I didn't. I only hoped. What does it say?'

Slowly he read it aloud, stumbling a little over the unfamiliar Latin. '*Gai sum peculiaris.*'

She took that in silence, her eyes distant and unseeing. 'Oh God, yes. Oh yes.'

'What? What does it mean?'

'What does it mean?' Her gaze shifted to him, and he saw that her eyes glittered with tears. 'It *means*, Patrick, it means: "I belong to Gaius".'

The hairs on the back of his neck stood on end.

'*Goddess,*' she quoted softly, as tears ran down her cheeks. '*I stand before Your sanctum, and pour the sweet, fresh Calenian wine for Your sacrifice. From the blood-red sardonyx flows the blood-red wine: a fitting gift, I think. And around my drinking-cup trots Your beloved horse. The horse with wings.*'

Patrick looked from Antonia to the *kántharos*, then back again.

I belong to Gaius. Gaius Cassius Vitalis.

'Oh God,' he said. 'It's his.'

Antonia stood at the mouth of the cave and watched the moon rise above the gorge. It was of that peculiar hue which is neither golden nor silver, but simply moon colour.

Over her shoulder she watched Patrick moving about the cave, gathering materials in which to pack the *kántharos* for the walk back to the mill. He had wrapped the *kántharos* in a plastic bag to keep the sand inside, then encased it in wadding plundered from the magnetometer crate. Now he was easing the bulky roll into his rucksack. He was absorbed in what he was doing, and unaware that she was watching. In the gaslight his face was thoughtful and grave. A face full of youth and certitude, like the young man on the cup.

But earlier, when Pegasus had first come to light, he hadn't been so assured. He had been deeply shaken. She loved him for that. He had tried not to show it, but she knew what he felt, for she felt it herself. A sense of something let loose, blowing through the cave.

She wanted to tell him how glad she was that it was he who had found the *kántharos*. Cassius would have been glad too, she thought. Oh, he would have liked you, Patrick. I know he would.

She turned back to the moonlight. The sky was a deep, soft indigo glittering with stars, and beneath it the cliff face shone like steel. A hot wind wafted up from the gorge, smelling faintly of dust and thyme.

Patrick emerged from the cave. He left the rucksack and lamp by the oak tree and came to stand beside her. 'I'm glad that's over,' he said. 'It sounds dumb, but I got spooked in there. I don't think she likes men.'

'Who?'

He nodded at the moon. 'The Goddess. Cybele. Artemis. Whoever she is.'

She made herself smile. 'Oh, I don't know. She's the goddess of little children, which I suppose includes boys. And of childbirth, I think . . .'

'Yeah, and also chastity, and sudden death. And doesn't she have a habit of peppering her admirers with arrows?'

She knew what he was trying to do. Get her to talk, so she wouldn't bottle everything up.

He looked down at her. 'Are you OK?'

'I—will be. It's just a bit much to take in. I've wanted something like this for so long. Since I was Modge's age.'

'I know.'

She wiped her eyes with her fingers. 'Sorry. I'll be all right in a minute.'

'It's OK. Take your time.'

After a while he said, 'What's that star over there? The really brilliant one, very low down?'

She sniffed. 'Um. Venus, I think. Actually, it's a planet—Sorry. You probably know that.'

He scuffed the dirt with his foot. 'You'd think I would, wouldn't you? Country boy and all.' His lip curled. 'Guess I just never learned.'

'Funnily enough, it was my mother who taught me.'

'Why funnily enough?'

'Well, it's not the sort of thing you'd associate with her.'

'What would you associate with her?'

'Oh. Tea at Fortnum's. A manicure at Harvey Nicks.' For a moment she wished she hadn't said it. Then she realised that it didn't matter. She no longer worried about him thinking her snobbish or overeducated. And it was amazing how much easier it was to talk to him in the dark.

Suddenly she had an idea. 'Look over there,' she said, touching his arm and turning to face southeast. 'Do you see that very bright star on the right, just above that line of trees?'

'No . . . Yeah. I've got it.'

'That's Vega. Now look across to your left, about the width of your palm when you hold it at arm's length. Just above the top of the cliff, to the right of that tree, do you see a big square made by four stars, one at each corner? The one at the top right is quite bright, but the other three are very faint, you've got to look for them.'

After a while he said, 'I see it.'

'That's the Great Square of Pegasus. The square's his body, and he's also got legs and a neck and a head, I think. But they're too faint to see without a telescope.'

'What about the wings?'

She frowned. 'You know, I don't think he's got any.'

'I guess we're supposed to infer them, huh? I mean, he must have them, if he managed to get all the way up there in the first place.'

She smiled. 'Isn't it amazing,' she murmured, looking up at the stars, 'that you just happened to find the *kántharos* at this particular time of year, just when—'

Patrick kissed her.

He took her by the shoulders and spun her round to face him, and kissed her dizzyingly. His mouth was warm and strong and incredibly tender. She opened her eyes and saw that his face was grave and intent, the dark brows drawn together in a frown.

After the first long astonishment, she clasped her arms about his neck and kissed him back.

They drew apart for breath, and his eyes met hers questioningly. *Do you want this? Do you want me?*

With her finger she traced the line of his brow. Then she raised herself and kissed his mouth. *Yes. I want you.*

The kiss deepened.

Never had she felt so absolutely and unreservedly wanted. And it was so easy and so natural to kiss him back. She felt no hesitation, no fear of doing it wrong. This was right, because it was Patrick.

He bore her back against the cliff face. A rock dug into her shoulder, and she flinched. He felt her recoil and turned them round so that he was against the rocks instead of her. Then he put his mouth to the tender place on her shoulder and gently sucked.

At the same moment, they drew apart. He leaned back against the rocks, and shut his eyes, and slowly shook his head.

She put her forehead to his chest. His heart was pounding like a turbine. 'It's Myles, isn't it?' she said in a low voice.

He took a deep breath. 'Yeah . . . It sounds crazy, but we have to tell him first.'

'I know.'

'The guy's my best friend. I'm living in his *house*, for Christ's sake. I can't do this behind his back. I wish I could.'

'I know. I feel the same.'

As they talked, their hands kept up a different dialogue: learning the contours of muscle and bone, the feel of hair and skin.

He took her head in his hands and kissed her once more. Then he said, 'Come on, let's go. If we don't get moving soon, I'll forget what I just said.'

They spoke little during the long walk down, and when they did, it was in whispers. Somehow that seemed to fit. The night was hushed, with only the song of the cicadas and the warm wind in the sage, and the frantic scurryings of lizards fleeing the beam of Patrick's torch.

A few hours earlier, Antonia thought, you were walking up this path and you were full of trepidation and self-doubt. Now you're back on the same path, and everything's different. You're not alone any more.

They stopped once, on the bridge across the Ravin de Verdura. Patrick's knee was giving him trouble after the hours of digging, and he needed to rest it for a while. Shoulder to shoulder, they leaned over the parapet and watched the river glow in the moonlight far below.

Antonia felt the warmth of his arm against hers, and the steady rise and fall of his breathing. I love you, I love you, I love you.

At length Patrick said, 'We'll tell Myles as soon as he gets back from Paris.'

'He'll be back some time today,' she said. 'Bound to be. He'll probably come straight to the mill. I'll tell him as soon as he arrives.'

'No. I think I should do it.'

She turned to him. 'Why?'

'He—might take it out on you.'

'He wouldn't get rough, if that's what you mean. He's not like that.'

'Maybe not. But still. I should be there.' He studied her face. 'As soon as we've told him, we'll go away for the weekend. We'll take the Jeep and just drive. Get the hell out of here.'

'Yes. Yes, we'll do that.'

His hand came up and traced the curve of her neck and shoulder. 'This is nuts,' he murmured. 'I can't believe we're holding back because of Myles. If the roles were reversed, he wouldn't think twice.'

She loved the way his lower lip thrust out when he was angry. She stood on tiptoe and kissed it. 'Only one day to go.'

'One day,' he said.

By five o'clock the following afternoon, the *kántharos* had been cleaned inside and out, and Antonia was in the pot-shed doing her best to make a line drawing of the reliefs—but she had made scant progress with any of it. Where was Myles? He should have been here hours ago.

She and Patrick had agreed not to see each other until Myles got back. But they had not envisaged waiting longer than a couple of hours. Now the wait had dragged on for most of the day, and Antonia was beginning to get worried. She kept picturing Myles trapped in the wreckage of the Panda. Or lying in a coma in some hospital bed.

Outside in the courtyard, the sound of Patrick's voice brought her back to the present. She went to the door.

He was standing on the kitchen steps, talking to her father. He wore his usual washed-out navy T-shirt and dusty jeans, and he was looking gravely down at the older man, as they discussed some detail about the dig. She remembered the hardness of his body against hers. She just wanted to be with him.

But where was Myles? If she had known the wait would last this long, maybe she would have acted differently the night before.

She and Patrick had reached the mill at about two, and he had left her at the kitchen door. He had handed her the rucksack without a word, then put his palm against her cheek, and turned and walked away, without looking back.

She had gone into the house and switched on the light—and the kitchen sprang to life in all its shocking normality. Taped to the fridge was an ill-tempered note from her father. *Since you didn't come back*, it said tersely, *I gave the child a sandwich and sent her to bed in the spare room.*

Not the product of a happy man, she thought dreamily, scrunching it up and tossing it in the bin.

She went to bed with Patrick's rucksack beside her, and fell into an exhausted sleep just before dawn.

The next morning she called her father, Modge, Simon and Nerissa into the kitchen, and showed them the *kántharos*.

Surprisingly, Simon was the only one to show unclouded enthusiasm. Nerissa said 'Oh how lovely' in a bored voice, and didn't the young man look like Patrick? Modge was awestruck at first, but when she heard where Antonia and Patrick had found the cup, her face closed, and her lower lip thrust out. Clearly she felt left out. Antonia's father said nothing at all. He went down on his knees, and studied the cup in silence. Then he reached out a hand—only to withdraw it, as she herself had done the night before. 'Magnificent,' he murmured, blinking furiously. The contrast between this miraculous object and his own dead-end dig was just too agonising to bear. She felt more sorry for him than she ever had before.

Eventually he shook himself out of his daze, and announced that they must make a video of those reliefs and he would go immediately to Toulouse and borrow a camcorder from his friend Professor Meriot at the university.

Antonia agreed with alacrity. They had a brief argument over whether he should take the Jeep, which she won, since he intended to stay for a couple of days, and not even he could justify depriving her of transport for so long. Then she drove him to the railway station at Foix. It was a relief and a sadness to see him go.

She put down her pencil, and rubbed the back of her neck. It was no good. She couldn't concentrate on anything as precise as a line drawing today. Not with Patrick so close by, and Myles so infuriatingly, worryingly absent. She pushed the drawing aside, and lost herself in the smooth, flowing lines of the *kántharos*.

It stood in a shaft of sunshine beneath the skylight, glowing with the intensity of fresh blood. There was something about it which inspired awe. The reliefs were miraculous: cut with subtlety and discipline to make skilful use of the natural colour variations in the stone. Pegasus's mane was streaked with ripples of deepest amber, so that it seemed to be floating on the wind. Bellerophon's toga had a flowing line of dark mulberry down the side, gracefully emphasising the young man's eager forward motion.

It was unquestionably the work of a master craftsman, and in Cassius's day it would have been of enormous value. He must have commissioned it specially, and it would probably have cost him his estate. Which in itself was a puzzle—for it was unlike Cassius to have squandered a fortune on such a treasure. So what had driven him to commission a prize such as this? And how had it found its way into a simple peasant sanctum in the hills? Was it possible that Plautius had put it there after his friend's death? Perhaps in his despair at failing to solve the riddle, the old man had done the next-best thing, and dedicated the poet's drinking-cup to the Goddess.

The riddle. It always came back to the riddle. *In poculo veritas.* The truth is in the cup.

Is it possible, she thought suddenly, that it doesn't mean what everyone thinks it means? Not 'seek the truth when you're drunk'—but 'the truth is, *literally*, in the cup'? In *this* cup. In Cassius's cup.

'The truth is in the cup,' she murmured, running her finger round the rim. She pictured Cassius drinking from it—from this cup—this one, that she was touching now. *Gai sum peculiaris*: 'I belong to Gaius'. She saw his face as she knew it from the marble bust in Rome's National Museum: thoughtful and high-browed, and frowning slightly, as if wrestling with some idea which needed all his concentration. She saw him standing at the mouth of the Source, pouring a sacrifice of blood-red wine from a sardonyx cup.

She felt a shiver of apprehension. Not merely anxiety or uncertainty, but something very close to fear. But of what? She tried to shrug it off.

This is what people mean, she told herself, when they talk about being overwrought. So much has happened, so quickly, that you can't take it all in. Besides, what do you expect, after only two hours' sleep?

But there was more to it than that.

'*When we love,*' Cassius had written 2,000 years before,

We hope and fear in equal measure.
Loving someone, and knowing how easily
they can be lost, is terrifying.
That's why I make this request of You, Goddess:
out of simple fear.
Grant us a little more time together.
Lycaris is young, she won't be content with
  memories.
And neither will I.
What's a year or two—or ten—
To an Immortal One like You?

The door creaked, and suddenly there was Patrick. He looked as exhausted as she felt. 'Hi,' he said. 'Are you OK? You look pale.'

She wrapped her arms about her waist. 'It's nothing. Ghost just walked over my grave.'

They exchanged tentative smiles.

He tapped the table with his fingertips and glanced at the *kántharos*, then back to her. 'Did you find anything inside?'

She shook her head. 'Only sand. So much for "the truth is in the cup".'

He gave her an enquiring look.

'The Cassius riddle,' she said. 'At least, I think that's what it means.'

She badly wanted to touch him, and he looked as if he wanted it too, for although he stayed on the other side of the table, his fingers moved slowly up and down the grain of the wood.

'Myles still isn't back yet,' she said.

'I know.'

'What's *happened* to him? He should've been back hours ago. He rang this morning, from somewhere on the autoroute, said he'd be back by noon at the latest. And it's past five now.'

'He'll be here,' he said. 'Listen, if he was in trouble, he'd have called. And if he'd been in an accident, we'd have heard by now. He's probably just playing games. You know what he's like.' But he did not sound entirely convinced, and his eyes betrayed the same concern that she felt. Then he asked her what Myles had said to her when he called.

She said, 'Just that he'd be back by noon.' She decided not to tell him what else Myles had said. It would only make him feel bad.

It had been a rushed call from a petrol station. Myles had sounded breathless and urgent, and curiously young. 'Sorry I'm such a shit,' he mumbled. 'Sorry. And I wanted you to know—you're not frigid.' In the silence which followed, she heard his breath coming fast and shallow, as it did when he was high. Then he said abruptly, 'I'm beginning to think I can't do without you,' and rang off.

She had felt achingly sorry for him. She shrank from the thought of telling him about Patrick.

Patrick was studying her face with an unreadable expression, and she wondered if he guessed that she was holding something back. She stood up and walked round to his side of the table.

He said softly, 'I'll stay and wait with you here.'

'No. Better if you go back to Les Limoniers. If you stayed here, I'd want to touch you all the time.'

He bit his lip. 'Try not to worry. He'll be here soon. And listen,' he added, 'whenever he does get in, call me. *Before* you tell him. OK?'

She nodded.

'Promise?'

'Promise.'

She touched his wristbone with her finger. Then she traced the thick, corded vein up his forearm.

He put a hand on the nape of her neck, and bent and kissed her. She closed her eyes. Took in the heat of his mouth. Smelt sage dust and clean sweat, and a dry, potent smell that was simply Patrick.

Abruptly, he turned on his heel and left.

After he had gone, she remained standing in the middle of the pot-shed for a long time. Then she took the line drawing, rolled it up, and tucked it inside the cup. She locked the *kántharos* in the only cupboard with a key, locked the pot-shed, put both keys on a cord round her neck, and walked across the courtyard to wait for Myles.

Modge couldn't sleep. She lay wide-eyed in the mill's spare room, staring at the luminous green face of the alarm clock that Antonia had given her for company. She wished Myles would come home, so that she could go back to her own room at Les Limoniers.

All day she had been feeling horribly lonely and left out, and when she went to bed, it only got worse. Patrick and Antonia had changed. She couldn't say exactly how, except that they were different. Even when they were right there in front of her they were really far away, somewhere together where she couldn't go.

Oh, they were still nice to her. They waited politely when she talked to them, and even made a stab at answering her. But they didn't really hear what she said.

She blamed that horrible cup thing which Patrick had dug up at the Source. To begin with, it had seemed like a miracle: so beautiful, and with Cassius's *name* on it. But when Antonia told her how she and Patrick had found it together at the Source, Modge knew in an instant that she had lost them both. It wasn't *fair*. She had been with Patrick at the Source to begin with, but then he'd sent her away without telling her about the cup, and made her fetch Antonia instead. And now she had lost them both, and it was all the fault of that cup thing. It had put a spell on them, and she hated it. She refused to believe that it had anything to do with Cassius. It was much too nasty for that.

She lay watching the hot wind sucking the curtains in and out, wondering when it would cool down so that she could sleep.

Some time later she was woken by voices, and a door slamming downstairs. She ran to the window, just in time to see the headlights of the Panda turning off. At last Myles had come home. Maybe now they could get back to normal.

But something was wrong. She could tell from the urgent tone of Antonia's whispers, and the stumbling noises on the stairs. She stood in the middle of the room, her heart thumping. When she couldn't bear it any longer, she opened the door.

At the end of the corridor, weak light poured from Antonia's room. Modge padded towards it. When she reached the doorway she froze.

Myles, her glamorous, wicked, infuriating older brother, was curled up on the bed with his head on Antonia's lap, shivering and crying like a baby. In the lamplight Myles's skin was clammy and white—even his lips were white—and he was gasping, really gasping, as if he couldn't get enough air. 'Oh God, oh God, help me, Toni, I'm going to die, I'm going to have a heart attack and die! Oh God oh God oh God!'

All the time Antonia was talking to him, very low and soft, and stroking his arm and telling him to breathe into the brown paper bag she was holding to his lips. You're not going to die, you're going to be all right. Just breathe into the bag, like the nurse showed us last time, remember? Just breathe in and out.

That made Modge feel a bit better. At least Antonia knew what to do.

Gradually, as the brown paper bag crackled in and out, Myles's breathing slowed. His shivering lessened to an occasional spasm. Antonia pulled the bedspread over him and settled back against the headboard, still with his head on her lap, still stroking his arm.

'God, Toni,' muttered Myles, 'I need you so *much*. Don't ever leave me.'

Modge had never heard him speak like that before, and it frightened her more than anything, for she could tell that he really meant it.

And she could tell from the look on Antonia's face as she sat staring into the darkness, that she knew that he meant it too.

345

CHAPTER SEVEN
A family tomb, Porta Capena,
Rome, July 25, 53 BC

SHE SHOULD HAVE TOLD HIM the moment they met that night, but she couldn't bring herself to do it. She needed to make love with him one last time before she ended it for ever.

And it would be for ever. She wasn't deceiving herself about that—as she had deceived herself about so much over the past few weeks.

Oh, she had been living in a fool's paradise! She saw that now. Hoping that time alone would solve everything: would allow him to find some way—through patronage, his own fame, anything—to make himself acceptable to her family.

But time had turned out to be not the solution, but the greatest enemy of all. It had waited for her like a thief in an alleyway, and then robbed her of everything at a single blow.

And now tonight—which was to have been their last night before he left for Gaul—would be their last night for ever.

She raised herself on one elbow to look at him.

He slept on his back as he always did, with his head turned towards her. His face was serene and young-looking. She knew each one of his scars: its exact shape and feel and provenance. Once, for a joke, she had plotted him like a map. Parthia. Britain. Syria. Anatolia.

That had made him laugh. He laughed a lot when he was with her. She made him happy. He made *her* happy.

Why couldn't it be as simple as that?

And now here she was, about to inflict on him the biggest wound of all. A great stabbing slash across the spirit, which would never heal. She knew how it would be for him, because it would be the same for her.

When she tried to think of what her life would be without him, she couldn't do it. The years stretched before her, a featureless blank.

But she could picture how it would be for him. He would ride away tomorrow on the long, hard road back to Gaul, not understanding why she had ended it between them. He would never understand. For she could never tell him the truth. That was the one certainty she clung to. If she told him, he would try to stop her, and get himself killed.

Lightly, she traced the new crescent scar on his shoulder, the one she had given him a month before. Had some part of her known, even then, that it would come to this? Was that why she had put the Goddess's mark upon him? To make sure that She would watch over him when she, Tacita, could not?

She settled against him and listened to his heart beat. He ran his fingers slowly through her hair, gently drawing out each lock from roots to ends, then letting it fall across her naked back.

'Gaius . . .'

'Mm?'

She swallowed. No. She couldn't do it yet. Quickly she got to her feet, snatching her under-tunic and dress from the flags and hastily pulling them on. With trembling fingers she fastened her belt in a slipshod knot. Then she went to the doorway and stood staring out at the road.

It was in the time of the moon's dark, so the marble tombs and urns along the Appian Way caught only a faint gleam of starlight. Albia was wise to bring extra lamps, she thought numbly. We'll need them on the way back.

Gaius caught her mood, as he always did. She heard him slipping on his tunic and coming up behind her. He put his hands on her shoulders, and rested his chin on the top of her head. 'I'll be back in three months.'

She turned into his arms and he held her tightly, as she needed to be held. She pressed her face to his chest to keep back the sobs, and his breastbone was hard beneath her forehead. His skin carried a faint scent of wine from the lees he used for mixing his ink. The fingertips of his left hand were always stained purple, and smelt faintly of grape.

A few words from me, she thought, and all I'll have left is memories. A few words. I can't bear it.

She took a step back and raised her head and said, 'I'm going to marry Lucius Cornelius Verus. The advocate.'

She watched his face go still.

She thought: now we can never go back to the way we were. Everything we had was before this moment.

'No,' he said calmly.

'Yes,' she said. 'It's all arranged. The betrothal ceremony was yesterday. The wedding's next week.'

His face was blank with shock. His hands hung at his sides. 'I don't—' he began, then broke off. Slowly he shook his head. 'You promised to wait for me. What's changed?'

'The wedding is next week,' she repeated unsteadily.

Her father had been overjoyed when she agreed so quickly to the match. Astonished, but overjoyed. So much so that he missed the fact that she had suggested it herself. But why should he question her motives, when she would be marrying one of the Cornelii?

'Tacita. *Why?*'

This deep, deep coldness in her bones. If only she could get rid of this coldness. She said, 'My father suspects that I have a lover.'

He took her by the shoulders. 'Look at me. No, *look* . . . You're lying.'

'No.'

'Yes. You can't meet my eyes.'

He was right. Her father suspected nothing. But he would. And soon, if she did not move fast.

'I'm doing this to save your life,' she said. That was the truth—for if her father and brothers found out that she had a lover, they would have him killed. And probably her as well.

He didn't believe her. 'You're frightened. That's it, isn't it? You're frightened, because I'm going away.'

'I'm frightened for *you*.'

He paced the length of the chamber. Then he turned. 'Come with me to Gaul.' She caught a flash of what made him such a good soldier. Assess the problem, then go for the solution nobody expects.

'I can't,' she said.

'Yes, you can. Come with me tonight.'

'They'd come after us. It'd be easy on the road. His men would find us. They'd slit your throat in front of me.'

He knew she was right. The bleakness in his eyes told her that. It was unbearable to watch. 'Don't do this, Tacita. Wait for me, as you promised. You promised to wait. Three months! What's three months? I'll be back. I'll sort things out. Don't do this—'

'I already have! Didn't you hear me? The wedding's next week!'

Again he paced the tomb, and this time he prowled like a caged animal. She watched the anger starting to work its way to the surface. Surely anger was a good sign? Surely it would help him get over this?

'You can't do this,' he muttered.

'Gaius, I—'

'*Cornelius?* The man's over fifty! He's got bad teeth, and a little bald patch which he gets his barber to dye with German herbs! No, it's impossible, absurd! Think what your life would be!'

'I don't care about that.'

He shook his head. 'I won't let this happen.'

'You can't stop me.'

'Then I'll beg,' he snarled.

'No.'

'Oh, yes. That's the one good thing about having peasant blood, as you insist on calling it. We have no pride, you see, no pride at all. I'm begging you, Tacita. Don't marry this man. Even if you never see me again, don't ruin your life. Don't do it.'

'I can't let them kill you!' she burst out. 'Hate me if you must, despise me for the rest of your life! But I won't let them kill you!'

She ran to where they had lain together, where his cloak was still spread out, rumpled from their lovemaking, and where hers was still rolled up as a pillow. Somehow she managed to throw it across her shoulders. 'Forgive me,' she said from the doorway.

'How can I forgive you? You're destroying our lives—'

'I have no choice—'

'—and you won't tell me why!'

'There isn't time, Gaius!' Her voice broke. 'We've run out of *time*!'

CHAPTER EIGHT
La Bastide,
September 24, 1988

'PATRICK?'

'Antonia? Is that you?—What time is it?'

'Seven in the morning. Sorry, did I wake you?'

'I—Christ, I guess I overslept! I was up all night.'

'Me too.'

'Is Myles . . .'

'He came back last night, very late.'

'I'll come down.'

'No. No. That's what I'm ringing about.'

'Why, what's wrong?'

'Nothing. It's just that—I haven't told him yet.'

'Good, I'll come down, we'll tell him together—'

'Patrick, listen. He was in a bad way when he got back. Really bad. Some kind of panic attack. It took me all night to get him over it.'

'Jesus. You should have called me.'

'No. You couldn't have done anything. And I knew what to do, it's happened before. Anyway, he's fine now, but he's still asleep. That's the point. He'll sleep for a few more hours, and then, when he's on an even keel—'

'Are you kidding? Myles Cantellow? On an even keel?'

'I know it sounds stupid . . .'

'It sounds like prevarication. We need to wake him up and talk to him.'

'It's not prevarication. All I'm saying is, we need to wait a bit longer. Just a couple of hours till he's awake and feeling better. Please, Patrick, I can't kick him when he's down. I just can't.'

'Hey. Hey. I'm sorry. I didn't mean to yell at you—Antonia? Are you still there?'

'Sorry. Sorry. I'm just a bit tired.'

'Take your time. Listen, I don't want to pressure you. If it makes you feel better to wait, we'll wait.'

As soon as Myles woke up, he knew without opening his eyes that he was in Toni's room at the mill.

He could tell from the creak of the bedstead when he stretched, and the roar of the river through the open window, and the way the pillow smelt of the peppermint shampoo she always used.

He rolled onto his side, and a piece of paper crackled under his cheek. There was a note on the pillow: *Gone to the dig, back by noon. Orange juice etc. in fridge. Have some. Hope you feel better soon. Toni.*

Her handwriting sprawled across the page, encapsulating everything about her which he was not. Elegant, forceful and straightforward.

And kind. He had never thought about that before, but now he felt the truth of it. Toni was kind.

He rolled onto his back and stared at the ceiling. Next to Toni, what was he, Myles Sebastian Cantellow? He was nothing. Not even bad enough to be truly *bad*. His only talent was to screw things up for other people. Look at him now, flat on his back because he couldn't even handle coke without screwing it up, while his girlfriend was out in the blazing sun making yet more epoch-making discoveries.

Last night she had told him about the find at the Source, talking to him in a low, soft voice as he lay with his head in her lap drifting in and out of consciousness, like a kid being lulled to sleep with fairy tales. He had never felt so peaceful and looked-after in his life.

Thank God he had Toni.

As always, his next thought was about what would happen when she left. A panicky sweat broke out on his forehead. Calm down. Don't think about her leaving. She won't leave. Like she said last night, the worst is over. You'll never touch the stuff again—and this time it's *true*, it really is. And because of that she'll stay, and you'll be fine.

He heard a noise at the door, and turned to see Nissa watching him from the corridor. She looked wonderful, in one of her floaty flowered dresses which only just skimmed the tops of her honey-coloured thighs.

'Hello, Nurse,' he murmured. 'Come to give the patient his morning blow job?'

'Get lost,' she said amiably. 'I hear you overdid it in Paris, even for you. You certainly look like crap.'

She sounded impressed, and he grinned. He was feeling better by the minute. 'Nurse,' he said, 'the patient could really murder a drink.'

She smiled. 'I thought you might say that.' From behind her back she produced a bottle of Côtes du Roussillon, two tumblers and a corkscrew.

'Nissa my darling, you are my angel of light.'

God, it tasted good. And alcohol slowed your heart, didn't it? So that was all right.

After filling her own tumbler, Nissa reached across his chest and deposited the bottle on the cabinet. Then she lay on her front beside him, sipping contentedly.

Looking at her made his pulse rise a couple of notches. He should probably send her away. But then again, she was nothing he couldn't handle. He could feel himself getting stronger all the time.

With his tumbler resting on his chest, he pulled down her panties and ran his palm lightly over her peachy buttocks.

'Mm,' she murmured, 'that's nice.'

'You must have been a cat in a former life,' he said.

'Yum. Definitely. I could do this all day.'

'*You're* not doing anything.'

'That's the point.'

After a minute he got bored and gave her a smack. 'Off you trot, step-sister. I want a shower.'

But she rolled onto her back and unbuttoned her dress and told him to do her front.

'Too much of a risk. Toni could come in at any minute.'

She snorted. 'Right now, Toni wouldn't notice if she found us working our way through the *Kama Sutra*.'

He rolled the wine around his mouth. 'What's that supposed to mean?'

'Oh, I forgot. You've been away for the last few days, so you don't know about it.'

'About what?'

'Well, it was bound to happen sooner or later. It's not exactly front-page news.'

'What isn't?'

351

'Toni and Patrick.'

Something inside him dropped like a stone. 'That's a fucking lie.'

'Why would I bother to make up a thing like that? I saw them yester-day in the pot-shed. They couldn't keep their hands off each other.'

He pressed his fingers to his throat. His pulse was racing. Toni and Patrick. Toni and Patrick. No no no no no.

'It must have started while you were in Paris,' she went on, 'because before then I never detected a thing, and I can always tell.'

He felt hot and prickly and cold. It was like lying on needles. He felt sick. Poor Patroclus, he told himself. It wasn't his fault, it couldn't have been, he wouldn't do this to his friend. She bowled him over. Stands to reason, doesn't it? Rich English girl. Clever. Talented. Beautiful. Country boy like him never stood a chance.

Ah, Toni! How could you *do* this? How could you *do* this to *me*?

But she had. She'd seduced his best friend behind his back, and now he had lost her, and Patroclus too.

'Who's Patroclus?' asked Nissa, and he realised he'd spoken aloud.

He ignored her. He thought about how he'd pleaded with Toni last night. How he'd begged her never to leave him. That made him shrink. He had been begging her not to leave him, but she already had.

No. Not possible. There must be some way to get her back. Reel her in, that was what he must do. Yes, definitely, it was time to reel her in. He had stayed in Paris too long, and she had got the bit between her teeth; now she needed to be reminded who was boss.

Already he knew how he would do it. It was only a matter of working out the details. 'Where's Modge?' he asked suddenly.

'How should I know? Around. I think I saw her in the kitchen, stuff-ing her face as usual.'

Good. Good. He would need his little sister's help. She could go places where he could not.

At half-past eleven Patrick straightened up in the sweltering trench where he'd been trowelling, and decided he'd had enough of this lunacy.

'I've had enough of this,' he told Antonia moments later, hunkering down beside her.

She made no reply. She looked exhausted, her eyes shadowed and huge. What had he been thinking of, letting things drag on like this?

'I'm going up to the house,' he went on, 'to shower and sling some stuff in a bag, then I'll meet you back at the mill. I don't care if he's awake or not, but we're out of here.'

She nodded.

He was often to think about that afterwards. About how different their lives would have been if they had managed to get away in time.

It was a little after twelve when he reached the mill. There was no one in the courtyard, and he sensed immediately that something was wrong. The kitchen door was ajar, and he pushed it open. He dropped his rucksack on the tiles. 'Myles? Antonia?'

Nothing. Not even the cat.

He went upstairs and found Antonia's room. It was empty, like all the others.

He had never been in her room before, but he knew it from the rainbow pile of clothes on the chair, and the tangle of jewel-coloured ribbons on the chest of drawers. Her bed was a chaos of brightly flowered sheets. He didn't want to look at it. That was where she and Myles—*no*. Uh-uh. Don't even *think* about it.

Then he noticed that her bedside cabinet was skewed, the door ajar. Myles had told him about the notes she kept in there, her big secret. At the time he had found that touching, for it showed a side of her he wouldn't have expected. Now, with a twinge of apprehension, he saw that the lock had been forced and the cabinet was empty.

Oh, shit. If Myles had messed with her notes it would flay her alive.

He found her in the pot-shed, turning the place upside-down. Her hair was wild, her face taut.

'He's taken everything,' she said dully. 'All the context sheets. From both digs. And—um—my papers.' She pressed her fingers to her mouth.

He remembered that she didn't know that he knew about her notes.

'He left a note.' Shakily she held it out to him.

Even for Myles, the writing was terrible. Something about a paper trail with a prize at the end.

An appalling thought occurred to him. He threw her a glance. 'The *kántharos*. He didn't . . .'

'Yes,' she said. 'He took that too.'

Myles's paper trail was insultingly easy to follow.

He had scattered the context sheets and the pages of Antonia's notes liberally along the track to the Source. Some were thumbtacked to trees, others tied to bushes with twine, and some had been impaled on Monsieur Panabière's barbed-wire fence.

He wants us to know exactly where it leads, thought Antonia numbly. Which probably means that he's put the *kántharos* somewhere else.

The *kántharos*. She couldn't bear to think of it. What if he'd dropped it? What if anything had happened to it?

'We'll take the Jeep,' Patrick had said between his teeth. 'You drive. I'll get out and collect the pages.'

'No,' she said quickly.

'Why not?'

'I'll do it.' She didn't want him to see any part of her translations, and particularly her Introductory Note—her pathetic, overblown, horribly personal theory about Cassius and Lycaris and the riddle.

Myles had excelled himself. He had jumbled up the context sheets from the main dig with those from the Source, then used pages from her notes, neatly folded into arrows, to point the way.

'D'you think he has any idea what he's done?' muttered Patrick.

She didn't answer. Of course Myles knew. If even a handful of context sheets was lost, the whole dig would be ruined. Twelve weeks' work lost beyond hope of retrieval. To say nothing of the wasted funds, and the recriminations her father would face at the faculty. Thank *God* he was safely in Toulouse.

Patrick wrenched the Jeep into gear, and she threw him a glance. From the set of his mouth she could tell how angry he was. She only hoped he wouldn't lose his temper when they caught up with Myles. Time enough for a fight once they had the *kántharos* safe and sound. Then maybe she too could allow herself the luxury of anger. Right now, it would only get in the way.

An hour and a half later, they had found the last of the context sheets. The knot in her stomach loosened fractionally, and she began to feel a glimmer of hope. At least that was one disaster averted.

Patrick cut the engine. They had just passed the turnoff to Le Figarol, and beyond this point the track was too narrow for the Jeep. They would have to continue to the Source on foot.

But to her surprise, Patrick made no move to get out. Instead he sat drumming his fingers on the steering wheel.

'Aren't you coming?' she asked.

'What for? We've got all the sheets and most of your notes.'

'But the *kán*—'

'I say we turn round and go back right now.'

She stared at him. 'What are you talking about?'

'Do you really think that when we get to the Source, we'll find the cup waiting for us, like the pot of gold at the end of the rainbow?'

She swallowed.

'He's got us where he wants us, Antonia. Halfway up a mountain, scurrying around like ants. He's angry and he's hurting, because he knows about us—God knows how—and he wants us to hurt too.'

'So what d'you think we should do?'

'Go back down and wait him out.'

'But—'

'We've got to show him he can't control us. When he knows that, he'll give us the damn cup.'

He was right. But what he suggested was impossible. 'I can't do it,' she said. 'I have to go to the Source. I have to make sure.'

He studied her face. 'OK. OK.'

He turned the Jeep round and parked in the usual place, just below the turn-off for the farm. Antonia put the context sheets on the passenger seat with a stone on top.

'Here,' Patrick tossed her the keys. 'You'd better hang on to these.'

She threw him a doubtful glance. 'You're not going to get into a fight, are you?'

'Who, me?' His lip curled. 'I'm just coming along to make sure *you* don't scratch his eyes out.'

Suddenly the whole exercise struck her as absurd. 'Try and stop me,' she muttered ruefully.

They rounded a bend and came upon three more pages of the Introductory Note tied to a juniper bush, and Modge.

She was stomping towards them down the track, red-faced and fuming. She looked like a small dusty goblin.

Antonia felt a twinge of guilt. She had completely forgotten about the eight-year-old. 'What's the matter, Modge?' she said. 'Where's your brother?'

Modge threw her a thunderous look. 'He told me to bugger off! He made *fun* of me! He says I can be his helper, then he's nasty and pretends it's a joke but it *isn't*, it's just a trick to make me cross so I'll go away! I wish somebody'd make fun of him for a change! Then he'd find out how *he* likes it!'

Her outburst confirmed Antonia's suspicions about how Myles had got into the pot-shed without breaking the lock. The upper window was too small for a man, but big enough for a child to squeeze through.

She asked Modge if Myles had taken the cup to the Source.

Modge glowered at the ground.

'Modge, it's OK,' Antonia said, 'I know it's not your fault. But we need to find the *kántharos*. The stone cup? He took it, didn't he?'

'We did a paper trail,' Modge said stubbornly.

Patrick threw Antonia a warning glance. 'Listen, honey,' he said to Modge, 'it's no big deal, it's just some dumb cup, OK? We're going on to the Source. How about you come too?'

Modge glanced from him to Antonia, then back again. She looked as if she might burst into tears. Then she shook her head. 'Two's company, three's a crowd,' she muttered, and started off down the track.

Patrick made to go after her, but Antonia held him back. 'Let her go. We'll catch up with her on the way down.'

'Wait for us by the Jeep,' Patrick called after Modge.

She did not turn round.

They trudged on up the track. Although it was only midafternoon, the light was worsening as a storm approached. The sky had turned a dirty grey, and a hot wind had begun to blow down the gorge.

They came on Myles without warning. They rounded a bend and there he was, perched on the slope above them. He was smoking a Montecristo, and swigging Veuve Clicquot from the bottle.

'*Hail, brother, and farewell!*' he called down to Patrick, raising the bottle in a mock salute. 'Haven't you done well, getting all the way up here in this heat? And what a *lovely* couple you make! Stupid of me not to notice that before!'

His eyes were red-rimmed and swollen. Antonia wondered if he'd been crying.

Patrick stood looking up at his friend. 'I'm sorry, man,' he said quietly. 'I didn't want this to happen.'

For a moment Myles's face worked. Then he snapped his fingers. '*De nada!* What's a fuck or two between friends?'

Antonia heard Patrick's sharp intake of breath. 'Myles,' she said. 'Tell us where you put the cup. Then we can all go home.'

'Fuck off,' he snarled.

'Come on, Antonia,' said Patrick. 'This is just a bloody waste of time.'

'Not without the cup,' she said.

'Antonia. Come. Now.'

'That's what *I'm* always telling her,' remarked Myles. 'Come now, for Christ's sake, because I am, and I'm fed up with waiting—but does she listen? Does she hell. Mind you,' he took another pull at the bottle, 'you didn't need much urging last night, did you, old girl? Jesus, that was one Godalmighty seeing-to I gave you, wasn't it? No wonder you're sore at me—as they say—'

'Ignore him,' she told Patrick, 'he's making it up. Myles, stop being an idiot and tell us where you put the cup.'

Myles didn't answer. Instead he raised the bottle in a mocking toast. '*A cup of wine for the afternoon,*' he quoted, '*and* don't *let the water-jug hear it. The Bacchus from these cellars flows* neat!' Then he drained the bottle and lobbed it over their heads into the gorge.

Antonia turned to Patrick. 'I'm going to the Source.'

'I told you,' he said, his face stony, 'that's what he wants.'

'I don't care.'

'*Jesus*, Antonia!' he burst out. 'Open your eyes! Can't you see you're playing into his hands? He's screwing you over, just like he's been doing all summer!'

'Well, not *all* summer,' put in Myles. 'If you remember, Patroclus, I've also been—'

'Oh yes,' said Patrick, 'I forgot, you've also been screwing Nerissa.'

Antonia froze.

'But you knew that, right, Antonia?' Patrick's face was taut and furious. 'I mean, you must have asked yourself why he only sleeps with you on certain days of the week? It's because the rest of the time he's screwing her brains out! And you know why? Because he gets *bored* with all that Cassius crap! Don't look like that. You think I didn't know about your notes until today? Your big secret? He told me, Antonia. Just like he told everyone else! Christ, girl, open your eyes!'

She stood there in the blazing sun while he hammered away at her, and her eyes were huge and dark in a face drained of blood.

Once he had started he couldn't stop. He was so angry—with Myles, with her, but mostly with himself, for letting this happen. For not saying the hell with it when they still had the chance, and getting her out of here. If he'd ignored all that crap about best friends, none of this would have happened. And beneath his anger was the worst feeling of all, a churning black doubt that what Myles had said about spending the night with her was not simply the ravings of a drunk, but true.

That's ridiculous, he told himself firmly; this is Antonia we're talking about. I will not let this come between us.

A few feet away from him, Antonia stood on the track twisting the pages she had collected into a roll. Her knuckles were white, and she was doing her best to ignore them both.

He went to her and told her he was sorry. She looked up and gave him a strained smile. She was struggling to keep a grip, and it hurt him to see the effort it took. 'That's OK,' she said. 'It doesn't matter.'

'Yes, it does. I got carried away. I'm sorry.' He wanted to say more, but Myles was watching them, feeding on the havoc he'd created. Patrick was damned if he was going to give him something else to laugh about.

And suddenly Patrick knew that if he didn't get out of there that minute, he would run up the slope and start pummelling his friend, and not stop until he'd killed him.

Antonia must have seen something in his face, for she put her hand on his chest and gave him a little shove and said, 'Go and find Modge.'

He said, 'Come with me,' and she said, 'Soon, but first I have to go up to the Source. It's just something I have to do.'

Then she touched his hand and smiled at him, and his heart leapt, for this time it was a real smile, and he thought, it's going to be all right. We're going to get through this mess.

After Patrick had gone, Myles came down the slope and sat beneath an olive tree with his head on his knees. If it hadn't been for the *kántharos*, Antonia would have pitied him.

Without a word she left him, and climbed the last few hundred yards to the cave. Patrick was right. The *kántharos* wasn't there. She had no choice but to go back to the Jeep and drive home, and hope that Myles would get bored and return the cup.

She found him where she had left him under the olive tree, and passed him, again without a word. A few minutes later he drew level with her, his face sullen and defeated.

Serves you bloody well right, she thought. I hope you get the mother of all hangovers.

She felt shaky and sick, her eyes scratchy with fatigue. And she wished she could stop the thoughts churning in her head. Nerissa. The *kántharos*. All that 'Cassius crap'. She wondered if Patrick felt the same way about that as Myles. Oh, but he didn't mean that, she told herself wearily. He's exhausted. You both are. It'll be all right. Everything will be all right.

But when they got back to the Jeep there was no sign of Patrick or Modge, and someone had shut Monsieur Panabière's gate and blocked the way home. The Jeep sat behind the gate, ready and waiting to head off downhill. But a hefty padlock and chain had put paid to that.

This was all she needed, thought Antonia exhaustedly. Now she faced a long walk down to the mill, with a sullen Myles. And still no *kántharos*.

Myles ran past the Jeep and gave the gate a furious shake. 'This is the last fucking straw! *Now* what do we do?'

Antonia snorted. 'I'd have thought that was obvious. We climb over and walk.'

'You walk if you like,' he snapped, 'I'm driving.'

'Oh, yes? And how do you propose getting the gate open?'

'I *propose* that you nip over to Le Fig and sweet-talk that stupid old fart into giving us the key.'

Antonia stared at him. 'Nip over? It's more than two miles! And why should I? I wouldn't even be here if it weren't for you.'

His eyes took on a dangerous glint. 'Right,' he snapped, 'I'll *drive* to the farm. Give me the keys.'

'Don't be ridiculous! That's not a track, it's a collection of potholes! I'm not letting you ruin my father's Jeep just because—'

'Give me the keys, you slimy little bitch, or I'll come and get them!'

'Fine,' she muttered, fumbling in her pocket. She chucked the keys at him, and he caught them in one hand.

She turned on her heel and made for the gate.

Behind her she heard him gun the engine hard, then yank the Jeep screamingly into gear.

'Don't force it, you idiot,' she shouted, 'you'll wreck the gearbox!'

Without looking up, he flipped her the finger.

She watched him back up jerkily past the farm track, then wrench the steering wheel round to make the turn. Again the gearbox shrieked as he ground it into first. Again she shouted at him to go easy.

He yelled at her to fuck off, and stepped on the gas.

Instead of going forwards, the Jeep stayed in reverse. In a single bound it lurched backwards across the track to the edge of the gorge.

A cry died in her throat. In disbelief she watched one rear wheel slide smoothly over the side of the cliff. Dust and gravel flew. The wheel spun over nothingness. Then, with a soft crumbling of earth, the other wheel went over.

Myles raised his head and met her eyes.

His face was blank, utterly blank, and the look they exchanged lasted for ever. Then the Jeep tipped slowly backwards and slid into the gorge.

She couldn't cry out. Her throat had closed. She heard the rattle of pebbles trickling into the gorge. She felt the hot wind buffeting her face. She saw the context sheets fluttering into the air where the jeep had been. They were dazzling white and weirdly peaceful as they twisted on the wind. Like white birds fluttering against a pewter sky.

Somewhere behind her, Modge began to scream. Then Patrick was running up and vaulting the gate, gripping her shoulder so hard that it hurt, and shouting at her to stay behind with Modge. Then he was scrambling down a goat track so steep that she screamed at him to stop, but he had already gone.

From far below came a terrific booming thunderclap, then a crackling like a forest fire. Suddenly black smoke was boiling up into the sky. Thick, bitter, oily black smoke. And a stink of petrol.

And always the context sheets: dazzling white and weirdly peaceful, fluttering like doves over the gorge.

CHAPTER NINE
17 Wilton Row, Belgravia,
October 24, 1988

ON THE MORNING OF THE INQUEST, the Passmores breakfasted earlier than usual, and Patrick was the last to come downstairs.

He had slept badly. Since the accident he always slept badly. And he felt tired all the time. Was that grief? It didn't feel like grief. More like disbelief. A deep-rooted sense that none of this was happening.

Myles's mother and stepfather and Modge were already in the beautiful blue and white breakfast room. As Patrick came in, all three looked up at him and smiled.

'You're looking rather peaky, old chap,' remarked Julian Passmore. 'Are those wretched burns giving you trouble again?'

'They're all right,' said Patrick. 'Thanks.' He took his seat, and poured coffee awkwardly into his cup with his right hand. These days he did everything awkwardly, but this morning felt worse than usual because he was in a suit and tie. He hadn't worn a suit since Finals.

Patrick drank his coffee, and watched Myles's mother buttering a slice of toast—to add to the two slices already on her plate, which she would also forget to eat.

Myles had nicknamed his mother the Queen of Sheba, and Patrick could understand why. She had dark eyes in a finely sculpted face, and when she spoke, her jaw clenched so tightly that the muscles knotted.

She was well groomed in a way which indicated that she wasn't interested in her appearance, but made the necessary effort because it mattered to those around her. Today, as always, she was dressed in a tailored suit, a slightly mannish striped blouse, and a matching bow tie.

From what little Myles had said about his mother, Patrick guessed that he had been in awe of her. He sympathised. He was in awe of her himself. But she had been briskly kind to him, as had her husband, ever since he had left the hospital after the accident.

Across the table, Julian Passmore frowned at his *Times*. He doesn't look like a judge, thought Patrick in bemusement. Although what do judges look like, anyhow?

He found himself wishing Nerissa was here to help him cope with all this. But Nerissa was in Paris with Simon, and would only be back for the funeral. Julian had remarked to Patrick with surprising sharpness that his daughter was probably staying away out of pique, because she hadn't been asked to give evidence at the inquest.

Lucky Nerissa, Patrick thought.

Looking at Myles's parents across the table, he felt more of an impostor than ever. No, impostor wasn't the right word. He felt worse than that. He was a *usurper*. He shouldn't be here. He didn't deserve this. Now he watched Modge put down her orange juice and quietly ask her mother if she could leave the table. Debra let her go with a tightening of the lips. She had made no secret of wanting her daughter to accompany them to the inquest, but the doctor had pronounced it 'most inadvisable', and for once Julian had gone against his wife and insisted that Modge should stay at home with the housekeeper.

Debra had taken some persuading. It was as if she failed to see why her daughter should be spared the forthcoming ordeal, when she was not. For Debra Passmore, grief was an angry business. Hers was a deep-burning anger which rarely surfaced, but nevertheless made the house crackle with tension.

And now Patrick was about to make it worse.

'If it's OK with you,' he began carefully, 'I'll meet you at the Coroner's Court just before the hearing? I've arranged to meet Antonia and her mother for a cup of coffee.'

Debra looked at him, then, in that clenched-jaw way of hers, she said the exact opposite of what she meant. 'Of course. What a good idea. We'll see you in court at about, say, nine forty-five?'

'Fine,' said Patrick.

'Good,' said Debra, and flashed him a brief smile, to reassure him that however much she might deplore his seeing Antonia, she did not hold it against *him*.

Why, he wondered, has she taken so violently against Antonia, but not against me? Right from the start, when she and her husband had stepped from the rented BMW on the morning after the accident, Debra had loathed Antonia with a hatred that was beyond all reason.

That girl, she would call her, when the iron clamps on her grief had been loosened by wine. 'If *that* girl hadn't thrown him the keys when he was *obviously* unfit to drive, he would be alive today!'

Patrick couldn't bear it when she talked like that. He wished he had the courage to say to her, OK, Debra, so Antonia threw him the keys. But she never meant for anything bad to happen. None of this is her fault! And if you think she's to blame, what about me? I was his friend, and I took everything from him. I took his trust and his hospitality. I took his girl. That's why he was drunk, Debra. That's why he couldn't handle the goddamned Jeep. That's why he died. Do you ever think about that? I do. Every minute of every day.

But how could you say such things to a woman whose only son has been crushed and incinerated beyond recognition? Whose only means of coping is to turn her rage outwards on someone else?

Oh, how he longed for Antonia. Since the accident he had hardly seen her, and never once alone. She had been at her mom's house in Suffolk all this time, and they got by on stilted telephone calls in which she assured him she was fine, in that very British way of hers which could mean anything from 'genuinely OK' to 'teetering on the edge of a nervous breakdown'.

These days, she rarely returned his calls. At first that had worried him, but now he was beginning to accept it. Maybe that was how it should be. After what had happened, how could he ride off into the sunset with Myles's girl?

Debra turned to Patrick. 'I forgot to tell you. We've arranged to go to the church on Wednesday at three, to go over the music for the service. You'll come, won't you?'

Patrick blinked. Today was Monday. Tomorrow he planned to return to Oxford. He wasn't sure what he would *do* there—apart from trying to find some kind of job—and of course, he had to return to London for the funeral, whenever that turned out to be. But he was certain he had told the Passmores that he was leaving tomorrow.

Debra picked up his hesitation. 'You'll stay for another couple of weeks, won't you?'

'Say yes, old chap,' said Julian. 'It would mean a lot to us. In fact, I don't think we can do without you. Modge certainly can't.' He softened that with one of his charming smiles, but he meant every word.

Patrick glanced from one to the other. He tried to return the smile, but his face felt stiff. Maybe that was the burns. 'Thank you,' he said. 'You're very kind.'

Before he left the house, he climbed to the top floor to say goodbye to Modge. She was in the playroom, crouching on the hearth-rug before a low table on which two Sindy dolls were having a furious row. A model Range Rover was parked beside them, perilously close to the edge. A roll of white paper protruded from its open boot, as if the Sindys had just bought a new rug and were bringing it home.

'No, *you* drive!' muttered Modge, butting the dolls' heads together. Her face was pinched and anxious. She was not enjoying the game.

'Hi,' said Patrick, pulling a chair closer to the table.

'Hi,' mumbled Modge without looking up.

He nodded at the Sindy dolls. 'Those guys look as if they're pretty mad at each other.'

Modge tightened her lips. 'It'll be all right. They're going to make friends again.'

'Sure. But you know, it's OK for them to be cross with each other for a while. Doesn't mean they're not still friends, and all.'

Which he had to admit was somewhat lacking in subtlety.

Apparently Modge thought so too, for she ignored him.

For several days after the accident she had been as clingy and dependent as a five-year-old, never letting Patrick or Antonia or her father out of her sight, and having screaming nightmares every night.

Then, a week later, she suddenly got better. She 'put it behind her', as Julian said, with undisguised relief. Now she spent most of her time in the playroom alone with her dolls. Julian talked of finding her a different boarding school, to help her make a complete break with the past.

One of the Sindys was now behind the wheel of the Range Rover, which teetered precariously on the edge of the table. The other Sindy shoved a rigid arm under the windscreen and yanked the car back to safety. The roll of paper slid from the boot and dropped onto the rug.

'Whoah, they've lost their load,' said Patrick. He reached for it.

'No!' cried Modge.

Her hand came down on his. Her grip was feverishly hot. He wondered what the roll represented to her. He turned it in his fingers, and three neat, pencilled initials caught his eye. 'AEH/88'.

Antonia Elizabeth Hunt.

Frowning, he slipped off the elastic band, spread the paper on the table, and found himself looking down at Antonia's half-finished line drawing of the *kántharos* reliefs. There in front of him was Pegasus, trotting joyfully towards Bellerophon.

He felt as if he were seeing them through deep water. Once, he had gazed on this young man's face and been awed into silence. But that had been a million years ago. It had happened to someone else.

His voice was hoarse as he asked Modge if Myles had given her the drawing.

The Range Rover completed a full circuit before she gave a slight nod.

'So he—uh—he got you to help take the cup, did he? As well as the other stuff?'

Another pause. Another imperceptible nod.

Oh, *Myles*. Getting your kid sister involved in something like this!

The context sheets were one thing—but the *kántharos*?

'Any idea where he put it?' he asked quietly. 'The cup, I mean?'

A vehement shake of the head.

'Because you see, Imogen, it's gone missing. Dr Hunt has looked all over, but he can't find it. And he really needs it, and Antonia too. Are you sure you don't know where it is?'

Her face became puffy. 'Cross my heart and hope to die.'

He winced at the grim schoolgirl oath. 'It's OK, honey, I believe you.'

The Range Rover did another circuit, then pulled up. 'Patrick?'

'Yeah?'

'Don't tell on me.'

'About what, honey?'

'That I helped Myles steal the cup thing.'

'Hey, it wasn't your fault! No one's going to blame you.'

The Range Rover started up again. 'If you tell on me, the policemen will come and take me away.'

'No they won't. Policemen don't take little girls away from their moms.'

She raised her head and gave him an unblinking stare. 'They will,' she said flatly. 'They'll ask questions and find out.'

'Find out what?'

A long pause. 'I was cross with him.'

He remembered the furious red-faced goblin marching down the track towards them. It wasn't hard to guess the way her mind worked. She'd had a fight with her brother, and he had been killed. Therefore it was her fault.

Patrick tried to tell Modge that bad thoughts can't hurt people, and that she hadn't caused the accident by being mad at her brother.

She didn't seem to hear him. So much for Patrick McMullan the would-be therapist.

The only thing that had any effect was when he rolled up the line drawing and put it in his pocket. For safe keeping, he said, if that was OK?

It was. In fact she seemed relieved that the drawing was no longer her responsibility. She sat on the rug looking more than ever like a small intense goblin, and fixed him with her long-lashed brown eyes. 'Promise you won't tell on me at the trial.'

'Honey, it's not a trial. It's an inquest. A kind of hearing they have when someone dies in an accident, to find out what happened. Nobody gets blamed. And no, I won't be saying anything about you, because none of this stuff will come up. They only want to know about the accident.'

She didn't even blink. 'Promise you won't tell.'

'If it makes you feel better, sure. I promise.'

'No doubt you'll think me old-fashioned,' remarked Evelyn Hunt as she wove Antonia's hair into a thick French plait, 'but I can't help thinking that some old traditions really made *sense*. In my mother's day when someone died, one went into mourning. Mourning dress makes sense. It gives people an indication of what one's going through. It's kinder to the bereaved, and so much less embarrassing for everyone else. These days, they have ribbons for AIDS and breast cancer, and heaven knows what else—but nothing for simple mourning.'

Simple mourning. Mourning Myles. It sounded bizarre. And not simple at all.

Antonia sat at the dressing table in her room in Montpelier Street and watched her mother's reflection as she fixed the plait which had defeated her. These days, the simplest tasks were beyond her grasp. She felt numb, and slightly sick. And cold all the time.

But the deeper feelings—like sorrow and pity and grief—eluded her. She couldn't feel them. She couldn't even cry.

Surprise, though, was something she could feel. She felt it now, at the comfort she took from being bossed around by her mother.

Evelyn Hunt had flown out the day after the accident and taken everything in hand. She had closed down the dig, paid off a bemused and shaken Simon, and found him lodgings in Paris with a friend of hers. Then she had shut up the mill, and briskly flown her husband and daughter home. She took Antonia with her to Suffolk, and dispatched her husband to her daughter Caroline in Gloucestershire, where he stayed—before, during and after his resignation from the faculty.

He had not been called to give evidence at the inquest, and would not be leaving his bolt hole to lend Antonia moral support. He had told his wife that he was not well enough to attend the hearing, and she had accepted that with the slightly impatient tolerance with which she met most of his pronouncements. But he did not fool Antonia. Since the accident, he could scarcely bring himself to speak to her. He blamed her for the wreck of his career. Curiously, it was not Myles's death which he found hardest to take, or even the ruin of the dig, but the loss of the *kántharos*. He seemed to have adopted it retrospectively as his own. It had become the Great Find which would have made his name. Until it had been lost through a daughter's negligence.

'Your young man phoned while you were in the bath,' said her mother, securing the finished plait with a black velvet ribbon. 'He said not to bother you, he just wanted to check that we knew which coffee shop to go to. I must say he sounds nice. And I do like the way he calls you Antonia rather than Toni.'

Antonia was surprised. 'So do I.'

'Finally!' Her mother rolled her eyes in exaggerated relief. Catching her daughter's enquiring glance in the mirror, she added, 'Well, I've always wondered how long you intended to cling to that horrendous nickname.'

'What do you mean? I never even liked it.'

'Darling, you were the one who chose it! Don't you remember?'

Antonia shook her head.

'One day when you were five, you declared, "I'm Toni. Nobody call me anything else." So that was that.'

'I don't remember.'

'Trust me, it happened. You absolutely *loathed* your name. Well, you *loathed* anything "girlish". Dolls. Dresses. I suppose it was because they reminded you of Caroline, and were therefore utterly beyond the pale.' She shook her head. 'I never could fathom you. Still can't. Caroline was always so much easier.'

And yet, her expression seemed to say, you're still my daughter, and you need me, so here I am.

Antonia's mother was a tall, slender, dark-haired woman who was still crisply beautiful at fifty-two. In honour of the inquest she wore a short boxy jacket in navy worsted, with wide trousers. She would be over-dressed for the Coroner's Court, but as far as she was concerned, one dressed 'properly' for all public occasions, and that included an inquest.

Mrs Hunt glanced at her watch, and her eyebrows shot up. 'Nearly eight already! We'd better hurry or we'll be late.'

Antonia stood up, and in her stomach a host of butterflies lifted off. In half an hour she would see Patrick again. Patrick, her lifeline to reality. She clung to the thought that some day, after all this ghastliness was over, they still had a chance to be together.

It had been terrible when he went incommunicado for those two weeks after the accident. She had been convinced that he was gone for good—that he had fallen off the edge of the world, like Myles. Even now, although she telephoned the house in Wilton Row every day, he didn't always call back. To begin with she had worried that he no longer wanted to speak to her, but recently she had begun to suspect that Mrs Passmore wasn't passing on her messages.

That struck Antonia as entirely understandable. After all, she had killed Debra Passmore's son.

Antonia waited with her mother in the Italian coffee bar. It was a pleasant office-workers' retreat, with gleaming green tiles, and marble-topped tables. Outside in the Horseferry Road, buses and taxis thundered past.

Suddenly Patrick was standing by the table, and her mother was smiling up at him and introducing herself, then serenely 'taking herself off' to find the court and wait for them there.

It was unbelievable to see him again. She had forgotten the light in his eyes, and how very blue they were.

He no longer wore the dressings on his face and neck, which now merely looked as if he had a mild case of sunburn down one side. His hair had been cut very short, presumably to get rid of the burnt bits, but his eyebrows and lashes no longer looked singed.

His right hand had the same smooth sunburn as his face, but the left was still encased in bulky dressings. The doctors said it was a serious burn, which might mean skin grafts, plastic surgery, and perhaps learning to write again.

She watched him go to the counter to buy their coffee. He wore what she guessed must be the suit in which he had sat his Finals. She had never seen him in a suit before. It made him look tall and rangy and intimidatingly elegant.

Patrick brought their coffee and sat down opposite her.

Antonia groped for something to say. 'Are you . . .' she began. 'I mean, is any of your family coming to the hearing?'

He looked at her blankly.

'I thought—your mother being English, she might come along? Or—you might have relatives here?'

He shook his head. 'My mom died a few years back. There's an aunt somewhere in the Midlands. I called her once, just after I came to Britain, but . . .' He shrugged.

She asked him how Modge was doing.

'OK, I guess. At least—' he broke off. 'To be honest, I don't know. I don't even know how _I_ am. None of this is real.'

They sat for a while in silence. Then he put out his good hand and touched hers. 'I've missed you,' he said, without looking at her.

'Me too.'

With his thumb he stroked the back of her hand. 'You know, it's weird, but I'm really nervous about this hearing.'

'I know. Me too.'

Abruptly, she couldn't look at him any more. She bowed her head over her coffee and felt the tears welling up. Her throat closed. The tears wouldn't come. It had been like that since the accident. She couldn't cry. Perhaps that was why she felt sick all the time.

'All I can think about,' she said in a strangled voice, 'is his face as the Jeep went over. I dream about it every night. He looked so blank. So utterly blank.' She drew a shaky breath. 'Then after the Jeep disappeared, there was the longest time till it hit the rocks. That endless silence while he fell. And all that time—all that *time*—he must have known he was going to die.'

Suddenly the coffee shop was unbearably hot. She couldn't breathe. 'I keep wondering when he lost consciousness. I tell myself it must have been when he hit the rocks. I mean, as *soon* as he hit? It would have been then, wouldn't it? Instantaneous. A blackout. He wouldn't have known . . . he wouldn't have—felt—anything. In the fire.'

He made no reply. He just went on gently stroking the back of her hand, while she sat with her head bent low, panting out her grief.

After a while she straightened and rubbed her dry eyes. Her head throbbed with unshed tears.

They sat together in silence, while office workers bought cappuccino and muffins, and the buses thundered past outside. Then Patrick glanced at the clock on the wall. Twenty to ten. 'We've got to go.'

She stood up. 'Let's get this over with,' she said.

They said goodbye on the steps outside the Coroner's Court. The Passmores would be waiting for him inside, and they both knew that Debra's presence would make further contact difficult.

As he held the door open for her, she looked up at him and said, 'After the hearing, can we—still see each other, do you think? Can we?'

He looked down at her. He tried to smile, but it wouldn't come.

'I—I mean,' she stammered, 'if you still want to?'

He opened his mouth. 'I still want to,' he said at last.

He reached into his breast pocket and brought out a folded sheet of notepaper and handed it to her: quickly, as if he might change his mind and take it back. On it he had set out his address and telephone number in Oxford, along with instructions on how to get there. He had been forced to type it, as his left hand was still in bandages.

Shakily she folded the notepaper and put it in her pocket. 'I'll call you after the hearing.'

'After the hearing. Right.'

It was only later, as she waited with her mother to go into the courtroom, that she realised that his answer had been equivocal. 'I still *want* to see you,' he had said.

Not: 'we still can'.

'The case we're going to hear,' said the coroner briskly, 'concerns the death of . . .' he consulted his files, 'Myles Sebastian Cantellow of 17 Wilton Row, London SW1: a death which occurred in France, but over which I have jurisdiction, as the body now lies in my district . . .'

Strange to hear 'Cantellow' mentioned after weeks of Passmores. On his mother's remarriage, Myles had chosen to retain his father's surname—not as a mark of affection, but simply to irritate Julian, whom he disliked marginally more than his own father. It seemed that Sheridan Cantellow felt the same way about his son, for he had not come down from Edinburgh for the inquest.

'. . . I have it in mind to admit eight items of documentary evidence,' said the coroner in his smooth consultant's voice. 'The statements of Monsieur Clovis Panabière (a local farmer), the French gendarme who was called to the scene, the representatives of the emergency medical and fire services, Dr Roger Gilbert (the pathologist), Dr Antonia Hunt, Patrick McMullan and Nerissa Passmore. I take it that no one objects?'

Beside him, Patrick felt Debra twitch. She seemed uncomfortable in the role of passive observer.

'Good,' said the coroner, flicking her a wary glance. 'Then can we go first to Patrick McMullan.'

Patrick stood up and the usher showed him how to take the oath. He was relieved that his voice didn't shake when he read the words.

The coroner read out Patrick's name and his new address in Oxford, and Patrick confirmed that they were correct.

'Now,' said the coroner. 'Firstly can we turn to the question of identity. I don't think this need detain us long, but I must ask one or two questions, as the dental evidence is inconclusive. I understand, Mr McMullan, that you were the first on the scene, having watched the Jeep go over the cliff with the deceased behind the wheel?'

'Yes, sir.'

'Now. As I understand it, you ran back up the track to assure yourself of Dr Hunt's safety, then took a narrow and extremely precipitous track down the face of the cliff to reach the Jeep. There you tried to rescue the deceased but were beaten back by the heat, sustaining some injury to yourself in the attempt.' His eyes flicked to Patrick's bandaged hand. 'Is that a fair summary of what happened?'

A fair summary? Patrick had followed the coroner's account with difficulty. The man's words were so divorced from his own experience that it was like listening to an account in Serbo-Croat and having to perform a simultaneous translation.

Everyone was waiting for him to answer. 'Yes, sir,' he said at last. 'That's how it was.'

The coroner nodded, then handed the usher a sheaf of papers and she gave a set to Patrick: two sheets of A4 stapled together, each bearing two glossy black and white photographs. 'We'll be discreet about these,' the coroner said, studying his own set, while Patrick struggled single-handedly with his. 'They're available to those who wish to examine them, but relatives of the deceased are warned that they may find them distressing. Now, Mr McMullan,' he said without raising his head, 'these were taken by the police after the fire had been extinguished. Clearly the deceased was terribly badly burned, completely unrecognisable, but does this approximate to what you saw when you arrived on the scene?'

Patrick focused on holding the pictures steady and keeping his features expressionless. He nodded.

'For the note, Mr McMullan—'

'Yes. Sir. It's what I saw.' Maybe he should have said *he*, not 'it'. But the thing in the photographs was very definitely an 'it'.

'Very good,' said the coroner, which struck Patrick as surreal. 'So to recap. You saw the Jeep go over with the deceased in it, and you saw him *in* the jeep when you reached the bottom of the gorge?'

Patrick said yes.

The coroner nodded. 'I think that's as far as we need go on identification. Usher, you may take back the photographs.'

Patrick glanced at Antonia. She caught his eye and gave him a slight smile, and though he didn't smile back, he could tell that she knew he would if he could. Suddenly he felt much less isolated.

'Let us pass to the cause of death,' said the coroner, scanning his file. 'Given the state of the body, the pathologist's report is naturally heavily qualified in many respects, but what emerges is that this was a young man of twenty-four, in good physical health, save for the fact that what remained of the liver showed signs of alcohol abuse . . .'

The liver. Jesus, did he *have* to put it like that? Patrick had been looking at Debra while the coroner was speaking, and he saw her sag and age before his eyes.

'. . . blood alcohol,' continued the coroner, reading from the report, 'could not be established with any accuracy, but was estimated at significantly above the legal limit of eighty milligrams per one hundred millilitres.' He sounded severe. Plainly, Myles was being docked points for bad behaviour. 'Now, Mr McMullan.' The coroner glanced up and fixed Patrick with serene brown eyes. 'About half an hour before the accident you saw the deceased consume an entire bottle of champagne.'

'Yes.'

'And in her statement, Ms Passmore tells of having seen him consume the better part of *another* bottle of wine that morning. Moreover, we know from the statement of Dr Hunt that the deceased had consumed a considerable amount of cocaine the night before. To your knowledge, did the deceased habitually make use of proscribed substances?'

Patrick licked his lips. He felt the heat of Debra Passmore's gaze. 'Yes,' he said at last.

'And was he also in the habit of combining them with excessive amounts of alcohol, or would that have been unusual for him?'

He cleared his throat. 'It was not unusual. Although he had recently made up his mind to quit the—'

'Confine yourself to the question, Mr McMullan. If you please.'

Patrick felt himself colouring.

'And had you ever seen him drive in this condition?'

'Yes, sir.'

'Often?'

'A few times, I guess.'

'So where does this take us?' asked the coroner with a touch of the amateur dramatics. 'We know the deceased was well over the legal limit when he got into the Jeep, and we know that he was seen first to *reverse* in order to make the turn, and then to attempt to move forwards in order to drive off down the hill—but instead, he remained in the wrong gear and backed over the cliff edge. I understand he had made a similar error once before in the same vehicle?'

'I believe so, sir. Those gears could be sticky, I'd noticed it myself when I drove it.'

'So it would seem that the deceased repeated an earlier mistake, his faculties being impaired by alcohol and cocaine. Would you agree?'

'Yes, sir,' murmured Patrick.

'Well, that all seems in order. Now finally on the medical evidence, it's clear that trauma from the crash was the principal cause of death, so we now come to the surrounding circumstances,' said the coroner, 'namely, *how* the deceased came to be driving, in his state of intoxication, halfway up a precipitous mountain track. Again I shall summarise from the statements, and you will please tell me if I've omitted anything material. You and Dr Hunt—the girlfriend of the deceased—had recently formed an "attachment"'—Patrick flinched—'of which the deceased had become aware—we know not how—and which prompted him to take revenge on Dr Hunt by laying a paper trail up the mountain track. There an altercation ensued. A fair summary?'

'Yes,' said Patrick.

'Now. After the altercation, Dr Hunt suggested that you go off in search of the deceased's eight-year-old sister, who was also on the mountainside at the time. This you did.'

'Yes.'

'And on your way you passed the Jeep, and noticed that a farm gate which had been open when you drove up the track was now closed and padlocked, thereby blocking the Jeep's exit.'

'Yes.'

'Now I want to ask you this. When you and Dr Hunt arrived earlier, why did you choose to park *uphill* from the gate, where you were at risk of being blocked in, if the gate were shut?'

Patrick blinked. 'There wasn't anywhere else to park, sir. We always parked there. It was the only place where the track was wide enough to let Monsieur Panabière's tractor pass, if he came by.'

'I see. And before you parked, you turned the Jeep round so that it was facing downhill. Was that also something you always did?'

'No,' he said uneasily. 'I guess that was the first time I did that.' Jesus, it sounded suspicious. Like he'd done it on purpose.

'So why did you do it this time?'

'Because I knew we'd be tired when we got back to the Jeep. Neither of us had slept much the night before—'oh boy, how good *that* sounded—'and I thought it'd be safer if we didn't have to do it on the return trip when we'd be even more tired.'

There was a silence while everyone thought about that, and Patrick wished he'd used any word in the dictionary but 'safe'.

'Now back to the gate. Did it strike you as odd that it should be closed and padlocked?'

'Perhaps a little. Though it had happened before. I mean, not the pad-locking, but it had been closed once or twice.'

'You see, Monsieur Panabière says in his statement that he definitely did *not* close *or* padlock the gate when he and his wife drove by at about two o'clock. Do you have any idea who shut and padlocked the gate?'

'No, sir, I don't.'

The coroner nodded. 'Well, I don't think we can take that any further. There doesn't seem to be anything out of the ordinary, no evidence of foul play. So,' he frowned at his papers, 'after climbing over the gate, you found the deceased's sister some distance further down the track, at which point you chanced to glance back, and caught sight of the deceased with Dr Hunt.'

'Yes, sir.'

'According to Dr Hunt's statement, after you left her she had a further altercation with the deceased, who demanded that she give him the keys of the Jeep. Did you see this altercation?'

'I couldn't see Anto—Dr Hunt, but I could see Myles.'

'But you say in your statement that you *saw* her give the keys to the deceased.'

'I saw him catch them, but I couldn't see her. There were bushes in the way.'

'Ah yes, quite so.' The coroner checked his file. 'She says in her statement that she *threw* the keys at the deceased.'

From the corner of his eye, Patrick saw Debra Passmore stiffen. 'I guess so,' he said reluctantly. 'But if she hadn't let him have them, he would have taken them from her anyway, so—'

A quelling glance from the coroner. 'Then you saw the deceased get into the Jeep.'

'Yes.'

'And the Jeep went over the edge.'

'Yes.'

'And we're back where we started. Very good.'

Patrick swayed. His back ached from standing for so long, and his left hand throbbed.

'I'm reaching the end of my questions, Mr McMullan,' said the coroner in a kindly voice. 'But I have to ask, did the deceased at any time seem excessively upset or depressed over what he had just discovered about your attachment with Dr Hunt?'

'Sir?'

'To the extent that he might have taken his own life, or been reckless as to whether he lived or died?'

Debra Passmore put her hands to her mouth.

How could he possibly answer that? He opened his mouth to speak but no sound came out. He swallowed. 'Myles,' he faltered, 'Myles *was* reckless. It's who he was. But that doesn't mean he—' he broke off. Started again. 'He would never try to kill himself. Absolutely not. He had too much to live for.'

Suddenly he had a picture of Myles hooting with laughter at the cliché. *'Too much to live for'? Jesus Christ, Patroclus, where did you get that one? "Eastenders"?*

They would have a laugh about that afterwards.

Then it hit him, as it was always hitting him, that he would never have a laugh with Myles again. The blood soughed in his ears. The courtroom misted over. 'I knew him,' he said. His voice cracked. 'He would never kill himself. He was my best friend.'

This time the coroner did not admonish him to confine himself to the question. He regarded Patrick in silence, as if mildly intrigued by this evidence of grief. Then he said, 'One last question. The deceased's younger sister was with you at the time of the accident, and witnessed it too. Understandably, she is too distressed to be questioned. But I must ask you. To your knowledge, could she add anything further to what we've heard today? Anything at all?'

Patrick thought about that. He thought about Myles enlisting his sister's help to take the *kántharos*. He thought about her pinched little face as she re-enacted the accident with her Sindies. He thought about his promise that he wouldn't 'tell on her', and his promise to Myles to look after his sister. 'No, sir,' he said. 'She couldn't add anything.'

'Thank you, Mr McMullan, that will be all.'

It was only when he had resumed his place next to Debra, and shut his eyes and taken a couple of deep, slow breaths, that he felt something crackle in his jacket pocket, and drew out Antonia's line drawing of the *kántharos* reliefs. He had intended to give it to her in the coffee bar.

Suddenly he wondered if he had made a mistake by protecting Modge just now. For the first time it struck him that nothing had been said about the *kántharos*. Surely that was a bit odd? Shouldn't he have said something?

Ah, but what good would it have done? It would only have meant all kinds of questions for poor little Modge, and what was the point? She didn't know where Myles hid the cup.

Cassius, the riddle, the *kántharos*. What did any of that matter now?

He stuffed the drawing back in his pocket.

The coroner went over the same ground with Antonia as he had with Patrick, but at greater speed. She did her best to answer, but found it hard to follow what he was saying. As a result her delivery was halting, and she frequently had to ask him to repeat the question. She suspected he found her uncooperative, perhaps even evasive.

The coroner had asked her another question. Something about the paper trail. She apologised and asked him to repeat it, which he did with slightly laboured patience.

'Yes,' she said, 'by the time Patrick and I reached the turnoff for Le Figarol, we had already collected all the context sheets.'

Her voice sounded cold and flat. She realised how she must appear to him. A hard, unfeeling career woman who had ruined the friendship between two young men, thrown a tantrum and hurled her car keys at her recently spurned and horribly drunk ex-boyfriend, then stood and watched him fall to his death without lifting a finger to help, while his best friend risked his neck to save him. No wonder two reporters in the back row were scribbling furiously.

And no wonder Debra Passmore was giving her that basilisk stare.

'. . . so why,' said the coroner, 'did you then think it necessary to leave the Jeep, and continue the search on foot? Since you now had all the papers, why did you not simply turn round and go home?'

'Because,' she began, 'we still had to find the *kántharos*.'

'The—?' The coroner frowned. 'I don't recall anything of that name being mentioned in the statements. Please explain.'

What does all this matter now? she wondered wearily. 'It was an artefact,' she said. 'A stone cup. Roman. Patrick found it a few days before the accident.'

'Roman, you say? Was it valuable?'

'Oh, yes. Because of its associations, it would have been priceless.'

The two reporters sat up straighter on their seats and exchanged knowing 'here it comes' glances.

'And why were you trying to find this artefact?'

'Well,' she said reluctantly, 'because Myles had taken it.'

An eruption in the Passmore camp. Julian looked aghast. Debra's face was an ivory mask.

'Dr Hunt,' said the coroner, 'I can find nothing in your statement about such an artefact, Roman or otherwise.'

'Really? I—I'm very sorry. Maybe I wasn't asked. I mean, the police only wanted to know about the accident.'

It was all so confusing, what with the local gendarmerie pestering her for details of the accident, and the French heritage authorities who were only interested in the *kántharos*. She had assumed that the two would have talked to one another.

The coroner wore a considering look. 'Very well,' he said at last. 'So now you say that the deceased had *taken* this item. How did you know this? Had he admitted it to you?'

'Not as such, no. But we knew he had.' She glanced at Patrick, but he had his head down, staring at the floor.

'This is outrageous!' cried Debra. 'The girl's lying! She's trying to use my son to cover up her own negligence—because he's dead and can't protect himself! My son was not a *thief*!'

'Mrs Passmore,' said the coroner firmly, 'I'm sure I don't need to remind you, of all people, of the penalties for disrupting court proceedings.'

'I'm not calling him a thief,' said Antonia stubbornly, 'and I'm not lying. I'm only saying that he took it, and that's why we didn't go back when we had the context sheets. We should have gone back, I know that now. But we didn't. Because he took it. Oh, of course he *meant* to give it back. He wasn't a thief. But he did take it. I'm certain of that.'

Reluctantly, the coroner instructed the usher to recall and reswear Patrick for further testimony.

'So, Mr McMullan,' the coroner said, 'just to clear up this small point for us. Did you gather from anything the deceased said or did that he had taken this—artefact?'

Patrick's eyes were fixed on a spot on the ground just in front of the coroner's desk. He frowned, then drew his thumb across his bottom lip. In a low voice, without looking up, he said, 'No, sir. I did not.'

The coroner watched the colour drain from Antonia's cheeks. She looked as if she had been struck across the face.

Patrick flicked her a glance and added, 'I mean, I don't know if he took it or not.'

'Just to be clear. You can't confirm that he took it?'

'No, sir. I can't.'

The coroner was astonished. The boy was quite clearly lying, and up till now he had been scrupulously truthful. Indeed, it had been painful to watch him struggling to leave nothing out, however unflattering it might be to himself. So why tell a falsehood now, on a point of only peripheral relevance? Perhaps, after all the damaging revelations he had been forced to make about his dead friend, he could not bring himself to brand him a thief as well.

Time to wrap this one up and go to lunch. He tidied his papers and prepared to deliver his finding. Accidental death.

Which would be no help whatsoever to all these tortured people. They would leave his court as he had seen hundreds of others before them: blaming themselves and others, in a desperate urge to make sense of the senseless. He bit back a yawn. It was all too familiar.

CHAPTER TEN
Upper Missenden,
Suffolk, five days later

ANTONIA WAS CHANGING HER CLOTHES for the fourth time when the crunch of wheels on gravel told her that Patrick's taxi had arrived.

She froze. Stared in panic at the mess of clothes on the bed. Told herself she was being ridiculous, it didn't *matter* what she wore. That was the least of her worries.

She grabbed the topmost jersey on the pile: a scratchy concrete-coloured crewneck which reminded her of school. It had shrunk in the wash, and only just reached the waistband of her jeans. She scrambled for her loafers beneath the bed. Tried to find a hair ribbon, failed, and scraped back her hair with an elastic band snatched from her desk.

Heart pounding, she ran out onto the landing, and the mirror at the top of the stairs stopped her short. A gaunt, unstable young woman stared back at her: cavernous dark eyes in a chalk-white face.

'Just to be clear,' said the coroner, 'you can't confirm that he took it?'

'No, sir,' said Patrick. 'I can't.'

She still couldn't believe it. She kept reliving the moment when he glanced at her across the courtroom, and the lie crackled between them.

The irony was, everyone believed him, and thought *she* was the liar. Why? Was it just a question of appearances? Did they prefer Patrick to her, simply because he was able to show his feelings, while she could not? Whatever the reason, the real question buzzed inside her head like an angry wasp. Why did he do it?

When she opened the door, he was standing with his back to her, looking out over the drive. He turned. 'Hi,' he said. He glanced briefly at her mouth, but made no move to kiss her. He didn't even touch her arm.

'Hi,' she replied.

He wore jeans, a skiing jacket, hiking boots, and an indigo cotton shirt that she hadn't seen before. She wondered if Debra Passmore had bought it for him.

'So you found us OK?' she asked.

He glanced up at the old house. 'Yes. It's some place you've got here.'

She was surprised. 'Is it? Um. Yes. I suppose it is.'

The blue shirt turned his eyes to cobalt. She wanted to put her arms around him and feel his hard warm chest against her, and smell the spicy scent of his skin.

But still he made no move towards her, and she could not bring herself to go to him. If he flinched she wouldn't be able to bear it.

A cold weight settled in the pit of her stomach.

She stepped back into the hall and he followed her, and she closed the door. 'The house is a bit dark on a day like this,' she said, sounding absurdly like a tour guide describing a stately home. 'So I thought we'd go into the garden. As long as the rain holds off.'

She grabbed a Barbour from the stand and led him across the echoing entrance hall, and through the drawing room and the French windows onto the terrace. He looked about him in that silent, watchful way he had when he felt unsure of himself, and she realised that asking him to

Holt Place had been a mistake. Feeling more and more like a tour guide, she led him through the rose garden and the heather garden, then down the steps and across the lawn to the river.

'Thanks for coming all this way,' she said awkwardly.

He glanced at her. 'I wanted to see you.'

She swallowed. 'I thought it'd be better to talk face to face. The phone's impossible. These days, Debra just cuts me off.' She threw him a glance to see how he had taken that, but his face remained blank.

'My mother's gone to town with my father, so we've got the place to ourselves.' She coloured. That sounded like a come-on. 'They're seeing a cardiologist,' she added. 'My father's not well.'

'Is that so.'

It stung her that he made no pretence of sympathy for her father. Suddenly she wanted to shake him. Here she was, making awkward one-sided conversation, hating herself for saying the wrong thing, when it was he who had created the distance between them. 'I suppose,' she said, 'you saw what they wrote about us in the newspaper?'

He turned to her. 'What?'

At last, a response. She felt a sick satisfaction. 'Tuesday's *Daily Mail*. Our cleaning lady brought it. It was just a couple of paragraphs. "Goings-on of the *jeunesse dorée* on the French Riviera". Wildly inaccurate, of course, but quite entertaining. As long as it's not about you.'

'Antonia, I—'

'They made me sound like a cross between Medea and Lady Macbeth. Ruthless treasure-seeker purloins priceless artefact for private sale . . .'

'*What?* They said you *stole* it?'

'Oh, not in so many words. But you know how good they are at innuendo.' She paused. 'They seem to think I took it, then tried to pin the blame on Myles, because he's dead.'

'Christ.'

'You came out of it well, though. A latter-day Gary Cooper, riding to the rescue of your dead friend by proclaiming the truth.'

He flinched.

'There's irony for you, don't you think?'

'Antonia, listen, I never expected—'

'Of course no one actually *believes* all that nonsense. But you can see them thinking about it. No smoke without fire. And when all's said and done, the wretched thing *is* missing, and I did royally screw up both digs. There's no getting away from that.'

'Myles did the screwing up. Not you.'

'I was in charge. That's what counts.' She snapped off a slip of willow and started stripping the sharp-scented bark. 'Oh, and I didn't get the Cambridge job, after all. They're giving it to someone else.'

'What? I thought you had it in the bag.'

'So did I, until all this came along.' She tossed the twig into the river and watched it glide off downstream. 'It doesn't matter. I've got something else lined up.' She didn't add that the 'something else' was gofering for a suspiciously unheard-of assistant professor in Tucson, Arizona, whose only claim to fame was a passion for neolithic shell middens too obscure to interest anyone else.

'I'm so sorry,' he said. 'I had no idea this would happen.'

She started on another twig. 'You can't imagine what it's like, reading lies about yourself in the paper. And the really horrible thing is the fact that I'm worrying about it at all. Worrying about myself, and my father, and our bloody careers, when Myles isn't even buried yet.'

'Antonia—'

'It makes me feel so mean and grasping. So *dirty*.' Suddenly she burst out, 'I just want to know why!'

'Why what?'

'Why did you lie?'

His face closed. 'I didn't lie.'

She was aghast. 'Patrick. Come on. This is me!'

'At no time did Myles say he'd taken it. At no time.' He sounded as if he'd been over it a hundred times in his head.

'But—'

'You were there, Antonia. You know that as well as I do.'

'How can you say that? Everything he *did*—the way he looked, what he *didn't* say, what he *didn't* do—it all shouted the fact that he'd taken it!'

He turned his head and stared at the river.

'Patrick. Please.' She struggled to keep her voice steady. 'It's your word against mine, and they prefer yours. After all, I had a reason to lie, didn't I? At least, that's how it looks. I mean, the bloody thing was my responsibility, and it disappeared, so obviously I needed to cook up a story, so obviously I blamed Myles. When you think about it, it actually does have a sick kind of logic. Can you imagine how it makes me feel?'

'I honestly had no idea it would turn out like this. But I had to think about Modge.'

'Modge? How does Modge come into this?'

He frowned. 'If I'd told the coroner that Myles took the cup, think what would have happened.'

Bewildered, she waited for him to go on.

'They'd be beating a path to her door. The police. The press: "So the kid helped the brother take it, did she? Well, hey, let's go question her! And if that only pushes her further into her traumatised little shell, gee, that's just tough, ma'am, we're only doing our job." And for what, Antonia? What good would it do? She doesn't know where it is.'

'That's not the point.'

'Then what is the point? What do you want me to do?'

'Tell the truth.'

'The truth. The truth. Antonia, she's only eight years old. Right now the truth is the last thing she needs!'

'What about me? What about what I need?'

He sighed. Then he turned and met her eyes. 'I'm sorry,' he said at last. 'He asked me to look after Modge, and I can't just walk away from that. Not even for you.'

Despite the warmth of the sun, she began to feel cold. She realised that she had lost him.

'This isn't about Modge, is it?' she said quietly. 'Or what you said at the hearing. It's about Myles. You've come to say goodbye. Because of Myles.'

His face was bleak.

'Patrick, it was an *accident*! It wasn't your fault.'

He would not look at her. 'If it hadn't been for us, he'd be alive.'

'But—'

'I'm sorry, Antonia . . . I'd better go,' he said. 'I'll miss my train.'

She stood looking up at him. His face was bereft and young, and she wanted to say something—anything—to make things better. But there was nothing left to say.

In silence they retraced their steps along the river walk and across the lawns, past the heather and the roses, and through the kitchen garden at the side of the house. At last they reached the carriage drive.

'So I guess you'll be coming on Tuesday,' he muttered. 'For the funeral.'

To stop her hands from shaking she jammed them into her pockets. 'No,' she said. 'I won't. Debra wrote and told me to stay away.'

He turned to her. 'What?'

'She doesn't want me there. She made it very clear.'

He shook his head. 'She didn't mean it. She's not herself, she doesn't know what she's—'

'Oh please!' she cried, unable to bear it any longer. 'Spare me the excuses for Debra Passmore! I don't *want* to come. All right? I don't want to slink around in dark glasses dodging the *Daily Mail*! And most of all, Patrick, I don't *want* to have to sit there and watch you turning into the surrogate son!'

He flinched as if she had struck him.

'I'm . . . sorry,' she said at last. 'I shouldn't have said that. I just—I can't come. That's all.'

He opened his mouth to speak, then closed it again. Then he glanced up at the big stone house behind her. 'I've got to go.'

She felt sick. 'I'll give you a lift to the station.'

'No. That's OK. I'll walk.'

'It's four miles.'

To soften his refusal, he forced a smile. 'Thanks. I'll be OK.'

In disbelief she watched him turn and walk away. She watched him until he disappeared from sight. He did not look back.

Six o'clock on a dank Tuesday afternoon in Belgravia.

Someone, thought Patrick, should write a book about What to Do After the Funeral. That's the crunch time. When you've done all the running around, and there's nothing left to do.

Of course, now would be the perfect time to call Antonia. Great excuse. Tell her about the service. The enormous echoing church. The cold hypocrisy of the speeches, including your own. The pathetically small clutch of people who bothered to turn up. And the dawning realisation that you had been his only friend.

'Didn't you know?' Nerissa had asked him coolly at the reception. She had arrived that morning, looking wonderful in something new and black which she'd obviously picked up in Paris.

'No,' he'd said, holding a glass of champagne which he didn't want, but felt obliged to drink, for Myles. 'I didn't know.'

So all things considered, now would be a good time to call Antonia. And when he was done telling her about the funeral, he could ask her why she hadn't changed her mind and come.

All through the service he had kept turning round to see if she was there. He kept hoping, right up until everyone started filing out into the rainswept churchyard. Until it hit him. She wasn't coming.

Not that he could blame her for that. Not after what she had told him about the newspapers, and Debra's note. Not after the way he had behaved in Suffolk.

The *surrogate son*. Ah, God, the way she had said it.

He leapt to his feet and prowled the room. Surely, *surely*, she didn't think he was sponging off the Passmores? Surely that wasn't what she meant? Although maybe it was.

No, it was good that he hadn't chickened out and called her. A clean break, that was the thing. It was only what he deserved.

He moved to the window and stood looking down at the street.

Now you're free, he told himself, squaring his shoulders. Free to pursue your goal. Whatever the hell that is. But you'd better think of something fast, boy—because you sure can't be a therapist now. Helping people doesn't seem to be your thing.

The way she had looked at him as he walked away down the drive.

Ah, *shit*, why can't you stop thinking about her? It's over. No going back now. Put the whole stupid mess behind you and move on.

A knock on the door. He jumped.

'Do you mind if I come in?' said Debra. 'I was sorting the last of Myles's things, and I found something you should have.'

As soon as he saw what lay in her palm, he recognised it, and his stomach turned over. It was the Roman coin that she had given Myles when he started at Oxford. A perfect silver *denarius*, with a profile of Constantine on one side, and a trireme slicing the waves on the other. Myles had kept it proudly on his desk, for he had clearly been flattered that his mother thought him capable of appreciating such a gift.

He cleared his throat. 'I'm sorry. I can't accept this.'

'Please. I insist.'

'No. I'm sorry. No.'

'I want you to have it.' She paused. 'For what you said at the hearing. You stood up for him. You told them all that he wasn't a thief.'

Patrick stared down at the coin lying on her palm. *Take this magic talisman*, quoth the wicked witch, *and you shall be my chosen one, and I will give you riches beyond price . . .*

If Antonia could see him now, what a chance for her to say, I told you so! The surrogate son being offered his reward for lying through his teeth. For giving her up.

His gaze moved to Debra's face.

The skin around her eyes was pinched, and her lipstick had faded into little plum-coloured creases. She was not the wicked witch, or the surrogate mother. She was merely a brittle, brilliant woman whose carapace of anger had not yet grown thick enough to hide her pain.

She looked exhausted. Maybe, like the rest of them, she had been playing the 'if' game. If only I'd spent more time with him. If only I'd got to know him better. If, if, if . . .

Well, all *right*, then, thought Patrick. From now on, this is the way it's going to be. You can't change it. You can't go back and start over. Myles is dead. You've got to live with that.

He took the coin from Debra's hand, and the metal felt hot and heavy in his palm.

'Thank you, Debra,' he said.

At six o'clock on the day of the funeral, Antonia finished clearing out her room at Upper Missenden.

She carried a large cardboard carton of papers down to the incinerator behind the rhubarb patch, along with a box of matches, a can of Bar-B-Blaze, and the other half of the bottle of Pinot Grigio with which she had drunk a toast to Myles when the service was due to begin.

She took another pull at the bottle. 'Now,' she told the rhubarb soberly. 'The final stage in the make-over of Antonia Hunt. Stage One: chuck out entire wardrobe and deposit with Oxfam. Stage Two: write smarmy Uriah Heep letter to Assistant *Per*fessor What's-His-Name, grovellingly accepting his crumby job. Stage Three: the Grand Finale. Assemble assorted Cassius crap, convey to garden, add assorted combustibles, stand well back—and *whoosh*. Adjust to desired temperature and leave till completely consumed.'

She upended the cardboard box over the incinerator, and books and papers tumbled out. First came the famous Cassius manuscript, including all copies and diskettes; then her entire collection of the *Poems*, in all known English translations: twelve, the product of years of trawling through secondhand bookshops.

Burn it. Burn the whole bloody lot.

A fire would do her good. It would be nice to be warm for a change. God, she was cold. Her teeth felt as if they hadn't stopped chattering since she had stood watching Patrick walk away.

At that moment, she had understood what it meant to be sick at heart. She had felt as if someone was inserting a pair of steel plates in her breastbone, and slowly drawing them apart, exposing her heart.

Tucking the Pinot Grigio awkwardly under her arm, she emptied the Bar-B-Blaze into the incinerator, struck a match with an unsteady flourish, and dropped it in. Orange flames whumped into life, and nearly took off her eyebrows.

'Way-hay!' she cried, staggering back. 'Welcome to the new Antonia Hunt!' She sank to her knees and settled down to watch.

She was glad she had resisted the temptation to call Patrick. What was there left to say? What was the point in thinking about him, when it only meant thinking about Myles, and her father, and Cassius, and the *kántharos*, and so on and on, until you were right back to Patrick again.

He had made his choice. He had chosen the Passmores over her. There was nothing left to say. And let's face it, Antonia, it was never more than a bad case of puppy love in the first place. OK, twenty-four is a bit late for puppy love, but you always were a slow starter, there's no getting away from that. So bite the bullet and tell the truth. You were desperate for love. Poor Myles made you feel worthless and frigid, till you just couldn't take any more. You'd have fallen for anyone. Then along comes this handsome Yank and, wonder of wonders, he actually pays you some attention—and *whammo*, you're hooked! Stands to reason, doesn't it? But that doesn't mean it was love!

'Anyway,' she muttered, waving the bottle at the fire, 'it's all over now. Patrick McMullan, I hereby consign you to the flames.'

All over now. From now on, the *work* is the thing. Your lodestone, your guiding star. As it was in the beginning, so shall it be for evermore. Now and for ever, unto the ending of the world. Amen.

She sat back on her heels. In her breast, the steel plates shifted painfully. Her shoulders sagged. Her head drooped. After five weeks, the dam finally burst. Great wrenching sobs tore through her.

PART TWO
CHAPTER ELEVEN
City of Perusia,
February 40 BC

TACITA AWOKE IN THE FREEZING darkness before dawn, huddled in her cloak, on the cold stone floor of the Etruscan tower. She felt frozen and stiff, and so weak with hunger that when she grasped the window ledge and hauled herself to her feet, the blood roared in her ears, and pin-pricks of light darted before her eyes.

All night long, the north wind had raged about the great beleaguered city. All night long, Tacita had begged the Goddess for an answer. Should she try to get a message down to Gaius in the enemy camp, imploring him to help her? Or should she cling to her pride, even if that meant condemning herself and her family to death?

But seeking his help would be such a risk! They had not spoken in thirteen years. And he was the enemy now.

Pulling her stool to the window, she sat and watched the darkness. Below her, the city of Perusia slept its uneasy sleep, bathed in the peculiar, hushed radiance that reigns after a heavy fall of snow. A thousand feet below, a sea of blue mist cloaked the valley of the Tiber. And beneath the mist, the enemy waited for Perusia to die.

She had not been surprised to learn of Gaius's presence in the besieging camp. It struck her as entirely natural that one day they should find themselves on different sides in a war: he fighting to crush the old

Republic and establish a new order; she—or rather, her husband—
siding with the republicans. What surprised her was that it had taken
thirteen years to reach this point.

Ah, *what* was she to do? Seek his help? Or starve?

If it were only for herself, she would not dream of asking him. But
there were others to think of. That was the dilemma.

Every time she thought about asking Gaius for help she flushed with
shame. Surely at best it would prove a humiliating waste of time—and
at worst, a catastrophe. Once he learned that she was in the city, what
might he not do? She knew from his poems that he had not forgiven her.
Surely this would only give him the perfect opportunity for revenge?

Besides, why *should* he help her—the enemy—when to do so might
put himself in danger? Surely Octavian would not tolerate treachery in
one of his own commanders? Not when the success of the entire campaign hinged upon crushing Perusia.

With its enormous walls of Etruscan stone, Perusia could never be
stormed, and Octavian knew it. He also knew that all he had to do was
wait. Another few weeks, and those still alive inside would be too weak
to spit at him. Already people were calling it the 'Perusine War', which
probably suited him very well. Waging a war sounded so much more
heroic than waiting patiently with an army of several thousand while a
few hundred men, women and children slowly starved to death.

Despair seized her. Even if she decided to send a message to Gaius,
how would it ever get through? Cleon, her slave, had assured her that he
had spied out a way. But how was that possible?

The sun was gathering strength. She must decide now. Cleon would
need the mist for cover on his journey down to the enemy camp.

If only she could decide. But still the Goddess withheld Her guid-
ance. Perhaps the Goddess was offended by the meanness of her sacrifice: a handful of dried trefoil leaves, two wizened black olives, and a
few drops of *posca*. But what did She expect after five months of siege?

In the early days of her marriage, it had astonished Tacita that she had
stumbled so easily upon the solace of worship, when she had spent her
girlhood earnestly debating the theory and finding it wanting. Then she
realised it was simply a matter of desperation. A woman needs something to fill a void.

Not that her husband was a bad man. Not really *bad*. Clever in a
narrow-minded way, unimaginative, infuriatingly pedantic, and menda-
cious when it suited him. In short, a lawyer. But at least he had left her
alone after the twins were born, and had the good sense to take a freed-
woman as a mistress. In recent years he had made much of his wife's

spotless reputation, which was indeed a rarity in their circle.

No, her husband was not a bad man. Merely a clever fool who had put them all in danger by backing the losing side. It was she who had seen disaster coming, and sent the twins to her brother's.

She realised that her mind was wandering. It was becoming harder and harder to focus. She wondered if Gaius knew she was in the city. Surely he must? Octavian's spies were said to be everywhere. And Gaius was now a general, after all. Perhaps he approved of her incarceration, a fitting punishment for what she had done.

She had only learned that he was part of the besieging forces four days before. Cleon had heard it from a scout who had just returned from the Flaminian Way. Thankfully, Cleon had had the good sense to tell his mistress privately, rather than blurting it out in front of her husband. Tacita had been astonished that the slave had known about her and Gaius at all, for she had never told anyone. It turned out that Albia had entrusted him with the secret a few weeks before she died.

In all their years apart, she had seen Gaius only once, seven years before, when he had given a reading in Rome. She had worn a heavy veil so that he couldn't possibly recognise her.

He had not aged, so much as hardened. The vertical lines at the sides of his mouth were now deeply etched, and sun and soldiering had burned him a dark bronze. It made his light grey eyes more startling still, and hard to look upon for long.

During the reading he did not smile once. Not even when the poem about the socialite and the gladiator convulsed the audience in fits.

But it was miraculous to see him again. Miraculous.

His voice was the one thing that hadn't changed. And he still had the ability to lose himself in the words, and let the feelings through.

Near the end, he gave them a new poem that hadn't yet been published. As he read it, it seemed to Tacita that the audience fell away, and he was speaking to her alone. They were back in the old days, in the moonlit tomb by the Porta Capena, lying together on his cloak.

I asked the gods to heal me,
but they only laughed. 'What, and spoil
all our fun? Come, Cassius, you
profit from this anguish as much as we!
Where would your poems be without Lycaris?
How would you earn your immortality?
Admit it, poet: she has been both
the summit and ruin of your life.'
And of course they're right.

But how strange that I
cannot write her out of my heart.
I've tried for years, but it can't be done.
I'm branded.
She's seared into that stubborn, beating muscle.
I cannot cut free from this love.

She had sat with the tears streaming down her cheeks. Was it possible that after all these years, after what she had done to him, he still loved her? And yet, even if that were true, there was no denying his pain. Year by year in the poems, she had watched him work his way through anger and bewilderment and contempt, until all those had burned away, leaving only the pain. He couldn't understand *why* she had left. She should have realised that for a man like him, not knowing would be slow torture.

She couldn't bear it.

So the next day, she wrote him a letter. She spent the whole morning on it, scribbling her way through several dozen drafts before finally arriving at a courteous, beautifully turned request for an interview.

The letter was returned the same afternoon, with the seal unbroken.

She was devastated. She did not even have the comfort of pretending that he hadn't known who the letter was from, for she had used her signet ring to seal it. He would have recognised her seal instantly.

She wore the ring still. That, and the crescent amulet were the only jewels she had left. A few more days, and she would not even have those.

'So you'd better hurry up and write the wretched letter, hadn't you,' she muttered under her breath, 'or you won't be able to seal it properly!'

Hmm. Apparently, she had made her decision without being aware of it. Maybe the Goddess had spoken, after all.

CHAPTER TWELVE
Chalk Farm,
early February, the Present

ANTONIA SAT OVER A MUG of coffee in her best friend's tiny bright orange kitchen. She had been staying at Kate's house for five days—ever since burst pipes had rendered her own small flat uninhabitable. Now she glanced around at all the paraphernalia of togetherness. A tottering pile of paperwork; nine-year-old Emma's latest 'project'—a Norman motte and bailey made of loo rolls; the fridge, covered in dinosaur magnets and shopping lists, and the little notes which Kate and her husband Phil left for each other when they were working late.

Her hands tightened on the mug.

'Aren't you going to open it?' said Kate, nodding at the envelope at Antonia's elbow.

'Mm,' Antonia said.

From the postmark, they both knew what it was: the letter from the solicitor, telling her how much she had inherited from her mother.

At best, she might get a half-share in the flat in Tooting, which was all that remained after the Lloyd's fiasco. It wasn't much, but a godsend as she had precisely £700 in the bank for her old age, and no job, once she finished ghosting poor old Professor Edgeware's monograph on pots.

But still she hesitated. She felt mean and grasping to be thinking of her mother in such a way. This was her *mother*. Her last link with the past. A cold white envelope on a plate.

'Go on,' said Kate, more gently.

Antonia picked up the envelope and tore it open. Rapidly she scanned the contents. Her hand went to her throat.

'What?' said Kate.

'She's—she's left the flat to my sister.'

'*What?*' said Kate. 'The whole thing? To Caroline?'

Antonia nodded.

'Jesus,' breathed Kate. 'Is that coals to Newcastle, or what?' Antonia's sister was married to a property developer who had made a fortune in the eighties, and managed to hang on to it through the recession.

'There's more,' said Antonia. She dropped the letter on the table and put her head in her hands. 'I get the mill at La Bastide.'

There was silence in the kitchen.

The *mill*? What had Mummy been thinking of? To leave the flat to Caroline, who didn't need it, and the great run-down white elephant to her. How exquisitely the wrong way round.

Come to that, how had her mother still owned the place at all, when Lloyd's had swallowed everything years ago? Perhaps it was in some kind of offshore trust which they couldn't get their hands on?

Suddenly she felt contrite. Her poor mother probably hadn't been thinking at all, just floating in a haze of anti-cancer drugs. She'd probably simply wanted to get the will out of the way quickly, and muddled up her daughters' names.

And of course, Antonia told herself, Mummy didn't *owe* you a thing. You were the one who ran away to Arizona and scarcely kept in touch.

Didn't even come home for Daddy's funeral. Mummy wasn't to know that you didn't have the fare. Not when your postcards told her breezily that you were 'doing fine'.

The mill. The mill. Oh, bloody hell.

You'll have to sell it, she told herself. Immediately, and from a distance. No point going over there. No point. No way.

Kate said, 'It could be worse. A place in the sun.'

'It's February,' muttered Antonia. 'There is no sun.'

'So? Nice and quiet. No tourists.'

'There aren't any tourists at La Bastide, even at the height of summer. Unless they're lost.'

'Well, just think,' said Kate, 'we can descend on you in the school holidays. I mean, if you haven't sold it by then.'

Antonia had a sudden vision of the hand-painted *à vendre* sign which had adorned the butcher's window for as long as anyone could remember. 'I'll be lucky to sell it by *next* summer,' she said. 'You're welcome to descend whenever you like, but you'll have to do without me.'

'So you won't be going out there yourself?'

Antonia shook her head.

Kate looked relieved, which irritated Antonia more than she would have imagined.

'So the next step,' Kate said briskly, 'is to find you a lawyer. Know any good *notaires*?'

'No,' Antonia replied. Then she added, 'But I know a man who does.' It was about time that her brother-in-law came in useful.

'Go on, then. No time like the present.'

Antonia threw her a glance. Dear, bossy, overprotective Kate. She had a pile of faxes at her elbow screaming for answers, but she gave no sign of impatience, and would be cross if Antonia tried to shoo her away. Antonia wished she had half her balance, generosity and kindness.

They had met during Antonia's first month in Arizona, when Kate was an embryo television researcher, and Antonia badly needed picking up off the floor. Kate had rolled up her sleeves and got on with it. Mrs Tiggywinkle to the rescue.

Sometimes Antonia wondered if her friend consciously fostered her resemblance to a hedgehog. She was naturally spherical, with beady dark eyes and razor-cut black hair that bore an uncanny resemblance to spines. Perhaps it was a look which helped in her work. Perhaps it distracted people, and made them easier to manage.

Half an hour later, Emma had been driven to school, Phil dispatched to his lab, the worst of the faxes neutralised, and Kate swept back into the kitchen just as Antonia slammed down the phone and decided to murder her sister. 'This,' Antonia said between her teeth, 'is too much.'

Kate pulled up a stool.

'I've got to go out there,' Antonia said.

'What, to the mill? Oh, I don't think that's a good idea. Oh no.'

'Oh yes.' She paced the kitchen. 'Apparently I *can't* sell the wretched place from here because it's full of "family stuff" which I've got to sort out first.'

'But—can't she go herself?'

'Oh, darling, of *course* not!' Antonia snarled in an exaggerated Knightsbridge accent. 'How could she possibly *spare* a couple of days, when she's got two au pairs and a live-in housekeeper to supervise? Not to mention her husband, whom she can't leave for five minutes without the poor sweetheart going into a decline! But then *you* wouldn't understand that, would you, Toni darling, because you're single, and childless, and unemployed, and—'

'Antonia,' Kate said firmly, 'stop it or you'll burst a blood vessel.'

Antonia came to a halt in the middle of the kitchen. 'Sorry. Sorry. It's amazing. She gets to me every time.' She kneaded her temples. 'But there's no getting away from it. I've got to go over there.'

'I really don't think that's a good idea.'

'Neither do I. But I'll manage. I've got enough for a cheap flight and a few days' car hire. Four days. Five at the most.'

Kate's hedgehog face became grave. 'I wasn't thinking about the money. It'll be the first time you've been back since the accident.'

Antonia stared at her. 'Good Lord, Kate, I'm not worried about *that*! I'll be fine! I *was* thinking about the money!'

'Really?'

'Of course! All that was twelve years ago. I'm a different person now.'

Kate studied her in silence.

'I'll be fine,' she repeated. 'Maybe I'll even get in a few days' work while I'm there.'

She picked up the phone and called Trailfinders, and five minutes later had a ticket to Toulouse for the first flight out on Friday morning.

'But that's the day after tomorrow!' said Kate.

Antonia gave her a tightlipped smile. 'The sooner I go, the sooner I'll be back.'

Antonia reached La Bastide at around two. Stopping the hire car on the bridge and stepping out into the teeth of an icy north wind, she was assailed by the scent of woodsmoke—a scent so familiar that it brought the tears to her eyes, and her childhood surging back.

Everything was as she remembered. There on the hill was the same little church where Mass was said once a month, when the travelling priest came through. And high above the village, there was the ruin of Castel Sarac, which she had once believed was inhabited by elves. And down on the main street she could just see the sign for the *dépôt de pain*, where she had once trotted, a self-important eight-year-old, to buy baguettes for her father.

An image of another eight-year-old superseded the picture. Modge in her tight yellow shorts, skipping in puppyish circles around Patrick as they walked down the rue de la Clouette. Firmly, Antonia closed the lid on that. She got back in the car and eased it gingerly down the track towards the mill.

The last time she had been on this road had been when her mother drove them to the airport the day after the accident. Then she had been shocked, in a daze. She heaved a shaky sigh, and realised that she had been holding her breath.

She parked in the courtyard and found the key under the stone where Monsieur Merou, the *gardien*, had said it would be, and let herself into the house. Another wave of relief. She inhaled only the mustiness of stale air, damp and cobwebs. The mill was free of ghosts.

It had the dead coldness of a house that has stood empty and unheated for years, and it was *dark*: she had forgotten how tiny the windows were—designed for retaining heat, rather than admitting light. At the height of summer, that had never mattered: on the contrary, they had welcomed the cool and the damp. Now it was like being in a grave.

A cold grave. Monsieur Merou had obligingly started the generator and lit the ancient boiler the day before, but the radiators were still struggling to get above blood heat. She turned up the thermostat, and down in the uncharted depths of the cellar, a boom like a nuclear explosion told her that the boiler was lurching into a higher gear.

The kitchen was appalling. Grey crocheted curtains rotting where they hung. Stained brown linoleum. Dismal yellow light from a lonely forty-watt bulb. She told herself firmly that she had been in shabbier digs in her career, so stop complaining. But she revised her stay from five days down to three. She might as well kiss goodbye to any thought of a rapid sale.

She went outside and brought in the groceries she had bought from a supermarket in Quillan from the car. Miraculously after its Rip Van Winkle sleep, the fridge-freezer was still shudderingly alive, although for how much longer she wouldn't like to bet. It didn't matter. If it packed in, she could survive on French toast.

She went upstairs, walked straight past her old room, and put her bag in the spare room. Her old room contained too many memories of Myles. Ghosts or no ghosts, there was no point in tempting fate.

She unpacked her laptop, and made her bed in thirty seconds by shaking out the sleeping-bag she had brought from her flat. Then, pulling on an extra fleece, she returned to the kitchen, found an old Star Trek mug under the sink, and half filled it with supermarket wine. OK, it was only two thirty in the afternoon, but that meant it was one thirty back in England, so this counted as a lunchtime drink.

Mug in hand, she made a swift review of what Caroline had described as 'good' pieces. They comprised two mahogany side-tables, an inlaid armoire in the dining room, and a reproduction Tudor desk in the sitting room. The whole lot would probably cost more to ship home than it was worth. *Damn* Caroline. Damn her to hell.

Another long swallow of wine put fresh heart into her, and on impulse she decided to take the bull by the horns and walk up to the Source.

'La Sourça, La Sourça,' she sang defiantly as she attacked the slope. But the track was steeper than she remembered, and she soon stopped singing and concentrated on the climb.

The noise of the river fell away, and her footsteps were loud in her ears. She realised with a shock that she had not trodden this path since the day of the accident. But to her enormous relief, it too harboured no ghosts. The past had happened to someone else. She felt as if she were on some tour, ticking off the sites from a long-ago fairy tale.

Here, at this turning in the path, a boy once had an accident and died. And here, on this narrow green bridge above this tributary gorge, another boy once stood shoulder to shoulder with a girl, and made plans with her in the moonlight. And here, by the mouth of this cave, the boy took the girl in his arms, and kissed her for the first time.

A glance inside confirmed the cave's non-spectral status. 'Nope,' she said aloud. 'No ghosts in here.'

Incredible to think that she had believed this was a magic place. Incredible to think that Cassius himself had worshipped here.

And incredible to think that all that had ever mattered to her.

The walk up to the Source had taken longer than she'd expected, and by the time she got back to the mill it was five o'clock, and already beginning to get dark.

As she let herself into the kitchen, the stillness engulfed her like a tomb. Her breath steamed. Clearly, the radiators had done all they could.

She decided then that she *must* make a start, or she'd never get the place sorted out in three days.

The kitchen cupboards yielded nothing that wouldn't benefit from a spell in a landfill site. The same went for the hall and the dining room. The understairs cupboard contained a prewar vacuum cleaner, a crate of empty wine bottles thick with dust, a decade's worth of mouse droppings, and two boxes, neatly labelled in her father's small, crabbed hand. One was a large tea chest entitled *Main dig finds, grids A035 to Z728*. The other was a cardboard carton of *Antonia's things*.

Antonia's things? But she hadn't left any things. Had she? She tried to remember, but the days after the accident were a blur.

Frowning, she carried the carton into the kitchen, placed it on the table, and stood staring down at it.

The mystery solved itself as soon as she summoned the courage to lift the lid. Inside, meticulously packed in cotton wadding, were the finds from the Source. Until now she had completely forgotten them. Fragments of earthenware; blackened fruit pips left by Gallic peasants 2,000 years before; a couple of Palaeolithic axe-heads; and, in a shoebox all to itself, the little Cybele lamp.

Her eyes misted over. Her father must have packed everything when he returned after the accident to make a last, fruitless search for the *kántharos*. He had packed it with care, indexing the finds on a neat, handwritten list taped inside the lid.

'Oh, Daddy,' she murmured. 'If only I'd known.'

She hated to think about him now. After the accident she had put him to the back of her mind, vaguely believing that one day she would make her peace with him. Then, in the spring of her fourth year in Arizona, his heart had given out while he was hurrying across the concourse at Waterloo to catch a train. Now, when she thought of him at all, it was with a grinding sense of guilt. A guilt which could never be assuaged.

At the bottom of the carton she found a red cardboard wallet labelled *Cassius Notes*.

Her mouth went dry.

But she had *burnt* all that. And yet here was a cardboard wallet full of God alone knew what, tidily labelled by her father. Frowning, she sat down on one of the chairs and drew out the contents of the wallet.

Her pulse steadied. It was harmless. A pocket Latin dictionary; a battered paperback edition of the *Poems*; a sheaf of jottings on the dig, still gritty with bronze-coloured dust; and an A4 page of handwritten 'Thoughts on the Cassius Riddle'—pompous title—penned by her twenty-four-year-old self.

The Cassius riddle. *In poculo veritas*.

God, she hadn't thought of that in years.

'*The truth is in the cup*', she declared, raising her mug of wine in a toast. 'Cassius, you never spoke a truer word!'

As if in reply, a postcard slid from the papers onto the floor, and suddenly Cassius was staring up at her.

She broke out in a chilly sweat. She hadn't looked upon that face for twelve years, and now here he was, gazing up at her—as if dispatched from the underworld by some malevolent little demon.

Heart thudding against her ribs, she met the thoughtful marble eyes across two millennia. It was a photograph of the bust which Plautius had commissioned at the time of his friend's death, and which was now in the National Museum in Rome. It was in the Republican style, which meant it was an accurate portrait, not an idealisation.

He had a broad, clear forehead, slightly furrowed by the drawing together of the vigorous arching brows; a wide mouth, firmly shut; a solid jaw. The modelling of the face was wonderful, the expression one of intense concentration, as if he were striving to work something out. One could tell that he had been a soldier. The hair and beard had been clipped pragmatically short, and the throat and shoulders were strong and muscular. As was customary with portraits of the time, he was dressed in the manner of a Greek orator: bare-chested, with a mantle flung across one shoulder. The other bore a small crescent-shaped mark just below the collarbone.

Down the centuries, that mark had been the focus of much scholarly debate. Was it some kind of ceremonial scar—perhaps a dedication to Luna or Cybele? Or was it a war wound, or a birthmark?

All of this flashed through Antonia's mind in the seconds while she crouched on her chair, staring down at the postcard on the floor.

Then she reached down and picked up the card by the edges. She turned it over. On the back, the Antonia of twelve years before had copied two lines of Cassius's verse.

I swear by the bones of my parents that I will be
yours, my life, until the ultimate darkness.

Suddenly she wanted to tear up the postcard into a thousand pieces. 'What the bloody *hell* possessed you to copy that out?' she cried. Her voice echoed bleakly in the empty kitchen. 'Surely you didn't actually *believe* all that rubbish? Christ, what a little idiot you were!'

She pushed the card, face down, into the middle of the sheaf of papers, and crammed the whole lot back in the wallet. Then she buried the wallet at the bottom of the box of '*Antonia's things*', shoved the box back in the understairs cupboard and slammed the door.

She woke up the next morning with a pounding headache and a strong desire to call Kate.

Not feeling feisty enough to do battle with the shower, she splashed rusty water on her face, and pulled on yesterday's jeans and fleece before setting out for the phone booth in the place de la Mairie.

Walking past what had once been the site of the main dig, she saw that the little house which had blighted her father's hopes had changed hands. The 'café' curtains and wrought-iron window screens had given way to sleek white shutters and venetian blinds, and the front door was flanked by a pair of elegant bay trees. The changes spoke of money and taste, as did the shiny black Land Rover Discovery parked outside.

Much too posh for locals, she mused. Must be weekenders from Bordeaux or Nice. Her hopes of a quick sale spluttered feebly back to life. Maybe the new owners had rich, stupid friends who were longing to sink their money in a ruin.

La Bastide's narrow streets were deserted and unwelcoming, all the windows securely shuttered. At her back a shutter creaked open, then rattled shut. The Catalan version of twitching net curtains.

Searching her pockets, she realised with a spurt of irritation that she'd forgotten to buy a phone-card at the airport. Oh well. It was one way of getting reacquainted with the locals.

The bar-tabac in the rue Bayadère was still run by the Vassals family, and had hardly changed. The same shelves of dusty plastic toys and curling magazines, the same fog of cigarette smoke and coffee.

At the back of the shop, two women studied magazines. At a table by the window, three old men in blue jackets nursed *coups de rouge* and crumpled roll-your-owns. As Antonia came in, they turned stiffly and gave her moist phlegmatic stares. She murmured '*Bonjour, messieurs*', and was rewarded with the briefest of nods.

Vassals *fils* was serving at the till: a soft-shouldered young man with whom she had once played. When he saw her, he registered astonished recognition, but said nothing. She bought her phone-card in disconcerted silence.

For the first time she wondered what the village would think of her. Would they welcome her as the daughter of once-regular visitors? Or had the accident changed all that? Who knew what garbled version had been handed down? And the Passmores had always been more popular than the Hunts. Far bigger spenders, even in the old days. She dismissed such thoughts as paranoia. She was probably irrelevant to La Bastide.

The women by the magazines were staring at her. Annoyed, she turned to repay the compliment, and found herself looking into the blankly astonished faces of Nerissa and Debra Passmore.

Of the three of them, Nerissa recovered first. '*Antonia?* Antonia Hunt?'

Antonia stood in the middle of the shop, blinking stupidly.

Nerissa came forward. With a brief smile she put her hand lightly on Antonia's arm, then leaned over and brushed her cheek with her own.

'Nerissa,' said Antonia dazedly. 'And—um, Debra. How are you? Both?'

'My God,' said Debra Passmore. 'My God. How extraordinary.'

Antonia could think of no answer to that. She felt obscurely as if she had been caught doing something wrong.

At the table by the window, the old men were sitting back in their chairs to enjoy the show. This, Antonia thought grimly, is probably as much fun as they've had all winter.

'Have you been here long?' Nerissa asked, sounding bizarrely as if they had just met at a cocktail party.

'Since yesterday. And—you?'

'The same. We arrived last night.' She opened her mouth to say something more, then seemed to think better of it, and flashed a wide smile instead. 'It's amazing to see you. You haven't changed a bit.'

Antonia could think of nothing to say to that, for it was manifestly untrue in her own case, and unnervingly accurate in Nerissa's.

'Are you staying at the mill?' Debra asked. She spoke with her jaws tightly clenched, as if they were wired together. Antonia remembered that from before.

'For a couple of days,' she replied hoarsely. 'I came out to sell the place.'

'Oh really?' Some of the tension left Debra's mouth. 'Well, I'm sure you'll find a buyer in no time. Such a wonderful location.'

Antonia mustered a wry smile. 'Nice of you to put it like that. I'm afraid it could most charitably be described as a picturesque ruin.'

Nerissa said, 'Someone told me you went to the States.'

Antonia told her she'd worked there for eleven years before returning to England, and they lapsed gratefully into comparing Arizona with the Home Counties.

Antonia hadn't seen Nerissa since the day of the accident, but she hadn't changed at all. Her skin was still smooth and honey-coloured, and she still wore that air of serene assurance which Antonia had once so envied. Although perhaps that had something to do with the spectacular diamond solitaire on her engagement finger. It was a little surprising that finding a husband had taken Nerissa so long, but from the size of the stone, he was probably worth the wait.

Debra, on the other hand, had changed enormously. The ivory skin was stretched like parchment over too-prominent bones, and the bridge of the nose looked painfully sharp.

Nerissa asked if Antonia ever bumped into Simon Toynbee, and she said yes, in fact they'd worked together in Tucson, until he'd given up archaeology for television journalism. Antonia then asked Nerissa what she had been doing with herself.

'Oh, this and that,' said Nerissa. 'Some television work. That sort of thing.'

Antonia gave a polite nod. 'I did a little myself a year ago. Just a schools programme. Nothing much.'

Nerissa gave her a considering look.

'Well,' Debra said briskly. 'We ought to be going. Lunch at Sainte Eulalie. And you know what dragons they are about arriving on time!' Again that tight smile, but warmer now. 'It's been extraordinary to see you again, Antonia. And I do wish you luck with the mill.'

Surprisingly, she sounded as if she meant it. Antonia was touched by her effort at friendliness.

To put some distance between them, she stayed behind to buy a newspaper. When she emerged onto the street, the clouds were closing in fast. The Castel Sarac had all but disappeared, and soft rain was beginning to make her hair frizz.

It occurred to her that perhaps her mother's legacy had not been as mistaken as she thought. Perhaps it hadn't sprung from a mix-up over names, but a desire to show her daughter that the past has no power to hurt the present.

If you can handle Debra Passmore you can handle anything, she told herself, and walked straight into Patrick.

The ground tilted beneath her as she slid back into the past.

'Hello, Antonia,' he said calmly.

He looked incredibly, agonisingly the same. The dark hair was still thick and shining, the blue eyes still full of light. They even had the same bruised-looking shadows beneath. And he appeared completely unruffled. As if bumping into her was an everyday occurrence.

She opened her mouth, but no sound came out. Cleared her throat, and started again. 'What—are you doing here?'

He blinked at the baldness of the question. 'I have a weekend place here. The first house in the village? Down by the bridge.'

Dear God. They were neighbours. At least, for the next couple of days. 'So—you're the new owner?' she floundered. 'I—was just admiring it. Looks like you've made some changes.'

'That wasn't me. That was Nerissa.'

Nerissa. She felt a falling sensation in the pit of her stomach. Nerissa. The engagement ring. Of course. Suddenly she knew why he wasn't surprised to see her. He had been forewarned. Nice of Nerissa not to do the same for her.

She pressed her lips together in a smile. 'Well. Congratulations. When's the wedding?'

'She didn't tell you?'

'We didn't talk for long.' He was giving her the detached appraisal of someone who has just come across an old book which they enjoyed in their youth but can't imagine reading now. It made her feel sharply aware of her lack of make-up, and her unwashed hair scraped back in an elastic band.

'You must have done well for yourself,' she said, thinking of the weekend place and the diamond solitaire.

A slight lift of the shoulders. 'I'm a barrister now.'

'A *barrister*?'

'Ain't that a blast? Me, with a tenancy at Hammond's Inn.'

Hammond's Inn. That was Debra's chambers.

He noticed that she noticed, and his features contracted slightly.

'So what kind of law do you do?' she asked.

'Personal injury litigation.'

She nodded, unable to think of a comment.

He certainly looked like a barrister. He had changed from a rangy and rather scruffy youth into a slender, confident man of unstudied elegance. Fishing jersey, cords, expensive skiing jacket, and an edge of striped City shirt which reminded her disturbingly of Myles.

'How about you?' he said. 'Are you still—'

'An archaeologist. Oh, yes.' She dug at the cobbles with her bootheel. 'Freelance, actually. Just about scraping by. In fact, that's why I came out. I'm selling the mill. I need the money.'

She decided that was all she would tell him about her career. Three years in shell middens, two terms as an assistant professor with no tenure at the end, then years of digging on other people's digs, writing up other people's research, and lecturing to bored tourists on cruise ships. Recently, Kate had pestered her to do another TV slot, but she'd turned it down. They wanted her to do a feature on Hadrian's Wall, but as far as she was concerned, Roman history was out of the question. Besides, she wanted the security of tenure. She wanted a roof over her head which didn't leak.

None of which she felt like sharing with this coolly elegant man standing before her. He wasn't interested. He hadn't even asked the obvious question: where did all the money go? Of course, there was no reason why he *should* ask, but she found his lack of curiosity dismaying.

Down by the bridge, a car hooted. He turned and raised a hand in acknowledgment. That would be Nerissa in the Discovery, chasing him up for 'lunch at Sainte Eulalie'.

'Gotta go,' he said.

'Of course.' She squared her shoulders, and borrowed Debra's line. 'Well, Patrick, it's been extraordinary to see you again.'

He gave her an unsmiling nod. 'Goodbye, Antonia.'

'**A** large glass of wine,' she muttered between her teeth as she headed back to the mill. 'A *large* glass. Then straight to work. The sooner you get out of this hellish place the better.'

She had given up all thought of calling Kate. She would not be able to hide her disarray from her friend, who would be on the first plane out. Kate loathed Patrick. True, she had never actually met him. But that had never stopped Kate.

It was all so surreal. She had always assumed that Debra would have sold Les Limoniers years ago. And yet here they were, playing Happy Families. And with Patrick. The surrogate son.

God, how he had changed. The romantic boy who had dreamed of becoming a therapist and helping people had morphed into a barrister. She wasn't sure what 'personal injury' was, but she was willing to bet it didn't have much to do with standing up for the underdog. At least, not at Hammond's Inn.

It was impossible to believe that such a man had ever memorised passages in the *Poems*, or been struck with superstitious awe on finding a stone cup in a cave. '*Spooked. So I guess the Goddess doesn't like men, huh?*'

She hadn't thought of that in years. Now it only made her sad.

Astonishing how people changed. No more *Poems*. No more *kántharos*. A barrister.

Letting herself into the mill, she was met with an exhalation of pure cold. It was like walking into a deep-freeze. She put her hand on the nearest radiator. It was glacial. Cursing aloud, she grabbed her torch, found the key to the cellars, and climbed down the near-vertical steps to find the boiler.

Fortunately, she did not have far to look. The boiler crouched at the bottom of the steps: a copper monolith the size of a small submarine. It had the menacing stillness of an unexploded missile.

For a single bleak moment she stood in the freezing darkness and thought of Patrick and Nerissa having lunch at Sainte Eulalie, then returning to their beautiful, well-lit, efficiently heated little house.

'*Stop* that!' she muttered angrily. 'Stop it right now. Fetch wood, get the range going, and you'll be *fine*. Hot coffee in no time.' Her voice sounded thin and shaky. An unconvincing display of bravado if ever there was one.

She was in the courtyard backing away from the woodpile with an armful of vine stumps, when she stepped on a rake which clanged against an old watering can, and startled a monster in the pot-shed. She screamed, the monster squealed, she fell backwards, and the vine stumps went flying. In the instant before the monster escaped, she saw flailing hoofs, a mane as coarse as rotten straw, and horrific wet mauve flesh where an eye should have been. Then the monster kicked up its heels and clattered out of the courtyard.

Bruised and shaken, she sat where she had fallen on the muddy cobbles, fighting back the tears.

First Cassius, then Patrick, and now *this*. A monster horse hiding in the pot-shed.

'Are you all right?' said a well-bred English voice a few feet away.

She opened her eyes, and saw Julian Passmore looking down at her with an expression of concern on his square, genial face.

'Not really,' she muttered. 'I've just been attacked by a rabid horse.'

Smiling, he reached down and pulled her gently to her feet. 'You know, I don't think horses get rabies. That was only Monsieur Panabière's little carthorse. His name's Hippolyte. You mustn't mind him. He had an altercation with a Percheron last year—hence the eye, or lack thereof—and since then he's been a tad grouchy.'

'Grouchy? He came straight for me!'

'Poor little fellow was probably startled.' He eyed the scattered vine stumps. 'I think I'd better bring those in before they get wet, don't you?'

She sniffed. She was embarrassingly glad to see him.

She had always liked Myles's stepfather. When she was a teenager he would sometimes come down to the mill and share a bottle of wine with her father, and ask her interesting questions about books, and listen to the answers. Even during the ghastliness of the accident he had been resolutely kind to her.

Accurately assuming that she had never made the Girl Guides, he suggested that he might just help her get the range going, if that was all right? She said it was. She also agreed when he suggested that he might just pop down into the cellar and take a look at that boiler—'My dear girl, I insist. We had one just like it for years. These contraptions and I are old adversaries!' And when he'd got it going again in a humiliatingly short time, he suggested that he might just help her boil some water for tea, and she agreed to that too.

'This is incredibly kind of you,' she said humbly, cradling her steaming mug and feeling about twelve.

He smiled. 'You looked as though you could do with a helping hand. Besides,' he paused, 'I dare say it was something of a shock, bumping into Debra like that.'

His directness surprised her. But that was one of the things she had liked about him as a child. 'A shock for her too,' she said. 'I should imagine.'

He sipped his tea and made no answer.

'You know,' she said carefully, 'I had no idea that any of you were still here. I'd have thought this was the last place you'd ever want to come.'

His face became grave. 'On the contrary. We spend all our spare time out here. Debra's converted one of the spare rooms into an office. Faxes, computers, scanners. I suppose for her this valley is . . .' he searched for words, 'it's where she feels closest to him.'

Antonia contemplated her tea. Despite the fact that they were sitting in her own kitchen, she felt like an intruder. 'I hadn't thought of that.'

He put down his mug and spread his hands on the table. 'I'm afraid I have a rather difficult favour to ask of you,' he said.

She waited, wondering what was coming next.

'Every year around this time, we give a drinks party for the village. Everyone's invited, and quite a few even turn up. It's tomorrow at seven.'

She looked around wildly for an excuse.

He raised a hand to ward off her protests. 'Before you say no, please hear me out. Reason the first: everyone else has been invited, so it would be jolly odd if you weren't too. Reason the second: there'll be hordes of people besides us, so you needn't fear an inquisition. The Passmores will be thoroughly diluted.' An apologetic smile of genuine warmth. 'And reason the third—which if I'm honest, is the only one that counts—I think it would help Modge enormously to see you.'

'Modge?' she echoed blankly.

'Imogen. Our daughter.'

'Yes, I—I remember her, of course. But I don't . . .' she trailed off.

His eyes crinkled in a smile which was painful to watch. 'She's had a bit of a rough time over the past few years. I don't know exactly why. Adolescence, I suppose. A phase. At least, that's what one hopes.' She could tell he didn't really believe it. 'Patrick's been marvellous. He's the only one she'll talk to. Of course, her mother and I are *completely* beyond the pale. Though I suppose that's natural enough at twenty. Isn't it?'

He looked at her doubtfully, as if seeking reassurance. She was touched that he should appeal to her, a woman in her thirties who had never had a child.

'I don't know what I could do,' she said helplessly.

'I just thought,' he went on, 'that as you're someone she's always admired—and liked, enormously—it might do her good to see you again.' He sighed. 'She always feels so terribly out of place at these events. Sometimes I think it might be better if we just let her stay upstairs with her videos and her computer, and whatnot. But I suppose Debra's right, and she's got to learn.'

Antonia had a sudden memory of her teenage self—lumpen, greasy-nosed, and on the edge of tears—standing on the landing listening to her parents debating her fate. 'But honestly, Evelyn, if the child doesn't *want* to attend this wretched tennis party, is it really necessary to compel her?' 'Yes, Charles, it really is. She's got to learn.'

History repeating itself. Poor Modge.

A drinks party at Les Limoniers with Debra and Nerissa and Patrick. Dear God, what would Kate say when she heard?

Julian Passmore spotted her hesitation and pounced. 'So you'll come?'

She raised her head and gave him a smile that she hoped didn't look too forced. 'Of course I will,' she said.

Modge snatched her overshirt from the clothes pile, and pulled it over her head. Then she wriggled into her leggings and squeezed her bare feet into the black stilettos.

There, she told her hateful reflection in the mirror. Now you're not just ugly, you're spectacularly ugly. She crammed on as many rings as each finger would take, but couldn't find her choke-chain anywhere. Oh well. Earstuds would do.

She heard Nerissa's voice downstairs in the hall, and her defiant mood evaporated. She sank to the floor with her back against the wall, and clutched her knees.

Nerissa would look amazing. She would be wearing that short sixties-style dress she'd picked up at Prada, which made her into a cross between Cindy Crawford and Claudia Schiffer. No wonder Patrick fancied her.

She moaned, and covered her face with her hands.

You're a joke, she told herself, rocking from side to side. You're *twenty years old*. You should be leaping about in Gap khakis and a stretchy top that doesn't reach your belly button. You should be backpacking with a boyfriend, or going to university, or driving fearlessly around in a new car, or having *kids*, for Christ's sake.

Instead, *look* at you. A pathetic, stay-at-home, failed-all-your-exams-*twice*, size sixteen freak. No wonder you're still a virgin. A twenty-year-old virgin who can't even drive.

And this drinks thing tonight! *God*. All those people staring at you. Smiling to your face, then shaking their heads behind your back.

Then she thought about seeing Antonia, and she felt hot and prickly, as if she was going to throw up.

Antonia had been with them on the hillside when it happened. Modge knew that because Daddy had told her, but she couldn't remember it herself. She couldn't remember much of what had happened that day. She remembered helping Myles take the cup thing, and lay the paper trail—but after that there was nothing, just a big blank until she was standing with Patrick, watching the Jeep sail out over the gorge. That single frozen moment. Those white papers fluttering against the grey sky.

Sometimes she wished she *could* remember. She knew Mummy resented it that she didn't. Mummy seemed to take her lack of memory as disloyalty to Myles. Myles the paragon. No one was allowed to forget anything about him.

She brought herself up short. What a cow you are to say a thing like that. And remember, if the thought of seeing Antonia again is getting to *you*, just think what it's doing to Mummy!

Will it always be like this? she wondered. Trapped in this horrible body, with no one to love you except Patrick, who's going to marry Nerissa. And always this grinding feeling that Mummy can't bear to have you around. That she'd rather you had died instead of Myles.

Won't someone help me?

But how could they? It was hopeless. It was no *use* going on a diet, because even if she lost stones and stones and became miraculously pretty, *and* got into university *and* learned to drive, Patrick would still marry Nerissa, and her mother would still resent her—for not being brilliant and successful and dead. For not being Myles.

'"**A**nd Daniel was cast into the lions' den,"' Antonia muttered as she waited on the Passmores' porch, '"but he felt no fear."'

Or something like that.

Easy for Daniel to say. He'd had a Supreme Being at his back.

Just remember, she told herself grimly. After tonight, you'll never have to see any of them again.

Then the doors were flung open and Julian was enveloping her in a bear hug—'You are a *darling* for coming'—and pressing a large glass of ruby Merlot into her hand. 'Let's pitch right in and see if we can find

Modge,' he murmured, shepherding her into a sea of noise and faces.

She had left it as late as she could, and the house was full. As they wove through the throng she recognised Vassals *fils* and the butcher's adopted daughter, and Monsieur Panabière, looking surprisingly small and frail, and Madame Merou from the *dépôt de pain*. She studied Antonia sourly, then muttered something to her husband from the corner of her mouth.

Antonia found such blatant rudeness unsettling. She wondered if her paranoia in the bar-tabac might have been justified. Certainly, none of the villagers made a move to welcome her.

Across the room, Debra nodded at her and smiled, stick-brittle in a plum-coloured silk shirt and black woollen slacks. Nerissa raised a hand from a doorway. To Antonia's relief, there was no sign of Patrick.

Julian read her mind with startling ease. Something had come up on one of Patrick's cases, he said. He'd be along later.

She made a mental note to be gone before 'later', and to take a circuitous route home. She didn't want a moonlit encounter in the rue de la Clouette.

Les Limoniers was startlingly different from what it had been twelve years before. It had been redecorated with expensive designer simplicity, and was now a haven of muted Etruscan reds, soft pooled lighting, and restful tropical plants, with tall pieces of abstract sculpture as focal points. The effect was serene and welcoming.

'Here she is,' murmured Julian, propelling Antonia into a corner behind an enormous date palm, where a plump black-clad figure was staring out of the French windows. Although the girl must have spotted their approach in the glass, her back remained resolutely turned.

Oh, great, thought Antonia. Someone else who isn't exactly overjoyed to see me. What the hell am I going to say to her?

Julian was no help. With the ease of a seasoned partygoer, he had already evaporated.

Then the girl turned, and Antonia forgot herself in pity.

The girl who stood blinking at her in the lamplight was unrecognisable as the quirky little goblin who used to dog her footsteps at the Source. She looked like a tart. Tight black leggings over bulging thighs, and an enormous black rayon overshirt smeared with make-up round the collar. Her face was white and puffy and pitted with blackheads, the eyes ringed with kohl beneath vestigial pencilled brows. The greasy shoulder-length hair had been dyed dead black, and was flecked with dandruff.

Antonia remembered how she had loathed false jocularity at that age. 'You've grown up,' she said flatly.

Modge blinked. 'Well, I've certainly grown.' She spoke with a nasal twang, in the estuary English often affected by well-heeled youth. 'You've changed too. What happened to all the bright colours and the parrot earrings?'

'I ditched them years ago. I'm not much into jewellery any more.' As she said it, she noticed the cheap silver-wire rings crammed onto the plump fingers. Modge caught her glance and raised a pencilled brow.

'Too expensive,' Antonia explained. 'I've got to watch the money.'

Another snort. 'Dad said that's why you're here. To sell the mill.'

'If I can. How about you?'

'How *about* me?'

'Why are you here? Do you like coming back to the valley all the time?'

Modge rolled her eyes. 'Did you, at my age?'

'At your age I didn't like anything.'

Modge threw her a suspicious glance to see if she was being humoured.

There was an awkward silence. Suddenly Antonia sympathised with all those thankless people who had tried to engage her in conversation at that age. She had no idea what Modge liked or disliked, and there seemed little point in trying to find out. Damn Julian. What did he think she was, a social worker?

'Did you know,' Modge said casually, 'that Myles is out here too?'

Antonia took that without blinking. At least, she hoped she did.

'It's true,' Modge said, watching her face. 'Mum brought his ashes back and chucked them in the gorge. So just think. When you're down there in that old mill, busily dusting away, you're actually brushing off little bits of my brother.'

Antonia took a long swallow of Merlot. 'I never dust,' she said.

That earned another snort, slightly less belligerent than the last.

So Julian had meant it literally when he said Debra felt closer to her son at La Bastide.

She felt hot and breathless, as if she was about to faint. A waiter passed with a tray, and she grabbed fresh drinks for herself and Modge, and downed most of hers in a single gulp. She was angry with herself for having succumbed to Julian's emotional blackmail. Who was he, that she should expose herself to this? And what gave any of these people the right to make her feel like an intruder? Here, in this valley which she had once loved? She had as much right to be here as they. It wasn't as though she'd committed some crime.

As if summoned by her dark thoughts, Patrick appeared in the corner of her vision. He was talking to Monsieur Panabière, stooping to bring his head level with the old man's. He wore cords, and a polo neck of some muted sea-green fleck, and he was blinking as if the light hurt his eyes.

Time to go.

'You know,' said Modge, 'Mum's absolutely desperate for you to leave.'

'Really?' she said, with exactly the same false jocularity which used to make her own hackles rise. 'I was just thinking I might.'

'Not this *drinks* bollocks,' said Modge with another roll of the eyes. 'The *village*. She wants you out of the village.'

Antonia gave the girl her full attention.

'She's been on the rampage all weekend,' Modge went on. 'Tearing up the house, and calling you "that creature". Is that because you slagged off my brother at the inquest?'

Antonia looked down at her empty glass. 'Probably.' She grabbed another drink, and knocked it back in one. She thought about Debra wishing her well in the bar-tabac, then 'tearing up the house' and calling her 'that creature'.

'People are such fucking hypocrites,' said Modge.

'Who's a hypocrite?' said Patrick with a smile, as he moved to join them.

'Not you,' said Modge quickly. 'I didn't mean you.' When she looked at him, she shed a decade. It was painful to watch.

So that's one thing which hasn't changed, thought Antonia. She's still got a massive crush on him.

She turned, and gave him what she hoped was an easy smile. 'Apparently you've got special status,' she remarked.

He did not return the smile. 'Hello, Antonia.'

He never used to drink, but now here he was knocking back the Merlot. Something else that had changed.

She watched him making Modge laugh with an account of a gibbering solicitor. He's done well for himself, she thought, no doubt about that. Weekends in France with the Head of Chambers. Engaged to a judge's daughter. She still couldn't believe it.

'I still can't believe you became a lawyer,' she said, when Modge had left them to go to the loo. 'You were going to be a psychologist, and help people. What happened?'

He gave her a lopsided smile. 'Sold my soul to the Devil.' He sounded as if he was only half joking.

'Do you enjoy it?' she asked.

He shrugged. 'Does anyone enjoy their work all the time?'

'God, you really *are* a lawyer,' she replied. 'That was a perfectly meaningless answer.'

He studied her. 'Why'd you come back, Antonia?'

That brought her up short. She had forgotten how direct he could be. 'I told you,' she said. 'To sell the mill.'

'Is that all?'

'Of course.'

He nodded.

She was annoyed to find herself becoming angry. 'I had no idea *you* were out here, if that's what you're thinking.'

'Just curious. That's all.'

She gave him an ill-tempered smile. She could feel her self-control slipping—hardly surprising, given the amount she had drunk.

Nerissa wandered over and gave her a brief smile, then glanced up at Patrick. 'Glad you could make it,' she told him. 'At last.'

'I've got to go back in a minute,' he replied.

'What, so soon?' She gave Antonia a long-suffering girlfriend grimace. 'He works *all* the time. It's such a bore.'

'I'll bet,' Antonia said, earning a sharp glance from Patrick.

Nerissa leaned against him with easy intimacy.

Antonia felt out of place. Time had stood still for her, with her shell middens and potsherds. But for Patrick and Nerissa it had moved on to grown-up things, like doing up houses and getting engaged.

God, she really had overdone the wine. It was time to leave before she smashed something.

Unfortunately, her hostess chose that moment to appear at Nerissa's elbow. 'I'm so *glad* you decided to come!' she said to Antonia, with a warmth that made what Modge had told her doubly surreal. 'From what Julian says, we're lucky to catch you at all! Apparently you're off tomorrow?'

Perhaps if Debra hadn't said that, everything would have turned out differently. Perhaps Antonia would have mouthed a few pleasantries, then made an excuse and slipped away. And perhaps next morning she would have flown meekly home, and never seen any of them again. But it was the way Debra said it. With such calm certainty. The Queen of the Valley, serenely assuming that the inconvenient intruder would go quietly, with the minimum of disruption to her realm.

'Not quite,' Antonia told Debra. 'I'm afraid I've changed my mind.'

Patrick's glass stopped on its way to his lips.

Debra did a wonderful job of looking faintly surprised. 'Oh? So you're not leaving tomorrow?'

Antonia shook her head. 'I thought that as I'm here, I might as well stay a couple of weeks. In fact,' she smiled, 'I thought I might see if I can find where Myles put the *kántharos*.'

CHAPTER THIRTEEN
A military camp outside Perusia, February 40 BC

SHE'S IN THE CITY, Cassius thought in disbelief.

Faenio had stoked the brazier before he left, and Cassius could feel its heat on his face, but it gave him no warmth. He was cold. So cold. He wondered how she kept warm up there. An idiotic thought. One did not keep warm in a siege in the middle of winter.

Her letter was propped up on the table against a bowl of dates. He hadn't summoned the courage to open it yet, and had turned it round so that he couldn't see the seal. That seal brought back too many memories. Images he had believed were long gone. Damn her to Hades. And damn her husband, Lucius Cornelius Verus for bringing her to this.

How easily memories revived. One glance at her seal, and all the pain, the anger, came flooding back. So much for getting over things.

He had thought he'd managed it at last. He remembered sitting up in bed one afternoon—he couldn't recall which afternoon, or whose bed—and putting his pounding head in his hands and telling himself to *stop*.

Stop playing the lovelorn fool. So you've lost her. So what? You're not the first man to lose a woman. The world won't come to an end because of this. Make a clean break.

And now here he was, right back where he started.

Once, several years before, he had received another letter from her. He had been in Rome, it was winter, the morning after a reading, and a note had arrived, bearing her seal. He knew it instantly. He guessed without opening it that she had been in the audience the day before. She had sat there and listened to him pouring out his heart. He found that peculiarly humiliating. Especially when he remembered the poem he had read. '*I cannot cut free from this love*'.

How she must have enjoyed that! *So he still loves me*, she must have thought smugly, as her litter carried her back to her husband's house.

It had been no effort at all to return the letter unopened. He had scarcely thought about it, and never regretted his decision.

And now here was another letter, just like the first.

He stood in the middle of the tent, looking down at the letter on the table. Then, quickly, he picked up the letter and broke the seal.

It did not take long to read. It was short, and obviously penned in haste. A bald request for him to help her and her family escape the siege.

Short and to the point. How like Tacita. No sentimental harking back to the past, no 'if you ever loved me, think of me now'. She was too proud for that. Her letter did not refer at all to what had once been between them, except for the two little words with which she addressed him at the start.

Mea vita, she began. My life.

Anger curdled inside him. How dare she address him like that after all these years? How *dare* she?

Mea vita. My life.

She used to call him that as they made love in the old tomb by the Porta Capena. She would whisper it against his chest. My life, my life.

He would feel her hands on his back. Her fingers digging into his shoulder blades. The moist warmth of her breath on his skin. *Mea vita, mea vita*. He tore up the letter and threw it on the fire.

CHAPTER FOURTEEN
La Bastide,
early February, the Present

WHAT A TRULY BRIGHT THING to say, thought Antonia, as she stood in the phone booth nursing a hangover.

'You told them *what*?' yelled Kate.

'I was angry. And drunk. And she acted like she owned the place.'

And you should have seen her face as I said it. Just that one tight little smile. It was terrifying.

'Besides,' she added as an afterthought, 'it's about time I had a crack at finding the wretched thing myself.'

Kate gave a disbelieving snort.

'What's that supposed to mean?'

'It means, how much of this is about a dead Roman, and how much is about Patrick McMullan?'

'Oh leave off, Kate! He's got nothing to do with it. He won't even be here most of the time.'

'I just think,' said Kate, relentlessly, 'you need to be clear about why you're staying. If it's to set the record straight about that cup thing and vindicate you and your dad—fine. If it's to give the Passmores and that man a bloody nose—*not* fine.'

Antonia told her not to be melodramatic, and rang off.

Two hours later, she sat at the kitchen table with her chin on her hand, contemplating the red cardboard wallet of Cassius notes. She had got as far as taking out the postcard of Cassius and sticking it on the fridge, but she still couldn't bring herself to make a start. A start on what, exactly? she asked herself. What on earth do you think you're doing?

To prevaricate, she cleaned the kitchen as best she could, moving cautiously to avoid stirring up the needles in her skull. Then she washed some bras and pants in the sink. She had almost run out of putting-off tasks, and was taking a bucket of water to the pot-shed in case the rabid horse returned, when Modge appeared in the gateway.

She wore the same black leggings as on the night before, with trainers and a heavy man's sweater—black, of course.

'Mum's pissed off with you,' she said.

'*I'm* pissed off with me,' Antonia replied.

Modge threw her a glance. 'Why?'

'I drank too much last night, and I feel terrible.'

Modge snorted. 'Patrick's pissed off with you too.'

If he was, he hadn't shown it last night. When she'd blurted out that she was going to find the *kántharos*, his face had been a careful study of non-response. God, he was self-controlled.

'He's all right, you know,' said Modge, picking up her train of thought. 'When I was at school he used to send me postcards from court. Sometimes he'd do a sketch. The judge snoozing, or something. He said I was the only one who could read his writing. He's got awful writing, he had to learn all over again when he burnt his hand.'

For Modge it was a speech of epic proportions. She caught Antonia's glance and flushed. Then she nodded at the bucket. 'What's that for?'

'Hippolyte. He and I got off to a bad start.'

'He's just jumpy because of his eye.'

'That's what your father said. It made me feel bad. Hence the bucket.'

'He'll never come back now that you're here. And if you want to know, horsenuts would be better than just water.'

'Horsenuts,' repeated Antonia, wondering what they were.

There was an awkward pause. For something to say, Antonia asked Modge if she liked horses.

She shrugged. 'They're all right. Least they don't order you about all the time.' After a pause she added, 'That's what I want to do, work with horses. There's this course at Newmarket. But I'll never get in.'

'Why not?'

'Mum wants me to go to Oxford—like the paragon.'

It took Antonia a moment to realise that she was talking about Myles. *Myles?* A paragon? Surely Debra hadn't done some kind of posthumous whitewash on him? Poor Myles. He would have hated that.

'What was he like?' asked Modge abruptly.

Antonia bit her lip, then said, 'Sometimes he could be a real prick.'

Modge lost her seen-it-all cool, and gasped.

'But the thing about Myles,' Antonia went on, 'was that he knew it. And when he was in the right mood, he could laugh at himself. He had a terrific sense of humour.'

Modge was pretending not to listen. She had gone back to attacking the gatepost with her thumbnail.

Antonia picked up the bucket. 'So where should I put this, then?'

Another shrug. 'I dunno. Just not so close to the mill.'

'Show me.'

Modge heaved a sigh. They left the mill. At the bridge, Antonia turned and started up the track towards the Source. Modge drew back. 'I'm not going up there,' she said accusingly, as if Antonia had tried to lure her into a trap.

'Why not?'

'I never go up there.'

Suddenly Antonia remembered an eight-year-old clutching her breast and keening like a puppy. 'Modge, I'm sorry. I should have thought.'

'Who *cares?*' Modge glowered. 'I don't even remember it.' At Antonia's surprised glance, she rolled her eyes. 'Well, why should I? I was only eight.' She paused. 'I s'pose you do. I s'pose you remember everything.'

'I—try not to think about it too much.'

'Then why'd you come back? That doesn't make sense.'

Antonia thought about that. Modge was right.

Modge pointed to a spot about twenty paces further up the track. 'Put it there. It's as good a place as any.'

Antonia crunched up the track and set the bucket in position. Modge had stayed where she was. Antonia called down to her, 'I'm going on for a bit. Why don't you just come part of the way?'

'I *told* you,' Modge shouted, 'I *never* go up there!'

Antonia sighed. She'd had about as much as she could take of maladjusted youth for one morning.

She was almost out of earshot when behind her Modge called out shrilly, 'Antonia! Did you mean what you said?'

'About what?'

The girl's face was white and pinched. 'You know what I mean! Last night. Did you mean what you said about looking for—that *thing*?'

Antonia stopped. 'Yes,' she said at last.

At least, she thought, I hadn't meant it then. But what about now?

This was no longer about defying the Passmores, or Patrick, or even vindicating her father and setting the record straight. It was too late for any of that. This was about regaining what she had lost.

A week later, the impossibility of finding the *kántharos* began to sink in.

The two favourites, the mill itself and the Source, had turned up nothing after extensive searches. Which meant that after a week Antonia had narrowed it down to anywhere on the cliff between the mill and the Source. Or in other words, half a mountainside.

She pushed back her chair, went to the range for her tenth mug of coffee that morning, and wondered what to do now.

The choice was a stark one. Either accept that the search was hopeless, pack her things and go home, or—what?

Do what you've been longing to do all along, said a voice in her head, and tackle the riddle. No more more putting off. Let's solve this thing.

In poculo veritas. The truth is in the cup.

She found her battered copy of Plautius's *Letters*, and turned up the old man's account of the riddle.

'*We sat outside his house in the warm spring sunshine,*' wrote Plautius, allowing himself a rare touch of lyricism,

> . . . *and Cassius turned the razor in his fingers so that the light caught it, and said, 'When I'm dead, I want you to make a libation to the Goddess. This must be for me and for Lycaris together, so that our spirits will be joined after death. This is important, my friend. I need to know it will be done.'*
>
> *At this I became greatly agitated. 'But how can I do this,' I said, 'for you've never told me her true name! You must tell me, or the Goddess won't hear the prayer.' Cassius gave a slight smile. 'That's a problem. But I'm afraid it's impossible.'*
>
> *Thoughtfully, he went to the edge of the terrace, pausing to admire his favourite wild pear tree, which was just coming into bloom. Then he turned back to me and said, 'What I can do is set you a riddle, which will only reveal her name when she too is gone.'*
>
> *He raised his new drinking-cup to his lips and drank, and said, 'The truth is in the cup.' Then he smiled again, and said, 'Not very clear, perhaps. But if the Goddess wills it, you or someone who comes after will solve it, I think.'*

Antonia sat back in her chair and gazed at the postcard on the fridge. Realistically, Cassius must have known that there was little chance of poor old Plautius—an octogenarian by then—outliving Lycaris and solving the riddle. So he must have been counting on the old man's pedantry as a lawyer to record his exact words, thereby giving posterity a chance.

'Because you *wanted* someone to solve it,' she told the postcard. 'Didn't you? "This is important . . . I need to know it will be done." You needed to know that someone, some time, would uncover the truth and make the libation, and bring your spirits together. Will it be me, Cassius? Will you help me to help you?'

Impassively the marble eyes gazed back at her, giving nothing away.

'*The truth is in the cup.* Or maybe it's *on* the cup. If only I had the bloody thing I might be able to work out which.'

She strained to picture it. She saw it in the pot-shed as it had looked on the afternoon before the accident. How it had glowed in the dusty sunlight. Like rubies, or fresh blood. How beautiful Pegasus had looked as he trotted joyfully towards Bellerophon. It seemed entirely natural that Pegasus should feature on a poet's drinking-cup, for to the Romans he had been a potent symbol of inspiration.

Unless, she thought suddenly, Pegasus himself is the key? Maybe the truth is, *literally*, in the reliefs?

She dredged up all she could remember about the Pegasus myth.

Bellerophon had tamed the magical horse, and over many adventures, a bond of love had grown between them. But then Bellerophon had become arrogant, and stormed Olympus, so Zeus had ordered Pegasus to topple his master from the skies and leave him to his fate. For the rest of his life, Bellerophon had wandered the earth alone—blind, crippled, yearning in vain for his miraculous companion.

So why, Antonia wondered suddenly, are Pegasus and Bellerophon reunited on the *kántharos*?

Nagged by a sense that she was missing something, she prowled round the kitchen table. Perhaps it was some tiny detail in the reliefs which had slipped her mind. If only she had the line drawing, she would have a chance. Damn Myles for taking that too.

Again she struggled to picture the *kántharos*.

But Patrick was in the pot-shed, and although he was keeping to his side of the table, she knew that he wanted to touch her, for his hand was moving slowly up and down the grain of the wood.

She walked round to him. Put her fingertips to his wristbone. Traced the thick corded vein up his forearm. He placed his warm hand on the nape of her neck and drew her to him, and bent his head to—

The phone rang. She jumped. Heart pounding, she stared at the new phone which had been installed only the day before.

No one had her number except for Kate, who was incommunicado on location for the next two days. So who could it be?

Debra? Nerissa? Patrick?

Warily she got to her feet and picked up the receiver. 'Hello?'

'Wow,' said Simon Toynbee, 'I must be out of touch. I thought it took months to get a phone in Europe. What'd you do, sleep with a phone engineer?'

She breathed out. 'Hello, Simon,' she said. 'I suppose Kate gave you my number?'

'Uh-huh.'

She had forgotten his love of Americanisms. That was one of the things which had irritated her towards the end.

'So what's with the phone?' he said. 'You staying out there a while?'

She told him that Kate had threatened to invade if she didn't get a phone with an answering machine, and Vassals *fils's* brother-in-law in France Télécom. She did not volunteer that Vassals *fils* had felt obliged to pull strings for her out of guilt at the coolness of the other villagers. He had even let her rent a cheap car from him.

She wrenched her mind back to the present. Simon was talking about his 'project', and as she had no idea what it was, she opted for silence rather than trying to make the right noises. Simon had a keen ear for when someone wasn't listening. As always when she spoke to him, she felt a twinge of guilt. They had got together in Arizona because they were the only English people in the Archaeology Department, he fancied her, and she had been alone for so long that she needed to know that that was still possible. Moreover he posed no threat to her, for there was never any danger of getting emotionally involved. Which was hardly fair on Simon—a fact he had been at pains to point out when they split up.

That had been three years ago. Since then, they had talked on the phone from time to time.

She realised he had asked her a question. Something about a conference in Bordeaux? 'Sorry,' she said, 'what was that?'

'I said, the conference is in a couple of weeks, so if you're still there, how about I drive over and we have dinner, for old times' sake?'

She winced. 'Oh, I don't know . . .'

'Can't even commit to dinner, huh? Same old Toni.'

She did not reply.

'So what are you doing out there, anyhow?' he said.

'Oh, this and that.'

'Kate says you're after that cup thing. But that can't be right. Right?'

'Why not?' she asked, nettled. 'That cup thing' was a deliberate trivialisation, designed to get under her skin.

'Jesus, Toni. I thought you got rid of that fixation years ago!'

'It's not a fixation, and can we please talk about this some other time? Why don't you give me your number and I'll ring you back? I've got work to do.'

That shut him up. He was sensitive about her work, and always on the lookout for signs that she was ahead of him—even though he had quit archaeology years ago for TV journalism.

He gave her his number and rang off.

Carefully, she replaced the receiver. Bloody Kate. She wondered if she had told Simon about Patrick. On the whole, she thought not. Simon had always loathed Patrick. If he had known that his old rival was back in the valley, he wouldn't have been able to resist a comment.

Bloody Kate. Bloody Simon. Bloody Patrick.

'Bloody hell,' she said.

Two weeks passed, and she decided not to call Simon back.

The Passmores came for weekends, but left her alone, and Patrick's house stayed empty and dark. He couldn't spare the time, said Modge, when Antonia bumped into her in the place de la Mairie. The girl looked worse than ever, pasty-faced and tired, and her eyes wouldn't meet Antonia's. Modge pointedly did not ask about her progress with the *kántharos*, and Antonia didn't volunteer an update. Besides, there wasn't much to tell.

For two weeks she had gone back to basics, and reread all she could find on Cassius. She'd haunted the museums and libraries of Narbonne, Toulouse and Béziers. She'd immersed herself in the *Poems*. And every day she wished that she hadn't incinerated her notes.

So far, all she had come up with was a clearer sense of the social gulf between Cassius and Lycaris.

Your suitors can give you ropes of deep-glowing
emeralds and yellow topazes.
I can't offer you anything.
Except perhaps immortality.

Yes, Lycaris had definitely been an uptown girl. But what *kind* of uptown girl? Was she already married when she met Cassius? Or a divorcée? Or an innocent? Or a high-class prostitute?

415

'Rule out the first,' Antonia said, circling the kitchen table, 'because reading between the lines, she and Cassius split up when she *got* married—to an older and richer man. And rule out the last, because if she'd been a whore, you'd have said, wouldn't you, Cassius? You were never one to mince your words.'

Which left either a divorcée or an innocent.

She sat down. Snatches of poetry drifted into her mind.

'Her breath yielded to mine, and mine to hers . . . We were sheeted in fire . . . My heart went up and sang in the sky . . . And now like Pegasus I ride the stars, I walk the spellbound moon . . .'

Wait. You're missing something. You've got the lines jumbled up. 'My heart went up' is from a different poem. But why does that matter? Her pulse quickened. She didn't know why it mattered. Just that it did.

Feverishly she flicked through the *Poems* till she found the line. It was where she least expected it. In the *last* poem. The one Cassius wrote on the day he killed himself. How could she have forgotten something as important as that?

Last night I dreamed of you again.
Beneath my eyelids you appeared for the final time,
and my heart went up and sang in the sky.
Now my death will not be bitter,
I won't drown in the river of darkness.
And when your own time comes, Beloved,
may the Goddess grant our plea,
and breathe your spirit into mine,
and mine into yours, for eternity.

That final poem, so famously different from the others he had written after the breakup with Lycaris. It was as if at last he had vanquished all the anger and the pain. As if he had finally come out into the light.

If Lycaris had caused the dark fatalism of the later poems, Antonia wondered, might she not also have caused the miraculous lightening at the end?

'You're onto something,' she breathed. She knew it. She had the same prickling sense of connection as she did in the moment before making a find, when a current seemed to ripple from the earth into her fingertips.

Think. *Think.*

Somehow, Lycaris had brought about a turnaround in Cassius—an alteration so profound that he had sat down and written that last, extraordinary poem. Then, *on the same day*, according to Plautius, he had opened his veins.

Therefore, there must be some connection between his death and Lycaris. Therefore, the key was to find out *why* he killed himself.

Once again, she turned up the old man's account in the *Letters*, but it gave no clue. Not even Plautius seemed to know why. All he could suggest was that Cassius had suffered a catastrophic fall from grace and taken the honourable way out, rather than face the dishonour of a sham trial.

So far, so Roman. But why? What had Cassius done to bring such disaster on his head? And why couldn't he have found another way out? By all accounts he had been a resourceful, highly experienced officer, who had for years successfully navigated the perilous political waters of the dying Republic. So why had he given up and taken his own life? It just didn't seem like Cassius. But clearly this was the question she must answer if she was going to solve the riddle.

To her surprise, she realised that in all her years with Cassius she had never focused on his death. Nor had anyone else. They had all been content to look no further than Plautius's account. And why shouldn't they? No one had ever regarded the poet's death as the key to Lycaris.

Three hours later, she had found nothing to add to the *Letters*, except for a vague recollection that somewhere in her old notes—the ones she'd incinerated in the rhubarb patch—there had been an obscure reference which might be of use. She shut her eyes and struggled to dredge it up. She remembered a note scribbled in green ink in her copy of Frontinus's *Stratagems*—a first-century compendium of underhand military tricks in which Cassius had been cited with approval. But infuriatingly, she couldn't remember what it said.

By six o'clock, just as the first chickens in the village were beginning to complain, she knew what she had to do. She had to retrace her steps: go back to Frontinus, review what she had once known about Roman military tactics, and hope that something in the trawl would jog her memory. The only place where she could do that was the British Library.

She had to go to London. There was just enough credit left on her card to cover a ticket, and she could stay with Kate to save the heating on her flat. Kate wouldn't mind. In fact, she had been pestering her to take a break. She would be delighted.

Kate wasn't. Kate was horrified.

'Exactly how much weight *have* you lost?' she demanded as soon as she opened the door. Then she reached out and unceremoniously pulled down Antonia's lower eyelid. 'I knew it,' she snapped. 'You're anaemic. Which is hardly surprising, when you're living on nothing but bread and wine.'

417

'No wine,' said Antonia, collapsing onto the sofa. 'It may surprise you to learn that I haven't had a drink in three weeks.'

Kate ignored her. 'And what sort of visit do you call this?' she demanded. '*Two days?*'

'A practical one,' Antonia replied. 'I need to get back, I've got work to do.'

Kate took the chair opposite. 'I still can't believe you're letting Patrick McMullan ruin your life all over again.'

'This is about *regaining* my life. Not ruining it. And Patrick has nothing to do with anything.'

Kate studied her with narrowed eyes. Then she gave a theatrical shrug. 'If that's the way you want it. To change the subject, a letter came for you yesterday, by courier. I think it's from that French lawyer of yours.' She held it out. 'I was going to call you last night,' she said, watching Antonia open it, 'but your line was busy.'

'Mm,' said Antonia, scanning the letter.

'Well? Is it good news?'

'Mm,' said Antonia again. 'You were right, it is from the lawyer . . . It seems he's found a buyer for the mill.'

'*What?* But that's *amazing!*'

Antonia nodded, and handed Kate the letter. She watched her friend reading it under her breath, ticking off the good points with little jerks of her spiky Mrs Tiggywinkle head.

A company owned by a consortium of Swiss tax exiles was looking for a site in the area to develop as a hotel. The money they were offering was more than generous, and they would let her stay on rent-free for a month or so to complete her research, provided she committed to the sale immediately—which the *notaire* clearly believed she should, for with his letter he had enclosed the papers for her to sign.

Kate was right, it was amazing news. Incredible, far better than she could have hoped.

'So why aren't you over the moon?' said Kate.

'Because I want to stay at the mill and solve the riddle.'

'But it says here that you can stay on for another month—'

'It could take longer than that.'

'So? You can continue when you're back in London.'

'No, I can't.'

'Why not?'

Antonia bit down on her irritation. Come on, she told herself, don't snap. This is the only friend you've got. 'I don't *know*,' she said at last. 'I just know that I need to be there. That's all.'

How like Antonia to make herself ill, thought Patrick as he watched Nerissa making her way towards him through the crowded restaurant.

'Acute anaemia,' the madwoman had ranted on the phone. 'The poor girl's making herself ill, and it's your fault for victimising her.'

He had tried to tell her that she was mistaken, but he hadn't got very far. 'Ms Walker—'

'Don't give me that *Miz* rubbish! It's *Mrs* Walker to you, thank you very much—'

'Fine,' said Patrick wearily. '*Mrs* Walker. I'm afraid I don't know what you're talking about. I haven't seen *Miss* Hunt for the past three weeks, and while I'm sorry that she's ill, it really has nothing to do with me.'

'Tell that to your horrible Marines,' snapped the madwoman, and rang off.

Heads turned as Nerissa came towards him, and two waiters hurried up to make sure she could manage her chair.

'How was the audition?' he asked.

She made a face and shook her head.

He wondered when she would get round to telling him what she actually did when she was supposed to be at these auditions. She had tried hard to begin with, but it had come as a shock to her that she hated talking in front of an audience. These days she pretended to go along to auditions, but her agent said she hadn't been to one in months. Maybe she had a lover. He found that he didn't really care. And instead of making him angry, that only made him feel sorry for her.

He ought to care. This wasn't fair on her. Or on Julian, or even on Debra, who, although she regarded her stepdaughter as an alien species, clearly approved of the engagement. Perhaps she saw it as some kind of dynastic coup.

'Excellent wife material,' he could imagine her saying. And she was right. Nerissa looked stunning, could run his social life superbly, and would no doubt give him beautiful children—while leaving him free to get on with his work. He was a bloody lucky man, as his colleagues were fond of telling him.

Suddenly he felt exhausted. He wondered if that was because of the headaches he had been suffering, or the Anderson case, or Antonia.

Probably Antonia. Why couldn't she just give up and go home? Because of her, Modge had retreated further and further into her frightened little shell, and Debra was punishing herself even more than usual and grinding the rest of chambers into the ground, and Julian was wandering around like one of his labradors, looking lost.

Nerissa was telling him something about her latest audition, but he couldn't hear, for the restaurant was the usual high-decibel nightmare.

He longed for the peace and solitude of the valley.

It was the beginning of March, so the first signs of spring would be softening the jagged edges of the Fenouillèdes. Great splashes of yellow broom would be lighting up the hillsides, the rosemary would be swarming with bees, and the almonds and mimosas would be bursting into bloom. He longed to be there.

And he needed to make sure that Antonia was all right.

Unfortunately for Antonia, Kate wasn't only correct about the anaemia. Two days turned out to be far too short to complete the research at the British Library. What had she been thinking of? Did anaemia muddle the brain? It took her two whole days just to track down the reference which she had scribbled on Frontinus—and then it turned out to be only a footnote in an obscure German text on Roman military strategy, which didn't advance things very far. All it contained was a cryptic reference to Cassius's legion having been involved in the Perusine War of 40 BC, the five-month siege which had marked a critical phase in the Civil War.

From Plautius, she knew that Cassius had been on active service throughout that time, so it was safe to assume that he had been with his legion during the terrible climax of the siege, when the city was torched, and 300 republicans massacred.

But that was as far as she could get—except for a throwaway reference to another, still more obscure German monograph on siege tactics, which might possibly contain something more promising.

That reference, the librarian told her, was in off-site storage, sorry, it would take a couple of days to retrieve. Antonia explained that she didn't *have* a couple of days, as she was returning to France today. The librarian thawed slightly. For a small fee, they could post her a photocopy in France, or maybe she'd like to try the pilot email scheme? Antonia chose the post. The mill's electricity was erratic. Her laptop had crashed twice already.

She went out into the Charing Cross Road and bought a bottle of iron pills and, on impulse, a small black nylon rucksack for Modge, along with two big fluorescent green plastic hair clips. She tucked one inside the rucksack with a note scribbled on the receipt: *I'll wear mine if you wear yours.* Maybe it would persuade Modge to wash her hair.

The moon was up by the time she reached La Bastide. It was a clear, cold night, and in the steely light the mill looked mysteriously beautiful.

It was freezing inside and she battled with the plumbing before pouring herself a mug of red wine. She then checked the answering machine, and was astonished to find that she had two messages.

'Antonia?' said Kate. 'It's Kate. Pick up the phone. You must be back by now. Pick up. Please.' She sounded agitated, and far less assured than usual. 'Listen, I did something OTT even for me, and I'm sorry—I rang your barrister and gave him a bit of an earful. About you. Yes, I know I shouldn't have done it, and I'm really sorry. Actually he was quite nice about it, considering. Anyway, sorry. Call me. Bye.'

Oh, *Kate*.

She glanced at her watch. Ten o'clock. Nine in London. There was only an outside chance that he'd still be in chambers.

She rang Enquiries and got the number of Hammond's Inn, and to her surprise, the clerk put her straight through to 'Mr McMullan'.

'Antonia?' he said quickly. 'What's wrong? Are you OK?'

'I'm fine. Listen, sorry to bother you at work, but I just called to apologise for Kate . . . My friend, Kate Walker? I understand she gave you a bit of a hard time.'

'Are you sure you're OK? She said you're ill.'

'I'm fine. Really. Kate always exaggerates.'

'She said the mill's barely habitable.'

'Ah well, that depends,' she said lightly.

He waited for her to elaborate, so she told him about the Boiler Monster in the basement, and the Russian roulette experience of taking a shower, as the water was either boiling or freezing, or not happening at all. That made him laugh.

There was another silence. She said, 'You're working late for a Friday, aren't you?'

'Not really. I've got a trial coming up.'

'Would that be the Anderson thing that's been in the papers?'

'Right.' He sounded wary. As well he might. The press was giving his clients a roasting.

'Well,' she said awkwardly. 'I'd better let you get on.'

'Listen, Antonia . . .'

'Yes?'

'. . . uh—if you need help out there, will you call me?'

For a moment she was too surprised to reply.

'Please.' He sounded as if he meant it.

'OK,' she said at last. 'Thanks.'

When she hung up, she found that she had been clutching the receiver so tightly that her knuckles were white.

Then she listened to the second message on the answering machine.

'This is Debra Passmore,' said a crisp, clenched voice. 'You'll shortly be receiving a letter from your lawyer, but I thought, for the avoidance of doubt, that I ought to ring and make sure that you understand the essentials.' She sounded friendly and calm, as she had done on that first day in the bar-tabac. 'It will no doubt come as a surprise to you to learn that I'm the majority shareholder in the company which is buying the mill. No doubt you'll be aware from the papers you've just signed that completion is set for the 24th of March. Which means that on that date I shall own the mill. And I'm sorry, Antonia, but I won't be able to let you stay. So do make sure that you're out by midnight on the 23rd at the latest. Without fail. Thank you so much. Goodbye.'

Antonia stood blinking down at the machine, struggling to take it in. Somehow, the friendliness of Debra's tone made it worse. *Do make sure that you're out by midnight on the 23rd at the latest. Without fail.*

The 23rd was ten days away. By then, the British Library's photocopy might not even have reached her. Or proved any use at all.

So that's that, she thought numbly.

She pressed the REWIND button and erased her messages. Then she sat on the kitchen floor and began to cry.

CHAPTER FIFTEEN
A military camp outside Perusia, February 21, 40 BC

IT COULD HARDLY BE a coincidence, thought Cassius, listening to the wind howl about his tent, that the day on which he had reached the cross-roads of his life should also be a public festival honouring the dead.

Was that just another instance of the gods' unfathomable sense of humour? Or was it a sign from the Goddess, pointing the way?

He didn't know. He didn't know. But that was the gods for you.

The only thing he knew for sure was that the road before him was forked. If he took one fork and ignored Tacita's letter, she would die in the siege. If he took the other fork he might succeed in rescuing her, but then he would be a traitor to his own side, and *he* must die.

Of course, when she wrote her letter, she couldn't have known about that. Doubtless she assumed that as a general, he was above punishment. She couldn't know how Octavian's attitude had hardened over the months, as he perceived that this starving city was the last obstacle between him and absolute power.

'Not one of them shall remain alive,' he had declared in his dull, methodical monotone. 'They are the enemies of Rome.'

Outside, the storm intensified. The walls of the tent bulged inwards with the weight of drifting snow.

Cassius looked about him, and all he could see were the symbols of death. A horse's head painted on a bowl of dates; a sky-blue cloth draping the table; even his signet ring, which he had slipped off and left on the pallet, as he always did before making an offering.

All the signs pointed to death. But whose death? Tacita's? Or his?

His throat tightened with sudden anger. What *right* had she to ask this of him? What right had she to ask anything at all?

'She has no right!' he cried aloud.

A corner of the tent-flap twitched, and Faenio put in his head. 'You called?' he said brightly, knowing very well that Cassius had not.

Cassius dismissed him with a jerk of the head.

'Seeing as I'm here,' said the Cretan slave, with a familiarity born of forty-five years of service, 'I thought I might bring you a bite to eat.'

'I don't want anything to eat.'

'Just a little porridge and cheese to keep out the chill.'

'I told you,' growled Cassius, 'I don't need food. Just tell my adjutant, Acilianus, to come to me at first light tomorrow.'

Surely by then, he thought, I'll have reached a decision? Surely the Goddess will have shown me the way?

'And you,' he said to the slave in Greek, so that the sentries wouldn't understand. 'Come to me two hours before first light. Alone. I may have work for you.'

'You—*may*?' The slave looked bemused.

'That's what I said,' he snapped. 'Now get out!'

But to his astonishment, the old Cretan hovered unhappily by the door.

'Didn't you hear me?' said Cassius between his teeth.

The slave swallowed. 'You'll be angry, but I must say something.'

'What?'

Again Faenio swallowed. Then it came out in a rush. 'Whatever you decide to do, I think you should see her one last time. Find out why she left. For your sake. I really think you must.'

Cassius went very still. 'What in Hades are you talking about?' he said, in the soft, quiet voice which his men had learned to fear.

'I—I recognised her seal,' stammered the slave. 'I guessed the rest. I'm sorry. I should be flogged. But this is too important, I had to speak out.'

'A flogging, you say? You're lucky I don't break your neck. Now get out. Before I change my mind.'

When the slave had gone, Cassius remained in the middle of the tent, clenching and unclenching his fists.

See her one last time. Find out why she left.

That is the one thing, he told himself, that I will never do. It would be too painful. And what would be the point?

But this was taking him nowhere.

He went to the table and poured wine into the libation bowl. With his foot he drew back a corner of one of the hides covering the ground, and carefully poured a ruby stream onto the cold rust-red earth.

Wine for the Great Mother. Drink deep, Goddess. It's the best I have. Then show me what I must do.

Next, he let a few drops fall upon the little mound of salt, wheat and green olives which at dawn that day—before he received Tacita's letter—he had placed by his pallet as an offering to his forebears.

Wine for the dead.

Finally, he pulled a chair close to the brazier, drew his bearskin cloak about him, and took a long swallow for himself.

Wine for the—how should I describe myself? The soon to be dead? Or the merely living? Which is it to be?

Ah, but she had been clever in that stark little note! She had not spelt out the consequences if he refused her extraordinary request. She didn't need to. They leapt from the page. *'Don't let us die like dogs in the street,'* she had written. *'I know you can find some way to help us to safety.'*

For if you don't, Gaius, continued the unwritten message beneath the words, *you must stand by and watch me butchered by your men. You might as well take your own sword and slit my throat yourself. Anything else would be cowardice.*

But what gall she had, to make this request of him! What did she imagine he owed her, that she could ask such a thing? He flung off the bearskin, put his elbows on the table, and pressed his brow to his clenched fists.

No, she wasn't cunning. There had been no guile in that hastily scribbled message. She was desperate. That was all. Doubtless she loved her children, and probably her husband as well. From what he had heard, it had been a happy marriage. Three healthy children, no rumours of divorce, and never a whiff of scandal to sully her name. These days in Rome that was something of a miracle.

So why, asked the small insistent voice inside his head, did she call you *mea vita* in that note? *Mea vita.* My life.

'To remind you, you fool,' he muttered, 'of what we once meant to one another. That's all it signifies. The poor girl's desperate. She only wants to live.'

Who could blame her for that? She must be—what? Twenty-nine? Only twenty-nine. She was still so young. Too young for all of this.

She had always been too young. That was the trouble. He should never have started with her. Small wonder that she hadn't had the strength to carry on, that she'd panicked and run back to her family. How could you expect anything more from a sixteen-year-old girl?

The wine began to steal through his veins, caressing his thoughts. He leaned back and gazed into the glowing heart of the brazier.

He picked up the flask, and poured wine into the *kántharos*.

What did it matter what—if anything—she still felt for him. What mattered was that he still loved her. He realised that now. And loving her, he must do everything in his power to save her. No matter what the cost.

Turning the *kántharos* in his hands, he studied the play of light on the smooth Corinthian bronze. Then he raised it to his lips and drank.

So the Goddess had answered him, after all.

Promptly at first light, Acilianus presented himself outside his general's tent, wondering what on earth this was all about.

The general looked tired, as if he hadn't slept at all, and as he walked to the table his limp was more noticeable than usual.

The general pulled up a chair and motioned Acilianus to do the same.

'Do you speak Greek?' the general asked abruptly.

Startled, Acilianus replied that he did.

'Good,' said the general in Greek. Then, without further preamble, he calmly proceeded to outline a plan to rescue four magistrates and their families from the siege. Acilianus's part would be to collect the little group from a meeting-point in the chestnut woods northwest of the city, and lead them five miles across country to a cluster of deserted farm buildings on the old road south of Lake Trasimeno. Thereafter, Acilianus's role would be at an end. The general was very clear about that.

Acilianus sat slack-jawed, with his hands between his knees. The analytical part of his brain couldn't help noting the excellence of the general's plan. It had all the boldness and cunning which made him so admire this man. But the *aim*! And yet, the general didn't look deranged. In fact, for all the lines of fatigue, his face was curiously serene.

Apparently, the same could not be said of his own. 'Marcus,' said the general with a curl of his lip, 'you look utterly bemused. Is there anything about your orders that you don't understand?'

Acilianus swallowed. 'Um—no, sir.'

'Good.'

'But—but, *sir*! What you're ordering me to do—what *you're* planning to do—it, it . . .'

'—contravenes what we're here for, yes, I know.' Calmly the grey eyes met his. 'The point is, will you carry out your orders?'

Acilianus squared his shoulders. 'I take my orders from you, sir. Nothing's changed about that. Of course I'll carry them out.'

'Good.' The general stood up. Clearly as far as he was concerned, the conversation was at an end.

Acilianus did not move.

The general shot him a glance. 'Was there something else?'

He bit his lip, uncertain how to begin. 'I—I feel it my duty, sir, to point out—not as a soldier to his commander, but as one man to another—that this has no chance of remaining a secret for long. I don't mean that *I'll* tell anyone, because I won't, your orders are very clear on that. But sooner or later it will come out. It's bound to.'

'I'm sure you're right,' agreed the general. 'We can only hope that it will be later rather than sooner.'

'But—don't you see, sir? This will have . . .' he searched for words, 'this will have consequences.'

'Of course,' said the general crisply, 'and I've provided for that.' He picked up a letter which had been propped against a bowl of dates, and handed it to Acilianus. The letter bore the general's personal seal. 'This,' said the general, 'absolves you of all responsibility in the affair.'

Acilianus was almost beside himself. 'No, no, *no*!' he cried. 'I wasn't thinking of me! I was thinking of you! The consequences for you!'

Again the grey eyes met his, but this time they were curiously distant. 'As regards myself,' the general said, 'I am aware of the consequences.'

Normally Acilianus wouldn't have dreamed of persisting. But this wasn't a normal conversation. 'But—sir,' he said unhappily, 'there'll be a trial. You'll be convicted. You'll be—'

'There will be no trial.' The general spoke with such certainty that Acilianus blinked. Then understanding dawned. His jaw went slack.

'It's only common sense,' said the general testily. 'If I lived, I'd be forced to reveal where they've gone, and then the whole bloody thing would be pointless, wouldn't it?'

'But they couldn't make you talk, sir. Not you.'

'Oh yes they could. At my age one has very few illusions left—least of all, I hope, about oneself.'

'But . . . what will happen?'

The general rubbed a hand over his face. Suddenly he looked exhausted. A man of forty-six who had lived a dangerous life, and was now confronting his own imminent death. 'I think the most I can hope for is to be allowed to return to my estate, and end things honourably there, by my own hand. I think he might grant me that. Yes,' he murmured to himself. 'It'll be good to get back to my valley. I've only a small place there, you know, it's hardly more than a farmhouse. But it has a fine view of the river. And there's a wild pear tree just below the terrace—' He broke off, his eyes distant, remembering. 'Ah, you should see the yellow broom at this time of year! The hills are aflame with it.'

There was a moment of silence between them.

Acilianus couldn't believe this was happening. Absurdly, he felt like bursting into tears.

The general tapped the tabletop with his fingertips. 'It won't be such a bad death, you know.' He sounded almost apologetic.

'I don't understand any of this!' Acilianus burst out. 'Can't you—can't you at least tell me *why*?'

The general studied him. 'Perhaps I can. Yes, I think I owe you that.'

He slipped off his signet ring and turned it in his fingers. It was of fine Alexandrian workmanship: a coiled serpent which Acilianus had often admired.

'A long time ago,' said the general, still studying the ring, 'someone very close to me did something which hurt me. I never understood why they did it. I still don't.' He frowned. 'And now I never will. That made it—somewhat hard to get over.'

Acilianus guessed that he must be talking about a woman, perhaps the 'Lycaris' of his poems. But as the general seemed reluctant to mention her directly—no doubt to protect her if she was still alive and still married—he decided to keep his supposition to himself.

'I spent the next thirteen years being angry,' the general went on. 'Trying to hate others, but really only succeeding in hating myself.' He shook his head. 'Perhaps that's the way of these things. I don't know. But yesterday, quite unexpectedly, I was given the chance to . . . to make things right, I suppose. Or at least, to make them as right as they can be after all this time.'

He glanced at Acilianus, and the light in his eyes was hard to bear. 'You see, Marcus, I've been presented with a choice. Either I cancel those orders I've given you, and when we break the siege and the prisoners are brought before me, I take my sword and kill them with my own hand. Or else your orders stand.' A corner of his mouth went up. 'So there we are. Not such a hard decision after all.'

CHAPTER SIXTEEN
La Bastide,
March 16, the Present

YOU SHOULD NOT BE HERE, thought Patrick, as he leaned over the bridge and watched the dark green water sliding by. This isn't fair on Nerissa. Or Antonia. Hell, it isn't even fair on Debra—although since you're here *because* of her, it's all getting pretty complicated.

He rubbed a hand over his face. The first twinges of a headache jabbed his temples.

Five o'clock on a Thursday afternoon, and already it was getting dark. He turned up his collar against the wind and started towards the mill. He had not been down this track in years, and had forgotten how much he hated the place. He could never think of the mill without reliving his headlong dash along the river to the phone after the accident. The panic as he realised he didn't know the number for the emergency services. The pain in his hands and face.

How did Antonia stand it?

The kitchen lights were on, but when he knocked on the door, nobody answered. Cautiously he went inside. There was no one about.

The kitchen was appalling, worse than anything he had imagined. Cobwebs festooned the empty shelves, and a pervasive smell of rot emanated from the curtains thumbtacked over the windows.

And it was freezing, actually *freezing*. His breath steamed, and when he put his hand on the ancient radiator, it was dead cold. 'Jesus, Antonia,' he murmured, 'can't you look after yourself better than this?'

Surely she could not be used to conditions such as these? And if she was, what on earth had her life been like?

Twelve years ago, the mill must already have been pretty rundown, but he had never noticed. It had been the height of summer, and they had lived outdoors. The mill had merely been a haven of coolness and shade for when the midday glare got too much.

He remembered how there always seemed to be food upon the great oak table in the kitchen, and in the evenings everyone would simply take what they wanted, and wander out to eat by the river. He remembered their long, wildly enthusiastic discussions, heated by bottles of rough *vin de pays*, and fuelled by great wedges of crusty village bread and wild boar pâté, and creamy local cheese, and apricots still warm from the sun. What had happened to all that? Where had it gone?

He wandered over to the fridge, which was feathered with yellow Post-it notes. In their midst, a postcard of Cassius frowned thoughtfully into the distance. The Post-its bore cryptic messages scrawled in Antonia's elegant spidery scrawl: *Perusia: C's earlier posting—signif? Milk, Dried apricots, Horse-nuts (what are they? where find?).*

The notice board in the pot-shed had looked like this: an eclectic mix of shopping lists and colour-charts and dig rotas, arranged around a reconstruction plan for the little Cybele lamp.

The Cybele lamp. He hadn't thought about that in years. Now he remembered sitting on a bench while Modge instructed him severely on the proper way of labelling finds. He remembered watching Antonia work. He remembered being unable to breathe. The slow strokes of her brush as she painted the edges of each shard with adhesive. The precision with which she fitted each piece into place. He hadn't wanted it to end.

He turned sharply away.

The kitchen table had lost a leg, and been unceremoniously upended against the wall. In place of the table, she had dragged in a heavy antique-looking desk, God alone knew how. Unlike the domestic chaos of the rest of the kitchen, the desk was an oasis of order. Two ancient crocheted blankets were neatly folded over the back of the chair, presumably to ensure that she didn't freeze to death. Tidy stacks of books and files were placed side by side according to subject matter. *The Perusine War: Causes and Consequences. Inventaire des mosaïques de la Gaule. Römische Staatsverwaltung. Anaemia: The Way Back.*

He picked up the anaemia book, and was leafing through a chapter when Antonia came in. She stood in the doorway, her face a mask of astonishment. She was bundled up in a padded jacket, with a dark blue scarf wound around her neck, and what looked like several sweaters underneath. Her face was thinner than when he had last seen her, and her eyelids were slightly reddened, as if she had been crying—although maybe that was the anaemia.

'I knocked,' he said, still with the book in his hands. 'I saw the lights and thought you must be somewhere around. So I waited.'

She closed the door and leaned against it.

He asked her how long the heating had been off.

'Um. Some time on Tuesday night. Something's wrong with the boiler.'

Two days? She had been without heat for two days?

She must have seen something in his face, for she added a little defensively, 'I had a hot-water bottle.'

He ignored that. 'You want me to take a look at the boiler?'

She shook her head. 'Thanks. I've got someone coming from Mazerans.'

He kept forgetting just how bad she was at asking for help. When Julian had sheepishly confessed to what he called Debra's 'little scheme' to buy the mill, Patrick had stayed near a phone all of Saturday, hoping Antonia would take him up on his offer and call for help. She had not, and he had cursed himself for a fool. He should have foreseen that. She had always been independent. And no matter how desperate she might become, she was unlikely to look to him.

'I thought you were in London for that trial,' she said.

'It's not for a few days. I came out this morning. Flying back tomorrow.'

She nodded, unwinding her scarf and emptying her pockets of a notebook, a pencil, and two baked potatoes. She caught him looking at them. 'I read about it once in *Cider with Rosie*. They keep your hands warm. Plus, you can eat them afterwards. Works well. D'you want coffee?'

'Sure.' He pulled up a chair.

'I can't remember, do you take it black? I don't think there's any milk.'

'Black's fine.'

There was an awkward silence while they waited for the kettle to boil and she spooned instant coffee into two plastic mugs that still had the prices on them. She passed his over, then pulled up a chair.

He said, 'Julian told me about Debra buying the mill.'

She cradled her mug in her hands. 'You know,' she said quietly, 'I'd never have guessed that she had such a sense of humour.'

'What do you mean?'

'Completion—if that's the right term—takes place at midnight on the 23rd of March.'

'I don't get it.'

'The twenty-*fourth* of March is the Roman Day of Blood. One of the chief festivals of the Mother Goddess. It was also the day on which Cassius killed himself.'

She threw him a glance, and he saw with a shock that her eyes glittered with tears. She gave him a watery smile. 'How bizarre all this must seem to you! Quite a change from doing battle for multinationals. But in a place like this it sort of—gets to you. Well. It gets to me.'

It would get to anyone, he was tempted to point out, if they locked themselves up in a ruin and forgot to eat. But she didn't look as though she could take that right now.

'The Day of Blood,' he repeated. 'I don't think Debra knows about things like that.'

'Oh, I'm sure she doesn't, it's just a coincidence. But still a bit odd, don't you think? Almost enough to make you believe in Fate.'

He could bear it no longer. 'Antonia, what are you doing out here?'

She blinked.

'The Perusine War?' he went on. 'How's that going to help you find the *kántharos*?'

'It isn't. Oh, I forgot. Since I last saw you, I've sort of—changed tack. I'm trying to solve the Cassius riddle.'

'The *Cassius* riddle?'

'Of course.' She said it as if no other existed.

'Wait, let me get this straight. You're trying to solve a two-thousand-year-old riddle that's baffled the best scholars for centuries—'

'Yes, but I don't think they appreciated—'

'—all by yourself, in this appalling old ruin, with no proper resources, and no heat. That's what you're trying to do?'

Two spots of colour appeared on her cheeks. She flashed him a grin. 'Well, someone's got to do it.'

He sat back in his chair. Suddenly he caught a glimpse of the girl he had fallen in love with twelve years before. The straight-backed Minoan priestess with the warm brown eyes and the bird-of-paradise clothes, and that curious mixture of fearlessness and vulnerability.

How could he ever have thought she had changed? She had not changed at all. She was the same girl.

For twelve years she had turned her back on what she had once cared about so passionately—and now here she was in this freezing subterranean hole, clawing her way back to the sunlight: confronting the wrong turnings in her life in a way he never had, and fighting to regain what she had lost. She took his breath away.

'I suppose I must seem pretty crazy to you,' she said.

Not crazy, he thought. Magnificent.

'Listen,' he said abruptly, 'I think I can help.'

It was the last thing she expected him to say.

'I mean it,' he said. He was leaning forward with his elbows on his knees, and his hands loosely clasped. His eyes were troubled, as if he feared she might turn him down.

'First,' he said, 'I need to see the paperwork on the sale.' He caught her puzzled glance. 'So I can figure out if there's some loophole to get you back the mill.'

When she did not move, he said gently, 'Antonia? May I see the papers?'

She swallowed. 'Yes, of course. They're upstairs. I'll get them.'

On the landing she caught sight of herself in the mirror. Her eyes were dark hollows, her cheeks gaunt. She looked like a witch. Hardly surprising if he thought her mad.

'Antonia,' he said when she got back to the kitchen. 'First I have to ask you something.' He met her eyes. 'You don't believe I knew anything about this, do you?'

She stared at him. 'You didn't, did you?'

'Of course not.' He took the papers from her hand. 'I just needed you to know that.'

He took off his jacket and pushed back his sleeves, and began to read. He sat very still and read slowly, with complete concentration. As she watched him, it hit her that he really was, in truth, a lawyer. Patrick McMullan, the scruffy, too-thin boy from Wyoming, with the dusty jeans and the black hair hanging in his eyes, was a barrister-at-law.

He was still reading, his eyelids moving back and forth. Watching him trying to help her made her want to cry.

He startled her by sitting back and meeting her eyes.

'I'm sorry,' he said, 'it's not good. Get your French lawyer to check it, but I can't find any holes. Everything's in place. It's a straightforward sale. No mortgage, no fancy *conditions suspensives*. And your guy did all the searches in advance, so there's nothing to stop it going through on time.' He paused. 'I guess you could renege on the deal, but you'd be in for a hefty penalty. I don't suppose you'd be able to afford—'

'I don't suppose I would.'

'Which means you're out of here in a week?'

She pressed her lips together and nodded.

'I guess the good thing, if there is a good thing, is that you'll come into quite a lot of money. You'll be able to stay pretty much wherever you like.'

'Except where I want to stay, which is right here.' She shook her head. 'No, the reality is, if I haven't made progress by then, I'll pack up and go home.'

'What?' He looked horrified. 'You can't do that! This is too important.'

She was surprised that he should understand that.

'Surely you could put up with someone in the village?'

She gave a hollow laugh. 'I've already asked about that. No room at the inn. I think the truth is, they're all a little afraid of the wicked witch of Les Limoniers. And who can blame them? She must be by far the biggest spender in the village.'

He closed the file with a snap. 'Well, one thing's for sure. You can't stay here another night.'

She opened her mouth to protest but he wouldn't let her.

'Face it, Antonia, this place is a ruin.'

'I'll be fine.'

'No. You won't. There's no heat, the plumbing's shot, and before you know it the electricity will be too.'

'I told you, I've got someone coming—'

'—from Mazerans, yeah, I know. Like, when, exactly? When he feels like making the trek out here?'

She did not reply.

'Listen. The answer's staring us in the face. Take my house.'

She sprang to her feet. 'That's a ridiculous idea.'

'It's perfect! I'll stay with Julian and Modge for tonight—I can say my fax has broken down or something—and you can move in right now.'

'What about Debra?' she said angrily. 'Imagine what she'll say! Not to mention Nerissa!'

'I'll handle that. Now listen. I'm not going back to London knowing you're down here in this subzero rabbit hole while there's a warm, dry house standing empty about five hundred yards from your front door.' He paused. 'Come on, Antonia. Get real. Say yes.'

Suddenly she felt exhausted. 'Is this how you handle witnesses?' she muttered. 'Hammer away until they cave in?'

He gave her his lopsided smile. 'It's not subtle, but it's effective.'

She stared at the floor. This was all wrong for about a dozen reasons. For one thing, he had underplayed the consequences of lending her his house. If Debra found out, she would probably excommunicate him on the spot, and as she was his Head of Chambers, the effect on his career would be significant. And as if that wasn't enough, what about Nerissa? What right had she to blunder into his life, irreparably damage his prospects, and cause trouble between him and the woman he wanted to marry? And what about the effect on herself? How could living in his house—the house he shared with Nerissa—do anything other than make things ten times worse?

She said yes.

First butterfly the fish,' said the recipe cryptically.

Modge glanced doubtfully at the turbot defrosting on the counter.

'Lightly steam, then set aside, and while fish is cooling, scald cream and make a roux flavoured with scallions . . .'

She bit her lip. She wanted lunch to be perfect, but she had a feeling that fish *quenelles* weren't going to happen.

Upstairs, the sitting-room door opened and she heard Patrick and her father coming downstairs.

She thought: here come the two people I love most in the whole world.

Patrick had arrived unexpectedly the previous afternoon, and to their great delight had been forced to stay at Les Limoniers, as his fax had gone on the blink. 'Stay the whole weekend,' her father had urged over breakfast. 'Come on, old chap. It's Friday. No point going back to the metropolis. You can work from here.' So Patrick had stayed.

It should always be like this, thought Modge.

And why *can't* it? We could stay here for ever, just the three of us. Patrick and Daddy could use Mummy's office for work, and fly to London for hearings, and you could look after them both. You wouldn't ever have to leave. And Mummy would be pleased too, because she could stay in London and work. Maybe she'll come for visits if she can spare the time, and you'll pick her up at the airport in your new car.

She pictured herself at the head of a candlelit table. This Modge is thin and pretty. Patrick is filling her glass with champagne and laughing at something she's said, and Mummy's murmuring, *Darling, these quenelles are delicious, you must give me the recipe*. And Nerissa's gone away somewhere, because she's finally realised that she can never compete with the special understanding which exists between Patrick and Modge.

Her father entered the kitchen, startling her out of her daydream. Smiling at her, he went to the fridge for the lunchtime bottle of wine. Patrick wandered over to the counter and studied the recipe book, his black hair flopping onto his forehead in the way she loved.

He glanced at the white slab on the plate, and shook his head. 'Looks like you've got a problem.'

She giggled. 'I was thinking of doing sandwiches instead. Is that OK?'

'Fine by me,' said her father, pouring three brimming glasses of wine. 'Patrick, what are you doing in the fridge?'

'Getting a Perrier. D'you want one?'

'I certainly don't! For heaven's sake, have a proper drink!'

'Thanks, but this afternoon I have to—'

'*Work!*' chorused Modge and her father.

Patrick smiled. 'Am I that predictable?'

'Hopeless,' said her father, passing him a glass.

Modge hoisted herself onto the counter and beamed.

The night before, knowing that Patrick was only two doors down the corridor, she had slept right through till morning for the first time since Antonia came, without having her recurring nightmare once.

Everything's going to be all right, she told herself. In a few days, Mummy will own the mill and Antonia will *have* to leave.

Thinking about Antonia set up a panicky fluttering in her stomach.

She liked Antonia, and wanting her gone made her feel bad. But it couldn't be helped. She had to go. It would be better for everyone. Already Patrick was happier than he'd been in years.

She took a big swallow of wine. Everything was going to be all right.

Patrick took a bottle of Perrier from the fridge and held it up with a questioning glance: *Do you want some of this?* She nodded, and passed him two tumblers from the shelf, feeling cool and sophisticated at being able to read his thoughts.

You see? We know each other so well that we don't need words.

Her heart swelled with such happiness that it hurt.

At ten o'clock on Friday morning Antonia drifted awake after a dreamless sleep of fifteen hours. She rolled onto her side and lay enjoying the warmth of the big, soft duvet and the play of slatted sunlight across the Mondrian prints on the wall. Then she padded into the bathroom and took the most wonderful bath of her life. She lay back and popped Nerissa's almond-scented bubbles beneath her fingers.

She knew it was Nerissa's, for Patrick and Nerissa had separate bathroom cabinets. Nerissa's held a comprehensive range of clinical frosted-glass bottles with Japanese labels. Patrick's was Spartan by comparison. He didn't even use aftershave. But he did go in for a lot of headache pills.

Wondering why he needed them, she sank beneath the surface. God, it was good to be warm again.

Wrapped in a fluffy blue towel the size of a bedspread, she padded downstairs to the kitchen. The marble tiles beneath her feet were smooth and level, and faintly warm. Everything *about* this house was smooth and level, and faintly warm. Recessed downlighters cast pools of silver onto gleaming granite work surfaces. She couldn't even hear the boiler. Maybe they had underfloor heating, like the Romans.

'Use everything,' Patrick had said when he showed her round the afternoon before. To give her the idea, he'd opened a couple of bottles of Crozes-Hermitage, then recorked them and left them on the kitchen table.

You are playing with fire, she had told herself as she watched him shoving sweaters in a holdall. Don't go down this road again. You'll only get hurt.

What would Kate say if she knew you were here?

But Kate didn't know. Nobody did. And in a strange way, that absolved her of responsibility. Or perhaps it was simply the hedonism of being warm and in beautiful surroundings. Clearly it didn't take much to lead her astray.

She got dressed, fixed herself brunch on a tray, and carried it out to the terrace. It was the first warm day of spring, and the sun was strong enough for her to sit at the big teak table in jeans and a sweatshirt.

On the hill behind the house, La Bastide was coming to life. She could hear chickens complaining in a yard, the velvety thrum of sparrows in the trees, and the creak of shutters flung wide. Below her on the slope, bees fumbled the cobalt flowers of rosemary. A mimosa's powdery yellow pompoms shivered in the breeze. An almond tree nodded pale pink blossom. Larches pushed new cones among the old: lime-green and succulent, like some new kind of vegetable.

Perhaps it was the half-glass of wine she had allowed herself, but when she began to eat, the food tasted miraculous. Coarse brown *pain de campagne* and Monsieur Vassals's *pâté de sanglier*. Then more bread, smothered in dark mountain honey so thick she had to cut it with a knife. Then another half-glass of fragrant Crozes-Hermitage, a wedge of creamy local *chèvre*, and a handful of juicy green olives. Lazily she lobbed the stones over the wall into a patch of level ground shaded by a clump of wild pear trees. It was the same patch of waste ground which her father had chosen for his ill-fated dig, and which had brought him up against the unpalatable truth that his longed-for Roman villa was buried beneath this very terrace. Twelve years on, Nature had taken back the site: dwarf oak, rosemary and juniper smothered it in aromatic profusion.

She was reminded of a poem by Cassius which she hadn't thought about in years.

My place in the hills is small and simple,
but it has a fine view over the river
to the golden broom beyond,
And a terrace where you can smell the rosemary in spring.

Idly, she wondered if she was standing on it.

She went back inside and wandered into Patrick's study, ostensibly to look for a pencil sharpener before starting work. It was lined with bookshelves, and intimidatingly orderly. The books were mostly law reports, although to her surprise the single row of fiction contained a hardback translation of the *Poems*.

The desk was a broad expanse of polished beech, with a flatscreen monitor, a laser printer, and very little else. An aluminium mesh in-tray, an answering machine, a ballpoint pen. No photograph of Nerissa. But you could make anything of that.

By the keyboard there was a silver coin which she recognised at once. Surely it had once belonged to Myles? She picked it up and turned it in her fingers. Yes, it was the same one. A present from his mother, of which he had been secretly proud. She read the inscription round the edge. *Fel. Temp. Reparatio.* The Roman version of: 'You *can* go home again.'

She wondered if Patrick believed that. She wondered if she did.

The phone rang. She froze. The answering machine clicked in, and Patrick told the caller to leave a message.

'It's me,' said Nerissa. 'Where are you?'

Antonia flinched.

'Your clerk said something about the fax being on the blink, but that can't be right, I thought you'd just got a new one. Anyway, I just wanted to remind you that we've got Suki Hemingway's lunch on Sunday, and *don't* tell me you've got to work because I've already said we can, and she won't take no for an answer. There'll be people there you should meet. Call me back.' She hung up.

Antonia breathed out.

Suddenly she felt ashamed. Nerissa's voice had been easy and famil-iar. They were getting *married*, for Christ's sake. And here she was, the lonely spinster, pathetically snooping through his things.

She replaced the sweater on the chair, fetched her coat and went quickly down to the mill to check her post.

Ten minutes later, breathless and shaking, she was ripping open the envelope from the British Library.

Kriegführung der Romer turned out to be an unremittingly turgid 1928 text on late republican siege tactics. But its authors claimed the distinc-tion of having trawled through more Roman papyri and military diplo-mas than virtually anyone else, and Antonia's A-level German—and a dictionary—allowed her swiftly to pinpoint what she had been hoping to find: a section on the Perusine War.

From a number of military diplomas and personal letters, the authors had established that in the spring of 40 BC someone had smuggled four magistrates and their wives and children out of the besieged city.

Her heart jerked. She knew as soon as she read it that the someone had been Cassius.

But what did that mean for Lycaris? For the riddle? Thoughtfully, she walked back up the track to Patrick's house. She paced the terrace. Then the pieces clicked into place.

Lycaris—whoever she was—had been trapped in the city, and Cassius had betrayed his own side to rescue her. Then, to avoid the inevitable trial—and perhaps to protect her as well—he had killed himself.

It all made sense. So the question now became: who were the women among the escapees, and which one was Lycaris?

The text listed the four magistrates by name, so it *might* be possible to trace their family histories and from that, to produce a short list of the women in the little group who might have been Lycaris. That would mean a trip to Toulouse for a couple of days. She would have to stay with Professor Meriot, her father's old friend.

An unwelcome thought brought her up short. Even if all went well and she came up with a short list, how would she ever discover which of them was Lycaris? She sank into a chair.

It would be appalling to get so close, only to fail at the final hurdle.

Then something dragged at her memory. Something that might help. She closed her eyes, willing it to return, but it had already slipped away.

The phone rang. She braced herself for Nerissa's voice on the answering machine. But it wasn't Nerissa. It was Patrick.

'Antonia it's me, pick up.'

She snatched up the cordless. 'Hello.'

'Hi.' A pause. 'How're you doing?'

'Fine. Actually, very fine.'

'You sound—excited.'

'I'm onto something. I really think I am.'

'That's terrific.' She could hear the smile in his voice.

'Um, before I forget,' she began, wishing she didn't have to spoil things, 'Nerissa rang. I didn't pick it up. She left a message—'

'I got it, she called here a while ago.'

There was an awkward silence. Antonia wondered why he had called.

'Antonia . . .' he began.

'Yes?'

'I—listen. I'm meeting old Panabière in the bar-tabac tonight. Every Friday he visits his wife in the cemetery, and he's always a bit low afterwards, so when I'm around we have a drink. I wondered—do you want to come?'

'Me?' she said stupidly.

'Yeah.'

'Um. Would he want me along? I don't think he likes me.'

'Sure he does. But maybe it wasn't such a good idea—'

'No, no. I'd like to.'

'Good. I'll come by around seven and pick you up. I think I forgot to show you how to jack up the heating.'

He had not forgotten, but she didn't feel like pointing that out.

Modge backed away from the doorway and stood in the corridor holding her breath. She heard Patrick ring off and return to the desk. She heard the creak of a chair as he sat down. But there was no scratch of his pen, no click of a keyboard. He must be staring into space. Thinking about Antonia.

Suddenly she understood. He was in love with Antonia. He always had been. They had fallen in love twelve years ago, and Myles had found out.

The thought of Patrick being in love with Antonia hurt terribly, far more than Nerissa.

She remembered her pathetic little daydream, and had to jam her fist in her mouth to keep from crying out. How could she ever have imagined that she had a chance?

Silently she made her way to the kitchen, took three tubs of Ben & Jerry's from the freezer, and went upstairs to her room. She curled up on her mattress and opened the first tub, mechanically spooning in Cherry Garcia without tasting it. She felt as if she were standing on a lava crust which was slowly cracking open. She and her mother were on one side, Patrick and Antonia on the other.

Her mother would never forgive him. It would be the end. She, Modge, would be left on the wrong side of the fault line with a mother who resented her, and she would never see Patrick again. The pain was so bad that she caught her breath. Grimly she worked her way through the second and third tubs.

It was the first warm night of spring, and as if to celebrate, half the village had crammed into the bar-tabac. The air was thick with the smell of freshly ground coffee and roll-your-owns and the rich, wet-leaf odour of muddy boots. Every table was packed.

Patrick, taking a call from chambers on his mobile, could hardly hear his clerk above the din. Something about the Anderson trial being brought forward, and an impossible deadline for skeleton arguments.

Only half listening to his clerk, he asked himself why he had invited Antonia along, when it could not help either of them to see each other again. Too much water had flowed under the bridge. It was way too late to change anything now. And it wouldn't be fair on her to try.

Across the table, she had just asked Monsieur Panabière why his cart-horse was called Hippolyte. Surprisingly the old man was telling her, his turquoise cardigan spectacularly mis-buttoned.

She was watching his lips, for the old man's Catalan accent became impenetrable as he worked his way deeper into a bottle, and her face was flushed, her lower lip caught between her teeth. Patrick thought she looked wonderful.

He desperately hoped that her research would turn up what she wanted, but it sounded like such a long shot that he couldn't imagine how. She had told him about it as they waited for Monsieur Panabière. He couldn't follow all of it, but he gathered she had unearthed some reference which proved that in 40 BC, the same year as Cassius's death, someone had smuggled a clutch of republicans out of a besieged city. 'And I'll stake my career,' she said, pushing back her springy black hair in a gesture he remembered, 'that the man behind it was Cassius.'

He cleared his throat. 'How do you know it was him?'

She spread her hands, as if the answer was written on the air. 'It makes sense for about a dozen reasons. He was there, in command of one of the units camped round the city. And it was exactly the kind of plan he'd go for. Frontinus calls it "bold and cunning": turning one of the chief strengths of the besieging army—its network of spies—against itself. And he knew the city like the back of his hand, he'd been stationed there before the Civil War, so he could have planned it in his sleep. And if she *was* inside the city, he'd have moved heaven and earth to save her. He wouldn't have let her die. Not Cassius. And last of all, it's the only thing which accounts for this amazingly upbeat final poem.'

'So you think Lycaris was definitely among them?'

'She had to be. The problem is, how do I find out *which* one she was.'

He turned his glass in his hands. 'If you had the cup, you'd know, wouldn't you? Something about it would tell you.'

She threw him a glance. 'It was nobody's fault, Patrick. It just happened.'

'Yeah.'

Vassals *fils* brought the wine: a heady, blackcurrant-layered Merlot. After he had gone, Antonia said, 'It's just a shame that poor old Myles took the wretched line drawing too.'

Patrick nearly dropped his glass. 'The—line drawing?'

'The one I made of the *kántharos*. I don't suppose you remember.'

'But—why—why would that help?'

She shrugged. 'Maybe it wouldn't. But it might. It would at least be some record of those reliefs.'

He felt dizzy. He should have seen this coming. He thought about what she would say if he told her he had the line drawing safely locked away in his desk. *You mean to tell me that you've had it all along?*

That was when Monsieur Panabière had arrived.

His mobile rang again and this time it was Julian, calling from a golfing crony's near Antibes. He sounded well into his umpteenth brandy, and had decided to stay the night, rather than risk the long drive home. Fine, said Patrick dazedly. No problem.

Patrick finished his drink. Myles would have loved an evening like this. Cigarettes, alcohol, and a comfortable crowd of villagers. Surprisingly, he had always got on well with them, particularly Monsieur Panabière. Perhaps he had felt that with the old man he didn't have to pretend.

Poor Myles. Poor, vain, selfish, insecure, lonely little bastard. Suddenly, Patrick wished savagely that his friend was still alive. *Achilles, my friend,* he would say to Myles, *I've got myself into a hole. Can't seem to find a way out that won't hurt someone. Any ideas?*

He gave himself a shake and called for the bill. Too much wine.

Antonia helped Monsieur Panabière into his jacket, and the old man went through his customary search for his keys. He was seventy-six and increasingly frail, with a spine so bent that he could only just see over the steering wheel of his *camionnette.* Whenever they met for a drink, Patrick argued about being allowed to drive him back to Le Figarol. He always lost.

Five minutes later they had waved off Monsieur Panabière and Patrick told Antonia he would walk her home. What the hell. He had made so many mistakes, one more couldn't make much difference.

When they reached the house they stood awkwardly by the gate. Patrick felt reluctant to leave, but inviting himself in for a nightcap was out of the question, as she would probably feel obliged to say yes. He noticed that she did not suggest it herself.

So instead, they sat on the low stone wall in front of the house and watched the little bats wheeling like scraps of black velvet across the stars. He smelt pine resin, and the drifting sweetness of almond blossom. For the first time in months, his temples were free of pain.

He put his hand on the cold smooth stone between them, and wished things could always be this simple.

What would have happened, he thought, if it hadn't all gone wrong? Would we be married? Would we have children? He would want a little girl like Antonia, with crinkly black hair and brown eyes and a straight Grecian nose.

That goddamned line drawing. He must give it to her, and soon. He wondered what he would say. *Listen, Antonia. After the inquest I meant to give it to you, but things got out of hand and I missed my chance. I miss a lot of chances. It's kind of my thing.*

How would she react? What would she say? Can you repair the past simply by saying you're sorry? To hell with it, it probably wasn't important, anyway. A horse with wings, trotting to meet a boy. What could that tell her about anything? Which of course was a typical lawyer's argument to let himself off the hook.

'Antonia,' he said quietly.

'Mm?'

'If you had to choose between solving the riddle and finding the cup, which would it be?'

She threw him a curious look. 'Solving the riddle.'

That surprised him. 'Why?'

She paused. 'D'you remember in Plautius, when Cassius says he wants a libation for him and Lycaris?'

'Sure. That's the point of the riddle, right?'

She looked up at the stars, and nodded. 'The Romans believed that when someone dies, the person closest to them must give them the last kiss—to take in the soul which passes with the final breath.' Again she paused. 'Cassius knew that Lycaris wouldn't be around to do that for him. So he needed someone to ask the Goddess directly, after they were both dead, to bring their spirits together.'

'A libation.'

'Yes.'

Suddenly it dawned on him. Her audacity took his breath away. 'Jesus. You want to be the one to make the libation.'

She picked at the moss on the wall. 'Sounds ridiculous, I know. But, when I was little, Cassius was sort of—my imaginary friend. When I was unhappy he helped me. So I always wanted to do something for him in return.'

She made it sound as straightforward as doing a favour for a friend, instead of fulfilling the dying wish of a poet who had lived 2,000 years before. But that was one of the things he loved about her, the way she could immerse herself in the past, fearlessly plunging in and bringing up great glittering handfuls of it. It was beautiful and unsettling and wildly unscientific. It was Antonia.

He thought back to when they had found the *kántharos* together. A hot, breathless night, spellbound with moonlight and wild sage, and the ancient murmuring voice of the Source. A night outside Time. He thought about that first incredible moment when he took her in his arms—his amazement and elation when she kissed him back. The softness of her lips, the minty fragrance of her hair. The unbelievably tender curve between shoulder and throat.

'Antonia?' he said after a while.

She crossed her arms about her. 'Mm?'

'I'm sorry.'

'For what?'

'For everything.'

She shook her head. 'It doesn't matter now.'

'It does. I screwed up. All the way down the line.'

She drew a shaky breath. 'So did I. All the way down the line.'

They sat side by side, in silence. He was so close that she could feel the rise and fall of his breathing.

'Do you think,' he began, 'do you think one can ever go back?'

She bit her lip. 'I don't know,' she said at last. She looked up at him. 'Do you?'

His phone rang. Patrick cursed aloud. 'Sorry,' he muttered.

Shakily, she moved away while he took the call.

After he rang off he was silent, rubbing his temple as if it hurt. 'It's Modge,' he said at last. 'The fuses have blown. She's in darkness up there.'

She pressed her lips together. 'Then you'd better go.'

He stood looking down at her.

She got to her feet. 'Thanks for the drink.' She forced a smile.

He did not return it. He left her standing by the gate, with the scent of almond blossom heavy on the night air.

Modge watched Patrick gazing unseeingly at his faxes, and thought, it's no good putting it off. You have to ask him *now*.

She was so nervous she could hardly breathe. She wondered if it showed. But what did it matter? In the mood he was in he probably wouldn't even notice. He hadn't even heard her anxiously concocted lie about fixing the fuse box herself. His face was distant and strangely raw-looking, as if he had just woken up after a long sleep.

She felt sick. Everything was unravelling before her eyes. That's why you've got to ask him, she told herself. A test.

She went to the desk, and sat in her mother's big leather chair. 'Patrick,' she said. 'Do you still have that drawing of the *kántharos* I gave you?'

The blue eyes fixed on her.

'I thought so,' she said. Amazing how calm she sounded. 'I want it back.'

Quietly, he asked her why.

She hadn't thought of a reason. The test was simply to see if he would give it to her. If he did not, she would know that she had lost him for ever. 'Does it matter?' she said at last. 'It's mine. Myles gave it to me.'

'It wasn't his to give,' he said evenly. 'You know that. It's Antonia's.'

She gripped the arms of the chair. 'Is that why you kept it all these years? Because it's hers?'

He touched the desk. 'You see, I have to give it back to her.'

'No. Give it to me.'

Their eyes met. He was looking at her as one adult to another, not as Patrick to Modge-Podge, the little sister. She wondered how much he understood. Then he said gently, 'I'm sorry, honey.'

Desolation opened up before her. 'You're still in love with her.'

'Modge—'

'My name is *Imogen*! Imogen Imogen *Imogen*! You used to get that right! When did you stop? When did you start talking like *them*?'

'I—'

'You can't give it back to her! What'll she say? What'll she think? She'll never forgive you. You know that!' She ran from the room.

An hour later, she had worked her way through two packets of chocolate biscuits, four choc-ices, and a family-sized tin of rice pudding. Her mattress was littered with wrappers and crumbs.

She felt completely alone.

On Saturday morning, after Patrick had waved goodbye to a hungover Julian and a stone-faced Modge, he went down to his house intending to retrieve the line drawing from his desk and give it to Antonia.

She wasn't there. Nor were her belongings. She had moved out. He pocketed the drawing and went down to the mill, but she wasn't there either, and her car was gone.

He dismissed the possibility that she had given up and gone back to London. Not Antonia. She had six days left to solve the riddle. She would do her utmost right up until midnight on Thursday night, when the mill became Debra's.

Besides, her answering machine was still hooked up, as he discovered when he called from Les Limoniers. He left a brief message asking her to call him, then spent a long fraught day thrashing out a stack of last-ditch witness statements and cross-examination notes, and calling the mill without success.

Antonia still hadn't returned on Sunday morning, by which time Debra was apoplectic about having him back *forthwith*, and Nerissa wasn't speaking to him because of Suki Hemingway's lunch. Around noon, with just under two hours before the last plane out from Perpignan, he loaded the Discovery, closed up both houses, and drove down to the mill. This time her car was in the courtyard.

'I need to see you,' he said, when she opened the door.

She blinked. 'I thought you had a trial.'

'It starts tomorrow.'

She let him in, and asked if he wanted coffee. He said he did, and took a seat at the desk.

'I'm sorry I didn't return your call,' she said over her shoulder, 'but I only got back a few minutes ago. I've been in Toulouse since yesterday morning. At the library, ordering up references from stacks.'

'Any good?'

'I don't know, they're not up yet. I'll go back tomorrow.'

She spooned coffee into the mugs. 'The thing is,' she said, 'I didn't feel right about being in your house. Creeping around avoiding the phone.'

He nodded.

Watching her go to the fridge for milk, he thought how extraordinary it was that a month ago he had believed he was doing just fine. Good job, surrogate family, beautiful fiancée. Not exactly happy, but then, who is? He thought he was doing all right. If anyone had asked about Antonia Hunt he'd have said, *Oh yeah, I remember her. But she's nothing to me now, hasn't been for years.* And yet here he was, ready to give it all up—to give it all up—and he didn't even know what she felt about him.

He wanted to tell her that he loved her, that he'd been a fool for not realising it sooner. That he would break up with Nerissa as soon as he got back to London, and could they try again? Could they?

But there was so little time, and his advocate's instinct warned him not to botch this by rushing her. *I'm sorry, Patrick, but it's too late to try again. Too much water under the bridge.* His stomach clenched at the thought.

He put his hands on the desk. 'I don't have much time,' he began. 'But I need to tell you something—I need to give you something.'

She put down the milk carton and looked at him.

'What I said at the inquest. That . . . lie. You know I did it because of Modge.'

'I know,' she said gently. 'It doesn't matter. Not any more. You must stop blaming yourself.'

'It matters. Because there's more.'

She waited, her face puzzled.

'What you don't know,' he went on, 'is that before the hearing, Modge gave me this.' He took the line drawing from his pocket and unrolled it on the desk. 'Myles gave it to her,' he said, 'and she gave it to me.'

Antonia stood staring down at it. Not moving. Not touching it. '*Before* the hearing,' she murmured at last. 'She gave it to you *before* the hearing?'

He nodded, watching her take that in. 'You should have had it years ago. I'm sorry.'

He wanted her to look at him, but she did not. 'Why now?' she said.

'I needed to set things straight.'

She did not reply.

He stood up. 'Call me,' he said, and left.

This time Modge's nightmare is very very bad. She is in a cellar, carpeted with soft, evil-smelling mould which gives underfoot, and lined with hundreds of wine bottles with blank black labels. On a table in the middle stands the *kántharos*, bloody and glowing in a shaft of dusty light.

Her chest heaves with panic. Suddenly the cellar is gone and she's out on the mountainside. The glare on the rocks is so bright that it hurts her eyes, and she's *furious* with Myles for sending her away. He made her steal, he made her scrape her tummy on the window-ledge, and then he laughed at her and told her to bugger off. *Pig*.

Still raging at him, she reaches the Jeep. Just beyond it, she sees Monsieur Panabière's beautiful new aluminium gate.

'That'll serve him right,' she says aloud, tugging at the stone which wedges the gate open. Serve him right if he has to walk all the way home. And if he trips as he's climbing over and bumps his knee, so much the better.

She expects the gate to be heavy, but it swings easily into place, and she even manages to fasten the padlock, which is new and shiny, and locks shut with a satisfying click. Serve him jolly well *right*.

Now she's with Patrick further down the slope, and they hear shouting behind them, and turn to see Myles in the Jeep, bumpily reversing across the track. Suddenly the back wheels are spinning over nothingness, and the edge is crumbling, and the Jeep is tipping backwards into the gorge. It's falling slowly, horribly slowly, and paper is fluttering all around it. Fluttering like pigeons' wings.

She screams. She goes on screaming.

She wakes curled in a ball with her knees under her chin and her hands over her ears to shut out her screams.

Oh god oh god oh god it was me. I *did it.* I *did it.*

Oh god oh god oh god.

I killed Myles.

It was six by the time Nerissa got back to the house which she shared with Patrick in Cornwall Gardens, after a ridiculously long lunch with an old flame. To her relief, Patrick had not yet arrived from the airport. That was good. She wanted to appear as if she had spent the weekend in. A long, dull weekend, being neglected by him. And of course, now she had the trump card in reserve.

The lunch had been a spur-of-the moment idea. The minute Debra put down the phone, she had cancelled Suki Hemingway and called Stephen Mackenzie instead. It had worked out beautifully. The champagne had soothed her nerves, and so had poor old Stephen.

Debra's call had been brief to the point of rudeness, although perhaps that was understandable under the circumstances. Did Nerissa know that Antonia Hunt had been staying at the house in La Bastide? Did she know that she had a rival?

No, she did not know about the house, and no thank you, Debra, Nerissa does not have a rival.

She had sat opposite poor Stephen in the restaurant, toying with her food in the way he adored, working out the best way to handle Patrick.

She *deserved* this marriage. She was so tired of going to friends' weddings and looking wonderful, and wondering why it wasn't her turn. She deserved to be married. And it was only right that her husband should be brilliant and good-looking and successful.

So, no thank you, Debra. Nerissa does not have a rival. She has never taken Antonia seriously, and she doesn't see why she should start now. On the other hand, this is not something that can be ignored.

Everything worked out beautifully. By the time she heard the taxi pull up outside the door she had showered and changed into a long, simple dress of cream cashmere which she knew Patrick liked.

She found him in the kitchen, adding water to a large whisky.

'You look awful,' she said, refusing his offer of a drink with a tiny shake of the head. 'If you want food I'm afraid you'll have to order something in. I haven't had time to shop.'

'I'm not hungry.'

'Neither am I. My agent rang yesterday, and I've been up to my ears in conference calls.'

That had occurred to her between courses at the restaurant, and she thought it rather good. Of course, once he knew about the trump card, he might think her a little callous to have been taking calls at a time like this, but she brushed that aside to explain away later. 'The audition's on Wednesday,' she said, knowing that he'd be in the middle of the trial. 'You will come with me, won't you? For moral support?'

'Nerissa,' he said abruptly. 'I have to talk to you.'

She licked her lips. She knew that tone. This might not be as straightforward as she'd thought. 'Can't it wait?' she said. 'I'm awfully tired.'

'I'm afraid it can't.'

She crossed her legs and waited.

'I guess you know what's coming,' he said. He paused. She could see he felt bad about this. Good. That would make him easier to handle.

He looked her in the eyes. 'I'm sorry, Nerissa, but I can't marry you.'

The important thing at times like this was to admit nothing. Admit nothing, accept nothing. It would soon blow over.

She crossed and recrossed her legs. 'I thought you might try something like this,' she said at last. 'Though I can't help feeling your timing is rather off.' At his puzzled glance she added, 'Poor Debra's beside herself. And as for Julian, well, you can imagine.'

Suddenly he was sick of her games. '*What*,' he said in a tone which made her nose turn pink.

'Modge tried to kill herself last night.'

'*Je suis désolée, mademoiselle*,' said the librarian cheerfully, '*mais vous devez patienter encore quelques jours.*'

'*Quelques jours*,' said Antonia between clenched teeth. 'Which takes us to, what? Wednesday? Thursday? Perhaps you could tell me why I have to wait *quelques jours* when you're the one who misread my request form and called up completely the wrong references?'

The librarian gave a shrug which had obviously been perfected by hundreds of similar confrontations. *Take it or leave it*, said the shrug,

Biting down on her frustration, Antonia filled in another form, then went to the canteen, bought coffee, and took it to a table in the corner. God, she was in a terrible mood.

Call me, he had said before he left.

What did that mean? 'Call me and we'll get together'? Or 'Call me and grant me absolution for past sins before I go off and marry Nerissa'? What did he think he was doing, dropping the drawing on her desk, then calmly flying back to London without another word?

Turning the plastic cup in her fingers, she plummeted from exasperation to dejection. He would never break free of the Passmores. He would never break free, because he believed he must take Myles's place. He had to be the perfect son, the perfect brother, the perfect fiancé.

There was no point in calling him back.

But why, she wondered, had he kept the line drawing all this time? For the twentieth time since he had given it to her, she took it from her bag.

Pegasus trotted joyfully towards Bellerophon, his head tilted, his nostrils dilated in a whinny of delight. About his hoofs curled a naturalistic confusion of acanthus. And beneath one overarching frond lay a small, coiled snake. She had recognised it at once. The coiled snake had been Cassius's personal seal. Like most educated Romans, he would have worn it on a ring and used it for sealing letters, and perhaps in his case, military orders. It *identified* him.

The wider implications had only struck her that morning as she lay in Professor Meriot's spare room gazing at the damp patches on the ceiling.

Cassius's seal—his identifying mark—had been carved at the feet of the winged horse. Surely that must mean that *Lycaris's* identifying mark would be found at the feet of Bellerophon, on the *other* side of the cup—which, a frantic re-examination of the line drawing revealed, Antonia had not, twelve years before, got round to sketching in.

In the bleak neon light of the canteen she stared at the blank patch of paper where Bellerophon's toga petered out. The blank patch which held the key to Lycaris.

Cassius and Lycaris.

The truth is in the cup.

She struggled to remember. What was on the other side of the cup? But nothing came.

And yet she knew she was right. Only this would explain why Cassius had told his friend that the riddle would be solved when Lycaris was dead. Because when Romans died, they were cremated, and their ashes placed in an urn, which, if they were wealthy, would be decorated with their seal.

So the task became to identify the seals of the women whom Cassius had rescued, and then to recall, somehow, if the cup had borne anything similar. It sounded simple. But it was complicated by the fact that some Roman women kept their seals on marriage, and some did not. And some didn't bother with seals at all.

After a day's trawl in the library, she had narrowed down the candidates to three. There had been twelve people in the little group which escaped Perusia, of whom five had been female. At first, Antonia had wondered why the group had been so large. Why rescue twelve people if you only wanted to save one? Then it dawned on her. Camouflage. If Lycaris was still married, Cassius would not have wanted to draw attention to their past liaison by singling her out.

Of the five females in the little group, *Kriegführung* mentioned that one had been in her sixties, and one a girl of ten. Which left three who might have been Lycaris.

Of these, the first, Aemilia Saturnina, had been a patrician who had married at fifteen, and would have been twenty-two in 53 BC, when the affair took place. At that time she could have been either a widow or a divorcée—and therefore quite possibly Cassius's lover.

Then there was Valeria Atilia, the daughter of a wealthy wine merchant from southern Spain, who had married well, and was about eighteen in 53 BC.

Finally there was Tacita Cornelia, another patrician, who at sixteen in 53 BC had been the youngest of the three—although since Roman girls married from the age of twelve, that by no means ruled her out.

Eenie, meenie, mynie, mo.

By a stroke of luck, she had learned that Aemilia's own cinerary urn lay somewhere in storage beneath the Glypototek in Copenhagen. She knew one of the assistant curators there, and he had promised to see if her seal was on it.

But as she sat in the canteen nursing her coffee, it occurred to her that even if a miracle happened—even if she uncovered all three seals, and one of them jogged her memory, so that she clapped her hand to her forehead and cried, *Eureka*, I remember, there was a four-leafed clover at Bellerophon's feet, *this* woman is the one!—she still wouldn't know for sure. Because memory plays tricks. Sometimes it serves up what you *want* to remember, rather than the truth. She would not know for sure that she had found Lycaris unless she held the *kántharos* in her hands and saw for herself the symbol at Bellerophon's feet.

Her spirits sank. What was she doing here, chasing after impossible dreams? The rational thing would be to go back to the mill, pack her bags, and return to London. Get on with her life.

And forget all about Patrick McMullan.

'How do you feel?' said Patrick, pulling up one of the hospital chairs.

He must have come straight from court, for instead of a tie he was still wearing his stock, and his hair was ruffled from his wig. Modge thought he looked exhausted.

She pulled the blanket under her chin and said, 'I feel like a fraud.'

He waited for her to go on.

'Pretty pathetic suicide bid,' she said. 'According to the nurses it was hardly enough aspirin to merit a stomach pump. The only reason they're keeping me in is because Mummy insisted, and that's just because she doesn't want me at home. How's the trial going?'

'It's going,' said Patrick, refusing to be sidetracked. 'How do you *feel*?'

She had been longing for him to come, but now that he was here, she wished he would go. How could she ever have fooled herself into thinking he could be more than a brother to her? Now all she wanted was for him to leave. It hurt too much to see him, when she knew she must begin facing life without him. 'I told you,' she mumbled. 'I feel like a fraud. I can't even kill myself properly. I should have had more guts.'

'What you did took guts. That note of yours got a whole lot of stuff out in the open for the first time in years. It was a brave thing to do.'

She looked at him. 'I wanted Mummy to know everything. Everything. Do you understand?'

'I understand.'

She blinked. 'I told her that Myles took the *kántharos*.'

'I know.'

'And now she'll hate me for ever.'

'No.'

Her eyes began to sting. 'She will,' she whispered at last. '*I* shut the gate. *I* killed Myles.'

'No, honey.'

'*Yes.*'

He leaned forward with his elbows on his knees and looked her steadily in the eyes. 'No one killed Myles. It was an accident. A whole lot of mistakes and missed chances and plain old bad luck had to come together for that Jeep to go into the gorge. Each one of us played a part in it. But only a part. It was an accident.' He paused. 'It's taken me years to accept that. I think that in time, you're going to be able to accept it too.'

She wiped her eyes with her fingers, and sniffed. 'Try telling that to Mummy.'

He glanced down at his hands. 'I don't think anyone can do that. It's something she'll have to come to on her own.'

'She never will.'

'You don't know that.'

But she did. Modge turned to find Patrick watching her. She said, 'Why did you bother to stick around all these years?'

He thought for a moment. 'Myles asked me to look after you. Plus, and I know you'll find this hard to believe, I've always liked you.'

Again her eyes filled. 'You've come to say goodbye, haven't you?'

He studied her face. 'For a little while. I think it's better.'

She rolled onto her side with her back to him. If he would leave now, this minute, she wouldn't break down. 'Go on then,' she muttered.

There was a pause. Then she heard him stand up. He placed something on the pillow in front of her.

'What's that?' she mumbled. But she knew what it was. It was Myles's Roman coin, which Mummy had given him years ago.

She fingered the coin; then pushed it way. 'I don't want it,' she declared. 'Take it away.'

'No. It's yours now. It should have come to you a long time ago.'

'I don't *want* it. Take it away or I'll chuck it in the bin.'

'You can do what you like with it. It's yours.'

'Right,' she muttered. Tears were sliding down her cheeks. She picked up the coin and threw it in the bin. 'Satisfied? Now go away.' She drew the blanket over her face and shut her eyes tight. *Go away, Patrick. Go away now. I can't bear this.*

'Maybe some time when you're better,' he said quietly, 'you'll give me a call? We'll go out for lunch. You'll drive up from Newmarket for the day, if the stables can spare you—'

She covered her ears with both hands.

'It'll happen, Imogen. You're going to make it happen. I know you. And you'll tell me all about Newmarket when we meet for lunch.'

'Get out. Get *out!*'

She heard him move to the door. 'I'll see you for that lunch, Imogen,' he said.

A long time later, when she had reached the hiccuping stage, she opened her eyes. Beneath her cheek there was a big damp patch, and her head was pounding. She got up and went to the basin and splashed cold water on her face. Then she sat on the edge of the bed.

The coin had landed on a pile of crumpled tissues and some half-eaten grapes which her father had brought from the hospital canteen. She sat contemplating it for a long time. Then she snatched it up, wrenched open the bottom drawer of the bedside cabinet, and shoved it in, on top of Antonia's green hair clip which she'd made her father bring from home. Right at the back, where she could pretend it wasn't there.

On Monday night when Antonia didn't call, Patrick told himself not to worry. Hadn't she said she would be in Toulouse? She would call on Tuesday, when she got back.

He immersed himself in the trial. Which was easy, for in the bizarre high-pressure world of High Court litigation, a thermonuclear war could break out, and no one would notice.

Debra was in her element, for victory was close at hand. Since the trial began, she and Patrick had rarely been out of each other's sight, yet not once had she mentioned his broken engagement, or Modge's bid for attention. He knew she must be aware of his feelings for Antonia, for Modge's 'suicide' note had been comprehensive—but she gave no sign of it.

Antonia did not call on Tuesday morning, so he did. She wasn't there. Just before he left for court, he left a message on her answering machine. 'Antonia, it's Patrick. Can we meet up? Call me, would you—please?'

She didn't call. He spent Tuesday night in Debra's war room with the litigation team. He watched himself reassuring clients, joking with solicitors, and debating with Debra over the best way to tackle each witness. The ease with which he could dissemble astonished him.

It was three in the morning by the time he got home, to find a note from Nerissa on his pillow—*audition now in Paris, back Thurs. (?)*—and no messages on the answering machine.

Early on Wednesday morning he called the mill again. Again there was no answer, so he left another message.

'Antonia, uh—could you call me? Please? This thing—this trial—it'll be over soon, I think they're going to settle, maybe today. Anyway, I'm going to catch the first plane out.'

At five to two, just before he left for court for the afternoon session, he called his travel service and bought a ticket on the first flight out in the morning. The hell with this. If she didn't want anything to do with him, she would have to tell him in person.

At a quarter to four the other side asked for a short adjournment, during which they accepted the settlement proposal they had been given on Saturday night. The judge was delighted: now he could go off and play golf. The clients were ecstatic. It was eight by the time Patrick and Debra managed to tear themselves away.

'I need to talk to you,' Patrick told Debra as they reached the clerks' room.

'Finally,' she said, walking into her room and shutting the door behind him. 'Would you care for a drink?'

He shook his head.

'I take it,' said Debra, pouring a generous measure of Scotch into a tumbler, 'that this is about Antonia Hunt?' Her face was as serene and unreadable as when she was running an impossible argument in court.

'It is,' he said smoothly. If she hoped to wrong-foot him, she would be disappointed. He had known she would try to seize the upper hand. She was a litigator, after all.

He added, 'I take it Julian also told you that I've split up with Nerissa?'

She gave him her small, tight smile.

He had told Julian that morning at breakfast, just before the older man left for the hospital. He had felt bad about burdening Julian at such a time, but he had no choice.

Julian had listened in silence. Then he slowly folded his *Times* and placed it on the table beside his plate. 'I was afraid this might happen. I suppose I always knew that Nerissa wasn't right for you.'

'It's not her fault.' He paused. 'I'm still in love with Antonia.'

How simple it sounded when you said it out loud. How simple. And suddenly everything fell into place. No more headaches. No more papering over the cracks and wondering why nothing felt right.

But plainly, Julian had not expected this. He looked shocked. 'Oh my dear boy, you can't! You must know how Debra will take this!'

'I can't help that, Julian. No one can.'

'I must say,' Debra was saying, 'I'm disappointed that you felt you had to mislead me all these years.'

'About?'

'You knew my son had taken that artefact, yet you covered it up. You knew my daughter had shut that gate, yet you never said. You—'

'I didn't know about the gate.'

'And now to resume your relations with that woman behind my back.' Debra reached for the decanter and poured herself another drink. 'So,' she said, 'it turns out I've been wrong all along—as my daughter was at pains to point out in her little note. My son was a thief, and that woman is in fact an angel of light, whom I'm expected to welcome into the fold with open arms.'

'No one expects you to do that,' said Patrick quietly. Then he said, 'May I speak now?'

She inclined her head with exaggerated courtesy.

'What I have to say won't take long. I'm leaving.'

'Leaving?' she echoed.

'Resigning my tenancy.'

She blinked. 'That's impossible.'

'No, it isn't. Not very usual, perhaps, but not impossible. I've made all the arrangements. My clerk will box up my things and send them round to Cornwall Gardens. He hasn't taken on any new cases for me recently, and as regards my current ones, they're all up-to-date. I'll prepare leaving notes tonight so that whoever takes over will be able to—'

'You can't just *leave*. You can't just throw everything away. Everything you've worked for.'

He was surprised. Clearly she had never envisaged this. 'Not everything,' he said. 'I'll still practise law.' His lip curled. 'Perversely, I get a kick out of it. But I'm thinking of changing allegiances.'

She laughed. 'You, a plaintiff's lawyer? Helping the underdog take on the multinationals? Oh, I don't think so!'

'Why not? I know enough about large companies to give them a run for their money.'

'Come off it, Patrick! We all get these sorts of doubts from time to time. But we get through them.'

'Maybe. But I'd still like to give it a try.'

She studied him. 'After all I've done for you.'

Calmly he met her eyes. 'I've learned a great deal from you, Debra.

For that I'll always be grateful. But we both know that what I've achieved, I've achieved myself.'

She looked down at her drink, and frowned. 'Don't leave, Patrick. I don't know if I could carry on without you.'

The personal appeal. He had been expecting that. Maybe she even meant it, too.

He stood up. 'Goodbye, Debra,' he said.

By the time Nerissa reached La Bastide on Wednesday afternoon, she had begun to feel more than merely irritated with Antonia. It was too much. The woman had to be made to face reality. And if that meant a trip out to this dreadful place, then so be it. Better to deal with it face to face. Point out how much Patrick needed a well-connected wife, how far he could go.

She rang the number Debra had given her, but either Antonia wasn't answering, or she wasn't at the mill. It hadn't occurred to Nerissa that Antonia might not be there.

She brought her bag in from the Discovery, locked the house again, and set off on foot for the mill. The old building was in darkness when she reached it, and Antonia's Citroën was gone. Nerissa tried the door. To her surprise, it opened. Antonia must have forgotten to lock it.

She went in. The kitchen was positively medieval, but on a counter by the sink was a phone and an answering machine. Antonia had four messages. Nerissa pressed PLAY.

When she heard Patrick's voice, she gasped.

She listened to all four messages. They were all from him. '. . . I'm going to catch the first plane out,' ran the final one. 'I think we can work this out, Antonia. I really do. That is, if you want to. I know I do. I—I love you. I don't think I ever stopped loving you.'

She was incredulous. She had never heard him talk like that.

Dear God. He had really meant it about splitting up. The thought appalled her. The *idea* of having to start all over again with someone else. It wasn't fair. She *deserved* this marriage.

She erased all four messages, and left the mill.

The Discovery was not in its usual place at the airport when Patrick reached Perpignan on Thursday morning.

He stood blinking at the oily spot on the concrete. It took him several minutes to work out that Nerissa must have got there before him. He wondered why that was so hard to figure out. Maybe it was lack of sleep. He had spent most of the night drafting leaving notes on his cases, then another couple of hours clearing his desk before catching a cab to the airport. Forty minutes' sleep on the plane had left him with a head like cotton wool.

Rain on his face pitched him back into the present. He returned to the terminal and rented a car, and reached La Bastide at around eleven thirty. The Discovery was parked outside the house. Oh, bloody hell. He didn't have the energy for another showdown with Nerissa.

The answering machine in the hall was blank, and there were no letters on the table. He swore under his breath. He had been counting on finding a message from Antonia.

He found Nerissa in the kitchen, writing him a note. 'I was just leaving,' she said, pocketing the note. 'I came to collect my things.'

Her face was serene. She seemed to have accepted that it was over between them.

He sat down and put his elbows on the table. He told her briefly about resigning from chambers and saying goodbye to Modge.

She raised an eyebrow. 'What's this, clean slate time?'

He tried to smile, but it wouldn't come. His face felt like cardboard.

She picked up her keys. 'I'll leave the car at the airport in the usual place.'

'Sure.'

He carried her bags out and loaded them in the back. As she opened the door, she turned and said, 'Oh, I almost forgot. I bumped into Antonia yesterday evening in the village. She said to say hi.'

Somehow he managed to take that without a flicker. 'Did—she say anything else?'

Nerissa was tying her scarf. She shook her head. 'She was in a hurry, she'd only come back from somewhere or other to collect her messages, then she was off again.'

He went cold. Yesterday evening. She had been here yesterday evening, she had collected his messages—and the only reply she had for him was 'hi'.

Well, you can't get much clearer than that, can you? Nice work, Patroclus. You've gone and lost her all over again.

At half past eleven on Thursday morning Antonia switched off her laptop, shouldered her bag, and left the university library in search of a proper cup of coffee.

Once inside the smoky little café which had become her haunt over the past four days, she sat with a *café américain* to contemplate defeat.

Over the past two days, she had learned a surprising amount about her three candidates, but it still wasn't enough to get her home.

Valeria Atilia, the wine merchant's daughter, seemed the least likely of them all. According to *Roman Inscriptions in Britain*, she had ended her life in Colchester, where a funeral plaque described her marriage by the conventional acronym *SVQ*. That was short for *Sine Una Querella*, or 'Without A Quarrel'. It didn't sound like a woman who had once bitten her lover's neck, as Cassius describes in the *Poems*.

Aemilia Saturnina remained the most likely candidate, for although Antonia knew little about her, the colleague in Copenhagen had at last called back and told her that the cinerary urn was decorated with a relief of pomegranates. To the Romans, the pomegranate had been a potent symbol of eternal life. Of course, it was a bit of a stretch to assume that the fruit had been Aemilia's personal seal rather than just a general motif for the afterlife. But pomegranates pointed the right way, and Antonia had a hunch that Aemilia was the one.

Finally, there was Tacita Cornelia, whom Antonia liked the best, even if she was probably not Lycaris. Her name turned up in a letter by Pliny the Elder written more than a century later, in which she was cited as an example of the influence which a strong, intelligent woman could have on her children. The young Cornelii had grown up in Athens. From an 1893 catalogue of Greek papyri, Antonia had learned that in later years they had adopted as their seal the crescent moon of their mother's family.

A pomegranate or a crescent moon.

Neither jogged her memory. She could not picture anything in the blank spot on the cup. It looked as if her stab at solving the riddle was doomed to remain just that. A stab in the dark.

Toying with her coffee, Antonia thought, how petty I am. To treat this riddle like some kind of intellectual puzzle. To be upset because *I'm* not the one who's going to solve it. It isn't a game. It never was.

Two thousand years ago, a man loved a woman. When he lost her, it blighted his life. Then, years later, she fell into danger, and he saved her life—at the cost of his own. But before he died, he did everything he could to ensure that one day their spirits would be together.

To him it was not a word game. It mattered. He believed in it.

She wondered if Lycaris had ever learned what Cassius had done for her. Did they meet again, one final time? Did they find some way to overcome whatever had separated them thirteen years before?

She watched the dancing shadows of the young leaves on the pavement, and thought about last chances, and mending the mistakes of the past. Then she got up and went inside, and dialled Patrick's number in chambers.

His clerk answered, sounding harried. No, Mr McMullan wasn't in chambers. And no, he wasn't at home either, they'd been trying to reach him there too. She could always try the hospital, although—

Antonia's heart lurched. 'The *hospital*?'

The clerk became evasive. Clearly if she did not know about that, he did not consider it his place to enlighten her. Perhaps she should speak to Mr Passmore or Mrs Passmore, although as Mrs Passmore was in conference, Mr Passmore was probably her best bet, he would be home around now, would she like the number?

Julian answered on the second ring, and did a valiant job of concealing his disappointment when he heard her voice. They had a brief, awkward conversation in which he did most of the talking, and when she put down the phone she needed a drink, a real one this time. When the waiter brought the *coup de rouge* it was an effort not to down it in one.

To try to *kill* herself? Poor little Modge. And poor Julian. And Debra. And Patrick.

Julian had sounded shattered, as well he might, and he had been vague about Patrick's whereabouts. He wished he knew, he said.

She had a sudden picture of a young man walking down the rue de la Clouette, while an eight-year-old skipped in circles round him and pestered him for *pain au chocolat*. Patrick in the pot-shed, sitting patiently on a bench while Modge instructed him in the art of numbering shards. She wondered how he was taking this.

She finished her drink and called for another.

'It's no one's *fault*,' Julian had said. 'In fact, it's time we got things out in the open. Rightly or wrongly, what Modge has done is a catalyst. We need to *deal* with things. For her sake. And perhaps also for ours.'

The waiter brought the second glass. She contemplated it. Another drink was hardly a good idea, given that she had to drive back to the village that afternoon, pack up her things, and be out—God knew where—by midnight, when the mill changed hands. The thought filled her with a great weariness. She just wanted to talk to Patrick and make sure he was all right.

She held up the wine glass, and watched the sunlight turn it to ruby. 'This is for you, Modge,' she murmured. 'And for you too, Patrick. Wherever you are. "A cup of wine for the afternoon . . ."'

A cup of wine . . .

She frowned. Where had she heard those words before?

Slowly she put down the wineglass. 'A cup of wine' . . . Then it came to her. Myles crouching on a sun-baked hillside, waving an empty champagne bottle as he shouted down an irreverent toast: '*A cup of wine*

*for the afternoon, and don't let the water-jug near it. The Bacchus from these
cellars flows neat!'*

Suddenly everything fell into place. Of course. How could she have
been so stupid? Myles had hidden the *kántharos* in the cellar—the one
place where neither she nor her father had thought to look. No one ever
went down there.

She glanced at her watch. It was shortly after noon. She had just
under twelve hours in which to hurry back to Professor Meriot's and
retrieve her things, drive down to La Bastide, search the cellars—*and*, on
top of all that, make contact with Patrick.

Just before she left the café, she tried his chambers again. This time
she was put straight through to the head clerk, who told her starchily
that no, Mr McMullan still wasn't in, and no, he was not expected back.
Mr McMullan had resigned.

They wouldn't tell her any more than that. She dialled the number
which—after considerable prevarication—they gave her for his house in
London, but all she got was an answering machine, and she didn't leave
a message in case Nerissa was there. The same thing happened when
she called the house in La Bastide. Where *was* he?

It was noon, and as Patrick had missed breakfast on the plane, he was
hungry, but he couldn't decide what to eat. Eventually he gave up the idea
altogether. Food was irrelevant. The important thing was to find Antonia.

One thing was certain: at midnight tonight, the mill would become
Debra's. Which meant that at some stage today, Antonia would have to
return to collect her belongings, or Debra's bailiffs would chuck them
out onto the road.

So what are you waiting for? he thought. Get down to the mill! Hell,
maybe she's already there! He threw on his jacket and left the house.

But there was no sign of anyone at the mill, although puzzlingly, the
door was unlocked. He went inside. No messages on the answering
machine. His last hope—that Nerissa had been lying, and Antonia had
not in fact been back and collected them—drained away.

On the floor he found a scattering of mail and a couriered envelope
from Paris, marked urgent. He wished he had thought of sending her a
couriered letter from London. Maybe she would have taken that more
seriously than a clutch of incoherent telephone messages.

He went over to the desk, tore a leaf from Antonia's memo pad, and
scribbled a note: *Antonia. I meant what I said. Every word. Patrick.* He
stuck it on the fridge beside the postcard of Cassius, where she was sure
to see it.

As he did so, his eye was caught by a fluorescent green Post-it underneath. KATE! it said in big red capitals, with a London number scrawled underneath. He pocketed it and left.

Back at his house he called the number, and somewhat to his relief, found himself speaking not to the mad friend herself, but to the mad friend's husband. No, said the husband, Antonia hadn't been in touch in the last couple of days, wasn't she overseas? Yes, he would tell his wife that Patrick needed to get in touch with Antonia *urgently*, and if she rang, they would be sure and pass on the message. The husband sounded more amenable than the wife, but worryingly vague.

Now Patrick found himself standing in the middle of the kitchen wondering what to do. It wasn't even two o'clock yet. It might be hours before she arrived at the mill. He could not face waiting in the house. He had to do something. He pulled on his jacket and left.

Despite the mildness of the afternoon, the track up to the Source had the stillness of midwinter. As he walked, inhaling the sweet resin-scented air, his mind cleared, as it always did when he approached the Source. You can't give up now, he told himself. If you do, you'll only be repeating the same mistake you made twelve years ago.

It was three o'clock by the time he reached the end of the track, and although fitful sunlight pierced the clouds, the Source was already a well of darkness.

He ducked his head and entered, and underfoot the ground was as dry as on the night they had found the *kántharos*. He knelt, and let a handful of dust trickle through his fingers. He remembered how Antonia had looked as they knelt in the dust before the *kántharos*. Her face transfigured, her dark eyes glittering with tears.

She was still the same girl. Why had it taken him so long to see that? She hadn't changed, and neither had he. You could try to convince yourself that people grew apart, that events got in the way—and maybe sometimes they did. But not this time. Not unless he let it happen.

On his way out, he cracked his head dizzyingly against a stalactite, which brought him smartly back to the present. *Watch your step, son*, the Goddess seemed to be warning him. *You're not out of the woods yet.*

His optimism drained away. No wonder Antonia hadn't called him. He should not have left her like that, with no indication of how he felt.

He emerged unsteadily into the sunshine. Black spots darted before his eyes, and when he put his fingers to his temple they came away covered in blood. Chastened, he started back down the track. But when he reached the little bridge where it branched off up the Ravin de Verdura, he came to a halt.

460

It was still only half past three. If he kept going, he would be back at the mill in half an hour. What if she still wasn't there? He didn't think he could face that. So to kill another hour he decided to take the side-track up to the ridge.

The track wound up through a beech wood carpeted in crisp, bronze-coloured leaves which made the sound of his passage loud in the still air. No wind stirred the bare grey branches. No cry of a hawk, no solitary piping wren. He was alone.

The track narrowed and became steeper. The leaf carpet deepened to knee-high drifts. This must be years of leaves, he thought as he ploughed through them. Years and years, maybe right back to that last summer. Right back to Myles.

Thinking about that, he stepped on a tree root that turned out to be a fallen branch, which upended and nearly pitched him off the track. He landed heavily on his right foot, and a bolt of pure white lightning shot through his knee.

The pain was worse than anything he had known. He fell, and for several heartbeats all he could do was roll in the leaves and fight it.

Panting and shivering, he lay staring at the tracery of naked branches against the sky. Of *all* the times for his knee to go.

One botched attempt at standing told him that he was in trouble. As soon as his foot touched the ground, the pain flared to a white, engulfing agony which felled him at once. He locked his jaws to keep from crying out. The cut on his head began to throb in unison with his knee. He forced himself to lie still and figure his options.

Obviously he couldn't stay here. Hikers did not come this way in March, and he doubted that hunters did either. Of course, he could always use his mobile, which—by sheer luck—he still had in his jacket pocket. But hell, this was hardly an emergency, he'd only buggered up the ligament in his knee. So forget about that.

How far was he from the mill? It must be about two miles back to the main track, then another mile and a half, maybe two, down to the mill. So say four miles in all. Which on two legs would be an easy one-hour hike. On one good leg and a couple of crutches, it would take maybe three hours, maybe four. OK, so say four hours at most, and you're back by seven thirty at the latest.

And maybe by then, said a snide little voice in his head, Antonia will already have been and gone. He told the voice to shut the hell up, and began looking around for crutches.

An hour later, he was not even halfway back to the main track, and already it was beginning to get dark. The branches he had found for crutches were helping, but they weren't really long enough, so it was slow going. And it hurt like hell.

He stopped to rest, noticing vaguely that the temperature had fallen sharply. Glancing up at the darkening sky, he wondered if there would be a moon tonight. If not, things might get tricky.

He hated the idea of calling for help. Who was he supposed to call? Antonia? Hers was the only local number he had, given that both his house and Les Limoniers were empty. So it looked like it was either Antonia, or the emergency services in Mazerans. But come off it, this wasn't an emergency.

He took out his mobile and punched in Antonia's name. Nothing happened. He tried again, with the same result. No reception. He bit back a laugh. Should have thought of that one, shouldn't you? That'll teach you to rely on technology.

Once again he struggled to his feet—foot—and began shuffling through the leaves like an elderly drunk.

Antonia reached the mill around four o'clock, and found it unlocked.

A rapid scan of her mail told her that none of it was from Patrick. To make matters worse, there were no messages on the answering machine.

She suppressed a flicker of exasperation. 'Call me,' he had said. Surely it wasn't beyond *him* to call her? Then she thought of Modge, and was contrite. He had other things to think about right now.

The official-looking envelope from Paris turned out to be from Debra's French lawyers, formally notifying her that if she stayed in the mill a minute past midnight, she would be evicted. She chucked it in the bin. If Debra wanted to waste money paying lawyers to tell her what she already knew, that was her problem.

Eight hours. What could she achieve in eight hours? The cellars would need five times as long for a proper search.

Wearily she went to the fridge for a Coke, and found a new Post-it stuck next to Cassius. *Patrick?* Patrick had been here and left a note?

The handwriting was terrible. She could barely decipher his name. *Antonia. I meant what I said. Every word. Patrick.* What did he mean, 'I meant what I said'? What he'd said about what? And when had he been here? Where had he gone? Had he flown back to London, or was he still in La Bastide?

She felt a prickle of unease. Was he all right? The writing was all over the place. Then she remembered Modge telling her about his scrawl, and how he'd had to learn how to write from scratch, because of the burns to his hand. So was this normal for him, or what?

She rang his house, but got no answer. Then she rang his house in London—again no answer. It's probably nothing, she told herself as she put down the receiver. He's probably just avoiding the phone—what with Modge, and resigning, and everything. He's probably in London right now, having a long, late, expensive lunch with Nerissa.

Telling herself severely not to overdramatise, she put together the Calor Gas lamp she'd bought in Toulouse, and started down to the cellars to begin the search. She had seven and a half hours in which to find the *kántharos*. And no one—not even Patrick—was going to get in the way.

Five minutes later she ran back upstairs, threw on her jacket, and set off at a run for his house. She had to know whether or not he was still in the valley.

The stars were out when Patrick came to.

He was lying on his back under the oak tree at the mouth of the Source. He had no recollection of how he had got there, although a quick inspection showed him that at some point he must have fallen and smashed his watch, for it had stopped at nine fifteen.

Nine fifteen? What had happened in between? Maybe that crack on the head had been worse than he thought. Or maybe he'd simply decided to catch up on some sleep.

Funny place to do it, though. And cold. Really cold. Hadn't there been piles of leaves somewhere? He remembered great drifts of dry, rustling leaves. Would've been better if he'd stopped for a nap in one of those.

Ah, the hell with it. He was too tired to worry about it now. And his head hurt like crazy.

'I haven't got *time* for this,' Antonia muttered as she ran up the road to Patrick's house.

To her relief it was lit up like a Christmas tree. Someone must be home. But instead of the Discovery she found a blue car with Hertz number plates parked in front. That can't be Nerissa, she thought, puzzled. A Nissan Primera is hardly her style.

She rang the bell, but no one answered. Then she saw that the door wasn't properly shut. 'Patrick?' she called. 'Nerissa?' Cautiously, she pushed it open and went inside.

On the kitchen table she found a scattering of loose change, some keys, an Air France ticket, a milk carton and a crumpled wad of car rental papers. The rental was in Patrick's name. So at least she knew he was still in the valley. But where?

She scrawled a quick note asking him to call her, propped it up against the milk carton, and left the house, running all the way to the bar-tabac to see if Patrick was there.

But wherever he was, he was not at the bar-tabac or anywhere else in La Bastide, according to the assembled drinkers. No one had seen him for days, and they all confidently assured her that he was in London.

He's probably fine, she told herself as she arrived back at the mill. He's probably just gone for a walk and forgotten the time.

It was half past six.

If she was going to make a start on the cellar, she must do it now. As far as Patrick was concerned, she had done all she could. From now on it was up to him.

Three and a half hours later, as she was struggling to shift a crate of ancient and extremely heavy empties, the phone rang. She fell upstairs and snatched the receiver. 'Where the hell have you *been*!' she cried. 'I've been calling your house every ten minutes for hours!'

'Ah,' said Kate. 'So he hasn't been in touch.'

'What? *What?*'

There was silence on the other end of the line. Then Kate said, 'Antonia, I'm really sorry. But my useless dork of a husband only just remembered that he took a message from your barrister hours ago. Apparently he said it was urgent, so I thought I'd better call.'

Antonia gripped the receiver. 'What did he say?'

'Phil can't remember exactly.'

'Oh, *Kate!*'

'I know, I know, he's getting sixty lashes in the morning. But he really can't remember, except that it was urgent, and could you call back as soon as possible.'

'When? When did he call?'

A whispered discussion on the other end of the line. 'Around lunchtime. Phil remembers, because he was eating a sandwich.'

Lunchtime. That was hours ago.

'Where was he calling from?'

More mutterings. 'Sorry. He didn't say.'

Antonia shut her eyes.

Kate sighed. 'Antonia, love, you can't go on like this. Why don't you just tell the man how you feel?'

She drew a ragged breath. 'Because I can't *find* him! I know it sounds bizarre, and there's probably a perfectly reasonable explanation, but I've been all over the place and I can't find him, and I can't shake off this horrible feeling that something's happened.'

There was another silence. Then Kate said in her most pragmatic and managing voice, 'Listen. I won't tell you not to worry, because it won't help. But if you haven't heard from him by midnight, call the police.'

When she rang off, the mill seemed very dark and quiet. Antonia stood by the fridge wondering what to do. It was half past ten, and she had barely scratched the surface of the cellar—which, as she had feared, was turning out to be an obstacle course of wine-boxes and unwieldy pieces of what looked like ancient farming equipment. The place must have been a paradise for Myles, he could have hidden the *kántharos* anywhere. And she had one and a half hours in which to find it.

Or looked at another way, she had one and a half hours in which to go stumbling around in the pitch darkness on a freezing mountainside making a complete idiot of herself, while the man she was trying to find was probably dining happily with his fiancée at the three-star Michelin in Sainte Eulalie.

She sat down wearily on her desk, and met Cassius's contemplative gaze on the fridge.

But that isn't the point, is it? she told him silently. *The point is, Cassius, I've got to go and find Patrick. And if that means giving up my last chance of helping you, I've still got to do it.*

She wiped her eyes with a grimy knuckle. 'I'm sorry, Cassius,' she said aloud. 'We were nearly there, weren't we? We were so close. So close.' She drew a ragged breath. 'But I have to do this. You understand, don't you? Wherever you are, you of all people understand. I have to make sure he's all right.'

Patrick was drifting in the sky somewhere around the moon, whose glaring brightness drilled savagely into his aching head.

Then someone was shaking him by the shoulders, and the moon resolved itself into a gas lamp with Antonia kneeling beside it, calling his name.

'Antonia,' he murmured, struggling into a sitting position which sent lightning shooting through his skull.

'What the *hell* are you doing up here?' she cried, gripping his shoulders with both hands.

'I was—'

'*Look* at you! Blood all over you! What d'you thinking you're *doing*, not telling anyone where you were going? Not even a note!'

She fished in her pocket for a handkerchief and ran inside to the spring, then ran back and started wiping the blood from his face. The water felt wonderful.

'What happened to you?' she demanded.

'Hit my head,' he mumbled. 'And my knee's kind of shot. Christ, but it's good to see you, I—'

'Your *knee*?' she exploded. 'Great God in Heaven, I can't *believe* you never got that fixed, you were supposed to do it years ago!'

That made him laugh. 'You're not going to give me a hard time about that now, are you?'

'It's not funny, you moron, I thought you were dead! What the fuck were you doing up here, wandering around in the dark? D'you know what time it is? It's a quarter past fucking *midnight*!'

She was swearing like a trooper, which she never did, and clutching his shoulders with both hands as if she never meant to let go. In the silvery gaslight her face was smooth and pale and glistening with tears, her lips as white as chiselled marble. She looked marvellous.

He told her so.

She sniffed, and wiped her nose on the back of her hand.

He touched her cheek with his fingers. 'Don't cry.' He struggled upright, ignoring the iron rings constricting his skull. 'Antonia—'

'Don't you move,' she said, pushing him down again. 'I'm going for help. Now you stay put. I won't be long.'

He grabbed her wrist. 'Wait. First I have to tell you something. It's important.'

'What?'

He searched for words. Shit, he was beginning to drift again. He knew that he had to tell her something and he knew it was incredibly important, but he couldn't remember what it was. So instead he asked her if she'd got his messages.

'The one on the fridge? What the hell was that supposed to mean?'

'No no, the other ones. On the phone.'

She looked at him blankly. 'You left messages?'

'Oh Christ. You didn't get them. That's why I came up here.'

Again she looked puzzled, and he realised that that didn't make any sense. 'I was waiting for you,' he explained. 'You hadn't answered my messages, but I knew you'd come up here to say goodbye. I mean, not to me, but—' He took a deep breath, then started again. The iron rings around his skull were tightening. 'I let everything get in the way,' he muttered. 'Shouldn't have let everything get in the way . . .'

He had a nagging feeling that there was a much, much simpler way of saying this, but his brain refused to tell him what it was.

Then he felt her put her arm round his shoulders and bring his head against her breast, and her warm hand was smoothing the hair back from his forehead, and her breath was heating his cheek. She bent close to him, and he caught the peppermint scent of her hair. 'Patrick,' she said softly. 'It's all right now. I understand.'

He was immensely tired. 'We let everything get in the way,' he mumbled. 'That has to end here, Antonia.'

'I know,' she whispered, and he felt her lips brush his, and tasted her salty tears. 'That ends here. You're going to be all right, Patrick. We're both going to be all right.'

CHAPTER SEVENTEEN
Near Lake Trasimeno, Umbria, March 1, 40 BC

TACITA DIDN'T KNOW WHAT she would do if he refused to see her.

She paced the barn, straining for the sound of footsteps in the courtyard. But all she heard was the drip, drip, drip of melting snow, and the occasional thump as an icicle dropped from the eaves.

Even if he came right now, they wouldn't have much time. In the farmhouse across the courtyard her husband and the others were still sleeping, exhausted by the terrors of their nocturnal flight through the hills. But she could not count on that for long.

If only he would come. Now more than ever, it was imperative that she should see him. He had to know the truth before—before he died.

She still could not believe it. Faenio had told her just after midnight, when they finally reached the deserted farm. The old slave couldn't help himself, it had come out in a rush. He had wept as he told her.

She had been too stunned to cry. What a fool she had been not to see at once what this rescue must cost him! What a fool! Although perhaps in her desperation, she had not *wanted* to see. Thinking about it, she had lain awake all night, while around her the others slept in the straw where they had dropped.

An hour before dawn she had risen silently and left the farmhouse, crossing the muddy courtyard to the barn, where Faenio had a fire blazing. Yes, he told her, he had got word to his master that she must see him. No, he didn't know what the response would be. She must wait and be patient.

She was not patient.

In the glow of the brazier she had washed as best she could, put up her hair, and tried to smooth the worst of the wrinkles from her dress. It was a cruel parody of those heady spring nights when, sick with excitement, she had crept from her father's house and run breathlessly through the streets to the Porta Capena, and into his arms.

A footstep in the courtyard. And there he was, standing in the doorway looking at her, his face expressionless. 'You wanted to see me,' he said. 'I can't stay long. It's too dangerous.'

She put a hand to her throat. Words deserted her.

He looked magnificent. Beneath a general's cloak of heavy scarlet wool he wore a doublet and kilt of gilded leather with buckles of burnished bronze. His half-boots were tooled in silver.

After that first long look, he did not glance at her again, but brusquely asked if she wanted wine. She did. She needed it.

He walked to the table beside the brazier, and she saw that his limp had worsened. She watched him pour wine into two bronze beakers, add hot water from the jug, and leave hers on the table for her to take. He doesn't want to touch me, she thought. Her heart contracted.

He held his cup in both hands and frowned at it. 'Your children,' he said at last, 'they are—coping with this?'

She picked up her cup and took a long swallow. It was good wine, and after months of sour *posca* it tasted ambrosial. She felt its warmth stealing down into her belly. 'The twins are with my brother on his estate,' she said. 'I only have my eldest with me.'

He nodded. 'That's good. It'll be a hard journey.'

'Gaius—'

'You need to make your way to Puteoli by the back roads,' he said, still without looking at her. 'Don't go anywhere near Spoletum. That's where our forces are massing for the final assault. When you get to Puteoli, take a ship for Corinth. Then another for Athens.'

He drained his cup and set it down, wiping his mouth on the back of his hand. 'I'm giving you my slave, Faenio. He'll see that you get there safely. He'll look after you.' He paused. 'My father gave him to me when I was a boy. You can trust him completely. He won't let you down.'

Thirteen years ago, as she lay in his arms, he had told her about the tricks he used to play on Faenio when he was ten. Did he think she had forgotten all that?

'You can't give me Faenio,' she said. 'He's been with you for so long—'

'Precisely. Besides, I won't be—' He cut himself short.

She knew what he had been going to say. *I won't be needing a slave for much longer. Not where I'm going.* She couldn't stand it any longer. 'Gaius, I can't let you do this!'

He shot her a glance. 'What do you mean?'

'I know what's going to happen to you. I know what you mean to do.'

His face hardened. 'Who told you? Who?'

'It doesn't matter—'

'That bloody Cretan! I expressly forbade him to say anything!'

She twisted her hands together. 'I've been such a fool. I never thought. You must believe that. I assumed that with your rank, you'd get away with it. I was such a fool!'

He waited awkwardly, while she brought herself under control.

'I'm sorry,' she muttered, 'it's the wine. I'm not used to it.' She went to the table and took another swallow, and put the cup down again. Then she said, 'I need you to know something.'

'I don't want—'

'I need you to *know*,' she repeated fiercely, 'that I've never loved any man but you. I never stopped loving you, Gaius. That's the truth.'

He looked stunned. He opened his mouth to speak, then closed it again. At last he said, 'I didn't know.'

She went to him and took his hands. They were rough and brown, and notched with scars: a soldier's hands. Beautiful, she thought. 'Well,' she said, 'now you do.'

His hands tightened on hers. 'Tacita. You haven't changed.'

'Neither have you.'

They stood like that for a long time. Then at last he drew her into his arms and held her tight. She put her head on his shoulder and in one breath she was back in the tomb in the Porta Capena. She couldn't bear it. 'It's not fair,' she said brokenly. 'We could have been happy.'

His arms tightened. 'No,' he murmured into her hair, 'not in this life.'

'Do you think there's another?'

'Oh, yes.'

'You sound so certain.'

'You used to tease me about my peasant faith. Remember?'

'But you weren't always so certain.'

'No.' He took her face in his hands and looked down into her eyes. 'It took me years to realise that what I felt for you—what I *feel*—is all the proof I'll ever need.'

Outside, an icicle hit the ground. They both started.

'We don't have much time,' he said. 'The others will wake up soon.'

She felt a rising tide of panic at the thought of leaving him. There was so much still to tell him, and she had scarcely begun. If they were interrupted now, how would she bear it?

She put her hands on his shoulders. 'Gaius, there's something else I must tell you. You need to understand why I left.'

To her dismay he shook his head. 'I don't want to know. That doesn't matter any more, it—'

'It matters,' she insisted. 'I tried to tell you once before, but—'

'I know, I sent back your letter. I'm sorry. That was wrong of me.'

She brushed that aside. 'I have to tell you, Gaius. We won't get another chance, and this is something you must know. Not for me, but for you.'

He watched in puzzlement as she ran to the door and called softly to Faenio. After a few moments the slave entered, gently pushing his charge before him. Then the old Cretan withdrew, to resume his watch outside the door.

Tacita turned back to Gaius, who had gone very still. She put her hands on the boy's shoulders and said simply, 'This is my son, Titus.'

Fearlessly, Titus stepped forward and extended his hand, and thanked the general for saving their lives.

Gaius did not move. He stood with his hands at his sides, gazing down into the twelve-year-old's face, into the startling grey eyes—his own eyes—gazing solemnly back at him.

Then he raised his head and looked at her over the dark, tousled curls of his son. His lips parted, but no words came. He cleared his throat. Started again. 'Why . . .' he began, 'why didn't you tell me?'

She licked her lips. 'How could I? You would have tried to stop me. You would have got yourself killed.'

She watched him take in the truth of that—and also the truth of what she had not said. If her father had discovered that his only daughter was carrying a provincial officer's child, he would have had her killed as well.

'And you never guessed?' she said.

Dazedly he shook his head. 'It—occurred to me, of course. But I thought—I thought I would have known. I thought one sensed these things. Somehow.'

Titus was glancing from one to the other, trying to follow what was going on, and scowling, because he couldn't. He looked exactly like Gaius when he was angry. The same lower lip thrust out, the same strong brows drawn together.

'What you did,' Gaius told her slowly, 'by leaving—you saved my life. And yours. And—his. All three of us.' He listened to the sound of that. 'And I thought you were *weak*! I thought you left because you were frightened!'

Slowly he went back to the table and sat down, and put his hand across his mouth.

He sat with his bad leg stretched before him. Intrigued, Titus edged closer. 'Are you wounded, sir?'

Still with his hand over his mouth, Gaius studied him. 'A long time ago.'

'Does it hurt?'

'Only sometimes . . . Come closer, will you?—Titus?'

Titus moved forward.

Gaius took the boy's small hand in his. Frowning, he turned it in his fingers, examining it as if it were some exotic and fragile object which he must commit to memory. At last he said, 'Titus, you have ink stains on your fingers.'

Titus gave a small smile. 'So have you, sir.'

'So I have. I was up late, writing.'

'You're lucky, sir! My mother won't let me stay up late.'

Still frowning, Gaius studied the boy's hand in his own.

Titus sucked in his lips. 'You're left-handed, sir,' he said.

'And you're observant, Titus.'

'I noticed, because I'm left-handed too.'

At last, Gaius released the boy's hand, took him gently by the shoulders, and looked into his face. 'And what do you write? Hm? Do you write poems?'

'Oh, no, sir. I write *plays*.'

'Ah, *plays*.' He nodded. 'That's good.'

'Father doesn't think so. He says writing isn't proper work, and I've got to be a magistrate when I grow up, but I won't. I'm going to be a playwright.'

'You stick to that.'

'That's what Mother says when Father isn't there.' He cast Tacita a doubtful glance to check that he hadn't overstepped the mark.

She nodded encouragement, and tried to smile.

'Your mother's right,' said Gaius. Over the boy's head, he met her eyes.

She said, 'I know I should have sent him to safety. He should be with the twins at my brother's—'

Titus rolled his eyes. 'Oh, *Mother*!'

'—but I couldn't. I couldn't bear to be parted from him.'

Gaius said to her, 'Will you tell him?'

'Of course. When he's sixteen.'

He nodded.

'Tell me what?' asked Titus.

'A secret,' Gaius replied.

'Why can't you tell me now?'

'Because it's too dangerous. Not just for you, but for your mother.'

471

Titus thrust out his lower lip rebelliously.

Tacita knew that look. It meant trouble. Gaius noticed it too, and said smoothly, 'But instead I can give you something, another kind of secret.'

Titus looked at him hopefully.

Gaius untied the pouch at his belt and brought out a small, figured bronze inkwell.

'Oh look, it's an owl!' cried Titus in delight.

'It's for travelling,' said Gaius. 'You'll be on the road for a while, so you'll need something to write with.' Again he fished in the pouch; he brought out a little bronze canister about the length of his middle finger, and snapped open the lid. 'And something to write *on*, of course. There's some paper already in there, to get you started. Have you a pen?'

Eagerly, Titus nodded.

'Well, then. You're ready to begin.' He put the canister and the inkwell into the boy's hands, and closed them with his own. For a moment he held the boy's hands in his. 'Keep these with you always,' he said with a catch in his voice.

'*Always*,' repeated Titus with satisfaction.

Suddenly Gaius raised his head and met her gaze. His eyes glittered. *Thank you*, he mouthed.

She gave him a shaky smile.

Outside the door, Faenio coughed.

Tacita caught her breath. It was time to go.

Gaius touched the boy's shoulder one last time. Then he passed his hand over the black curls. 'Titus,' he said, getting stiffly to his feet.

'Yes, sir?'

'Promise me you'll write your plays.'

Titus looked up at him and smiled. 'I promise, sir.' He caught his lip between his teeth. Then he said, 'And when I do, will you read it, and tell me *honestly* what you think?'

Tacita pressed her hands to her mouth.

Gaius stood looking down at his son with a longing which would never be satisfied. Then he made himself smile, and said, 'I'd like to, Titus. Very much.'

I can't bear it, she thought. She went to Gaius and said quickly, 'Come with us. Come with us tonight.'

'Oh, *yes*!' cried Titus.

'I can't,' said Gaius.

'*Why* not—' she began.

'It's impossible. You know that.'

'No I don't!'

'Tacita. It would put you all in danger.'

She shook her head. She could no longer speak for the tears.

Titus went to her and took her hand. 'Why are you crying, Mother?'

'Because I'm sad.'

Gaius put his hands on her shoulders and gave her a little shake. 'You mustn't be sad. This is how it was meant to be.'

The tears were running down her cheeks, and she made no attempt to keep them back.

Faenio put his head round the door, and then withdrew.

Gaius's hands tightened on her shoulders. 'This is how it was meant to be, Tacita. We weren't meant to be together in this life. But we've had this time, which I never expected. And now, after all these years, I can do something for you at last. For you both. You've given me that.' He paused. 'Some day we will be together.'

'How can you say that!' she burst out passionately.

'Because I know it's true.'

'*How?* How do you know?'

'If the Goddess wills it,' he said simply, 'it will be so.'

CHAPTER EIGHTEEN
Mazerans Hospital, 2.00pm, March 24, the Present

PATRICK WAS STANDING at the window in a hospital dressing gown when Antonia entered the room. He was talking on the phone. His face was grave. 'Yes. Yes.—No. It'll be all right.'

When he heard her come in, he turned awkwardly on his crutches.

She gave him a brief smile, which he did not return. Obviously it was not an easy call.

The doctor said he had been extraordinarily lucky. Apart from the crutches, and a sticking plaster on his temple, there was nothing to show that he had walked into a rock, hobbled two miles with a torn ligament, and spent half the night on a freezing mountainside.

He put down the phone. Then he shook his head and murmured, 'Son of a bitch.'

She waited, but he did not enlighten her.

Feeling unaccountably shy, she picked up the bag she had brought from his house, and put it on the bed. 'Clothes and shaving things. The doctor says you're free to go, and you're lucky it wasn't worse.'

He gave her a strange look she couldn't read, then picked up the bag and hobbled into the bathroom. She sat on the bed and listened to the splash of water as he started to shave.

The events of the previous night felt increasingly unreal. After several hours at the hospital, she had got a lift back to Patrick's house and spent a bizarre few hours trying to sleep. He had called at six to check that she was all right, and she had been awkward and tongue-tied.

'How did it go at the mill?' he called from the bathroom.

'Fine,' she replied. It was not fine, but she didn't feel like going into that. During the night, Debra's minions had emptied the place and dumped everything in the courtyard, where a thin rain had given it a thorough soaking. Her sister's 'good' pieces were ruined, but luckily one of the minions had taken pity on Antonia's laptop and notes, and shoved them in a plastic bin-liner under the eaves.

'I almost forgot,' she said. 'There was a message from Modge on your answering machine. She wants you to call.'

'Uh-huh. That was her just now.'

She was on the point of asking how Modge knew where to reach him, when she remembered Julian. She had called him that morning, to tell him that she had found Patrick and that he was OK. Julian had sounded so worried when she spoke to him the night before that she hadn't the heart to leave him in the dark.

She went to stand in the doorway.

Patrick had jettisoned the dressing gown, and wore the jeans she had brought from the house, and nothing else. She wished he would put on his shirt.

She asked hoarsely how Modge was doing.

'I think she's going to be all right. Given time.'

'What did she want?'

He tapped his razor on the edge of the basin. Then he met her eyes in the mirror and said, 'We need to go to Le Figarol.'

She wondered if the doctors had got it wrong, and he did have concussion after all. 'What are you talking about?'

'We need to go and see old Panabière. Right now.'

'Now? But—why? Surely it can wait till tomorrow?'

He shook his head. 'Today's the 24th. The Day of Blood, right?'

She had been trying not to think about that. The anniversary of Cassius's death had very nearly claimed Patrick, too.

In bemusement she helped him on with his shirt. Visiting Clovis

Panabière was not how she had imagined they would spend their first day together. Patrick ought to be home in bed. They both ought to be home in bed. Preferably the same bed.

He leaned down and kissed her gently on the mouth. 'I can't tell you any more in case it doesn't come off. Just trust me. OK?'

She met his eyes. Then she reached up and brushed the black hair from his forehead. 'OK,' she said.

Monsieur Panabière had been foraging in his wine cellar for what seemed like hours, hunting out a special vintage of Pic-St-Loup which he insisted they should try.

He had been delighted to see them, for he took a proprietorial interest in Patrick's recovery. Antonia had run to *his* farm in the middle of the night, and *his camionnette* had brought them back to the farm, where they had called for help on *his* phone.

At last he emerged triumphantly from the cellar. In his arms he carried two dusty and extremely serious-looking bottles of Pic-St-Loup—and a large, apparently prewar tin of patent hair restorative: TONIQUE AMIEUX: LE PLUS EFFECTIF DU MONDE POUR RESTITUER LES CHEVEUX.

With a flourish he placed the tin on the kitchen table in front of Antonia, then took three tumblers from the draining board, and poured them all a drink.

'*Santé*,' he said.

'*Santé*,' they replied.

The wine was wonderful: punchy, with a peppery undercurrent.

Antonia indicated the tin. 'What's that?'

Patrick and Monsieur Panabière exchanged glances.

'That,' said Patrick, 'is why Modge called.' He turned his glass in his fingers. 'It's taken her a while to get up the courage to tell me.'

Antonia looked at him. Then she understood. 'I got the wrong cellar.'

'What?' said Patrick.

'I got the *wrong* cellar! I was on the right track, but in the wrong place.'

'You? Wrong?' Patrick smiled. 'Not possible.'

When she made no move to touch the tin, he pushed it towards her. 'Go on. Open it.'

Looking back on it afterwards, it seemed to Antonia that at the moment when she opened the tin, a stillness descended on the kitchen. The little black cat by the stove stopped licking its paws. The chickens outside fell silent. The sun went in.

'It's even more beautiful than I remembered,' she said as she lifted the *kántharos* from its nest of wadding.

She held it in both hands and turned it slowly, and the light caught the reliefs and brought them alive.

Pegasus trotted joyfully over a field of waving acanthus, where a small coiled snake sheltered beneath an overarching frond. Bellerophon walked like a young prince, his face serene and joyful, his palm outstretched to greet his long-lost companion. And behind his shoulder, a crescent moon rose into the evening sky.

With her finger, Antonia traced the outline of the moon. 'Her name was Tacita,' she said softly. 'Tacita Cornelia.' She swallowed. 'After the escape from Perusia she went to Athens. She stayed there until she died. That's where her children grew up.'

Carefully, she set the *kántharos* on the table. Then she glanced from Patrick to Monsieur Panabière. Steadily he returned her gaze.

'*Monsieur. Pourquoi ne m'avez vous jamais parlé de ceci?*'

Monsieur Panabière regarded her with the eyes of a man who has seen seven decades of human wickedness and folly, and learned not to take anything too seriously. He lifted his thin shoulders in a shrug.

'*Parce que, mademoiselle, vous ne m'avez jamais demandé.*'

It was half past four by the time the Citroën emerged from the turnoff to Le Figarol. Antonia had no choice but to park where they always used to park, in the widest part of the track, just uphill from Monsieur Panabière's aluminium gate. Neither of them spoke as they sat in the car fifteen feet from the site of the accident.

You've done it, she thought. You've found the cup and you've solved the riddle. Now all that's left is to make the libation.

Ever since she could remember, she had wanted this day to come. But now that it had, she felt bereft. It was too much.

Patrick sat beside her in silence. She wondered if he guessed what she was feeling. Or perhaps he was thinking about Myles.

They got out of the car, Patrick moving awkwardly on his crutches. She opened the back and took out the elderly hunting-satchel which Monsieur Panabière had donated, and the tin with the *kántharos* inside, and the second bottle of Pic-St-Loup, which the old man had opened for them, and then recorked.

She glanced at Patrick. He was leaning against the bonnet, looking pale. Her heart sank. She needed him with her for this. She didn't want to face it on her own. But plainly he was in no state to walk up to the Source. 'I think you'd better wait here,' she said.

He shook his head. 'I'll come. I don't want you to do this alone.'

'I'll be fine.'

'That's what you always say.'

She made herself smile. 'I will. Really.' She tried to make light of it. 'And the Goddess prefers women. Remember?'

He inclined his head. 'She looked after me pretty well last night.'

Their eyes met. She didn't want to think about what would have happened if she had not found him.

He took hold of her wrist and glanced at her watch. 'I figure you have just under an hour to get up there, make that libation, and get back here before I start worrying and come after you.'

'Fine,' she said.

Unfortunately, Monsieur Panabière's hunting-satchel was not big enough to take the tin of hair restorative. Patrick held the satchel open while she lifted the *kántharos* from its nest of wadding.

It was a clear, warm day, and although the Catalan sun was already low in the sky, it still shone brightly. For a moment Antonia held up the *kántharos*, and they watched it fill with light.

'You be careful up there,' Patrick said.

She did not reply.

Something inside the rim had caught the light. She brought it closer. Her mouth went dry.

'What is it?' said Patrick. 'What?'

She cleared her throat. 'He didn't leave as much to chance as we thought.'

'What do you mean?'

'The truth is *in* the cup,' she said quietly. She placed the *kántharos* on the bonnet of the car, and with her forefinger traced the inscription hidden just under the lip. She spelled it aloud: '"C. et T. et f."'

Patrick said, 'What does the last bit mean?' Then he turned to her. 'Jesus. *Jesus.*'

'Cassius and Tacita. And son.'

Again she touched the letters.

She knew who had made it. In contrast to the professionally executed inscription on the base, this had been roughly cut. It was the sort of carving which might be done by a man with no special expertise in stonecutting, using his own knife. He would have needed a good knife, and a lot of determination, for this was sardonyx, and as hard as nails.

Antonia thought of him carving the initials on the miraculous cup which he had commissioned, so that someone—he didn't know who—would, at some future time, make the libation he needed. She thought of him carving the initials with his knife. Like a boy scratching his sweetheart's name on a tree trunk.

'We drank wine,' ran the famous passage in Plautius's letter, 'and I followed my young friend out onto the terrace. I struggled to keep back the tears, but he seemed almost serene. "Why, Plautius," he said, "I hadn't realised until now, but today is the Day of Blood." Then he astonished me by breaking into a smile. "But how fitting that is! It's a good sign, don't you think?"'

The setting sun filled the *kántharos* with ruby light. Sunset on the Day of Blood, thought Antonia. A good time for a libation. Again that sense of disbelief. It was too much. Her eyes began to sting.

Patrick leaned against the bonnet of the car and put his hands on her shoulders, and drew her into his arms. 'I'm coming with you,' he said.

She shook her head. 'You can't. Your knee—'

'I'll manage.'

'But—'

'What you've got to get used to,' he said gently, 'is that you're not alone any more.'

He looked down into her face, as she took in the truth of that.

She wiped her eyes with her knuckles, and blinked at him. Finally, she nodded. 'Come on, then,' she said.

MICHELLE PAVER

Just over two years ago, Michelle Paver was working as a partner in a prestigious London law firm, dreaming of becoming a full-time writer. Now, hard at work on her third novel, with her second, *A Place in the Hills* just published, that dream has become reality. Making the change and giving up a successful well-paid career for the uncertain life of a writer wasn't easy, but it was something she felt she had to do. 'I have always wanted to write,' she says, 'and as a child spent my time making up stories.' She wrote in her spare time while she was at Oxford studying for a degree in biochemistry, and then later while holding down her high-pressure legal job.

Courageously, she resigned from the partnership before she got a contract for her first published novel, *Without Charity*. 'It was a stupid thing to do,' she says of the timing, 'the same impulse as when people jump off cliffs. But I had reached the point where I just had to give my writing a chance.' When she heard that she had got a publishing contract she says she was so thrilled that she 'whooped like a ten-year-old'. And now, two years on, she says, 'although sometimes I find writing hard, when I'm just staring at a blank piece of paper and the words won't come, I have never regretted my decision to give up law.'

While writing *A Place in the Hills,* Michelle Paver was able to draw upon another childhood interest—her fascination with ancient Roman history. She says that a great deal of what happens to her modern-day character, Antonia, is wish fulfilment. 'I've always wanted to have the kind of direct link with the past that Antonia has when she finds the *kántharos* that belonged to Cassius. I really enjoyed working on that scene, and found it very moving.' She found writing the Roman sections of the novel easiest and had a clear picture of what Cassius looked like. 'Just after I'd started the book I went along to the British Museum and I saw a bust of a Roman man who looked exactly as I imagined Cassius to look. I popped in to see him quite a few times when I was writing the book,' she said with a laugh.

She loves doing the research for her books, not least because it has often involved travel. Her father's family come from South Africa and she spent some time there researching *Without Charity,* which is partly set during the Boer War. *A Place in the Hills* took her on a short trip to the French Pyrenees and her next novel, which is set in Jamaica just after the end of slavery, took her out to the Caribbean. 'It was wonderful,' she said, 'much better than commuting every day to the city.'

Sally Cummings

601-010-1